THE
HUNCHBACK OF
NOTRE-DAME

THE HUNCHBACK OF NOTRE-DAME

VICTOR HUGO

The Hunchback of Notre-Dame was first published in 1831.

This edition published by Tess Press, an imprint of
Black Dog & Leventhal Publishers, Inc.
151 West 19th Street, New York, NY 10011

Design by Lindsay Wolff
Manufactured in the U.S.A.

ISBN-10: 1-57912-672-3
ISBN-13: 978-1-57912-672-8

h g f e d c b a

Contents

❀

BOOK FIFTH

BOOK SIXTH

BOOK SEVENTH

BOOK EIGHTH

Preface

A FEW YEARS ago, while visiting or, rather, rummaging about Notre-Dame, the author of this book found, in an obscure nook of one of the towers, the following word, engraved by hand upon the wall:—

ἈΝΆΓΚΗ

These Greek capitals, black with age, and quite deeply graven in the stone, with I know not what signs peculiar to Gothic calligraphy imprinted upon their forms and upon their attitudes, as though with the purpose of revealing that it had been a hand of the Middle Ages which had inscribed them there, and especially the fatal and melancholy meaning contained in them, struck the author deeply.

He questioned himself; he sought to divine who could have been that soul in torment which had not been willing to quit this world without leaving this stigma of crime or unhappiness upon the brow of the ancient church.

Afterwards, the wall was whitewashed or scraped down, I know not which, and the inscription disappeared. For it is thus that people have been in the habit of proceeding with the marvellous churches of the Middle Ages for the last two hundred years. Mutilations come to them from every quarter, from within as well as from without. The priest whitewashes them, the archdeacon scrapes them down; then the populace arrives and demolishes them.

Thus, with the exception of the fragile memory which the author of this book here consecrates to it, there remains today nothing whatever of the mysterious word engraved within the gloomy tower of Notre-Dame—nothing of the destiny which it so sadly summed up.

The man who wrote that word upon the wall disappeared from the midst of the generations of man many centuries ago; the word, in its turn, has been effaced from the wall of the church; the church will, perhaps, itself soon disappear from the face of the earth.

It is upon this word that this book is founded.

March 1831

Book First

CHAPTER 1

The Grand Hall

THREE HUNDRED AND forty-eight years, six months, and nineteen days ago today, the Parisians awoke to the sound of all the bells in the triple circuit of the city, the university, and the town ringing a full peal.

The sixth of January, 1482, is not, however, a day of which history has preserved the memory. There was nothing notable in the event which thus set the bells and the bourgeois of Paris in a ferment from early morning. It was neither an assault by the Picards nor the Burgundians, nor a hunt led along in procession, nor a revolt of scholars in the town of Laas, nor an entry of "our much dread lord, monsieur the king," nor even a pretty hanging of male and female thieves by the courts of Paris. Neither was it the arrival, so frequent in the fifteenth century, of some plumed and bedizened embassy. It was barely two days since the last cavalcade of that nature, that of the Flemish ambassadors charged with concluding the marriage between the dauphin and Marguerite of Flanders, had made its entry into Paris, to the great annoyance of M. le Cardinal de Bourbon, who, for the sake of pleasing the king, had been obliged to assume an amiable mien toward this whole rustic rabble of Flemish burgomasters, and to regale them at his Hôtel de Bourbon, with a very "pretty morality, allegorical satire, and farce," while a driving rain drenched the magnificent tapestries at his door.

What put the "whole population of Paris in commotion," as Jehan de Troyes expresses it, on the sixth of January, was the double solemnity, united from time immemorial, of the Epiphany and the Feast of Fools.

On that day, there was to be a bonfire on the Place de Grève, a maypole at the Chapelle de Braque, and a mystery at the Palais de

Justice. It had been cried, to the sound of the trumpet, the preceding evening at all the cross roads, by the provost's men, clad in handsome, short, sleeveless coats of violet camelot, with large white crosses upon their breasts.

So the crowd of citizens, male and female, having closed their houses and shops, thronged from every direction, at early morn, toward some one of the three spots designated.

Each had made his choice; one, the bonfire; another, the maypole; another, the mystery play. It must be stated, in honor of the good sense of the loungers of Paris, that the greater part of this crowd directed their steps toward the bonfire, which was quite in season, or toward the mystery play, which was to be presented in the grand hall of the Palais de Justice (the courts of law), which was well roofed and walled; and that the curious left the poor, scantily flowered maypole to shiver all alone beneath the sky of January, in the cemetery of the Chapel of Braque.

The populace thronged the avenues of the law courts in particular, because they knew that the Flemish ambassadors, who had arrived two days before, intended to be present at the representation of the mystery, and at the election of the Pope of the Fools, which was also to take place in the grand hall.

It was no easy matter on that day to force one's way into that grand hall, although it was then reputed to be the largest covered enclosure in the world (it is true that Sauval had not yet measured the grand hall of the Château of Montargis). The palace place, encumbered with people, offered to the curious gazers at the windows the aspect of a sea; into which five or six streets, like so many mouths of rivers, discharged every moment fresh floods of heads. The waves of this crowd, augmented incessantly, dashed against the angles of the houses which projected here and there, like so many promontories, into the irregular basin of the place. In the centre of the lofty Gothic* façade of the palace, the grand staircase, incessantly ascended and descended by a double current, which, after parting on the intermediate landing-place,

---

*The word Gothic, in the sense in which it is generally employed, is wholly unsuitable, but wholly consecrated. Hence we accept it and we adopt it, like all the rest of the world, to characterize the architecture of the second half of the Middle Ages, where the ogive is the principle which succeeds the architecture of the first period, of which the semi-circle is the father.

flowed in broad waves along its lateral slopes, the grand staircase, I say, trickled incessantly into the place, like a cascade into a lake. The cries, the laughter, the trampling of those thousands of feet, produced a great noise and a great clamor. From time to time, this noise and clamor redoubled; the current that drove the crowd toward the grand staircase flowed backwards, became troubled, formed whirlpools. This was produced by the buffet of an archer, or the horse of one of the provost's sergeants, which kicked to restore order; an admirable tradition which the provostship has bequeathed to the constablery, the constablery to the *maréchaussée*, the *maréchaussée* to our *gendarmerie* of Paris.

Thousands of good, calm, bourgeois faces thronged the windows, the doors, the dormer windows, the roofs, gazing at the palace, gazing at the populace, and asking nothing more; for many Parisians content themselves with the spectacle of the spectators, and a wall behind which something is going on becomes at once, for us, a very curious thing indeed.

If it could be granted to us, the men of 1830, to mingle in thought with those Parisians of the fifteenth century, and to enter with them, jostled, elbowed, pulled about, into that immense hall of the palace, which was so cramped on that sixth of January, 1482, the spectacle would not be devoid of either interest or charm, and we should have about us only things that were so old that they would seem new.

With the reader's consent, we will endeavor to retrace in thought, the impression which he would have experienced in company with us on crossing the threshold of that grand hall, in the midst of that tumultuous crowd in surcoats, short, sleeveless jackets, and doublets.

And, first of all, there is a buzzing in the ears, a dazzlement in the eyes. Above our heads is a double ogive vault, panelled with wood carving, painted azure, and sown with golden fleurs-de-lis; beneath our feet a pavement of black and white marble, alternating. A few paces distant, an enormous pillar, then another, then another; seven pillars in all, down the length of the hall, sustaining the spring of the arches of the double vault, in the centre of its width. Around four of the pillars, stalls of merchants, all sparkling with glass and tinsel; around the last three, benches of oak, worn and polished by the trunk hose of the litigants, and the robes of the attorneys. Around the hall, along the lofty wall, between the doors, between the windows, between the pillars, the interminable row of all the kings of France, from Pharamond down: the lazy kings, with pendent arms and downcast eyes; the valiant and combative kings, with heads and arms raised boldly heavenward.

Then in the long, pointed windows, glass of a thousand hues; at the wide entrances to the hall, rich doors, finely sculptured; and all, the vaults, pillars, walls, jambs, panelling, doors, statues, covered from top to bottom with a splendid blue and gold illumination, which, a trifle tarnished at the epoch when we behold it, had almost entirely disappeared beneath dust and spiders in the year of grace, 1549, when du Breul still admired it from tradition.

Let the reader picture to himself now, this immense, oblong hall, illuminated by the pallid light of a January day, invaded by a motley and noisy throng which drifts along the walls, and eddies round the seven pillars, and he will have a confused idea of the whole effect of the picture, whose curious details we shall make an effort to indicate with more precision.

It is certain, that if Ravaillac had not assassinated Henri IV, there would have been no documents in the trial of Ravaillac deposited in the clerk's office of the Palais de Justice, no accomplices interested in causing the said documents to disappear; hence, no incendiaries obliged, for lack of better means, to burn the clerk's office in order to burn the documents, and to burn the Palais de Justice in order to burn the clerk's office; consequently, in short, no conflagration in 1618. The old Palais would be standing still, with its ancient grand hall; I should be able to say to the reader, "Go and look at it," and we should thus both escape the necessity, I of making, and he of reading, a description of it, such as it is. Which demonstrates a new truth: that great events have incalculable results.

It is true that it may be quite possible, in the first place, that Ravaillac had no accomplices; and in the second, that if he had any, they were in no way connected with the fire of 1618. Two other very plausible explanations exist: First, the great flaming star, a foot broad, and a cubit high, which fell from heaven, as every one knows, upon the law courts, after midnight on the seventh of March; second, Théophile's quatrain—

> Sure, 'twas but a sorry game
> When at Paris, Dame Justice,
> Through having eaten too much spice,
> Set the palace all aflame.

Whatever may be thought of this triple explanation, political, physical, and poetical, of the burning of the law courts in 1618, the unfortunate fact of the fire is certain. Very little today remains, thanks to this catastrophe—thanks, above all, to the successive restorations which have completed what it spared—very little remains of that first dwelling of the kings of France, of that elder palace of the Louvre, already so old in the time of Philip the Handsome, that they sought there for the traces of the magnificent buildings erected by King Robert and described by Helgaldus. Nearly everything has disappeared. What has become of the chamber of the chancellery, where Saint Louis consummated his marriage? The garden where he administered justice, "clad in a coat of camelot, a surcoat of linsey-woolsey, without sleeves, and a sur-mantle of black sandal, as he lay upon the carpet with Joinville?" Where is the chamber of the Emperor Sigismond? And that of Charles IV? That of Jean the Landless? Where is the staircase, from which Charles VI promulgated his edict of pardon? The slab where Marcel cut the throats of Robert de Clermont and the Marshal of Champagne, in the presence of the dauphin? The wicket where the bulls of Pope Benedict were torn, and whence those who had brought them departed decked out, in derision, in copes and mitres, and making an apology through all Paris? And the grand hall, with its gilding, its azure, its statues, its pointed arches, its pillars, its immense vault, all fretted with carvings? And the gilded chamber? And the stone lion, which stood at the door, with lowered head and tail between his legs, like the lions on the throne of Solomon, in the humiliated attitude which befits force in the presence of justice? And the beautiful doors? And the stained glass? And the chased ironwork, which drove Biscornette to despair? And the delicate woodwork of Hancy? What has time, what have men done with these marvels? What have they given us in return for all this Gallic history, for all this Gothic art? The heavy flattened arches of M. de Brosse, that awkward architect of the Saint-Gervais portal. So much for art; and, as for history, we have the gossiping reminiscences of the great pillar, still ringing with the tattle of the Patru.

It is not much. Let us return to the veritable grand hall of the veritable old palace. The two extremities of this gigantic parallelogram were occupied, the one by the famous marble table, so long, so broad, and so thick that, as the ancient land rolls—in a style that would have given Gargantua an appetite—say, "such a slice of marble as was never beheld in the world"; the other by the chapel where Louis XI had himself sculptured on his knees before the Virgin, and whither he caused to be brought, without heeding the two gaps thus made in the row of royal statues, the statues of Charlemagne and of Saint Louis, two saints whom he supposed to be great in favor in heaven, as kings of France. This chapel, quite new, having been built only six years, was entirely in that charming taste of delicate architecture, of marvellous sculpture, of fine and deep chasing, which marks with us the end of the Gothic era, and which is perpetuated to about the middle of the sixteenth century in the fairylike fancies of the Renaissance. The little open-work rose window, pierced above the portal, was, in particular, a masterpiece of lightness and grace; one would have pronounced it a star of lace.

In the middle of the hall, opposite the great door, a platform of gold brocade, placed against the wall, a special entrance to which had been effected through a window in the corridor of the gold chamber, had been erected for the Flemish emissaries and the other great personages invited to the presentation of the mystery play.

It was upon the marble table that the mystery was to be enacted, as usual. It had been arranged for the purpose, early in the morning; its rich slabs of marble, all scratched by the heels of law clerks, supported a cage of carpenter's work of considerable height, the upper surface of which, within view of the whole hall, was to serve as the theatre, and whose interior, masked by tapestries, was to take the place of dressing-rooms for the personages of the piece. A ladder, naively placed on the outside, was to serve as means of communication between the dressing-room and the stage, and lend its rude rungs to entrances as well as to exits. There was no personage, however unexpected, no sudden change, no theatrical effect, which was not obliged to mount that ladder. Innocent and venerable infancy of art and contrivances!

Four of the bailiff's palace sergeants, perfunctory guardians of all the pleasures of the people, on days of festival as well as on days of execution, stood at the four corners of the marble table.

The piece was only to begin with the twelfth stroke of the great palace clock sounding midday. It was very late, no doubt, for a theatrical representation, but they had been obliged to fix the hour to suit the convenience of the ambassadors.

Now, this whole multitude had been waiting since morning. A goodly number of curious, good people had been shivering since daybreak before the grand staircase of the palace; some even affirmed that they had passed the night across the threshold of the great door, in order to make sure that they should be the first to pass in. The crowd grew more dense every moment, and, like water, which rises above its normal level, began to mount along the walls, to swell around the pillars, to spread out on the entablatures, on the cornices, on the window-sills, on all the salient points of the architecture, on all the reliefs of the sculpture. Hence, discomfort, impatience, weariness, the liberty of a day of cynicism and folly, the quarrels which break forth for all sorts of causes—a pointed elbow, an iron-shod shoe, the fatigue of long waiting—had already, long before the hour appointed for the arrival of the ambassadors, imparted a harsh and bitter accent to the clamor of these people who were shut in, fitted into each other, pressed, trampled upon, stifled. Nothing was to be heard but imprecations on the Flemish, the provost of the merchants, the Cardinal de Bourbon, the bailiff of the courts, Madame Marguerite of Austria, the sergeants with their rods, the cold, the heat, the bad weather, the Bishop of Paris, the Pope of the Fools, the pillars, the statues, that closed door, that open window; all to the vast amusement of a band of scholars and lackeys scattered through the mass, who mingled with all this discontent their teasing remarks, and their malicious suggestions, and pricked the general bad temper with a pin, so to speak.

Among the rest there was a group of those merry imps, who, after smashing the glass in a window, had seated themselves hardily on the entablature, and from that point despatched their gaze and their railleries both within and without, upon the throng in the hall, and the throng upon the Place. It was easy to see, from their parodied gestures, their ringing laughter, the bantering appeals which they exchanged with their comrades, from one end of the hall to the other, that these young clerks did not share the weariness and fatigue of the rest of the spectators, and that they understood very well the art of extracting, for their own private diversion from that which they had under their eyes, a spectacle which made them await the other with patience.

"Upon my soul, so it's you, Joannes Frollo de Molendino!" cried one of them, to a sort of little, light-haired imp, with a well-favored and malign countenance, clinging to the acanthus leaves of a capital; "you are well named John of the Mill, for your two arms and your two legs have the air of four wings fluttering on the breeze. How long have you been here?"

"By the mercy of the devil," retorted Joannes Frollo, "these four hours and more; and I hope that they will be reckoned to my credit in purgatory. I heard the eight singers of the King of Sicily intone the first verse of seven o'clock mass in the Sainte-Chapelle."

"Fine singers!" replied the other, "with voices even more pointed than their caps! Before founding a mass for Monsieur Saint John, the king should have inquired whether Monsieur Saint John likes Latin droned out in a Provençal accent."

"He did it for the sake of employing those accursed singers of the King of Sicily!" cried an old woman sharply from among the crowd beneath the window. "I just put it to you! A thousand *livres parisi* for a mass! And out of the tax on sea fish in the markets of Paris, to boot!"

"Peace, old crone," said a tall, grave person, stopping up his nose on the side toward the fishwife; "a mass had to be founded. Would you wish the king to fall ill again?"

"Bravely spoken, Sire Gilles Lecornu, master furrier of king's robes!" cried the little student, clinging to the capital.

A shout of laughter from all the students greeted the unlucky name of the poor furrier of the king's robes.

"Lecornu! Gilles Lecornu!" said some.

"*Cornutus et hirsutus*, horned and hairy," another went on.

"He, of course!" continued the small imp on the capital. "What are they laughing at? An honorable man is Gilles Lecornu, brother of Master Jehan Lecornu, provost of the king's house, son of Master Mahiet Lecornu, first porter of the Bois de Vincennes—all bourgeois of Paris, all married, from father to son."

The gayety redoubled. The big furrier, without uttering a word in reply, tried to escape all the eyes riveted upon him from all sides; but he perspired and panted in vain; like a wedge entering the wood, his efforts served only to bury still more deeply in the shoulders of his neighbors, his large, apoplectic face, purple with spite and rage.

At length one of these, as fat, short, and venerable as himself, came to his rescue.

"Abomination! Scholars addressing a bourgeois in that fashion in my day would have been flogged with a fagot, which would have afterwards been used to burn them."

The whole band burst into laughter.

"Hallo! Who is scolding so? Who is that screech owl of evil fortune?"

"Hold, I know him," said one of them; "'tis Master Andry Musnier."

"Because he is one of the four sworn booksellers of the university!" said the other.

"Everything goes by fours in that shop," cried a third; "the four nations, the four faculties, the four feasts, the four procurators, the four electors, the four booksellers."

"Well," began Jehan Frollo once more, "we must play the devil with them."

"Musnier, we'll burn your books."

"Musnier, we'll beat your lackeys."

"Musnier, we'll kiss your wife."

"That fine, big Mademoiselle Oudarde."

"Who is as fresh and as gay as though she were a widow."

"Devil take you!" growled Master Andry Musnier.

"Master Andry," pursued Jehan, still clinging to his capital, "hold your tongue, or I'll drop on your head!"

Master Andry raised his eyes, seemed to measure in an instant the height of the pillar, the weight of the scamp, mentally multiplied that weight by the square of the velocity and remained silent.

Jehan, master of the field of battle, pursued triumphantly:

"That's what I'll do, even if I am the brother of an archdeacon!"

"Fine gentry are our people of the university, not to have caused our privileges to be respected on such a day as this! However, there is a maypole and a bonfire in the town; a mystery, Pope of the Fools, and Flemish ambassadors in the city; and, at the university, nothing!"

"Nevertheless, the Place Maubert is sufficiently large!" interposed one of the clerks established on the window-sill.

"Down with the rector, the electors, and the procurators!" cried Joannes.

"We must have a bonfire this evening in the Champ-Gaillard," went on the other, "made of Master Andry's books."

"And the desks of the scribes!" added his neighbor.

"And the beadles' wands!"

"And the spittoons of the deans!"

"And the cupboards of the procurators!"

"And the hutches of the electors!"

"And the stools of the rector!"

"Down with them!" put in little Jehan, as counterpoint; "down with Master Andry, the beadles and the scribes; the theologians, the doctors and the decretists; the procurators, the electors and the rector!"

"The end of the world has come!" muttered Master Andry, stopping up his ears.

"By the way, there's the rector! See, he is passing through the Place," cried one of those in the window.

Each rivalled his neighbor in his haste to turn toward the Place.

"Is it really our venerable rector, Master Thibaut?" demanded Jehan Frollo du Moulin, who, as he was clinging to one of the inner pillars, could not see what was going on outside.

"Yes, yes," replied all the others, "it is really he, Master Thibaut, the rector."

It was, in fact, the rector and all the dignitaries of the university, who were marching in procession in front of the embassy, and at that moment traversing the Place. The students crowded into the window, saluted them as they passed with sarcasms and ironical applause. The rector, who was walking at the head of his company, had to support the first broadside; it was severe.

"Good day, monsieur le recteur! Hallo! Good day there!"

"How does he manage to be here, the old gambler? Has he abandoned his dice?"

"How he trots along on his mule! Her ears are not so long as his!"

"Hallo, good day, monsieur le recteur Thibaut! *Tybalde aleator!* Old fool! Old gambler!"

"God preserve you! Did you throw double six often last night?"

"Oh, what a decrepit face, livid and haggard and drawn with the love of gambling and of dice!"

"Where are you bound for in that fashion, Thibaut, *Tybalde ad dados*, with your back turned to the university, and trotting toward the town?"

"He is on his way, no doubt, to seek a lodging in the Rue Thibautodé?"* cried Jehan du M. Moulin.

The entire band repeated this quip in a voice of thunder, clapping their hands furiously.

"You are going to seek a lodging in the Rue Thibautodé, are you not, monsieur le recteur, gamester on the side of the devil?"

Then came the turns of the other dignitaries.

"Down with the beadles! Down with the mace-bearers!"

"Tell me, Robin Pouissepain, who is that yonder?"

"He is Gilbert de Suilly, *Gilbertus de Soliaco*, the chancellor of the College of Autun."

---

* Thibaut au des: Thibaut of the dice.

"Hold on, here's my shoe; you are better placed than I, fling it in his face."

"*Saturnalitias mittimus ecce nuces.*"

"Down with the six theologians, with their white surplices!"

"Are those the theologians? I thought they were the white geese given by Sainte-Geneviève to the city, for the fief of Roogny."

"Down with the doctors!"

"Down with the cardinal disputations, and quibblers!"

"My cap to you, Chancellor of Sainte-Geneviève! You have done me a wrong. 'Tis true; he gave my place in the nation of Normandy to little Ascanio Falzapada, who comes from the province of Bourges, since he is an Italian."

"That is an injustice," said all the scholars. "Down with the Chancellor of Sainte-Geneviève!"

"Hey Master Joachim de Ladehors! Hey Louis Dahuille! Hey Lambert Hoctement!"

"May the devil stifle the procurator of the German nation!"

"And the chaplains of the Sainte-Chapelle, with their gray *amices; cum tunices grisis!*"

"*Seu de pellibus grisis fourratis!*"

"Hallo! Masters of Arts! All the beautiful black copes! All the fine red copes!"

"They make a fine tail for the rector."

"One would say that he was a Doge of Venice on his way to his bridal with the sea."

"Say, Jehan, here are the canons of Sainte-Geneviève!"

"To the deuce with the whole set of canons!"

"Abbé Claude Choart! Doctor Claude Choart! Are you in search of Marie la Giffarde?"

"She is in the Rue de Glatigny."

"She is making the bed of the king of the debauchees. She is paying her four deniers, *quatuor denarios.*"

"*Aut unum bombum.*"

"Would you like to have her pay you in the face?"

"Comrades! Master Simon Sanguin, the Elector of Picardy, with his wife on the crupper!"

"*Post equitem seclet atra eura*—behind the horseman sits black care."

"Courage, Master Simon!"

"Good day, Mister Elector!"

"Good night, Madame Electress!"

"How happy they are to see all that!" sighed Joannes de Molendino, still perched in the foliage of his capital.

Meanwhile, the sworn bookseller of the university, Master Andry Musnier, was inclining his ear to the furrier of the king's robes, Master Gilles Lecornu.

"I tell you, sir, that the end of the world has come. No one has ever beheld such outbreaks among the students! It is the accursed inventions of this century that are ruining everything—artilleries, bombards, and, above all, printing, that other German pest. No more manuscripts, no more books! printing will kill bookselling. It is the end of the world that is drawing nigh."

"I see that plainly, from the progress of velvet stuffs," said the fur-merchant.

At this moment, midday sounded.

"Ha!" exclaimed the entire crowd, in one voice.

The scholars held their peace. Then a great hurly-burly ensued; a vast movement of feet, hands, and heads; a general outbreak of coughs and handkerchiefs; each one arranged himself, assumed his post, raised himself up, and grouped himself. Then came a great silence; all necks remained outstretched, all mouths remained open, all glances were directed toward the marble table. Nothing made its appearance there. The bailiff's four sergeants were still there, stiff, motionless, as painted statues. All eyes turned to the estrade reserved for the Flemish envoys. The door remained closed, the platform empty. This crowd had been waiting since daybreak for three things: noonday, the embassy from Flanders, the mystery play. Noonday alone had arrived on time.

On this occasion, it was too much.

They waited one, two, three, five minutes, a quarter of an hour; nothing came. The dais remained empty, the theatre dumb. In the meantime, wrath had succeeded to impatience. Irritated words circulated in a low tone, still, it is true. "The mystery! The mystery!" they murmured, in hollow voices. Heads began to ferment. A tempest, which was only rumbling in the distance as yet, was floating on the surface of this crowd. It was Jehan du Moulin who struck the first spark from it.

"The mystery, and to the devil with the Flemings!" he exclaimed at the full force of his lungs, twining like a serpent around his pillar.

The crowd clapped their hands.

"The mystery!" it repeated, "and may all the devils take Flanders!"

"We must have the mystery instantly," resumed the student; "or else, my advice is that we should hang the bailiff of the courts, by way of a morality and a comedy."

"Well said," cried the people, "and let us begin the hanging with his sergeants."

A grand acclamation followed. The four poor fellows began to turn pale, and to exchange glances. The crowd hurled itself toward them, and they already beheld the frail wooden railing, which separated them from it, giving way and bending before the pressure of the throng.

It was a critical moment.

"To the sack, to the sack!" rose the cry on all sides.

At that moment, the tapestry of the dressing-room, which we have described above, was raised, and afforded passage to a personage, the mere sight of whom suddenly stopped the crowd, and changed its wrath into curiosity as by enchantment.

"Silence, silence!"

The personage, but little reassured, and trembling in every limb, advanced to the edge of the marble table with a vast amount of bows, which, in proportion as he drew nearer, more and more resembled genuflections.

In the meanwhile, tranquillity had gradually been restored. All that remained was that slight murmur which always rises above the silence of a crowd.

"Messieurs the bourgeois," said he, "and mesdemoiselles the bourgeoises, we shall have the honor of declaiming and representing, before his eminence, monsieur the cardinal, a very beautiful morality which has for its title, 'The Good Judgment of Madame the Virgin Mary.' I am to play Jupiter. His eminence is, at this moment, escorting the very honorable embassy of the Duke of Austria; which is detained, at present, listening to the harangue of monsieur the rector of the university, at the gate Baudets. As soon as his illustrious eminence, the cardinal, arrives, we will begin."

It is certain, that nothing less than the intervention of Jupiter was required to save the four unfortunate sergeants of the bailiff of the courts. If we had the happiness of having invented this very veracious tale, and of being, in consequence, responsible for it before our Lady

Criticism, it is not against us that the classic precept, *Nec deus intersit*, could be invoked. Moreover, the costume of Seigneur Jupiter, was very handsome, and contributed not a little toward calming the crowd, by attracting all its attention. Jupiter was clad in a coat of mail, covered with black velvet, with gilt nails; and had it not been for the rouge, and the huge red beard, each of which covered one-half of his face, had it not been for the roll of gilded cardboard, spangled, and all bristling with strips of tinsel, which he held in his hand, and in which the eyes of the initiated easily recognized thunderbolts, had not his feet been flesh-colored, and banded with ribbons in Greek fashion, he might have borne comparison, so far as the severity of his mien was concerned, with a Breton archer from the guard of Monsieur de Berry.

Chapter 2

Pierre Gringoire

NEVERTHELESS, AS HE harangued them, the satisfaction and admiration unanimously excited by his costume were dissipated by his words; and when he reached that untoward conclusion: "As soon as his illustrious eminence, the cardinal, arrives, we will begin," his voice was drowned in a thunder of hooting.

"Begin instantly! The mystery, the mystery immediately!" shrieked the people. And above all the voices, Joannes de Molendino's was audible, piercing the uproar like the fife's derisive serenade: "Commence instantly!" yelped the scholar.

"Down with Jupiter and the Cardinal de Bourbon!" vociferated Robin Poussepain and the other clerks perched in the window.

"The morality this very instant!" repeated the crowd; "this very instant! The sack and the rope for the comedians, and the cardinal!"

Poor Jupiter, haggard, frightened, pale beneath his rouge, dropped his thunderbolt, took his cap in his hand; then he bowed and trembled and stammered: "His eminence—the ambassadors—Madame Marguerite of Flanders—" He did not know what to say. In truth, he was afraid of being hung.

Hung by the populace for waiting, hung by the cardinal for not having waited, he saw between the two dilemmas only an abyss; that is to say, a gallows.

Luckily, some one came to rescue him from his embarrassment, and assume the responsibility.

An individual who was standing beyond the railing, in the free space around the marble table, and whom no one had yet caught sight of, since his long, thin body was completely sheltered from every visual ray by the diameter of the pillar against which he was leaning; this individual, we say, tall, gaunt, pallid, blond, still young, although already wrinkled about the brow and cheeks, with brilliant eyes and a smiling mouth, clad in garments of black serge, worn and shining with age, approached the marble table, and made a sign to the poor sufferer. But the other was so confused that he did not see him. The new comer advanced another step.

"Jupiter," said he, "my dear Jupiter!"

The other did not hear.

At last, the tall blond, driven out of patience, shrieked almost in his face, "Michel Giborne!"

"Who calls me?" said Jupiter, as though awakened with a start.

"I," replied the person clad in black.

"Ah!" said Jupiter.

"Begin at once," went on the other. "Satisfy the populace; I undertake to appease the bailiff, who will appease monsieur the cardinal."

Jupiter breathed once more.

"Messeigneurs the bourgeois," he cried, at the top of his lungs to the crowd, which continued to hoot him, "we are going to begin at once."

"*Evoe Jupiter! Plaudite cives*! All hail, Jupiter! Applaud, citizens!" shouted the scholars.

"Noel! Noel! Good, good," shouted the people.

The hand clapping was deafening, and Jupiter had already withdrawn under his tapestry, while the hall still trembled with acclamations.

In the meanwhile, the personage who had so magically turned the tempest into dead calm, as our old and dear Corneille puts it, had modestly retreated to the half-shadow of his pillar, and would, no doubt, have remained invisible there, motionless, and mute as before, had he not been plucked by the sleeve by two young women, who, standing in the front row of the spectators, had noticed his colloquy with Michel Giborne-Jupiter.

"Master," said one of them, making him a sign to approach. "Hold your tongue, my dear Liénarde," said her neighbor, pretty, fresh, and very brave, in consequence of being dressed up in her best attire. "He is not a clerk, he is a layman; you must not say master to him, but messire."

"Messire," said Liénarde.

The stranger approached the railing.

"What would you have of me, damsels?" he asked, with alacrity.

"Oh, nothing," replied Liénarde, in great confusion; "it is my neighbor, Gisquette la Gencienne, who wishes to speak with you."

"Not so," replied Gisquette, blushing; "it was Liénarde who called you master; I only told her to say messire."

The two young girls dropped their eyes. The man, who asked nothing better than to enter into conversation, looked at them with a smile.

"So you have nothing to say to me, damsels?"

"Oh, nothing at all," replied Gisquette.

"Nothing," said Liénarde.

The tall, light-haired young man retreated a step; but the two curious maidens had no mind to let slip their prize.

"Messire," said Gisquette, with the impetuosity of an open sluice, or of a woman who has made up her mind, "do you know that soldier who is to play the part of Madame the Virgin in the mystery?"

"You mean the part of Jupiter?" replied the stranger.

"Oh, yes," said Liénarde, "isn't she stupid? So you know Jupiter?"

"Michel Giborne?" replied the unknown; "yes, madam."

"He has a fine beard!" said Liénarde.

"Will what they are about to say here be fine?" inquired Gisquette, timidly.

"Very fine, mademoiselle," replied the unknown, without the slightest hesitation.

"What is it to be?" said Liénarde.

"'The Good Judgment of Madame the Virgin,'—a morality, if you please, damsel."

"Ah, that makes a difference," responded Liénarde.

A brief silence ensued—broken by the stranger.

"It is a perfectly new morality, and one which has never yet been played."

"Then it is not the same one," said Gisquette, "that was given two years ago, on the day of the entrance of monsieur the legate, and where three handsome maids played the parts—"

"Of sirens," said Liénarde.

"And all naked," added the young man.

Liénarde lowered her eyes modestly. Gisquette glanced at her and did the same. He continued, with a smile, "It was a very pleasant thing to see. Today it is a morality made expressly for Madame the Demoiselle of Flanders."

"Will they sing shepherd songs?" inquired Gisquette.

"Fie!" said the stranger, "in a morality? You must not confound styles. If it were a farce, well and good."

"That is a pity," resumed Gisquette. "That day, at the Ponceau Fountain, there were wild men and women, who fought and assumed many aspects, as they sang little motets and bergerettes."

"That which is suitable for a legate," returned the stranger, with a good deal of dryness, "is not suitable for a princess."

"And beside them," resumed Liénarde, "played many brass instruments, making great melodies."

"And for the refreshment of the passers-by," continued Gisquette, "the fountain spouted through three mouths, wine, milk, and hippocrass, of which every one drank who wished."

"And a little below the Ponceau, at the Trinity," pursued Liénarde, "there was a passion performed, and without any speaking."

"How well I remember that!" exclaimed Gisquette; "God on the cross, and the two thieves on the right and the left." Here the young gossips, growing warm at the memory of the entrance of monsieur the legate, both began to talk at once.

"And, further on, at the Painters' Gate, there were other personages, very richly clad."

"And at the fountain of Saint-Innocent, that huntsman, who was chasing a hind with great clamor of dogs and hunting-horns."

"And, at the Paris slaughter-houses, stages, representing the fortress of Dieppe!"

"And when the legate passed, you remember, Gisquette? They made the assault, and the English all had their throats cut."

"And against the gate of the Châtelet, there were very fine personages!"

"And on the Port au Change, which was all draped above!"

"And when the legate passed, they let fly on the bridge more than two hundred sorts of birds; wasn't it beautiful, Liénarde?"

"It will be better today," finally resumed their interlocutor, who seemed to listen to them with impatience.

"Do you promise us that this mystery will be fine?" said Gisquette.

"Without doubt," he replied; then he added, with a certain emphasis, "I am the author of it, damsels."

"Truly?" said the young girls, quite taken aback.

"Truly!" replied the poet, bridling a little; "that is, to say, there are two of us; Jehan Marchand, who has sawed the planks and erected the framework of the theatre and the woodwork; and I, who have made the piece. My name is Pierre Gringoire."

The author of the "Cid" could not have said "Pierre Corneille" with more pride.

Our readers have been able to observe, that a certain amount of time must have already elapsed from the moment when Jupiter had retired beneath the tapestry to the instant when the author of the new morality had thus abruptly revealed himself to the innocent admiration of Gisquette and Liénarde. Remarkable fact: that whole crowd, so tumultuous but a few moments before, now waited amiably on the word of the comedian; which proves the eternal truth, still experienced every day in our theatres, that the best means of making the public wait patiently is to assure them that one is about to begin instantly.

However, scholar Joannes had not fallen asleep.

"Hey!" he shouted suddenly, in the midst of the peaceable waiting which had followed the tumult. "Jupiter, Madame the Virgin, buffoons of the devil! Are you jeering at us? The piece! The piece! Commence or we will commence again!"

This was all that was needed.

The music of high and low instruments immediately became audible from the interior of the stage; the tapestry was raised; four personages, in motley attire and painted faces, emerged from it, climbed the steep ladder of the theatre, and, arrived upon the upper platform, arranged themselves in a line before the public, whom they saluted with profound reverences; then the symphony ceased.

The mystery was about to begin.

The four personages, after having reaped a rich reward of applause for their reverences, began, in the midst of profound silence, a prologue, which we gladly spare the reader. Moreover, as happens in our own day, the public was more occupied with the costumes that the actors wore than with the roles that they were enacting; and, in truth, they were right. All four were dressed in parti-colored robes of yellow and white, which were distinguished from each other only by the nature of the stuff; the first was of gold and silver brocade; the second, of silk; the third, of wool; the fourth, of linen. The first of these personages carried in his right hand a sword; the second, two golden keys; the third, a pair of scales; the fourth, a spade: and, in order to aid sluggish minds which would not have seen clearly through the transparency of these attributes, there was to be read, in large, black letters, on the hem of the robe of brocade, MY NAME IS NOBILITY; on the hem of the silken robe, MY NAME IS CLERGY; on the hem of the woolen robe, MY NAME IS MERCHANDISE; on the hem of the linen robe, MY NAME IS LABOR. The sex of the two male characters was briefly indicated to every judicious spectator, by their shorter robes, and by the cap that they wore on their heads; while the two female characters, less briefly clad, were covered with hoods.

Much ill-will would also have been required, not to comprehend, through the medium of the poetry of the prologue, that Labor was wedded to Merchandise, and Clergy to Nobility, and that the two happy couples possessed in common a magnificent golden dolphin, which they desired to adjudge to the fairest only. So they were roaming about the world seeking and searching for this beauty, and, after having successively rejected the Queen of Golconda, the Princess of Trebizonde, the daughter of the Grand Khan of Tartary, etc., Labor and Clergy, Nobility and Merchandise, had come to rest upon the marble table of the Palais de Justice, and to utter, in the presence of the honest audience, as many sentences and maxims as could then be dispensed at the Faculty of Arts, at examinations, sophisms, determinances, figures, and acts, where the masters took their degrees.

All this was, in fact, very fine.

Nevertheless, in that throng, upon which the four allegories vied with each other in pouring out floods of metaphors, there was no ear more attentive, no heart that palpitated more, not an eye was more haggard, no neck more outstretched, than the eye, the ear, the neck, and the heart of the author, of the poet, of that brave Pierre Gringoire, who had not been able to resist, a moment before, the joy of telling his name to two pretty girls. He had retreated a few paces from them, behind his pillar, and there he listened, looked, enjoyed. The amiable applause that had greeted the beginning of his prologue was still echoing in his bosom, and he was completely absorbed in that species of ecstatic contemplation with which an author beholds his ideas fall, one by one, from the mouth of the actor into the vast silence of the audience. Worthy Pierre Gringoire!

It pains us to say it, but this first ecstasy was speedily disturbed. Hardly had Gringoire raised this intoxicating cup of joy and triumph to his lips, when a drop of bitterness was mingled with it.

A tattered mendicant, who could not collect any coins, lost as he was in the midst of the crowd, and who had not probably found sufficient indemnity in the pockets of his neighbors, had hit upon the idea of perching himself upon some conspicuous point, in order to attract looks and alms. He had, accordingly, hoisted himself, during the first verses of the prologue, with the aid of the pillars of the reserve gallery, to the cornice which ran round the balustrade at its lower edge; and there he had seated himself, soliciting the attention and the pity of the multitude, with his rags and a hideous sore which covered his right arm. However, he uttered not a word.

The silence that he preserved allowed the prologue to proceed without hindrance, and no perceptible disorder would have ensued, if ill-luck had not willed that the scholar Joannes should catch sight, from the heights of his pillar, of the mendicant and his grimaces. A wild fit of laughter took possession of the young scamp, who, without caring that he was interrupting the spectacle, and disturbing the universal composure, shouted boldly, "Look! See that sickly creature asking alms!"

Any one who has thrown a stone into a frog pond, or fired a shot into a covey of birds, can form an idea of the effect produced by these incongruous words, in the midst of the general attention. It made Gringoire shudder as though it had been an electric shock. The prologue stopped short, and all heads turned tumultuously toward the beggar, who, far from being disconcerted by this, saw, in this incident, a good opportunity for reaping his harvest, and who began to whine in a doleful way, half closing his eyes the while, "Charity, please!"

"Well—upon my soul," resumed Joannes, "it's Clopin Trouillefou! Hallo my friend, did your sore bother you on the leg, that you have transferred it to your arm?" So saying, with the dexterity of a monkey, he flung a bit of silver into the gray felt hat that the beggar held in his ailing arm. The mendicant received both the alms and the sarcasm without wincing, and continued, in lamentable tones, "Charity, please!"

This episode considerably distracted the attention of the audience; and a goodly number of spectators, among them Robin Poussepain, and all the clerks at their head, gayly applauded this eccentric duet, which the scholar, with his shrill voice, and the mendicant had just improvised in the middle of the prologue.

Gringoire was highly displeased. On recovering from his first stupefaction, he bestirred himself to shout, to the four personages on the stage, "Go on! What the devil—go on!" without even deigning to cast a glance of disdain upon the two interrupters.

At that moment, he felt some one pluck at the hem of his surtout; he turned round, and not without ill-humor, and found considerable difficulty in smiling; but he was obliged to do so, nevertheless. It was the pretty arm of Gisquette la Gencienne, which, passed through the railing, was soliciting his attention in this manner.

"Monsieur," said the young girl, "are they going to continue?"

"Of course," replied Gringoire, a good deal shocked by the question.

"In that case, messire," she resumed, "would you have the courtesy to explain to me—"

"What they are about to say?" interrupted Gringoire. "Well, listen."

"No," said Gisquette, "but what they have said so far."

Gringoire started, like a man whose wound has been probed to the quick.

"A plague on the stupid and dull-witted little girl!" he muttered, between his teeth.

From that moment forth, Gisquette was nothing to him.

In the meantime, the actors had obeyed his injunction, and the public, seeing that they were beginning to speak again, began once more to listen, not without having lost many beauties in the sort of soldered joint which was formed between the two portions of the piece thus abruptly cut short. Gringoire commented on it bitterly to himself. Nevertheless, tranquillity was gradually restored, the scholar held his peace, the mendicant counted over some coins in his hat, and the piece resumed the upper hand.

It was, in fact, a very fine work, and one that, as it seems to us, might be put to use today, by the aid of a little rearrangement. The exposition, rather long and rather empty, that is to say, according to the rules, was simple; and Gringoire, in the candid sanctuary of his own conscience, admired its clearness. As the reader may surmise, the four allegorical personages were somewhat weary with having traversed the three sections of the world, without having found suitable opportunity for getting rid of their golden dolphin. Thereupon a eulogy of the marvellous fish, with a thousand delicate allusions to the young betrothed of Marguerite of Flanders, then sadly cloistered in at Amboise, and without a suspicion that Labor and Clergy, Nobility and Merchandise had just made the circuit of the world in his behalf. The said dauphin was then young, was handsome, was stout, and, above all (magnificent origin of all royal virtues), he was the son of the Lion of France. I declare that this bold metaphor is admirable, and that the natural history of the theatre, on a day of allegory and royal marriage songs, is not in the least startled by a dolphin who is the son of a lion. It is precisely these rare and Pindaric mixtures that prove the poet's enthusiasm. Nevertheless, in order to play the part of critic also, the poet might have developed this beautiful idea in something less than two hundred lines. It is true that the mystery was to last from noon until four o'clock, in accordance with the orders of monsieur the provost, and that it was necessary to say something. Besides, the people listened patiently.

All at once, in the very middle of a quarrel between Mademoiselle Merchandise and Madame Nobility, at the moment when Monsieur Labor was giving utterance to this wonderful line—

In forest ne'er was seen a more triumphant beast;

—the door of the reserved gallery which had hitherto remained so inopportunely closed, opened still more inopportunely; and the ringing voice of the usher announced abruptly, "His eminence, Monseigneur the Cardinal de Bourbon."

Chapter 3

Monsieur the Cardinal

Poor Gringoire! The din of all the great double petards of the Saint-Jean, the discharge of twenty arquebuses on supports, the detonation of that famous serpentine of the Tower of Billy, which, during the siege of Paris, on Sunday, the twenty-sixth of September, 1465, killed seven Burgundians at one blow, the explosion of all the powder stored at the gate of the Temple, would have rent his ears less rudely at that solemn and dramatic moment, than these few words, which fell from the lips of the usher, "His eminence, Monseigneur the Cardinal de Bourbon."

It is not that Pierre Gringoire either feared or disdained monsieur the cardinal. He had neither the weakness nor the audacity for that. A true eclectic, as it would be expressed nowadays, Gringoire was one of those firm and lofty, moderate and calm spirits, which always know how to bear themselves amid all circumstances (*stare in dimidio rerum*), and who are full of reason and of liberal philosophy, while still setting store by cardinals. A rare, precious, and never interrupted race of philosophers to whom wisdom, like another Ariadne, seems to have given a clew of thread which they have been walking along unwinding since the beginning of the world, through the labyrinth of human affairs. One finds them in all ages, ever the same; that is to say, always according to all times. And, without reckoning our Pierre Gringoire, who may represent them in the fifteenth century if we succeed in bestowing upon him the distinction which he deserves, it certainly was their spirit which animated Father du Breul, when he wrote, in the sixteenth, these naively sublime words, worthy of all centuries: "I am a Parisian by nation, and a Parrhisian in language, for *parrhisia* in Greek signifies liberty of speech; of which I have made use even toward messeigneurs the cardinals, uncle and brother to Monsieur the Prince de Conty, always with respect to their greatness, and without offending any one of their suite, which is much to say."

There was then neither hatred for the cardinal, nor disdain for his presence, in the disagreeable impression produced upon Pierre Gringoire. Quite the contrary; our poet had too much good sense and too threadbare a coat, not to attach particular importance to having the numerous allusions in his prologue, and, in particular, the glorification of the dauphin, son of the Lion of France, fall upon the most eminent ear. But it is not interest that predominates in the noble nature of poets. I suppose that the entity of the poet may be represented by the number ten; it is certain that a chemist on analyzing and pharmacopolizing it, as Rabelais says, would find it composed of one part interest to nine parts of self-esteem.

Now, at the moment when the door had opened to admit the cardinal, the nine parts of self-esteem in Gringoire, swollen and expanded by the breath of popular admiration, were in a state of prodigious augmentation, beneath which disappeared, as though stifled, that imperceptible molecule of which we have just remarked upon in the constitution of poets; a precious ingredient, by the way, a ballast of reality and humanity, without which they would not touch the earth. Gringoire enjoyed seeing, feeling, fingering, so to speak an entire assembly (of knaves, it is true, but what matters that?) stupefied, petrified, and as though asphyxiated in the presence of the incommensurable tirades which welled up every instant from all parts of his bridal song. I affirm that he shared the general beatitude, and that, quite the reverse of La Fontaine, who, at the presentation of his comedy of the "Florentine," asked, "Who is the ill-bred lout who made that rhapsody?" Gringoire would gladly have inquired of his neighbor, "Whose masterpiece is this?"

The reader can now judge of the effect produced upon him by the abrupt and unseasonable arrival of the cardinal.

That which he had to fear was only too fully realized. The entrance of his eminence upset the audience. All heads turned toward the gallery. It was no longer possible to hear one's self. "The cardinal! The cardinal!" repeated all mouths. The unhappy prologue stopped short for the second time.

The cardinal halted for a moment on the threshold of the estrade. While he was sending a rather indifferent glance around the audience, the tumult redoubled. Each person wished to get a better view of him. Each man vied with the other in thrusting his head over his neighbor's shoulder.

He was, in fact, an exalted personage, the sight of whom was well worth any other comedy. Charles, Cardinal de Bourbon, Archbishop and Comte of Lyon, Primate of the Gauls, was allied both to Louis XI, through his brother, Pierre, Seigneur de Beaujeu, who had married the king's eldest daughter, and to Charles the Bold through his mother, Agnes of Burgundy. Now, the dominating trait, the peculiar and distinctive trait of the character of the Primate of the Gauls, was the spirit of the courtier, and devotion to the powers that be. The reader can form an idea of the numberless embarrassments which this double relationship had caused him, and of all the temporal reefs among which his spiritual bark had been forced to tack, in order not to suffer shipwreck on either Louis or Charles, that Scylla and that Charybdis which had devoured the Duc de Nemours and the Constable de Saint-Pol. Thanks to Heaven's mercy, he had made the voyage successfully, and had reached home without hindrance. But although he was in port, and precisely because he was in port, he never recalled without disquiet the varied haps of his political career, so long uneasy and laborious. Thus, he was in the habit of saying that the year 1476 had been "white and black" for him—meaning thereby, that in the course of that year he had lost his mother, the Duchesse de la Bourbonnais, and his cousin, the Duke of Burgundy, and that one grief had consoled him for the other.

Nevertheless, he was a fine man; he led a joyous cardinal's life, liked to enliven himself with the royal vintage of Challuau, did not hate Richarde la Garmoise and Thomasse la Saillarde, bestowed alms on pretty girls rather than on old women, and for all these reasons was very agreeable to the populace of Paris. He never went about otherwise than surrounded by a small court of bishops and abbés of high lineage, gallant, jovial, and given to carousing on occasion; and more than once the good and devout women of Saint Germain d' Auxerre, when passing at night beneath the brightly illuminated windows of Bourbon, had been scandalized to hear the same voices which had intoned vespers for them during the day carolling, to the clinking of glasses, the bacchic proverb of Benedict XII, that pope who had added a third crown to the Tiara—*Bibamus papaliter.*

It was this justly acquired popularity, no doubt, which preserved him on his entrance from any bad reception at the hands of the mob, which had been so displeased but a moment before, and very little disposed to respect a cardinal on the very day when it was to elect a pope. But the Parisians cherish little rancor; and then, having forced the beginning of the play by their authority, the good bourgeois had got the upper hand of the cardinal, and this triumph was sufficient for them. Moreover, the Cardinal de Bourbon was a handsome man—he wore a fine scarlet robe, which he carried off very well—that is to say, he had all the women on his side, and, consequently, the best half of the audience. Assuredly, it would be injustice and bad taste to hoot a cardinal for having come late to the spectacle, when he is a handsome man, and when he wears his scarlet robe well.

He entered, then, bowed to those present with the hereditary smile of the great for the people, and directed his course slowly toward his scarlet velvet armchair, with the air of thinking of something quite different. His cortege—what we should nowadays call his staff—of bishops and abbés invaded the estrade in his train, not without causing redoubled tumult and curiosity among the audience. Each man vied with his neighbor in pointing them out and naming them, in seeing who should recognize at least one of them: this one, the Bishop of Marseilles (Alaudet, if my memory serves me right); this one, the primicier of Saint-Denis; this one, Robert de Lespinasse, Abbé of Saint-Germain des Prés, that libertine brother of a mistress of Louis XI; all with many errors and absurdities. As for the scholars, they swore. This was their day, their feast of fools, their saturnalia, the annual orgy of the corporation of Law clerks and of the school. There was no turpitude that was not sacred on that day. And then there were gay gossips in the crowd—Simone Quatrelivres, Agnes la Gadine, and Rabine Piédebou. Was it not the least that one could do to swear at one's ease and revile the name of God a little, on so fine a day, in such good company as dignitaries of the church and loose women? So they did not abstain; and, in the midst of the uproar, there was a frightful concert of blasphemies and enormities of all the unbridled tongues, the tongues of clerks and students restrained during the rest of the year, by the fear of the hot iron of Saint Louis. Poor Saint Louis! How they set him at defiance in his own court of law! Each one of them selected from the newcomers on the platform, a black, gray, white, or violet cassock as his target. Joannes Frollo de Molendin, in his quality of brother to an archdeacon, boldly attacked the scarlet; he sang in deafening tones, with his impudent eyes fastened on the cardinal, "*Cappa repleta mero!*"

All these details that we here lay bare for the edification of the reader, were so covered by the general uproar, that they were lost in it before reaching the reserved platforms; moreover, they would have moved the cardinal but little, so much a part of the customs were the liberties of that day. Moreover, he had another cause for solicitude, and his mien as wholly preoccupied with it, which entered the estrade the same time as himself; this was the embassy from Flanders.

Not that he was a profound politician, nor was he borrowing trouble about the possible consequences of the marriage of his cousin Marguerite de Bourgoyne to his cousin Charles, Dauphin de Vienne; nor as to how long the good understanding which had been patched up between the Duke of Austria and the King of France would last; nor how the King of England would take this disdain of his daughter. All that troubled him but little; and he gave a warm reception every evening to the wine of the royal vintage of Chaillot, without a suspicion that several flasks of that same wine (somewhat revised and corrected, it is true, by Doctor Coictier), cordially offered to Edward IV by Louis XI, would, some fine morning, rid Louis XI of Edward IV. "The much honored embassy of Monsieur the Duke of Austria," brought the cardinal none of these cares, but it troubled him in another direction. It was, in fact, somewhat hard, and we have already hinted at it on the second page of this book—for him, Charles de Bourbon, to be obliged to feast and receive cordially no one knows what bourgeois—for him, a cardinal, to receive aldermen—for him, a Frenchman, and a jolly companion, to receive Flemish beer-drinkers—and that in public! This was, certainly, one of the most irksome parts that he had ever executed for the good pleasure of the king.

So he turned toward the door, with the best grace in the world (so well had he trained himself to it), when the usher announced, in a sonorous voice, "Messieurs the Envoys of Monsieur the Duke of Austria." It is useless to add that the whole hall did the same.

Then arrived, two by two, with a gravity which made a contrast in the midst of the frisky ecclesiastical escort of Charles de Bourbon, the eight and forty ambassadors of Maximilian of Austria, having at their head the reverend Father in God, Jehan, Abbot of Saint-Bertin, Chancellor of the Golden Fleece, and Jacques de Goy, Sieur Dauby, Grand Bailiff of Ghent. A deep silence settled over the assembly, accompanied by stifled laughter at the preposterous names and all the bourgeois designations which each of these personages transmitted with imperturbable gravity to the usher, who then tossed names and titles pell-mell and mutilated to the crowd below. There were Master Loys Roelof, alderman of the city of Louvain; Messire Clays d'Etuelde, alderman of Brussels; Messire Paul de Baeust, Sieur de Voirmizelle, President of Flanders; Master Jehan Coleghens, burgomaster of the city of Antwerp; Master George de la Moere, first alderman of the kuere of the city of Ghent; Master Gheldolf van der Hage, first alderman of the *parchous* of the said town; and the Sieur de Bierbecque, and Jehan Pinnock, and Jehan Dymaerzelle, etc., etc., etc.; bailiffs, aldermen, burgomasters; burgomasters, aldermen, bailiffs—all stiff, affectedly grave, formal, dressed out in velvet and damask, hooded with caps of black velvet, with great tufts of Cyprus gold thread; good Flemish heads, after all, severe and worthy faces, of the family which Rembrandt makes to stand out so strong and grave from the black background of his "Night Patrol"; personages all of whom bore, written on their brows, that Maximilian of Austria had done well in "trusting implicitly," as the manifest ran, "in their sense, valor, experience, loyalty, and good wisdom."

There was one exception, however. It was a subtle, intelligent, crafty-looking face, a sort of combined monkey and diplomat phiz, before whom the cardinal made three steps and a profound bow, and whose name, nevertheless, was only, "Guillaume Rym, counsellor and pensioner of the City of Ghent."

Few persons were then aware who Guillaume Rym was. A rare genius who in a time of revolution would have made a brilliant appearance on the surface of events, but who in the fifteenth century was reduced to cavernous intrigues, and to "living in mines," as the Duc de Saint-Simon expresses it. Nevertheless, he was appreciated by the "miner" of Europe; he plotted familiarly with Louis XI, and often lent a hand to the king's secret jobs. All which things were quite unknown to that throng, who were amazed at the cardinal's politeness to that frail figure of a Flemish bailiff.

CHAPTER 4

Master Jacques Coppenole

WHILE THE PENSIONER of Ghent and his eminence were exchanging very low bows and a few words in voices still lower, a man of lofty stature, with a large face and broad shoulders, presented himself, in order to enter abreast with Guillaume Rym; one would have pronounced him a bull-dog by the side of a fox. His felt doublet and leather jerkin made a spot on the velvet and silk that surrounded him. Presuming that he was some groom who had stolen in, the usher stopped him.

"Hold, my friend, you cannot pass!"

The man in the leather jerkin shouldered him aside.

"What does this knave want with me?" said he, in stentorian tones, which rendered the entire hall attentive to this strange colloquy. "Don't you see that I am one of them?"

"Your name?" demanded the usher.

"Jacques Coppenole."

"Your titles?"

"Hosier at the sign of the Three Little Chains, of Ghent."

The usher recoiled. One might bring one's self to announce aldermen and burgomasters, but a hosier was too much. The cardinal was on thorns. All the people were staring and listening. For two days his eminence had been exerting his utmost efforts to lick these Flemish bears into shape, and to render them a little more presentable to the public, and this freak was startling. But Guillaume Rym, with his polished smile, approached the usher.

"Announce Master Jacques Coppenole, clerk of the aldermen of the city of Ghent," he whispered, very low.

"Usher," interposed the cardinal, aloud, "announce Master Jacques Coppenole, clerk of the aldermen of the illustrious city of Ghent."

This was a mistake. Guillaume Rym alone might have conjured away the difficulty, but Coppenole had heard the cardinal.

"No, cross of God?" he exclaimed, in his voice of thunder, "Jacques Coppenole, hosier. Do you hear, usher? Nothing more, nothing less. Cross of God! Hosier; that's fine enough. Monsieur the Archduke has more than once sought his *gant* in my hose." [Wordplay upon *gant*, glove, pronounced just like *Ghent*, the town in Flanders.]

Laughter and applause burst forth. A jest is always understood in Paris, and, consequently, always applauded.

Let us add that Coppenole was of the people, and that the auditors that surrounded him were also of the people. Thus the communication between him and them had been prompt, electric, and, so to speak, on a level. The haughty air of the Flemish hosier, by humiliating the courtiers, had touched in all these plebeian souls that latent sentiment of dignity still vague and indistinct in the fifteenth century.

This hosier was an equal, who had just held his own before monsieur the cardinal. A very sweet reflection to poor fellows habituated to respect and obedience toward the underlings of the sergeants of the bailiff of Sainte-Geneviève, the cardinal's train-bearer.

Coppenole proudly saluted his eminence, who returned the salute of the all-powerful bourgeois feared by Louis XI. Then, while Guillaume Rym, a "sage and malicious man," as Philippe de Comines puts it, watched them both with a smile of raillery and superiority, each sought his place, the cardinal quite abashed and troubled, Coppenole tranquil and haughty, and thinking, no doubt, that his title of hosier was as good as any other, after all, and that Marie of Burgundy, mother to that Marguerite whom Coppenole was today bestowing in marriage, would have been less afraid of the cardinal than of the hosier; for it is not a cardinal who would have stirred up a revolt among the men of Ghent against the favorites of the daughter of Charles the Bold; it is not a cardinal who could have fortified the populace with a word against her tears and prayers, when the Maid of Flanders came to supplicate her people in their behalf, even at the very foot of the scaffold; while the hosier had only to raise his leather elbow, in order to cause to fall your two heads, most illustrious seigneurs, Guy d'Hymbercourt and Chancellor Guillaume Hugonet.

Nevertheless, all was over for the poor cardinal, and he was obliged to quaff to the dregs the bitter cup of being in such bad company.

The reader has, probably, not forgotten the impudent beggar who had been clinging fast to the fringes of the cardinal's gallery ever since the beginning of the prologue. The arrival of the illustrious guests had by no means caused him to relax his hold, and, while the prelates and ambassadors were packing themselves into the stalls—like genuine Flemish herrings—he settled himself at his ease, and boldly crossed his legs on the architrave. The insolence of this proceeding was extraordinary, yet no one noticed it at first, the attention of all being directed elsewhere. He, on his side, perceived nothing that was going on in the hall; he wagged his head with the unconcern of a Neapolitan, repeating from time to time, amid the clamor, as from a mechanical habit, "Charity, please!" And, assuredly, he was, out of all those present, the only one who had not deigned to turn his head at the altercation between Coppenole and the usher. Now, chance ordained that the master hosier of Ghent, with whom the people were already in lively sympathy, and upon whom all eyes were riveted—should come and seat himself in the front row of the gallery, directly above the mendicant; and people were not a little amazed to see the Flemish ambassador, on concluding his inspection of the knave thus placed beneath his eyes, bestow a friendly tap on that ragged shoulder. The beggar turned round; there was surprise, recognition, a lighting up of the two countenances, and so forth; then, without paying the slightest heed in the world to the spectators, the hosier and the wretched being began to converse in a low tone, holding each other's hands, in the meantime, while the rags of Clopin Trouillefou, spread out upon the cloth of gold of the dais, produced the effect of a caterpillar on an orange.

The novelty of this singular scene excited such a murmur of mirth and gayety in the hall, that the cardinal was not slow to perceive it; he half bent forward, and, as from the point where he was placed he could catch only an imperfect view of Trouillefou's ignominious doublet, he very naturally imagined that the mendicant was asking alms, and, disgusted with his audacity, he exclaimed: "Bailiff of the Courts, toss me that knave into the river!"

"Cross of God! Monseigneur the cardinal," said Coppenole, without quitting Clopin's hand, "he's a friend of mine."

"Good! Good!" shouted the populace. From that moment, Master Coppenole enjoyed in Paris as in Ghent, "Great favor with the people; for men of that sort do enjoy it," says Philippe de Comines, "when they are thus disorderly." The cardinal bit his lips. He bent toward his neighbor, the Abbé of Saint Geneviéve, and said to him in a low tone, "Fine ambassadors monsieur the archduke sends here, to announce to us Madame Marguerite!"

"Your eminence," replied the abbé, "wastes your politeness on these Flemish swine. *Margaritas ante porcos*, pearls before swine."

"Say rather," retorted the cardinal, with a smile, "*Porcos ante Margaritam*, swine before the pearl."

The whole little court in cassocks went into ecstacies over this play upon words. The cardinal felt a little relieved; he was quits with Coppenole, he also had had his jest applauded.

Now, will those of our readers who possess the power of generalizing an image or an idea, as the expression runs in the style of today, permit us to ask them if they have formed a very clear conception of the spectacle presented at this moment, upon which we have arrested their attention, by the vast parallelogram of the grand hall of the palace.

In the middle of the hall, backed against the western wall, a large and magnificent gallery draped with cloth of gold, into which enter in procession, through a small, arched door, grave personages, announced successively by the shrill voice of an usher. On the front benches were already a number of venerable figures, muffled in ermine, velvet, and scarlet. Around the dais—which remains silent and dignified—below, opposite, everywhere, a great crowd and a great murmur. Thousands of glances directed by the people on each face upon the dais, a thousand whispers over each name. Certainly, the spectacle is curious, and well deserves the attention of the spectators. But yonder, quite at the end, what is that sort of trestle work with four motley puppets upon it, and more below? Who is that man beside the trestle, with a black doublet and a pale face? Alas, my dear reader, it is Pierre Gringoire and his prologue.

We have all forgotten him completely.

This is precisely what he feared.

From the moment of the cardinal's entrance, Gringoire had never ceased to tremble for the safety of his prologue. At first he had enjoined the actors, who had stopped in suspense, to continue, and to raise their voices; then, perceiving that no one was listening, he had stopped them; and, during the entire quarter of an hour that the interruption lasted, he had not ceased to stamp, to flounce about, to appeal to Gisquette and Liénarde, and to urge his neighbors to the continuance of the prologue; all in vain. No one quitted the cardinal, the embassy, and the gallery—sole centre of this vast circle of visual rays. We must also believe, and we say it with regret, that the prologue had begun slightly to weary the audience at the moment when his eminence had arrived, and created a diversion in so terrible a fashion. After all, on the gallery as well as on the marble table, the spectacle was the same: the conflict of Labor and Clergy, of Nobility and Merchandise. And many people preferred to see them alive, breathing, moving, elbowing each other in flesh and blood, in this Flemish embassy, in this Episcopal court, under the cardinal's robe, under Coppenole's jerkin, than painted, decked out, talking in verse, and, so to speak, stuffed beneath the yellow amid white tunics in which Gringoire had so ridiculously clothed them.

Nevertheless, when our poet beheld quiet reestablished to some extent, he devised a stratagem that might have redeemed all.

"Monsieur," he said, turning toward one of his neighbors, a fine, big man, with a patient face, "suppose we begin again."

"What?" said his neighbor.

"The Mystery!" said Gringoire.

"As you like," returned his neighbor.

This semi-approbation sufficed for Gringoire, and, conducting his own affairs, he began to shout, confounding himself with the crowd as much as possible: "Begin the mystery again! Begin again!"

"The devil!" said Joannes de Molendino, "what are they jabbering down yonder, at the end of the hall?" (for Gringoire was making noise enough for four). "Say, comrades, isn't that mystery finished? They want to begin it all over again. That's not fair!"

"No, no!" shouted all the scholars. "Down with the mystery! Down with it!"

But Gringoire had multiplied himself, and only shouted the more vigorously: "Begin again! Begin again!"

These clamors attracted the attention of the cardinal.

"Monsieur Bailiff of the Courts," said he to a tall, black man, placed a few paces from him, "are those knaves in a holy-water vessel, that they make such a hellish noise?"

The bailiff of the courts was a sort of amphibious magistrate, a sort of bat of the judicial order, related to both the rat and the bird, the judge and the soldier.

He approached his eminence, and not without a good deal of fear of the latter's displeasure, he awkwardly explained to him the seeming disrespect of the audience: that noonday had arrived before his eminence, and that the comedians had been forced to begin without waiting for his eminence.

The cardinal burst into a laugh.

"On my faith, the rector of the university ought to have done the same. What say you, Master Guillaume Rym?"

"Monseigneur," replied Guillaume Rym, "let us be content with having escaped half of the comedy. There is at least that much gained."

"Can these rascals continue their farce?" asked the bailiff.

"Continue, continue," said the cardinal, "it's all the same to me. I'll read my breviary in the meantime."

The bailiff advanced to the edge of the estrade, and cried, after having invoked silence by a wave of the hand, "Bourgeois, rustics, and citizens, in order to satisfy those who wish the play to begin again, and those who wish it to end, his eminence orders that it be continued."

Both parties were forced to resign themselves. But the public and the author long cherished a grudge against the cardinal.

So the personages on the stage took up their parts, and Gringoire hoped that the rest of his work, at least, would be listened to. This hope was speedily dispelled like his other illusions; silence had indeed, been restored in the audience, after a fashion; but Gringoire had not observed that at the moment when the cardinal gave the order to continue, the gallery was far from full, and that after the Flemish envoys there had arrived new personages forming part of the cortege, whose names and ranks, shouted out in the midst of his dialogue by the intermittent cry of the usher, produced considerable ravages in it. Let the reader imagine the effect in the midst of a theatrical piece, of the yelping of an usher, flinging in between two rhymes, and often in the middle of a line, parentheses like the following, "Master Jacques Charmolue, procurator to the king in the Ecclesiastical Courts!"

"Jehan de Harlay, equerry guardian of the office of chevalier of the night watch of the city of Paris!"

"Messire Galiot de Genoilhac, chevalier, seigneur de Brussac, master of the king's artillery!"

"Master Dreux-Raguier, surveyor of the woods and forests of the king our sovereign, in the land of France, Champagne and Brie!"

"Messire Louis de Graville, chevalier, councillor, and chamberlain of the king, admiral of France, keeper of the Forest of Vincennes!"

"Master Denis le Mercier, guardian of the house of the blind at Paris!" etc., etc., etc.

This was becoming unbearable.

This strange accompaniment, which rendered it difficult to follow the piece, made Gringoire all the more indignant because he could not conceal from himself the fact that the interest was continually increasing, and that all his work required was a chance of being heard.

It was, in fact, difficult to imagine a more ingenious and more dramatic composition. The four personages of the prologue were bewailing themselves in their mortal embarrassment, when Venus in person (*vera incessa patuit dea*) presented herself to them, clad in a fine robe bearing the heraldic device of the ship of the city of Paris. She had come herself to claim the dolphin promised to the most beautiful. Jupiter, whose thunder could be heard rumbling in the dressing-room, supported her claim, and Venus was on the point of carrying it off,—that is to say, without allegory, of marrying monsieur the dauphin, when a young child clad in white damask, and holding in her hand a daisy (a transparent personification of Mademoiselle Marguerite of Flanders) came to contest it with Venus.

Theatrical effect and change.

After a dispute, Venus, Marguerite, and the assistants agreed to submit to the good judgment of the holy Virgin. There was another good part, that of the king of Mesopotamia; but through so many interruptions, it was difficult to make out what end he served. All these persons had ascended by the ladder to the stage.

But all was over; none of these beauties had been felt nor understood. On the entrance of the cardinal, one would have said that an invisible magic thread had suddenly drawn all glances from the marble table to the gallery, from the southern to the western extremity of the hall. Nothing could disenchant the audience; all eyes remained fixed there, and the newcomers and their accursed names, and their faces, and their costumes, afforded a continual diversion. This was very distressing. With the exception of Gisquette and Liénarde, who turned round from time to time when Gringoire plucked them by the sleeve; with the exception of the big, patient neighbor, no one listened, no one looked at the poor, deserted morality full face. Gringoire saw only profiles.

With what bitterness did he behold his whole erection of glory and of poetry crumble away bit by bit! And to think that these people had been upon the point of instituting a revolt against the bailiff through impatience to hear his work; now that they had it they did not care for it! This same representation that had been begun amid so unanimous an acclamation! Eternal flood and ebb of popular favor! To think that they had been on the point of hanging the bailiff's sergeant! What would he not have given to be still at that hour of honey!

But the usher's brutal monologue came to an end; every one had arrived, and Gringoire breathed freely once more; the actors continued bravely. But Master Coppenole, the hosier, must needs rise of a sudden, and Gringoire was forced to listen to him deliver, amid universal attention, the following abominable harangue.

"Messieurs the bourgeois and squires of Paris, I don't know, cross of God, what we are doing here! I certainly do see yonder in the corner on that stage, some people who appear to be fighting. I don't know whether that is what you call a "mystery," but it is not amusing; they quarrel with their tongues and nothing more. I have been waiting for the first blow this quarter of an hour; nothing comes; they are cowards who only scratch each other with insults. You ought to send for the fighters of London or Rotterdam; and, I can tell you! You would have had blows of the fist that could be heard in the Place; but these men excite our pity. They ought at least, to give us a moorish dance, or some other mummer! That is not what was told me; I was promised a feast of fools, with the election of a pope. We have our pope of fools at Ghent also; we're not behindhand in that, cross of God! But this is the way we manage it; we collect a crowd like this one here, then each person in turn passes his head through a hole, and makes a grimace at the rest; the one who makes the ugliest, is elected pope by general acclamation; that's the way it is. It is very diverting. Would you like to make your pope after the fashion of my country? At all events, it will be less wearisome than to listen to chatterers. If they wish to come and make their grimaces through the hole, they can join the game. What say you, Messieurs les bourgeois? You have here enough grotesque specimens of both sexes, to allow of laughing in Flemish fashion, and there are enough of us ugly in countenance to hope for a fine grinning match."

Gringoire would have liked to retort; stupefaction, rage, indignation, deprived him of words. Moreover, the suggestion of the popular hosier was received with such enthusiasm by these bourgeois who were flattered at being called "squires," that all resistance was useless. There was nothing to be done but to allow one's self to drift with the torrent. Gringoire hid his face between his two hands, not being so fortunate as to have a mantle with which to veil his head, like Agamemnon of Timantis.

CHAPTER 5

Quasimodo

IN THE TWINKLING of an eye, all was ready to execute Coppenole's idea. Bourgeois, scholars and law clerks all set to work. The little chapel situated opposite the marble table was selected for the scene of the grinning match. A pane broken in the pretty rose window above the door, left free a circle of stone through which it was agreed that the competitors should thrust their heads. In order to reach it, it was only necessary to mount upon a couple of hogsheads, which had been produced from I know not where, and perched one upon the other, after a fashion. It was settled that each candidate, man or woman (for it was possible to choose a female pope), should, for the sake of leaving the impression of his grimace fresh and complete, cover his face and remain concealed in the chapel until the moment of his appearance. In less than an instant, the chapel was crowded with competitors, upon whom the door was then closed.

Coppenole, from his post, ordered all, directed all, arranged all. During the uproar, the cardinal, no less abashed than Gringoire, had retired with all his suite, under the pretext of business and vespers, without the crowd which his arrival had so deeply stirred being in the least moved by his departure. Guillaume Rym was the only one who noticed his eminence's discomfiture. The attention of the populace, like the sun, pursued its revolution; having set out from one end of the hall, and halted for a space in the middle, it had now reached the other end. The marble table, the brocaded gallery had each had their day; it was now the turn of the chapel of Louis XI. Henceforth, the field was open to all folly. There was no one there now, but the Flemings and the rabble.

The grimaces began. The first face that appeared at the aperture, with eyelids turned up to the reds, a mouth open like a maw, and a brow wrinkled like our hussar boots of the Empire, evoked such an inextinguishable peal of laughter that Homer would have taken all these louts for gods. Nevertheless, the grand hall was anything but Olympus, and Gringoire's poor Jupiter knew it better than any one else. A second and third grimace followed, then another and another; and the laughter and transports of delight went on increasing. There was in this spectacle, a peculiar power of intoxication and fascination, of which it would be difficult to convey to the reader of our day and our salons any idea.

Let the reader picture to himself a series of visages presenting successively all geometrical forms, from the triangle to the trapezium, from the cone to the polyhedron; all human expressions, from wrath to lewdness; all ages, from the wrinkles of the new-born babe to the wrinkles of the aged and dying; all religious phantasmagories, from Faun to Beelzebub; all animal profiles, from the maw to the beak, from the jowl to the muzzle. Let the reader imagine all these grotesque figures of the Pont Neuf, those nightmares petrified beneath the hand of Germain Pilon, assuming life and breath, and coming in turn to stare you in the face with burning eyes; all the masks of the Carnival of Venice passing in succession before your glass—in a word, a human kaleidoscope.

The orgy grew more and more Flemish. Teniers could have given but a very imperfect idea of it. Let the reader picture to himself in bacchanal form, Salvator Rosa's battle. There were no longer either scholars or ambassadors or bourgeois or men or women; there was no longer any Clopin Trouillefou, nor Gilles Lecornu, nor Marie Quatrelivres, nor Robin Poussepain. All was universal license. The grand hall was no longer anything but a vast furnace of effrontry and joviality, where every mouth was a cry, every individual a posture; everything shouted and howled. The strange visages that came, in turn, to gnash their teeth in the rose window, were like so many brands cast into the brazier; and from the whole of this effervescing crowd, there escaped, as from a furnace, a sharp, piercing, stinging noise, hissing like the wings of a gnat.

"Oh, curse it!"

"Just look at that face!"

"It's not good for anything."

"Guillemette Maugerepuis, just look at that bull's muzzle; it only lacks the horns. It can't be your husband."

"Another!"

"Belly of the pope! What sort of a grimace is that?"

"Hey! That's cheating. One must show only one's face."

"That damned Perrette Callebotte! She's capable of that!"

"Good! Good!"

"I'm stifling!"

"There's a fellow whose ears won't go through!" Etc., etc.

But we must do justice to our friend Jehan. In the midst of this witches' sabbath, he was still to be seen on the top of his pillar, like the cabin-boy on the topmast. He floundered about with incredible fury. His mouth was wide open, and from it there escaped a cry which no one heard, not that it was covered by the general clamor, great as that was but because it attained, no doubt, the limit of perceptible sharp sounds, the thousand vibrations of Sauveur, or the eight thousand of Biot.

As for Gringoire, the first moment of depression having passed, he had regained his composure. He had hardened himself against adversity. "Continue!" he had said for the third time, to his comedians, speaking machines; then as he was marching with great strides in front of the marble table, a fancy seized him to go and appear in his turn at the aperture of the chapel, were it only for the pleasure of making a grimace at that ungrateful populace. "But no, that would not be worthy of us; no, vengeance! Let us combat until the end," he repeated to himself; "the power of poetry over people is great; I will bring them back. We shall see which will carry the day, grimaces or polite literature."

Alas, he had been left the sole spectator of his piece! It was far worse than it had been a little while before. He no longer beheld anything but backs.

I am mistaken. The big, patient man, whom he had already consulted in a critical moment, had remained with his face turned toward the stage. As for Gisquette and Liénarde, they had deserted him long ago.

Gringoire was touched to the heart by the fidelity of his only spectator. He approached him and addressed him, shaking his arm slightly; for the good man was leaning on the balustrade and dozing a little.

"Monsieur," said Gringoire, "I thank you!"

"Monsieur," replied the big man with a yawn, "for what?"

"I see what wearies you," resumed the poet; "'tis all this noise which prevents your hearing comfortably. But be at ease! Your name shall descend to posterity! Your name, if you please?"

"Renauld Chateau, guardian of the seals of the Châtelet of Paris, at your service."

"Monsieur, you are the only representative of the muses here," said Gringoire.

"You are too kind, sir," said the guardian of the seals at the Châtelet.

"You are the only one," resumed Gringoire, "who has listened to the piece decorously. What do you think of it?"

"He, he!" replied the fat magistrate, half aroused, "it's tolerably jolly, that's a fact."

Gringoire was forced to content himself with this eulogy; for a thunder of applause, mingled with a prodigious acclamation, cut their conversation short. The Pope of the Fools had been elected.

"Noël! Noël! Noël!" shouted the people on all sides. That was, in fact, a marvellous grimace which was beaming at that moment through the aperture in the rose window. After all the pentagonal, hexagonal, and whimsical faces, which had succeeded each other at that hole without realizing the ideal of the grotesque which their imaginations, excited by the orgy, had constructed, nothing less was needed to win their suffrages than the sublime grimace which had just dazzled the assembly. Master Coppenole himself applauded, and Clopin Trouillefou, who had been among the competitors (and God knows what intensity of ugliness his visage could attain), confessed himself conquered: We will do the same. We shall not try to give the reader an idea of that tetrahedral nose, that horseshoe mouth; that little left eye obstructed with a red, bushy, bristling eyebrow, while the right eye disappeared entirely beneath an enormous wart; of those teeth in disarray, broken here and there, like the embattled parapet of a fortress; of that callous lip, upon which one of these teeth encroached, like the tusk of an elephant; of that forked chin; and above all, of the expression spread over the whole; of that mixture of malice, amazement, and sadness. Let the reader dream of this whole, if he can.

The acclamation was unanimous; people rushed toward the chapel. They made the lucky Pope of the Fools come forth in triumph. But it was then that surprise and admiration attained their highest pitch; the grimace was his face.

Or rather, his whole person was a grimace. A huge head, bristling with red hair; between his shoulders an enormous hump, a counterpart perceptible in front; a system of thighs and legs so strangely astray that they could touch each other only at the knees, and, viewed from the front, resembled the crescents of two scythes joined by the handles; large feet, monstrous hands; and, with all this deformity, an indescribable and redoubtable air of vigor, agility, and courage, strange exception to the eternal rule which wills that force as well as beauty shall be the result of harmony. Such was the pope whom the fools had just chosen for themselves.

One would have pronounced him a giant who had been broken and badly put together again.

When this species of cyclops appeared on the threshold of the chapel, motionless, squat, and almost as broad as he was tall; squared on the base, as a great man says; with his doublet half red, half violet, sown with silver bells, and, above all, in the perfection of his ugliness, the populace recognized him on the instant, and shouted with one voice, "'Tis Quasimodo, the bellringer! 'Tis Quasimodo, the hunchback of Notre-Dame! Quasimodo, the one-eyed! Quasimodo, the bandy-legged! Noel! Noel!"

It will be seen that the poor fellow had a choice of surnames.

"Let the women with child beware!" shouted the scholars.

"Or those who wish to be," resumed Joannes.

The women did, in fact, hide their faces.

"Oh, the horrible monkey!" said one of them.

"As wicked as he is ugly," retorted another.

"He's the devil," added a third.

"I have the misfortune to live near Notre-Dame; I hear him prowling round the eaves by night."

"With the cats."

"He's always on our roofs."

"He throws spells down our chimneys."

"The other evening, he came and made a grimace at me through my attic window. I thought that it was a man. Such a fright as I had!"

"I'm sure that he goes to the witches' sabbath. Once he left a broom on my leads."

"Oh, what a displeasing hunchback's face!"

"Oh, what an ill-favored soul!"

"Whew!"

The men, on the contrary, were delighted and applauded. Quasimodo, the object of the tumult, still stood on the threshold of the chapel, sombre and grave, and allowed them to admire him.

One scholar (Robin Poussepain, I think), came and laughed in his face, and too close. Quasimodo contented himself with taking him by the girdle, and hurling him ten paces off amid the crowd; all without uttering a word.

Master Coppenole, in amazement, approached him.

"Cross of God! Holy Father! You possess the handsomest ugliness that I have ever beheld in my life. You would deserve to be pope at Rome, as well as at Paris."

So saying, he placed his hand gayly on his shoulder. Quasimodo did not stir. Coppenole went on, "You are a rogue with whom I have a fancy for carousing, were it to cost me a new dozen of twelve livres of Tours. How does it strike you?"

Quasimodo made no reply.

"Cross of God!" said the hosier, "are you deaf?"

He was, in truth, deaf.

Nevertheless, he began to grow impatient with Coppenole's behavior, and suddenly turned toward him with so formidable a gnashing of teeth, that the Flemish giant recoiled, like a bull-dog before a cat.

Then there was created around that strange personage, a circle of terror and respect, whose radius was at least fifteen geometrical feet. An old woman explained to Coppenole that Quasimodo was deaf.

"Deaf!" said the hosier, with his great Flemish laugh. "Cross of God! He's a perfect pope!"

"He! I recognize him," exclaimed Jehan, who had, at last, descended from his capital, in order to see Quasimodo at closer quarters. "He's the bellringer of my brother, the archdeacon. Good-day, Quasimodo!"

"What a devil of a man!" said Robin Poussepain, still all bruised with his fall. "He shows himself; he's a hunchback. He walks; he's bandy-legged. He looks at you; he's one-eyed. You speak to him; he's deaf. And what does this Polyphemus do with his tongue?"

"He speaks when he chooses," said the old woman; "he became deaf through ringing the bells. He is not dumb."

"That he lacks," remarks Jehan.

"And he has one eye too many," added Robin Poussepain.

"Not at all," said Jehan wisely. "A one-eyed man is far less complete than a blind man. He knows what he lacks."

In the meantime, all the beggars, all the lackeys, all the cutpurses, joined with the scholars, had gone in procession to seek, in the cupboard of the law clerks' company, the cardboard tiara, and the derisive robe of the Pope of the Fools. Quasimodo allowed them to array him in them without wincing, and with a sort of proud docility. Then they made him seat himself on a motley litter. Twelve officers of the fraternity of fools raised him on their shoulders; and a sort of bitter and disdainful joy lighted up the morose face of the cyclops, when he beheld beneath his deformed feet all those heads of handsome, straight, well-made men. Then the ragged and howling procession set out on its march, according to custom, around the inner galleries of the Courts, before making the circuit of the streets and squares.

CHAPTER 6

Esmeralda

WE ARE DELIGHTED to be able to inform the reader, that during the whole of this scene, Gringoire and his piece had stood firm. His actors, spurred on by him, had not ceased to spout his comedy, and he had not ceased to listen to it. He had made up his mind about the tumult, and was determined to proceed to the end, not giving up the hope of a return of attention on the part of the public. This gleam of hope acquired fresh life, when he saw Quasimodo, Coppenole, and the deafening escort of the pope of the procession of fools quit the hall amid great uproar. The throng rushed eagerly after them. "Good," he said to himself, "there go all the mischief-makers." Unfortunately, all the mischief-makers constituted the entire audience. In the twinkling of an eye, the grand hall was empty.

To tell the truth, a few spectators still remained, some scattered, others in groups around the pillars, women, old men, or children, who had had enough of the uproar and tumult. Some scholars were still perched astride of the window-sills, engaged in gazing into the Place.

"Well," thought Gringoire, "here are still as many as are required to hear the end of my mystery. They are few in number, but it is a choice audience, a lettered audience."

An instant later, a symphony that had been intended to produce the greatest effect on the arrival of the Virgin, was lacking. Gringoire perceived that his music had been carried off by the procession of the Pope of the Fools. "Skip it," said he, stoically.

He approached a group of bourgeois, who seemed to him to be discussing his piece. This is the fragment of conversation which he caught: "You know, Master Cheneteau, the Hôtel de Navarre, which belonged to Monsieur de Nemours?"

"Yes, opposite the Chapelle de Braque."

"Well, the treasury has just let it to Guillaume Alixandre, historian, for six livres, eight sols, parisis, a year."

"How rents are going up!"

"Come," said Gringoire to himself, with a sigh, "the others are listening."

"Comrades," suddenly shouted one of the young scamps from the window, "La Esmeralda! La Esmeralda in the Place!"

This word produced a magical effect. Every one who was left in the hall flew to the windows, climbing the walls in order to see, and repeating, "La Esmeralda! La Esmeralda!" At the same time, a great sound of applause was heard from without.

"What's the meaning of this, of la Esmeralda?" said Gringoire, wringing his hands in despair. "Ah, good heavens! It seems to be the turn of the windows now."

He returned toward the marble table, and saw that the representation had been interrupted. It was precisely at the instant when Jupiter should have appeared with his thunder. But Jupiter was standing motionless at the foot of the stage.

"Michel Giborne!" cried the irritated poet, "what are you doing there? Is that your part? Come up!"

"Alas!" said Jupiter, "a scholar has just seized the ladder."

Gringoire looked. It was but too true. All communication between his plot and its solution was intercepted.

"The rascal," he murmured. "And why did he take that ladder?"

"In order to go and see the Esmeralda," replied Jupiter piteously. "He said, 'Come, here's a ladder that's of no use!' and he took it."

This was the last blow. Gringoire received it with resignation.

"May the devil fly away with you!" he said to the comedian, "and if I get my pay, you shall receive yours."

Then he beat a retreat, with drooping head, but the last in the field, like a general who has fought well.

And as he descended the winding stairs of the courts: "A fine rabble of asses and dolts these Parisians!" he muttered between his teeth; "they come to hear a mystery and don't listen to it at all! They are engrossed by every one, by Chopin Trouillefou, by the cardinal, by Coppenole, by Quasimodo, by the devil! But by Madame the Virgin Mary, not at all. If I had known, I'd have given you Virgin Mary; you ninnies! And I! To come to see faces and behold only backs! To be a poet, and to reap the success of an apothecary! It is true that Homerus begged through the Greek towns, and that Naso died in exile among the Muscovites. But may the devil flay me if I understand what they mean with their Esmeralda! What is that word, in the first place? 'Tis Egyptian!"

Book Second

CHAPTER 1

From Charybdis to Scylla

NIGHT COMES ON early in January. The streets were already dark when Gringoire issued forth from the Courts. This gloom pleased him; he was in haste to reach some obscure and deserted alley, in order there to meditate at his ease, and in order that the philosopher might place the first dressing upon the wound of the poet. Philosophy, moreover, was his sole refuge, for he did not know where he was to lodge for the night. After the brilliant failure of his first theatrical venture, he dared not return to the lodging which he occupied in the Rue Grenier-sur-l'Eau, opposite to the Port-au-Foin, having depended upon receiving from monsieur the provost for his epithalamium, the wherewithal to pay Master Guillaume Doulx-Sire, farmer of the taxes on cloven-footed animals in Paris, the rent which he owed him, that is to say, twelve sols parisis; twelve times the value of all that he possessed in the world, including his trunk-hose, his shirt, and his cap. After reflecting a moment, temporarily sheltered beneath the little wicket of the prison of the treasurer of the Sainte-Chappelle, as to the shelter which he would select for the night, having all the pavements of Paris to choose from, he remembered to have noticed the week previously in the Rue de la Savaterie, at the door of a councillor of the parliament, a stepping stone for mounting a mule, and to have said to himself that that stone would furnish, on occasion, a very excellent pillow for a mendicant or a poet. He thanked Providence for having sent this happy idea to him; but, as he was preparing to cross the Place, in order to reach the tortuous labyrinth of the city, where meander all those old sister streets, the Rues de la Barillerie, de la Vielle-Draperie, de la Savaterie, de la Juiverie, etc., still extant today, with their nine-story houses, he saw the procession of the Pope of the Fools, which was also emerging from the court house, and rushing across the courtyard, with great cries, a great flashing of torches, and the music which belonged to him, Gringoire. This sight revived the pain of his self-love; he fled. In the bitterness of his dramatic misadventure, everything that reminded him of the festival of that day irritated his wound and made it bleed.

He was on the point of turning to the Pont Saint-Michel; children were running about here and there with fire lances and rockets.

"Pest on firework candles!" said Gringoire; and he fell back on the Pont au Change. To the house at the head of the bridge there had been affixed three small banners, representing the king, the dauphin, and Marguerite of Flanders, and six little pennons on which were portrayed the Duke of Austria, the Cardinal de Bourbon, M. de Beaujeu, and Madame Jeanne de France, and Monsieur the Bastard of Bourbon, and I know not whom else; all being illuminated with torches. The rabble were admiring.

"Happy painter, Jehan Fourbault!" said Gringoire with a deep sigh; and he turned his back upon the bannerets and pennons. A street opened before him; he thought it so dark and deserted that he hoped to there escape from all the rumors as well as from all the gleams of the festival. At the end of a few moments his foot came in contact with an obstacle; he stumbled and fell. It was the May truss, which the clerks of the clerks' law court had deposited that morning at the door of a president of the parliament, in honor of the solemnity of the day. Gringoire bore this new disaster heroically; he picked himself up, and reached the water's edge. After leaving behind him the civic Tournelle [a chamber of the ancient parliament of Paris] and the criminal tower, and skirted the great walls of the king's garden, on that unpaved strand where the mud reached to his ankles, he reached the western point of the city, and considered for some time the islet of the Passeur-aux-Vaches, which has disappeared beneath the bronze horse of the Pont Neuf. The islet appeared to him in the shadow like a black mass, beyond the narrow strip of whitish water that separated him from it. One could divine by the ray of a tiny light the sort of hut in the form of a beehive where the ferryman of cows took refuge at night.

"Happy ferryman!" thought Gringoire; "you do not dream of glory, and you do not make marriage songs! What matters it to you, if kings and Duchesses of Burgundy marry? You know no other daisies than those that your April greensward gives your cows to browse upon; while I, a poet, am hooted, and shiver, and owe twelve sous, and the soles of my shoes are so transparent, that they might serve as glasses for your lantern! Thanks, ferryman, your cabin rests my eyes, and makes me forget Paris!"

He was roused from his almost lyric ecstacy, by a big double Saint-Jean cracker, which suddenly went off from the happy cabin. It was the cow ferryman, who was taking his part in the rejoicings of the day, and letting off fireworks.

This cracker made Gringoire's skin bristle up all over.

"Accursed festival!" he exclaimed, "wilt thou pursue me everywhere? Oh, good God! Even to the ferryman's!"

Then he looked at the Seine at his feet, and a horrible temptation took possession of him:

"Oh!" said he, "I would gladly drown myself, were the water not so cold!"

Then a desperate resolution occurred to him. It was, since he could not escape from the Pope of the Fools, from Jehan Fourbault's bannerets, from May trusses, from squibs and crackers, to go to the Place de Grève.

"At least," he said to himself, "I shall there have a firebrand of joy wherewith to warm myself, and I can sup on some crumbs of the three great armorial bearings of royal sugar which have been erected on the public refreshment-stall of the city."

Chapter 2

The Place de Grève

THERE REMAINS TODAY but a very imperceptible vestige of the Place de Grève, such as it existed then; it consists in the charming little turret, which occupies the angle north of the Place, and which, already enshrouded in the ignoble plaster which fills with paste the delicate lines of its sculpture, may soon have disappeared, perhaps submerged by that flood of new houses which so rapidly devours all the ancient façades of Paris.

The persons who, like ourselves, never cross the Place de Grève without casting a glance of pity and sympathy on that poor turret strangled between two hovels of the time of Louis XV, can easily reconstruct in their minds the aggregate of edifices to which it belonged, and find again entire in it the ancient Gothic place of the fifteenth century.

It was then, as it is today, an irregular trapezoid, bordered on one side by the quay, and on the other three by a series of lofty, narrow, and gloomy houses. By day, one could admire the variety of its edifices, all sculptured in stone or wood, and already presenting complete specimens of the different domestic architectures of the Middle Ages, running back from the fifteenth to the eleventh century, from the casement which had begun to dethrone the arch, to the Roman semicircle, which had been supplanted by the ogive, and which still occupies, below it, the first story of that ancient house de la Tour Roland, at the corner of the Place upon the Seine, on the side of the street with the Tannerie. At night, one could distinguish nothing of all that mass of buildings, except the black indentation of the roofs, unrolling their chain of acute angles round the place; for one of the radical differences between the cities of that time, and the cities of the present day, lay in the façades which looked upon the places and streets, and which were then gables. For the last two centuries the houses have been turned round.

In the centre of the eastern side of the Place, rose a heavy and hybrid construction, formed of three buildings placed in juxtaposition. It was called by three names which explain its history, its destination, and its architecture: "The House of the Dauphin," because Charles V, when Dauphin, had inhabited it; "The Marchandise," because it had served as town hall; and "The Pillared House" (*domus ad piloria*), because of a series of large pillars which sustained the three stories. The city found there all that is required for a city like Paris; a chapel in which to pray to God; a *plaidoyer*, or pleading room, in which to hold hearings, and to repel, at need, the King's people; and under the roof, an *arsenac* full of artillery. For the bourgeois of Paris were aware that it is not sufficient to pray in every conjuncture, and to plead for the franchises of the city, and they had always in reserve, in the garret of the town hall, a few good rusty arquebuses. The Grève had then that sinister aspect which it preserves today from the execrable ideas that it awakens, and from the sombre town hall of Dominique Bocador, which has replaced the Pillared House. It must be admitted that a permanent gibbet and a pillory, "a justice and a ladder," as they were called in that day, erected side by side in the centre of the pavement, contributed not a little to cause eyes to be turned away from that fatal place, where so many beings full of life and health have agonized; where, fifty years later, that fever of Saint Vallier was destined to have its birth, that terror of the scaffold, the most monstrous of all maladies because it comes not from God, but from man.

It is a consoling idea (let us remark in passing), to think that the death penalty, which three hundred years ago still encumbered with its iron wheels, its stone gibbets, and all its paraphernalia of torture, permanent and riveted to the pavement, the Grève, the Halles, the Place Dauphine, the Cross du Trahoir, the Marché aux Pourceaux, that hideous Montfauçon, the barrier des Sergents, the Place aux Chats, the Porte Saint-Denis, Champeaux, the Porte Baudets, the Porte Saint Jacques, without reckoning the innumerable ladders of the provosts, the bishop of the chapters, of the abbots, of the priors, who had the decree of life and death,—without reckoning the judicial drownings in the river Seine; it is consoling today, after having lost successively all the pieces of its armor, its luxury of torment, its penalty of imagination and fancy, its torture for which it reconstructed every five years a leather bed at the Grand Châtelet, that ancient suzerain of feudal society almost expunged from our laws and our cities, hunted from code to code, chased from place to place, has no longer, in our immense Paris, any more than a dishonored corner of the Grève, than a miserable guillotine, furtive, uneasy, shameful, which seems always afraid of being caught in the act, so quickly does it disappear after having dealt its blow.

CHAPTER 3

Kisses for Blows

WHEN PIERRE GRINGOIRE arrived on the Place de Grève, he was
paralyzed. He had directed his course across the Pont aux Meuniers, in
order to avoid the rabble on the Pont au Change, and the pennons of
Jehan Fourbault; but the wheels of all the bishop's mills had splashed
him as he passed, and his doublet was drenched; it seemed to him
besides, that the failure of his piece had rendered him still more sensible
to cold than usual. Hence he made haste to draw near the bonfire,
which was burning magnificently in the middle of the Place. But a
considerable crowd formed a circle around it.

"Accursed Parisians!" he said to himself (for Gringoire, like
a true dramatic poet, was subject to monologues), "there they are
obstructing my fire! Nevertheless, I am greatly in need of a chimney
corner; my shoes drink in the water, and all those cursed mills wept
upon me! That devil of a Bishop of Paris, with his mills! I'd just like
to know what use a bishop can make of a mill! Does he expect to
become a miller instead of a bishop? If only my malediction is needed
for that, I bestow it upon him! And his cathedral, and his mills! Just
see if those boobies will put themselves out! Move aside! I'd like
to know what they are doing there! They are warming themselves,
much pleasure may it give them! They are watching a hundred fagots
burn; a fine spectacle!"

On looking more closely, he perceived that the circle was much
larger than was required simply for the purpose of getting warm at the
king's fire, and that this concourse of people had not been attracted
solely by the beauty of the hundred fagots which were burning.

In a vast space left free between the crowd and the fire, a young
girl was dancing.

Whether this young girl was a human being, a fairy, or an angel, is what Gringoire, sceptical philosopher and ironical poet that he was, could not decide at the first moment, so fascinated was he by this dazzling vision.

She was not tall, though she seemed so, so boldly did her slender form dart about. She was swarthy of complexion, but one divined that, by day, her skin must possess that beautiful golden tone of the Andalusians and the Roman women. Her little foot, too, was Andalusian, for it was both pinched and at ease in its graceful shoe. She danced, she turned, she whirled rapidly about on an old Persian rug, spread negligently under her feet; and each time that her radiant face passed before you, as she whirled, her great black eyes darted a flash of lightning at you.

All around her, all glances were riveted, all mouths open; and, in fact, when she danced thus, to the humming of the Basque tambourine, which her two pure, rounded arms raised above her head, slender, frail and vivacious as a wasp, with her corsage of gold without a fold, her variegated gown puffing out, her bare shoulders, her delicate limbs, which her petticoat revealed at times, her black hair, her eyes of flame, she was a supernatural creature.

"In truth," said Gringoire to himself, "she is a salamander, she is a nymph, she is a goddess, she is a bacchante of the Menelean Mount!"

At that moment, one of the salamander's braids of hair became unfastened, and a piece of yellow copper which was attached to it, rolled to the ground.

"Oh, no!" said he, "she is a gypsy!"

All illusions had disappeared.

She began her dance once more; she took from the ground two swords, whose points she rested against her brow, and which she made to turn in one direction, while she turned in the other; it was a purely gypsy effect. But, disenchanted though Gringoire was, the whole effect of this picture was not without its charm and its magic; the bonfire illuminated, with a red flaring light, which trembled, all alive, over the circle of faces in the crowd, on the brow of the young girl, and at the background of the Place cast a pallid reflection, on one side upon the ancient, black, and wrinkled façade of the House of Pillars, on the other, upon the old stone gibbet.

Among the thousands of visages which that light tinged with scarlet, there was one which seemed, even more than all the others, absorbed in contemplation of the dancer. It was the face of a man, austere, calm, and sombre. This man, whose costume was concealed by the crowd which surrounded him, did not appear to be more than five and thirty years of age; nevertheless, he was bald; he had merely a few tufts of thin, gray hair on his temples; his broad, high forehead had begun to be furrowed with wrinkles, but his deep-set eyes sparkled with extraordinary youthfulness, an ardent life, a profound passion. He kept them fixed incessantly on the gypsy, and, while the giddy young girl of sixteen danced and whirled, for the pleasure of all, his revery seemed to become more and more sombre. From time to time, a smile and a sigh met upon his lips, but the smile was more melancholy than the sigh.

The young girl, stopped at length, breathless, and the people applauded her lovingly.

"Djali!" said the gypsy.

Then Gringoire saw come up to her, a pretty little white goat, alert, wide-awake, glossy, with gilded horns, gilded hoofs, and gilded collar, which he had not hitherto perceived, and which had remained lying curled up on one corner of the carpet watching his mistress dance.

"Djali!" said the dancer, "it is your turn."

And, seating herself, she gracefully presented her tambourine to the goat.

"Djali," she continued, "what month is this?"

The goat lifted its fore foot, and struck one blow upon the tambourine. It was the first month in the year, in fact.

"Djali," pursued the young girl, turning her tambourine round, "what day of the month is this?"

Djali raised his little gilt hoof, and struck six blows on the tambourine.

"Djali," pursued the Egyptian, with still another movement of the tambourine, "what hour of the day is it?"

Djali struck seven blows. At that moment, the clock of the Pillar House rang out seven.

The people were amazed.

"There's sorcery at the bottom of it," said a sinister voice in the crowd. It was that of the bald man, who never removed his eyes from the gypsy.

She shuddered and turned round; but applause broke forth and drowned the morose exclamation.

It even effaced it so completely from her mind that she continued to question her goat.

"Djali, what does Master Guichard Grand-Remy, captain of the pistoliers of the town do, at the procession of Candlemas?"

Djali reared himself on his hind legs, and began to bleat, marching along with so much dainty gravity, that the entire circle of spectators burst into a laugh at this parody of the interested devoutness of the captain of pistoliers.

"Djali," resumed the young girl, emboldened by her growing success, "how preaches Master Jacques Charmolue, procurator to the king in the ecclesiastical court?"

The goat seated himself on his hind quarters, and began to bleat, waving his fore feet in so strange a manner, that, with the exception of the bad French, and worse Latin, Jacques Charmolue was there complete—gesture, accent, and attitude.

And the crowd applauded louder than ever.

"Sacrilege! Profanation!" resumed the voice of the bald man.

The gypsy turned round once more.

"Ah!" said she, "'tis that villanous man!" Then, thrusting her lower lip out beyond the upper, she made a little pout, which appeared to be familiar to her, executed a pirouette on her heel, and set about collecting in her tambourine the gifts of the multitude.

Big coins, little coins—*grands, blancs, petit blancs, targes, liards a l'aigle*—showered into it. All at once, she passed in front of Gringoire. Gringoire put his hand so recklessly into his pocket that she halted. "The devil!" said the poet, finding at the bottom of his pocket the reality, that is to say, a void. In the meantime, the pretty girl stood there, gazing at him with her big eyes, and holding out her tambourine to him and waiting. Gringoire broke into a violent perspiration.

If he had all Peru in his pocket, he would certainly have given it to the dancer; but Gringoire had not Peru, and, moreover, America had not yet been discovered.

Happily, an unexpected incident came to his rescue.

"Will you take yourself off, you Egyptian grasshopper?" cried a sharp voice, which proceeded from the darkest corner of the Place.

The young girl turned round in affright. It was no longer the voice of the bald man; it was the voice of a woman, bigoted and malicious.

However, this cry, which alarmed the gypsy, delighted a troop of children who were prowling about there.

"It is the recluse of the Tour-Roland," they exclaimed, with wild laughter, "it is the sacked nun who is scolding! Hasn't she supped? Let's carry her the remains of the city refreshments!"

All rushed toward the Pillar House.

In the meanwhile, Gringoire had taken advantage of the dancer's embarrassment, to disappear. The children's shouts had reminded him that he, also, had not supped, so he ran to the public buffet. But the little rascals had better legs than he; when he arrived, they had stripped the table. There remained not so much as a miserable *camichon* at five sous the pound. Nothing remained upon the wall but slender fleurs-de-lis, mingled with rose bushes, painted in 1434 by Mathieu Biterne. It was a meagre supper.

It is an unpleasant thing to go to bed without supper, it is a still less pleasant thing not to sup and not to know where one is to sleep. That was Gringoire's condition. No supper, no shelter; he saw himself pressed on all sides by necessity, and he found necessity very crabbed. He had long ago discovered the truth, that Jupiter created men during a fit of misanthropy, and that during a wise man's whole life, his destiny holds his philosophy in a state of siege. As for himself, he had never seen the blockade so complete; he heard his stomach sounding a parley, and he considered it very much out of place that evil destiny should capture his philosophy by famine.

This melancholy revery was absorbing him more and more, when a song, quaint but full of sweetness, suddenly tore him from it. It was the young gypsy who was singing.

Her voice was like her dancing, like her beauty. It was indefinable and charming; something pure and sonorous, aerial, winged, so to speak. There were continual outbursts, melodies, unexpected cadences, then simple phrases strewn with aerial and hissing notes; then floods of scales which would have put a nightingale to rout, but in which harmony was always present; then soft modulations of octaves which rose and fell, like the bosom of the young singer. Her beautiful face followed, with singular mobility, all the caprices of her song, from the wildest inspiration to the chastest dignity. One would have pronounced her now a mad creature, now a queen.

The words which she sang were in a tongue unknown to Gringoire, and which seemed to him to be unknown to herself, so little relation did the expression which she imparted to her song bear to the sense of the words. Thus, these four lines, in her mouth, were madly gay—

Un cofre de gran riqueza
Hallaron dentro un pilar,
Dentro del, nuevas banderas
Con figuras de espantar.

And an instant afterwards, at the accents which she imparted to this stanza—

Alarabes de cavallo
Sin poderse menear,
Con espadas, y los cuellos,
Ballestas de buen echar.

Gringoire felt the tears come to his eyes. Nevertheless, her song breathed joy, most of all, and she seemed to sing like a bird, from serenity and heedlessness.

The gypsy's song had disturbed Gringoire's revery as the swan disturbs the water. He listened in a sort of rapture, and forgetfulness of everything. It was the first moment in the course of many hours when he did not feel that he suffered.

The moment was brief.

The same woman's voice, which had interrupted the gypsy's dance, interrupted her song.

"Will you hold your tongue, you cricket of hell?" it cried, still from the same obscure corner of the place.

The poor "cricket" stopped short. Gringoire covered up his ears.

"Oh!" he exclaimed, "accursed saw with missing teeth, which comes to break the lyre!"

Meanwhile, the other spectators murmured like himself. "To the devil with the sacked nun!" said some of them. And the old invisible kill-joy might have had occasion to repent of her aggressions against the gypsy had their attention not been diverted at this moment by the procession of the Pope of the Fools, which, after having traversed many streets and squares, debouched on the Place de Grève, with all its torches and all its uproar.

This procession, which our readers have seen set out from the Palais de Justice, had organized on the way, and had been recruited by all the knaves, idle thieves, and unemployed vagabonds in Paris; so that it presented a very respectable aspect when it arrived at the Grève.

First came Egypt. The Duke of Egypt headed it, on horseback, with his counts on foot holding his bridle and stirrups for him; behind them, the male and female Egyptians, pell-mell, with their little children crying on their shoulders; all—duke, counts, and populace—in rags and tatters. Then came the Kingdom of Argot; that is to say, all the thieves of France, arranged according to the order of their dignity; the minor people walking first. Thus defiled by fours, with the divers insignia of their grades, in that strange faculty, most of them lame, some cripples, others one-armed, shop clerks, pilgrim, *hubins*, bootblacks, thimble-riggers, street arabs, beggars, the blear-eyed beggars, thieves, the weakly, vagabonds, merchants, sham soldiers, goldsmiths, passed masters of pickpockets, isolated thieves. A catalogue that would weary Homer. In the centre of the conclave of the passed masters of pickpockets, one had some difficulty in distinguishing the King of Argot, the grand coësre, so called, crouching in a little cart drawn by two big dogs. After the kingdom of the Argotiers, came the Empire of Galilee. Guillaume Rousseau, Emperor of the Empire of Galilee, marched majestically in his robe of purple, spotted with wine, preceded by buffoons wrestling and executing military dances; surrounded by his macebearers, his pickpockets and clerks of the chamber of accounts. Last of all came the corporation of law clerks, with its maypoles crowned with flowers, its black robes, its music worthy of the orgy, and its large candles of yellow wax. In the centre of this crowd, the grand officers of the Brotherhood of Fools bore on their shoulders a litter more loaded down with candles than the reliquary of Sainte-Geneviève in time of pest; and on this litter shone resplendent, with crosier, cope, and mitre, the new Pope of the Fools, the bellringer of Notre-Dame, Quasimodo the hunchback.

Each section of this grotesque procession had its own music. The Egyptians made their drums and African tambourines resound. The slang men, not a very musical race, still clung to the goat's horn trumpet and the Gothic rubebbe of the twelfth century. The Empire of Galilee was not much more advanced; among its music one could hardly distinguish some miserable rebec, from the infancy of the art, still imprisoned in the *re-la-mi*. But it was around the Pope of the Fools that all the musical riches of the epoch were displayed in a magnificent discord. It was nothing but soprano rebecs, counter-tenor rebecs, and tenor rebecs, not to reckon the flutes and brass instruments. Alas! our readers will remember that this was Gringoire's orchestra.

It is difficult to convey an idea of the degree of proud and blissful expansion to which the sad and hideous visage of Quasimodo had attained during the transit from the Palais de Justice, to the Place de Grève. It was the first enjoyment of self-love that he had ever experienced. Down to that day, he had known only humiliation, disdain for his condition, disgust for his person. Hence, deaf though he was, he enjoyed, like a veritable pope, the acclamations of that throng, which he hated because he felt that he was hated by it. What mattered it that his people consisted of a pack of fools, cripples, thieves, and beggars? It was still a people and he was its sovereign. And he accepted seriously all this ironical applause, all this derisive respect, with which the crowd mingled, it must be admitted, a good deal of very real fear. For the hunchback was robust; for the bandy-legged fellow was agile; for the deaf man was malicious: three qualities that temper ridicule.

We are far from believing, however, that the new Pope of the Fools understood both the sentiments that he felt and the sentiments he inspired. The spirit that was lodged in this failure of a body had, necessarily, something incomplete and deaf about it. Thus, what he felt at the moment was to him, absolutely vague, indistinct, and confused. Only joy made itself felt, only pride dominated. Around that sombre and unhappy face, there hung a radiance.

It was, then, not without surprise and alarm, that at the very moment when Quasimodo was passing the Pillar House, in that semi-intoxicated state, a man was seen to dart from the crowd, and to tear from his hands, with a gesture of anger, his crosier of gilded wood, the emblem of his mock popeship.

This man, this rash individual, was the man with the bald brow, who, a moment earlier, standing with the gypsy's group had chilled the poor girl with his words of menace and of hatred. He was dressed in an eccleslastical costume. At the moment when he stood forth from the crowd, Gringoire, who had not noticed him up to that time, recognized him: "Hold!" he said, with an exclamation of astonishment. "Eh! 'Tis my master in Hermes, Dom Claude Frollo, the archdeacon! What the devil does he want of that old one-eyed fellow? He'll get himself devoured!"

A cry of terror arose, in fact. The formidable Quasimodo had hurled himself from the litter, and the women turned aside their eyes in order not to see him tear the archdeacon asunder.

He made one bound as far as the priest, looked at him, and fell upon his knees.

The priest tore off his tiara, broke his crozier, and rent his tinsel cope.

Quasimodo remained on his knees, with head bent and hands clasped. Then there was established between them a strange dialogue of signs and gestures, for neither of them spoke. The priest, erect on his feet, irritated, threatening, imperious; Quasimodo, prostrate, humble, suppliant. And, nevertheless, it is certain that Quasimodo could have crushed the priest with his thumb.

At length the archdeacon, giving Quasimodo's powerful shoulder a rough shake, made him a sign to rise and follow him.

Quasimodo rose.

Then the Brotherhood of Fools, their first stupor having passed off, wished to defend their pope, so abruptly dethroned. The Egyptians, the men of slang, and all the fraternity of law clerks, gathered howling round the priest.

Quasimodo placed himself in front of the priest, set in play the muscles of his athletic fists, and glared upon the assailants with the snarl of an angry tiger.

The priest resumed his sombre gravity, made a sign to Quasimodo, and retired in silence.

Quasimodo walked in front of him, scattering the crowd as he passed.

When they had traversed the populace and the Place, the cloud of curious and idle were minded to follow them. Quasimodo then constituted himself the rearguard, and followed the archdeacon, walking backwards, squat, surly, monstrous, bristling, gathering up his limbs, licking his boar's tusks, growling like a wild beast, and imparting to the crowd immense vibrations, with a look or a gesture.

Both were allowed to plunge into a dark and narrow street, where no one dared to venture after them; so thoroughly did the mere chimera of Quasimodo gnashing his teeth bar the entrance.

"Here's a marvellous thing," said Gringoire; "but where the deuce shall I find some supper?"

CHAPTER 4

The Inconveniences of Following a Pretty Woman Through the Streets in the Evening

GRINGOIRE SET OUT to follow the gypsy at all hazards. He had seen her, accompanied by her goat, take to the Rue de la Coutellerie; he took the Rue de la Coutellerie.

"Why not?" he said to himself.

Gringoire, a practical philosopher of the streets of Paris, had noticed that nothing is more propitious to revery than following a pretty woman without knowing whither she is going. There was in this voluntary abdication of his free will, in this fancy submitting itself to another fancy, which suspects it not, a mixture of fantastic independence and blind obedience, something indescribable, intermediate between slavery and liberty, which pleased Gringoire, a spirit essentially compound, undecided, and complex, holding the extremities of all extremes, incessantly suspended between all human propensities, and neutralizing one by the other. He was fond of comparing himself to Mahomet's coffin, attracted in two different directions by two lodestones, and hesitating eternally between the heights and the depths, between the vault and the pavement, between fall and ascent, between zenith and nadir.

If Gringoire had lived in our day, what a fine middle course he would hold between classicism and romanticism!

But he was not sufficiently primitive to live three hundred years, and 'tis a pity. His absence is a void that is but too sensibly felt today.

Moreover, for the purpose of thus following passers-by (and especially female passers-by) in the streets, which Gringoire was fond of doing, there is no better disposition than ignorance of where one is going to sleep.

So he walked along, very thoughtfully, behind the young girl, who hastened her pace and made her goat trot as she saw the bourgeois returning home and the taverns—the only shops that had been open that day—closing.

"After all," he half thought to himself, "she must lodge somewhere; gypsies have kindly hearts. Who knows?"

And in the points of suspense that he placed after this reticence in his mind, there lay I know not what flattering ideas.

Meanwhile, from time to time, as he passed the last groups of bourgeois closing their doors, he caught some scraps of their conversation, which broke the thread of his pleasant hypotheses.

Now it was two old men accosting each other.

"Do you know that it is cold, Master Thibaut Fernicle?" (Gringoire had been aware of this since the beginning of the winter.)

"Yes, indeed, Master Boniface Disome! Are we going to have a winter such as we had three years ago, in '80, when wood cost eight sous the measure?"

"Bah! That's nothing, Master Thibaut, compared with the winter of 1407, when it froze from St. Martin's Day until Candlemas! And so cold that the pen of the registrar of the parliament froze every three words, in the Grand Chamber, which interrupted the registration of justice!"

Further on there were two female neighbors at their windows, holding candles, which the fog caused to sputter.

"Has your husband told you about the mishap, Mademoiselle la Boudraque?"

"No. What is it, Mademoiselle Turquant?"

"The horse of M. Gilles Godin, the notary at the Châtelet, took fright at the Flemings and their procession, and overturned Master Philippe Avrillot, lay monk of the Célestins."

"Really?"

"Actually."

"A bourgeois horse 'tis rather too much! If it had been a cavalry horse, well and good!"

And the windows were closed. But Gringoire had lost the thread of his ideas, nevertheless.

Fortunately, he speedily found it again, and he knotted it together without difficulty, thanks to the gypsy, thanks to Djali, who still walked in front of him; two fine, delicate, and charming creatures, whose tiny feet, beautiful forms, and graceful manners he was engaged in admiring, almost confusing them in his contemplation; believing them to be both young girls, from their intelligence and good friendship; regarding them both as goats, so far as the lightness, agility, and dexterity of their walk were concerned.

But the streets were becoming blacker and more deserted every moment. The curfew had sounded long ago, and it was only at rare intervals now that they encountered a passer-by in the street, or a light in the windows. Gringoire had become involved, in his pursuit of the gypsy, in that inextricable labyrinth of alleys, squares, and closed courts which surround the ancient sepulchre of the Saints-Innocents, and which resembles a ball of thread tangled by a cat. "Here are streets which possess but little logic!" said Gringoire, lost in the thousands of circuits which returned upon themselves incessantly, but where the young girl pursued a road which seemed familiar to her, without hesitation and with a step which became ever more rapid. As for him, he would have been utterly ignorant of his situation had he not espied, in passing, at the turn of a street, the octagonal mass of the pillory of the fish markets, the open-work summit of which threw its black, fretted outlines clearly upon a window which was still lighted in the Rue Verdelet.

The young girl's attention had been attracted to him for the last few moments; she had repeatedly turned her head toward him with uneasiness; she had even once come to a standstill, and taking advantage of a ray of light which escaped from a half-open bakery to survey him intently, from head to foot, then, having cast this glance, Gringoire had seen her make that little pout which he had already noticed, after which she passed on.

This little pout had furnished Gringoire with food for thought. There was certainly both disdain and mockery in that graceful grimace. So he dropped his head, began to count the paving-stones, and to follow the young girl at a little greater distance, when, at the turn of a street, which had caused him to lose sight of her, he heard her utter a piercing cry.

He hastened his steps.

The street was full of shadows. Nevertheless, a twist of tow soaked in oil, which burned in a cage at the feet of the Holy Virgin at the street corner, permitted Gringoire to make out the gypsy struggling in the arms of two men, who were endeavoring to stifle her cries. The poor little goat, in great alarm, lowered his horns and bleated.

"Help, gentlemen of the watch!" shouted Gringoire, and advanced bravely. One of the men who held the young girl turned toward him. It was the formidable visage of Quasimodo.

Gringoire did not take to flight, but neither did he advance another step.

Quasimodo came up to him, tossed him four paces away on the pavement with a backward turn of the hand, and plunged rapidly into the gloom, bearing the young girl folded across one arm like a silken scarf. His companion followed him, and the poor goat ran after them all, bleating plaintively.

"Murder! Murder!" shrieked the unhappy gypsy.

"Halt, rascals, and yield me that wench!" suddenly shouted in a voice of thunder, a cavalier who appeared suddenly from a neighboring square.

It was a captain of the king's archers, armed from head to foot, with his sword in his hand.

He tore the gypsy from the arms of the dazed Quasimodo, threw her across his saddle, and at the moment when the terrible hunchback, recovering from his surprise, rushed upon him to regain his prey, fifteen or sixteen archers, who followed their captain closely, made their appearance, with their two-edged swords in their fists. It was a squad of the king's police, which was making the rounds, by order of Messire Robert d'Estouteville, guard of the provostship of Paris.

Quasimodo was surrounded, seized, garroted; he roared, he foamed at the mouth, he bit; and had it been broad daylight, there is no doubt that his face alone, rendered more hideous by wrath, would have put the entire squad to flight. But by night he was deprived of his most formidable weapon, his ugliness.

His companion had disappeared during the struggle.

The gypsy gracefully raised herself upright upon the officer's saddle, placed both hands upon the young man's shoulders, and gazed fixedly at him for several seconds, as though enchanted with his good looks and with the aid which he had just rendered her. Then breaking silence first, she said to him, making her sweet voice still sweeter than usual, "What is your name, monsieur le gendarme?"

"Captain Phoebus de Châteaupers, at your service, my beauty!" replied the officer, drawing himself up.

"Thanks," said she.

And while Captain Phoebus was turning up his moustache in Burgundian fashion, she slipped from the horse, like an arrow falling to earth, and fled.

A flash of lightning would have vanished less quickly.

"Nombrill of the Pope!" said the captain, causing Quasimodo's straps to be drawn tighter, "I should have preferred to keep the wench."

"What would you have, captain?" said one gendarme. "The warbler has fled, and the bat remains."

CHAPTER 5

Result of the Dangers

GRINGOIRE, THOROUGHLY STUNNED by his fall, remained on the pavement in front of the Holy Virgin at the street corner. Little by little, he regained his senses; at first, for several minutes, he was floating in a sort of half-somnolent revery, which was not without its charm, in which aerial figures of the gypsy and her goat were coupled with Quasimodo's heavy fist. This state lasted but a short time. A decidedly vivid sensation of cold in the part of his body which was in contact with the pavement, suddenly aroused him and caused his spirit to return to the surface.

"Whence comes this chill?" he said abruptly, to himself. He then perceived that he was lying half in the middle of the gutter.

"That devil of a hunchbacked cyclops!" he muttered between his teeth; and he tried to rise. But he was too much dazed and bruised; he was forced to remain where he was. Moreover, his hand was tolerably free; he stopped up his nose and resigned himself.

"The mud of Paris," he said to himself—for decidedly he thought that he was sure that the gutter would prove his refuge for the night; and what can one do in a refuge, except dream? "The mud of Paris is particularly stinking; it must contain a great deal of volatile and nitric salts. That, moreover, is the opinion of Master Nicholas Flamel, and of the alchemists—"

The word "alchemists" suddenly suggested to his mind the idea of Archdeacon Claude Frollo. He recalled the violent scene which he had just witnessed in part; that the gypsy was struggling with two men, that Quasimodo had a companion; and the morose and haughty face of the archdeacon passed confusedly through his memory. "That would be strange!" he said to himself. And on that fact and that basis he began to construct a fantastic edifice of hypothesis, that card-castle of philosophers; then, suddenly returning once more to reality, "Come! I'm freezing!" he ejaculated.

The place was, in fact, becoming less and less tenable. Each molecule of the gutter bore away a molecule of heat radiating from Gringoire's loins, and the equilibrium between the temperature of his body and the temperature of the brook, began to be established in rough fashion.

Quite a different annoyance suddenly assailed him. A group of children, those little bare-footed savages who have always roamed the pavements of Paris under the eternal name of *gamins*, and who, when we were also children ourselves, threw stones at all of us in the afternoon, when we came out of school, because our trousers were not torn—a swarm of these young scamps rushed toward the square where Gringoire lay, with shouts and laughter which seemed to pay but little heed to the sleep of the neighbors. They were dragging after them some sort of hideous sack; and the noise of their wooden shoes alone would have roused the dead. Gringoire who was not quite dead yet, half raised himself.

"Oh, Hennequin Dandéche! Oh, Jehan Pincebourde!" they shouted in deafening tones, "old Eustache Moubon, the merchant at the corner, has just died. We've got his straw pallet, we're going to have a bonfire out of it. It's the turn of the Flemish today!"

And behold, they flung the pallet directly upon Gringoire, beside whom they had arrived, without espying him. At the same time, one of them took a handful of straw and set off to light it at the wick of the good Virgin.

"S'death!" growled Gringoire, "am I going to be too warm now?"

It was a critical moment. He was caught between fire and water; he made a superhuman effort, the effort of a counterfeiter of money who is on the point of being boiled, and who seeks to escape. He rose to his feet, flung aside the straw pallet upon the street urchins, and fled.

"Holy Virgin!" shrieked the children; "'tis the merchant's ghost!" And they fled in their turn.

The straw mattress remained master of the field. Belleforet, Father Le Juge, and Corrozet affirm that it was picked up on the morrow, with great pomp, by the clergy of the quarter, and borne to the treasury of the church of Saint Opportune, where the sacristan, even as late as 1789, earned a tolerably handsome revenue out of the great miracle of the Statue of the Virgin at the corner of the Rue Mauconseil, which had, by its mere presence, on the memorable night between the sixth and seventh of January, 1482, exorcised the defunct Eustache Moubon, who, in order to play a trick on the devil, had at his death maliciously concealed his soul in his straw pallet.

CHAPTER 6

The Broken Jug

AFTER HAVING RUN for some time at the top of his speed, without knowing whither, knocking his head against many a street corner, leaping many a gutter, traversing many an alley, many a court, many a square, seeking flight and passage through all the meanderings of the ancient passages of the Halles, exploring in his panic terror what the fine Latin of the maps calls *tota via, cheminum et viaria*, our poet suddenly halted for lack of breath in the first place, and in the second, because he had been collared, after a fashion, by a dilemma which had just occurred to his mind. "It strikes me, Master Pierre Gringoire," he said to himself, placing his finger to his brow, "that you are running like a madman. The little scamps are no less afraid of you than you are of them. It strikes me, I say, that you heard the clatter of their wooden shoes fleeing southward, while you were fleeing northward. Now, one of two things, either they have taken flight, and the pallet, which they must have forgotten in their terror, is precisely that hospitable bed in search of which you have been running ever since morning, and which madame the Virgin miraculously sends you, in order to recompense you for having made a morality in her honor, accompanied by triumphs and mummeries; or the children have not taken flight, and in that case they have put the brand to the pallet, and that is precisely the good fire which you need to cheer, dry, and warm you. In either case, good fire or good bed, that straw pallet is a gift from heaven. The blessed Virgin Marie who stands at the corner of the Rue Mauconseil, could only have made Eustache Moubon die for that express purpose; and it is folly on your part to flee thus zigzag, like a Picard before a Frenchman, leaving behind you what you seek before you; and you are a fool!"

Then he retraced his steps, and feeling his way and searching, with his nose to the wind and his ears on the alert, he tried to find the blessed pallet again, but in vain. There was nothing to be found but intersections of houses, closed courts, and crossings of streets, in the midst of which he hesitated and doubted incessantly, being more perplexed and entangled in this medley of streets than he would have been even in the labyrinth of the Hôtel des Tournelles. At length he lost patience, and exclaimed solemnly: "Cursed be cross roads! 'tis the devil who has made them in the shape of his pitchfork!"

This exclamation afforded him a little solace, and a sort of reddish reflection which he caught sight of at that moment, at the extremity of a long and narrow lane, completed the elevation of his moral tone. "God be praised!" said he, "There it is yonder! There is my pallet burning." And comparing himself to the pilot who suffers shipwreck by night, "*Salve*," he added piously, "*salve, maris stella!*"

Did he address this fragment of litany to the Holy Virgin, or to the pallet? We are utterly unable to say.

He had taken but a few steps in the long street, which sloped downwards, was unpaved, and more and more muddy and steep, when he noticed a very singular thing. It was not deserted; here and there along its extent crawled certain vague and formless masses, all directing their course toward the light which flickered at the end of the street, like those heavy insects which drag along by night, from blade to blade of grass, toward the shepherd's fire.

Nothing renders one so adventurous as not being able to feel the place where one's pocket is situated. Gringoire continued to advance, and had soon joined that one of the forms that dragged along most indolently, behind the others. On drawing near, he perceived that it was nothing else than a wretched legless cripple in a bowl, who was hopping along on his two hands like a wounded field-spider that has but two legs left. At the moment when he passed close to this species of spider with a human countenance, it raised toward him a lamentable voice: "*La buona mancia, signor! La buona mancia!*"

"Deuce take you," said Gringoire, "and me with you, if I know what you mean!"

And he passed on.

He overtook another of these itinerant masses, and examined it. It was an impotent man, both halt and crippled, and halt and crippled to such a degree that the complicated system of crutches and wooden legs which sustained him, gave him the air of a mason's scaffolding on the march. Gringoire, who liked noble and classical comparisons, compared him in thought to the living tripod of Vulcan.

This living tripod saluted him as he passed, but stopping his hat on a level with Gringoire's chin, like a shaving dish, while he shouted in the latter's ears: *"Senor cabellero, para comprar un pedaso de pan!"*

"It appears," said Gringoire, "that this one can also talk; but 'tis a rude language, and he is more fortunate than I if he understands it." Then, smiting his brow, in a sudden transition of ideas: "By the way, what the deuce did they mean this morning with their Esmeralda?"

He was minded to augment his pace, but for the third time something barred his way. This something or, rather, some one was a blind man, a little blind fellow with a bearded, Jewish face, who, rowing away in the space about him with a stick, and towed by a large dog, droned through his nose with a Hungarian accent: *"Facitote caritatem!"*

"Well, now," said Gringoire, "here's one at last who speaks a Christian tongue. I must have a very charitable aspect, since they ask alms of me in the present lean condition of my purse. My friend," and he turned toward the blind man, "I sold my last shirt last week; that is to say, since you understand only the language of Cicero: *Vendidi hebdomade nuper transita meam ultimam chemisan.*"

That said, he turned his back upon the blind man, and pursued his way. But the blind man began to increase his stride at the same time; and, behold! The cripple and the legless man, in his bowl, came up on their side in great haste, and with great clamor of bowl and crutches, upon the pavement. Then all three, jostling each other at poor Gringoire's heels, began to sing their song to him. "*Caritatem!*" chanted the blind man.

"*La buona mancia!*" chanted the cripple in the bowl.

And the lame man took up the musical phrase by repeating: "*Un pedaso de pan!*"

Gringoire stopped up his ears. "Oh, tower of Babel!" he exclaimed.

He set out to run. The blind man ran! The lame man ran! The cripple in the bowl ran!

And then, in proportion as he plunged deeper into the street, cripples in bowls, blind men and lame men, swarmed about him, and men with one arm, and with one eye, and the leprous with their sores, some emerging from little streets adjacent, some from the air-holes of cellars, howling, bellowing, yelping, all limping and halting, all flinging themselves toward the light, and humped up in the mire, like snails after a shower.

Gringoire, still followed by his three persecutors, and not knowing very well what was to become of him, marched along in terror among them, turning out for the lame, stepping over the cripples in bowls, with his feet imbedded in that ant-hill of lame men, like the English captain who got caught in the quicksand of a swarm of crabs.

The idea occurred to him of making an effort to retrace his steps. But it was too late. This whole legion had closed in behind him, and his three beggars held him fast. So he proceeded, impelled both by this irresistible flood, by fear, and by a vertigo which converted all this into a sort of horrible dream.

At last he reached the end of the street. It opened upon an immense place, where a thousand scattered lights flickered in the confused mists of night. Gringoire flew thither, hoping to escape, by the swiftness of his legs, from the three infirm spectres who had clutched him.

"*Onde vas, hombre?*" cried the cripple, flinging away his crutches, and running after him with the best legs that ever traced a geometrical step upon the pavements of Paris.

In the meantime the legless man, erect upon his feet, crowned Gringoire with his heavy iron bowl, and the blind man glared in his face with flaming eyes!

"Where am I?" said the terrified poet.

"In the Court of Miracles," replied a fourth spectre, who had accosted them.

"Upon my soul," resumed Gringoire, "I certainly do behold the blind who see, and the lame who walk, but where is the Saviour?"

They replied by a burst of sinister laughter.

The poor poet cast his eyes about him. It was, in truth, that redoubtable Cour des Miracles, whither an honest man had never penetrated at such an hour; the magic circle where the officers of the Châtelet and the sergeants of the provostship, who ventured thither, disappeared in morsels; a city of thieves, a hideous wart on the face of Paris; a sewer, from which escaped every morning, and whither returned every night to crouch, that stream of vices, of mendicancy and vagabondage which always overflows in the streets of capitals; a monstrous hive, to which returned at nightfall, with their booty, all the drones of the social order; a lying hospital where the bohemian, the disfrocked monk, the ruined scholar, the ne'er-do-wells of all nations, Spaniards, Italians, Germans,—of all religions, Jews, Christians, Mahometans, idolaters, covered with painted sores, beggars by day, were transformed by night into brigands; an immense dressing-room, in a word, where, at that epoch, the actors of that eternal comedy, which theft, prostitution, and murder play upon the pavements of Paris, dressed and undressed.

It was a vast place, irregular and badly paved, like all the squares of Paris at that date. Fires, around which swarmed strange groups, blazed here and there. Every one was going, coming, and shouting. Shrill laughter was to be heard, the wailing of children, the voices of women. The hands and heads of this throng, black against the luminous background, outlined against it a thousand eccentric gestures. At times, upon the ground, where trembled the light of the fires, mingled with large, indefinite shadows, one could behold a dog passing, which resembled a man, a man who resembled a dog. The limits of races and species seemed effaced in this city, as in a pandemonium. Men, women, beasts, age, sex, health, maladies, all seemed to be in common among these people; all went together, they mingled, confounded, superposed; each one there participated in all.

The poor and flickering flames of the fire permitted Gringoire to distinguish, amid his trouble, all around the immense place, a hideous frame of ancient houses, whose wormeaten, shrivelled, stunted façades, each pierced with one or two lighted attic windows, seemed to him, in the darkness, like enormous heads of old women, ranged in a circle, monstrous and crabbed, winking as they looked on at the Witches' Sabbath.

It was like a new world, unknown, unheard of, misshapen, creeping, swarming, fantastic.

Gringoire, more and more terrified, clutched by the three beggars as by three pairs of tongs, dazed by a throng of other faces which frothed and yelped around him, unhappy Gringoire endeavored to summon his presence of mind, in order to recall whether it was a Saturday. But his efforts were vain; the thread of his memory and of his thought was broken; and, doubting everything, wavering between what he saw and what he felt, he put to himself this unanswerable question: "If I exist, does this exist? If this exists, do I exist?"

At that moment, a distinct cry arose in the buzzing throng that surrounded him, "Let's take him to the king! Let's take him to the king!"

"Holy Virgin!" murmured Gringoire, "the king here must be a ram."

"To the king! To the king!" repeated all voices.

They dragged him off. Each vied with the other in laying his claws upon him. But the three beggars did not loose their hold and tore him from the rest, howling, "He belongs to us!"

The poet's already sickly doublet yielded its last sigh in this struggle.

While traversing the horrible place, his vertigo vanished. After taking a few steps, the sentiment of reality returned to him. He began to become accustomed to the atmosphere of the place. At the first moment there had arisen from his poet's head, or, simply and prosaically, from his empty stomach, a mist, a vapor, so to speak, which, spreading between objects and himself, permitted him to catch a glimpse of them only in the incoherent fog of nightmare, in those shadows of dreams which distort every outline, agglomerating objects into unwieldy groups, dilating things into chimeras, and men into phantoms. Little by little, this hallucination was succeeded by a less bewildered and exaggerating view. Reality made its way to the light around him, struck his eyes, struck his feet, and demolished, bit by bit, all that frightful poetry with which he had, at first, believed himself to be surrounded. He was forced to perceive that he was not walking in the Styx, but in mud, that he was elbowed not by demons, but by thieves; that it was not his soul which was in question, but his life (since he lacked that precious conciliator, which places itself so effectually between the bandit and the honest man—a purse). In short, on examining the orgy more closely, and with more coolness, he fell from the Witches' Sabbath to the dram-shop.

The Cour des Miracles was, in fact, merely a dram-shop; but a brigand's dram-shop, reddened quite as much with blood as with wine.

The spectacle that presented itself to his eyes, when his ragged escort finally deposited him at the end of his trip, was not fitted to bear him back to poetry, even to the poetry of hell. It was more than ever the prosaic and brutal reality of the tavern. Were we not in the fifteenth century, we would say that Gringoire had descended from Michael Angelo to Callot.

Around a great fire that burned on a large, circular flagstone, the flames of which had heated red-hot the legs of a tripod, which was empty for the moment, some wormeaten tables were placed, here and there, haphazard, no lackey of a geometrical turn having deigned to adjust their parallelism, or to see to it that they did not make too unusual angles. Upon these tables gleamed several dripping pots of wine and beer, and round these pots were grouped many bacchic visages, purple with the fire and the wine. There was a man with a huge belly and a jovial face, noisily kissing a woman of the town, thickset and brawny. There was a sort of sham soldier, a *"naquois,"* as the slang expression runs, who was whistling as he undid the bandages from his fictitious wound, and removing the numbness from his sound and vigorous knee, which had been swathed since morning in a thousand ligatures. On the other hand, there was a wretched fellow, preparing with celandine and beef's blood, his "leg of God," for the next day. Two tables further on, a palmer, with his pilgrim's costume complete, was practising the lament of the Holy Queen, not forgetting the drone and the nasal drawl. Further on, a young scamp was taking a lesson in epilepsy from an old pretender, who was instructing him in the art of foaming at the mouth, by chewing a morsel of soap. Beside him, a man with the dropsy was getting rid of his swelling, and making four or five female thieves, who were disputing at the same table, over a child who had been stolen that evening, hold their noses. All circumstances which, two centuries later, "seemed so ridiculous to the court," as Sauval says, "that they served as a pastime to the king, and as an introduction to the royal ballet of Night, divided into four parts and danced on the theatre of the Petit-Bourbon." "Never," adds an eye witness of 1653, "have the sudden metamorphoses of the Court of Miracles been more happily presented. Benserade prepared us for it by some very gallant verses."

Loud laughter everywhere, and obscene songs. Each one held his own course, carping and swearing, without listening to his neighbor. Pots clinked, and quarrels sprang up at the shock of the pots, and the broken pots made rents in the rags.

A big dog, seated on his tail, gazed at the fire. Some children were mingled in this orgy. The stolen child wept and cried. Another, a big boy four years of age, seated with legs dangling, upon a bench that was too high for him, before a table that reached to his chin, and uttering not a word. A third, gravely spreading out upon the table with his finger the melted tallow that dripped from a candle. Last of all, a little fellow crouching in the mud, almost lost in a cauldron, which he was scraping with a tile, and from which he was evoking a sound that would have made Stradivarius swoon.

Near the fire was a hogshead, and on the hogshead a beggar. This was the king on his throne.

The three who had Gringoire in their clutches led him in front of this hogshead, and the entire bacchanal rout fell silent for a moment, with the exception of the cauldron inhabited by the child.

Gringoire dared neither breathe nor raise his eyes.

"*Hombre, quita tu sombrero!*" said one of the three knaves, in whose grasp he was, and, before he had comprehended the meaning, the other had snatched his hat—a wretched headgear, it is true, but still good on a sunny day or when there was but little rain. Gringoire sighed.

Meanwhile the king addressed him, from the summit of his cask, "Who is this rogue?"

Gringoire shuddered. That voice, although accentuated by menace, recalled to him another voice, which, that very morning, had dealt the deathblow to his mystery, by drawling, nasally, in the midst of the audience, "Charity, please!" He raised his head. It was indeed Clopin Trouillefou.

Clopin Trouillefou, arrayed in his royal insignia, wore neither one rag more nor one rag less. The sore upon his arm had already disappeared. He held in his hand one of those whips made of thongs of white leather, which police sergeants then used to repress the crowd, and which were called *boullayes*. On his head he wore a sort of headgear, bound round and closed at the top. But it was difficult to make out whether it was a child's cap or a king's crown, the two things bore so strong a resemblance to each other.

Meanwhile Gringoire, without knowing why, had regained some hope, on recognizing in the King of the Cour des Miracles his accursed mendicant of the Grand Hall.

"Master," stammered he; "monseigneur—sire—how ought I to address you?" he said at length, having reached the culminating point of his crescendo, and knowing neither how to mount higher, nor to descend again.

"Monseigneur, his majesty, or comrade, call me what you please. But make haste. What have you to say in your own defence?"

"In your own defence?" thought Gringoire, "that displeases me." He resumed, stuttering, "I am he, who this morning—"

"By the devil's claws!" interrupted Clopin, "your name, knave, and nothing more. Listen. You are in the presence of three powerful sovereigns: myself, Clopin Trouillefou, King of Thunes, successor to the Grand Coësre, supreme suzerain of the Realm of Argot; Mathias Hunyadi Spicali, Duke of Egypt and of Bohemia, the old yellow fellow whom you see yonder, with a dish clout round his head; Guillaume Rousseau, Emperor of Galilee, that fat fellow who is not listening to us but caressing a wench. We are your judges. You have entered the Kingdom of Argot, without being an *argotier*; you have violated the privileges of our city. You must be punished unless you are a *capon*, a *franc-mitou* or a *rifodé*; that is to say, in the slang of honest folks, a thief, a beggar, or a vagabond. Are you anything of that sort? Justify yourself; announce your titles."

"Alas!" said Gringoire, "I have not that honor. I am the author—"

"That is sufficient," resumed Trouillefou, without permitting him to finish. "You are going to be hanged. 'Tis a very simple matter, gentlemen and honest bourgeois! As you treat our people in your abode, so we treat you in ours! The law that you apply to vagabonds, vagabonds apply to you. 'Tis your fault if it is harsh. One really must behold the grimace of an honest man above the hempen collar now and then; that renders the thing honorable. Come, friend, divide your rags gayly among these damsels. I am going to have you hanged to amuse the vagabonds, and you are to give them your purse to drink your health. If you have any mummery to go through with, there's a very good God the Father in that mortar yonder, in stone, which we stole from Saint-Pierre aux Boeufs. You have four minutes in which to fling your soul at his head."

The harangue was formidable.

"Well said, upon my soul! Clopin Trouillefou preaches like the Holy Father the Pope!" exclaimed the Emperor of Galilee, smashing his pot in order to prop up his table.

"Messeigneurs, emperors, and kings," said Gringoire coolly (for I know not how, firmness had returned to him, and he spoke with resolution), "don't think of such a thing; my name is Pierre Gringoire. I am the poet whose morality was presented this morning in the grand hall of the Courts."

"Ah! So it was you, master!" said Clopin. "I was there, *tête-Dieu!* Well, comrade, is that any reason, because you bored us to death this morning, that you should not be hung this evening?"

"I shall find difficulty in getting out of it," said Gringoire to himself. Nevertheless, he made one more effort: "I don't see why poets are not classed with vagabonds," said he. "Vagabond, Aesopus certainly was; Homerus was a beggar; Mercurius was a thief—"

Clopin interrupted him: "I believe that you are trying to blarney us with your jargon. Zounds! Let yourself be hung, and don't kick up such a row over it!"

"Pardon me, monseigneur, the King of Thunes," replied Gringoire, disputing the ground foot by foot. "It is worth trouble—one moment! Listen to me. You are not going to condemn me without having heard me—"

His unlucky voice was, in fact, drowned in the uproar that rose around him. The little boy scraped away at his cauldron with more spirit than ever; and, to crown all, an old woman had just placed on the tripod a frying-pan of grease, which hissed away on the fire with a noise similar to the cry of a troop of children in pursuit of a masker.

In the meantime, Clopin Trouillefou appeared to hold a momentary conference with the Duke of Egypt, and the Emperor of Galilee, who was completely drunk. Then he shouted shrilly: "Silence!" and, as the cauldron and the frying-pan did not heed him, and continued their duet, he jumped down from his hogshead, gave a kick to the boiler, which rolled ten paces away bearing the child with it, a kick to the frying-pan, which upset in the fire with all its grease, and gravely remounted his throne, without troubling himself about the stifled tears of the child, or the grumbling of the old woman, whose supper was wasting away in a fine white flame.

Trouillefou made a sign, and the duke, the emperor, and the passed masters of pickpockets, and the isolated robbers, came and ranged themselves around him in a horseshoe, of which Gringoire, still roughly held by the body, formed the centre. It was a semicircle of rags, tatters, tinsel, pitchforks, axes, legs staggering with intoxication, huge, bare arms, faces sordid, dull, and stupid. In the midst of this Round Table of beggary, Clopin Trouillefou—as the doge of this senate, as the king of this peerage, as the pope of this conclave—dominated; first by virtue of the height of his hogshead, and next by virtue of an indescribable, haughty, fierce, and formidable air, which caused his eyes to flash, and corrected in his savage profile the bestial type of the race of vagabonds. One would have pronounced him a boar amid a herd of swine.

"Listen," said he to Gringoire, fondling his misshapen chin with his horny hand. "I don't see why you should not be hung. It is true that it appears to be repugnant to you; and it is very natural, for you bourgeois are not accustomed to it. You form for yourselves a great idea of the thing. After all, we don't wish you any harm. Here is a means of extricating yourself from your predicament for the moment. Will you become one of us?"

The reader can judge of the effect that this proposition produced upon Gringoire, who beheld life slipping away from him, and who was beginning to lose his hold upon it. He clutched at it again with energy.

"Certainly I will, and right heartily," said he.

"Do you consent," resumed Clopin, "to enroll yourself among the people of the knife?"

"Of the knife, precisely," responded Gringoire.

"You recognize yourself as a member of the free bourgeoisie?" added the King of Thunes.

"Of the free bourgeoisie."

"Subject of the Kingdom of Argot?"

"Of the Kingdom of Argot" [thieves].

"A vagabond?"

"A vagabond."

"In your soul?"

"In my soul."

"I must call your attention to the fact," continued the king, "that you will be hung all the same."

"The devil!" said the poet.

"Only," continued Clopin imperturbably, "you will be hung later on, with more ceremony, at the expense of the good city of Paris, on a handsome stone gibbet, and by honest men. That is a consolation."

"Just so," responded Gringoire.

"There are other advantages. In your quality of a high-toned sharper, you will not have to pay the taxes on mud, or the poor, or lanterns, to which the bourgeois of Paris are subject."

"So be it," said the poet. "I agree. I am a vagabond, a thief, a sharper, a man of the knife, anything you please; and I am all that already, monsieur, King of Thunes, for I am a philosopher; *et omnia in philosophia, omnes in philosopho continentur*—all things are contained in philosophy, all men in the philosopher, as you know."

The King of Thunes scowled.

"What do you take me for, my friend? What Hungarian Jew patter are you jabbering at us? I don't know Hebrew. One isn't a Jew because one is a bandit. I don't even steal any longer. I'm above that; I kill. Cut-throat, yes; cutpurse, no."

Gringoire tried to slip in some excuse between these curt words, which wrath rendered more and more jerky.

"I ask your pardon, monseigneur. It is not Hebrew; 'tis Latin."

"I tell you," resumed Clopin angrily, "that I'm not a Jew, and that I'll have you hung, belly of the synagogue, like that little shopkeeper of Judea, who is by your side, and whom I entertain strong hopes of seeing nailed to a counter one of these days, like the counterfeit coin that he is!"

So saying, he pointed his finger at the little, bearded Hungarian Jew who had accosted Gringoire with his *facitote caritatem*, and who, understanding no other language beheld with surprise the King of Thunes's ill-humor overflow upon him.

At length Monsieur Clopin calmed down.

"So you will be a vagabond, you knave?" he said to our poet.

"Of course," replied the poet.

"Willing is not all," said the surly Clopin; "good will doesn't put one onion the more into the soup, and 'tis good for nothing except to go to Paradise with; now, Paradise and the thieves' band are two different things. In order to be received among the thieves, you must prove that you are good for something, and for that purpose, you must search the manikin."

"I'll search anything you like," said Gringoire.

Clopin made a sign. Several thieves detached themselves from the circle, and returned a moment later. They brought two thick posts, terminated at their lower extremities in spreading timber supports, which made them stand readily upon the ground; to the upper extremity of the two posts they fitted a cross-beam, and the whole constituted a very pretty portable gibbet, which Gringoire had the satisfaction of beholding rise before him, in a twinkling. Nothing was lacking, not even the rope, which swung gracefully over the cross-beam.

"What are they going to do?" Gringoire asked himself with some uneasiness. A sound of bells, which he heard at that moment, put an end to his anxiety; it was a stuffed manikin, which the vagabonds were suspending by the neck from the rope, a sort of scarecrow dressed in red, and so hung with mule-bells and larger bells, that one might have tricked out thirty Castilian mules with them. These thousand tiny bells quivered for some time with the vibration of the rope, then gradually died away, and finally became silent when the manikin had been brought into a state of immobility by that law of the pendulum which has dethroned the water clock and the hour-glass. Then Clopin, pointing out to Gringoire a rickety old stool placed beneath the manikin, "Climb up there."

"Death of the devil!" objected Gringoire; "I shall break my neck. Your stool limps like one of Martial's distiches; it has one hexameter leg and one pentameter leg."

"Climb!" repeated Clopin.

Gringoire mounted the stool, and succeeded, not without some oscillations of head and arms, in regaining his centre of gravity.

"Now," went on the King of Thunes, "twist your right foot round your left leg, and rise on the tip of your left foot."

"Monseigneur," said Gringoire, "so you absolutely insist on my breaking some one of my limbs?"

Clopin tossed his head.

"Hark ye, my friend, you talk too much. Here's the gist of the matter in two words: you are to rise on tiptoe, as I tell you; in that way you will be able to reach the pocket of the manikin, you will rummage it, you will pull out the purse that is there—and if you do all this without our hearing the sound of a bell, all is well: you shall be a vagabond. All we shall then have to do, will be to thrash you soundly for the space of a week."

"*Ventre-Dieu*! I will be careful," said Gringoire. "And suppose I do make the bells sound?"

"Then you will be hanged. Do you understand?"

"I don't understand at all," replied Gringoire.

"Listen, once more. You are to search the manikin, and take away its purse; if a single bell stirs during the operation, you will be hung. Do you understand that?"

"Good," said Gringoire; "I understand that. And then?"

"If you succeed in removing the purse without our hearing the bells, you are a vagabond, and you will be thrashed for eight consecutive days. You understand now, no doubt?"

"No, monseigneur; I no longer understand. Where is the advantage to me? Hanged in one case, cudgelled in the other?"

"And a vagabond," resumed Clopin, "and a vagabond; is that nothing? It is for your interest that we should beat you, in order to harden you to blows."

"Many thanks," replied the poet.

"Come, make haste," said the king, stamping upon his cask, which resounded like a huge drum! "Search the manikin, and let there be an end to this! I warn you for the last time, that if I hear a single bell, you will take the place of the manikin."

The band of thieves applauded Clopin's words, and arranged themselves in a circle round the gibbet, with a laugh so pitiless that Gringoire perceived that he amused them too much not to have everything to fear from them. No hope was left for him, accordingly, unless it were the slight chance of succeeding in the formidable operation which was imposed upon him; he decided to risk it, but it was not without first having addressed a fervent prayer to the manikin he was about to plunder, and who would have been easier to move to pity than the vagabonds. These myriad bells, with their little copper tongues, seemed to him like the mouths of so many asps, open and ready to sting and to hiss.

"Oh!" he said, in a very low voice, "is it possible that my life depends on the slightest vibration of the least of these bells? Oh!" he added, with clasped hands, "bells, do not ring, hand-bells do not clang, mule-bells do not quiver!"

He made one more attempt upon Trouillefou.

"And if there should come a gust of wind?"

"You will be hanged," replied the other, without hesitation.

Perceiving that no respite, nor reprieve, nor subterfuge was possible, he bravely decided upon his course of action; he wound his right foot round his left leg, raised himself on his left foot, and stretched out his arm: but at the moment when his hand touched the manikin, his body, which was now supported upon one leg only, wavered on the stool which had but three; he made an involuntary effort to support himself by the manikin, lost his balance, and fell heavily to the ground, deafened by the fatal vibration of the thousand bells of the manikin, which, yielding to the impulse imparted by his hand, described first a rotary motion, and then swayed majestically between the two posts.

"Malediction!" he cried as he fell, and remained as though dead, with his face to the earth.

Meanwhile, he heard the dreadful peal above his head, the diabolical laughter of the vagabonds, and the voice of Trouillefou saying, "Pick me up that knave, and hang him without ceremony." He rose. They had already detached the manikin to make room for him.

The thieves made him mount the stool, Clopin came to him, passed the rope about his neck, and, tapping him on the shoulder, "Adieu, my friend. You can't escape now, even if you digested with the pope's guts."

The word "Mercy!" died away upon Gringoire's lips. He cast his eyes about him; but there was no hope: all were laughing.

"Bellevigne de l'Etoile," said the King of Thunes to an enormous vagabond, who stepped out from the ranks, "climb upon the cross beam."

Bellevigne de l'Etoile nimbly mounted the transverse beam, and in another minute, Gringoire, on raising his eyes, beheld him, with terror, seated upon the beam above his head.

"Now," resumed Clopin Trouillefou, "as soon as I clap my hands, you, Andry the Red, will fling the stool to the ground with a blow of your knee; you, François Chante-Prune, will cling to the feet of the rascal; and you, Bellevigne, will fling yourself on his shoulders; and all three at once, do you hear?"

Gringoire shuddered.

"Are you ready?" said Clopin Trouillefou to the three thieves, who held themselves in readiness to fall upon Gringoire. A moment of horrible suspense ensued for the poor victim, during which Clopin tranquilly thrust into the fire with the tip of his foot, some bits of vine shoots which the flame had not caught. "Are you ready?" he repeated, and opened his hands to clap. One second more and all would have been over.

But he paused, as though struck by a sudden thought.

"One moment!" said he; "I forgot! It is our custom not to hang a man without inquiring whether there is any woman who wants him. Comrade, this is your last resource. You must wed either a female vagabond or the noose."

This law of the vagabonds, singular as it may strike the reader, remains today written out at length, in ancient English legislation.

Gringoire breathed again. This was the second time that he had returned to life within an hour. So he did not dare to trust to it too implicitly.

"Hallo!" cried Clopin, mounted once more upon his cask, "hallo women, females, is there among you, from the sorceress to

her cat, a wench who wants this rascal? Hey Colette la Charonne!
Elisabeth Trouvain! Simone Jodouyne! Marie Piédebou! Thonne la
Longue! Bérarde Fanouel! Michelle Genaille! Claude Rouge-oreille!
Mathurine Girorou! Hey! Isabeau-la-Thierrye! Come and see! A man
for nothing! Who wants him?"

Gringoire, no doubt, was not very appetizing in this miserable
condition. The female vagabonds did not seem to be much affected
by the proposition. The unhappy wretch heard them answer: "No, no!
Hang him; there'll be the more fun for us all!"

Nevertheless, three emerged from the throng and came to smell of
him. The first was a big wench, with a square face. She examined the
philosopher's deplorable doublet attentively. His garment was worn,
and more full of holes than a stove for roasting chestnuts. The girl
made a wry face. "Old rag!" she muttered, and addressing Gringoire,
"Let's see your cloak!" "I have lost it," replied Gringoire. "Your hat?"
"They took it away from me." "Your shoes?" "They have hardly any
soles left." "Your purse?" "Alas!" stammered Gringoire, "I have not
even a sou." "Let them hang you, then, and say 'Thank you!'" retorted
the vagabond wench, turning her back on him.

The second, old, black, wrinkled, hideous, with an ugliness
conspicuous even in the Cour des Miracles, trotted round Gringoire.
He almost trembled lest she should want him. But she mumbled
between her teeth, "He's too thin," and went off.

The third was a young girl, quite fresh, and not too ugly. "Save
me!" said the poor fellow to her, in a low tone. She gazed at him for
a moment with an air of pity, then dropped her eyes, made a plait
in her petticoat, and remained in indecision. He followed all these
movements with his eyes; it was the last gleam of hope. "No," said the
young girl, at length, "no! Guillaume Longuejoue would beat me."
She retreated into the crowd.

"You are unlucky, comrade," said Clopin.

Then rising to his feet, upon his hogshead. "No one wants him," he
exclaimed, imitating the accent of an auctioneer, to the great delight of
all; "no one wants him? Once, twice, three times!" and, turning toward
the gibbet with a sign of his hand, "Gone!"

Bellevigne de l'Etoile, Andry the Red, François Chante-Prune,
stepped up to Gringoire.

At that moment a cry arose among the thieves: "La Esmeralda! La
Esmeralda!"

Gringoire shuddered, and turned toward the side whence the clamor proceeded.

The crowd opened, and gave passage to a pure and dazzling form.

It was the gypsy.

"La Esmeralda!" said Gringoire, stupefied in the midst of his emotions, by the abrupt manner in which that magic word knotted together all his reminiscences of the day.

This rare creature seemed, even in the Cour des Miracles, to exercise her sway of charm and beauty. The vagabonds, male and female, ranged themselves gently along her path, and their brutal faces beamed beneath her glance.

She approached the victim with her light step. Her pretty Djali followed her. Gringoire was more dead than alive. She examined him for a moment in silence.

"You are going to hang this man?" she said gravely, to Clopin.

"Yes, sister," replied the King of Thunes, "unless you will take him for your husband."

She made her pretty little pout with her under lip. "I'll take him," said she.

Gringoire firmly believed that he had been in a dream ever since morning, and that this was the continuation of it.

The change was, in fact, violent, though a gratifying one. They undid the noose, and made the poet step down from the stool. His emotion was so lively that he was obliged to sit down.

The Duke of Egypt brought an earthenware crock, without uttering a word. The gypsy offered it to Gringoire: "Fling it on the ground," said she.

The crock broke into four pieces.

"Brother," then said the Duke of Egypt, laying his hands upon their foreheads, "she is your wife; sister, he is your husband for four years. Go."

CHAPTER 7

A Bridal Night

A FEW MOMENTS later our poet found himself in a tiny arched chamber, very cosy, very warm, seated at a table which appeared to ask nothing better than to make some loans from a larder hanging near by, having a good bed in prospect, and alone with a pretty girl. The adventure smacked of enchantment. He began seriously to take himself for a personage in a fairy tale; he cast his eyes about him from time to time to time, as though to see if the chariot of fire, harnessed to two-winged chimeras, which alone could have so rapidly transported him from Tartarus to Paradise, were still there. At times, also, he fixed his eyes obstinately upon the holes in his doublet, in order to cling to reality, and not lose the ground from under his feet completely. His reason, tossed about in imaginary space, now hung only by this thread.

The young girl did not appear to pay any attention to him; she went and came, displaced a stool, talked to her goat, and indulged in a pout now and then. At last she came and seated herself near the table, and Gringoire was able to scrutinize her at his ease.

You have been a child, reader, and you would, perhaps, be very happy to be one still. It is quite certain that you have not, more than once (and for my part, I have passed whole days, the best employed of my life, at it) followed from thicket to thicket, by the side of running water, on a sunny day, a beautiful green or blue dragon-fly, breaking its flight in abrupt angles, and kissing the tips of all the branches. You recollect with what amorous curiosity your thought and your gaze were riveted upon this little whirlwind, hissing and humming with wings of purple and azure, in the midst of which floated an imperceptible body, veiled by the very rapidity of its movement. The aerial being that was dimly outlined amid this quivering of wings, appeared to you chimerical, imaginary, impossible to touch, impossible to see. But when, at length, the dragon-fly alighted on the tip of a reed, and, holding your breath the while, you were able to examine the long, gauze wings, the long enamel robe, the two globes of crystal, what astonishment you felt, and what fear lest you should again behold the form disappear into a shade, and the creature into a chimera! Recall these impressions, and you will readily appreciate what Gringoire felt on contemplating, beneath her visible and palpable form, that Esmeralda of whom, up to that time, he had only caught a glimpse, amidst a whirlwind of dance, song, and tumult.

Sinking deeper and deeper into his revery: "So this," he said to himself, following her vaguely with his eyes, "is la Esmeralda! A celestial creature! A street dancer! So much, and so little! 'Twas she who dealt the death-blow to my mystery this morning, 'tis she who saves my life this evening! My evil genius! My good angel! A pretty woman, on my word! And who must needs love me madly to have taken me in that fashion. By the way," said he, rising suddenly, with that sentiment of the true that formed the foundation of his character and his philosophy, "I don't know very well how it happens, but I am her husband!"

With this idea in his head and in his eyes, he stepped up to the young girl in a manner so military and so gallant that she drew back.

"What do you want of me?" said she.

"Can you ask me, adorable Esmeralda?" replied Gringoire, with so passionate an accent that he was himself astonished at it on hearing himself speak.

The gypsy opened her great eyes. "I don't know what you mean."

"What!" resumed Gringoire, growing warmer and warmer, and supposing that, after all, he had to deal merely with a virtue of the Cour des Miracles; "am I not thine, sweet friend, art thou not mine?"

And, quite ingenuously, he clasped her waist.

The gypsy's corsage slipped through his hands like the skin of an eel. She bounded from one end of the tiny room to the other, stooped down, and raised herself again, with a little poniard in her hand, before Gringoire had even had time to see whence the poniard came; proud and angry, with swelling lips and inflated nostrils, her cheeks as red as an api apple [a dessert apple], and her eyes darting lightnings. At the same time, the white goat placed itself in front of her, and presented to Gringoire a hostile front, bristling with two pretty horns, gilded and very sharp. All this took place in the twinkling of an eye.

The dragon-fly had turned into a wasp, and asked nothing better than to sting.

Our philosopher was speechless, and turned his astonished eyes from the goat to the young girl. "Holy Virgin!" he said at last, when surprise permitted him to speak, "here are two hearty dames!"

The gypsy broke the silence on her side.

"You must be a very bold knave!"

"Pardon, mademoiselle," said Gringoire, with a smile. "But why did you take me for your husband?"

"Should I have allowed you to be hanged?"

"So," said the poet, somewhat disappointed in his amorous hopes. "You had no other idea in marrying me than to save me from the gibbet?"

"And what other idea did you suppose that I had?"

Gringoire bit his lips. "Come," said he, "I am not yet so triumphant in Cupido, as I thought. But then, what was the good of breaking that poor jug?"

Meanwhile Esmeralda's dagger and the goat's horns were still upon the defensive.

"Mademoiselle Esmeralda," said the poet, "let us come to terms. I am not a clerk of the court, and I shall not go to law with you for thus carrying a dagger in Paris, in the teeth of the ordinances and prohibitions of M. the Provost. Nevertheless, you are not ignorant of the fact that Noel Lescrivain was condemned, a week ago, to pay ten Parisian sous, for having carried a cutlass. But this is no affair of mine, and I will come to the point. I swear to you, upon my share of Paradise, not to approach you without your leave and permission, but do give me some supper."

The truth is, Gringoire was, like M. Despreaux, "not very voluptuous." He did not belong to that chevalier and musketeer species who take young girls by assault. In the matter of love, as in all other affairs, he willingly assented to temporizing and adjusting terms; and a good supper, and an amiable tête-a-tête appeared to him, especially when he was hungry, an excellent interlude between the prologue and the catastrophe of a love adventure.

The gypsy did not reply. She made her disdainful little grimace, drew up her head like a bird, then burst out laughing, and the tiny poniard disappeared as it had come, without Gringoire being able to see where the wasp concealed its sting.

A moment later, there stood upon the table a loaf of rye bread, a slice of bacon, some wrinkled apples and a jug of beer. Gringoire began to eat eagerly. One would have said, to hear the furious clashing of his iron fork and his earthenware plate, that all his love had turned to appetite.

The young girl seated opposite him, watched him in silence, visibly preoccupied with another thought, at which she smiled from time to time, while her soft hand caressed the intelligent head of the goat, gently pressed between her knees.

A candle of yellow wax illuminated this scene of voracity and revery.

Meanwhile, the first cravings of his stomach having been stilled, Gringoire felt some false shame at perceiving that nothing remained but one apple.

"You do not eat, Mademoiselle Esmeralda?"

She replied by a negative sign of the head, and her pensive glance fixed itself upon the vault of the ceiling.

"What the deuce is she thinking of?" thought Gringoire, staring at what she was gazing at; "'tis impossible that it can be that stone dwarf carved in the keystone of that arch, which thus absorbs her attention. What the deuce! I can bear the comparison!"

He raised his voice, "Mademoiselle!"

She seemed not to hear him.

He repeated, still more loudly, "Mademoiselle Esmeralda!"

Trouble wasted. The young girl's mind was elsewhere, and Gringoire's voice had not the power to recall it. Fortunately, the goat interfered. She began to pull her mistress gently by the sleeve.

"What dost thou want, Djali?" said the gypsy, hastily, as though suddenly awakened.

"She is hungry," said Gringoire, charmed to enter into conversation. Esmeralda began to crumble some bread, which Djali ate gracefully from the hollow of her hand.

Moreover, Gringoire did not give her time to resume her revery. He hazarded a delicate question.

"So you don't want me for your husband?"

The young girl looked at him intently, and said, "No."

"For your lover?" went on Gringoire.

She pouted, and replied, "No."

"For your friend?" pursued Gringoire.

She gazed fixedly at him again, and said, after a momentary reflection, "Perhaps."

This "perhaps," so dear to philosophers, emboldened Gringoire.

"Do you know what friendship is?" he asked.

"Yes," replied the gypsy; "it is to be brother and sister; two souls which touch without mingling, two fingers on one hand."

"And love?" pursued Gringoire.

"Oh, love!" said she, and her voice trembled, and her eye beamed. "That is to be two and to be but one. A man and a woman mingled into one angel. It is heaven."

The street dancer had a beauty as she spoke thus, that struck Gringoire singularly, and seemed to him in perfect keeping with the almost oriental exaltation of her words. Her pure, red lips half smiled; her serene and candid brow became troubled, at intervals, under her thoughts, like a mirror under the breath; and from beneath her long, drooping, black eyelashes, there escaped a sort of ineffable light, which gave to her profile that ideal serenity which Raphael found at the mystic point of intersection of virginity, maternity, and divinity.

Nevertheless, Gringoire continued, "What must one be then, in order to please you?"

"A man."

"And I—" said he, "what, then, am I?"

"A man has a hemlet on his head, a sword in his hand, and golden spurs on his heels."

"Good," said Gringoire, "without a horse, no man. Do you love any one?"

"As a lover?"

"Yes."

She remained thoughtful for a moment, then said with a peculiar expression: "That I shall know soon."

"Why not this evening?" resumed the poet tenderly. "Why not me?"

She cast a grave glance upon him and said, "I can never love a man who cannot protect me."

Gringoire colored, and took the hint. It was evident that the young girl was alluding to the slight assistance that he had rendered her in the critical situation in which she had found herself two hours previously. This memory, effaced by his own adventures of the evening, now recurred to him. He smote his brow.

"By the way, mademoiselle, I ought to have begun there. Pardon my foolish absence of mind. How did you contrive to escape from the claws of Quasimodo?"

This question made the gypsy shudder.

"Oh! The horrible hunchback," said she, hiding her face in her hands. And she shuddered as though with violent cold.

"Horrible, in truth," said Gringoire, who clung to his idea; "but how did you manage to escape him?"

La Esmeralda smiled, sighed, and remained silent.

"Do you know why he followed you?" began Gringoire again, seeking to return to his question by a circuitous route.

"I don't know," said the young girl, and she added hastily, "but you were following me also, why were you following me?"

"In good faith," responded Gringoire, "I don't know either."

Silence ensued. Gringoire slashed the table with his knife. The young girl smiled and seemed to be gazing through the wall at something. All at once she began to sing in a barely articulate voice:

> Quando las pintadas aves,
> Mudas estan, y la tierra—

She broke off abruptly, and began to caress Djali.

"That's a pretty animal of yours," said Gringoire.

"She is my sister," she answered.

"Why are you called 'la Esmeralda'?" asked the poet.

"I do not know."

"But why?"

She drew from her bosom a sort of little oblong bag, suspended from her neck by a string of adrézarach beads. This bag exhaled a strong odor of camphor. It was covered with green silk, and bore in its centre a large piece of green glass, in imitation of an emerald.

"Perhaps it is because of this," said she.

Gringoire was on the point of taking the bag in his hand. She drew back.

"Don't touch it! It is an amulet. You would injure the charm or the charm would injure you."

The poet's curiosity was more and more aroused.

"Who gave it to you?"

She laid one finger on her mouth and concealed the amulet in her bosom. He tried a few more questions, but she hardly replied.

"What is the meaning of the words, 'la Esmeralda'?"

"I don't know," said she.

"To what language do they belong?"

"They are Egyptian, I think."

"I suspected as much," said Gringoire, "you are not a native of France?"

"I don't know."

"Are your parents alive?"

She began to sing, to an ancient air:

> *Mon père est oiseau,*
> *Ma mère est oiselle.*
> *Je passe l'eau sans nacelle,*
> *Je passe l'eau sans bateau,*
> *Ma mère est oiselle,*
> *Mon père est oiseau.*

"Good," said Gringoire. "At what age did you come to France?"

"When I was very young."

"And when to Paris?"

"Last year. At the moment when we were entering the papal gate I saw a reed warbler flit through the air, that was at the end of August; I said, it will be a hard winter."

"So it was," said Gringoire, delighted at this beginning of a conversation. "I passed it in blowing my fingers. So you have the gift of prophecy?"

She retired into her laconics again.

"Is that man whom you call the Duke of Egypt, the chief of your tribe?"

"Yes."

"But it was he who married us," remarked the poet timidly.

She made her customary pretty grimace.

"I don't even know your name."

"My name? If you want it, here it is—Pierre Gringoire."

"I know a prettier one," said she.

"Naughty girl!" retorted the poet. "Never mind, you shall not provoke me. Wait, perhaps you will love me more when you know me better; and then, you have told me your story with so much confidence,

that I owe you a little of mine. You must know, then, that my name
is Pierre Gringoire, and that I am a son of the farmer of the notary's
office of Gonesse. My father was hung by the Burgundians, and my
mother disembowelled by the Picards, at the siege of Paris, twenty
years ago. At six years of age, therefore, I was an orphan, without a sole
to my foot except the pavements of Paris. I do not know how I passed
the interval from six to sixteen. A fruit dealer gave me a plum here,
a baker flung me a crust there; in the evening I got myself taken up
by the watch, who threw me into prison, and there I found a bundle
of straw. All this did not prevent my growing up and growing thin, as
you see. In the winter I warmed myself in the sun, under the porch
of the Hôtel de Sens, and I thought it very ridiculous that the fire on
Saint John's Day was reserved for the dog days. At sixteen, I wished
to choose a calling. I tried all in succession. I became a soldier; but
I was not brave enough. I became a monk; but I was not sufficiently
devout; and then I'm a bad hand at drinking. In despair, I became an
apprentice of the woodcutters, but I was not strong enough; I had
more of an inclination to become a schoolmaster; 'tis true that I did
not know how to read, but that's no reason. I perceived at the end of
a certain time, that I lacked something in every direction; and seeing
that I was good for nothing, of my own free will I became a poet
and rhymester. That is a trade that one can always adopt when one
is a vagabond, and it's better than stealing, as some young brigands
of my acquaintance advised me to do. One day I met by luck, Dom
Claude Frollo, the reverend archdeacon of Notre-Dame. He took an
interest in me, and it is to him that I today owe it that I am a veritable
man of letters, who knows Latin from the *de Officiis* of Cicero to
the mortuology of the Celestine Fathers, and a barbarian neither in
scholastics, nor in politics, nor in rhythmics, that sophism of sophisms.
I am the author of the Mystery which was presented today with great
triumph and a great concourse of populace, in the grand hall of the
Palais de Justice. I have also made a book that will contain six hundred
pages, on the wonderful comet of 1465, which sent one man mad.
I have enjoyed still other successes. Being somewhat of an artillery
carpenter, I lent a hand to Jean Mangue's great bombard, which burst,
as you know, on the day when it was tested, on the Pont de Charenton,
and killed four and twenty curious spectators. You see that I am not
a bad match in marriage. I know a great many sorts of very engaging
tricks, which I will teach your goat; for example, to mimic the Bishop

of Paris, that cursed Pharisee whose mill wheels splash passers-by the whole length of the Pont aux Meuniers. And then my mystery will bring me in a great deal of coined money, if they will only pay me. And finally, I am at your orders, I and my wits, and my science and my letters, ready to live with you, damsel, as it shall please you, chastely or joyously; husband and wife, if you see fit; brother and sister, if you think that better."

Gringoire ceased, awaiting the effect of his harangue on the young girl. Her eyes were fixed on the ground.

"'Phoebus,'" she said in a low voice. Then, turning toward the poet, "'Phoebus,' what does that mean?"

Gringoire, without exactly understanding what the connection could be between his address and this question, was not sorry to display his erudition. Assuming an air of importance, he replied, "It is a Latin word which means 'sun.'"

"Sun!" she repeated.

"It is the name of a handsome archer, who was a god," added Gringoire.

"A god!" repeated the gypsy, and there was something pensive and passionate in her tone.

At that moment, one of her bracelets became unfastened and fell. Gringoire stooped quickly to pick it up; when he straightened up, the young girl and the goat had disappeared. He heard the sound of a bolt. It was a little door, communicating, no doubt, with a neighboring cell, which was being fastened on the outside.

"Has she left me a bed, at least?" said our philosopher.

He made the tour of his cell. There was no piece of furniture adapted to sleeping purposes, except a tolerably long wooden coffer; and its cover was carved, to boot; which afforded Gringoire, when he stretched himself out upon it, a sensation somewhat similar to that which Micromégas would feel if he were to lie down on the Alps.

"Come!" said he, adjusting himself as well as possible, "I must resign myself. But here's a strange nuptial night. 'Tis a pity. There was something innocent and antediluvian about that broken crock, which quite pleased me."

Book Third

Chapter 1

Notre-Dame

THE CHURCH OF Notre-Dame de Paris is still no doubt, a majestic and sublime edifice. But, beautiful as it has been preserved in growing old, it is difficult not to sigh, not to wax indignant, before the numberless degradations and mutilations which time and men have both caused the venerable monument to suffer, without respect for Charlemagne, who laid its first stone, or for Philip Augustus, who laid the last.

On the face of this aged queen of our cathedrals, by the side of a wrinkle, one always finds a scar. *Tempus edax, homo edacior;* which I should be glad to translate thus: time is blind, man is stupid.

If we had leisure to examine with the reader, one by one, the diverse traces of destruction imprinted upon the old church, time's share would be the least, the share of men the most, especially the men of art, since there have been individuals who assumed the title of architects during the last two centuries.

And, in the first place, to cite only a few leading examples, there certainly are few finer architectural pages than this façade, where, successively and at once, the three portals hollowed out in an arch; the broidered and dentated cordon of the eight and twenty royal niches; the immense central rose window, flanked by its two lateral windows, like a priest by his deacon and subdeacon; the frail and lofty gallery of trefoil arcades, which supports a heavy platform above its fine, slender columns; and lastly, the two black and massive towers with their slate penthouses, harmonious parts of a magnificent whole, superposed in five gigantic stories; develop themselves before the eye, in a mass and without confusion, with their innumerable details of statuary, carving, and sculpture, joined powerfully to the tranquil grandeur of the whole; a vast symphony in stone, so to speak; the colossal work of one man and one people, all together one and complex, like the Iliads and the Romanceros, whose sister it is; prodigious product of the grouping together of all the forces of an epoch, where, upon each stone, one sees the fancy of the workman disciplined by the genius of the artist start forth in a hundred fashions; a sort of human creation, in a word, powerful and fecund as the divine creation of which it seems to have stolen the double character—variety, eternity.

And what we here say of the façade must be said of the entire church; and what we say of the cathedral church of Paris, must be said of all the churches of Christendom in the Middle Ages. All things are in place in that art, self-created, logical, and well proportioned. To measure the great toe of the foot is to measure the giant.

Let us return to the façade of Notre-Dame, as it still appears to us, when we go piously to admire the grave and puissant cathedral, which inspires terror, so its chronicles assert: *quoe mole sua terrorem incutit spectantibus.*

Three important things are today lacking in that façade: in the first place, the staircase of eleven steps which formerly raised it above the soil; next, the lower series of statues which occupied the niches of the three portals; and lastly the upper series, of the twenty-eight most ancient kings of France, which garnished the gallery of the first story, beginning with Childebert, and ending with Phillip Augustus, holding in his hand "the imperial apple."

Time has caused the staircase to disappear, by raising the soil of the city with a slow and irresistible progress; but, while thus causing the eleven steps which added to the majestic height of the edifice, to be devoured, one by one, by the rising tide of the pavements of Paris—time has bestowed upon the church perhaps more than it has taken away, for it is time which has spread over the façade that sombre hue of the centuries which makes the old age of monuments the period of their beauty.

But who has thrown down the two rows of statues? Who has left the niches empty? Who has cut, in the very middle of the central portal, that new and bastard arch? Who has dared to frame therein that commonplace and heavy door of carved wood, à la Louis XV, beside the arabesques of Biscornette? The men, the architects, the artists of our day.

And if we enter the interior of the edifice, who has overthrown that colossus of Saint Christopher, proverbial for magnitude among statues, as the grand hall of the Palais de Justice was among halls, as the spire of Strasbourg among spires? And those myriads of statues, which peopled all the spaces between the columns of the nave and the choir, kneeling, standing, equestrian, men, women, children, kings, bishops, gendarmes, in stone, in marble, in gold, in silver, in copper, in wax even—who has brutally swept them away? It is not time.

And who substituted for the ancient gothic altar, splendidly encumbered with shrines and reliquaries, that heavy marble sarcophagus, with angels' heads and clouds, which seems a specimen pillaged from the Val-de-Grâce or the Invalides? Who stupidly sealed that heavy anachronism of stone in the Carlovingian pavement of Hercandus? Was it not Louis XIV, fulfilling the request of Louis XIII?

And who put the cold, white panes in the place of those windows, "high in color," which caused the astonished eyes of our fathers to hesitate between the rose of the grand portal and the arches of the apse? And what would a sub-chanter of the sixteenth century say, on beholding the beautiful yellow wash, with which our archiepiscopal vandals have desmeared their cathedral? He would remember that it was the color with which the hangman smeared "accursed" edifices; he would recall the Hôtel du Petit-Bourbon, all smeared thus, on account of the constable's treason. "Yellow, after all, of so good a quality," said Sauval, "and so well recommended, that more than a century has not yet caused it to lose its color." He would think that the sacred place had become infamous, and would flee.

And if we ascend the cathedral, without mentioning a thousand barbarisms of every sort—what has become of that charming little bell tower, which rested upon the point of intersection of the cross-roofs, and which, no less frail and no less bold than its neighbor (also destroyed), the spire of the Sainte-Chapelle, buried itself in the sky, farther forward than the towers, slender, pointed, sonorous, carved in open work. An architect of good taste amputated it (1787), and considered it sufficient to mask the wound with that large, leaden plaster, which resembles a pot cover.

'Tis thus that the marvellous art of the Middle Ages has been treated in nearly every country, especially in France. One can distinguish on its ruins three sorts of lesions, all three of which cut into it at different depths; first, time, which has insensibly notched its surface here and there, and gnawed it everywhere; next, political and religious revolution, which, blind and wrathful by nature, have flung themselves tumultuously upon it, torn its rich garment of carving and sculpture, burst its rose windows, broken its necklace of arabesques and tiny figures, torn out its statues, sometimes because of their mitres, sometimes because of their crowns; lastly, fashions, even more grotesque and foolish, which, since the anarchical and splendid deviations of the Renaissance, have followed each other in the necessary decadence of architecture. Fashions have wrought more harm than revolutions. They have cut to the quick; they have attacked the very bone and framework of art; they have cut, slashed, disorganized, killed the edifice, in form as in the symbol, in its consistency as well as in its beauty. And then they have made it over; a presumption of which neither time nor revolutions at least have been guilty. They have audaciously adjusted, in the name of "good taste," upon the wounds of Gothic architecture, their miserable gewgaws of a day, their ribbons of marble, their pompons of metal, a veritable leprosy of egg-shaped ornaments, volutes, whorls, draperies, garlands, fringes, stone flames, bronze clouds, pudgy cupids, chubby-cheeked cherubim, which begin to devour the face of art in the oratory of Catherine de Medicis, and cause it to expire, two centuries later, tortured and grimacing, in the boudoir of the Dubarry.

Thus, to sum up the points that we have just indicated, three sorts of ravages today disfigure Gothic architecture. Wrinkles and warts on the epidermis; this is the work of time. Deeds of violence, brutalities, contusions, fractures; this is the work of the revolutions from Luther to Mirabeau. Mutilations, amputations, dislocation of the joints, "restorations"; this is the Greek, Roman, and barbarian work of professors according to Vitruvius and Vignole. This magnificent art produced by the Vandals has been slain by the academies. The centuries, the revolutions, which at least devastate with impartiality and grandeur, have been joined by a cloud of school architects, licensed, sworn, and bound by oath; defacing with the discernment and choice of bad taste, substituting the *chicorées* of Louis XV for the Gothic lace, for the greater glory of the Parthenon. It is the kick of the ass at the dying lion. It is the old oak crowning itself, and which, to heap the measure full, is stung, bitten, and gnawed by caterpillars.

How far it is from the epoch when Robert Cenalis, comparing Notre-Dame de Paris to the famous temple of Diana at Ephesus, so much lauded by the ancient pagans, which Erostatus has immortalized, found the Gallic temple "more excellent in length, breadth, height, and structure" [*Histoire Gallicane*, liv. II. Periode III. f. 130, p. 1].

Notre-Dame is not, moreover, what can be called a complete, definite, classified monument. It is no longer a Romanesque church; nor is it a Gothic church. This edifice is not a type. Notre-Dame de Paris has not, like the Abbey of Tournus, the grave and massive frame, the large and round vault, the glacial bareness, the majestic simplicity of the edifices that have the rounded arch for their progenitor. It is not, like the Cathedral of Bourges, the magnificent, light, multiform, tufted, bristling efflorescent product of the pointed arch. Impossible to class it in that ancient family of sombre, mysterious churches, low and crushed as it were by the round arch, almost Egyptian, with the exception of the ceiling; all hieroglyphics, all sacerdotal, all symbolical, more loaded in their ornaments, with lozenges and zigzags, than with flowers, with flowers than with animals, with animals than with men; the work of the architect less than of the bishop; first transformation of art, all impressed with theocratic and military discipline, taking root in the Lower Empire, and stopping with the time of William the Conqueror. Impossible to place our Cathedral in that other family of lofty, aerial churches, rich in painted windows and sculpture; pointed in form, bold in attitude; communal and bourgeois as political symbols; free, capricious, lawless, as a work of art; second transformation of architecture, no longer hieroglyphic, immovable and sacerdotal, but artistic, progressive, and popular, which begins at the return from the crusades, and ends with Louis IX. Notre-Dame de Paris is not of pure Romanesque, like the first; nor of pure Arabian race, like the second.

It is an edifice of the transition period. The Saxon architect completed the erection of the first pillars of the nave, when the pointed arch, which dates from the Crusade, arrived and placed itself as a conqueror upon the large Romanesque capitals that should support only round arches. The pointed arch, mistress since that time, constructed the rest of the church. Nevertheless, timid and inexperienced at the start, it sweeps out, grows larger, restrains itself, and dares no longer dart upwards in spires and lancet windows, as it did later on, in so many marvellous cathedrals. One would say that it were conscious of the vicinity of the heavy Romanesque pillars.

However, these edifices of the transition from the Romanesque to the Gothic, are no less precious for study than the pure types. They express a shade of the art that would be lost without them. It is the graft of the pointed upon the round arch.

Notre-Dame de Paris is, in particular, a curious specimen of this variety. Each face, each stone of the venerable monument, is a page not only of the history of the country, but of the history of science and art as well. Thus, in order to indicate here only the principal details, while the little Red Door almost attains to the limits of the Gothic delicacy of the fifteenth century, the pillars of the nave, by their size and weight, go back to the Carlovingian Abbey of Saint-Germain des Prés. One would suppose that six centuries separated these pillars from that door. There is no one, not even the hermetics, who does not find in the symbols of the grand portal a satisfactory compendium of their science, of which the Church of Saint-Jacques de la Boucherie was so complete a hieroglyph. Thus, the Roman abbey, the philosophers' church, the Gothic art, Saxon art, the heavy, round pillar, which recalls Gregory VII, the hermetic symbolism, with which Nicolas Flamel played the prelude to Luther, papal unity, schism, Saint-Germain des Prés, Saint-Jacques de la Boucherie—all are mingled, combined, amalgamated in Notre-Dame. This central mother church is, among the ancient churches of Paris, a sort of chimera; it has the head of one, the limbs of another, the haunches of another, something of all.

We repeat it, these hybrid constructions are not the least interesting for the artist, for the antiquarian, for the historian. They make one feel to what a degree architecture is a primitive thing, by demonstrating (what is also demonstrated by the cyclopean vestiges, the pyramids of Egypt, the gigantic Hindoo pagodas) that the greatest products of architecture are less the works of individuals than of society; rather the offspring of a nation's effort, than the inspired flash of a man of genius; the deposit left by a whole people; the heaps accumulated by centuries; the residue of successive evaporations of human society, in a word, species of formations. Each wave of time contributes its alluvium, each race deposits its layer on the monument, each individual brings his stone. Thus do the beavers, thus do the bees, thus do men. The great symbol of architecture, Babel, is a hive.

Great edifices, like great mountains, are the work of centuries. Art often undergoes a transformation while they are pending, *pendent opera interrupta*; they proceed quietly in accordance with the transformed art. The new art takes the monument where it finds it, incrusts itself there, assimilates it to itself, develops it according to its fancy, and finishes it if it can. The thing is accomplished without trouble, without effort, without reaction, following a natural and tranquil law. It is a graft that shoots up, a sap that circulates, a vegetation that starts forth anew. Certainly there is matter here for many large volumes, and often the universal history of humanity in the successive engrafting of many arts at many levels, upon the same monument. The man, the artist, the individual, is effaced in these great masses, which lack the name of their author; human intelligence is there summed up and totalized. Time is the architect; the nation is the builder.

Not to consider here anything except the Christian architecture of Europe, that younger sister of the great masonries of the Orient, it appears to the eyes as an immense formation divided into three well-defined zones, which are superposed, the one upon the other: the Romanesque zone,★ the Gothic zone, the zone of the Renaissance, which we would gladly call the Greco-Roman zone. The Roman layer, which is the most ancient and deepest, is occupied by the round arch, which reappears, supported by the Greek column, in the modern and upper layer of the Renaissance. The pointed arch is found between the two. The edifices that belong exclusively to any one of these three layers are perfectly distinct, uniform, and complete. There is the Abbey of Jumiéges, there is the Cathedral of Reims, there is the Sainte-Croix of Orleans. But the three zones mingle and amalgamate along the edges, like the colors in the solar spectrum. Hence, complex monuments, edifices of gradation and transition. One is Roman at the base, Gothic in the middle, Greco-Roman at the top. It is because it was six hundred years in building. This variety is rare. The donjon keep of d'Etampes is a specimen of it. But monuments of two formations are more frequent. There is Notre-Dame de Paris, a pointed-arch edifice, which is imbedded by its pillars in that Roman zone, in which are plunged the portal of Saint-Denis, and the nave of Saint-Germain des Prés. There is the charming, half-Gothic chapter-house of Bocherville, where the Roman layer extends half way up. There is the cathedral of Rouen, which would be entirely Gothic if it did not bathe the tip of its central spire in the zone of the Renaissance.★★

★ This is the same that is called, according to locality, climate, and races, Lombard, Saxon, or Byzantine. There are four sister and parallel architectures, each having its special character, but derived from the same origin, the round arch.

★★ This portion of the spire, which was of woodwork, is precisely that which was consumed by lightning, in 1823.

However, all these shades, all these differences, do not affect the surfaces of edifices only. It is art that has changed its skin. The very constitution of the Christian church is not attacked by it. There is always the same internal woodwork, the same logical arrangement of parts. Whatever may be the carved and embroidered envelope of a cathedral, one always finds beneath it—in the state of a germ, and of a rudiment at the least—the Roman basilica. It is eternally developed upon the soil according to the same law. There are, invariably, two naves, which intersect in a cross, and whose upper portion, rounded into an apse, forms the choir; there are always the side aisles, for interior processions, for chapels, a sort of lateral walks or promenades where the principal nave discharges itself through the spaces between the pillars. That settled, the number of chapels, doors, bell towers, and pinnacles are modified to infinity, according to the fancy of the century, the people, and art. The service of religion once assured and provided for, architecture does what she pleases. Statues, stained glass, rose windows, arabesques, denticulations, capitals, bas-reliefs, she combines all these imaginings according to the arrangement which best suits her. Hence, the prodigious exterior variety of these edifices, at whose foundation dwells so much order and unity. The trunk of a tree is immovable; the foliage is capricious.

Chapter 2

A Bird's-Eye View of Paris

WE HAVE JUST attempted to restore, for the reader's benefit, that admirable church of Notre-Dame de Paris. We have briefly pointed out the greater part of the beauties which it possessed in the fifteenth century, and which it lacks today; but we have omitted the principal thing—the view of Paris which was then to be obtained from the summits of its towers.

That was, in fact, when, after having long groped one's way up the dark spiral which perpendicularly pierces the thick wall of the belfries, one emerged, at last abruptly, upon one of the lofty platforms inundated with light and air, that was, in fact, a fine picture which spread out, on all sides at once, before the eye; a spectacle *sui generis*, of which those of our readers who have had the good fortune to see a Gothic city entire, complete, homogeneous—a few of which still remain, Nuremberg in Bavaria and Vittoria in Spain—can readily form an idea; or even smaller specimens, provided that they are well preserved—Vitré in Brittany, Nordhausen in Prussia.

The Paris of three hundred and fifty years ago—the Paris of the fifteenth century—was already a gigantic city. We Parisians generally make a mistake as to the ground that we think that we have gained, since Paris has not increased much over one-third since the time of Louis XI. It has certainly lost more in beauty than it has gained in size.

Paris had its birth, as the reader knows, in that old island of the City that has the form of a cradle. The strand of that island was its first boundary wall, the Seine its first moat. Paris remained for many centuries in its island state, with two bridges, one on the north, the other on the south; and two bridge heads, which were at the same time its gates and its fortresses—the Grand-Châtelet on the right bank, the Petit-Châtelet on the left. Then, from the date of the kings of the first race, Paris, being too cribbed and confined in its island, and unable to return thither, crossed the water. Then, beyond the Grand, beyond the Petit-Châtelet, a first circle of walls and towers began to infringe upon the country on the two sides of the Seine. Some vestiges of this ancient enclosure still remained in the last century; today, only the memory of it is left, and here and there a tradition, the Baudets or Baudoyer gate, "Porte Bagauda."

Little by little, the tide of houses, always thrust from the heart of the city outwards, overflows, devours, wears away, and effaces this wall. Philip Augustus makes a new dike for it. He imprisons Paris in a circular chain of great towers, both lofty and solid. For the period of more than a century, the houses press upon each other, accumulate, and raise their level in this basin, like water in a reservoir. They begin to deepen; they pile story upon story; they mount upon each other; they gush forth at the top, like all laterally compressed growth, and there is a rivalry as to which shall thrust its head above its neighbors, for the sake of getting a little air. The street grows narrower and deeper, every space is overwhelmed and disappears. The houses finally leap the wall of Philip Augustus, and scatter joyfully over the plain, without order, and all askew, like runaways. There they plant themselves squarely, cut themselves gardens from the fields, and take their ease. Beginning with 1367, the city spreads to such an extent into the suburbs, that a new wall becomes necessary, particularly on the right bank; Charles V builds it. But a city like Paris is perpetually growing. It is only such cities that become capitals. They are funnels, into which all the geographical, political, moral, and intellectual water-sheds of a country, all the natural slopes of a people, pour; wells of civilization, so to speak, and also sewers, where commerce, industry, intelligence, population,—all that is sap, all that is life, all that is the soul of a nation, filters and amasses unceasingly, drop by drop, century by century.

So Charles V's wall suffered the fate of that of Philip Augustus. At the end of the fifteenth century, the Faubourg strides across it, passes beyond it, and runs farther. In the sixteenth, it seems to retreat visibly, and to bury itself deeper and deeper in the old city, so thick had the new city already become outside of it. Thus, beginning with the fifteenth century, where our story finds us, Paris had already outgrown the three concentric circles of walls which, from the time of Julian the Apostate, existed, so to speak, in germ in the Grand-Châtelet and the Petit-Châtelet. The mighty city had cracked, in succession, its four enclosures of walls, like a child grown too large for his garments of last year. Under Louis XI, this sea of houses was seen to be pierced at intervals by several groups of ruined towers, from the ancient wall, like the summits of hills in an inundation, like archipelagos of the old Paris submerged beneath the new. Since that time Paris has undergone yet another transformation, unfortunately for our eyes; but it has passed only one more wall, that of Louis XV, that miserable wall of mud and spittle, worthy of the king who built it, worthy of the poet who sung it:

Le mur murant Paris rend Paris murmurant.

In the fifteenth century, Paris was still divided into three wholly distinct and separate towns, each having its own physiognomy, its own specialty, its manners, customs, privileges, and history: the City, the University, the Town. The City, which occupied the island, was the most ancient, the smallest, and the mother of the other two, crowded in between them like (may we be pardoned the comparison) a little old woman between two large and handsome maidens. The University covered the left bank of the Seine, from the Tournelle to the Tour de Nesle, points which correspond in the Paris of today, the one to the wine market, the other to the mint. Its wall included a large part of that plain where Julian had built his hot baths. The hill of Sainte-Geneviève was enclosed in it. The culminating point of this sweep of walls was the Papal gate, that is to say, near the present site of the Pantheon. The Town, which was the largest of the three fragments of Paris, held the right bank. Its quay, broken or interrupted in many places, ran along the Seine, from the Tour de Billy to the Tour du Bois; that is to say, from the place where the granary stands today, to the present site of the Tuileries. These four points, where the Seine intersected the wall of the capital, the Tournelle and the Tour de Nesle on the right, the Tour de Billy and the Tour du Bois on the left, were called preeminently, "the four towers of Paris." The Town encroached still more extensively upon the fields than the University. The culminating point of the Town wall (that of Charles V) was at the gates of Saint-Denis and Saint-Martin, whose situation has not been changed.

As we have just said, each of these three great divisions of Paris was a town, but too special a town to be complete, a city that could not get along without the other two. Hence three entirely distinct aspects: churches abounded in the City; palaces, in the Town; and colleges, in the University. Neglecting here the originalities, of secondary importance in old Paris, and the capricious regulations regarding the public highways, we will say, from a general point of view, taking only masses and the whole group, in this chaos of communal jurisdictions, that the island belonged to the bishop, the right bank to the provost of the merchants, the left bank to the Rector; over all ruled the provost of Paris, a royal not a municipal official. The City had Notre-Dame; the Town, the Louvre and the Hôtel de Ville; the University, the Sorbonne. The Town had the markets (Halles); the city, the Hospital; the University, the Pré-aux-Clercs. Offences committed by the scholars on the left bank were tried in the law courts on the island, and were punished on the right bank at Montfauçon; unless the rector, feeling the university to be strong and the king weak, intervened; for it was the students' privilege to be hanged on their own grounds.

The greater part of these privileges, it may be noted in passing, and there were some even better than the above, had been extorted from the kings by revolts and mutinies. It is the course of things from time immemorial; the king only lets go when the people tear away. There is an old charter which puts the matter naively: apropos of fidelity: *Civibus fidelitas in reges, quoe tamen aliquoties seditionibus interrypta, multa peperit privileyia.*

In the fifteenth century, the Seine bathed five islands within the walls of Paris: Louviers island, where there were then trees, and where there is no longer anything but wood; l'ile aux Vaches, and l'ile Notre-Dame, both deserted, with the exception of one house, both fiefs of the bishop—in the seventeenth century, a single island was formed out of these two, which was built upon and named l'ile Saint-Louis, lastly the City, and at its point, the little islet of the cow tender, which was afterwards engulfed beneath the platform of the Pont-Neuf. The City then had five bridges: three on the right, the Pont Notre-Dame, and the Pont au Change, of stone, the Pont aux Meuniers, of wood; two on the left, the Petit Pont, of stone, the Pont Saint-Michel, of wood; all loaded with houses.

The University had six gates, built by Philip Augustus; there were, beginning with la Tournelle, the Porte Saint-Victor, the Porte Bordelle, the Porte Papale, the Porte Saint-Jacques, the Porte Saint-Michel, the Porte Saint-Germain. The Town had six gates, built by Charles V; beginning with the Tour de Billy they were: the Porte Saint-Antoine, the Porte du Temple, the Porte Saint-Martin, the Porte Saint-Denis, the Porte Montmartre, the Porte Saint-Honoré. All these gates were strong, and also handsome, which does not detract from strength. A large, deep moat, with a brisk current during the high water of winter, bathed the base of the wall round Paris; the Seine furnished the water. At night, the gates were shut, the river was barred at both ends of the city with huge iron chains, and Paris slept tranquilly.

From a bird's-eye view, these three burgs, the City, the Town, and the University, each presented to the eye an inextricable skein of eccentrically tangled streets. Nevertheless, at first sight, one recognized the fact that these three fragments formed but one body. One immediately perceived three long parallel streets, unbroken, undisturbed, traversing, almost in a straight line, all three cities, from one end to the other; from North to South, perpendicularly, to the Seine, which bound them together, mingled them, infused them in each other, poured and transfused the people incessantly, from one to the other, and made one out of the three. The first of these streets ran from the Porte Saint-Martin: it was called the Rue Saint-Jacques in the University, Rue de la Juiverie in the City, Rue Saint-Martin in the Town; it crossed the water twice, under the name of the Petit Pont and the Pont Notre-Dame. The second, which was called the Rue de la Harpe on the left bank, Rue de la Barillerié in the island, Rue Saint-Denis on the right bank, Pont Saint-Michel on one arm of the Seine, Pont au Change on the other, ran from the Porte Saint-Michel in the University, to the Porte Saint-Denis in the Town. However, under all these names, there were but two streets, parent streets, generating streets, the two arteries of Paris. All the other veins of the triple city either derived their supply from them or emptied into them.

Independently of these two principal streets, piercing Paris diametrically in its whole breadth, from side to side, common to the entire capital, the City and the University had also each its own great special street, which ran lengthwise by them, parallel to the Seine, cutting, as it passed, at right angles, the two arterial thoroughfares. Thus, in the Town, one descended in a straight line from the Porte Saint-Antoine to the Porte Saint-Honoré; in the University from the Porte Saint-Victor to the Porte Saint-Germain. These two great thoroughfares intersected by the two first, formed the canvas upon which reposed, knotted and crowded together on every hand, the labyrinthine network of the streets of Paris. In the incomprehensible plan of these streets, one distinguished likewise, on looking attentively, two clusters of great streets, like magnified sheaves of grain, one in the University, the other in the Town, which spread out gradually from the bridges to the gates.

Some traces of this geometrical plan still exist today.

Now, what aspect did this whole present, when, as viewed from the summit of the towers of Notre-Dame, in 1482? That we shall try to describe.

For the spectator who arrived, panting, upon that pinnacle, it was first a dazzling confusing view of roofs, chimneys, streets, bridges, places, spires, bell towers. Everything struck your eye at once: the carved gable, the pointed roof, the turrets suspended at the angles of the walls; the stone pyramids of the eleventh century, the slate obelisks of the fifteenth; the round, bare tower of the donjon keep; the square and fretted tower of the church; the great and the little, the massive and the aerial. The eye was, for a long time, wholly lost in this labyrinth, where there was nothing which did not possess its originality, its reason, its genius, its beauty, nothing which did not proceed from art; beginning with the smallest house, with its painted and carved front, with external beams, elliptical door, with projecting stories, to the royal Louvre, which then had a colonnade of towers. But these are the principal masses that were then to be distinguished when the eye began to accustom itself to this tumult of edifices.

In the first place, the City—"the island of the City," as Sauval says, who, in spite of his confused medley, sometimes has such happy turns of expression—"the island of the city is made like a great ship, stuck in the mud and run aground in the current, near the centre of the Seine."

We have just explained that, in the fifteenth century, this ship was anchored to the two banks of the river by five bridges. This form of a ship had also struck the heraldic scribes; for it is from that, and not from the siege by the Normans, that the ship which blazons the old shield of Paris, comes, according to Favyn and Pasquier. For him who understands how to decipher them, armorial bearings are algebra, armorial bearings have a tongue. The whole history of the second half of the Middle Ages is written in armorial bearings—the first half is in the symbolism of the Roman churches. They are the hieroglyphics of feudalism, succeeding those of theocracy.

Thus the City first presented itself to the eye, with its stern to the east, and its prow to the west. Turning toward the prow, one had before one an innumerable flock of ancient roofs, over which arched broadly the lead-covered apse of the Sainte-Chapelle, like an elephant's haunches loaded with its tower. Only here, this tower was the most audacious, the most open, the most ornamented spire of cabinet-maker's work that ever let the sky peep through its cone of lace. In front of Notre-Dame, and very near at hand, three streets opened into the cathedral square—a fine square, lined with ancient houses. Over the south side of this place bent the wrinkled and sullen façade of the Hôtel Dieu, and its roof, which seemed covered with warts and pustules. Then, on the right and the left, to east and west, within that wall of the City, which was yet so contracted, rose the bell towers of its one and twenty churches, of every date, of every form, of every size, from the low and wormeaten belfry of Saint-Denis du Pas (*Carcer Glaucini*) to the slender needles of Saint-Pierre aux Boeufs and Saint-Landry.

Behind Notre-Dame, the cloister and its Gothic galleries spread out toward the north; on the south, the half-Roman palace of the bishop; on the east, the desert point of the Terrain. In this throng of houses the eye also distinguished, by the lofty open-work mitres of stone which then crowned the roof itself, even the most elevated windows of the palace, the Hôtel given by the city, under Charles VI, to Juvénal des Ursins; a little farther on, the pitch-covered sheds of the Palus Market; in still another quarter the new apse of Saint-Germain le Vieux, lengthened in 1458, with a bit of the Rue aux Febves; and then, in places, a square crowded with people; a pillory, erected at the corner of a street; a fine fragment of the pavement of Philip Augustus, a magnificent flagging, grooved for the horses' feet, in the middle of the road, and so badly replaced in the sixteenth century by the miserable cobblestones, called the "pavement of the League"; a deserted back courtyard, with one of those diaphanous staircase turrets, such as were erected in the fifteenth century, one of which is still to be seen in the Rue des Bourdonnais. Lastly, at the right of the Sainte-Chapelle, toward the west, the Palais de Justice rested its group of towers at the edge of the water. The thickets of the king's gardens, which covered the western point of the City, masked the Island du Passeur. As for the water, from the summit of the towers of Notre-Dame one hardly saw it, on either side of the City; the Seine was hidden by bridges, the bridges by houses.

And when the glance passed these bridges, whose roofs were visibly green, rendered mouldy before their time by the vapors from the water, if it was directed to the left, toward the University, the first edifice which struck it was a large, low sheaf of towers, the Petit-Châtelet, whose yawning gate devoured the end of the Petit-Pont. Then, if your view ran along the bank, from east to west, from the Tournelle to the Tour de Nesle, there was a long cordon of houses, with carved beams, stained-glass windows, each story projecting over that beneath it, an interminable zigzag of bourgeois gables, frequently interrupted by the mouth of a street, and from time to time also by the front or angle of a huge stone mansion, planted at its ease, with courts and gardens, wings and detached buildings, amid this populace of crowded and narrow houses, like a grand gentleman among a throng of rustics. There were five or six of these mansions on the quay, from the house of Lorraine, which shared with the Bernardins the grand enclosure adjoining the Tournelle, to the Hôtel de Nesle, whose principal tower ended Paris, and whose pointed roofs were in a position, during three months of the year, to encroach, with their black triangles, upon the scarlet disk of the setting sun.

This side of the Seine was, however, the least mercantile of the two. Students furnished more of a crowd and more noise there than artisans, and there was not, properly speaking, any quay, except from the Pont Saint-Michel to the Tour de Nesle. The rest of the bank of the Seine was now a naked strand, the same as beyond the Bernardins; again, a throng of houses, standing with their feet in the water, as between the two bridges.

There was a great uproar of laundresses; they screamed, and talked, and sang from morning till night along the beach, and beat a great deal of linen there, just as in our day. This is not the least of the gayeties of Paris.

The University presented a dense mass to the eye. From one end to the other, it was homogeneous and compact. The thousand roofs, dense, angular, clinging to each other, composed, nearly all, of the same geometrical element, offered, when viewed from above, the aspect of a crystallization of the same substance.

The capricious ravine of streets did not cut this block of houses into too disproportionate slices. The forty-two colleges were scattered about in a fairly equal manner, and there were some everywhere. The amusingly varied crests of these beautiful edifices were the product of the same art as the simple roofs that they overshot, and were, actually, only a multiplication of the square or the cube of the same geometrical figure. Hence they complicated the whole effect, without disturbing

it; completed, without overloading it. Geometry is harmony. Some
fine mansions here and there made magnificent outlines against
the picturesque attics of the left bank. The house of Nevers, the house
of Rome, the house of Reims, which have disappeared; the Hôtel de
Cluny, which still exists, for the consolation of the artist, and whose
tower was so stupidly deprived of its crown a few years ago. Close to
Cluny, that Roman palace, with fine round arches, were once the hot
baths of Julian. There were a great many abbeys, of a beauty more
devout, of a grandeur more solemn than the mansions, but not less
beautiful, not less grand. Those which first caught the eye were the
Bernardins, with their three bell towers; Sainte-Geneviève, whose
square tower, which still exists, makes us regret the rest; the Sorbonne,
half college, half monastery, of which so admirable a nave survives; the
fine quadrilateral cloister of the Mathurins; its neighbor, the cloister
of Saint-Benoit, within whose walls they have had time to cobble up
a theatre, between the seventh and eighth editions of this book; the
Cordeliers, with their three enormous adjacent gables; the Augustins,
whose graceful spire formed, after the Tour de Nesle, the second
denticulation on this side of Paris, starting from the west. The colleges,
which are, in fact, the intermediate ring between the cloister and the
world, hold the middle position in the monumental series between the
Hôtels and the abbeys, with a severity full of elegance, sculpture less
giddy than the palaces, an architecture less severe than the convents.
Unfortunately, hardly anything remains of these monuments, where
Gothic art combined with so just a balance, richness and economy.
The churches (and they were numerous and splendid in the University,
and they were graded there also in all the ages of architecture, from the
round arches of Saint-Julian to the pointed arches of Saint-Séverin),
the churches dominated the whole; and, like one harmony more in
this mass of harmonies, they pierced in quick succession the multiple
open work of the gables with slashed spires, with open-work bell
towers, with slender pinnacles, whose line was also only a magnificent
exaggeration of the acute angle of the roofs.

The ground of the University was hilly; Mount Sainte-Geneviève
formed an enormous mound to the south; and it was a sight to see
from the summit of Notre-Dame how that throng of narrow and
tortuous streets (today the Latin Quarter), those bunches of houses
which, spread out in every direction from the top of this eminence,
precipitated themselves in disorder, and almost perpendicularly down

its flanks, nearly to the water's edge, having the air, some of falling, others of clambering up again, and all of holding to one another. A continual flux of a thousand black points which passed each other on the pavements made everything move before the eyes; it was the populace seen thus from aloft and afar.

Lastly, in the intervals of these roofs, of these spires, of these accidents of numberless edifices, which bent and writhed, and jagged in so eccentric a manner the extreme line of the University, one caught a glimpse, here and there, of a great expanse of moss-grown wall, a thick, round tower, a crenellated city gate, shadowing forth the fortress; it was the wall of Philip Augustus. Beyond, the fields gleamed green; beyond, fled the roads, along which were scattered a few more suburban houses, which became more infrequent as they became more distant. Some of these faubourgs were important: there were, first, starting from la Tournelle, the Bourg Saint-Victor, with its one arch bridge over the Bièvre, its abbey where one could read the epitaph of Louis le Gros, *epitaphium Ludovici Grossi*, and its church with an octagonal spire, flanked with four little bell towers of the eleventh century (a similar one can be seen at Etampes; it is not yet destroyed); next, the Bourg Saint-Marceau, which already had three churches and one convent; then, leaving the mill of the Gobelins and its four white walls on the left, there was the Faubourg Saint-Jacques with the beautiful carved cross in its square; the church of Saint-Jacques du Haut-Pas, which was then Gothic, pointed, charming; Saint-Magloire, a fine nave of the fourteenth century, which Napoleon turned into a hayloft; Notre-Dame des Champs, where there were Byzantine mosaics; lastly, after having left behind, full in the country, the Monastery des Chartreux, a rich edifice contemporary with the Palais de Justice, with its little garden divided into compartments, and the haunted ruins of Vauvert, the eye fell, to the west, upon the three Roman spires of Saint-Germain des Prés. The Bourg Saint-Germain, already a large community, formed fifteen or twenty streets in the rear; the pointed bell tower of Saint-Sulpice marked one corner of the town. Close beside it one descried the quadrilateral enclosure of the fair of Saint-Germain, where the market is situated today; then the abbot's pillory, a pretty little round tower, well capped with a leaden cone; the brickyard was further on, and the Rue du Four, which led to the common bakehouse, and the mill on its hillock, and the lazar house, a tiny house, isolated and half seen.

But that which attracted the eye most of all, and fixed it for a long time on that point, was the abbey itself. It is certain that this monastery, which had a grand air, both as a church and as a seignory; that abbatial palace, where the bishops of Paris counted themselves happy if they could pass the night; that refectory, upon which the architect had bestowed the air, the beauty, and the rose window of a cathedral; that elegant chapel of the Virgin; that monumental dormitory; those vast gardens; that portcullis; that drawbridge; that envelope of battlements which notched to the eye the verdure of the surrounding meadows; those courtyards, where gleamed men at arms, intermingled with golden copes;—the whole grouped and clustered about three lofty spires, with round arches, well planted upon a Gothic apse, made a magnificent figure against the horizon.

When, at length, after having contemplated the University for a long time, you turned toward the right bank, toward the Town, the character of the spectacle was abruptly altered. The Town, in fact much larger than the University, was also less of a unit. At the first glance, one saw that it was divided into many masses, singularly distinct. First, to the eastward, in that part of the town that still takes its name from the marsh where Camulogènes entangled Caesar, was a pile of palaces. The block extended to the very water's edge. Four almost contiguous Hôtels, Jouy, Sens, Barbeau, the house of the Queen, mirrored their slate peaks, broken with slender turrets, in the Seine.

These four edifices filled the space from the Rue des Nonaindières, to the abbey of the Celestins, whose spire gracefully relieved their line of gables and battlements. A few miserable, greenish hovels, hanging over the water in front of these sumptuous Hôtels, did not prevent one from seeing the fine angles of their façades, their large, square windows with stone mullions, their pointed porches overloaded with statues, the vivid outlines of their walls, always clear cut, and all those charming accidents of architecture, which cause Gothic art to have the air of beginning its combinations afresh with every monument.

Behind these palaces, extended in all directions, now broken, fenced in, battlemented like a citadel, now veiled by great trees like a Carthusian convent, the immense and multiform enclosure of that miraculous Hôtel de Saint-Pol, where the King of France possessed the means of lodging superbly two and twenty princes of the rank of the dauphin and the Duke of Burgundy, with their domestics and their suites, without counting the great lords, and the emperor when he came to view Paris, and the lions, who had their separate Hôtel at the royal Hôtel. Let us say here that a prince's apartment was then composed of never less than eleven large rooms, from the chamber of state to the oratory, not to mention the galleries, baths, vapor-baths, and other "superfluous places," with which each apartment was provided; not to mention the private gardens for each of the king's guests; not to mention the kitchens, the cellars, the domestic offices, the general refectories of the house, the poultry-yards, where there were twenty-two general laboratories, from the bakehouses to the wine-cellars; games of a thousand sorts, malls, tennis, and riding at the ring; aviaries, fishponds, menageries, stables, barns, libraries, arsenals and foundries. This was what a king's palace, a Louvre, a Hôtel de Saint-Pol was then. A city within a city.

From the tower where we are placed, the Hôtel Saint-Pol, almost half hidden by the four great houses of which we have just spoken, was still very considerable and very marvellous to see. One could there distinguish, very well, though cleverly united with the principal building by long galleries, decked with painted glass and slender columns, the three Hôtels which Charles V had amalgamated with his palace: the Hôtel du Petit-Muce, with the airy balustrade, which formed a graceful border to its roof; the Hôtel of the Abbe de Saint-Maur, having the vanity of a stronghold, a great tower, machicolations, loopholes, iron gratings, and over the large Saxon door, the armorial bearings of the abbé, between the two mortises of the drawbridge; the Hôtel of the Comte d' Etampes, whose donjon keep, ruined at its summit, was rounded and notched like a cock's comb; here and there, three or four ancient oaks, forming a tuft together like enormous cauliflowers; gambols of swans, in the clear water of the fishponds, all in folds of light and shade; many courtyards of which one beheld picturesque bits; the Hôtel of the Lions, with its low, pointed arches on short, Saxon pillars, its iron gratings and its perpetual roar; shooting up above the whole, the scale-ornamented spire of the Ave-Maria; on the left, the house of the Provost of Paris, flanked by four small towers, delicately grooved, in the middle; at the extremity, the Hôtel Saint-Pol, properly speaking, with its multiplied façades, its successive enrichments from the time of Charles V, the hybrid excrescences, with which the fancy of the architects had loaded it during the last two centuries, with all the apses of its chapels, all the gables of its galleries, a thousand weathercocks for the four winds, and its two lofty contiguous towers, whose conical roof, surrounded by battlements at its base, looked like those pointed caps which have their edges turned up.

Continuing to mount the stories of this amphitheatre of palaces spread out afar upon the ground, after crossing a deep ravine hollowed out of the roofs in the Town, which marked the passage of the Rue Saint-Antoine, the eye reached the house of Angoulême, a vast construction of many epochs, where there were perfectly new and very white parts, which melted no better into the whole than a red patch on a blue doublet. Nevertheless, the remarkably pointed and lofty roof of the modern palace, bristling with carved eaves, covered with sheets of lead, where coiled a thousand fantastic arabesques of sparkling incrustations of gilded bronze, that roof, so curiously damascened, darted upwards gracefully from the midst of the brown ruins of the ancient edifice; whose huge and ancient towers, rounded by age like casks, sinking together with old age, and rending themselves from top to bottom, resembled great bellies unbuttoned. Behind rose the forest of spires of the Palais des Tournelles. Not a view in the world, either at Chambord or at the Alhambra, is more magic, more aerial, more enchanting, than that thicket of spires, tiny bell towers, chimneys, weather-vanes, winding staircases, lanterns through which the daylight makes its way, which seem cut out at a blow, pavilions, spindle-shaped turrets, or, as they were then called, "tournelles," all differing in form, in height, and attitude. One would have pronounced it a gigantic stone chess-board.

To the right of the Tournelles, that truss of enormous towers, black as ink, running into each other and tied, as it were, by a circular moat; that donjon keep, much more pierced with loopholes than with windows; that drawbridge, always raised; that portcullis, always lowered, is the Bastille. Those sorts of black beaks which project from between the battlements, and which you take from a distance to be cave spouts, are cannons.

Beneath them, at the foot of the formidable edifice, behold the Porte Sainte-Antoine, buried between its two towers.

Beyond the Tournelles, as far as the wall of Charles V, spread out, with rich compartments of verdure and of flowers, a velvet carpet of cultivated land and royal parks, in the midst of which one recognized, by its labyrinth of trees and alleys, the famous Daedalus garden which Louis XI had given to Coictier. The doctor's observatory rose above the labyrinth like a great isolated column, with a tiny house for a capital. Terrible astrologies took place in that laboratory.

There today is the Place Royale.

As we have just said, the quarter of the palace, of which we have just endeavored to give the reader some idea by indicating only the chief points, filled the angle that Charles V's wall made with the Seine on the east. The centre of the Town was occupied by a pile of houses for the populace. It was there, in fact, that the three bridges disgorged upon the right bank, and bridges lead to the building of houses rather than palaces. That congregation of bourgeois habitations, pressed together like the cells in a hive, had a beauty of its own. It is with the roofs of a capital as with the waves of the sea—they are grand. First the streets, crossed and entangled, forming a hundred amusing figures in the block; around the market-place, it was like a star with a thousand rays.

The Rues Saint-Denis and Saint-Martin, with their innumerable ramifications, rose one after the other, like trees intertwining their branches; and then the tortuous lines, the Rues de la Plâtrerie, de la Verrerie, de la Tixeranderie, etc., meandered over all. There were also fine edifices that pierced the petrified undulations of that sea of gables. At the head of the Pont aux Changeurs, behind which one beheld the Seine foaming beneath the wheels of the Pont aux Meuniers, there was the Chalelet, no longer a Roman tower, as under Julian the Apostate, but a feudal tower of the thirteenth century, and of a stone so hard that the pickaxe could not break away so much as the thickness of the fist in a space of three hours; there was the rich square bell tower of Saint-Jacques de la Boucherie, with its angles all frothing with carvings, already admirable, although it was not finished in the fifteenth century. (It lacked, in particular, the four monsters, which, still perched today on the corners of its roof, have the air of so many sphinxes who are propounding to new Paris the riddle of the ancient Paris. Rault, the sculptor, only placed them in position in 1526, and received twenty francs for his pains.) There was the Maison-aux-Piliers, the Pillar House, opening upon that Place de Grève of which we have given the reader some idea; there was Saint-Gervais, which a front "in good taste" has since spoiled; Saint-Méry, whose ancient pointed arches were still almost round arches; Saint-Jean, whose magnificent spire was proverbial; there were twenty other monuments, which did not disdain to bury their wonders in that chaos of black, deep, narrow streets. Add the crosses of carved stone, more lavishly scattered through the squares than even the gibbets; the cemetery of the Innocents, whose architectural wall could be seen in the distance above the roofs; the pillory of the Markets, whose top was visible between two chimneys of the Rue de la Cossonnerie; the ladder of the Croix-du-Trahoir, in its square always black with people; the circular buildings of the wheat mart; the fragments of Philip Augustus's ancient wall, which could be made out here and there, drowned among the houses, its towers gnawed by ivy, its gates in ruins, with crumbling and deformed stretches of wall; the quay with its thousand shops, and its bloody knacker's yards; the Seine encumbered with boats, from the Port au Foin to Port-l'Evêque, and you will have a confused picture of what the central trapezium of the Town was like in 1482.

With these two quarters, one of Hôtels, the other of houses, the third feature of aspect presented by the city was a long zone of abbeys, which bordered it in nearly the whole of its circumference, from the rising to the setting sun, and, behind the circle of fortifications which hemmed in Paris, formed a second interior enclosure of convents and chapels. Thus, immediately adjoining the park des Tournelles, between the Rue Saint-Antoine and the Vielle Rue du Temple, there stood Sainte-Catherine, with its immense cultivated lands, which were terminated only by the wall of Paris. Between the old and the new Rue du Temple, there was the Temple, a sinister group of towers, lofty, erect, and isolated in the middle of a vast, battlemented enclosure. Between the Rue Neuve-du-Temple and the Rue Saint-Martin, there was the Abbey of Saint-Martin, in the midst of its gardens, a superb fortified church, whose girdle of towers, whose diadem of bell towers, yielded in force and splendor only to Saint-Germain des Prés. Between the Rue Saint-Martin and the Rue Saint-Denis, spread the enclosure of the Trinité.

Lastly, between the Rue Saint-Denis, and the Rue Montorgueil, stood the Filles-Dieu. On one side, the rotting roofs and unpaved enclosure of the Cour des Miracles could be descried. It was the sole profane ring that was linked to that devout chain of convents.

Finally, the fourth compartment, which stretched itself out in the agglomeration of the roofs on the right bank, and which occupied the western angle of the enclosure, and the banks of the river down stream, was a fresh cluster of palaces and Hôtels pressed close about the base of the Louvre. The old Louvre of Philip Augustus, that immense edifice whose great tower rallied about it three and twenty chief towers, not to reckon the lesser towers, seemed from a distance to be enshrined in the Gothic roofs of the Hôtel d'Alençon, and the Petit-Bourbon. This hydra of towers, giant guardian of Paris, with its four and twenty heads, always erect, with its monstrous haunches, loaded or scaled with slates, and all streaming with metallic reflections, terminated with wonderful effect the configuration of the Town toward the west.

Thus an immense block, which the Romans called *insula*, or island, of bourgeois houses, flanked on the right and the left by two blocks of palaces, crowned, the one by the Louvre, the other by the Tournelles, bordered on the north by a long girdle of abbeys and cultivated enclosures, all amalgamated and melted together in one view; upon these thousands of edifices, whose tiled and slated roofs outlined upon each other so many fantastic chains, the bell towers, tattooed, fluted, and ornamented with twisted bands, of the four and forty churches on the right bank; myriads of cross streets; for boundary on one side, an enclosure of lofty walls with square towers (that of the University had round towers); on the other, the Seine, cut by bridges, and bearing on its bosom a multitude of boats; behold the Town of Paris in the fifteenth century.

Beyond the walls, several suburban villages pressed close about the gates, but less numerous and more scattered than those of the University. Behind the Bastille there were twenty hovels clustered round the curious sculptures of the Croix-Faubin and the flying buttresses of the Abbey of Saint-Antoine des Champs; then Popincourt, lost amid wheat fields; then la Courtille, a merry village of wine-shops; the hamlet of Saint-Laurent with its church whose bell tower, from afar, seemed to add itself to the pointed towers of the Porte Saint-Martin; the Faubourg Saint-Denis, with the vast enclosure of Saint-Ladre; beyond the Montmartre Gate, the Grange-Batelière, encircled with white walls; behind it, with its chalky slopes, Montmartre, which had then almost as many churches as windmills, and which has kept only the windmills, for society no longer demands anything but bread for the body. Lastly, beyond the Louvre, the Faubourg Saint-Honoré, already considerable at that time, could be seen stretching away into the fields, and Petit-Bretagne gleaming green, and the Marché aux Pourceaux spreading abroad, in whose centre swelled the horrible apparatus used for boiling counterfeiters. Between la Courtille and Saint-Laurent, your eye had already noticed, on the summit of an eminence crouching amid desert plains, a sort of edifice which resembled from a distance a ruined colonnade, mounted upon a basement with its foundation laid bare. This was neither a Parthenon, nor a temple of the Olympian Jupiter. It was Montfauçon.

Now, if the enumeration of so many edifices, summary as we have endeavored to make it, has not shattered in the reader's mind the general image of old Paris, as we have constructed it, we will recapitulate it in a few words. In the centre, the island of the City, resembling as to form an enormous tortoise, and throwing out its bridges with tiles for scales; like legs from beneath its gray shell of roofs. On the left, the monolithic trapezium, firm, dense, bristling, of the University; on the right, the vast semicircle of the Town, much more intermixed with gardens and monuments. The three blocks, city, university, and town, marbled with innumerable streets. Across all, the Seine, "foster-mother Seine," as says Father Du Breul, blocked with islands, bridges, and boats. All about an immense plain, patched with a thousand sorts of cultivated plots, sown with fine villages. On the left, Issy, Vanvres, Vaugirarde, Montrouge, Gentilly, with its round tower and its square tower, etc.; on the right, twenty others, from Conflans to Ville-l'Evêque. On the horizon, a border of hills arranged in a circle like the rim of the basin. Finally, far away to the east, Vincennes, and its seven quadrangular towers to the south, Bicêtre and its pointed turrets; to the north, Saint-Denis and its spire; to the west, Saint Cloud and its donjon keep. Such was the Paris that the ravens, who lived in 1482, beheld from the summits of the towers of Notre-Dame.

Nevertheless, Voltaire said of this city, that "before Louis XIV, it possessed but four fine monuments": the dome of the Sorbonne, the Val-de-Grâce, the modern Louvre, and I know not what the fourth was—the Luxembourg, perhaps. Fortunately, Voltaire was the author of *Candide* in spite of this, and in spite of this, he is, among all the men who have followed each other in the long series of humanity, the one who has best possessed the diabolical laugh. Moreover, this proves that one can be a fine genius, and yet understand nothing of an art to which one does not belong. Did not Molière imagine that he was doing Raphael and Michaelangelo a very great honor, by calling them "those Mignards of their age"?

Let us return to Paris and to the fifteenth century.

It was not then merely a handsome city; it was a homogeneous city, an architectural and historical product of the Middle Ages, a chronicle in stone. It was a city formed of two layers only; the Romanesque layer and the Gothic layer; for the Roman layer had disappeared long before, with the exception of the Hot Baths of Julian, where it still pierced through the thick crust of the Middle Ages. As for the Celtic layer, no specimens were any longer to be found, even when sinking wells.

Fifty years later, when the Renaissance began to mingle with this unity which was so severe and yet so varied, the dazzling luxury of its fantasies and systems, its debasements of Roman round arches, Greek columns, and Gothic bases, its sculpture which was so tender and so ideal, its peculiar taste for arabesques and acanthus leaves, its architectural paganism, contemporary with Luther, Paris, was perhaps, still more beautiful, although less harmonious to the eye, and to the thought.

But this splendid moment lasted only for a short time; the Renaissance was not impartial; it did not content itself with building, it wished to destroy; it is true that it required the room. Thus Gothic Paris was complete only for a moment. Saint-Jacques de la Boucherie had barely been completed when the demolition of the old Louvre was begun.

After that, the great city became more disfigured every day. Gothic Paris, beneath which Roman Paris was effaced, was effaced in its turn; but can any one say what Paris has replaced it?

There is the Paris of Catherine de Medicis at the Tuileries;* the Paris of Henri II, at the Hôtel de Ville, two edifices still in fine taste; the Paris of Henri IV, at the Place Royale: façades of brick with stone corners, and slated roofs, tri-colored houses; the Paris of Louis XIII, at the Val-de-Grace: a crushed and squat architecture, with vaults like basket-handles, and something indescribably pot-bellied in the column, and thickset in the dome; the Paris of Louis XIV, in the Invalides: grand, rich, gilded, cold; the Paris of Louis XV, in Saint-Sulpice: volutes, knots of ribbon, clouds, vermicelli and chiccory leaves, all in stone; the Paris

---

*We have seen with sorrow mingled with indignation, that it is the intention to increase, to recast, to make over, that is to say, to destroy this admirable palace. The architects of our day have too heavy a hand to touch these delicate works of the Renaissance. We still cherish a hope that they will not dare. Moreover, this demolition of the Tuileries now, would be not only a brutal deed of violence, which would make a drunken vandal blush—it would be an act of treason. The Tuileries is not simply a masterpiece of the art of the sixteenth century, it is a page of the history of the nineteenth. This palace no longer belongs to the king, but to the people. Let us leave it as it is. Our revolution has twice set its seal upon its front. On one of its two façades, there are the cannon-balls of the 10th of August; on the other, the balls of the 29th of July. It is sacred. Paris, April 1, 1831. [Note to the fifth edition.]

of Louis XVI, in the Pantheon: Saint Peter of Rome, badly copied (the edifice is awkwardly heaped together, which has not amended its lines); the Paris of the Republic, in the School of Medicine: a poor Greek and Roman taste, which resembles the Coliseum or the Parthenon as the constitution of the year III, resembles the laws of Minos—it is called in architecture, "the Messidor" taste—the Paris of Napoleon in the Place Vendome: this one is sublime, a column of bronze made of cannons; the Paris of the Restoration, at the Bourse: a very white colonnade supporting a very smooth frieze; the whole is square and cost twenty millions.

To each of these characteristic monuments there is attached by a similarity of taste, fashion, and attitude, a certain number of houses scattered about in different quarters and which the eyes of the connoisseur easily distinguishes and furnishes with a date. When one knows how to look, one finds the spirit of a century, and the physiognomy of a king, even in the knocker on a door.

The Paris of the present day has then, no general physiognomy. It is a collection of specimens of many centuries, and the finest have disappeared. The capital grows only in houses, and what houses! At the rate at which Paris is now proceeding, it will renew itself every fifty years.

Thus the historical significance of its architecture is being effaced every day. Monuments are becoming rarer and rarer, and one seems to see them gradually engulfed, by the flood of houses. Our fathers had a Paris of stone; our sons will have one of plaster.

So far as the modern monuments of new Paris are concerned, we would gladly be excused from mentioning them. It is not that we do not admire them as they deserve. The Sainte-Geneviève of M. Soufflot is certainly the finest Savoy cake that has ever been made in stone. The Palace of the Legion of Honor is also a very distinguished bit of pastry. The dome of the wheat market is an English jockey cap, on a grand scale. The towers of Saint-Sulpice are two huge clarinets, and the form is as good as any other; the telegraph, contorted and grimacing, forms an admirable accident upon their roofs. Saint-Roch has a door that, for magnificence, is comparable only to that of Saint-Thomas d'Aquin. It has, also, a crucifixion in high relief, in a cellar, with a sun of gilded wood. These things are fairly marvellous. The lantern of the labyrinth of the Jardin des Plantes is also very ingenious.

As for the Palace of the Bourse, which is Greek as to its colonnade, Roman in the round arches of its doors and windows, of the Renaissance by virtue of its flattened vault, it is indubitably a very correct and very pure monument; the proof is that it is crowned with an attic, such as was never seen in Athens, a beautiful, straight line, gracefully broken here and there by stovepipes. Let us add that if it is according to rule that the architecture of a building should be adapted to its purpose in such a manner that this purpose shall be immediately apparent from the mere aspect of the building, one cannot be too much amazed at a structure which might be indifferently—the palace of a king, a chamber of communes, a town-hall, a college, a riding-school, an academy, a warehouse, a court-house, a museum, a barracks, a sepulchre, a temple, or a theatre. However, it is an Exchange. An edifice ought to be, moreover, suitable to the climate. This one is evidently constructed expressly for our cold and rainy skies. It has a roof almost as flat as roofs in the East, which involves sweeping the roof in winter, when it snows; and of course roofs are made to be swept. As for its purpose, of which we just spoke, it fulfils it to a marvel; it is a bourse in France as it would have been a temple in Greece. It is true that the architect was at a good deal of trouble to conceal the clock face, which would have destroyed the purity of the fine lines of the façade; but, on the other hand, we have that colonnade which circles round the edifice and under which, on days of high religious ceremony, the theories of the stock-brokers and the courtiers of commerce can be developed so majestically.

These are very superb structures. Let us add a quantity of fine, amusing, and varied streets, like the Rue de Rivoli, and I do not despair of Paris presenting to the eye, when viewed from a balloon, that richness of line, that opulence of detail, that diversity of aspect, that grandiose something in the simple, and unexpected in the beautiful, which characterizes a checker-board.

However, admirable as the Paris of today may seem to you, reconstruct the Paris of the fifteenth century, call it up before you in thought; look at the sky athwart that surprising forest of spires, towers, and belfries; spread out in the centre of the city, tear away at the point of the islands, fold at the arches of the bridges, the Seine, with its broad green and yellow expanses, more variable than the skin of a serpent; project clearly against an azure horizon the Gothic profile of this ancient Paris. Make its contour float in a winter's mist which clings to its numerous chimneys; drown it in profound night and watch the odd play of lights and shadows in that sombre labyrinth of edifices; cast upon it a ray of light which shall vaguely outline it and cause to emerge from the fog the great heads of the towers; or take that black silhouette again, enliven with shadow the thousand acute angles of the spires and gables, and make it start out more toothed than a shark's jaw against a copper-colored western sky—and then compare.

And if you wish to receive of the ancient city an impression with which the modern one can no longer furnish you, climb—on the morning of some grand festival, beneath the rising sun of Easter or of Pentecost—climb upon some elevated point, whence you command the entire capital; and be present at the wakening of the chimes. Behold, at a signal given from heaven, for it is the sun that gives it, all those churches quiver simultaneously. First come scattered strokes, running from one church to another, as when musicians give warning that they are about to begin. Then, all at once, behold! For it seems at times, as though the ear also possessed a sight of its own, behold, rising from each bell tower, something like a column of sound, a cloud of harmony. First, the vibration of each bell mounts straight upwards, pure and, so to speak, isolated from the others, into the splendid morning sky; then, little by little, as they swell they melt together, mingle, are lost in each other, and amalgamate in a magnificent concert. It is no longer anything but a mass of sonorous vibrations incessantly sent forth from the numerous belfries; floats, undulates, bounds, whirls over the city, and prolongs far beyond the horizon the deafening circle of its oscillations.

Nevertheless, this sea of harmony is not a chaos; great and profound as it is, it has not lost its transparency; you behold the windings of each group of notes which escapes from the belfries. You can follow the dialogue, by turns grave and shrill, of the treble and the bass; you can see the octaves leap from one tower to another; you watch them spring forth, winged, light, and whistling, from the silver bell, to fall, broken and limping from the bell of wood; you admire in their midst the rich gamut which incessantly ascends and re-ascends the seven bells of Saint-Eustache; you see light and rapid notes running across it, executing three or four luminous zigzags, and vanishing like flashes of lightning. Yonder is the Abbey of Saint-Martin, a shrill, cracked singer; here the gruff and gloomy voice of the Bastille; at the other end, the great tower of the Louvre, with its bass. The royal chime of the palace scatters on all sides, and without relaxation, resplendent trills, upon which fall, at regular intervals, the heavy strokes from the belfry of Notre-Dame, which makes them sparkle like the anvil under the hammer. At intervals you behold the passage of sounds of all forms that come from the triple peal of Saint-Germaine des Prés. Then, again, from time to time, this mass of sublime noises opens and gives passage to the beats of the Ave Maria, which bursts forth and sparkles like an aigrette of stars. Below, in the very depths of the concert, you confusedly distinguish the interior chanting of the churches, which exhales through the vibrating pores of their vaulted roofs.

Assuredly, this is an opera that it is worth the trouble of listening to. Ordinarily, the noise which escapes from Paris by day is the city speaking; by night, it is the city breathing; in this case, it is the city singing. Lend an ear, then, to this concert of bell towers; spread over all the murmur of half a million men, the eternal plaint of the river, the infinite breathings of the wind, the grave and distant quartette of the four forests arranged upon the hills, on the horizon, like immense stacks of organ pipes; extinguish, as in a half shade, all that is too hoarse and too shrill about the central chime, and say whether you know anything in the world more rich and joyful, more golden, more dazzling, than this tumult of bells and chimes—than this furnace of music—than these ten thousand brazen voices chanting simultaneously in the flutes of stone, three hundred feet high—than this city which is no longer anything but an orchestra—than this symphony which produces the noise of a tempest.

Book Fourth

CHAPTER 1

Good Souls

SIXTEEN YEARS PREVIOUS to the epoch when this story takes place, one fine morning, on Quasimodo Sunday, a living creature had been deposited, after mass, in the church of Notre-Dame, on the wooden bed securely fixed in the vestibule on the left, opposite that great image of Saint Christopher, which the figure of Messire Antoine des Essarts, chevalier, carved in stone, had been gazing at on his knees since 1413, when they took it into their heads to overthrow the saint and the faithful follower. Upon this bed of wood it was customary to expose foundlings for public charity. Whoever cared to take them did so. In front of the wooden bed was a copper basin for alms.

The sort of living being which lay upon that plank on the morning of Quasimodo, in the year of the Lord, 1467, appeared to excite to a high degree, the curiosity of the numerous group that had congregated about the wooden bed. The group was formed for the most part of the fair sex. Hardly any one was there except old women.

In the first row, and among those who were most bent over the bed, four were noticeable, who, from their gray *cagoule*, a sort of cassock, were recognizable as attached to some devout sisterhood. I do not see why history has not transmitted to posterity the names of these four discreet and venerable damsels. They were Agnes la Herme, Jehanne de la Tarme, Henriette la Gaultière, Gauchère la Violette, all four widows, all four dames of the Chapel Etienne Haudry, who had quitted their house with the permission of their mistress, and in conformity with the statutes of Pierre d'Ailly, in order to come and hear the sermon.

However, if these good Haudriettes were, for the moment, complying with the statutes of Pierre d'Ailly, they certainly violated with joy those of Michel de Brache, and the Cardinal of Pisa, which so inhumanly enjoined silence upon them.

"What is this, sister?" said Agnes to Gauchère, gazing at the little creature exposed, which was screaming and writhing on the wooden bed, terrified by so many glances.

"What is to become of us," said Jehanne, "if that is the way children are made now?"

"I'm not learned in the matter of children," resumed Agnes, "but it must be a sin to look at this one."

"'Tis not a child, Agnes."

"'Tis an abortion of a monkey," remarked Gauchère.

"'Tis a miracle," interposed Henriette la Gaultière.

"Then," remarked Agnes, "it is the third since the Sunday of the *Lœtare*: for, in less than a week, we had the miracle of the mocker of pilgrims divinely punished by Notre-Dame d'Aubervilliers, and that was the second miracle within a month."

"This pretended foundling is a real monster of abomination," resumed Jehanne.

"He yells loud enough to deafen a chanter," continued Gauchère. "Hold your tongue, you little howler!"

"To think that Monsieur of Reims sent this enormity to Monsieur of Paris," added la Gaultière, clasping her hands.

"I imagine," said Agnes la Herme, "that it is a beast, an animal, the fruit of a Jew and a sow; something not Christian, in short, which ought to be thrown into the fire or into the water."

"I really hope," resumed la Gaultière, "that nobody will apply for it."

"Ah, good heavens!" exclaimed Agnes; "those poor nurses yonder in the foundling asylum, which forms the lower end of the lane as you go to the river, just beside Monseigneur the bishop! What if this little monster were to be carried to them to suckle? I'd rather give suck to a vampire."

"How innocent that poor la Herme is!" resumed Jehanne; "don't you see, sister, that this little monster is at least four years old, and that he would have less appetite for your breast than for a turnspit."

The "little monster" we should find it difficult ourselves to describe him otherwise, was, in fact, not a newborn child. It was a very angular and very lively little mass, imprisoned in its linen sack, stamped with the cipher of Messire Guillaume Chartier, then bishop of Paris, with a head projecting. That head was deformed enough; one beheld only a forest of red hair, one eye, a mouth, and teeth. The eye wept, the mouth cried, and the teeth seemed to ask only to be allowed to bite. The whole struggled in the sack, to the great consternation of the crowd, which increased and was renewed incessantly around it.

Dame Aloise de Gondelaurier, a rich and noble woman, who held by the hand a pretty girl about five or six years of age, and dragged a long veil about, suspended to the golden horn of her headdress, halted as she passed the wooden bed, and gazed for a moment at the wretched creature, while her charming little daughter, Fleur-de-Lys de Gondelaurier, spelled out with her tiny, pretty finger, the permanent inscription attached to the wooden bed: "Foundlings."

"Really," said the dame, turning away in disgust, "I thought that they only exposed children here."

She turned her back, throwing into the basin a silver florin, which rang among the liards, and made the poor goodwives of the chapel of Etienne Haudry open their eyes.

A moment later, the grave and learned Robert Mistricolle, the king's protonotary, passed, with an enormous missal under one arm and his wife on the other (Damoiselle Guillemette la Mairesse), having thus by his side his two regulators, spiritual and temporal.

"Foundling!" he said, after examining the object; "found, apparently, on the banks of the river Phlegethon."

"One can only see one eye," observed Damoiselle Guillemette; "there is a wart on the other."

"It's not a wart," returned Master Robert Mistricolle, "it is an egg which contains another demon exactly similar, who bears another little egg which contains another devil, and so on."

"How do you know that?" asked Guillemette la Mairesse.

"I know it pertinently," replied the protonotary.

"Monsieur le protonotare," asked Gauchère, "what do you prognosticate of this pretended foundling?"

"The greatest misfortunes," replied Mistricolle.

"Ah! Good heavens!" said an old woman among the spectators, "and that besides our having had a considerable pestilence last year, and that they say that the English are going to disembark in a company at Harfleur."

"Perhaps that will prevent the queen from coming to Paris in the month of September," interposed another; "trade is so bad already."

"My opinion is," exclaimed Jehanne de la Tarme, "that it would be better for the louts of Paris, if this little magician were put to bed on a fagot than on a plank."

"A fine, flaming fagot," added the old woman.

"It would be more prudent," said Mistricolle.

For several minutes, a young priest had been listening to the reasoning of the Haudriettes and the sentences of the notary. He had a severe face, with a large brow, a profound glance. He thrust the crowd silently aside, scrutinized the "little magician," and stretched out his hand upon him. It was high time, for all the devotees were already licking their chops over the "fine, flaming fagot."

"I adopt this child," said the priest.

He took it in his cassock and carried it off. The spectators followed him with frightened glances. A moment later, he had disappeared through the "Red Door," which then led from the church to the cloister.

When the first surprise was over, Jehanne de la Tarme bent down to the ear of la Gaultière, "I told you so, sister, that young clerk, Monsieur Claude Frollo, is a sorcerer."

CHAPTER 2

Claude Frollo

IN FACT, CLAUDE Frollo was no common person.

He belonged to one of those middle-class families that were called indifferently, in the impertinent language of the last century, the high *bourgeoise* or the petty nobility. This family had inherited from the brothers Paclet the fief of Tirechappe, which was dependent upon the Bishop of Paris, and whose twenty-one houses had been in the thirteenth century the object of so many suits before the official. As possessor of this fief, Claude Frollo was one of the twenty-seven seigneurs keeping claim to a manor in fee in Paris and its suburbs; and for a long time, his name was to be seen inscribed in this quality, between the Hôtel de Tancarville, belonging to Master François Le Rez, and the college of Tours, in the records deposited at Saint Martin des Champs.

Claude Frollo had been destined from infancy, by his parents, to the ecclesiastical profession. He had been taught to read in Latin; he had been trained to keep his eyes on the ground and to speak low. While still a child, his father had cloistered him in the college of Torchi in the University. There it was that he had grown up, on the missal and the lexicon.

Moreover, he was a sad, grave, serious child, who studied ardently, and learned quickly; he never uttered a loud cry in recreation hour, mixed but little in the bacchanals of the Rue du Fouarre, did not know what it was to *dare alapas et capillos laniare*, and had cut no figure in that revolt of 1463, which the annalists register gravely, under the title of "The sixth trouble of the University." He seldom rallied the poor students of Montaigu on the *cappettes* from which they derived their name, or the bursars of the college of Dormans on their shaved tonsure, and their surtout parti-colored of bluish-green, blue, and violet cloth, *azurini coloris et bruni*, as says the charter of the Cardinal des Quatre-Couronnes.

On the other hand, he was assiduous at the great and the small schools of the Rue Saint Jean de Beauvais. The first pupil whom the Abbé de Saint Pierre de Val, at the moment of beginning his reading on canon law, always perceived, glued to a pillar of the school Saint-Vendregesile, opposite his rostrum, was Claude Frollo, armed with his horn ink-bottle, biting his pen, scribbling on his threadbare knee, and, in winter, blowing on his fingers. The first auditor whom Messire Miles d'Isliers, doctor in decretals, saw arrive every Monday morning, all breathless, at the opening of the gates of the school of the Chef-Saint-Denis, was Claude Frollo. Thus, at sixteen years of age, the young clerk might have held his own, in mystical theology, against a father of the church; in canonical theology, against a father of the councils; in scholastic theology, against a doctor of Sorbonne.

Theology conquered, he had plunged into decretals. From the *Master of Sentences*, he had passed to the *Capitularies of Charlemagne*; and he had devoured in succession, in his appetite for science, decretals upon decretals, those of Theodore, Bishop of Hispalus; those of Bouchard, Bishop of Worms; those of Yves, Bishop of Chartres; next the decretal of Gratian, which succeeded the capitularies of Charlemagne; then the collection of Gregory IX; then the Epistle of *Superspecula*, of Honorius III. He rendered clear and familiar to himself that vast and tumultuous period of civil law and canon law in conflict and at strife with each other, in the chaos of the Middle Ages—a period which Bishop Theodore opens in 618, and which Pope Gregory closes in 1227.

Decretals digested, he flung himself upon medicine, on the liberal arts. He studied the science of herbs, the science of unguents; he became an expert in fevers and in contusions, in sprains and abcesses. Jacques d' Espars would have received him as a physician; Richard Hellain, as a surgeon. He also passed through all the degrees of licentiate, master, and doctor of arts. He studied the languages, Latin, Greek, Hebrew, a triple sanctuary then very little frequented. His was a veritable fever for acquiring and hoarding, in the matter of science. At the age of eighteen, he had made his way through the four faculties; it seemed to the young man that life had but one sole object: learning.

It was toward this epoch, that the excessive heat of the summer of 1466 caused that grand outburst of the plague which carried off more than forty thousand souls in the vicomty of Paris, and among others, as Jean de Troyes states, "Master Arnoul, astrologer to the king, who was a very fine man, both wise and pleasant." The rumor spread in the University that the Rue Tirechappe was especially devastated by the malady. It was there that Claude's parents resided, in the midst of their fief. The young scholar rushed in great alarm to the paternal mansion. When he entered it, he found that both father and mother had died on the preceding day. A very young brother of his, who was in swaddling clothes, was still alive and crying abandoned in his cradle. This was all that remained to Claude of his family; the young man took the child under his arm and went off in a pensive mood. Up to that moment, he had lived only in science; he now began to live in life.

This catastrophe was a crisis in Claude's existence. Orphaned, the eldest, head of the family at the age of nineteen, he felt himself rudely recalled from the reveries of school to the realities of this world. Then, moved with pity, he was seized with passion and devotion toward that child, his brother; a sweet and strange thing was a human affection to him, who had hitherto loved his books alone.

This affection developed to a singular point; in a soul so new, it was like a first love. Separated since infancy from his parents, whom he had hardly known; cloistered and immured, as it were, in his books; eager above all things to study and to learn; exclusively attentive up to that time, to his intelligence which broadened in science, to his imagination, which expanded in letters—the poor scholar had not yet had time to feel the place of his heart.

This young brother, without mother or father, this little child that had fallen abruptly from heaven into his arms, made a new man of him. He perceived that there was something else in the world besides the speculations of the Sorbonne, and the verses of Homer; that man needed affections; that life without tenderness and without love was only a set of dry, shrieking, and rending wheels. Only, he imagined, for he was at the age when illusions are as yet replaced only by illusions, that the affections of blood and family were the sole ones necessary, and that a little brother to love sufficed to fill an entire existence.

He threw himself, therefore, into the love for his little Jehan with the passion of a character already profound, ardent, concentrated; that poor frail creature, pretty, fair-haired, rosy, and curly, that orphan with another orphan for his only support, touched him to the bottom of his heart; and grave thinker as he was, he set to meditating upon Jehan with an infinite compassion. He kept watch and ward over him as over something very fragile, and very worthy of care. He was more than a brother to the child; he became a mother to him.

Little Jehan had lost his mother while he was still at the breast; Claude gave him to a nurse. Besides the fief of Tirechappe, he had inherited from his father the fief of Moulin, which was a dependency of the square tower of Gentilly; it was a mill on a hill, near the château of Winchestre (Bicêtre). There was a miller's wife there who was nursing a fine child; it was not far from the university, and Claude carried the little Jehan to her in his own arms.

From that time forth, feeling that he had a burden to bear, he took life very seriously. The thought of his little brother became not only his recreation, but the object of his studies. He resolved to consecrate himself entirely to a future for which he was responsible in the sight of God, and never to have any other wife, any other child than the happiness and fortune of his brother. Therefore, he attached himself more closely than ever to the clerical profession. His merits, his learning, his quality of immediate vassal of the Bishop of Paris, threw the doors of the church wide open to him. At the age of twenty, by special dispensation of the Holy See, he was a priest, and served as the youngest of the chaplains of Notre-Dame the altar that is called, because of the late mass which is said there, *altare pigrorum*.

There, plunged more deeply than ever in his dear books, which he quitted only to run for an hour to the fief of Moulin, this mixture of learning and austerity, so rare at his age, had promptly acquired for him the respect and admiration of the monastery. From the cloister, his reputation as a learned man had passed to the people, among whom it had changed a little, a frequent occurrence at that time, into reputation as a sorcerer.

It was at the moment when he was returning, on Quasimodo day, from saying his mass at the Altar of the Lazy, which was by the side of the door leading to the nave on the right, near the image of the Virgin, that his attention had been attracted by the group of old women chattering around the bed for foundlings.

Then it was that he approached the unhappy little creature, which was so hated and so menaced. That distress, that deformity, that abandonment, the thought of his young brother, the idea which suddenly occurred to him, that if he were to die, his dear little Jehan might also be flung miserably on the plank for foundlings, all this had gone to his heart simultaneously; a great pity had moved in him, and he had carried off the child.

When he removed the child from the sack, he found it greatly deformed, in very sooth. The poor little wretch had a wart on his left eye, his head placed directly on his shoulders, his spinal column was crooked, his breast bone prominent, and his legs bowed; but he appeared to be lively; and although it was impossible to say in what language he lisped, his cry indicated considerable force and health. Claude's compassion increased at the sight of this ugliness; and he made a vow in his heart to rear the child for the love of his brother, in order that, whatever might be the future faults of the little Jehan, he should have beside him that charity done for his sake. It was a sort of investment of good works, which he was effecting in the name of his young brother; it was a stock of good works which he wished to amass in advance for him, in case the little rogue should some day find himself short of that coin, the only sort which is received at the toll-bar of paradise.

He baptized his adopted child, and gave him the name of Quasimodo, either because he desired thereby to mark the day, when he had found him, or because he wished to designate by that name to what a degree the poor little creature was incomplete, and hardly sketched out. In fact, Quasimodo, blind, hunchbacked, knock-kneed, was only an "almost."

CHAPTER 3

Immanis Pecoris Custos, Immanior Ipse

Now, in 1482, Quasimodo had grown up. He had become a few years previously the bellringer of Notre-Dame, thanks to his father by adoption, Claude Frollo, who had become archdeacon of Josas, thanks to his suzerain, Messire Louis de Beaumont, who had become Bishop of Paris, at the death of Guillaume Chartier in 1472, thanks to his patron, Olivier Le Daim, barber to Louis XI, king by the grace of God.

So Quasimodo was the ringer of the chimes of Notre-Dame.

In the course of time there had been formed a certain peculiarly intimate bond which united the ringer to the church. Separated forever from the world, by the double fatality of his unknown birth and his natural deformity, imprisoned from his infancy in that impassable double circle, the poor wretch had grown used to seeing nothing in this world beyond the religious walls that had received him under their shadow. Notre-Dame had been to him successively, as he grew up and developed, the egg, the nest, the house, the country, the universe.

There was certainly a sort of mysterious and pre-existing harmony between this creature and this church. When, still a little fellow, he had dragged himself tortuously and by jerks beneath the shadows of its vaults, he seemed, with his human face and his bestial limbs, the natural reptile of that humid and sombre pavement, upon which the shadow of the Romanesque capitals cast so many strange forms.

Later on, the first time that he caught hold, mechanically, of the ropes to the towers, and hung suspended from them, and set the bell to clanging, it produced upon his adopted father, Claude, the effect of a child whose tongue is unloosed and who begins to speak.

It is thus that, little by little, developing always in sympathy with the cathedral, living there, sleeping there, hardly ever leaving it, subject every hour to the mysterious impress, he came to resemble it, he incrusted himself in it, so to speak, and became an integral part of it. His salient angles fitted into the retreating angles of the cathedral (if we may be allowed this figure of speech), and he seemed not only its inhabitant but more than that, its natural tenant. One might almost say that he had assumed its form, as the snail takes on the form of its shell. It was his dwelling, his hole, his envelope. There existed between him and the old church so profound an instinctive sympathy, so many magnetic affinities, so many material affinities, that he adhered to it somewhat as a tortoise adheres to its shell. The rough and wrinkled cathedral was his shell.

It is useless to warn the reader not to take literally all the similes which we are obliged to employ here to express the singular, symmetrical, direct, almost consubstantial union of a man and an edifice. It is equally unnecessary to state to what a degree that whole cathedral was familiar to him, after so long and so intimate a cohabitation. That dwelling was peculiar to him. It had no depths to which Quasimodo had not penetrated, no height which he had not scaled. He often climbed many stones up the front, aided solely by the uneven points of the carving. The towers, on whose exterior surface he was frequently seen clambering, like a lizard gliding along a perpendicular wall, those two gigantic twins, so lofty, so menacing, so formidable, possessed for him neither vertigo, nor terror, nor shocks of amazement.

To see them so gentle under his hand, so easy to scale, one would have said that he had tamed them. By dint of leaping, climbing, gambolling amid the abysses of the gigantic cathedral he had become, in some sort, a monkey and a goat, like the Calabrian child who swims before he walks, and plays with the sea while still a babe.

Moreover, it was not his body alone that seemed fashioned after the Cathedral, but his mind also. In what condition was that mind? What bent had it contracted, what form had it assumed beneath that knotted envelope, in that savage life? This it would be hard to determine. Quasimodo had been born one-eyed, hunchbacked, lame. It was with great difficulty, and by dint of great patience that Claude Frollo had succeeded in teaching him to talk. But a fatality was attached to the poor foundling. Bellringer of Notre-Dame at the age of fourteen, a new infirmity had come to complete his misfortunes: the bells had broken the drums of his ears; he had become deaf. The only gate which nature had left wide open for him had been abruptly closed, and forever.

In closing, it had cut off the only ray of joy and of light which still made its way into the soul of Quasimodo. His soul fell into profound night. The wretched being's misery became as incurable and as complete as his deformity. Let us add that his deafness rendered him to some extent dumb. For, in order not to make others laugh, the very moment that he found himself to be deaf, he resolved upon a silence that he only broke when he was alone. He voluntarily tied that tongue which Claude Frollo had taken so much pains to unloose. Hence, it came about, that when necessity constrained him to speak, his tongue was torpid, awkward, and like a door whose hinges have grown rusty.

If now we were to try to penetrate to the soul of Quasimodo through that thick, hard rind; if we could sound the depths of that badly constructed organism; if it were granted to us to look with a torch behind those non-transparent organs to explore the shadowy interior of that opaque creature, to elucidate his obscure corners, his absurd no-thoroughfares, and suddenly to cast a vivid light upon the soul enchained at the extremity of that cave, we should, no doubt, find the unhappy Psyche in some poor, cramped, and ricketty attitude, like those prisoners beneath the Leads of Venice, who grew old bent double in a stone box which was both too low and too short for them.

It is certain that the mind becomes atrophied in a defective body. Quasimodo was barely conscious of a soul cast in his own image, moving blindly within him. The impressions of objects underwent a considerable refraction before reaching his mind. His brain was a peculiar medium; the ideas that passed through it issued forth completely distorted. The reflection that resulted from this refraction was, necessarily, divergent and perverted.

Hence a thousand optical illusions, a thousand aberrations of judgment, a thousand deviations, in which his thought strayed, now mad, now idiotic.

The first effect of this fatal organization was to trouble the glance that he cast upon things. He received hardly any immediate perception of them. The external world seemed much farther away to him than it does to us.

The second effect of his misfortune was to render him malicious.

He was malicious, in fact, because he was savage; he was savage because he was ugly. There was logic in his nature, as there is in ours.

His strength, so extraordinarily developed, was a cause of still greater malevolence: "*Malus puer robustus*," says Hobbes.

This justice must, however be rendered to him. Malevolence was not, perhaps, innate in him. From his very first steps among men, he had felt himself, later on he had seen himself, spewed out, blasted, rejected. Human words were, for him, always a raillery or a malediction. As he grew up, he had found nothing but hatred around him. He had caught the general malevolence. He had picked up the weapon with which he had been wounded.

After all, he turned his face toward men only with reluctance; his cathedral was sufficient for him. It was peopled with marble figures— kings, saints, bishops—who at least did not burst out laughing in his face, and who gazed upon him only with tranquillity and kindliness. The other statues, those of the monsters and demons, cherished no hatred for him, Quasimodo. He resembled them too much for that. They seemed rather, to be scoffing at other men. The saints were his friends, and blessed him; the monsters were his friends and guarded him. So he held long communion with them. He sometimes passed whole hours crouching before one of these statues, in solitary conversation with it. If any one came, he fled like a lover surprised in his serenade.

And the cathedral was not only society for him, but the universe, and all nature beside. He dreamed of no other hedgerows than the painted windows, always in flower; no other shade than that of the foliage of stone which spread out, loaded with birds, in the tufts of the Saxon capitals; of no other mountains than the colossal towers of the church; of no other ocean than Paris, roaring at their bases.

What he loved above all else in the maternal edifice, that which aroused his soul, and made it open its poor wings, which it kept so miserably folded in its cavern, that which sometimes rendered him even happy, was the bells. He loved them, fondled them, talked to them, understood them. From the chime in the spire, over the intersection of the aisles and nave, to the great bell of the front, he cherished a tenderness for them all. The central spire and the two towers were to him as three great cages, whose birds, reared by himself, sang for him alone. Yet it was these very bells which had made him deaf; but mothers often love best that child which has caused them the most suffering.

It is true that their voice was the only one that he could still hear. On this score, the big bell was his beloved. It was she whom he preferred out of all that family of noisy girls that bustled above him, on festival days. This bell was named Marie. She was alone in the southern tower, with her sister Jacqueline, a bell of lesser size, shut up in a smaller cage beside hers. This Jacqueline was so called from the name of the wife of Jean Montagu, who had given it to the church, which had not prevented his going and figuring without his head at Montfauçon. In the second tower there were six other bells, and, finally, six smaller ones inhabited the belfry over the crossing, with the wooden bell, which rang only between after dinner on Good Friday and the morning of the day before Easter. So Quasimodo had fifteen bells in his seraglio; but big Marie was his favorite.

No idea can be formed of his delight on days when the grand peal was sounded. At the moment when the archdeacon dismissed him, and said, "Go!" he mounted the spiral staircase of the clock tower faster than any one else could have descended it. He entered perfectly breathless into the aerial chamber of the great bell; he gazed at her a moment, devoutly and lovingly; then he gently addressed her and patted her with his hand, like a good horse, which is about to set out on a long journey. He pitied her for the trouble that she was about to suffer. After these first caresses, he shouted to his assistants, placed in the lower story of the tower, to begin. They grasped the ropes, the wheel creaked, the enormous capsule of metal started slowly into motion. Quasimodo followed it with his glance and trembled. The first shock of the clapper and the brazen wall made the framework upon which it was mounted quiver. Quasimodo vibrated with the bell.

"Vah!" he cried, with a senseless burst of laughter. However, the movement of the bass was accelerated, and, in proportion as it described a wider angle, Quasimodo's eye opened also more and more widely, phosphoric and flaming. At length the grand peal began; the whole tower trembled; woodwork, leads, cut stones, all groaned at once, from the piles of the foundation to the trefoils of its summit. Then Quasimodo boiled and frothed; he went and came; he trembled from head to foot with the tower. The bell, furious, running riot, presented to the two walls of the tower alternately its brazen throat, whence escaped that tempestuous breath, which is audible leagues away. Quasimodo stationed himself in front of this open throat; he crouched and rose with the oscillations of the bell, breathed in this overwhelming breath, gazed by turns at the deep place, which swarmed with people, two hundred feet below him, and at that enormous, brazen tongue which came, second after second, to howl in his ear.

It was the only speech that he understood, the only sound that broke for him the universal silence. He swelled out in it as a bird does in the sun. All of a sudden, the frenzy of the bell seized upon him; his look became extraordinary; he lay in wait for the great bell as it passed, as a spider lies in wait for a fly, and flung himself abruptly upon it, with might and main. Then, suspended above the abyss, borne to and fro by the formidable swinging of the bell, he seized the brazen monster by the ear-laps, pressed it between both knees, spurred it on with his heels, and redoubled the fury of the peal with the whole shock and weight of his body. Meanwhile, the tower trembled; he shrieked and gnashed his teeth, his red hair rose erect, his breast heaving like a bellows, his eye flashed flames, the monstrous bell neighed, panting, beneath him; and then it was no longer the great bell of Notre-Dame nor Quasimodo: it was a dream, a whirlwind, a tempest, dizziness mounted astride of noise; a spirit clinging to a flying crupper, a strange centaur, half man, half bell; a sort of horrible Astolphus, borne away upon a prodigious hippogriff of living bronze.

The presence of this extraordinary being caused, as it were, a breath of life to circulate throughout the entire cathedral. It seemed as though there escaped from him, at least according to the growing superstitions of the crowd, a mysterious emanation that animated all the stones of Notre-Dame, and made the deep bowels of the ancient church to palpitate. It sufficed for people to know that he was there, to make them believe that they beheld the thousand statues of the galleries and the fronts in motion. And the cathedral did indeed seem a docile and obedient creature beneath his hand; it waited on his will to raise its great voice; it was possessed and filled with Quasimodo, as with a familiar spirit. One would have said that he made the immense edifice breathe. He was everywhere about it; in fact, he multiplied himself on all points of the structure. Now one perceived with affright at the very top of one of the towers, a fantastic dwarf climbing, writhing, crawling on all fours, descending outside above the abyss, leaping from projection to projection, and going to ransack the belly of some sculptured gorgon; it was Quasimodo dislodging the crows. Again, in some obscure corner of the church one came in contact with a sort of living chimera, crouching and scowling; it was Quasimodo engaged in thought. Sometimes one caught sight, upon a bell tower, of an enormous head and a bundle of disordered limbs swinging furiously at the end of a rope; it was Quasimodo ringing vespers or the Angelus.

Often at night a hideous form was seen wandering along the frail balustrade of carved lacework, which crowns the towers and borders the circumference of the apse; again it was the hunchback of Notre-Dame. Then, said the women of the neighborhood, the whole church took on something fantastic, supernatural, horrible; eyes and mouths were opened, here and there; one heard the dogs, the monsters, and the gargoyles of stone, which keep watch night and day, with outstretched neck and open jaws, around the monstrous cathedral, barking. And, if it was a Christmas Eve, while the great bell, which seemed to emit the death rattle, summoned the faithful to the midnight mass, such an air was spread over the sombre façade that one would have declared that the grand portal was devouring the throng, and that the rose window was watching it. And all this came from Quasimodo. Egypt would have taken him for the god of this temple; the Middle Ages believed him to be its demon: he was in fact its soul.

To such an extent was this disease that for those who know that Quasimodo has existed, Notre-Dame is today deserted, inanimate, dead. One feels that something has disappeared from it. That immense body is empty; it is a skeleton; the spirit has quitted it, one sees its place and that is all. It is like a skull which still has holes for the eyes, but no longer sight.

CHAPTER 4

The Dog and His Master

NEVERTHELESS, THERE WAS one human creature whom Quasimodo excepted from his malice and from his hatred for others, and whom he loved even more, perhaps, than his cathedral: this was Claude Frollo.

The matter was simple; Claude Frollo had taken him in, had adopted him, had nourished him, had reared him. When a little lad, it was between Claude Frollo's legs that he was accustomed to seek refuge, when the dogs and the children barked after him. Claude Frollo had taught him to talk, to read, to write. Claude Frollo had finally made him the bellringer. Now, to give the big bell in marriage to Quasimodo was to give Juliet to Romeo.

Hence Quasimodo's gratitude was profound, passionate, boundless; and although the visage of his adopted father was often clouded or severe, although his speech was habitually curt, harsh, imperious, that gratitude never wavered for a single moment. The archdeacon had in Quasimodo the most submissive slave, the most docile lackey, the most vigilant of dogs. When the poor bellringer became deaf, there had been established between him and Claude Frollo, a language of signs, mysterious and understood by themselves alone. In this manner the archdeacon was the sole human being with whom Quasimodo had preserved communication. He was in sympathy with but two things in this world: Notre-Dame and Claude Frollo.

There is nothing that can be compared with the empire of the archdeacon over the bellringer; with the attachment of the bellringer for the archdeacon. A sign from Claude and the idea of giving him pleasure would have sufficed to make Quasimodo hurl himself headlong from the summit of Notre-Dame. It was a remarkable thing—all that physical strength which had reached in Quasimodo such an extraordinary development, and which was placed by him blindly at the disposition of another. There was in it, no doubt, filial devotion, domestic attachment; there was also the fascination of one spirit by another spirit. It was a poor, awkward, and clumsy organization, which stood with lowered head and supplicating eyes before a lofty and profound, a powerful and superior intellect. Lastly, and above all, it was gratitude. Gratitude so pushed to its extremest limit, that we do not know to what to compare it. This virtue is not one of those of which the finest examples are to be met with among men. We will say then, that Quasimodo loved the archdeacon as never a dog, never a horse, never an elephant loved his master.

CHAPTER 5

More About Claude Frollo

IN 1482, QUASIMODO WAS about twenty years of age; Claude Frollo, about thirty-six. One had grown up, the other had grown old.

Claude Frollo was no longer the simple scholar of the college of Torch, the tender protector of a little child, the young and dreamy philosopher who knew many things and was ignorant of many. He was a priest, austere, grave, morose; one charged with souls; monsieur the archdeacon of Josas, the bishop's second acolyte, having charge of the two deaneries of Montlhéry, and Châteaufort, and one hundred and seventy-four country curacies. He was an imposing and sombre personage, before whom the choir boys in alb and in jacket trembled, as well as the *machicos*, and the brothers of Saint-Augustine and the matutinal clerks of Notre-Dame, when he passed slowly beneath the lofty arches of the choir, majestic, thoughtful, with arms folded and his head so bent upon his breast that all one saw of his face was his large, bald brow.

Dom Claude Frollo had, however, abandoned neither science nor the education of his young brother, those two occupations of his life. But as time went on, some bitterness had been mingled with these things that were so sweet. In the long run, says Paul Diacre, the best lard turns rancid. Little Jehan Frollo, surnamed *du Moulin* because of the place where he had been reared, had not grown up in the direction that Claude would have liked to impose upon him. The big brother counted upon a pious, docile, learned, and honorable pupil. But the little brother, like those young trees which deceive the gardener's hopes and turn obstinately to the quarter whence they receive sun and air, the little brother did not grow and did not multiply, but only put forth fine bushy and luxuriant branches on the side of laziness, ignorance, and debauchery. He was a regular devil, and a very disorderly one, who made Dom Claude scowl; but very droll and very subtle, which made the big brother smile.

Claude had confided him to that same college of Torchi where he had passed his early years in study and meditation; and it was a grief to him that this sanctuary, formerly edified by the name of Frollo, should today be scandalized by it. He sometimes preached Jehan very long and severe sermons, which the latter intrepidly endured. After all, the young scapegrace had a good heart, as can be seen in all comedies. But the sermon over, he none the less tranquilly resumed his course of seditions and enormities. Now it was a *bejaune* or yellow beak (as they called the new arrivals at the university), whom he had been mauling by way of welcome; a precious tradition which has been carefully preserved to our own day. Again, he had set in movement a band of scholars, who had flung themselves upon a wine-shop in classic fashion, quasi *classico excitati*, had then beaten the tavern-keeper "with offensive cudgels," and joyously pillaged the tavern, even to smashing in the hogsheads of wine in the cellar. And then it was a fine report in Latin, which the sub-monitor of Torchi carried piteously to Dom Claude with this dolorous marginal comment,—*Rixa; prima causa vinum optimum potatum.* Finally, it was said, a thing quite horrible in a boy of sixteen, that his debauchery often extended as far as the Rue de Glatigny.

Claude, saddened and discouraged in his human affections, by all this, had flung himself eagerly into the arms of learning, that sister which, at least does not laugh in your face, and which always pays you, though in money that is sometimes a little hollow, for the attention which you have paid to her. Hence, he became more and more learned, and, at the same time, as a natural consequence, more and more rigid as a priest, more and more sad as a man. There are for each of us several parallelisms between our intelligence, our habits, and our character, which develop without a break, and break only in the great disturbances of life.

As Claude Frollo had passed through nearly the entire circle of human learning—positive, exterior, and permissible—since his youth, he was obliged, unless he came to a halt, *ubi defuit orbis*, to proceed further and seek other aliments for the insatiable activity of his intelligence. The antique symbol of the serpent biting its tail is, above all, applicable to science. It would appear that Claude Frollo had experienced this. Many grave persons affirm that, after having exhausted the *fas* of human learning, he had dared to penetrate into the *nefas*. He had, they said, tasted in succession all the apples of the tree of knowledge, and, whether from hunger or disgust, had ended by tasting the forbidden fruit. He had taken his place by turns, as the reader has seen, in the conferences of the theologians in Sorbonne, in the assemblies of the doctors of art, after the manner of Saint-Hilaire, in the disputes of the decretalists, after the manner of Saint-Martin, in the congregations of physicians at the holy water font of Notre-Dame, *ad cupam Nostroe-Dominoe*. All the dishes permitted and approved, which those four great kitchens called the four faculties could elaborate and serve to the understanding, he had devoured, and had been satiated with them before his hunger was appeased. Then he had penetrated further, lower, beneath all that finished, material, limited knowledge; he had, perhaps, risked his soul, and had seated himself in the cavern at that mysterious table of the alchemists, of the astrologers, of the hermetics, of which Averroès, Gillaume de Paris, and Nicolas Flamel hold the end in the Middle Ages; and which extends in the East, by the light of the seven-branched candlestick, to Solomon, Pythagoras, and Zoroaster.

That is, at least, what was supposed, whether rightly or not. It is certain that the archdeacon often visited the cemetery of the Saints-Innocents, where, it is true, his father and mother had been buried, with other victims of the plague of 1466; but that he appeared far less devout before the cross of their grave than before the strange figures with which the tomb of Nicolas Flamel and Claude Pernelle, erected just beside it, was loaded.

It is certain that he had frequently been seen to pass along the Rue des Lombards, and furtively enter a little house that formed the corner of the Rue des Ecrivans and the Rue Marivault. It was the house which Nicolas Flamel had built, where he had died about 1417, and which, constantly deserted since that time, had already begun to fall in ruins, so greatly had the hermetics and the alchemists of all countries wasted away the walls, merely by carving their names upon them. Some neighbors even affirm that they had once seen, through an air-hole, Archdeacon Claude excavating, turning over, digging up the earth in the two cellars, whose supports had been daubed with numberless couplets and hieroglyphics by Nicolas Flamel himself. It was supposed that Flamel had buried the philosopher's stone in the cellar; and the alchemists, for the space of two centuries, from Magistri to Father Pacifique, never ceased to worry the soil until the house, so cruelly ransacked and turned over, ended by falling into dust beneath their feet.

Again, it is certain that the archdeacon had been seized with a singular passion for the symbolical door of Notre-Dame, that page of a conjuring book written in stone, by Bishop Guillaume de Paris, who has, no doubt, been damned for having affixed so infernal a frontispiece to the sacred poem chanted by the rest of the edifice. Archdeacon Claude had the credit also of having fathomed the mystery of the colossus of Saint Christopher, and of that lofty, enigmatical statue which then stood at the entrance of the vestibule, and which the people, in derision, called "Monsieur Legris." But, what every one might have noticed was the interminable hours which he often employed, seated upon the parapet of the area in front of the church, in contemplating the sculptures of the front; examining now the foolish virgins with their lamps reversed, now the wise virgins with their lamps upright; again, calculating the angle of vision of that raven which belongs to the left front, and which is looking at a mysterious point inside the church, where is concealed the philosopher's stone, if it be not in the cellar of Nicolas Flamel.

It was, let us remark in passing, a singular fate for the Church of Notre-Dame at that epoch to be so beloved, in two different degrees, and with so much devotion, by two beings so dissimilar as Claude and Quasimodo. Beloved by one, a sort of instinctive and savage half-man, for its beauty, for its stature, for the harmonies which emanated from its magnificent ensemble; beloved by the other, a learned and passionate imagination, for its myth, for the sense which it contains, for the symbolism scattered beneath the sculptures of its front—like the first text underneath the second in a palimpsest—in a word, for the enigma which it is eternally propounding to the understanding.

Furthermore, it is certain that the archdeacon had established himself in that one of the two towers which looks upon the Grève, just beside the frame for the bells, a very secret little cell, into which no one, not even the bishop, entered without his leave, it was said. This tiny cell had formerly been made almost at the summit of the tower, among the ravens' nests, by Bishop Hugo de Besançon, who had wrought sorcery there in his day. What that cell contained, no one knew; but from the strand of the Terrain, at night, there was often seen to appear, disappear, and reappear at brief and regular intervals, at a little dormer window opening upon the back of the tower, a certain red, intermittent, singular light which seemed to follow the panting breaths of a bellows, and to proceed from a flame, rather than from a light. In the darkness, at that height, it produced a singular effect; and the goodwives said: "There's the archdeacon blowing! Hell is sparkling up yonder!"

There were no great proofs of sorcery in that, after all, but there was still enough smoke to warrant a surmise of fire, and the archdeacon bore a tolerably formidable reputation. We ought to mention however, that the sciences of Egypt, that necromancy and magic, even the whitest, even the most innocent, had no more envenomed enemy, no more pitiless denunciator before the gentlemen of the officialty of Notre-Dame. Whether this was sincere horror, or the game played by the thief who shouts, "Stop thief!" at all events, it did not prevent the archdeacon from being considered by the learned heads of the chapter, as a soul who had ventured into the vestibule of hell, who was lost in the caves of the cabal, groping amid the shadows of the occult sciences. Neither were the people deceived thereby; with any one who possessed any sagacity, Quasimodo passed for the demon; Claude Frollo, for the sorcerer. It was evident that the bellringer was to serve the archdeacon for a given time, at the end of which he would carry away the latter's soul, by way of payment. Thus the archdeacon, in spite of the excessive austerity of his life, was in bad odor among all pious souls; and there was no devout nose so inexperienced that it could not smell him out to be a magician.

And if, as he grew older, abysses had formed in his science, they had also formed in his heart. That at least, is what one had grounds for believing on scrutinizing that face upon which the soul was only seen to shine through a sombre cloud. Whence that large, bald brow? That head forever bent? That breast always heaving with sighs? What secret thought caused his mouth to smile with so much bitterness, at the same moment that his scowling brows approached each other like two bulls on the point of fighting? Why was what hair he had left already gray? What was that internal fire which sometimes broke forth in his glance, to such a degree that his eye resembled a hole pierced in the wall of a furnace?

These symptoms of a violent moral preoccupation, had acquired an especially high degree of intensity at the epoch when this story takes place. More than once a choir-boy had fled in terror at finding him alone in the church, so strange and dazzling was his look. More than once, in the choir, at the hour of the offices, his neighbor in the stalls had heard him mingle with the plain song, *ad omnem tonum*, unintelligible parentheses. More than once the laundress of the Terrain charged "with washing the chapter" had observed, not without affright, the marks of nails and clenched fingers on the surplice of monsieur the archdeacon of Josas.

However, he redoubled his severity, and had never been more exemplary. By profession as well as by character, he had always held himself aloof from women; he seemed to hate them more than ever. The mere rustling of a silken petticoat caused his hood to fall over his eyes. Upon this score he was so jealous of austerity and reserve, that when the Dame de Beaujeu, the king's daughter, came to visit the cloister of Notre-Dame, in the month of December, 1481, he gravely opposed her entrance, reminding the bishop of the statute of the Black Book, dating from the vigil of Saint-Barthélemy, 1334, which interdicts access to the cloister to "any woman whatever, old or young, mistress or maid." Upon which the bishop had been constrained to recite to him the ordinance of Legate Odo, which excepts certain great dames, *aliquœ magnates mulieres, quoe sine scandalo vitari non possunt.* And again the archdeacon had protested, objecting that the ordinance of the legate, which dated back to 1207, was anterior by a hundred and twenty-seven years to the Black Book, and consequently was abrogated in fact by it. And he had refused to appear before the princess.

It was also noticed that his horror for Bohemian women and gypsies had seemed to redouble for some time past. He had petitioned the bishop for an edict which expressly forbade the Bohemian women to come and dance and beat their tambourines on the place of the Parvis; and for about the same length of time, he had been ransacking the mouldy placards of the officialty, in order to collect the cases of sorcerers and witches condemned to fire or the rope, for complicity in crimes with rams, sows, or goats.

Chapter 6

Unpopularity

THE ARCHDEACON AND the bellringer, as we have already said, were but little loved by the populace great and small, in the vicinity of the cathedral. When Claude and Quasimodo went out together, which frequently happened, and when they were seen traversing in company, the valet behind the master, the cold, narrow, and gloomy streets of the block of Notre-Dame, more than one evil word, more than one ironical quaver, more than one insulting jest greeted them on their way, unless Claude Frollo, which was rarely the case, walked with head upright and raised, showing his severe and almost august brow to the dumbfounded jeerers.

Both were in their quarter like "the poets" of whom Régnier speaks—

> All sorts of persons run after poets,
> As warblers fly shrieking after owls.

Sometimes a mischievous child risked his skin and bones for the ineffable pleasure of driving a pin into Quasimodo's hump. Again, a young girl, more bold and saucy than was fitting, brushed the priest's black robe, singing in his face the sardonic ditty, "niche, niche, the devil is caught." Sometimes a group of squalid old crones, squatting in a file under the shadow of the steps to a porch, scolded noisily as the archdeacon and the bellringer passed, and tossed them this encouraging welcome, with a curse: "Hum! There's a fellow whose soul is made like the other one's body!" Or a band of schoolboys and street urchins, playing hop-scotch, rose in a body and saluted him classically, with some cry in Latin: "*Eia! Eia! Claudius cum claudo!*"

But the insult generally passed unnoticed both by the priest and the bellringer. Quasimodo was too deaf to hear all these gracious things, and Claude was too dreamy.

Book Fifth

Chapter 1

Abbas Beati Martini

Dom Claude's fame had spread far and wide. It procured for him, at about the epoch when he refused to see Madame de Beaujeu, a visit that he long remembered.

It was in the evening. He had just retired, after the office, to his canon's cell in the cloister of Notre-Dame. This cell, with the exception, possibly, of some glass phials, relegated to a corner, and filled with a decidedly equivocal powder, which strongly resembled the alchemist's "powder of projection," presented nothing strange or mysterious. There were, indeed, here and there, some inscriptions on the walls, but they were pure sentences of learning and piety, extracted from good authors. The archdeacon had just seated himself, by the light of a three-jetted copper lamp, before a vast coffer crammed with manuscripts. He had rested his elbow upon the open volume of *Honorius d'Autun, De predestinatione et libero arbitrio,* and he was turning over, in deep meditation, the leaves of a printed folio which he had just brought, the sole product of the press which his cell contained. In the midst of his revery there came a knock at his door. "Who's there?" cried the learned man, in the gracious tone of a famished dog, disturbed over his bone.

A voice without replied, "Your friend, Jacques Coictier." He went to open the door.

It was, in fact, the king's physician; a person about fifty years of age, whose harsh physiognomy was modified only by a crafty eye. Another man accompanied him. Both wore long slate-colored robes, furred with minever, girded and closed, with caps of the same stuff and hue. Their hands were concealed by their sleeves, their feet by their robes, their eyes by their caps.

"God help me, messieurs!" said the archdeacon, showing them in; "I was not expecting distinguished visitors at such an hour." And while speaking in this courteous fashion he cast an uneasy and scrutinizing glance from the physician to his companion.

"'Tis never too late to come and pay a visit to so considerable a learned man as Dom Claude Frollo de Tirechappe," replied Dr. Coictier, whose Franche-Comté accent made all his phrases drag along with the majesty of a train-robe.

There then ensued between the physician and the archdeacon one of those congratulatory prologues which, in accordance with custom, at that epoch preceded all conversations between learned men, and which did not prevent them from detesting each other in the most cordial manner in the world. However, it is the same nowadays; every wise man's mouth complimenting another wise man is a vase of honeyed gall.

Claude Frollo's felicitations to Jacques Coictier bore reference principally to the temporal advantages which the worthy physician had found means to extract, in the course of his much envied career, from each malady of the king, an operation of alchemy much better and more certain than the pursuit of the philosopher's stone.

"In truth, Monsieur le Docteur Coictier, I felt great joy on learning of the bishopric given your nephew, my reverend seigneur Pierre Verse. Is he not Bishop of Amiens?"

"Yes, monsieur Archdeacon; it is a grace and mercy of God."

"Do you know that you made a great figure on Christmas Day at the head of your company of the chamber of accounts, Monsieur President?"

"Vice-President, Dom Claude. Alas, nothing more!"

"How is your superb house in the Rue Saint-André des Arcs coming on? 'Tis a Louvre. I love greatly the apricot tree which is carved on the door, with this play of words: 'A L'ABRI-COTIER'" [sheltered from reefs].

"Alas! Master Claude, all that masonry costeth me dear. In proportion as the house is erected, I am ruined."

"Hey! Have you not your revenues from the jail, and the bailiwick of the Palais, and the rents of all the houses, sheds, stalls, and booths of the enclosure? 'Tis a fine breast to suck."

"My castellany of Poissy has brought me in nothing this year."

"But your tolls of Triel, of Saint-James, of Saint-Germainen-Laye are always good."

"Six score livres, and not even Parisian livres at that."

"You have your office of counsellor to the king. That is fixed."

"Yes, brother Claude; but that accursed seigneury of Poligny, which people make so much noise about, is worth not sixty gold crowns, year out and year in."

In the compliments which Dom Claude addressed to Jacques Coictier, there was that sardonical, biting, and covertly mocking accent, and the sad cruel smile of a superior and unhappy man who toys for a moment, by way of distraction, with the dense prosperity of a vulgar man. The other did not perceive it.

"Upon my soul," said Claude at length, pressing his hand, "I am glad to see you and in such good health."

"Thanks, Master Claude."

"By the way," exclaimed Dom Claude, "how is your royal patient?"

"He payeth not sufficiently his physician," replied the doctor, casting a side glance at his companion.

"Think you so, Gossip Coictier," said the latter.

These words, uttered in a tone of surprise and reproach, drew upon this unknown personage the attention of the archdeacon which, to tell the truth, had not been diverted from him a single moment since the stranger had set foot across the threshold of his cell. It had even required all the thousand reasons that he had for handling tenderly Dr. Jacques Coictier, the all-powerful physician of King Louis XI, to induce him to receive the latter thus accompanied. Hence, there was nothing very cordial in his manner when Jacques Coictier said to him, "By the way, Dom Claude, I bring you a colleague who has desired to see you on account of your reputation."

"Monsieur belongs to science?" asked the archdeacon, fixing his piercing eye upon Coictier's companion. He found beneath the brows of the stranger a glance no less piercing or less distrustful than his own.

He was, so far as the feeble light of the lamp permitted one to judge, an old man about sixty years of age and of medium stature, who appeared somewhat sickly and broken in health. His profile, although of a very ordinary outline, had something powerful and severe about it; his eyes sparkled beneath a very deep superciliary arch, like a light in the depths of a cave; and beneath his cap which was well drawn down and fell upon his nose, one recognized the broad expanse of a brow of genius.

He took it upon himself to reply to the archdeacon's question, "Reverend master," he said in a grave tone, "your renown has reached my ears, and I wish to consult you. I am but a poor provincial gentleman, who removeth his shoes before entering the dwellings of the learned. You must know my name. I am called Gossip Tourangeau."

"Strange name for a gentleman," said the archdeacon to himself.

Nevertheless, he had a feeling that he was in the presence of a strong and earnest character. The instinct of his own lofty intellect made him recognize an intellect no less lofty under Gossip Tourangeau's furred cap, and as he gazed at the solemn face, the ironical smile which Jacques Coictier's presence called forth on his gloomy face, gradually disappeared as twilight fades on the horizon of night. Stern and silent, he had resumed his seat in his great armchair; his elbow rested as usual, on the table, and his brow on his hand. After a few moments of reflection, he motioned his visitors to be seated, and, turning to Gossip Tourangeau he said, "You come to consult me, master, and upon what science?"

"Your reverence," replied Tourangeau, "I am ill, very ill. You are said to be great Aesculapius, and I am come to ask your advice in medicine."

"Medicine!" said the archdeacon, tossing his head. He seemed to meditate for a moment, and then resumed: "Gossip Tourangeau, since that is your name, turn your head, you will find my reply already written on the wall."

Gossip Tourangeau obeyed, and read this inscription engraved above his head: "Medicine is the daughter of dreams.—JAMBLIQUE."

Meanwhile, Dr. Jacques Coictier had heard his companion's question with a displeasure that Dom Claude's response had but redoubled. He bent down to the ear of Gossip Tourangeau, and said to him, softly enough not to be heard by the archdeacon: "I warned you that he was mad. You insisted on seeing him."

"'Tis very possible that he is right, madman as he is, Dr. Jacques," replied his comrade in the same low tone, and with a bitter smile.

"As you please," replied Coictier dryly. Then, addressing the archdeacon: "You are clever at your trade, Dom Claude, and you are no more at a loss over Hippocrates than a monkey is over a nut. Medicine a dream! I suspect that the pharmacopolists and the master physicians would insist upon stoning you if they were here. So you deny the influence of philtres upon the blood, and unguents on the skin! You deny that eternal pharmacy of flowers and metals, which is called the world, made expressly for that eternal invalid called man!"

"I deny," said Dom Claude coldly, "neither pharmacy nor the invalid. I reject the physician."

"Then it is not true," resumed Coictier hotly, "that gout is an internal eruption; that a wound caused by artillery is to be cured by the application of a young mouse roasted; that young blood, properly injected, restores youth to aged veins; it is not true that two and two make four, and that emprostathonos follows opistathonos."

The archdeacon replied without perturbation: "There are certain things of which I think in a certain fashion."

Coictier became crimson with anger.

"There, there, my good Coictier, let us not get angry," said Gossip Tourangeau. "Monsieur the archdeacon is our friend."

Coictier calmed down, muttering in a low tone, "After all, he's mad."

"*Pasque-dieu*, Master Claude," resumed Gossip Tourangeau, after a silence, "You embarrass me greatly. I had two things to consult you upon, one touching my health and the other touching my star."

"Monsieur," returned the archdeacon, "if that be your motive, you would have done as well not to put yourself out of breath climbing my staircase. I do not believe in Medicine. I do not believe in Astrology."

"Indeed!" said the man, with surprise.

Coictier gave a forced laugh.

"You see that he is mad," he said, in a low tone, to Gossip Tourangeau. "He does not believe in astrology."

"The idea of imagining," pursued Dom Claude, "that every ray of a star is a thread which is fastened to the head of a man!"

"And what then, do you believe in?" exclaimed Gossip Tourangeau.

The archdeacon hesitated for a moment, then he allowed a gloomy smile to escape, which seemed to give the lie to his response: "*Credo in Deum*."

"*Dominum nostrum*," added Gossip Tourangeau, making the sign of the cross.

"Amen," said Coictier.

"Reverend master," resumed Tourangeau, "I am charmed in soul to see you in such a religious frame of mind. But have you reached the point, great savant as you are, of no longer believing in science?"

"No," said the archdeacon, grasping the arm of Gossip Tourangeau, and a ray of enthusiasm lighted up his gloomy eyes, "no, I do not reject science. I have not crawled so long, flat on my belly, with my nails in the earth, through the innumerable ramifications of its caverns, without perceiving far in front of me, at the end of the obscure gallery, a light, a flame, a something, the reflection, no doubt, of the dazzling central laboratory where the patient and the wise have found out God."

"And in short," interrupted Tourangeau, "what do you hold to be true and certain?"

"Alchemy."

Coictier exclaimed, "Pardieu, Dom Claude, alchemy has its use, no doubt, but why blaspheme medicine and astrology?"

"Naught is your science of man, naught is your science of the stars," said the archdeacon, commandingly.

"That's driving Epidaurus and Chaldea very fast," replied the physician with a grin.

"Listen, Messire Jacques. This is said in good faith. I am not the king's physician, and his majesty has not given me the Garden of Daedalus in which to observe the constellations. Don't get angry, but listen to me. What truth have you deduced, I will not say from medicine, which is too foolish a thing, but from astrology? Cite to me the virtues of the vertical boustrophedon, the treasures of the number ziruph and those of the number zephirod!"

"Will you deny," said Coictier, "the sympathetic force of the collar bone, and the cabalistics which are derived from it?"

"An error, Messire Jacques! None of your formulas end in reality. Alchemy on the other hand has its discoveries. Will you contest results like this? Ice confined beneath the earth for a thousand years is transformed into rock crystals. Lead is the ancestor of all metals. For gold is not a metal, gold is light. Lead requires only four periods of two hundred years each, to pass in succession from the state of lead, to the state of red arsenic, from red arsenic to tin, from tin to silver. Are not these facts? But to believe in the collar bone, in the full line and in the stars, is as ridiculous as to believe with the inhabitants of Grand-Cathay that the golden oriole turns into a mole, and that grains of wheat turn into fish of the carp species."

"I have studied hermetic science!" exclaimed Coictier, "and I affirm—"

The fiery archdeacon did not allow him to finish: "And I have studied medicine, astrology, and hermetics. Here alone is the truth." (As he spoke thus, he took from the top of the coffer a vial filled with the powder which we have mentioned above.) "Here alone is light! Hippocrates is a dream; Urania is a dream; Hermes, a thought. Gold is the sun; to make gold is to be God. Herein lies the one and only science. I have sounded the depths of medicine and astrology, I tell you! Naught, nothingness! The human body, shadows! The planets, shadows!"

And he fell back in his armchair in a commanding and inspired attitude. Gossip Touraugeau watched him in silence. Coictier tried to grin, shrugged his shoulders imperceptibly, and repeated in a low voice, "A madman!"

"And," said Tourangeau suddenly, "the wondrous result, have you attained it, have you made gold?"

"If I had made it," replied the archdeacon, articulating his words slowly, like a man who is reflecting, "the king of France would be named Claude and not Louis."

The stranger frowned.

"What am I saying?" resumed Dom Claude, with a smile of disdain. "What would the throne of France be to me when I could rebuild the empire of the Orient?"

"Very good!" said the stranger.

"Oh, the poor fool!" murmured Coictier.

The archdeacon went on, appearing to reply now only to his thoughts, "But no, I am still crawling; I am scratching my face and knees against the pebbles of the subterranean pathway. I catch a glimpse, I do not contemplate! I do not read, I spell out!"

"And when you know how to read!" demanded the stranger, "will you make gold?"

"Who doubts it?" said the archdeacon.

"In that case Our Lady knows that I am greatly in need of money, and I should much desire to read in your books. Tell me, reverend master, is your science inimical or displeasing to Our Lady?"

"Whose archdeacon I am?" Dom Claude contented himself with replying, with tranquil hauteur.

"That is true, my master. Well! Will it please you to initiate me? Let me spell with you."

Claude assumed the majestic and pontifical attitude of a Samuel.

"Old man, it requires longer years than remain to you, to undertake this voyage across mysterious things. Your head is very gray! One comes forth from the cavern only with white hair, but only those with dark hair enter it. Science alone knows well how to hollow, wither, and dry up human faces; she needs not to have old age bring her faces already furrowed. Nevertheless, if the desire possesses you of putting yourself under discipline at your age, and of deciphering the formidable alphabet of the sages, come to me; 'tis well, I will make the effort. I will not tell you, poor old man, to go and visit the sepulchral chambers of the pyramids, of which ancient Herodotus speaks, nor the brick tower of Babylon, nor the immense white marble sanctuary of the Indian temple of Eklinga. I, no more than yourself, have seen the Chaldean masonry works constructed according to the sacred form of the Sikra, nor the temple of Solomon, which is destroyed, nor the stone doors of the sepulchre of the kings of Israel, which are broken. We will content ourselves with the fragments of the book of Hermes that we have here. I will explain to you the statue of Saint Christopher, the symbol of the sower, and that of the two angels which are on the front of the Sainte-Chapelle, and one of which holds in his hands a vase, the other, a cloud—"

Here Jacques Coictier, who had been unhorsed by the archdeacon's impetuous replies, regained his saddle, and interrupted him with the triumphant tone of one learned man correcting another, "*Erras amice Claudi*. The symbol is not the number. You take Orpheus for Hermes."

"'Tis you who are in error," replied the archdeacon, gravely. "Daedalus is the base; Orpheus is the wall; Hermes is the edifice, that is all. You shall come when you will," he continued, turning to Tourangeau, "I will show you the little parcels of gold which remained at the bottom of Nicholas Flamel's alembic, and you shall compare them with the gold of Guillaume de Paris. I will teach you the secret virtues of the Greek word, *peristera*. But, first of all, I will make you read, one after the other, the marble letters of the alphabet, the granite pages of the book. We shall go to the portal of Bishop Guillaume and of Saint-Jean le Rond at the Sainte-Chapelle, then to the house of Nicholas Flamel, Rue Manvault, to his tomb, which is at the Saints-Innocents, to his two hospitals, Rue de Montmorency. I will make you read the hieroglyphics that cover the four great iron cramps on the portal of the hospital Saint-Gervais, and of the Rue de la Ferronnerie. We will spell out in company, also, the façade of Saint-Come, of Sainte-Geneviève-des-Ardents, of Saint Martin, of Saint-Jacques de la Boucherie—"

For a long time, Gossip Tourangeau, intelligent as was his glance, had appeared not to understand Dom Claude. He interrupted.

"*Pasque-dieu!* What are your books, then?"

"Here is one of them," said the archdeacon.

And opening the window of his cell he pointed out with his finger the immense church of Notre-Dame, which, outlining against the starry sky the black silhouette of its two towers, its stone flanks, its monstrous haunches, seemed an enormous two-headed sphinx, seated in the middle of the city.

The archdeacon gazed at the gigantic edifice for some time in silence, then extending his right hand, with a sigh, toward the printed book which lay open on the table, and his left toward Notre-Dame, and turning a sad glance from the book to the church. "Alas," he said, "this will kill that."

Coictier, who had eagerly approached the book, could not repress an exclamation. "Hey now, what is there so formidable in this: 'GLOSSA IN EPISTOLAS D. PAULI, *Norimbergoe, Antonius Koburger*, 1474.' This is not new. 'Tis a book of Pierre Lombard, the Master of Sentences. Is it because it is printed?"

"You have said it," replied Claude, who seemed absorbed in a profound meditation, and stood resting, his forefinger bent backward on the folio that had come from the famous press of Nuremberg. Then he added these mysterious words: "Alas! Alas! Small things come at the end of great things; a tooth triumphs over a mass. The Nile rat kills the crocodile, the swordfish kills the whale, the book will kill the edifice."

The curfew of the cloister sounded at the moment when Master Jacques was repeating to his companion in low tones, his eternal refrain, "He is mad!" To which his companion this time replied, "I believe that he is."

It was the hour when no stranger could remain in the cloister. The two visitors withdrew. "Master," said Gossip Tourangeau, as he took leave of the archdeacon, "I love wise men and great minds, and I hold you in singular esteem. Come tomorrow to the Palace des Tournelles, and inquire for the Abbé de Sainte-Martin, of Tours."

The archdeacon returned to his chamber dumbfounded, comprehending at last who Gossip Tourangeau was, and recalling that passage of the register of Sainte-Martin, of Tours: *Abbas beati Martini, SCILICET REX FRANCIAE, est canonicus de consuetudine et habet parvam proebendam quam habet sanctus Venantius, et debet sedere in sede thesaurarii.*

It is asserted that after that epoch the archdeacon had frequent conferences with Louis XI, when his majesty came to Paris, and that Dom Claude's influence quite overshadowed that of Olivier le Daim and Jacques Coictier, who, as was his habit, rudely took the king to task on that account.

CHAPTER 2

This Will Kill That

OUR LADY READERS will pardon us if we pause for a moment to seek what could have been the thought concealed beneath those enigmatic words of the archdeacon: "This will kill that. The book will kill the edifice."

To our mind, this thought had two faces. In the first place, it was a priestly thought. It was the affright of the priest in the presence of a new agent, the printing press. It was the terror and dazzled amazement of the men of the sanctuary, in the presence of the luminous press of Gutenberg. It was the pulpit and the manuscript taking the alarm at the printed word: something similar to the stupor of a sparrow that should behold the angel Legion unfold his six million wings. It was the cry of the prophet who already hears emancipated humanity roaring and swarming; who beholds in the future, intelligence sapping faith, opinion dethroning belief, the world shaking off Rome. It was the prognostication of the philosopher who sees human thought, volatilized by the press, evaporating from the theocratic recipient. It was the terror of the soldier who examines the brazen battering ram, and says: "The tower will crumble." It signified that one power was about to succeed another power. It meant, "The press will kill the church."

But underlying this thought, the first and most simple one, no doubt, there was in our opinion another, newer one, a corollary of the first, less easy to perceive and more easy to contest, a view as philosophical and belonging no longer to the priest alone but to the savant and the artist. It was a presentiment that human thought, in changing its form, was about to change its mode of expression; that the dominant idea of each generation would no longer be written with the same matter, and in the same manner; that the book of stone, so solid and so durable, was about to make way for the book of paper, more solid and still more durable. In this connection the archdeacon's vague formula had a second sense. It meant, "Printing will kill architecture."

In fact, from the origin of things down to the fifteenth century of the Christian era, inclusive, architecture is the great book of humanity, the principal expression of man in his different stages of development, either as a force or as an intelligence.

When the memory of the first races felt itself overloaded, when the mass of reminiscences of the human race became so heavy and so confused that speech naked and flying, ran the risk of losing them on the way, men transcribed them on the soil in a manner which was at once the most visible, most durable, and most natural. They sealed each tradition beneath a monument.

The first monuments were simple masses of rock, "which the iron had not touched," as Moses says. Architecture began like all writing. It was first an alphabet. Men planted a stone upright, it was a letter, and each letter was a hieroglyph, and upon each hieroglyph rested a group of ideas, like the capital on the column. This is what the earliest races did everywhere, at the same moment, on the surface of the entire world. We find the "standing stones" of the Celts in Asian Siberia; in the pampas of America.

Later on, they made words; they placed stone upon stone, they coupled those syllables of granite, and attempted some combinations. The Celtic dolmen and cromlech, the Etruscan tumulus, the Hebrew galgal, are words. Some, especially the tumulus, are proper names. Sometimes even, when men had a great deal of stone, and a vast plain, they wrote a phrase. The immense pile of Karnac is a complete sentence.

At last they made books. Traditions had brought forth symbols, beneath which they disappeared like the trunk of a tree beneath its foliage; all these symbols in which humanity placed faith continued to grow, to multiply, to intersect, to become more and more complicated; the first monuments no longer sufficed to contain them, they were overflowing in every part; these monuments hardly expressed now the primitive tradition, simple like themselves, naked and prone upon the earth. The symbol felt the need of expansion in the edifice. Then architecture was developed in proportion with human thought; it became a giant with a thousand heads and a thousand arms, and fixed all this floating symbolism in an eternal, visible, palpable form. While Daedalus, who is force, measured; while Orpheus, who is intelligence, sang; the pillar, which is a letter; the arcade, which is a syllable; the pyramid, which is a word, all set in movement at once by a law of geometry and by a law of poetry, grouped themselves, combined, amalgamated, descended, ascended, placed themselves side by side on the soil, ranged themselves in stories in the sky, until they had written under the dictation of the general idea of an epoch, those marvellous books which were also marvellous edifices: the Pagoda of Eklinga, the Rhamseion of Egypt, the Temple of Solomon.

The generating idea, the word, was not only at the foundation of all these edifices, but also in the form. The temple of Solomon, for example, was not alone the binding of the holy book; it was the holy book itself. On each one of its concentric walls, the priests could read the word translated and manifested to the eye, and thus they followed its transformations from sanctuary to sanctuary, until they seized it in its last tabernacle, under its most concrete form, which still belonged to architecture: the arch. Thus the word was enclosed in an edifice, but its image was upon its envelope, like the human form on the coffin of a mummy.

And not only the form of edifices, but the sites selected for them, revealed the thought which they represented, according as the symbol to be expressed was graceful or grave. Greece crowned her mountains with a temple harmonious to the eye; India disembowelled hers, to chisel therein those monstrous subterranean pagodas, borne up by gigantic rows of granite elephants.

Thus, during the first six thousand years of the world, from the most immemorial pagoda of Hindustan, to the cathedral of Cologne, architecture was the great handwriting of the human race. And this is so true, that not only every religious symbol, but every human thought, has its page and its monument in that immense book.

All civilization begins in theocracy and ends in democracy. This law of liberty following unity is written in architecture. For, let us insist upon this point, masonry must not be thought to be powerful only in erecting the temple and in expressing the myth and sacerdotal symbolism; in inscribing in hieroglyphs upon its pages of stone the mysterious tables of the law. If it were thus, as there comes in all human society a moment when the sacred symbol is worn out and becomes obliterated under freedom of thought, when man escapes from the priest, when the excrescence of philosophies and systems devour the face of religion, architecture could not reproduce this new state of human thought; its leaves, so crowded on the face, would be empty on the back; its work would be mutilated; its book would he incomplete. But no.

Let us take as an example the Middle Ages, where we see more clearly because it is nearer to us. During its first period, while theocracy is organizing Europe, while the Vatican is rallying and reclassing about itself the elements of a Rome made from the Rome which lies in ruins around the Capitol, while Christianity is seeking all the stages of society amid the rubbish of anterior civilization, and rebuilding with its ruins a new hierarchic universe, the keystone to whose vault is the priest—one first hears a dull echo from that chaos, and then, little by little, one sees, arising from beneath the breath of Christianity, from beneath the hand of the barbarians, from the fragments of the dead Greek and Roman architectures, that mysterious Romanesque architecture, sister of the theocratic masonry of Egypt and of India, inalterable emblem of pure catholicism, unchangeable hieroglyph of the papal unity. All the thought of that day is written, in fact, in this sombre, Romanesque style. One feels everywhere in it authority, unity, the impenetrable, the absolute, Gregory VII; always the priest, never the man; everywhere caste, never the people.

But the Crusades arrive. They are a great popular movement, and every great popular movement, whatever may be its cause and object, always sets free the spirit of liberty from its final precipitate. New things spring into life every day. Here opens the stormy period of the Jacqueries, Pragueries, and Leagues. Authority wavers, unity is divided. Feudalism demands to share with theocracy, while awaiting the inevitable arrival of the people, who will assume the part of the lion: *Quia nominor leo*. Seignory pierces through sacerdotalism; the commonality, through seignory. The face of Europe is changed. Well! The face of architecture is changed also. Like civilization, it has turned a page, and the new spirit of the time finds her ready to write at its dictation. It returns from the crusades with the pointed arch, like the nations with liberty.

Then, while Rome is undergoing gradual dismemberment, Romanesque architecture dies. The hieroglyph deserts the cathedral, and betakes itself to blazoning the donjon keep, in order to lend prestige to feudalism. The cathedral itself, that edifice formerly so dogmatic, invaded henceforth by the bourgeoisie, by the community, by liberty, escapes the priest and falls into the power of the artist. The artist builds it after his own fashion. Farewell to mystery, myth, law. Fancy and caprice, welcome. Provided the priest has his basilica and his altar, he has nothing to say. The four walls belong to the artist. The architectural book belongs no longer to the priest, to religion, to Rome; it is the property of poetry, of imagination, of the people. Hence the rapid and innumerable transformations of that architecture which owns but three centuries, so striking after the stagnant immobility of the Romanesque architecture, which owns six or seven. Nevertheless, art marches on with giant strides. Popular genius amid originality accomplish the task which the bishops formerly fulfilled. Each race writes its line upon the book, as it passes; it erases the ancient Romanesque hieroglyphs on the frontispieces of cathedrals, and at the most one only sees dogma cropping out here and there, beneath the new symbol which it has deposited. The popular drapery hardly permits the religious skeleton to be suspected. One cannot even form an idea of the liberties that the architects then take, even toward the Church. There are capitals knitted of nuns and monks, shamelessly coupled, as on the hall of chimney pieces in the Palais de Justice, in Paris. There is Noah's adventure carved to the last detail, as under the great portal of Bourges. There is a bacchanalian monk, with ass's ears and glass in hand, laughing in the face of a whole community, as on the lavatory of the Abbey of Bocherville. There exists at that epoch, for thought written in stone, a privilege exactly comparable to our present liberty of the press. It is the liberty of architecture.

This liberty goes very far. Sometimes a portal, a façade, an entire church, presents a symbolical sense absolutely foreign to worship, or even hostile to the Church. In the thirteenth century, Guillaume de Paris, and Nicholas Flamel, in the fifteenth, wrote such seditious pages. Saint-Jacques de la Boucherie was a whole church of the opposition.

Thought was then free only in this manner; hence it never wrote itself out completely except on the books called edifices. Thought, under the form of edifice, could have beheld itself burned in the public square by the hands of the executioner, in its manuscript form, if it had been sufficiently imprudent to risk itself thus; thought, as the door of a church, would have been a spectator of the punishment of thought as a book. Having thus only this resource, masonry, in order to make its way to the light, flung itself upon it from all quarters. Hence the immense quantity of cathedrals that have covered Europe—a number so prodigious that one can hardly believe it even after having verified it. All the material forces, all the intellectual forces of society converged toward the same point: architecture. In this manner, under the pretext of building churches to God, art was developed in its magnificent proportions.

Then whoever was born a poet became an architect. Genius, scattered in the masses, repressed in every quarter under feudalism as under a *testudo* of brazen bucklers, finding no issue except in the direction of architecture, gushed forth through that art, and its Iliads assumed the form of cathedrals. All other arts obeyed, and placed themselves under the discipline of architecture. They were the workmen of the great work. The architect, the poet, the master, summed up in his person the sculpture which carved his façades, painting which illuminated his windows, music which set his bells to pealing, and breathed into his organs. There was nothing down to poor poetry, properly speaking, that which persisted in vegetating in manuscripts, which was not forced, in order to make something of itself, to come and frame itself in the edifice in the shape of a hymn or of prose; the same part, after all, which the tragedies of Aeschylus had played in the sacerdotal festivals of Greece; Genesis, in the temple of Solomon.

Thus, down to the time of Gutenberg, architecture is the principal writing, the universal writing. In that granite book, begun by the Orient, continued by Greek and Roman antiquity, the Middle Ages wrote the last page. Moreover, this phenomenon of an architecture of the people following an architecture of caste, which we have just been observing in the Middle Ages, is reproduced with every analogous movement in the human intelligence at the other great epochs of history. Thus, in order to enunciate here only summarily, a law which it would require volumes to develop: in the high Orient, the cradle of primitive times, after Hindoo architecture came Phoenician architecture, that opulent mother of Arabian architecture; in antiquity, after Egyptian architecture, of which Etruscan style and cyclopean monuments are but one variety, came Greek architecture (of which the Roman style is only a continuation), surcharged with the Carthaginian dome; in modern times, after Romanesque architecture came Gothic architecture. And by separating there three series into their component parts, we shall find in the three eldest sisters, Hindoo architecture, Egyptian architecture, Romanesque architecture, the same symbol;

that is to say, theocracy, caste, unity, dogma, myth, God: and for the three younger sisters, Phoenician architecture, Greek architecture, Gothic architecture, whatever, nevertheless, may be the diversity of form inherent in their nature, the same signification also; that is to say, liberty, the people, man.

In the Hindu, Egyptian, or Romanesque architecture, one feels the priest, nothing but the priest, whether he calls himself Brahmin, Magian, or Pope. It is not the same in the architectures of the people. They are richer and less sacred. In the Phoenician, one feels the merchant; in the Greek, the republican; in the Gothic, the citizen.

The general characteristics of all theocratic architecture are immutability, horror of progress, the preservation of traditional lines, the consecration of the primitive types, the constant bending of all the forms of men and of nature to the incomprehensible caprices of the symbol. These are dark books, which the initiated alone understand how to decipher. Moreover, every form, every deformity even, has there a sense that renders it inviolable. Do not ask of Hindu, Egyptian, Romanesque masonry to reform their design, or to improve their statuary. Every attempt at perfecting is an impiety to them. In these architectures it seems as though the rigidity of the dogma had spread over the stone like a sort of second petrifaction. The general characteristics of popular masonry, on the contrary, are progress, originality, opulence, perpetual movement. They are already sufficiently detached from religion to think of their beauty, to take care of it, to correct without relaxation their parure of statues or arabesques. They are of the age. They have something human, which they mingle incessantly with the divine symbol under which they still produce. Hence, edifices comprehensible to every soul, to every intelligence, to every imagination, symbolical still, but as easy to understand as nature. Between theocratic architecture and this there is the difference that lies between a sacred language and a vulgar language, between hieroglyphics and art, between Solomon and Phidias.

If the reader will sum up what we have hitherto briefly, very briefly, indicated, neglecting a thousand proofs and also a thousand objections of detail, be will be led to this: that architecture was, down to the fifteenth century, the chief register of humanity; that in that interval not a thought which is in any degree complicated made its appearance in the world, which has not been worked into an edifice; that every popular idea, and every religious law, has had its monumental records; that the human race has, in short, had no important thought which it has not written in stone. And why? Because every thought, either philosophical or religious, is interested in perpetuating itself; because the idea which has moved one generation wishes to move others also, and leave a trace. Now, what a precarious immortality is that of the manuscript! How much more solid, durable, unyielding, is a book of stone! In order to destroy the written word, a torch and a Turk are sufficient. To demolish the constructed word, a social revolution, a terrestrial revolution are required. The barbarians passed over the Coliseum; the deluge, perhaps, passed over the Pyramids.

In the fifteenth century everything changes.

Human thought discovers a mode of perpetuating itself, not only more durable and more resisting than architecture, but still more simple and easy. Architecture is dethroned. Gutenberg's letters of lead are about to supersede Orpheus's letters of stone.

The invention of printing is the greatest event in history. It is the mother of revolution. It is the mode of expression of humanity that is totally renewed; it is human thought stripping off one form and donning another; it is the complete and definitive change of skin of that symbolical serpent which since the days of Adam has represented intelligence.

In its printed form, thought is more imperishable than ever; it is volatile, irresistible, indestructible. It is mingled with the air. In the days of architecture it made a mountain of itself, and took powerful possession of a century and a place. Now it converts itself into a flock of birds, scatters itself to the four winds, and occupies all points of air and space at once.

We repeat, who does not perceive that in this form it is far more indelible? It was solid, it has become alive. It passes from duration in time to immortality. One can demolish a mass; how can one extirpate ubiquity? If a flood comes, the mountains will have long disappeared beneath the waves, while the birds will still be flying about; and if a single ark floats on the surface of the cataclysm, they will alight upon it, will float with it, will be present with it at the ebbing of the waters; and the new world which emerges from this chaos will behold, on its awakening, the thought of the world which has been submerged soaring above it, winged and living.

And when one observes that this mode of expression is not only the most conservative, but also the most simple, the most convenient, the most practicable for all; when one reflects that it does not drag after it bulky baggage, and does not set in motion a heavy apparatus; when one compares thought forced, in order to transform itself into an edifice, to put in motion four or five other arts and tons of gold, a whole mountain of stones, a whole forest of timber-work, a whole nation of workmen; when one compares it to the thought which becomes a book, and for which a little paper, a little ink, and a pen suffice,—how can one be surprised that human intelligence should have quitted architecture for printing? Cut the primitive bed of a river abruptly with a canal hollowed out below its level, and the river will desert its bed.

Behold how, beginning with the discovery of printing, architecture withers away little by little, becomes lifeless and bare. How one feels the water sinking, the sap departing, the thought of the times and of the people withdrawing from it! The chill is almost imperceptible in the fifteenth century; the press is, as yet, too weak, and, at the most, draws from powerful architecture a superabundance of life. But practically beginning with the sixteenth century, the malady of architecture is visible; it is no longer the expression of society; it becomes classic art in a miserable manner; from being Gallic, European, indigenous, it becomes Greek and Roman; from being true and modern, it becomes pseudo-classic. It is this decadence that is called the Renaissance. A magnificent decadence, however, for the ancient Gothic genius, that sun which sets behind the gigantic press of Mayence, still penetrates for a while longer with its rays that whole hybrid pile of Latin arcades and Corinthian columns.

It is that setting sun which we mistake for the dawn.

Nevertheless, from the moment when architecture is no longer anything but an art like any other; as soon as it is no longer the total art, the sovereign art, the tyrant art, it has no longer the power to retain the other arts. So they emancipate themselves, break the yoke of the architect, and take themselves off, each one in its own direction. Each one of them gains by this divorce. Isolation aggrandizes everything. Sculpture becomes statuary, the image trade becomes painting, the canon becomes music. One would pronounce it an empire dismembered at the death of its Alexander, and whose provinces become kingdoms.

Hence Raphael, Michaelangelo, Jean Goujon, Palestrina, those splendors of the dazzling sixteenth century.

Thought emancipates itself in all directions at the same time as the arts. The arch-heretics of the Middle Ages had already made large incisions into Catholicism. The sixteenth century breaks religious unity. Before the invention of printing, reform would have been merely a schism; printing converted it into a revolution. Take away the press; heresy is enervated. Whether it be Providence or Fate, Gutenburg is the precursor of Luther.

Nevertheless, when the sun of the Middle Ages is completely set, when the Gothic genius is forever extinct upon the horizon, architecture grows dim, loses its color, becomes more and more effaced. The printed book, the gnawing worm of the edifice, sucks and devours it. It becomes bare, denuded of its foliage, and grows visibly emaciated. It is petty, it is poor, it is nothing. It no longer expresses anything, not even the memory of the art of another time. Reduced to itself, abandoned by the other arts, because human thought is abandoning it, it summons bunglers in place of artists. Glass replaces the painted windows. The stone-cutter succeeds the sculptor. Farewell all sap, all originality, all life, all intelligence. It drags along, a lamentable workshop mendicant, from copy to copy. Michaelangelo, who, no doubt, felt even in the sixteenth century that it was dying, had a last idea, an idea of despair. That Titan of art piled the Pantheon on the Parthenon, and made Saint-Peter's at Rome. A great work, which deserved to remain unique, the last originality of architecture, the signature of a giant artist at the bottom of the colossal register of stone that was closed forever. With Michaelangelo dead, what does this miserable architecture, which survived itself in the state of a spectre, do? It takes Saint-Peter in Rome, copies it and parodies it. It is a mania. It is a pity. Each century has its Saint-Peter's of Rome; in the seventeenth century, the Val-de-Grâce; in the eighteenth, Sainte-Geneviève. Each country has its Saint-Peter's of Rome. London has one; Petersburg has another; Paris has two or three. The insignificant testament, the last dotage of a decrepit grand art falling back into infancy before it dies.

If, in place of the characteristic monuments that we have just described, we examine the general aspect of art from the sixteenth to the eighteenth century, we notice the same phenomena of decay and phthisis. Beginning with François II, the architectural form of the edifice effaces itself more and more, and allows the geometrical form, like the bony structure of an emaciated invalid, to become prominent. The fine lines of art give way to the cold and inexorable lines of geometry. An edifice is no longer an edifice; it is a polyhedron. Meanwhile, architecture is tormented in her struggles to conceal this nudity. Look at the Greek pediment inscribed upon the Roman pediment, and vice versa. It is still the Pantheon on the Parthenon: Saint-Peter's of Rome. Here are the brick houses of Henri IV, with their stone corners; the Place Royale, the Place Dauphine. Here are the churches of Louis XIII, heavy, squat, thickset, crowded together, loaded with a dome like a hump. Here is the Mazarin architecture, the wretched Italian pasticcio of the Four Nations. Here are the palaces of Louis XIV, long barracks for courtiers, stiff, cold, tiresome. Here, finally, is Louis XV, with chiccory leaves and vermicelli, and all the warts, and all the fungi, which disfigure that decrepit, toothless, and coquettish old architecture. From François II to Louis XV, the evil has increased in geometrical progression. Art has no longer anything but skin upon its bones. It is miserably perishing.

Meanwhile what becomes of printing? All the life that is leaving architecture comes to it. In proportion as architecture ebbs, printing swells and grows. That capital of forces which human thought had been expending in edifices, it henceforth expends in books. Thus, from the sixteenth century onward, the press, raised to the level of decaying architecture, contends with it and kills it. In the seventeenth century it is already sufficiently the sovereign, sufficiently triumphant, sufficiently established in its victory, to give to the world the feast of a great literary century. In the eighteenth, having reposed for a long time at the Court of Louis XIV, it seizes again the old sword of Luther, puts it into the hand of Voltaire, and rushes impetuously to the attack of that ancient Europe, whose architectural expression it has already killed. At the moment when the eighteenth century comes to an end, it has destroyed everything. In the nineteenth, it begins to reconstruct.

Now, we ask, which of the three arts has really represented human thought for the last three centuries? Which translates it? Which expresses not only its literary and scholastic vagaries, but its vast, profound, universal movement? Which constantly superposes itself, without a break, without a gap, upon the human race, which walks a monster with a thousand legs? Architecture or printing?

It is printing. Let the reader make no mistake; architecture is dead; irretrievably slain by the printed book, slain because it endures for a shorter time, slain because it costs more. Every cathedral represents millions. Let the reader now imagine what an investment of funds it would require to rewrite the architectural book; to cause thousands of edifices to swarm once more upon the soil; to return to those epochs when the throng of monuments was such, according to the statement of an eye witness, "that one would have said that the world in shaking itself, had cast off its old garments in order to cover itself with a white vesture of churches." *Erat enim ut si mundus, ipse excutiendo semet, rejecta vetustate, candida ecclesiarum vestem indueret* (Glaber Radolphus).

A book is so soon made, costs so little, and can go so far! How can it surprise us that all human thought flows in this channel? This does not mean that architecture will not still have a fine monument, an isolated masterpiece, here and there. We may still have from time to time, under the reign of printing, a column made I suppose, by a whole army from melted cannon, as we had under the reign of architecture, Iliads and Romanceros, Mahabâhrata, and Nibelungen Lieds, made by a whole people, with rhapsodies piled up and melted together. The great accident of an architect of genius may happen in the twentieth century, like that of Dante in the thirteenth. But architecture will no longer be the social art, the collective art, the dominating art. The grand poem, the grand edifice, the grand work of humanity will no longer be built: it will be printed.

And henceforth, if architecture should arise again accidentally, it will no longer be mistress. It will be subservient to the law of literature, which formerly received the law from it. The respective positions of the two arts will be inverted. It is certain that in architectural epochs, the poems, rare it is true, resemble the monuments. In India, Vyasa is branching, strange, impenetrable as a pagoda. In Egyptian Orient, poetry has like the edifices, grandeur and tranquillity of line; in antique Greece, beauty, serenity, calm; in Christian Europe, the Catholic majesty, the popular naivete, the rich and luxuriant vegetation of an epoch of renewal. The Bible resembles the Pyramids; the Iliad, the Parthenon; Homer, Phidias. Dante in the thirteenth century is the last Romanesque church; Shakespeare in the sixteenth, the last Gothic cathedral.

Thus, to sum up what we have hitherto said, in a fashion which is necessarily incomplete and mutilated, the human race has two books, two registers, two testaments: masonry and printing; the Bible of stone and the Bible of paper. No doubt, when one contemplates these two Bibles, laid so broadly open in the centuries, it is permissible to regret the visible majesty of the writing of granite, those gigantic alphabets formulated in colonnades, in pylons, in obelisks, those sorts of human mountains which cover the world and the past, from the pyramid to the bell tower, from Cheops to Strasburg. The past must be reread upon these pages of marble. This book, written by architecture, must be admired and perused incessantly; but the grandeur of the edifice which printing erects in its turn must not be denied.

That edifice is colossal. Some compiler of statistics has calculated, that if all the volumes which have issued from the press since Gutenberg's day were to be piled one upon another, they would fill the space between the earth and the moon; but it is not that sort of grandeur of which we wished to speak. Nevertheless, when one tries to collect in one's mind a comprehensive image of the total products of printing down to our own days, does not that total appear to us like an immense construction, resting upon the entire world, at which humanity toils without relaxation, and whose monstrous crest is lost in the profound mists of the future? It is the anthill of intelligence. It is the hive whither come all imaginations, those golden bees, with their honey.

The edifice has a thousand stories. Here and there one beholds on its staircases the gloomy caverns of science that pierce its interior. Everywhere upon its surface, art causes its arabesques, rosettes, and laces to thrive luxuriantly before the eyes. There, every individual work, however capricious and isolated it may seem, has its place and its projection. Harmony results from the whole. From the cathedral of Shakespeare to the mosque of Byron, a thousand tiny bell towers are piled pell-mell above this metropolis of universal thought. At its base are written some ancient titles of humanity which architecture had not registered. To the left of the entrance has been fixed the ancient bas-relief, in white marble, of Homer; to the right, the polyglot Bible rears its seven heads. The hydra of the Romancero and some other hybrid forms, the Vedas and the Nibelungen bristle further on.

Nevertheless, the prodigious edifice still remains incomplete. The press, that giant machine, which incessantly pumps all the intellectual sap of society, belches forth without pause fresh materials for its work. The whole human race is on the scaffoldings. Each mind is a mason. The humblest fills his hole, or places his stone. Retif dè le Bretonne brings his hod of plaster. Every day a new course rises. Independently of the original and individual contribution of each writer, there are collective contingents. The eighteenth century gives the *Encyclopedia*, the revolution gives the *Moniteur*. Assuredly, it is a construction that increases and piles up in endless spirals; there also are confusion of tongues, incessant activity, indefatigable labor, eager competition of all humanity, refuge promised to intelligence, a new Flood against an overflow of barbarians. It is the second tower of Babel of the human race.

Book Sixth

Chapter 1

An Impartial Glance at the Ancient Magistracy

A VERY HAPPY personage in the year of grace 1482, was the noble gentleman Robert d'Estouteville, chevalier, Sieur de Beyne, Baron d'Ivry and Saint Andry en la Marche, counsellor and chamberlain to the king, and guard of the provostship of Paris. It was already nearly seventeen years since he had received from the king, on November 7, 1465, the comet year,* that fine charge of the provostship of Paris, which was reputed rather a seigneury than an office. *Dignitas*, says Joannes Loemnoeus, *quoe cum non exigua potestate politiam concernente, atque proerogativis multis et juribus conjuncta est.* A marvellous thing in '82 was a gentleman bearing the king's commission, and whose letters of institution ran back to the epoch of the marriage of the natural daughter of Louis XI with Monsieur the Bastard of Bourbon. The same day on which Robert d'Estouteville took the place of Jacques de Villiers in the provostship of Paris, Master Jehan Dauvet replaced Messire Helye de Thorrettes in the first presidency of the Court of Parliament, Jehan Jouvenel des Ursins supplanted Pierre de Morvilliers in the office of chancellor of France, Regnault des Dormans ousted Pierre Puy from the charge of master of requests in ordinary of the king's household. Now, upon how many heads had the presidency, the chancellorship, the mastership passed since Robert d'Estouteville had held the provostship of Paris. It had been "granted to him for safekeeping," as the letters patent said; and certainly he kept it well. He had clung to it, he had incorporated himself with it, he had so

---

*This comet against which Pope Calixtus, uncle of Borgia, ordered public prayers, is the same that reappeared in 1835.

identified himself with it that he had escaped that fury for change which possessed Louis XI, a tormenting and industrious king, whose policy it was to maintain the elasticity of his power by frequent appointments and revocations. More than this; the brave chevalier had obtained the reversion of the office for his son, and for two years already, the name of the noble man Jacques d'Estouteville, equerry, had figured beside his at the head of the register of the salary list of the provostship of Paris. A rare and notable favor indeed! It is true that Robert d'Estouteville was a good soldier, that he had loyally raised his pennon against "the league of public good," and that he had presented to the queen a very marvellous stag in confectionery on the day of her entrance to Paris in 14—. Moreover, he possessed the good friendship of Messire Tristan l'Hermite, provost of the marshals of the king's household. Hence a very sweet and pleasant existence was that of Messire Robert. In the first place, very good wages, to which were attached, and from which hung, like extra bunches of grapes on his vine, the revenues of the civil and criminal registries of the provostship, plus the civil and criminal revenues of the tribunals of Embas of the Châtelet, without reckoning some little toll from the bridges of Mantes and of Corbeil, and the profits on the craft of Shagreen-makers of Paris, on the corders of firewood and the measurers of salt. Add to this the pleasure of displaying himself in rides about the city, and of making his fine military costume, which you may still admire sculptured on his tomb in the abbey of Valmont in Normandy, and his morion, all embossed at Montlhéry, stand out a contrast against the parti-colored red and tawny robes of the aldermen and police. And then, was it nothing to wield absolute supremacy over the sergeants of the police, the porter and watch of the Châtelet, the two auditors of the Châtelet, *auditores castelleti*, the sixteen commissioners of the sixteen quarters, the jailer of the Châtelet, the four enfeoffed sergeants, the hundred and twenty mounted sergeants, with maces, the chevalier of the watch with his watch, his sub-watch, his counter-watch and his rear-watch? Was it nothing to exercise high and low justice, the right to interrogate, to hang and to draw, without reckoning petty jurisdiction in the first resort (*in prima instantia*, as the charters say), on that viscomty of Paris, so nobly appanaged with seven noble bailiwicks? Can anything sweeter be imagined than rendering judgments and decisions, as Messire Robert d'Estouteville daily did in the Grand Châtelet, under the large and flattened arches of Philip Augustus? And going, as he was wont to do every evening, to that charming house situated in the Rue Galilee, in the enclosure of the royal palace, which he held in right of his wife, Madame Ambroise de Lore, to repose after the fatigue of having sent some poor wretch to pass the night in "that little cell of the Rue de Escorcherie, which the provosts and aldermen of Paris used to make their prison; the same being eleven feet long, seven feet and four inches wide, and eleven feet high?"*

And not only had Messire Robert d'Estouteville his special court as provost and vicomte of Paris; but in addition he had a share, both for eye and tooth, in the grand court of the king. There was no head in the least elevated that had not passed through his hands before it came to the headsman. It was he who went to seek M. de Nemours at the Bastille Saint Antoine, in order to conduct him to the Halles; and to conduct to the Grève M. de Saint-Pol, who clamored and resisted, to the great joy of the provost, who did not love monsieur the constable.

Here, assuredly, is more than sufficient to render a life happy and illustrious, and to deserve some day a notable page in that interesting history of the provosts of Paris, where one learns that Oudard de Villeneuve had a house in the Rue des Boucheries, that Guillaume de Hangest purchased the great and the little Savoy, that Guillaume Thiboust gave the nuns of Sainte-Geneviève his houses in the Rue Clopin, that Hugues Aubriot lived in the Hôtel du Pore-Epic, and other domestic facts.

Nevertheless, with so many reasons for taking life patiently and joyously, Messire Robert d'Estouteville woke up on the morning of the seventh of January, 1482, in a very surly and peevish mood. Whence came this ill temper? He could not have told himself. Was it because the sky was gray? Or was the buckle of his old belt of Montlhéry badly fastened, so that it confined his provostal portliness too closely? Had he beheld ribald fellows, marching in bands of four, beneath his window, and setting him at defiance, in doublets but no shirts, hats without crowns, with wallet and bottle at their side? Was it a vague presentiment of the three hundred and seventy livres, sixteen sous, eight farthings, which the future King Charles VII was to cut off from the provostship in the following year? The reader can take his choice; we, for our part, are much inclined to believe that he was in a bad humor, simply because he was in a bad humor.

---

*Comptes du domaine, 1383.

Moreover, it was the day after a festival, a tiresome day for every one, and above all for the magistrate who is charged with sweeping away all the filth, properly and figuratively speaking, which a festival day produces in Paris. And then he had to hold a sitting at the Grand Châtelet. Now, we have noticed that judges in general so arrange matters that their day of audience shall also be their day of bad humor, so that they may always have some one upon whom to vent it conveniently, in the name of the king, law, and justice.

However, the audience had begun without him. His lieutenants, civil, criminal, and private, were doing his work, according to usage; and from eight o'clock in the morning, some scores of bourgeois and bourgeoises, heaped and crowded into an obscure corner of the audience chamber of Embas du Châtelet, between a stout oaken barrier and the wall, had been gazing blissfully at the varied and cheerful spectacle of civil and criminal justice dispensed by Master Florian Barbedienne, auditor of the Châtelet, lieutenant of monsieur the provost, in a somewhat confused and utterly haphazard manner.

The hall was small, low, vaulted. A table studded with fleurs-de-lis stood at one end, with a large armchair of carved oak, which belonged to the provost and was empty, and a stool on the left for the auditor, Master Florian. Below sat the clerk of the court, scribbling; opposite was the populace; and in front of the door, and in front of the table were many sergeants of the provostship in sleeveless jackets of violet camlet, with white crosses. Two sergeants of the Parloir-aux-Bourgeois, clothed in their jackets of Toussaint, half red, half blue, were posted as sentinels before a low, closed door, which was visible at the extremity of the hall, behind the table. A single pointed window, narrowly encased in the thick wall, illuminated with a pale ray of January sun two grotesque figures,—the capricious demon of stone carved as a tail-piece in the keystone of the vaulted ceiling, and the judge seated at the end of the hall on the fleurs-de-lis.

Imagine, in fact, at the provost's table, leaning upon his elbows between two bundles of documents of cases, with his foot on the train of his robe of plain brown cloth, his face buried in his hood of white lamb's skin, of which his brows seemed to be of a piece, red, crabbed, winking, bearing majestically the load of fat on his cheeks which met under his chin, Master Florian Barbedienne, auditor of the Châtelet.

Now, the auditor was deaf. A slight defect in an auditor. Master Florian delivered judgment, none the less, without appeal and very suitably. It is certainly quite sufficient for a judge to have the air of listening; and the venerable auditor fulfilled this condition, the sole one in justice, all the better because his attention could not be distracted by any noise.

Moreover, he had in the audience, a pitiless censor of his deeds and gestures, in the person of our friend Jehan Frollo du Moulin, that little student of yesterday, that "stroller," whom one was sure of encountering all over Paris, anywhere except before the rostrums of the professors.

"Stay," he said in a low tone to his companion, Robin Poussepain, who was grinning at his side, while he was making his comments on the scenes which were being unfolded before his eyes, "yonder is Jehanneton du Buisson. The beautiful daughter of the lazy dog at the Marché-Neuf! Upon my soul, he is condemning her, the old rascal! He has no more eyes than ears. Fifteen sous, four farthings, parisis, for having worn two rosaries! 'Tis somewhat dear. *Lex duri carminis.* Who's that? Robin Chief-de-Ville, hauberkmaker. For having been passed and received master of the said trade! That's his entrance money. Hey! Two gentlemen among these knaves! Aiglet de Soins, Hutin de Mailly, two equerries, *Corpus Christi!* Ah, they have been playing at dice! When shall I see our rector here? A hundred livres parisis, fine to the king! That Barbedienne strikes like a deaf man—as he is! I'll be my brother the archdeacon, if that keeps me from gaming; gaming by day, gaming by night, living at play, dying at play, and gaming away my soul after my shirt. Holy Virgin, what damsels! One after the other, my lambs. Ambroise Lécuyere, Isabeau la Paynette, Bérarde Gironin! I know them all, by Heavens! A fine! A fine! That's what will teach you to wear gilded girdles! Ten sous parisis! You coquettes! Oh! The old snout of a judge, deaf and imbecile! Oh! Florian the dolt! Oh! Barbedienne the blockhead! There he is at the table! He's eating the plaintiff, he's eating the suits, he eats, he chews, he crams, he fills himself. Fines, lost goods, taxes, expenses, loyal charges, salaries, damages, and interests, Gehenna, prison, and jail, and fetters with expenses are Christmas spice cake and marchpanes of Saint-John to him! Look at him, the pig! Come! Good! Another amorous woman! Thibaud-la-Thibaude, neither more nor less! For having come from the Rue Glatigny! What fellow is this? Gieffroy Mabonne, gendarme bearing the crossbow. He has cursed the name of the Father. A fine for la Thibaude! A fine for Gieffroy! A fine for them both! The deaf old fool! He must have mixed up the two cases! Ten to one that he makes the wench pay for the oath and the gendarme for the amour! Attention, Robin Poussepain! What are they going to bring in? Here are many sergeants! By Jupiter! All the bloodhounds of the pack are there. It must be the great beast of the hunt—a wild boar. And 'tis one, Robin, 'tis one. And a fine one too! *Hercle*, 'tis our prince of yesterday, our Pope of the Fools, our bellringer, our one-eyed man, our hunchback, our grimace! 'Tis Quasimodo!"

It was he indeed.

It was Quasimodo, bound, encircled, roped, pinioned, and under good guard. The squad of policemen who surrounded him was assisted by the chevalier of the watch in person, wearing the arms of France embroidered on his breast, and the arms of the city on his back. There was nothing, however, about Quasimodo, except his deformity, which could justify the display of halberds and arquebuses; he was gloomy, silent, and tranquil. Only now and then did his single eye cast a sly and wrathful glance upon the bonds with which he was loaded.

He cast the same glance about him, but it was so dull and sleepy that the women only pointed him out to each other in derision.

Meanwhile Master Florian, the auditor, turned over attentively the document in the complaint entered against Quasimodo, which the clerk handed him, and, having thus glanced at it, appeared to reflect for a moment. Thanks to this precaution, which he always was careful to take at the moment when on the point of beginning an examination, he knew beforehand the names, titles, and misdeeds of the accused, made cut and dried responses to questions foreseen, and succeeded in extricating himself from all the windings of the interrogation without allowing his deafness to be too apparent. The written charges were to him what the dog is to the blind man. If his deafness did happen to betray him here and there, by some incoherent apostrophe or some unintelligible question, it passed for profundity with some, and for imbecility with others. In neither case did the honor of the magistracy sustain any injury; for it is far better that a judge should be reputed imbecile or profound than deaf. Hence he took great care to conceal his deafness from the eyes of all, and he generally succeeded so well that he had reached the point of deluding himself, which is, by the way, easier than is supposed. All hunchbacks walk with their heads held high, all stutterers harangue, all deaf people speak low. As for him, he believed, at the most, that his ear was a little refractory. It was the sole concession that he made on this point to public opinion, in his moments of frankness and examination of his conscience.

Having, then, thoroughly ruminated Quasimodo's affair, he threw back his head and half closed his eyes, for the sake of more majesty and impartiality, so that, at that moment, he was both deaf and blind. A double condition, without which no judge is perfect. It was in this magisterial attitude that he began the examination.

"Your name?"

Now this was a case which had not been "provided for by law," where a deaf man should be obliged to question a deaf man.

Quasimodo, whom nothing warned that a question had been addressed to him, continued to stare intently at the judge, and made no reply. The judge, being deaf, and being in no way warned of the deafness of the accused, thought that the latter had answered, as all accused do in general, and therefore he pursued, with his mechanical and stupid self-possession, "Very well. And your age?"

Again Quasimodo made no reply to this question. The judge supposed that it had been replied to, and continued, "Now, your profession?"

Still the same silence. The spectators had begun, meanwhile, to whisper together, and to exchange glances.

"That will do," went on the imperturbable auditor, when he supposed that the accused had finished his third reply. "You are accused before us, *primo*, of nocturnal disturbance; *secundo*, of a dishonorable act of violence upon the person of a foolish woman, *in proejudicium meretricis; tertio*, of rebellion and disloyalty toward the archers of the police of our lord, the king. Explain yourself upon all these points. Clerk, have you written down what the prisoner has said thus far?"

At this unlucky question, a burst of laughter rose from the clerk's table caught by the audience, so violent, so wild, so contagious, so universal, that the two deaf men were forced to perceive it. Quasimodo turned round, shrugging his hump with disdain, while Master Florian, equally astonished, and supposing that the laughter of the spectators had been provoked by some irreverent reply from the accused, rendered visible to him by that shrug of the shoulders, apostrophized him indignantly, "You have uttered a reply, knave, which deserves the halter. Do you know to whom you are speaking?"

This sally was not fitted to arrest the explosion of general merriment. It struck all as so whimsical, and so ridiculous, that the wild laughter even attacked the sergeants of the Parloi-aux-Bourgeois, a sort of pikemen, whose stupidity was part of their uniform. Quasimodo alone preserved his seriousness, for the good reason that he understood nothing of what was going on around him. The judge, more and more irritated, thought it his duty to continue in the same tone, hoping thereby to strike the accused with a terror that should react upon the audience, and bring it back to respect.

"So this is as much as to say, perverse and thieving knave that you are, that you permit yourself to be lacking in respect toward the Auditor of the Châtelet, to the magistrate committed to the popular police of Paris, charged with searching out crimes, delinquencies, and evil conduct; with controlling all trades, and interdicting monopoly; with maintaining the pavements; with debarring the hucksters of chickens, poultry, and water- fowl; of superintending the measuring of fagots and other sorts of wood; of purging the city of mud, and the air of contagious maladies; in a word, with attending continually to public affairs, without wages or hope of salary! Do you know that I am called Florian Barbedienne, actual lieutenant to monsieur the provost, and, moreover, commissioner, inquisitor, controller, and examiner, with equal power in provostship, bailiwick, preservation, and inferior court of judicature?"

There is no reason why a deaf man talking to a deaf man should stop. God knows where and when Master Florian would have landed, when thus launched at full speed in lofty eloquence, if the low door at the extreme end of the room had not suddenly opened, and given entrance to the provost in person. At his entrance Master Florian did not stop short, but, making a half-turn on his heels, and aiming at the provost the harangue with which he had been withering Quasimodo a moment before, "Monseigneur," said he, "I demand such penalty as you shall deem fitting against the prisoner here present, for grave and aggravated offence against the court."

And he seated himself, utterly breathless, wiping away the great drops of sweat that fell from his brow and drenched, like tears, the parchments spread out before him. Messire Robert d'Estouteville frowned and made a gesture so imperious and significant to Quasimodo, that the deaf man in some measure understood it.

The provost addressed him with severity, "What have you done that you have been brought hither, knave?"

The poor fellow, supposing that the provost was asking his name, broke the silence which he habitually preserved, and replied, in a harsh and guttural voice, "Quasimodo."

The reply matched the question so little that the wild laugh began to circulate once more, and Messire Robert exclaimed, red with wrath, "Are you mocking me also, you arrant knave?"

"Bellringer of Notre-Dame," replied Quasimodo, supposing that what was required of him was to explain to the judge who he was.

"Bellringer!" interpolated the provost, who had waked up early enough to be in a sufficiently bad temper, as we have said, not to require to have his fury inflamed by such strange responses. "Bellringer! I'll play you a chime of rods on your back through the squares of Paris! Do you hear, knave?"

"If it is my age that you wish to know," said Quasimodo, "I think that I shall be twenty at Saint Martin's day."

This was too much; the provost could no longer restrain himself.

"Ah! You are scoffing at the provostship, wretch! Messieurs the sergeants of the mace, you will take me this knave to the pillory of the Grève, you will flog him, and turn him for an hour. He shall pay me for it, *tête Dieu*! And I order that the present judgment shall be cried, with the assistance of four sworn trumpeters, in the seven castellanies of the viscomty of Paris."

The clerk set to work incontinently to draw up the account of the sentence.

"*Ventre Dieu*! 'Tis well adjudged!" cried the little scholar, Jehan Frollo du Moulin, from his corner.

The provost turned and fixed his flashing eyes once more on Quasimodo. "I believe the knave said '*Ventre Dieu*.' Clerk, add twelve deniers parisis for the oath, and let the vestry of Saint Eustache have the half of it; I have a particular devotion for Saint Eustache."

In a few minutes the sentence was drawn up. Its tenor was simple and brief. The customs of the provostship and the viscomty had not yet been worked over by President Thibaut Baillet, and by Roger Barmne, the king's advocate; they had not been obstructed, at that time, by that lofty hedge of quibbles and procedures, which the two jurisconsults planted there at the beginning of the sixteenth century. All was clear, expeditious, explicit. One went straight to the point then, and at the end of every path there was immediately visible, without thickets and without turnings; the wheel, the gibbet, or the pillory. One at least knew whither one was going.

The clerk presented the sentence to the provost, who affixed his seal to it, and departed to pursue his round of the audience hall, in a frame of mind which seemed destined to fill all the jails in Paris that day. Jehan Frollo and Robin Poussepain laughed in their sleeves. Quasimodo gazed on the whole with an indifferent and astonished air.

However, at the moment when Master Florian Barbedienne was reading the sentence in his turn, before signing it, the clerk felt himself moved with pity for the poor wretch of a prisoner, and, in the hope of obtaining some mitigation of the penalty, he approached as near the auditor's ear as possible, and said, pointing to Quasimodo, "That man is deaf."

He hoped that this community of infirmity would awaken Master Florian's interest in behalf of the condemned man. But, in the first place, we have already observed that Master Florian did not care to have his deafness noticed. In the next place, he was so hard of hearing that he did not catch a single word of what the clerk said to him; nevertheless, he wished to have the appearance of hearing, and replied, "Ah, ah! That is different; I did not know that. An hour more of the pillory, in that case."

And he signed the sentence thus modified.

"'Tis well done," said Robin Poussepain, who cherished a grudge against Quasimodo. "That will teach him to handle people roughly."

Chapter 2

The Rat-Hole

THE READER MUST permit us to take him back to the Place de Grève, which we quitted yesterday with Gringoire, in order to follow la Esmeralda.

It is ten o'clock in the morning; everything is indicative of the day after a festival. The pavement is covered with rubbish; ribbons, rags, feathers from tufts of plumes, drops of wax from the torches, crumbs of the public feast. A goodly number of bourgeois are "sauntering," as we say, here and there, turning over with their feet the extinct brands of the bonfire, going into raptures in front of the Pillar House, over the memory of the fine hangings of the day before, and today staring at the nails that secured them a last pleasure. The venders of cider and beer are rolling their barrels among the groups. Some busy passers-by come and go. The merchants converse and call to each other from the thresholds of their shops. The festival, the ambassadors, Coppenole, the Pope of the Fools, are in all mouths; they vie with each other, each trying to criticise it best and laugh the most. And, meanwhile, four mounted sergeants, who have just posted themselves at the four sides of the pillory, have already concentrated around themselves a goodly proportion of the populace scattered on the Place, who condemn themselves to immobility and fatigue in the hope of a small execution.

If the reader, after having contemplated this lively and noisy scene which is being enacted in all parts of the Place, will now transfer his gaze toward that ancient demi-Gothic, demi-Romanesque house of the Tour-Roland, which forms the corner on the quay to the west, he will observe, at the angle of the façade, a large public breviary, with rich illuminations, protected from the rain by a little penthouse, and from thieves by a small grating, which, however, permits of the leaves being turned. Beside this breviary is a narrow, arched window, closed by two iron bars in the form of a cross, and looking on the square; the only opening which admits a small quantity of light and air to a little cell without a door, constructed on the ground-floor, in the thickness of the walls of the old house, and filled with a peace all the more profound, with a silence all the more gloomy, because a public place, the most populous and most noisy in Paris swarms and shrieks around it.

This little cell had been celebrated in Paris for nearly three centuries, ever since Madame Rolande de la Tour-Roland, in mourning for her father who died in the Crusades, had caused it to be hollowed out in the wall of her own house, in order to immure herself there forever, keeping of all her palace only this lodging whose door was walled up, and whose window stood open, winter and summer, giving all the rest to the poor and to God. The afflicted damsel had, in fact, waited twenty years for death in this premature tomb, praying night and day for the soul of her father, sleeping in ashes, without even a stone for a pillow, clothed in a black sack, and subsisting on the bread and water which the compassion of the passers-by led them to deposit on the ledge of her window, thus receiving charity after having bestowed it. At her death, at the moment when she was passing to the other sepulchre, she had bequeathed this one in perpetuity to afflicted women, mothers, widows, or maidens, who should wish to pray much for others or for themselves, and who should desire to inter themselves alive in a great grief or a great penance. The poor of her day had made her a fine funeral, with tears and benedictions; but, to their great regret, the pious maid had not been canonized, for lack of influence. Those among them who were a little inclined to impiety, had hoped that the matter might be accomplished in Paradise more easily than at Rome, and had frankly besought God, instead of the pope, in behalf of the deceased. The majority had contented themselves with holding the memory of Rolande sacred, and converting her rags into relics. The city, on its side, had founded in honor of the damoiselle, a public breviary, which had been fastened near the window of the cell, in order that passers-by might halt there from time to time, were it only to pray; that prayer might remind them of alms, and that the poor recluses, heiresses of Madame Rolande's vault, might not die outright of hunger and forgetfulness.

Moreover, this sort of tomb was not so very rare a thing in the cities of the Middle Ages. One often encountered in the most frequented street, in the most crowded and noisy market, in the very middle, under the feet of the horses, under the wheels of the carts, as it were, a cellar, a well, a tiny walled and grated cabin, at the bottom of which a human being prayed night and day, voluntarily devoted to some eternal lamentation, to some great expiation. And all the reflections which that strange spectacle would awaken in us today; that horrible cell, a sort of intermediary link between a house and the tomb, the cemetery and the city; that living being cut off from the human community, and thenceforth reckoned among the dead; that lamp consuming its last drop of oil in the darkness; that remnant of life flickering in the grave; that breath, that voice, that eternal prayer in a box of stone; that face forever turned toward the other world; that eye already illuminated with another sun; that ear pressed to the walls of a tomb; that soul a prisoner in that body; that body a prisoner in that dungeon cell, and beneath that double envelope of flesh and granite, the murmur of that soul in pain;—nothing of all this was perceived by the crowd. The piety of that age, not very subtle nor much given to reasoning, did not see so many facets in an act of religion. It took the thing in the block, honored, venerated, hallowed the sacrifice at need, but did not analyze the sufferings, and felt but moderate pity for them. It brought some pittance to the miserable penitent from time to time, looked through the hole to see whether he were still living, forgot his name, hardly knew how many years ago he had begun to die, and to the stranger, who questioned them about the living skeleton who was perishing in that cellar, the neighbors replied simply, "It is the recluse."

Everything was then viewed without metaphysics, without exaggeration, without magnifying glass, with the naked eye. The microscope had not yet been invented, either for things of matter or for things of the mind.

Moreover, although people were but little surprised by it, the examples of this sort of cloistration in the hearts of cities were in truth frequent, as we have just said. There were in Paris a considerable number of these cells, for praying to God and doing penance; they were nearly all occupied. It is true that the clergy did not like to have them empty, since that implied lukewarmness in believers, and that lepers were put into them when there were no penitents on hand. Besides the cell on the Grève, there was one at Montfauçon, one at the

Charnier des Innocents, another I hardly know where, at the Clichon House, I think; others still at many spots where traces of them are found in traditions, in default of memorials. The University had also its own. On Mount Sainte-Geneviève a sort of Job of the Middle Ages, for the space of thirty years, chanted the seven penitential psalms on a dunghill at the bottom of a cistern, beginning anew when he had finished, singing loudest at night, *magna voce per umbras*, and today, the antiquary fancies that he hears his voice as he enters the Rue du Puits-qui-parle—the street of the "Speaking Well."

To confine ourselves to the cell in the Tour-Roland, we must say that it had never lacked recluses. After the death of Madame Rolande, it had stood vacant for a year or two, though rarely. Many women had come thither to mourn, until their death, for relatives, lovers, faults. Parisian malice, which thrusts its finger into everything, even into things that concern it the least, affirmed that it had beheld but few widows there.

In accordance with the fashion of the epoch, a Latin inscription on the wall indicated to the learned passer-by the pious purpose of this cell. The custom was retained until the middle of the sixteenth century of explaining an edifice by a brief device inscribed above the door. Thus, one still reads in France, above the wicket of the prison in the seignorial mansion of Tourville, *Sileto et spera*; in Ireland, beneath the armorial bearings which surmount the grand door to Fortescue Castle, *Forte scutum, salus ducum*; in England, over the principal entrance to the hospitable mansion of the Earls Cowper: *Tuum est*. At that time every edifice was a thought.

As there was no door to the walled cell of the Tour-Roland, these two words had been carved in large Roman capitals over the window:

TU, ORA

And this caused the people, whose good sense does not perceive so much refinement in things, and likes to translate *Ludovico Magno* by "Porte Saint-Denis," to give to this dark, gloomy, damp cavity, the name of "The Rat-Hole." An explanation less sublime, perhaps, than the other; but, on the other hand, more picturesque.

Chapter 3

History of a Leavened Cake of Maize

AT THE EPOCH of this history, the cell in the Tour-Roland was occupied. If the reader desires to know by whom, he has only to lend an ear to the conversation of three worthy gossips, who, at the moment when we have directed his attention to the Rat-Hole, were directing their steps toward the same spot, coming up along the water's edge from the Châtelet, toward the Grève.

Two of these women were dressed like good *bourgeoises* of Paris. Their fine white ruffs; their petticoats of linsey-woolsey, striped red and blue; their white knitted stockings, with clocks embroidered in colors, well drawn upon their legs; the square-toed shoes of tawny leather with black soles, and, above all, their headgear, that sort of tinsel horn, loaded down with ribbons and laces, which the women of Champagne still wear, in company with the grenadiers of the imperial guard of Russia, announced that they belonged to that class wives which holds the middle ground between what the lackeys call a woman and what they term a lady. They wore neither rings nor gold crosses, and it was easy to see that, in their ease, this did not proceed from poverty, but simply from fear of being fined. Their companion was attired in very much the same manner; but there was that indescribable something about her dress and bearing which suggested the wife of a provincial notary. One could see, by the way in which her girdle rose above her hips, that she had not been long in Paris.—Add to this a plaited tucker, knots of ribbon on her shoes—and that the stripes of her petticoat ran horizontally instead of vertically, and a thousand other enormities which shocked good taste.

The two first walked with that step peculiar to Parisian ladies, showing Paris to women from the country. The provincial held by the hand a big boy, who held in his a large, flat cake.

We regret to be obliged to add, that, owing to the rigor of the season, he was using his tongue as a handkerchief.

The child was making them drag him along, *non passibus Cequis*, as Virgil says, and stumbling at every moment, to the great indignation of his mother. It is true that he was looking at his cake more than at the pavement. Some serious motive, no doubt, prevented his biting it (the cake), for he contented himself with gazing tenderly at it. But the mother should have rather taken charge of the cake. It was cruel to make a Tantalus of the chubby-checked boy.

Meanwhile, the three demoiselles (for the name of dames was then reserved for noble women) were all talking at once.

"Let us make haste, Demoiselle Mahiette," said the youngest of the three, who was also the largest, to the provincial, "I greatly fear that we shall arrive too late; they told us at the Châtelet that they were going to take him directly to the pillory."

"Ah, bah! What are you saying, Demoiselle Oudarde Musnier?" interposed the other Parisienne. "There are two hours yet to the pillory. We have time enough. Have you ever seen any one pilloried, my dear Mahiette?"

"Yes," said the provincial, "at Reims."

"Ah, bah! What is your pillory at Reims? A miserable cage into which only peasants are turned. A great affair, truly!"

"Only peasants!" said Mahiette, "at the cloth market in Reims! We have seen very fine criminals there, who have killed their father and mother! Peasants! For what do you take us, Gervaise?"

It is certain that the provincial was on the point of taking offence, for the honor of her pillory. Fortunately, that discreet damoiselle, Oudarde Musnier, turned the conversation in time.

"By the way, Damoiselle Mahiette, what say you to our Flemish Ambassadors? Have you as fine ones at Reims?"

"I admit," replied Mahiette, "that it is only in Paris that such Flemings can be seen."

"Did you see among the embassy, that big ambassador who is a hosier?" asked Oudarde.

"Yes," said Mahiette. "He has the eye of a Saturn."

"And the big fellow whose face resembles a bare belly?" resumed Gervaise. "And the little one, with small eyes framed in red eyelids, pared down and slashed up like a thistle head?"

"'Tis their horses that are worth seeing," said Oudarde, "caparisoned as they are after the fashion of their country!"

"Ah my dear," interrupted provincial Mahiette, assuming in her turn an air of superiority, "what would you say then, if you had seen in '61, at the consecration at Reims, eighteen years ago, the horses of the princes and of the king's company? Housings and caparisons of all sorts; some of damask cloth, of fine cloth of gold, furred with sables; others of velvet, furred with ermine; others all embellished with goldsmith's work and large bells of gold and silver! And what money that had cost! And what handsome boy pages rode upon them!"

"That," replied Oudarde dryly, "does not prevent the Flemings having very fine horses, and having had a superb supper yesterday with monsieur, the provost of the merchants, at the Hôtel-de-Ville, where they were served with comfits and hippocras, and spices, and other singularities."

"What are you saying, neighbor!" exclaimed Gervaise. "It was with monsieur the cardinal, at the Petit Bourbon that they supped."

"Not at all. At the Hôtel-de-Ville.

"Yes, indeed. At the Petit Bourbon!"

"It was at the Hôtel-de-Ville," retorted Oudarde sharply, "and Dr. Scourable addressed them a harangue in Latin, which pleased them greatly. My husband, who is sworn bookseller, told me."

"It was at the Petit Bourbon," replied Gervaise, with no less spirit, "and this is what monsieur the cardinal's procurator presented to them: twelve double quarts of hippocras, white, claret, and red; twenty-four boxes of double Lyons marchpane, gilded; as many torches, worth two livres a piece; and six demi-queues of Beaune wine, white and claret, the best that could be found. I have it from my husband, who is a cinquantenier [a captain of fifty men], at the Parloir-aux Bourgeois, and who was this morning comparing the Flemish ambassadors with those of Prester John and the Emperor of Trebizond, who came from Mesopotamia to Paris, under the last king, and who wore rings in their ears."

"So true is it that they supped at the Hôtel-de-Ville," replied Oudarde but little affected by this catalogue, "that such a triumph of viands and comfits has never been seen."

"I tell you that they were served by Le Sec, sergeant of the city, at the Hôtel du Petit-Bourbon, and that that is where you are mistaken."

"At the Hôtel-de-Ville, I tell you!"

"At the Petit-Bourbon, my dear! And they had illuminated with magic glasses the word hope, which is written on the grand portal."

"At the Hôtel-de-Ville! At the Hôtel-de-Ville! And Husson-le-Voir played the flute!"

"I tell you, no!"

"I tell you, yes!"

"I say, no!"

Plump and worthy Oudarde was preparing to retort, and the quarrel might, perhaps, have proceeded to a pulling of caps, had not Mahiette suddenly exclaimed, "Look at those people assembled yonder at the end of the bridge! There is something in their midst that they are looking at!"

"In sooth," said Gervaise, "I hear the sounds of a tambourine. I believe 'tis the little Esmeralda, who plays her mummeries with her goat. Eh, be quick, Mahiette! Redouble your pace and drag along your boy. You are come hither to visit the curiosities of Paris. You saw the Flemings yesterday; you must see the gypsy today."

"The gypsy!" said Mahiette, suddenly retracing her steps, and clasping her son's arm forcibly. "God preserve me from it! She would steal my child from me! Come, Eustache!"

And she set out on a run along the quay toward the Grève, until she had left the bridge far behind her. In the meanwhile, the child whom she was dragging after her fell upon his knees; she halted breathless. Oudarde and Gervaise rejoined her.

"That gypsy steal your child from you!" said Gervaise. "That's a singular freak of yours!"

Mahiette shook her head with a pensive air.

"The singular point is," observed Oudarde, "that *la sachette* has the same idea about the Egyptian woman."

"What is *la sachette*?" asked Mahiette.

"Oh!" said Oudarde, "Sister Gudule."

"And who is Sister Gudule?" persisted Mahiette.

"You are certainly ignorant of all but your Reims, not to know that!" replied Oudarde. "'Tis the recluse of the Rat-Hole."

"What!" demanded Mahiette, "that poor woman to whom we are carrying this cake?"

Oudarde nodded affirmatively.

"Precisely. You will see her presently at her window on the Grève. She has the same opinion as yourself of these vagabonds of Egypt, who play the tambourine and tell fortunes to the public. No one knows whence comes her horror of the gypsies and Egyptians. But you, Mahiette—why do you run so at the mere sight of them?"

"Oh!" said Mahiette, seizing her child's round head in both hands, "I don't want that to happen to me which happened to Paquette la Chantefleurie."

"Oh! You must tell us that story, my good Mahiette," said Gervaise, taking her arm.

"Gladly," replied Mahiette, "but you must be ignorant of all but your Paris not to know that! I will tell you then (but 'tis not necessary for us to halt that I may tell you the tale), that Paquette la Chantefleurie was a pretty maid of eighteen when I was one myself, that is to say, eighteen years ago, and 'tis her own fault if she is not today, like me, a good, plump, fresh mother of six and thirty, with a husband and a son. However, after the age of fourteen, it was too late! Well, she was the daughter of Guybertant, minstrel of the barges at Reims, the same who had played before King Charles VII, at his coronation, when he descended our river Vesle from Sillery to Muison, when Madame the Maid of Orleans was also in the boat. The old father died when Paquette was still a mere child; she had then no one but her mother, the sister of M. Pradon, master-brazier and coppersmith in Paris, Rue Farm-Garlin, who died last year. You see she was of good family. The mother was a good simple woman, unfortunately, and she taught Paquette nothing but a bit of embroidery and toy-making which did not prevent the little one from growing very large and remaining very poor. They both dwelt at Reims, on the river front, Rue de Folle-Peine. Mark this: For I believe it was this that brought misfortune to Paquette. In '61, the year of the coronation of our King Louis XI, whom God preserve! Paquette was so gay and so pretty that she was called everywhere by no other name than "la Chantefleurie"—blossoming song. Poor girl! She had handsome teeth, she was fond of laughing and displaying them. Now, a maid who loves to laugh is on the road to weeping; handsome teeth ruin handsome eyes. So she was la Chantefleurie. She and her mother earned a precarious living; they had been very destitute since the death of the minstrel; their embroidery did not bring them in more than six farthings a week, which does not amount to quite two eagle liards. Where were the days when Father Guybertant had earned twelve sous parisis, in a single coronation, with a song? One winter (it was in that same year of '61), when the two women had neither

fagots nor firewood, it was very cold, which gave la Chantefleurie such
a fine color that the men called her Paquette [ox-eye daisy] and many
called her Pàquerette [easter daisy] and she was ruined! Eustache, just
let me see you bite that cake if you dare! We immediately perceived
that she was ruined, one Sunday when she came to church with a
gold cross about her neck. At fourteen years of age! Do you see? First
it was the young Vicomte de Cormontreuil, who has his bell tower
three leagues distant from Reims; then Messire Henri de Triancourt,
equerry to the King; then less than that, Chiart de Beaulion, sergeant-
at-arms; then, still descending, Guery Aubergeon, carver to the King;
then, Mace de Frépus, barber to monsieur the dauphin; then, Thévenin
le Moine, King's cook; then, the men growing continually younger
and less noble, she fell to Guillaume Racine, minstrel of the hurdy
gurdy; and to Thierry de Mer, lamplighter. Then, poor Chantefleurie,
she belonged to every one: she had reached the last sou of her gold
piece. What shall I say to you, my damoiselles? At the coronation, in
the same year, '61, 'twas she who made the bed of the king of the
debauchees! In the same year!"

Mahiette sighed, and wiped away a tear that trickled from her
eyes.

"This is no very extraordinary history," said Gervaise, "and in the
whole of it I see nothing of any Egyptian women or children."

"Patience!" resumed Mahiette, "you will see one child. In '66,
'twill be sixteen years ago this month, at Sainte-Paule's day, Paquette
was brought to bed of a little girl. The unhappy creature! It was a great
joy to her; she had long wished for a child. Her mother, good woman,
who had never known what to do except to shut her eyes, her mother
was dead. Paquette had no longer any one to love in the world or any
one to love her. La Chantefleurie had been a poor creature during the
five years since her fall. She was alone, alone in this life, fingers were
pointed at her, she was hooted at in the streets, beaten by the sergeants,
jeered at by the little boys in rags. And then, twenty had arrived: and
twenty is an old age for amorous women. Folly began to bring her
in no more than her trade of embroidery in former days; for every
wrinkle that came, a crown fled; winter became hard to her once more,
wood became rare again in her brazier, and bread in her cupboard.
She could no longer work because, in becoming voluptuous, she had
grown lazy; and she suffered much more because, in growing lazy, she
had become voluptuous. At least, that is the way in which monsieur

the cure of Saint-Remy explains why these women are colder and
hungrier than other poor women, when they are old."

"Yes," remarked Gervaise, "but the gypsies?"

"One moment, Gervaise!" said Oudarde, whose attention was less
impatient. "What would be left for the end if all were in the beginning?
Continue, Mahiette, I entreat you. That poor Chantefleurie!"

Mahiette went on.

"So she was very sad, very miserable, and furrowed her cheeks
with tears. But in the midst of her shame, her folly, her debauchery, it
seemed to her that she should be less wild, less shameful, less dissipated,
if there were something or some one in the world whom she could
love, and who could love her. It was necessary that it should be a child,
because only a child could be sufficiently innocent for that. She had
recognized this fact after having tried to love a thief, the only man
who wanted her; but after a short time, she perceived that the thief
despised her. Those women of love require either a lover or a child to
fill their hearts. Otherwise, they are very unhappy. As she could not
have a lover, she turned wholly toward a desire for a child, and as she
had not ceased to be pious, she made her constant prayer to the good
God for it. So the good God took pity on her, and gave her a little
daughter. I will not speak to you of her joy; it was a fury of tears, and
caresses, and kisses. She nursed her child herself, made swaddling-bands
for it out of her coverlet, the only one that she had on her bed, and
no longer felt either cold or hunger. She became beautiful once more,
in consequence of it. An old maid makes a young mother. Gallantry
claimed her once more; men came to see la Chantefleurie; she found
customers again for her merchandise, and out of all these horrors she
made baby clothes, caps and bibs, bodices with shoulder-straps of lace,
and tiny bonnets of satin, without even thinking of buying herself
another coverlet. —Master Eustache, I have already told you not to
eat that cake. It is certain that little Agnes, that was the child's name,
a baptismal name, for it was a long time since la Chantefleurie had
had any surname—it is certain that that little one was more swathed
in ribbons and embroideries than a dauphiness of Dauphiny! Among
other things, she had a pair of little shoes, the like of which King Louis
XI certainly never had! Her mother had stitched and embroidered
them herself; she had lavished on them all the delicacies of her art of
embroideress, and all the embellishments of a robe for the good Virgin.
They certainly were the two prettiest little pink shoes that could be

seen. They were no longer than my thumb, and one had to see the child's little feet come out of them, in order to believe that they had been able to get into them. 'Tis true that those little feet were so small, so pretty, so rosy! Rosier than the satin of the shoes! When you have children, Oudarde, you will find that there is nothing prettier than those little hands and feet."

"I ask no better," said Oudarde with a sigh, "but I am waiting until it shall suit the good pleasure of M. Andry Musnier."

"However, Paquette's child had more that was pretty about it besides its feet. I saw her when she was only four months old; she was a love! She had eyes larger than her mouth, and the most charming black hair, which already curled. She would have been a magnificent brunette at the age of sixteen! Her mother became more crazy over her every day. She kissed her, caressed her, tickled her, washed her, decked her out, devoured her! She lost her head over her, she thanked God for her. Her pretty, little rosy feet above all were an endless source of wonderment, they were a delirium of joy! She was always pressing her lips to them, and she could never recover from her amazement at their smallness. She put them into the tiny shoes, took them out, admired them, marvelled at them, looked at the light through them, was curious to see them try to walk on her bed, and would gladly have passed her life on her knees, putting on and taking off the shoes from those feet, as though they had been those of an Infant Jesus."

"The tale is fair and good," said Gervaise in a low tone; "but where do gypsies come into all that?"

"Here," replied Mahiette. "One day there arrived in Reims a very queer sort of people. They were beggars and vagabonds who were roaming over the country, led by their duke and their counts. They were browned by exposure to the sun, they had closely curling hair, and silver rings in their ears. The women were still uglier than the men. They had blacker faces, which were always uncovered, a miserable frock on their bodies, an old cloth woven of cords bound upon their shoulder, and their hair hanging like the tail of a horse. The children who scrambled between their legs would have frightened as many monkeys. A band of excommunicates. All these persons came direct from lower Egypt to Reims through Poland. The Pope had confessed them, it was said, and had prescribed to them as penance to roam through the world for seven years, without sleeping in a bed; and so they were called penancers, and smelt horribly. It appears that

they had formerly been Saracens, which was why they believed in
Jupiter, and claimed ten livres of Tournay from all archbishops, bishops,
and mitred abbots with croziers. A bull from the Pope empowered
them to do that. They came to Reims to tell fortunes in the name
of the King of Algiers, and the Emperor of Germany. You can readily
imagine that no more was needed to cause the entrance to the town
to be forbidden them. Then the whole band camped with good grace
outside the gate of Braine, on that hill where stands a mill, beside the
cavities of the ancient chalk pits. And everybody in Reims vied with
his neighbor in going to see them. They looked at your hand, and told
you marvellous prophecies; they were equal to predicting to Judas that
he would become Pope. Nevertheless, ugly rumors were in circulation
in regard to them; about children stolen, purses cut, and human flesh
devoured. The wise people said to the foolish: "Don't go there!" and
then went themselves on the sly. It was an infatuation. The fact is, that
they said things fit to astonish a cardinal. Mothers triumphed greatly
over their little ones after the Egyptians had read in their hands all
sorts of marvels written in pagan and in Turkish. One had an emperor;
another, a pope; another, a captain. Poor Chantefleurie was seized with
curiosity; she wished to know about herself, and whether her pretty
little Agnes would not become some day Empress of Armenia, or
something else. So she carried her to the Egyptians; and the Egyptian
women fell to admiring the child, and to caressing it, and to kissing
it with their black mouths, and to marvelling over its little hand, alas
to the great joy of the mother. They were especially enthusiastic over
her pretty feet and shoes. The child was not yet a year old. She already
lisped a little, laughed at her mother like a little mad thing, was plump
and quite round, and possessed a thousand charming little gestures of
the angels of paradise.

"She was very much frightened by the Egyptians, and wept. But
her mother kissed her more warmly and went away enchanted with
the good fortune which the soothsayers had foretold for her Agnes. She
was to be a beauty, virtuous, a queen. So she returned to her attic in the
Rue Folle-Peine, very proud of bearing with her a queen. The next day
she took advantage of a moment when the child was asleep on her bed
(for they always slept together), gently left the door a little way open,
and ran to tell a neighbor in the Rue de la Séchesserie, that the day
would come when her daughter Agnes would be served at table by the
King of England and the Archduke of Ethiopia, and a hundred other

marvels. On her return, hearing no cries on the staircase, she said to herself: 'Good! the child is still asleep!' She found her door wider open than she had left it, but she entered, poor mother, and ran to the bed. The child was no longer there, the place was empty. Nothing remained of the child, but one of her pretty little shoes. She flew out of the room, dashed down the stairs, and began to beat her head against the wall, crying: 'My child! Who has my child? Who has taken my child?' The street was deserted, the house isolated; no one could tell her anything about it. She went about the town, searched all the streets, ran hither and thither the whole day long, wild, beside herself, terrible, snuffing at doors and windows like a wild beast which has lost its young. She was breathless, dishevelled, frightful to see, and there was a fire in her eyes that dried her tears. She stopped the passers-by and cried: 'My daughter! My daughter! My pretty little daughter! If any one will give me back my daughter, I will be his servant, the servant of his dog, and he shall eat my heart if he will.' She met M. le Curé of Saint-Remy, and said to him: 'Monsieur, I will till the earth with my finger-nails, but give me back my child!' It was heartrending, Oudarde; and I saw a very hard man, Master Ponce Lacabre, the procurator, weep. Ah! Poor mother! In the evening she returned home. During her absence, a neighbor had seen two gypsies ascend up to it with a bundle in their arms, then descend again, after closing the door. After their departure, something like the cries of a child were heard in Paquette's room. The mother, burst into shrieks of laughter, ascended the stairs as though on wings, and entered. A frightful thing to tell, Oudarde! Instead of her pretty little Agnes, so rosy and so fresh, who was a gift of the good God, a sort of hideous little monster, lame, one-eyed, deformed, was crawling and squalling over the floor. She hid her eyes in horror. 'Oh!' said she, 'have the witches transformed my daughter into this horrible animal?' They hastened to carry away the little club-foot; he would have driven her mad. It was the monstrous child of some gypsy woman, who had given herself to the devil. He appeared to be about four years old, and talked a language that was no human tongue; there were words in it that were impossible. La Chantefleurie flung herself upon the little shoe, all that remained to her of all that she loved. She remained so long motionless over it, mute, and without breath, that they thought she was dead. Suddenly she trembled all over, covered her relic with furious kisses, and burst out sobbing as though her heart were broken. I assure you that we were all weeping also. She said: 'Oh, my little daughter!

My pretty little daughter, where art thou?'—and it wrung your very heart. I weep still when I think of it. Our children are the marrow of our bones, you see. My poor Eustache! Thou art so fair! If you only knew how nice he is! Yesterday he said to me: 'I want to be a gendarme, that I do.' Oh! My Eustache! If I were to lose thee! All at once la Chantefleurie rose, and set out to run through Reims, screaming: 'To the gypsies' camp! To the gypsies' camp! Police, to burn the witches!' The gypsies were gone. It was pitch dark. They could not be followed. On the morrow, two leagues from Reims, on a heath between Gueux and Tilloy, the remains of a large fire were found, some ribbons that had belonged to Paquette's child, drops of blood, and the dung of a ram. The night just past had been a Saturday. There was no longer any doubt that the Egyptians had held their Sabbath on that heath, and that they had devoured the child in company with Beelzebub, as the practice is among the Mahometans. When La Chantefleurie learned these horrible things, she did not weep, she moved her lips as though to speak, but could not. On the morrow, her hair was gray. On the second day, she had disappeared.

"'Tis in truth, a frightful tale," said Oudarde, "and one which would make even a Burgundian weep."

"I am no longer surprised," added Gervaise, "that fear of the gypsies should spur you on so sharply."

"And you did all the better," resumed Oudarde, "to flee with your Eustache just now, since these also are gypsies from Poland."

"No," said Gervais, "'tis said that they come from Spain and Catalonia."

"Catalonia? 'Tis possible," replied Oudarde. "Pologne, Catalogue, Valogne, I always confound those three provinces, one thing is certain, that they are gypsies."

"Who certainly," added Gervaise, "have teeth long enough to eat little children. I should not be surprised if la Esmeralda ate a little of them also, though she pretends to be dainty. Her white goat knows tricks that are too malicious for there not to be some impiety underneath it all."

Mahiette walked on in silence. She was absorbed in that revery which is, in some sort, the continuation of a mournful tale, and which ends only after having communicated the emotion, from vibration to vibration, even to the very last fibres of the heart. Nevertheless, Gervaise addressed her, "And did they ever learn what became of la Chantefleurie?" Mahiette made no reply. Gervaise repeated her question, and shook her arm, calling her by name. Mahiette appeared to awaken from her thoughts.

"What became of la Chantefleurie?" she said, repeating mechanically the words whose impression was still fresh in her ear; then, making an effort to recall her attention to the meaning of her words, "Ah!" she continued briskly, "no one ever found out."

She added, after a pause, "Some said that she had been seen to quit Reims at nightfall by the Fléchembault gate; others, at daybreak, by the old Basée gate. A poor man found her gold cross hanging on the stone cross in the field where the fair is held. It was that ornament which had wrought her ruin, in '61. It was a gift from the handsome Vicomte de Cormontreuil, her first lover. Paquette had never been willing to part with it, wretched as she had been. She had clung to it as to life itself. So, when we saw that cross abandoned, we all thought that she was dead. Nevertheless, there were people of the Cabaret les Vantes, who said that they had seen her pass along the road to Paris, walking on the pebbles with her bare feet. But, in that case, she must have gone out through the Porte de Vesle, and all this does not agree. Or, to speak more truly, I believe that she actually did depart by the Porte de Vesle, but departed from this world."

"I do not understand you," said Gervaise.

"La Vesle," replied Mahiette, with a melancholy smile, "is the river."

"Poor Chantefleurie!" said Oudarde, with a shiver. "Drowned!"

"Drowned!" resumed Mahiette, "who could have told good Father Guybertant, when he passed under the bridge of Tingueux with the current, singing in his barge, that one day his dear little Paquette would also pass beneath that bridge, but without song or boat."

"And the little shoe?" asked Gervaise.

"Disappeared with the mother," replied Mahiette.

"Poor little shoe!" said Oudarde.

Oudarde, a big and tender woman, would have been well pleased to sigh in company with Mahiette. But Gervaise, more curious, had not finished her questions.

"And the monster?" she said suddenly, to Mahiette.

"What monster?" inquired the latter.

"The little gypsy monster left by the sorceresses in Chantefleurie's chamber, in exchange for her daughter. What did you do with it? I hope you drowned it also."

"No," replied Mahiette.

"What? You burned it then? In sooth, that is more just. A witch child!"

"Neither the one nor the other, Gervaise. Monseigneur the archbishop interested himself in the child of Egypt, exorcised it, blessed it, removed the devil carefully from its body, and sent it to Paris, to be exposed on the wooden bed at Notre-Dame, as a foundling."

"Those bishops!" grumbled Gervaise, "because they are learned, they do nothing like anybody else. I just put it to you, Oudarde, the idea of placing the devil among the foundlings! For that little monster was assuredly the devil. Well, Mahiette, what did they do with it in Paris? I am quite sure that no charitable person wanted it."

"I do not know," replied the Rémoise, "'twas just at that time that my husband bought the office of notary, at Bern, two leagues from the town, and we were no longer occupied with that story; besides, in front of Bern, stand the two hills of Cernay, which hide the towers of the cathedral in Reims from view."

While chatting thus, the three worthy *bourgeoises* had arrived at the Place de Grève. In their absorption, they had passed the public breviary of the Tour-Roland without stopping, and took their way mechanically toward the pillory around which the throng was growing more dense with every moment. It is probable that the spectacle which at that moment attracted all looks in that direction, would have made them forget completely the Rat-Hole, and the halt which they intended to make there, if big Eustache, six years of age, whom Mahiette was dragging along by the hand, had not abruptly recalled the object to them: "Mother," said he, as though some instinct warned him that the Rat-Hole was behind him, "can I eat the cake now?"

If Eustache had been more adroit, that is to say, less greedy, he would have continued to wait, and would only have hazarded that simple question, "Mother, can I eat the cake, now?" on their return to the University, to Master Andry Musnier's, Rue Madame la Valence, when he had the two arms of the Seine and the five bridges of the city between the Rat-Hole and the cake.

This question, highly imprudent at the moment when Eustache put it, aroused Mahiette's attention.

"By the way," she exclaimed, "we are forgetting the recluse! Show me the Rat-Hole, that I may carry her her cake."

"Immediately," said Oudarde, "'tis a charity."

But this did not suit Eustache.

"Stop! My cake!" said he, rubbing both ears alternatively with his shoulders, which, in such cases, is the supreme sign of discontent.

The three women retraced their steps, and, on arriving in the vicinity of the Tour-Roland, Oudarde said to the other two, "We must not all three gaze into the hole at once, for fear of alarming the recluse. Do you two pretend to read the *Dominus* in the breviary, while I thrust my nose into the aperture; the recluse knows me a little. I will give you warning when you can approach."

She proceeded alone to the window. At the moment when she looked in, a profound pity was depicted on all her features, and her frank, gay visage altered its expression and color as abruptly as though it had passed from a ray of sunlight to a ray of moonlight; her eye became humid; her mouth contracted, like that of a person on the point of weeping. A moment later, she laid her finger on her lips, and made a sign to Mahiette to draw near and look.

Mahiette, much touched, stepped up in silence, on tiptoe, as though approaching the bedside of a dying person.

It was, in fact, a melancholy spectacle that presented itself to the eyes of the two women, as they gazed through the grating of the Rat-Hole, neither stirring nor breathing.

The cell was small, broader than it was long, with an arched ceiling, and viewed from within, it bore a considerable resemblance to the interior of a huge bishop's mitre. On the bare flagstones that formed the floor, in one corner, a woman was sitting, or rather, crouching. Her chin rested on her knees, which her crossed arms pressed forcibly to her breast. Thus doubled up, clad in a brown sack, which enveloped her entirely in large folds, her long, gray hair pulled over in front, falling over her face and along her legs nearly to her feet, she presented, at the first glance, only a strange form outlined against the dark background of the cell, a sort of dusky triangle, which the ray of daylight falling through the opening, cut roughly into two shades, the one sombre, the other illuminated. It was one of those spectres, half light, half shadow, such as one beholds in dreams and in the extraordinary work of Goya, pale, motionless, sinister, crouching over a tomb, or leaning against the grating of a prison cell.

It was neither a woman, nor a man, nor a living being, nor a definite form; it was a figure, a sort of vision, in which the real and the fantastic intersected each other, like darkness and day. It was with difficulty that one distinguished, beneath her hair which spread to the ground, a gaunt and severe profile; her dress barely allowed the extremity of a bare foot to escape, which contracted on the hard, cold pavement. The little of human form of which one caught a sight beneath this envelope of mourning, caused a shudder.

That figure, which one might have supposed to be riveted to the flagstones, appeared to possess neither movement, nor thought, nor breath. Lying, in January, in that thin, linen sack, lying on a granite floor, without fire, in the gloom of a cell whose oblique air-hole allowed only the cold breeze, but never the sun, to enter from without, she did not appear to suffer or even to think. One would have said that she had turned to stone with the cell, ice with the season. Her hands were clasped, her eyes fixed. At first sight one took her for a spectre; at the second, for a statue.

Nevertheless, at intervals, her blue lips half opened to admit a breath, and trembled, but as dead and as mechanical as the leaves that the wind sweeps aside.

Nevertheless, from her dull eyes there escaped a look, an ineffable look, a profound, lugubrious, imperturbable look, incessantly fixed upon a corner of the cell which could not be seen from without; a gaze which seemed to fix all the sombre thoughts of that soul in distress upon some mysterious object.

Such was the creature who had received, from her habitation, the name of the "recluse"; and, from her garment, the name of "the sacked nun."

The three women, for Gervaise had rejoined Mahiette and Oudarde, gazed through the window. Their heads intercepted the feeble light in the cell, without the wretched being whom they thus deprived of it seeming to pay any attention to them. "Do not let us trouble her," said Oudarde, in a low voice, "she is in her ecstasy; she is praying."

Meanwhile, Mahiette was gazing with ever-increasing anxiety at that wan, withered, dishevelled head, and her eyes filled with tears. "This is very singular," she murmured.

She thrust her head through the bars, and succeeded in casting a glance at the corner where the gaze of the unhappy woman was immovably riveted.

When she withdrew her head from the window, her countenance was inundated with tears.

"What do you call that woman?" she asked Oudarde.

Oudarde replied, "We call her Sister Gudule."

"And I," returned Mahiette, "call her Paquette la Chantefleurie."

Then, laying her finger on her lips, she motioned to the astounded Oudarde to thrust her head through the window and look.

Oudarde looked and beheld, in the corner where the eyes of the recluse were fixed in that sombre ecstasy, a tiny shoe of pink satin, embroidered with a thousand fanciful designs in gold and silver.

Gervaise looked after Oudarde, and then the three women, gazing upon the unhappy mother, began to weep.

But neither their looks nor their tears disturbed the recluse. Her hands remained clasped; her lips mute; her eyes fixed; and that little shoe, thus gazed at, broke the heart of any one who knew her history.

The three women had not yet uttered a single word; they dared not speak, even in a low voice. This deep silence, this deep grief, this profound oblivion in which everything had disappeared except one thing, produced upon them the effect of the grand altar at Christmas or Easter. They remained silent, they meditated, they were ready to kneel. It seemed to them that they were ready to enter a church on the day of Tenebrae.

At length Gervaise, the most curious of the three, and consequently the least sensitive, tried to make the recluse speak:

"Sister! Sister Gudule!"

She repeated this call three times, raising her voice each time. The recluse did not move; not a word, not a glance, not a sigh, not a sign of life.

Oudarde, in her turn, in a sweeter, more caressing voice, "Sister!" said she, "Sister Sainte-Gudule!"

The same silence; the same immobility.

"A singular woman!" exclaimed Gervaise, "and one not to be moved by a catapult!"

"Perchance she is deaf," said Oudarde.

"Perhaps she is blind," added Gervaise.

"Dead, perchance," returned Mahiette.

It is certain that if the soul had not already quitted this inert, sluggish, lethargic body, it had at least retreated and concealed itself in depths whither the perceptions of the exterior organs no longer penetrated.

"Then we must leave the cake on the window," said Oudarde; "some scamp will take it. What shall we do to rouse her?"

Eustache, who, up to that moment had been diverted by a little carriage drawn by a large dog, which had just passed, suddenly perceived that his three conductresses were gazing at something through the window, and, curiosity taking possession of him in his turn, he climbed upon a stone post, elevated himself on tiptoe, and applied his fat, red face to the opening, shouting, "Mother, let me see too!"

At the sound of this clear, fresh, ringing child's voice, the recluse trembled; she turned her head with the sharp, abrupt movement of a steel spring, her long, fleshless hands cast aside the hair from her brow, and she fixed upon the child, bitter, astonished, desperate eyes. This glance was but a lightning flash.

"Oh my God!" she suddenly exclaimed, hiding her head on her knees, and it seemed as though her hoarse voice tore her chest as it passed from it, "do not show me those of others!"

"Good day, madam," said the child, gravely.

Nevertheless, this shock had, so to speak, awakened the recluse. A long shiver traversed her frame from head to foot; her teeth chattered; she half raised her head and said, pressing her elbows against her hips, and clasping her feet in her hands as though to warm them, "Oh, how cold it is!"

"Poor woman!" said Oudarde, with great compassion, "would you like a little fire?"

She shook her head in token of refusal.

"Well," resumed Oudarde, presenting her with a flagon; "here is some hippocras that will warm you—drink it."

Again she shook her head, looked at Oudarde fixedly and replied, "Water."

Oudarde persisted, "No, sister, that is no beverage for January. You must drink a little hippocras and eat this leavened cake of maize, which we have baked for you."

She refused the cake which Mahiette offered to her, and said, "Black bread."

"Come," said Gervaise, seized in her turn with an impulse of charity, and unfastening her woolen cloak, "here is a cloak which is a little warmer than yours."

She refused the cloak as she had refused the flagon and the cake, and replied, "A sack."

"But," resumed the good Oudarde, "you must have perceived to some extent, that yesterday was a festival."

"I do perceive it," said the recluse; "'tis two days now since I have had any water in my crock."

She added, after a silence, "'Tis a festival, I am forgotten. People do well. Why should the world think of me, when I do not think of it? Cold charcoal makes cold ashes."

And as though fatigued with having said so much, she dropped her head on her knees again. The simple and charitable Oudarde, who fancied that she understood from her last words that she was complaining of the cold, replied innocently, "Then you would like a little fire?"

"Fire!" said the sacked nun, with a strange accent; "and will you also make a little for the poor little one who has been beneath the sod for these fifteen years?"

Every limb was trembling, her voice quivered, her eyes flashed, she had raised herself upon her knees; suddenly she extended her thin, white hand toward the child, who was regarding her with a look of astonishment. "Take away that child!" she cried. "The Egyptian woman is about to pass by."

Then she fell face downward on the earth, and her forehead struck the stone, with the sound of one stone against another stone. The three women thought her dead. A moment later, however, she moved, and they beheld her drag herself, on her knees and elbows, to the corner where the little shoe was. Then they dared not look; they no longer saw her; but they heard a thousand kisses and a thousand sighs, mingled with heartrending cries, and dull blows like those of a head in contact with a wall. Then, after one of these blows, so violent that all three of them staggered, they heard no more.

"Can she have killed herself?" said Gervaise, venturing to pass her head through the air-hole. "Sister! Sister Gudule!"

"Sister Gudule!" repeated Oudarde.

"Ah! Good heavens! She no longer moves!" resumed Gervaise; "is she dead? Gudule! Gudule!"

Mahiette, choked to such a point that she could not speak, made an effort. "Wait," said she. Then bending toward the window, "Paquette!" she said, "Paquette le Chantefleurie!"

A child who innocently blows upon the badly ignited fuse of a bomb, and makes it explode in his face, is no more terrified than was

Mahiette at the effect of that name, abruptly launched into the cell of Sister Gudule.

The recluse trembled all over, rose erect on her bare feet, and leaped at the window with eyes so glaring that Mahiette and Oudarde, and the other woman and the child recoiled even to the parapet of the quay.

Meanwhile, the sinister face of the recluse appeared pressed to the grating of the air-hole. "Oh, oh!" she cried, with an appalling laugh; "'tis the Egyptian who is calling me!"

At that moment, a scene that was passing at the pillory caught her wild eye. Her brow contracted with horror, she stretched her two skeleton arms from her cell, and shrieked in a voice which resembled a death-rattle, "So 'tis thou once more, daughter of Egypt! 'Tis thou who callest me, stealer of children! Well! Be thou accursed! Accursed! Accursed! Accursed!"

CHAPTER 4

A Tear for a Drop of Water

THESE WORDS WERE, so to speak, the point of union of two scenes, which had, up to that time, been developed in parallel lines at the same moment, each on its particular theatre; one, that which the reader has just perused, in the Rat-Hole; the other, which he is about to read, on the ladder of the pillory. The first had for witnesses only the three women with whom the reader has just made acquaintance; the second had for spectators all the public that we have seen above, collecting on the Place de Grève, around the pillory and the gibbet.

That crowd which the four sergeants posted at nine o'clock in the morning at the four corners of the pillory had inspired with the hope of some sort of an execution, no doubt, not a hanging, but a whipping, a cropping of ears, something, in short, that crowd had increased so rapidly that the four policemen, too closely besieged, had had occasion to "press" it, as the expression then ran, more than once, by sound blows of their whips, and the haunches of their horses.

This populace, disciplined to waiting for public executions, did not manifest very much impatience. It amused itself with watching the pillory, a very simple sort of monument, composed of a cube of masonry about six feet high and hollow in the interior. A very steep staircase, of unhewn stone, which was called by distinction "the ladder," led to the upper platform, upon which was visible a horizontal wheel of solid oak. The victim was bound upon this wheel, on his knees, with his hands behind his back. A wooden shaft, which set in motion a capstan concealed in the interior of the little edifice, imparted a rotatory motion to the wheel, which always maintained its horizontal position, and in this manner presented the face of the condemned man to all quarters of the square in succession. This was what was called "turning" a criminal.

As the reader perceives, the pillory of the Grève was far from presenting all the recreations of the pillory of the Halles. Nothing architectural, nothing monumental. No roof to the iron cross, no octagonal lantern, no frail, slender columns spreading out on the edge of the roof into capitals of acanthus leaves and flowers, no waterspouts of chimeras and monsters, on carved woodwork, no fine sculpture, deeply sunk in the stone.

They were forced to content themselves with those four stretches of rubble work, backed with sandstone, and a wretched stone gibbet, meagre and bare, on one side.

The entertainment would have been but a poor one for lovers of Gothic architecture. It is true that nothing was ever less curious on the score of architecture than the worthy gapers of the Middle Ages, and that they cared very little for the beauty of a pillory.

The victim finally arrived, bound to the tail of a cart, and when he had been hoisted upon the platform, where he could be seen from all points of the Place, bound with cords and straps upon the wheel of the pillory, a prodigious hoot, mingled with laughter and acclamations, burst forth upon the Place. They had recognized Quasimodo.

It was he, in fact. The change was singular. Pilloried on the very place where, on the day before, he had been saluted, acclaimed, and proclaimed Pope and Prince of Fools, in the cortege of the Duke of Egypt, the King of Thunes, and the Emperor of Galilee! One thing is certain, and that is, that there was not a soul in the crowd, not even himself, though in turn triumphant and the sufferer, who set forth this combination clearly in his thought. Gringoire and his philosophy were missing at this spectacle.

Soon Michel Noiret, sworn trumpeter to the king, our lord, imposed silence on the louts, and proclaimed the sentence, in accordance with the order and command of monsieur the provost. Then he withdrew behind the cart, with his men in livery surcoats.

Quasimodo, impassible, did not wince. All resistance had been rendered impossible to him by what was then called, in the style of the criminal chancellery, "the vehemence and firmness of the bonds" which means that the thongs and chains probably cut into his flesh; moreover, it is a tradition of jail and wardens, which has not been lost, and which the handcuffs still preciously preserve among us, a civilized, gentle, humane people (the galleys and the guillotine in parentheses).

He had allowed himself to be led, pushed, carried, lifted, bound, and bound again. Nothing was to be seen upon his countenance but the astonishment of a savage or an idiot. He was known to be deaf; one might have pronounced him to be blind.

They placed him on his knees on the circular plank; he made no resistance. They removed his shirt and doublet as far as his girdle; he allowed them to have their way. They entangled him under a fresh system of thongs and buckles; he allowed them to bind and buckle him. Only from time to time he snorted noisily, like a calf whose head is hanging and bumping over the edge of a butcher's cart.

"The dolt," said Jehan Frollo of the Mill, to his friend Robin Poussepain (for the two students had followed the culprit, as was to have been expected), "he understands no more than a cockchafer shut up in a box!"

There was wild laughter among the crowd when they beheld Quasimodo's hump, his camel's breast, his callous and hairy shoulders laid bare. During this gayety, a man in the livery of the city, short of stature and robust of mien, mounted the platform and placed himself near the victim. His name speedily circulated among the spectators. It was Master Pierrat Torterue, official torturer to the Châtelet.

He began by depositing on an angle of the pillory a black hourglass, the upper lobe of which was filled with red sand, which it allowed to glide into the lower receptacle; then he removed his parti-colored surtout, and there became visible, suspended from his right hand, a thin and tapering whip of long, white, shining, knotted, plaited thongs, armed with metal nails. With his left hand, he negligently folded back his shirt around his right arm, to the very armpit.

In the meantime, Jehan Frollo, elevating his curly blonde head above the crowd (he had mounted upon the shoulders of Robin Poussepain for the purpose), shouted: "Come and look, gentle ladies and men! They are going to peremptorily flagellate Master Quasimodo, the bellringer of my brother, monsieur the archdeacon of Josas, a knave of oriental architecture, who has a back like a dome, and legs like twisted columns!"

And the crowd burst into a laugh, especially the boys and young girls.

At length the torturer stamped his foot. The wheel began to turn. Quasimodo wavered beneath his bonds. The amazement that was suddenly depicted upon his deformed face caused the bursts of laughter to redouble around him.

All at once, at the moment when the wheel in its revolution presented to Master Pierrat, the humped back of Quasimodo, Master Pierrat raised his arm; the fine thongs whistled sharply through the air, like a handful of adders, and fell with fury upon the wretch's shoulders.

Quasimodo leaped as though awakened with a start. He began to understand. He writhed in his bonds; a violent contraction of surprise and pain distorted the muscles of his face, but he uttered not a single sigh. He merely turned his head backward, to the right, then to the left, balancing it as a bull does who has been stung in the flanks by a gadfly.

A second blow followed the first, then a third, and another and another, and still others. The wheel did not cease to turn, nor the blows to rain down.

Soon the blood burst forth, and could be seen trickling in a thousand threads down the hunchback's black shoulders; and the slender thongs, in their rotatory motion which rent the air, sprinkled drops of it upon the crowd.

Quasimodo had resumed, to all appearance, his first imperturbability. He had at first tried, in a quiet way and without much outward movement, to break his bonds. His eye had been seen to light up, his muscles to stiffen, his members to concentrate their force, and the straps to stretch. The effort was powerful, prodigious, desperate; but the provost's seasoned bonds resisted. They cracked, and that was all. Quasimodo fell back exhausted. Amazement gave way, on his features, to a sentiment of profound and bitter discouragement. He closed his single eye, allowed his head to droop upon his breast, and feigned death.

From that moment forth, he stirred no more. Nothing could force a movement from him. Neither his blood, which did not cease to flow, nor the blows which redoubled in fury, nor the wrath of the torturer, who grew excited himself and intoxicated with the execution, nor the sound of the horrible thongs, more sharp and whistling than the claws of scorpions.

At length a bailiff from the Châtelet clad in black, mounted on a black horse, who had been stationed beside the ladder since the beginning of the execution, extended his ebony wand toward the hour-glass. The torturer stopped. The wheel stopped. Quasimodo's eye opened slowly.

The scourging was finished. Two lackeys of the official torturer bathed the bleeding shoulders of the patient, anointed them with some unguent which immediately closed all the wounds, and threw upon his back a sort of yellow vestment, in cut like a chasuble. In the meanwhile, Pierrat Torterue allowed the thongs, red and gorged with blood, to drip upon the pavement.

All was not over for Quasimodo. He had still to undergo that hour of pillory which Master Florian Barbedienne had so judiciously added to the sentence of Messire Robert d'Estouteville; all to the greater glory of the old physiological and psychological play upon words of Jean de Cumène, *Surdus absurdus*: a deaf man is absurd.

So the hour-glass was turned over once more, and they left the hunchback fastened to the plank, in order that justice might be accomplished to the very end.

The populace, especially in the Middle Ages, is in society what the child is in the family. As long as it remains in its state of primitive ignorance, of moral and intellectual minority, it can be said of it as of the child, 'Tis the pitiless age. We have already shown that Quasimodo was generally hated, for more than one good reason, it is true. There was hardly a spectator in that crowd who had not or who did not believe that he had reason to complain of the malevolent hunchback of Notre-Dame. The joy at seeing him appear thus in the pillory had been universal; and the harsh punishment which he had just suffered, and the pitiful condition in which it had left him, far from softening the populace had rendered its hatred more malicious by arming it with a touch of mirth.

Hence, the "public prosecution" satisfied, as the bigwigs of the law still express it in their jargon, the turn came of a thousand private vengeances. Here, as in the Grand Hall, the women rendered themselves particularly prominent. All cherished some rancor against him, some for his malice, others for his ugliness. The latter were the most furious.

"Oh! Mask of Antichrist!" said one.

"Rider on a broom handle!" cried another.

"What a fine tragic grimace," howled a third, "and who would make him Pope of the Fools if today were yesterday?"

"'Tis well," struck in an old woman. "This is the grimace of the pillory. When shall we have that of the gibbet?"

"When will you be coiffed with your big bell a hundred feet under ground, cursed bellringer?"

"But 'tis the devil who rings the Angelus!"

"Oh! The deaf man! The one-eyed creature! The hunchback! The monster!"

"A face to make a woman miscarry better than all the drugs and medicines!"

And the two scholars, Jehan du Moulin, and Robin Poussepain, sang at the top of their lungs, the ancient refrain—

> A rope for the gallows bird!
> A fagot for the ape.

A thousand other insults rained down upon him, and hoots and imprecations, and laughter, and now and then, stones.

Quasimodo was deaf but his sight was clear, and the public fury was no less energetically depicted on their visages than in their words. Moreover, the blows from the stones explained the bursts of laughter.

At first he held his ground. But little by little that patience that had borne up under the lash of the torturer, yielded and gave way before all these stings of insects. The bull of the Asturias who has been but little moved by the attacks of the picador grows irritated with the dogs and banderilleras.

He first cast around a slow glance of hatred upon the crowd. But bound as he was, his glance was powerless to drive away those flies that were stinging his wound. Then he moved in his bonds, and his furious exertions made the ancient wheel of the pillory shriek on its axle. All this only increased the derision and hooting.

Then the wretched man, unable to break his collar, like that of a chained wild beast, became tranquil once more; only at intervals a sigh of rage heaved the hollows of his chest. There was neither shame nor redness on his face. He was too far from the state of society, and too near the state of nature to know what shame was. Moreover, with such a degree of deformity, is infamy a thing that can be felt? But wrath, hatred, despair, slowly lowered over that hideous visage a cloud which grew ever more and more sombre, ever more and more charged with electricity, which burst forth in a thousand lightning flashes from the eye of the cyclops.

Nevertheless, that cloud cleared away for a moment, at the passage of a mule that traversed the crowd, bearing a priest. As far away as he could see that mule and that priest, the poor victim's visage grew gentler. The fury that had contracted it was followed by a strange smile full of ineffable sweetness, gentleness, and tenderness. In proportion as the priest approached, that smile became more clear, more distinct, more radiant. It was like the arrival of a Saviour, which the unhappy man was greeting. But as soon as the mule was near enough to the pillory to allow of its rider recognizing the victim, the priest dropped his eyes, beat a hasty retreat, spurred on rigorously, as though in haste to rid himself of humiliating appeals, and not at all desirous of being saluted and recognized by a poor fellow in such a predicament.

This priest was Archdeacon Dom Claude Frollo.

The cloud descended more blackly than ever upon Quasimodo's brow. The smile was still mingled with it for a time, but was bitter, discouraged, profoundly sad.

Time passed on. He had been there at least an hour and a half, lacerated, maltreated, mocked incessantly, and almost stoned.

All at once he moved again in his chains with redoubled despair, which made the whole framework that bore him tremble, and, breaking the silence which he had obstinately preserved hitherto, he cried in a hoarse and furious voice, which resembled a bark rather than a human cry, and which was drowned in the noise of the hoots—"Drink!"

This exclamation of distress, far from exciting compassion, only added amusement to the good Parisian populace who surrounded the ladder, and who, it must be confessed, taken in the mass and as a multitude, was then no less cruel and brutal than that horrible tribe of robbers among whom we have already conducted the reader, and which was simply the lower stratum of the populace. Not a voice was raised around the unhappy victim, except to jeer at his thirst. It is certain that at that moment he was more grotesque and repulsive than pitiable, with his face purple and dripping, his eye wild, his mouth foaming with rage and pain, and his tongue lolling half out. It must also be stated that if a charitable soul of a bourgeois or bourgeoise, in the rabble, had attempted to carry a glass of water to that wretched creature in torment, there reigned around the infamous steps of the pillory such a prejudice of shame and ignominy, that it would have sufficed to repulse the good Samaritan.

At the expiration of a few moments, Quasimodo cast a desperate glance upon the crowd, and repeated in a voice still more heartrending: "Drink!"

And all began to laugh.

"Drink this!" cried Robin Poussepain, throwing in his face a sponge that had been soaked in the gutter. "There, you deaf villain, I'm your debtor."

A woman hurled a stone at his head. "That will teach you to wake us up at night with your peal of a dammed soul."

"Hey, good, my son!" howled a cripple, making an effort to reach him with his crutch, "will you cast any more spells on us from the top of the towers of Notre-Dame?"

"Here's a drinking cup!" chimed in a man, flinging a broken jug at his breast. "'Twas you that made my wife, simply because she passed near you, give birth to a child with two heads!"

"And my cat bring forth a kitten with six paws!" yelped an old crone, launching a brick at him.

"Drink!" repeated Quasimodo panting, and for the third time.

At that moment he beheld the crowd give way. A young girl, fantastically dressed, emerged from the throng. She was accompanied by a little white goat with gilded horns, and carried a tambourine in her hand.

Quasimodo's eyes sparkled. It was the gypsy whom he had attempted to carry off on the preceding night, a misdeed for which he was dimly conscious that he was being punished at that very moment; which was not in the least the case, since he was being chastised only for the misfortune of being deaf, and of having been judged by a deaf man. He doubted not that she had come to wreak her vengeance also, and to deal her blow like the rest.

He saw her, in fact, mount the ladder rapidly. Wrath and spite suffocated him. He would have liked to make the pillory crumble into ruins, and if the lightning of his eye could have dealt death, the gypsy would have been reduced to powder before she reached the platform.

She approached, without uttering a syllable, the victim who writhed in a vain effort to escape her, and detaching a gourd from her girdle, she raised it gently to the parched lips of the miserable man.

Then, from that eye which had been, up to that moment, so dry and burning, a big tear was seen to fall, and roll slowly down that deformed visage so long contracted with despair. It was the first, in all probability, that the unfortunate man had ever shed.

Meanwhile, he had forgotten to drink. The gypsy made her little pout, from impatience, and pressed the spout to the tusked mouth of Quasimodo, with a smile.

He drank with deep draughts. His thirst was burning.

When he had finished, the wretch protruded his black lips, no doubt, with the object of kissing the beautiful hand that had just succoured him. But the young girl, who was, perhaps, somewhat distrustful, and who remembered the violent attempt of the night, withdrew her hand with the frightened gesture of a child who is afraid of being bitten by a beast.

Then the poor deaf man fixed on her a look full of reproach and inexpressible sadness.

It would have been a touching spectacle anywhere, this beautiful, fresh, pure, and charming girl, who was at the same time so weak, thus hastening to the relief of so much misery, deformity, and malevolence. On the pillory, the spectacle was sublime.

The very populace were captivated by it, and began to clap their hands, crying,—

"Noel! Noel!"

It was at that moment that the recluse caught sight, from the window of her bole, of the gypsy on the pillory, and hurled at her her sinister imprecation,—

"Accursed be thou, daughter of Egypt! Accursed! Accursed!"

CHAPTER 5

End of the Story of the Cake

LA ESMERALDA TURNED pale and descended from the pillory, staggering as she went. The voice of the recluse still pursued her, "Descend! Descend! Thief of Egypt, thou shalt ascend it once more!"

"The sacked nun is in one of her tantrums," muttered the populace; and that was the end of it. For that sort of woman was feared, which rendered them sacred. People did not then willingly attack one who prayed day and night.

The hour had arrived for removing Quasimodo. He was unbound, the crowd dispersed.

Near the Grand Pont, Mahiette, who was returning with her two companions, suddenly halted, "By the way, Eustache! What did you do with that cake?"

"Mother," said the child, "while you were talking with that lady in the hole, a big dog took a bite of my cake, and then I bit it also."

"What, sir, did you eat the whole of it?" she went on.

"Mother, it was the dog. I told him, but he would not listen to me. Then I bit into it, also."

"'Tis a terrible child!" said the mother, smiling and scolding at one and the same time. "Do you see, Oudarde? He already eats all the fruit from the cherry-tree in our orchard of Charlerange. So his grandfather says that be will be a captain. Just let me catch you at it again, Master Eustache. Come along, you greedy fellow!"

Book Seventh

Chapter 1

The Danger of Confiding One's Secret to a Goat

Many weeks had elapsed.

The first of March had arrived. The sun, which Dubartas, that classic ancestor of periphrase, had not yet dubbed the "Grand-duke of Candles," was none the less radiant and joyous on that account. It was one of those spring days that possesses so much sweetness and beauty, that all Paris turns out into the squares and promenades and celebrates them as though they were Sundays. In those days of brilliancy, warmth, and serenity, there is a certain hour above all others, when the façade of Notre-Dame should be admired. It is the moment when the sun, already declining toward the west, looks the cathedral almost full in the face. Its rays, growing more and more horizontal, withdraw slowly from the pavement of the square, and mount up the perpendicular façade, whose thousand bosses in high relief they cause to start out from the shadows, while the great central rose window flames like the eye of a cyclops, inflamed with the reflections of the forge.

This was the hour.

Opposite the lofty cathedral, reddened by the setting sun, on the stone balcony built above the porch of a rich Gothic house, which formed the angle of the square and the Rue du Parvis, several young girls were laughing and chatting with every sort of grace and mirth. From the length of the veil which fell from their pointed coif, twined with pearls, to their heels, from the fineness of the embroidered chemisette which covered their shoulders and allowed a glimpse, according to the pleasing custom of the time, of the swell of their fair virgin bosoms, from the opulence of their under-petticoats still more precious than their overdress (marvellous refinement), from the gauze, the silk, the velvet, with which all this was composed, and, above all,

249

from the whiteness of their hands, which certified to their leisure and idleness, it was easy to divine they were noble and wealthy heiresses. They were, in fact, Damoiselle Fleur-de-Lys de Gondelaurier and her companions, Diane de Christeuil, Amelotte de Montmichel, Colombe de Gaillefontaine, and the little de Champchevrier maiden; all damsels of good birth, assembled at that moment at the house of the dame widow de Gondelaurier, on account of Monseigneur de Beaujeu and Madame his wife, who were to come to Paris in the month of April, there to choose maids of honor for the Dauphiness Marguerite, who was to be received in Picardy from the hands of the Flemings. Now, all the squires for twenty leagues around were intriguing for this favor for their daughters, and a goodly number of the latter had been already brought or sent to Paris. These four maidens had been confided to the discreet and venerable charge of Madame Aloise de Gondelaurier, widow of a former commander of the king's cross-bowmen, who had retired with her only daughter to her house in the Place du Parvis, Notre-Dame, in Paris.

The balcony on which these young girls stood opened from a chamber richly tapestried in fawn-colored Flanders leather, stamped with golden foliage. The beams, which cut the ceiling in parallel lines, diverted the eye with a thousand eccentric painted and gilded carvings. Splendid enamels gleamed here and there on carved chests; a boar's head in faience crowned a magnificent dresser, whose two shelves announced that the mistress of the house was the wife or widow of a knight banneret. At the end of the room, by the side of a lofty chimney blazoned with arms from top to bottom, in a rich red velvet armchair, sat Dame de Gondelaurier, whose five and fifty years were written upon her garments no less distinctly than upon her face.

Beside her stood a young man of imposing mien, although partaking somewhat of vanity and bravado—one of those handsome fellows whom all women agree to admire, although grave men learned in physiognomy shrug their shoulders at them. This young man wore the garb of a captain of the king's unattached archers, which bears far too much resemblance to the costume of Jupiter, which the reader has already been enabled to admire in the first book of this history, for us to inflict upon him a second description.

The damoiselles were seated, a part in the chamber, a part in the balcony, some on square cushions of Utrecht velvet with golden corners, others on stools of oak carved in flowers and figures. Each of them held on her knee a section of a great needlework tapestry, on which they were working in company, while one end of it lay upon the rush mat that covered the floor.

They were chatting together in that whispering tone and with the half-stifled laughs peculiar to an assembly of young girls in whose midst there is a young man. The young man whose presence served to set in play all these feminine self-conceits, appeared to pay very little heed to the matter, and, while these pretty damsels were vying with one another to attract his attention, he seemed to be chiefly absorbed in polishing the buckle of his sword belt with his doeskin glove. From time to time, the old lady addressed him in a very low tone, and he replied as well as he was able, with a sort of awkward and constrained politeness.

From the smiles and significant gestures of Dame Aloise, from the glances which she threw toward her daughter, Fleur-de-Lys, as she spoke low to the captain, it was easy to see that there was here a question of some betrothal concluded, some marriage near at hand no doubt, between the young man and Fleur-de-Lys. From the embarrassed coldness of the officer, it was easy to see that on his side, at least, love had no longer any part in the matter. His whole air was expressive of constraint and weariness, which our lieutenants of the garrison would today translate admirably as, "What a beastly bore!"

The poor dame, very much infatuated with her daughter, like any other silly mother, did not perceive the officer's lack of enthusiasm, and strove in low tones to call his attention to the infinite grace with which Fleur-de-Lys used her needle or wound her skein.

"Come, little cousin," she said to him, plucking him by the sleeve, in order to speak in his ear, "Look at her, do! See her stoop."

"Yes, truly," replied the young man, and fell back into his glacial and absent-minded silence.

A moment later, he was obliged to bend down again, and Dame Aloise said to him, "Have you ever beheld a more gay and charming face than that of your betrothed? Can one be more white and blonde? Are not her hands perfect? And that neck—does it not assume all the curves of the swan in ravishing fashion? How I envy you at times! And how happy you are to be a man, naughty libertine that you are! Is not my Fleur-de-Lys adorably beautiful, and are you not desperately in love with her?"

"Of course," he replied, still thinking of something else.

"But do say something," said Madame Aloise, suddenly giving his shoulder a push; "you have grown very timid."

We can assure our readers that timidity was neither the captain's virtue nor his defect. But he made an effort to do what was demanded of him.

"Fair cousin," he said, approaching Fleur-de-Lys, "what is the subject of this tapestry work which you are fashioning?"

"Fair cousin," responded Fleur-de-Lys, in an offended tone, "I have already told you three times. 'Tis the grotto of Neptune."

It was evident that Fleur-de-Lys saw much more clearly than her mother through the captain's cold and absent-minded manner. He felt the necessity of making some conversation.

"And for whom is this Neptunerie destined?"

"For the Abbey of Saint-Antoine des Champs," answered Fleur-de-Lys, without raising her eyes.

The captain took up a corner of the tapestry.

"Who, my fair cousin, is this big gendarme, who is puffing out his cheeks to their full extent and blowing a trumpet?"

"'Tis Triton," she replied.

There was a rather pettish intonation in Fleur-de-Lys's laconic words. The young man understood that it was indispensable that he should whisper something in her ear, a commonplace, a gallant compliment, no matter what. Accordingly he bent down, but he could find nothing in his imagination more tender and personal than this, "Why does your mother always wear that surcoat with armorial designs, like our grandmothers of the time of Charles VII? Tell her, fair cousin, that 'tis no longer the fashion, and that the embroidery on her robe all emblazoned in that way gives her the air of a walking mantlepiece. In truth, people no longer sit thus on their banners, I assure you."

Fleur-de-Lys raised her beautiful eyes, full of reproach, "Is that all of which you can assure me?" she said, in a low voice.

In the meantime, Dame Aloise, delighted to see them thus bending toward each other and whispering, said as she toyed with the clasps of her prayer-book, "Touching picture of love!"

The captain, more and more embarrassed, fell back upon the subject of the tapestry, "'Tis, in sooth, a charming work!" he exclaimed.

Whereupon Colombe de Gaillefontaine, another beautiful blonde, with a white skin, dressed to the neck in blue damask, ventured a timid remark that she addressed to Fleur-de-Lys, in the hope that the handsome captain would reply to it, "My dear Gondelaurier, have you seen the tapestries of the Hôtel de la Roche-Guyon?"

"Is not that the hotel in which is enclosed the garden of the Lingère du Louvre?" asked Diane de Christeuil with a laugh; for she had handsome teeth, and consequently laughed on every occasion.

"And where there is that big, old tower of the ancient wall of Paris," added Amelotte de Montmichel, a pretty fresh and curly-headed brunette, who had a habit of sighing just as the other laughed, without knowing why.

"My dear Colombe," interpolated Dame Aloise, "do you not mean the hotel which belonged to Monsieur de Bacqueville, in the reign of King Charles VI? There are indeed many superb high warp tapestries there."

"Charles VI! Charles VI!" muttered the young captain, twirling his moustache. "Good heavens, what old things the good dame does remember!"

Madame de Gondelaurier continued, "Fine tapestries, in truth. A work so esteemed that it passes as unrivalled."

At that moment Bérangère de Champchevrier, a slender little maid of seven years, who was peering into the square through the trefoils of the balcony, exclaimed, "Oh look, fair Godmother Fleur-de-Lys, at that pretty dancer who is dancing on the pavement and playing the tambourine in the midst of the loutish bourgeois!"

The sonorous vibration of a tambourine was, in fact, audible. "Some gypsy from Bohemia," said Fleur-de-Lys, turning carelessly toward the square.

"Look, look!" exclaimed her lively companions; and they all ran to the edge of the balcony, while Fleur-de-Lys, rendered thoughtful by the coldness of her betrothed, followed them slowly, and the latter, relieved by this incident, which put an end to an embarrassing conversation, retreated to the farther end of the room, with the satisfied air of a soldier released from duty. Nevertheless, the fair Fleur-de-Lys's was a charming and noble service, and such it had formerly appeared to him; but the captain had gradually become blasé; the prospect of a speedy marriage cooled him more every day. Moreover, he was of a fickle disposition, and, must we say it, rather vulgar in taste. Although of very noble birth, he had contracted in his official harness more than one habit of the common trooper. The tavern and its accompaniments pleased him. He was only at his ease amid gross language, military gallantries, facile beauties, and successes yet more easy. He had, nevertheless, received from his family some education and some politeness of manner; but he had been thrown on the world too young, he had been in garrison at too early an age, and every day the polish of a gentleman became more and more effaced by the rough friction of his gendarme's cross-belt. While still continuing to visit her from time to time, from a remnant of common respect, he felt doubly embarrassed with Fleur-de-Lys; in the first place, because, in consequence of having scattered his love in all sorts of places, he had reserved very little for her; in the next place, because, amid so many stiff, formal, and decent ladies, he was in constant fear lest his mouth, habituated to oaths, should suddenly take the bit in its teeth, and break out into the language of the tavern. The effect can be imagined!

Moreover, all this was mingled in him, with great pretentions to elegance, toilet, and a fine appearance. Let the reader reconcile these things as best he can. I am simply the historian.

He had remained, therefore, for several minutes, leaning in silence against the carved jamb of the chimney, and thinking or not thinking, when Fleur-de-Lys suddenly turned and addressed him. After all, the poor young girl was pouting against the dictates of her heart.

"Fair cousin, did you not speak to us of a little Bohemian whom you saved a couple of months ago, while making the patrol with the watch at night, from the hands of a dozen robbers?"

"I believe so, fair cousin," said the captain.

"Well," she resumed, "perchance 'tis that same gypsy girl who is dancing yonder, on the church square. Come and see if you recognize her, fair Cousin Phoebus."

A secret desire for reconciliation was apparent in this gentle invitation that she gave him to approach her, and in the care which she took to call him by name. Captain Phoebus de Châteaupers (for it is he whom the reader has had before his eyes since the beginning of this chapter) slowly approached the balcony. "Stay," said Fleur-de-Lys, laying her hand tenderly on Phoebus's arm; "look at that little girl yonder, dancing in that circle. Is she your Bohemian?"

Phoebus looked, and said, "Yes, I recognize her by her goat."

"Oh, in fact, what a pretty little goat!" said Amelotte, clasping her hands in admiration.

"Are his horns of real gold?" inquired Bérangère.

Without moving from her armchair, Dame Aloise interposed, "Is she not one of those gypsy girls who arrived last year by the Gibard gate?"

"Madame my mother," said Fleur-de-Lys gently, "that gate is now called the Porte d'Enfer."

Mademoiselle de Gondelaurier knew how her mother's antiquated mode of speech shocked the captain. In fact, he began to sneer, and muttered between his teeth: "Porte Gibard! Porte Gibard! 'Tis enough to make King Charles VI pass by."

"Godmother!" exclaimed Bérangère, whose eyes, incessantly in motion, had suddenly been raised to the summit of the towers of Notre-Dame, "who is that black man up yonder?"

All the young girls raised their eyes. A man was, in truth, leaning on the balustrade that surmounted the northern tower, looking on the Grève. He was a priest. His costume could be plainly discerned, and his face resting on both his hands. But he stirred no more than if he had been a statue. His eyes, intently fixed, gazed into the Place.

It was something like the immobility of a bird of prey, who has just discovered a nest of sparrows, and is gazing at it.

"'Tis monsieur the archdeacon of Josas," said Fleur-de-Lys.

"You have good eyes if you can recognize him from here," said the Gaillefontaine.

"How he is staring at the little dancer!" went on Diane de Christeuil.

"Let the gypsy beware!" said Fleur-de-Lys, "for he loves not Egypt."

"'Tis a great shame for that man to look upon her thus," added Amelotte de Montmichel, "for she dances delightfully."

"Fair cousin Phoebus," said Fleur-de-Lys suddenly, "Since you know this little gypsy, make her a sign to come up here. It will amuse us."

"Oh, yes!" exclaimed all the young girls, clapping their hands.

"Why, 'tis not worth while!" replied Phoebus. "She has forgotten me, no doubt, and I know not so much as her name. Nevertheless, as you wish it, young ladies, I will make the trial." And leaning over the balustrade of the balcony, he began to shout, "Little one!"

The dancer was not beating her tambourine at the moment. She turned her head toward the point whence this call proceeded, her brilliant eyes rested on Phoebus, and she stopped short.

"Little one!" repeated the captain; and he beckoned her to approach.

The young girl looked at him again, then she blushed as though a flame had mounted into her cheeks, and, taking her tambourine under her arm, she made her way through the astonished spectators toward the door of the house where Phoebus was calling her, with slow, tottering steps, and with the troubled look of a bird which is yielding to the fascination of a serpent.

A moment later, the tapestry portière was raised, and the gypsy appeared on the threshold of the chamber, blushing, confused, breathless, her large eyes drooping, and not daring to advance another step.

Bérangère clapped her hands.

Meanwhile, the dancer remained motionless upon the threshold. Her appearance had produced a singular effect upon these young girls. It is certain that a vague and indistinct desire to please the handsome officer animated them all, that his splendid uniform was the target of all their coquetries, and that from the moment he presented himself, there existed among them a secret, suppressed rivalry, which they hardly acknowledged even to themselves, but which broke forth, none the less, every instant, in their gestures and remarks. Nevertheless, as they were all very nearly equal in beauty, they contended with equal arms, and each could hope for the victory. The arrival of the gypsy suddenly destroyed this equilibrium. Her beauty was so rare, that, at the moment when she appeared at the entrance of the apartment, it seemed as though she diffused a sort of light that was peculiar to herself. In that narrow chamber, surrounded by that sombre frame of hangings and woodwork, she was incomparably more beautiful and more radiant than on the public square. She was like a torch that has suddenly been brought from broad daylight into the dark. The noble damsels were dazzled by her in spite of themselves. Each one felt herself, in some sort, wounded in her beauty. Hence, their battle front (may we be allowed the expression?) was immediately altered, although they exchanged not a single word. But they understood each other perfectly. Women's instincts comprehend and respond to each other more quickly than the intelligences of men. An enemy had just arrived; all felt it—all rallied together. One drop of wine is sufficient to tinge a glass of water red; to diffuse a certain degree of ill temper throughout a whole assembly of pretty women, the arrival of a prettier woman suffices, especially when there is but one man present.

Hence the welcome accorded to the gypsy was marvellously glacial. They surveyed her from head to foot, then exchanged glances, and all was said; they understood each other. Meanwhile, the young girl was waiting to be spoken to, in such emotion that she dared not raise her eyelids.

The captain was the first to break the silence. "Upon my word," said he, in his tone of intrepid fatuity, "here is a charming creature! What think you of her, fair cousin?"

This remark, which a more delicate admirer would have uttered in a lower tone, at least was not of a nature to dissipate the feminine jealousies that were on the alert before the gypsy.

Fleur-de-Lys replied to the captain with a bland affectation of disdain, "Not bad."

The others whispered.

At length, Madame Aloise, who was not the less jealous because she was so for her daughter, addressed the dancer, "Approach, little one."

"Approach, little one!" repeated, with comical dignity, little Bérangère, who would have reached about as high as her hips.

The gypsy advanced toward the noble dame.

"Fair child," said Phoebus, with emphasis, taking several steps toward her, "I do not know whether I have the supreme honor of being recognized by you."

She interrupted him, with a smile and a look full of infinite sweetness, "Oh, yes!" said she.

"She has a good memory," remarked Fleur-de-Lys.

"Come, now," resumed Phoebus, "you escaped nimbly the other evening. Did I frighten you!"

"Oh, no!" said the gypsy.

There was in the intonation of that "Oh, no!" uttered after that "Oh, yes!," an ineffable something which wounded Fleur-de-Lys.

"You left me in your stead, my beauty," pursued the captain, whose tongue was unloosed when speaking to a girl out of the street, "a crabbed knave, one-eyed and hunchbacked, the bishop's bellringer, I believe. I have been told that by birth he is the bastard of an archdeacon and a devil. He has a pleasant name: he is called *Quatre-Temps* [Ember Days], *Paques-Fleuries* [Palm Sunday], *Mardi-Gras* [Shrove Tuesday], I know not what! The name of some festival when the bells are pealed! So he took the liberty of carrying you off, as though you were made for beadles! 'Tis too much. What the devil did that screech-owl want with you? Hey, tell me!"

"I do not know," she replied.

"The inconceivable impudence! A bellringer carrying off a wench, like a vicomte, a lout poaching on the game of gentlemen! That is a rare piece of assurance. However, he paid dearly for it. Master Pierrat

Torterue is the harshest groom that ever curried a knave; and I can tell you, if it will be agreeable to you, that your bellringer's hide got a thorough dressing at his hands."

"Poor man!" said the gypsy, in whom these words revived the memory of the pillory.

The captain burst out laughing.

"Corne-de-boeuf! Here's pity as well placed as a feather in a pig's tail! May I have as big a belly as a pope, if—"

He stopped short. "Pardon me, ladies; I believe that I was on the point of saying something foolish."

"Fie, sir" said la Gaillefontaine.

"He talks to that creature in her own tongue!" added Fleur-de-Lys, in a low tone, her irritation increasing every moment. This irritation was not diminished when she beheld the captain, enchanted with the gypsy, and, most of all, with himself, execute a pirouette on his heel, repeating with coarse, naïve, and soldierly gallantry, "A handsome wench, upon my soul!"

"Rather savagely dressed," said Diane de Christeuil, laughing to show her fine teeth.

This remark was a flash of light to the others. Not being able to impugn her beauty, they attacked her costume.

"That is true," said la Montmichel; "what makes you run about the streets thus, without guimpe or ruff?"

"That petticoat is so short that it makes one tremble," added la Gaillefontaine.

"My dear," continued Fleur-de-Lys, with decided sharpness, "You will get yourself taken up by the sumptuary police for your gilded girdle."

"Little one, little one;" resumed la Christeuil, with an implacable smile, "if you were to put respectable sleeves upon your arms they would get less sunburned."

It was, in truth, a spectacle worthy of a more intelligent spectator than Phoebus, to see how these beautiful maidens, with their envenomed and angry tongues, wound, serpent-like, and glided and writhed around the street dancer. They were cruel and graceful; they searched and rummaged maliciously in her poor and silly toilet of spangles and tinsel. There was no end to their laughter, irony, and humiliation. Sarcasms rained down upon the gypsy, and haughty condescension and malevolent looks. One would have thought they were young Roman dames thrusting golden pins into the breast of a beautiful slave. One would have pronounced them elegant grayhounds, circling, with inflated nostrils, round a poor woodland fawn, whom the glance of their master forbade them to devour.

After all, what was a miserable dancer on the public squares in the presence of these high-born maidens? They seemed to take no heed of her presence, and talked of her aloud, to her face, as of something unclean, abject, and yet, at the same time, passably pretty.

The gypsy was not insensible to these pin-pricks. From time to time a flush of shame, a flash of anger inflamed her eyes or her cheeks; with disdain she made that little grimace with which the reader is already familiar, but she remained motionless; she fixed on Phoebus a sad, sweet, resigned look. There was also happiness and tenderness in that gaze. One would have said that she endured for fear of being expelled.

Phoebus laughed, and took the gypsy's part with a mixture of impertinence and pity.

"Let them talk, little one!" he repeated, jingling his golden spurs. "No doubt your toilet is a little extravagant and wild, but what difference does that make with such a charming damsel as yourself?"

"Good gracious!" exclaimed the blonde Gaillefontaine, drawing up her swan-like throat, with a bitter smile. "I see that messieurs the archers of the king's police easily take fire at the handsome eyes of gypsies!"

"Why not?" said Phoebus.

At this reply uttered carelessly by the captain, like a stray stone, whose fall one does not even watch, Colombe began to laugh, as well as Diane, Amelotte, and Fleur-de-Lys, into whose eyes at the same time a tear started.

The gypsy, who had dropped her eyes on the floor at the words of Colombe de Gaillefontaine, raised them beaming with joy and pride and fixed them once more on Phoebus. She was very beautiful at that moment.

The old dame, who was watching this scene, felt offended, without understanding why.

"Holy Virgin!" she suddenly exclaimed, "what is it moving about my legs? Ah, the villanous beast!"

It was the goat, who had just arrived, in search of his mistress, and who, in dashing toward the latter, had begun by entangling his horns in the pile of stuffs that the noble dame's garments heaped up on her feet when she was seated.

This created a diversion. The gypsy disentangled his horns without uttering a word.

"Oh, here's the little goat with golden hoofs!" exclaimed Bérangère, dancing with joy.

The gypsy crouched down on her knees and leaned her cheek against the fondling head of the goat. One would have said that she was asking pardon for having quitted it thus.

Meanwhile, Diane had bent down to Colombe's ear.

"Ah, good heavens! Why did not I think of that sooner? 'Tis the gypsy with the goat. They say she is a sorceress, and that her goat executes very miraculous tricks."

"Well!" said Colombe, "the goat must now amuse us in its turn, and perform a miracle for us."

Diane and Colombe eagerly addressed the gypsy.

"Little one, make your goat perform a miracle."

"I do not know what you mean," replied the dancer.

"A miracle, a piece of magic, a bit of sorcery, in short."

"I do not understand." And she fell to caressing the pretty animal, repeating, "Djali! Djali!"

At that moment Fleur-de-Lys noticed a little bag of embroidered leather suspended from the neck of the goat, "What is that?" she asked of the gypsy.

The gypsy raised her large eyes upon her and replied gravely, "That is my secret."

"I should really like to know what your secret is," thought Fleur-de-Lys.

Meanwhile, the good dame had risen angrily, "Come now, gypsy, if neither you nor your goat can dance for us, what are you doing here?"

The gypsy walked slowly toward the door, without making any reply. But the nearer she approached it, the more her pace slackened. An irresistible magnet seemed to hold her. Suddenly she turned her eyes, wet with tears, toward Phoebus, and halted.

"True God!" exclaimed the captain, "that's not the way to depart. Come back and dance something for us. By the way, my sweet love, what is your name?"

"La Esmeralda," said the dancer, never taking her eyes from him.

At this strange name, a burst of wild laughter broke from the young girls.

"Here's a terrible name for a young lady," said Diane.

"You see well enough," retorted Amelotte, "that she is an enchantress."

"My dear," exclaimed Dame Aloise solemnly, "your parents did not commit the sin of giving you that name at the baptismal font."

In the meantime, several minutes previously, Bérangère had coaxed the goat into a corner of the room with a marzipan cake, without any one having noticed her. In an instant they had become good friends. The curious child had detached the bag from the goat's neck, had opened it, and had emptied out its contents on the rush matting; it was an alphabet, each letter of which was separately inscribed on a tiny block of boxwood. Hardly had these playthings been spread out on the matting, when the child, with surprise, beheld the goat (one of whose "miracles" this was no doubt), draw out certain letters with its golden hoof, and arrange them, with gentle pushes, in a certain order. In a moment they constituted a word, which the goat seemed to have been trained to write, so little hesitation did it show in forming it, and Bérangère suddenly exclaimed, clasping her hands in admiration, "Godmother Fleur-de-Lys, see what the goat has just done!"

Fleur-de-Lys ran up and trembled. The letters arranged upon the floor formed this word:

PHOEBUS

"Did the goat write that?" she inquired in a changed voice.

"Yes, godmother," replied Bérangère.

It was impossible to doubt it; the child did not know how to write.

"This is the secret!" thought Fleur-de-Lys.

Meanwhile, at the child's exclamation, all had hastened up, the mother, the young girls, the gypsy, and the officer.

The gypsy beheld the piece of folly that the goat had committed. She turned red, then pale, and began to tremble like a culprit before the captain, who gazed at her with a smile of satisfaction and amazement.

"Phoebus!" whispered the young girls, stupefied: "'tis the captain's name!"

"You have a marvellous memory!" said Fleur-de-Lys, to the petrified gypsy. Then, bursting into sobs: "Oh!" she stammered mournfully, hiding her face in both her beautiful hands, "she is a magician!" And she heard another and a still more bitter voice at the bottom of her heart, saying, "She is a rival!"

She fell fainting.

"My daughter, my daughter!" cried the terrified mother. "Begone, you gypsy of hell!"

In a twinkling, la Esmeralda gathered up the unlucky letters, made a sign to Djali, and went out through one door, while Fleur-de-Lys was being carried out through the other.

Captain Phoebus, on being left alone, hesitated for a moment between the two doors, then he followed the gypsy.

Chapter 2

A Priest and a Philosopher Are Two Different Things

THE PRIEST WHOM the young girls had observed at the top of the North tower, leaning over the Place and so attentive to the dance of the gypsy, was, in fact, Archdeacon Claude Frollo.

Our readers have not forgotten the mysterious cell that the archdeacon had reserved for himself in that tower. (I do not know, by the way, whether it be not the same, the interior of which can be seen today through a little square window, opening to the east at the height of a man above the platform from which the towers spring; a bare and dilapidated den, whose badly plastered walls are ornamented here and there, at the present day, with some wretched yellow engravings representing the façades of cathedrals. I presume that this hole is jointly inhabited by bats and spiders, and that, consequently, it wages a double war of extermination on the flies.)

Every day, an hour before sunset, the archdeacon ascended the staircase to the tower, and shut himself up in this cell, where he sometimes passed whole nights. That day, at the moment when, standing before the low door of his retreat, he was fitting into the lock the complicated little key which he always carried about him in the purse suspended to his side, a sound of tambourine and castanets had reached his ear. These sounds came from the Place du Parvis. The cell, as we have already said, had only one window opening upon the rear of the church. Claude Frollo had hastily withdrawn the key, and an instant later, he was on the top of the tower, in the gloomy and pensive attitude in which the maidens had seen him.

There he stood, grave, motionless, absorbed in one look and one thought. All Paris lay at his feet, with the thousand spires of its edifices and its circular horizon of gentle hills—with its river winding under its bridges, and its people moving to and fro through its streets, with the clouds of its smoke, with the mountainous chain of its roofs which presses Notre-Dame in its doubled folds; but out of all the city, the archdeacon gazed at one corner only of the pavement, the Place du Parvis; in all that throng at but one figure, the gypsy.

It would have been difficult to say what was the nature of this look, and whence proceeded the flame that flashed from it. It was a fixed gaze, which was, nevertheless, full of trouble and tumult. And, from the profound immobility of his whole body, barely agitated at intervals by an involuntary shiver, as a tree is moved by the wind; from the stiffness of his elbows, more marble than the balustrade on which they leaned; or the sight of the petrified smile which contracted his face, one would have said that nothing living was left about Claude Frollo except his eyes.

The gypsy was dancing; she was twirling her tambourine on the tip of her finger, and tossing it into the air as she danced Provençal sarabands; agile, light, joyous, and unconscious of the formidable gaze that descended perpendicularly upon her head.

The crowd was swarming around her; from time to time, a man accoutred in red and yellow made them form into a circle, and then returned, seated himself on a chair a few paces from the dancer, and took the goat's head on his knees. This man seemed to be the gypsy's companion. Claude Frollo could not distinguish his features from his elevated post.

From the moment when the archdeacon caught sight of this stranger, his attention seemed divided between him and the dancer, and his face became more and more gloomy. All at once he rose upright, and a quiver ran through his whole body: "Who is that man?" he muttered between his teeth: "I have always seen her alone before!"

Then he plunged down beneath the tortuous vault of the spiral staircase, and once more descended. As he passed the door of the bell chamber, which was ajar, be saw something that struck him; he beheld Quasimodo, who, leaning through an opening of one of those slate penthouses that resemble enormous blinds, appeared also to be gazing at the Place. He was engaged in so profound a contemplation, that he did not notice the passage of his adopted father. His savage eye had a singular expression; it was a charmed, tender look. "This is strange!" murmured Claude. "Is it the gypsy at whom he is thus gazing?" He continued his descent. At the end of a few minutes, the anxious archdeacon entered upon the Place from the door at the base of the tower.

"What has become of the gypsy girl?" he said, mingling with the group of spectators that the sound of the tambourine had collected.

"I know not," replied one of his neighbors, "I think that she has gone to make some of her fandangoes in the house opposite, whither they have called her."

In the place of the gypsy, on the carpet, whose arabesques had seemed to vanish but a moment previously by the capricious figures of her dance, the archdeacon no longer beheld any one but the red and yellow man, who, in order to earn a few testers in his turn, was walking round the circle, with his elbows on his hips, his head thrown back, his face red, his neck outstretched, with a chair between his teeth. To the chair he had fastened a cat, which a neighbor had lent, and which was spitting in great affright.

"Notre-Dame!" exclaimed the archdeacon, at the moment when the juggler, perspiring heavily, passed in front of him with his pyramid of chair and his cat, "What is Master Pierre Gringoire doing here?"

The harsh voice of the archdeacon threw the poor fellow into such a commotion that he lost his equilibrium, together with his whole edifice, and the chair and the cat tumbled pell-mell upon the heads of the spectators, in the midst of inextinguishable hootings.

It is probable that Master Pierre Gringoire (for it was indeed he) would have had a sorry account to settle with the neighbor who owned the cat, and all the bruised and scratched faces which surrounded him, if he had not hastened to profit by the tumult to take refuge in the church, whither Claude Frollo had made him a sign to follow him.

The cathedral was already dark and deserted; the side-aisles were full of shadows, and the lamps of the chapels began to shine out like stars, so black had the vaulted ceiling become. Only the great rose window of the façade, whose thousand colors were steeped in a ray of horizontal sunlight, glittered in the gloom like a mass of diamonds, and threw its dazzling reflection to the other end of the nave.

When they had advanced a few paces, Dom Claude placed his back against a pillar, and gazed intently at Gringoire. The gaze was not the one which Gringoire feared, ashamed as he was of having been caught by a grave and learned person in the costume of a buffoon. There was nothing mocking or ironical in the priest's glance, it was serious, tranquil, piercing. The archdeacon was the first to break the silence.

"Come now, Master Pierre. You are to explain many things to me. And first of all, how comes it that you have not been seen for two months, and that now one finds you in the public squares, in a fine equipment in truth! Motley red and yellow, like a Caudebec apple?"

"Messire," said Gringoire, piteously, "it is, in fact, an amazing accoutrement. You see me no more comfortable in it than a cat coiffed with a calabash. 'Tis very ill done, I am conscious, to expose messieurs the sergeants of the watch to the liability of cudgelling beneath this cassock the humerus of a Pythagorean philosopher. But what would you have, my reverend master? 'Tis the fault of my ancient jerkin, which abandoned me in cowardly wise, at the beginning of the winter, under the pretext that it was falling into tatters, and that it required repose in the basket of a rag-picker. What is one to do? Civilization has not yet arrived at the point where one can go stark naked, as ancient Diogenes wished. Add that a very cold wind was blowing, and 'tis not in the month of January that one can successfully attempt to make humanity take this new step. This garment presented itself, I took it, and I left my ancient black smock, which, for a hermetic like myself, was far from being hermetically closed. Behold me then, in the garments of a stage-player, like Saint Genest. What would you have? 'Tis an eclipse. Apollo himself tended the flocks of Admetus."

"'Tis a fine profession that you are engaged in!" replied the archdeacon.

"I agree, my master, that 'tis better to philosophize and poetize, to blow the flame in the furnace, or to receive it from carry cats on a shield. So, when you addressed me, I was as foolish as an ass before a turnspit. But what would you have, messire? One must eat every day, and the finest Alexandrine verses are not worth a bit of Brie cheese. Now, I made for Madame Marguerite of Flanders, that famous epithalamium, as you know, and the city will not pay me, under the pretext that it was not excellent; as though one could give a tragedy of Sophocles for four crowns! Hence, I was on the point of dying with hunger. Happily, I found that I was rather strong in the jaw; so I said to this jaw, perform some feats of strength and of equilibrium: nourish thyself. *Ale te ipsam.* A pack of beggars who have become my good friends, have taught me twenty sorts of herculean feats, and now I give to my teeth every evening the bread that they have earned during the day by the sweat of my brow. After all, concede, I grant that it is a sad employment for my intellectual faculties, and that man is not made to pass his life in beating the tambourine and biting chairs. But, reverend master, it is not sufficient to pass one's life, one must earn the means for life."

Dom Claude listened in silence. All at once his deep-set eye assumed so sagacious and penetrating an expression, that Gringoire felt himself, so to speak, searched to the bottom of the soul by that glance.

"Very good, Master Pierre; but how comes it that you are now in company with that gypsy dancer?"

"In faith!" said Gringoire, "'tis because she is my wife and I am her husband."

The priest's gloomy eyes flashed into flame.

"Have you done that, you wretch!" he cried, seizing Gringoire's arm with fury; "have you been so abandoned by God as to raise your hand against that girl?"

"On my chance of paradise, monseigneur," replied Gringoire, trembling in every limb, "I swear to you that I have never touched her, if that is what disturbs you."

"Then why do you talk of husband and wife?" said the priest. Gringoire made haste to relate to him as succinctly as possible, all that the reader already knows, his adventure in the Court of Miracles and the broken-crock marriage. It appeared, moreover, that this marriage had led to no results whatever, and that each evening the gypsy girl cheated him of his nuptial right as on the first day. "'Tis a mortification," he said in conclusion, "but that is because I have had the misfortune to wed a virgin."

"What do you mean?" demanded the archdeacon, who had been gradually appeased by this recital.

"'Tis very difficult to explain," replied the poet. "It is a superstition. My wife is, according to what an old thief, who is called among us the Duke of Egypt, has told me, a foundling or a lost child, which is the same thing. She wears on her neck an amulet which, it is affirmed, will cause her to meet her parents some day, but which will lose its virtue if the young girl loses hers. Hence it follows that both of us remain very virtuous."

"So," resumed Claude, whose brow cleared more and more, "you believe, Master Pierre, that this creature has not been approached by any man?"

"What would you have a man do, Dom Claude, as against a superstition? She has got that in her head. I assuredly esteem as a rarity this nunlike prudery that is preserved untamed amid those Bohemian girls who are so easily brought into subjection. But she has three things to protect her: the Duke of Egypt, who has taken her under his safeguard, reckoning, perchance, on selling her to some gay abbé; all his tribe, who hold her in singular veneration, like a Notre-Dame; and a certain tiny poignard, which the buxom dame always wears about her, in some nook, in spite of the ordinances of the provost, and which one causes to fly out into her hands by squeezing her waist. 'Tis a proud wasp, I can tell you!"

The archdeacon pressed Gringoire with questions.

La Esmeralda, in the judgment of Gringoire, was an inoffensive and charming creature, pretty, with the exception of a pout which was peculiar to her; a naïve and passionate damsel, ignorant of everything and enthusiastic about everything; not yet aware of the difference between a man and a woman, even in her dreams; made like that; wild especially over dancing, noise, the open air; a sort of woman bee, with invisible wings on her feet, and living in a whirlwind. She owed this nature to the wandering life that she had always led. Gringoire had succeeded in learning that, while a mere child, she had traversed Spain and Catalonia, even to Sicily; he believed that she had even been taken by the caravan of Zingari, of which she formed a part, to the kingdom of Algiers, a country situated in Achaia, which country adjoins, on one side Albania and Greece; on the other, the Sicilian Sea, which is the road to Constantinople. The Bohemians, said Gringoire, were vassals of the King of Algiers, in his quality of chief of the White Moors. One thing is certain, that la Esmeralda had come to France while still very young, by way of Hungary. From all these countries the young girl had brought back fragments of queer jargons, songs, and strange ideas, which made her language as motley as her costume, half Parisian, half African. However, the people of the quarters that she frequented loved her for her gayety, her daintiness, her lively manners, her dances, and her songs. She believed herself to be hated, in all the city, by but two persons, of whom she often spoke in terror: the sacked nun of the Tour-Roland, a villanous recluse who cherished some secret grudge against these gypsies, and who cursed the poor dancer every time that the latter passed before her window; and a priest, who never met her without casting at her looks and words which frightened her.

The mention of this last circumstance disturbed the archdeacon greatly, though Gringoire paid no attention to his perturbation; to such an extent had two months sufficed to cause the heedless poet to forget the singular details of the evening on which he had met the gypsy, and the presence of the archdeacon in it all. Otherwise, the little dancer feared nothing; she did not tell fortunes, which protected her against those trials for magic that were so frequently instituted against gypsy women. And then, Gringoire held the position of her brother, if not of her husband. After all, the philosopher endured this sort of platonic marriage very patiently. It meant a shelter and bread at least. Every morning, he set out from the lair of the thieves, generally with the gypsy; he helped her make her collections of *targes* and *petits-blancs* in the squares; each evening he returned to the same roof with her, allowed her to bolt herself into her little chamber, and slept the sleep of the just. A very sweet existence, taking it all in all, he said, and well adapted to revery. And then, on his soul and conscience, the philosopher was not very sure that he was madly in love with the gypsy. He loved her goat almost as dearly. It was a charming animal, gentle, intelligent, clever; a learned goat. Nothing was more common in the Middle Ages than these learned animals, which amazed people greatly, and often led their instructors to the stake. But the witchcraft of the goat with the golden hoofs was a very innocent species of magic. Gringoire explained them to the archdeacon, whom these details seemed to interest deeply. In the majority of cases, it was sufficient to present the tambourine to the goat in such or such a manner, in order to obtain from him the trick desired. He had been trained to this by the gypsy, who possessed, in these delicate arts, so rare a talent that two months had sufficed to teach the goat to write, with movable letters, the word "Phoebus."

"'Phoebus!'" said the priest; "why 'Phoebus'?"

"I know not," replied Gringoire. "Perhaps it is a word that she believes to be endowed with some magic and secret virtue. She often repeats it in a low tone when she thinks that she is alone."

"Are you sure," persisted Claude, with his penetrating glance, "that it is only a word and not a name?"

"The name of whom?" said the poet.

"How should I know?" said the priest.

"This is what I imagine, messire. These Bohemians are something like Guebrs, and adore the sun. Hence, Phoebus."

"That does not seem so clear to me as to you, Master Pierre."

"After all, that does not concern me. Let her mumble her Phoebus at her pleasure. One thing is certain, that Djali loves me almost as much as he does her."

"Who is Djali?"

"The goat."

The archdeacon dropped his chin into his hand, and appeared to reflect for a moment. All at once he turned abruptly to Gringoire once more.

"And do you swear to me that you have not touched her?"

"Whom?" said Gringoire; "the goat?"

"No, that woman."

"My wife? I swear to you that I have not."

"You are often alone with her?"

"A good hour every evening."

Claude frowned.

"Oh, oh! *Solus cum sola non cogitabuntur orare Pater Noster.*"

"Upon my soul, I could say the *Pater*, and the *Ave Maria*, and the *Credo in Deum patrem omnipotentem* without her paying any more attention to me than a chicken to a church."

"Swear to me, by the body of your mother," repeated the archdeacon violently, "that you have not touched that creature with even the tip of your finger."

"I will also swear it by the head of my father, for the two things have more affinity between them. But, my reverend master, permit me a question in my turn."

"Speak, sir."

"What concern is it of yours?"

The archdeacon's pale face became as crimson as the cheek of a young girl. He remained for a moment without answering; then, with visible embarrassment, "Listen, Master Pierre Gringoire. You are not yet damned, so far as I know. I take an interest in you, and wish you well. Now the least contact with that Egyptian of the demon would make you the vassal of Satan. You know that 'tis always the body which ruins the soul. Woe to you if you approach that woman! That is all."

"I tried once," said Gringoire, scratching his ear; "it was the first day: but I got stung."

"You were so audacious, Master Pierre?" and the priest's brow clouded over again.

"On another occasion," continued the poet, with a smile, "I peeped through the keyhole, before going to bed, and I beheld the most delicious dame in her shift that ever made a bed creak under her bare foot."

"Go to the devil!" cried the priest, with a terrible look; and, giving the amazed Gringoire a push on the shoulders, he plunged, with long strides, under the gloomiest arcades of the cathedral.

CHAPTER 3

The Bells

AFTER THE MORNING in the pillory, the neighbors of Notre-Dame thought they noticed that Quasimodo's ardor for ringing had grown cool. Formerly, there had been peals for every occasion, long morning serenades, which lasted from prime to compline; peals from the belfry for a high mass, rich scales drawn over the smaller bells for a wedding, for a christening, and mingling in the air like a rich embroidery of all sorts of charming sounds. The old church, all vibrating and sonorous, was in a perpetual joy of bells. One was constantly conscious of the presence of a spirit of noise and caprice, who sang through all those mouths of brass. Now that spirit seemed to have departed; the cathedral seemed gloomy, and gladly remained silent; festivals and funerals had the simple peal, dry and bare, demanded by the ritual, nothing more. Of the double noise that constitutes a church, the organ within, the bell without, the organ alone remained. One would have said that there was no longer a musician in the belfry. Quasimodo was always there, nevertheless; what, then, had happened to him? Was it that the shame and despair of the pillory still lingered in the bottom of his heart, that the lashes of his tormentor's whip reverberated unendingly in his soul, and that the sadness of such treatment had wholly extinguished in him even his passion for the bells? Or was it that Marie had a rival in the heart of the bellringer of Notre-Dame, and that the great bell and her fourteen sisters were neglected for something more amiable and more beautiful?

It chanced that, in the year of grace 1482, Annunciation Day fell on Tuesday, the twenty-fifth of March. That day the air was so pure and light that Quasimodo felt some returning affection for his bells. He therefore ascended the northern tower while the beadle below was opening wide the doors of the church, which were then enormous panels of stout wood, covered with leather, bordered with nails of gilded iron, and framed in carvings "very artistically elaborated."

On arriving in the lofty bell chamber, Quasimodo gazed for some time at the six bells and shook his head sadly, as though groaning over some foreign element that had interposed itself in his heart between them and him. But when he had set them to swinging, when he felt that cluster of bells moving under his hand, when he saw, for he did not hear it, the palpitating octave ascend and descend that sonorous scale, like a bird hopping from branch to branch; when the demon Music, that demon who shakes a sparkling bundle of strette, trills and arpeggios, had taken possession of the poor deaf man, he became happy once more, he forgot everything, and his heart expanding, made his face beam.

He went and came, he beat his hands together, he ran from rope to rope, he animated the six singers with voice and gesture, like the leader of an orchestra who is urging on intelligent musicians.

"Go on," said he, "go on, go on, Gabrielle, pour out all thy noise into the Place, 'tis a festival today. No laziness, Thibauld; thou art relaxing; go on, go on, then, art thou rusted, thou sluggard? That is well! Quick! Quick! Let not thy clapper be seen! Make them all deaf like me. That's it, Thibauld, bravely done! Guillaume! Guillaume! Thou art the largest, and Pasquier is the smallest, and Pasquier does best. Let us wager that those who hear him will understand him better than they understand thee. Good, good, my Gabrielle, stoutly, more stoutly! Eli, what are you doing up aloft there, you two sparrows? I do not see you making the least little shred of noise. What is the meaning of those beaks of copper that seem to be gaping when they should sing? Come, work now, 'tis the Feast of the Annunciation. The sun is fine; the chime must be fine also. Poor Guillaume, thou art all out of breath, my big fellow!"

He was wholly absorbed in spurring on his bells, all six of which vied with each other in leaping and shaking their shining haunches, like a noisy team of Spanish mules, pricked on here and there by the apostrophes of the muleteer.

All at once, on letting his glance fall between the large slate scales which cover the perpendicular wall of the bell tower at a certain height, he beheld on the square a young girl, fantastically dressed, stop, spread out on the ground a carpet, on which a small goat took up its post, and a group of spectators collect around her. This sight suddenly changed the course of his ideas, and congealed his enthusiasm as a breath of air congeals melted rosin. He halted, turned his back to the bells, and crouched down behind the projecting roof of slate, fixing upon the dancer that dreamy, sweet, and tender look which had already astonished the archdeacon on one occasion. Meanwhile, the forgotten bells died away abruptly and all together, to the great disappointment of the lovers of bell ringing, who were listening in good faith to the peal from above the Pont du Change, and who went away dumbfounded, like a dog who has been offered a bone and given a stone.

CHAPTER 4

ἈΝΆΓΚΗ

IT CHANCED THAT upon a fine morning in this same month of March, I think it was on Saturday the 29th, Saint Eustache's day, our young friend the student, Jehan Frollo du Moulin, perceived, as he was dressing himself, that his breeches, which contained his purse, gave out no metallic ring. "Poor purse," he said, drawing it from his fob, "what, not the smallest parisis! How cruelly the dice, beer-pots, and Venus have depleted thee! How empty, wrinkled, limp, thou art! Thou resemblest the throat of a fury! I ask you, Messer Cicero, and Messer Seneca, copies of whom, all dog's-eared, I behold scattered on the floor, what profits it me to know, better than any governor of the mint, or any Jew on the Pont aux Changeurs, that a golden crown stamped with a crown is worth thirty-five unzains of twenty-five sous, and eight deniers parisis apiece, and that a crown stamped with a crescent is worth thirty-six unzains of twenty-six sous, six deniers tournois apiece, if I have not a single wretched black liard to risk on the double-six! Oh! Consul Cicero! This is no calamity from which one extricates one's self with periphrases, *quemadmodum*, and *verum enim vero*!"

He dressed himself sadly. An idea had occurred to him as he laced his boots, but he rejected it at first; nevertheless, it returned, and he put on his waistcoat wrong side out, an evident sign of violent internal combat. At last he dashed his cap roughly on the floor, and exclaimed: "So much the worse! Let come of it what may. I am going to my brother! I shall catch a sermon, but I shall catch a crown."

Then be hastily donned his long jacket with furred half-sleeves, picked up his cap, and went out like a man driven to desperation.

He turned down the Rue de la Harpe toward the City. As he passed the Rue de la Huchette, the odor of those admirable spits, which were incessantly turning, tickled his olfactory apparatus, and he bestowed a loving glance toward the Cyclopean roast, which one day drew from the Franciscan friar, Calatagirone, this pathetic exclamation: *Veramente, queste rotisserie sono cosa stupenda*! But Jehan had not the wherewithal to buy a breakfast, and he plunged, with a profound sigh, under the gateway of the Petit-Châtelet, that enormous double trefoil of massive towers which guarded the entrance to the City.

He did not even take the trouble to cast a stone in passing, as was the usage, at the miserable statue of that Périnet Leclerc who had delivered up the Paris of Charles VI to the English, a crime which his effigy, its face battered with stones and soiled with mud, expiated for three centuries at the corner of the Rue de la Harpe and the Rue de Buci, as in an eternal pillory.

The Petit-Pont traversed, the Rue Neuve-Sainte-Geneviève crossed, Jehan de Molendino found himself in front of Notre-Dame. Then indecision seized upon him once more, and he paced for several minutes round the statue of M. Legris, repeating to himself with anguish: "The sermon is sure, the crown is doubtful."

He stopped a beadle who emerged from the cloister, "Where is monsieur the archdeacon of Josas?"

"I believe that he is in his secret cell in the tower," said the beadle; "I should advise you not to disturb him there, unless you come from some one like the pope or monsieur the king."

Jehan clapped his hands.

"*Bédiable*! Here's a magnificent chance to see the famous sorcery cell!"

This reflection having brought him to a decision, he plunged resolutely into the small black doorway, and began the ascent of the spiral of Saint-Gilles, which leads to the upper stories of the tower. "I am going to see," he said to himself on the way. "By the ravens of the Holy Virgin it must need be a curious thing, that cell which my reverend brother hides so secretly! 'Tis said that he lights up the kitchens of hell there, and that he cooks the philosopher's stone there over a hot fire. *Bédieu*! I care no more for the philosopher's stone than for a pebble, and I would rather find over his furnace an omelette of Easter eggs and bacon, than the biggest philosopher's stone in the world.'"

On arriving at the gallery of slender columns, he took breath for a moment, and swore against the interminable staircase by I know not how many million cartloads of devils; then he resumed his ascent through the narrow door of the north tower, now closed to the public. Several moments after passing the bell chamber, he came upon a little landing-place, built in a lateral niche, and under the vault of a low, pointed door, whose enormous lock and strong iron bars he was enabled to see through a loophole pierced in the opposite circular wall of the staircase. Persons desirous of visiting this door at the present day will recognize it by this inscription engraved in white letters on the black wall: "J'ADORE CORALIE, 1823. SIGNE UGENE." "Signé" stands in the text.

"Ugh!" said the scholar; "'tis here, no doubt."

The key was in the lock, the door was very close to him; he gave it a gentle push and thrust his head through the opening.

The reader cannot have failed to turn over the admirable works of Rembrandt, that Shakespeare of painting. Amid so many marvellous engravings, there is one etching in particular, which is supposed to represent Doctor Faust, and which it is impossible to contemplate without being dazzled. It represents a gloomy cell; in the centre is a table loaded with hideous objects; skulls, spheres, alembics, compasses, hieroglyphic parchments. The doctor is before this table clad in his large coat and covered to the very eyebrows with his furred cap. He is visible only to his waist. He has half risen from his immense armchair, his clenched fists rest on the table, and he is gazing with curiosity and terror at a large luminous circle, formed of magic letters, which gleams from the wall beyond, like the solar spectrum in a dark chamber. This cabalistic sun seems to tremble before the eye, and fills the wan cell with its mysterious radiance. It is horrible and it is beautiful.

Something very similar to Faust's cell presented itself to Jehan's view, when he ventured his head through the half-open door. It also was a gloomy and sparsely lighted retreat. There also stood a large armchair and a large table, compasses, alembics, skeletons of animals suspended from the ceiling, a globe rolling on the floor, hippocephali mingled promiscuously with drinking cups, in which quivered leaves of gold, skulls placed upon vellum checkered with figures and characters, huge manuscripts piled up wide open, without mercy on the cracking corners of the parchment; in short, all the rubbish of science, and everywhere on this confusion dust and spiders' webs; but there was no circle of luminous letters, no doctor in an ecstasy contemplating the flaming vision, as the eagle gazes upon the sun.

Nevertheless, the cell was not deserted. A man was seated in the armchair, and bending over the table. Jehan, to whom his back was turned, could see only his shoulders and the back of his skull; but he had no difficulty in recognizing that bald head, which nature had provided with an eternal tonsure, as though desirous of marking, by this external symbol, the archdeacon's irresistible clerical vocation.

Jehan accordingly recognized his brother; but the door had been opened so softly, that nothing warned Dom Claude of his presence. The inquisitive scholar took advantage of this circumstance to examine the cell for a few moments at his leisure. A large furnace, which he had not at first observed, stood to the left of the armchair, beneath the window. The ray of light that penetrated through this aperture made its way through a spider's circular web, which tastefully inscribed its delicate rose in the arch of the window, and in the centre of which the insect architect hung motionless, like the hub of this wheel of lace. Upon the furnace were accumulated in disorder, all sorts of vases, earthenware bottles, glass retorts, and mattresses of charcoal. Jehan observed, with a sigh, that there was no frying-pan. "How cold the kitchen utensils are!" he said to himself.

In fact, there was no fire in the furnace, and it seemed as though none had been lighted for a long time. A glass mask, which Jehan noticed among the utensils of alchemy, and which served no doubt, to protect the archdeacon's face when he was working over some substance to be dreaded, lay in one corner covered with dust and apparently forgotten. Beside it lay a pair of bellows no less dusty, the upper side of which bore this inscription incrusted in copper letters: SPIRA SPERA.

Other inscriptions were written, in accordance with the fashion of the hermetics, in great numbers on the walls; some traced with ink, others engraved with a metal point. There were, moreover, Gothic letters, Hebrew letters, Greek letters, and Roman letters, pell-mell; the inscriptions overflowed at haphazard, on top of each other, the more recent effacing the more ancient, and all entangled with each other, like the branches in a thicket, like pikes in an affray. It was, in fact, a strangely confused mingling of all human philosophies, all reveries, all human wisdom. Here and there one shone out from among the rest like a banner among lance heads. Generally, it was a brief Greek or Roman device, such as the Middle Ages knew so well how to formulate. *Undè? Indè? Homo homini monstrum. Astra, castra, nomen, numen.* Μεʹγα βιςλιʹον, μεʹγα χαχνοʹ. *Sapere aude. Flat ubi vult,* etc.; sometimes a word devoid of all apparent sense, Ανάγχοφαγί'α, which possibly contained a bitter allusion to the regime of the cloister; sometimes a simple maxim of clerical discipline formulated in a regular hexameter *Caelestem dominum, terrestrem dicito domnum*. There was also Hebrew jargon, of which Jehan, who as yet knew but little Greek, understood nothing; and all were traversed in every direction by stars, by figures of men or animals, and by intersecting triangles; and this contributed not a little to make the scrawled wall of the cell resemble a sheet of paper over which a monkey had drawn back and forth a pen filled with ink.

The whole chamber, moreover, presented a general aspect of abandonment and dilapidation; and the bad state of the utensils induced the supposition that their owner had long been distracted from his labors by other preoccupations. Meanwhile, this master, bent over a vast manuscript, ornamented with fantastical illustrations, appeared to be tormented by an idea that incessantly mingled with his meditations. That at least was Jehan's idea, when he heard him exclaim, with the thoughtful breaks of a dreamer thinking aloud, "Yes, Manou said it, and Zoroaster taught it! The sun is born from fire, the moon from the sun; fire is the soul of the universe; its elementary atoms pour forth and flow incessantly upon the world through infinite channels! At the point where these currents intersect each other in the heavens, they produce light; at their points of intersection on earth, they produce gold. Light, gold; the same thing! From fire to the concrete state. The difference between the visible and the palpable, between the fluid and the solid in the same substance, between water and ice, nothing more. These are no dreams; it is the general law of nature. But what is one to do in order to extract from science the secret of this general law? What! This light that inundates my hand is gold! These same atoms dilated in accordance with a certain law need only be condensed in accordance with another law. How is it to be done? Some have fancied by burying a ray of sunlight, Averroës, yes, 'tis Averroës, Averroës buried one under the first pillar on the left of the sanctuary of the Koran, in the great Mahometan mosque of Cordova; but the vault cannot he opened for the purpose of ascertaining whether the operation has succeeded, until after the lapse of eight thousand years.

"The devil!" said Jehan, to himself, "'tis a long while to wait for a crown!"

"Others have thought," continued the dreamy archdeacon, "that it would be better worth while to operate upon a ray of Sirius. But 'tis exceeding hard to obtain this ray pure, because of the simultaneous presence of other stars whose rays mingle with it. Flamel esteemed it more simple to operate upon terrestrial fire. Flamel! There's predestination in the name! *Flamma*! Yes, fire. All lies there. The diamond is contained in the carbon, gold is in the fire. But how to extract it? Magistri affirms that there are certain feminine names, which possess a charm so sweet and mysterious, that it suffices to pronounce them during the operation. Let us read what Manon says on the matter: 'Where women are honored, the divinities are rejoiced; where they are despised, it is useless to pray to God. The mouth of a woman is constantly pure; it is a running water, it is a ray of sunlight. The name of a woman should be agreeable, sweet, fanciful; it should end in long vowels, and resemble words of benediction.' Yes, the sage is right; in truth, Maria, Sophia, la Esmeral—Damnation, always that thought!"

And he closed the book violently.

He passed his hand over his brow, as though to brush away the idea that assailed him; then he took from the table a nail and a small hammer, whose handle was curiously painted with cabalistic letters.

"For some time," he said with a bitter smile, "I have failed in all my experiments! One fixed idea possesses me, and sears my brain like fire. I have not even been able to discover the secret of Cassiodorus, whose lamp burned without wick and without oil. A simple matter, nevertheless—"

"The deuce!" muttered Jehan in his beard.

"Hence," continued the priest, "one wretched thought is sufficient to render a man weak and beside himself! Oh, how Claude Pernelle would laugh at me. She who could not turn Nicholas Flamel aside, for one moment, from his pursuit of the great work! What! I hold in my hand the magic hammer of Zéchiélé at every blow dealt by the formidable rabbi, from the depths of his cell, upon this nail, that one of his enemies whom he had condemned, were he a thousand leagues away, was buried a cubit deep in the earth which swallowed him. The King of France himself, in consequence of once having inconsiderately knocked at the door of the thermaturgist, sank to the knees through the pavement of his own Paris. This took place three centuries ago. Well! I possess the hammer and the nail, and in my hands they are utensils no more formidable than a club in the hands of a maker of edge tools. And yet all that is required is to find the magic word which Zéchiélé pronounced when he struck his nail."

"What nonsense!" thought Jehan.

"Let us see, let us try!" resumed the archdeacon briskly. "Were I to succeed, I should behold the blue spark flash from the head of the nail. Emen-Hétan! Emen-Hétan! That's not it. Sigéani! Sigéani! May this nail open the tomb to any one who bears the name of Phoebus! A curse upon it! Always and eternally the same idea!"

And he flung away the hammer in a rage. Then he sank down so deeply on the armchair and the table, that Jehan lost him from view behind the great pile of manuscripts. For the space of several minutes, all that he saw was his fist convulsively clenched on a book. Suddenly, Dom Claude sprang up, seized a compass and engraved in silence upon the wall in capital letters, this Greek word

ἈΝΆΓΚΗ

"My brother is mad," said Jehan to himself; "it would have been far more simple to write *Fatum*, every one is not obliged to know Greek."

The archdeacon returned and seated himself in his armchair, and placed his head on both his hands, as a sick man does, whose head is heavy and burning.

The student watched his brother with surprise. He did not know, he who wore his heart on his sleeve, he who observed only the good old law of Nature in the world, he who allowed his passions to follow their inclinations, and in whom the lake of great emotions was always dry, so freely did he let it off each day by fresh drains, he did not know with what fury the sea of human passions ferments and boils when all egress is denied to it, how it accumulates, how it swells, how it overflows, how it hollows out the heart; how it breaks in inward sobs, and dull convulsions, until it has rent its dikes and burst its bed. The austere and glacial envelope of Claude Frollo, that cold surface of steep and inaccessible virtue, had always deceived Jehan. The merry scholar had never dreamed that there was boiling lava, furious and profound, beneath the snowy brow of Aetna.

We do not know whether he suddenly became conscious of these things; but, giddy as he was, he understood that he had seen what he ought not to have seen, that he had just surprised the soul of his elder brother in one of its most secret altitudes, and that Claude must not be allowed to know it. Seeing that the archdeacon had fallen back into his former immobility, he withdrew his head very softly, and made some noise with his feet outside the door, like a person who has just arrived and is giving warning of his approach.

"Enter!" cried the archdeacon, from the interior of his cell; "I was expecting you. I left the door unlocked expressly; enter Master Jacques!"

The scholar entered boldly. The archdeacon, who was very much embarrassed by such a visit in such a place, trembled in his armchair. "What! 'tis you, Jehan?"

"'Tis a J, all the same," said the scholar, with his ruddy, merry, and audacious face.

Dom Claude's visage had resumed its severe expression.

"What are you come for?"

"Brother," replied the scholar, making an effort to assume a decent, pitiful, and modest mien, and twirling his cap in his hands with an innocent air; "I am come to ask of you—"

"What?"

"A little lecture on morality, of which I stand greatly in need." Jehan did not dare to add aloud, "And a little money of which I am in still greater need." This last member of his phrase remained unuttered.

"Monsieur," said the archdeacon, in a cold tone, "I am greatly displeased with you."

"Alas!" sighed the scholar.

Dom Claude made his armchair describe a quarter circle, and gazed intently at Jehan.

"I am very glad to see you."

This was a formidable exordium. Jehan braced himself for a rough encounter.

"Jehan, complaints are brought me about you every day. What affray was that in which you bruised with a cudgel a little vicomte, Albert de Ramonchamp?"

"Oh!" said Jehan, "a vast thing that! A malicious page amused himself by splashing the scholars, by making his horse gallop through the mire!"

"Who," pursued the archdeacon, "is that Mahiet Fargel, whose gown you have torn? *Tunicam dechiraverunt*, saith the complaint."

"Ah bah! A wretched cap of a Montaigu! Isn't that it?"

"The complaint says *tunicam* and not *cappettam*. Do you know Latin?"

Jehan did not reply.

"Yes," pursued the priest shaking his head, "that is the state of learning and letters at the present day. The Latin tongue is hardly understood, Syriac is unknown, Greek so odious that 'tis accounted no ignorance in the most learned to skip a Greek word without reading it, and to say, '*Græcum est non legitur.*'"

The scholar raised his eyes boldly. "Monsieur my brother, doth it please you that I shall explain in good French vernacular that Greek word which is written yonder on the wall?"

"What word?"

ἈΝΆΓΚΗ

A slight flush spread over the cheeks of the priest with their high bones, like the puff of smoke that announces on the outside the secret commotions of a volcano. The student hardly noticed it.

"Well, Jehan," stammered the elder brother with an effort, "What is the meaning of yonder word?"

"FATE."

Dom Claude turned pale again, and the scholar pursued carelessly.

"And that word below it, graved by the same hand, Ἀναγνεία, signifies 'impurity.' You see that people do know their Greek."

And the archdeacon remained silent. This Greek lesson had rendered him thoughtful.

Master Jehan, who possessed all the artful ways of a spoiled child, judged that the moment was a favorable one in which to risk his request. Accordingly, he assumed an extremely soft tone and began, "My good brother, do you hate me to such a degree as to look savagely upon me because of a few mischievous cuffs and blows distributed in a fair war to a pack of lads and brats, *quibusdam marcosetis?* You see, good Brother Claude, that people know their Latin."

But all this caressing hypocrisy did not have its usual effect on the severe elder brother. Cerberus did not bite at the honey cake. The archdeacon's brow did not lose a single wrinkle.

"What are you driving at?" he said dryly.

"Well, in point of fact, this!" replied Jehan bravely, "I stand in need of money."

At this audacious declaration, the archdeacon's visage assumed a thoroughly pedagogical and paternal expression.

"You know, Monsieur Jehan, that our fief of Tirechappe, putting the direct taxes and the rents of the nine and twenty houses in a block, yields only nine and thirty livres, eleven sous, six deniers, parisis. It is one half more than in the time of the brothers Paclet, but it is not much."

"I need money," said Jehan stoically.

"You know that the official has decided that our twenty-one houses should he moved full into the fief of the Bishopric, and that we could redeem this homage only by paying the reverend bishop two marks of silver gilt of the price of six livres parisis. Now, these two marks I have not yet been able to get together. You know it."

"I know that I stand in need of money," repeated Jehan for the third time.

"And what are you going to do with it?"

This question caused a flash of hope to gleam before Jehan's eyes. He resumed his dainty, caressing air.

"Stay, dear Brother Claude, I should not come to you, with any evil motive. There is no intention of cutting a dash in the taverns with your unzains, and of strutting about the streets of Paris in a caparison of gold brocade, with a lackey, *cum meo laquasio*. No, brother, 'tis for a good work."

"What good work?" demanded Claude, somewhat surprised.

"Two of my friends wish to purchase an outfit for the infant of a poor Haudriette widow. It is a charity. It will cost three forms, and I should like to contribute to it."

"What are names of your two friends?"

"Pierre l'Assommeur and Baptiste Croque-Oison" [Peter the Slaughterer; and Baptist Crack-Gosling].

"Hum," said the archdeacon; "those are names as fit for a good work as a catapult for the chief altar."

It is certain that Jehan had made a very bad choice of names for his two friends. He realized it too late.

"And then," pursued the sagacious Claude, "what sort of an infant's outfit is it that is to cost three forms, and that for the child of a Haudriette? Since when have the Haudriette widows taken to having babes in swaddling-clothes?"

Jehan broke the ice once more.

"Eh, well! Yes! I need money in order to go and see Isabeau la Thierrye to-night; in the Val-d' Amour!"

"Impure wretch!" exclaimed the priest.

"Ἀναγνεία!" said Jehan.

This quotation, which the scholar borrowed with malice, perchance, from the wall of the cell, produced a singular effect on the archdeacon. He bit his lips and his wrath was drowned in a crimson flush.

"Begone," he said to Jehan. "I am expecting some one."

The scholar made one more effort.

"Brother Claude, give me at least one little parisis to buy something to eat."

"How far have you gone in the Decretals of Gratian?" demanded Dom Claude.

"I have lost my copy books."

"Where are you in your Latin humanities?"

"My copy of Horace has been stolen."

"Where are you in Aristotle?"

"In faith! Brother, what father of the church is it, who says that the errors of heretics have always had for their lurking place the thickets of Aristotle's metaphysics? A plague on Aristotle! I care not to tear my religion on his metaphysics."

"Young man," resumed the archdeacon, "at the king's last entry, there was a young gentleman, named Philippe de Comines, who wore embroidered on the housings of his horse this device, upon which I counsel you to meditate: *Qui non laborat, non manducet.*"

The scholar remained silent for a moment, with his finger in his ear, his eyes on the ground, and a discomfited mien.

All at once he turned round to Claude with the agile quickness of a wagtail.

"So, my good brother, you refuse me a sou parisis, wherewith to buy a crust at a baker's shop?"

"*Qui non laborat, non manducet.*"

At this response of the inflexible archdeacon, Jehan hid his head in his hands, like a woman sobbing, and exclaimed with an expression of despair: "Ὀ τοτοτοτο-τοι!"

"What is the meaning of this, sir?" demanded Claude, surprised at this freak.

"What indeed!" said the scholar; and he lifted to Claude his impudent eyes into which he had just thrust his fists in order to communicate to them the redness of tears. "'Tis Greek! 'Tis an anapaest of Æschylus which expresses grief perfectly."

And here he burst into a laugh so droll and violent that it made the archdeacon smile. It was Claude's fault, in fact: why had he so spoiled that child?

"Oh, good Brother Claude," resumed Jehan, emboldened by this smile. "Look at my worn-out boots. Is there a cothurnus in the world more tragic than these boots, whose soles are hanging out their tongues?"

The archdeacon promptly returned to his original severity.

"I will send you some new boots, but no money."

"Only a poor little parisis, brother," continued the suppliant Jehan. "I will learn Gratian by heart, I will believe firmly in God, I will be a regular Pythagoras of science and virtue. But one little parisis, in mercy! Would you have famine bite me with its jaws which are gaping in front of me, blacker, deeper, and more noisome than a Tartarus or the nose of a monk?"

Dom Claude shook his wrinkled head: "*Qui non laborat—*"

Jehan did not allow him to finish.

"Well," he exclaimed, "to the devil then! Long live joy! I will live in the tavern, I will fight, I will break pots and I will go and see the wenches." And thereupon, he hurled his cap at the wall, and snapped his fingers like castanets.

The archdeacon surveyed him with a gloomy air.

"Jehan, you have no soul."

"In that case, according to Epicurius, I lack a something made of another something which has no name."

"Jehan, you must think seriously of amending your ways."

"Oh, come now," cried the student, gazing in turn at his brother and the alembics on the furnace, "everything is preposterous here, both ideas and bottles!"

"Jehan, you are on a very slippery downward road. Do you know whither you are going?"

"To the wine-shop," said Jehan.

"The wine-shop leads to the pillory."

"'Tis as good a lantern as any other, and perchance with that one, Diogenes would have found his man."

"The pillory leads to the gallows."

"The gallows is a balance which has a man at one end and the whole earth at the other. 'Tis fine to be the man."

"The gallows leads to hell."

"'Tis a big fire."

"Jehan, Jehan, the end will be bad."

"The beginning will have been good."

At that moment, the sound of a footstep was heard on the staircase.

"Silence!" said the archdeacon, laying his finger on his mouth, "here is Master Jacques. Listen, Jehan," he added, in a low voice; "have a care never to speak of what you shall have seen or heard here. Hide yourself quickly under the furnace, and do not breathe."

The scholar concealed himself; just then a happy idea occurred to him.

"By the way, Brother Claude, a form for not breathing."

"Silence! I promise."

"You must give it to me."

"Take it, then!" said the archdeacon angrily, flinging his purse at him.

Jehan darted under the furnace again, and the door opened.

CHAPTER 5

The Two Men Clothed in Black

THE PERSONAGE WHO entered wore a black gown and a gloomy mien. The first point which struck the eye of our Jehan (who, as the reader will readily surmise, had ensconced himself in his nook in such a manner as to enable him to see and hear everything at his good pleasure) was the perfect sadness of the garments and the visage of this new-comer. There was, nevertheless, some sweetness diffused over that face, but it was the sweetness of a cat or a judge, an affected, treacherous sweetness. He was very gray and wrinkled, and not far from his sixtieth year, his eyes blinked, his eyebrows were white, his lip pendulous, and his hands large. When Jehan saw that it was only this, that is to say, no doubt a physician or a magistrate, and that this man had a nose very far from his mouth, a sign of stupidity, he nestled down in his hole, in despair at being obliged to pass an indefinite time in such an uncomfortable attitude, and in such bad company.

The archdeacon, in the meantime, had not even risen to receive this personage. He had made the latter a sign to seat himself on a stool near the door, and, after several moments of a silence which appeared to be a continuation of a preceding meditation, he said to him in a rather patronizing way, "Good day, Master Jacques."

"Greeting, master," replied the man in black.

There was in the two ways in which "Master Jacques" was pronounced on the one hand, and the "master" by preeminence on the other, the difference between monseigneur and monsieur, between *domine* and *domne*. It was evidently the meeting of a teacher and a disciple.

"Well!" resumed the archdeacon, after a fresh silence which Master Jacques took good care not to disturb, "how are you succeeding?"

"Alas, master," said the other, with a sad smile, "I am still seeking the stone. Plenty of ashes. But not a spark of gold."

Dom Claude made a gesture of impatience. "I am not talking to you of that, Master Jacques Charmolue, but of the trial of your magician. Is it not Marc Cenaine that you call him? The butler of the Court of Accounts? Does he confess his witchcraft? Have you been successful with the torture?"

"Alas, no!" replied Master Jacques, still with his sad smile. "We have not that consolation. That man is a stone. We might have him boiled in the Marché aux Pourceaux, before he would say anything. Nevertheless, we are sparing nothing for the sake of getting at the truth; he is already thoroughly dislocated, we are applying all the herbs of Saint John's day; as saith the old comedian Plautus,—

'*Advorsum stimulos, laminas, crucesque, cimpedesque,*
Nervos, catenas, carceres, numellas, pedicas, boias'

"Nothing answers; that man is terrible. I am at my wit's end over him."

"You have found nothing new in his house?"

"In faith, yes," said Master Jacques, fumbling in his pouch. "This parchment. There are words in it that we cannot comprehend. The criminal advocate, Monsieur Philippe Lheulier, nevertheless, knows a little Hebrew, which he learned in that matter of the Jews of the Rue Kantersten, at Brussels."

So saying, Master Jacques unrolled a parchment. "Give it here," said the archdeacon. And casting his eyes upon this writing: "Pure magic, Master Jacques!" he exclaimed. "'Emen-Hétan!' 'Tis the cry of the vampires when they arrive at the Witches' Sabbath. *Per ipsum, et cum ipso, et in ipso!* 'Tis the command that chains the devil in hell. *Hax, pax, max!* That refers to medicine. A formula against the bite of mad dogs. Master Jacques! You are procurator to the king in the Ecclesiastical Courts: this parchment is abominable."

"We will put the man to the torture once more. Here again," added Master Jacques, fumbling afresh in his pouch, "is something that we have found at Marc Cenaine's house."

It was a vessel belonging to the same family as those which covered Dom Claude's furnace.

"Ah," said the archdeacon, "a crucible for alchemy!"

"I will confess to you," continued Master Jacques, with his timid and awkward smile, "that I have tried it over the furnace, but I have succeeded no better than with my own."

The archdeacon began an examination of the vessel. "What has he engraved on his crucible? *Och! Och!* The word that expels fleas! That Marc Cenaine is an ignoramus! I verily believe that you will never make gold with this! 'Tis good to set in your bedroom in summer and that is all!"

"Since we are talking about errors," said the king's procurator, "I have just been studying the figures on the portal below before ascending hither; is your reverence quite sure that the opening of the work of physics is there portrayed on the side toward the Hôtel-Dieu, and that among the seven nude figures which stand at the feet of Notre-Dame, that which has wings on his heels is Mercurius?"

"Yes," replied the priest; "'tis Augustin Nypho who writes it, that Italian doctor who had a bearded demon who acquainted him with all things. However, we will descend, and I will explain it to you with the text before us."

"Thanks, master," said Charmolue, bowing to the earth. "By the way, I was on the point of forgetting. When doth it please you that I shall apprehend the little sorceress?"

"What sorceress?"

"That gypsy girl you know, who comes every day to dance on the church square, in spite of the official's prohibition! She hath a demoniac goat with horns of the devil, which reads, which writes, which knows mathematics like Picatrix, and which would suffice to hang all Bohemia. The prosecution is all ready; 'twill soon be finished, I assure you! A pretty creature, on my soul, that dancer! The handsomest black eyes! Two Egyptian carbuncles! When shall we begin?"

The archdeacon was excessively pale.

"I will tell you that hereafter," he stammered, in a voice that was barely articulate; then he resumed with an effort, "Busy yourself with Marc Cenaine."

"Be at ease," said Charmolue with a smile; "I'll buckle him down again for you on the leather bed when I get home. But 'tis a devil of a man; he wearies even Pierrat Torterue himself, who hath hands larger than my own. As that good Plautus saith:

'Nudus vinctus, centum pondo,
es quando pendes per pedes.'

"The torture of the wheel and axlè! 'Tis the most effectual! He shall taste it!"

Dom Claude seemed absorbed in gloomy abstraction. He turned to Charmolue, "Master Pierrat—Master Jacques, I mean, busy yourself with Marc Cenaine."

"Yes, yes, Dom Claude. Poor man! He will have suffered like Mummol. What an idea to go to the Witches' Sabbath! A butler of the Court of Accounts, who ought to know Charlemagne's text; *Stryga vel masca*! In the matter of the little girl, Smelarda, as they call her, I will await your orders. Ah! As we pass through the portal, you will explain to me also the meaning of the gardener painted in relief, which one sees as one enters the church. Is it not the Sower? Hey master, of what are you thinking, pray?"

Dom Claude, buried in his own thoughts, no longer listened to him. Charmolue, following the direction of his glance, perceived that it was fixed mechanically on the great spider's web that draped the window. At that moment, a bewildered fly seeking the March sun, flung itself through the net and became entangled there. On the agitation of his web, the enormous spider made an abrupt move from his central cell, then with one bound, rushed upon the fly, which he folded together with his fore antennae, while his hideous proboscis dug into the victim's head. "Poor fly!" said the king's procurator in the ecclesiastical court; and he raised his hand to save it. The archdeacon, as though roused with a start, withheld his arm with convulsive violence.

"Master Jacques," he cried, "let fate take its course!" The procurator wheeled round in affright; it seemed to him that pincers of iron had clutched his arm. The priest's eye was staring, wild, flaming, and remained riveted on the horrible little group of the spider and the fly.

"Oh, yes!" continued the priest, in a voice which seemed to proceed from the depths of his being, "behold here a symbol of all. She flies, she is joyous, she is just born; she seeks the spring, the open air, liberty: oh, yes! But let her come in contact with the fatal network, and the spider issues from it, the hideous spider! Poor dancer, poor predestined fly! Let things take their course, Master Jacques, 'tis fate! Alas! Claude, thou art the spider! Claude, thou art the fly also! Thou wert flying toward learning, light, the sun. Thou hadst no other care than to reach the open air, the full daylight of eternal truth; but in precipitating thyself toward the dazzling window which opens upon the other world,— upon the world of brightness, intelligence, and science—blind fly!

senseless, learned man! Thou hast not perceived that subtle spider's web, stretched by destiny betwixt the light and thee—thou hast flung thyself headlong into it, and now thou art struggling with head broken and mangled wings between the iron antennae of fate! Master Jacques! Master Jacques! Let the spider work its will!"

"I assure you," said Charmolue, who was gazing at him without comprehending him, "that I will not touch it. But release my arm, master, for pity's sake! You have a hand like a pair of pincers."

The archdeacon did not hear him. "Oh, madman!" he went on, without removing his gaze from the window. "And even couldst thou have broken through that formidable web, with thy gnat's wings, thou believest that thou couldst have reached the light? Alas, that pane of glass that is further on, that transparent obstacle, that wall of crystal, harder than brass, which separates all philosophies from the truth, how wouldst thou have overcome it? Oh, vanity of science! How many wise men come flying from afar, to dash their heads against thee! How many systems vainly fling themselves buzzing against that eternal pane!"

He became silent. These last ideas, which had gradually led him back from himself to science, appeared to have calmed him. Jacques Charmolue recalled him wholly to a sense of reality by addressing to him this question: "Come, now, master, when will you come to aid me in making gold? I am impatient to succeed."

The archdeacon shook his head, with a bitter smile. "Master Jacques read Michel Psellus' *Dialogus de Energia et Operatione Daemonum*. What we are doing is not wholly innocent."

"Speak lower, master! I have my suspicions of it," said Jacques Charmolue. "But one must practise a bit of hermetic science when one is only procurator of the king in the ecclesiastical court, at thirty crowns tournois a year. Only speak low."

At that moment the sound of jaws in the act of mastication, which proceeded from beneath the furnace, struck Charmolue's uneasy ear.

"What's that?" he inquired.

It was the scholar, who, ill at ease, and greatly bored in his hiding-place, had succeeded in discovering there a stale crust and a triangle of mouldy cheese, and had set to devouring the whole without ceremony, by way of consolation and breakfast. As he was very hungry, he made a great deal of noise, and he accented each mouthful strongly, which startled and alarmed the procurator.

"'Tis a cat of mine," said the archdeacon, quickly, "who is regaling herself under there with a mouse,"

This explanation satisfied Charmolue.

"In fact, master," he replied, with a respectful smile, "all great philosophers have their familiar animal. You know what Servius saith: '*Nullus enim locus sine genio est*—for there is no place that hath not its spirit.'"

But Dom Claude, who stood in terror of some new freak on the part of Jehan, reminded his worthy disciple that they had some figures on the façade to study together, and the two quitted the cell, to the accompaniment of a great "ouf!" from the scholar, who began to seriously fear that his knee would acquire the imprint of his chin.

CHAPTER 6

The Effect That Seven Oaths in the Open Air Can Produce

"Te Deum Laudamus!" exclaimed Master Jehan, creeping out from his hole, "the screech-owls have departed. Och! Och! Hax! Pax! Max! Fleas! Mad dogs! The devil! I have had enough of their conversation! My head is humming like a bell tower. And mouldy cheese to boot! Come on! Let us descend, take the big brother's purse and convert all these coins into bottles!"

He cast a glance of tenderness and admiration into the interior of the precious pouch, readjusted his toilet, rubbed up his boots, dusted his poor half sleeves, all gray with ashes, whistled an air, indulged in a sportive pirouette, looked about to see whether there were not something more in the cell to take, gathered up here and there on the furnace some amulet in glass which might serve to bestow, in the guise of a trinket, on Isabeau la Thierrye, finally pushed open the door which his brother had left unfastened, as a last indulgence, and which he, in his turn, left open as a last piece of malice, and descended the circular staircase, skipping like a bird.

In the midst of the gloom of the spiral staircase, he elbowed something which drew aside with a growl; he took it for granted that it was Quasimodo, and it struck him as so droll that he descended the remainder of the staircase holding his sides with laughter. On emerging upon the Place, he laughed yet more heartily.

He stamped his foot when he found himself on the ground once again. "Oh!" said he, "good and honorable pavement of Paris, cursed staircase, fit to put the angels of Jacob's ladder out of breath! What was I thinking of to thrust myself into that stone gimlet which pierces the sky; all for the sake of eating bearded cheese, and looking at the bell towers of Paris through a hole in the wall!"

He advanced a few paces, and caught sight of the two screech owls, that is to say, Dom Claude and Master Jacques Charmolue, absorbed in contemplation before a carving on the façade. He approached them on tiptoe, and heard the archdeacon say in a low tone to Charmolue: "'Twas Guillaume de Paris who caused a Job to be carved upon this stone of the hue of lapis-lazuli, gilded on the edges. Job represents the philosopher's stone, which must also be tried and martyrized in order to become perfect, as saith Raymond Lulle: *Sub conservatione formoe speciftoe salva anima.*"

"That makes no difference to me," said Jehan, "'tis I who have the purse."

At that moment he heard a powerful and sonorous voice articulate behind him a formidable series of oaths. "*Sang Dieu! Ventre-Dieu! Bé-Dieu! Corps de Dieu! Nombril de Belzebuth! Nom d'un pape! Corne et tonnerre.*"

"Upon my soul!" exclaimed Jehan, "that can only be my friend, Captain Phoebus!"

This name of Phoebus reached the ears of the archdeacon at the moment when he was explaining to the king's procurator the dragon which is hiding its tail in a bath, from which issue smoke and the head of a king. Dom Claude started, interrupted himself and, to the great amazement of Charmolue, turned round and beheld his brother Jehan accosting a tall officer at the door of the Gondelaurier mansion.

It was, in fact, Captain Phoebus de Châteaupers. He was backed up against a corner of the house of his betrothed and swearing like a heathen.

"By my faith! Captain Phoebus," said Jehan, taking him by the hand, "you are cursing with admirable vigor."

"Horns and thunder!" replied the captain.

"Horns and thunder yourself!" replied the student. "Come now, fair captain, whence comes this overflow of fine words?"

"Pardon me, good comrade Jehan," exclaimed Phoebus, shaking his hand, "a horse going at a gallop cannot halt short. Now, I was swearing at a hard gallop. I have just been with those prudes, and when I come forth, I always find my throat full of curses, I must spit them out or strangle, *ventre et tonnerre!*"

"Will you come and drink?" asked the scholar.

This proposition calmed the captain.

"I'm willing, but I have no money."

"But I have!"

"Bah! Let's see it!"

Jehan spread out the purse before the captain's eyes, with dignity and simplicity. Meanwhile, the archdeacon, who had abandoned the dumbfounded Charmolue where he stood, had approached them and halted a few paces distant, watching them without their noticing him, so deeply were they absorbed in contemplation of the purse.

Phoebus exclaimed: "A purse in your pocket, Jehan! 'Tis the moon in a bucket of water, one sees it there but 'tis not there. There is nothing but its shadow. Pardieu, let us wager that these are pebbles!"

Jehan replied coldly: "Here are the pebbles wherewith I pave my pocket!"

And without adding another word, he emptied the purse on a neighboring post, with the air of a Roman saving his country.

"True God!" muttered Phoebus, "*targes, grand blancs, petit blancs, mailles*, every two worth one of Tournay, farthings of Paris, real eagle liards! 'Tis dazzling!"

Jehan remained dignified and immovable. Several liards had rolled into the mud; the captain in his enthusiasm stooped to pick them up. Jehan restrained him.

"Fye, Captain Phoebus de Châteaupers!"

Phoebus counted the coins, and turning toward Jehan with solemnity, "Do you know, Jehan, that there are three and twenty sous parisis! Whom have you plundered to-night, in the Rue Coupe-Guele?"

Jehan flung back his blonde and curly head, and said, half-closing his eyes disdainfully, "We have a brother who is an archdeacon and a fool."

"*Corne de Dieu!*" exclaimed Phoebus, "the worthy man!"

"Let us go and drink," said Jehan.

"Where shall we go?" said Phoebus; "To the Pomme d'Eve?"

"No, captain, to the Vieille Science. Une *vieille* qui *scie* une *anse*— 'tis a rebus, and I like that."

"A plague on rebuses, Jehan! The wine is better at 'Eve's Apple'; and then, beside the door there is a vine in the sun which cheers me while I am drinking."

"Well, here goes for Eve and her apple!" said the student, taking Phoebus's arm. "By the way, my dear captain, you just mentioned the Rue Coupe-Gueule. That is a very bad form of speech; people are no longer so barbarous. They say, Rue Coupe-Gorge" [cutthroat street].

The two friends set out toward the Pomme d'Eve. It is unnecessary to mention that they had first gathered up the money, and that the archdeacon followed them.

The archdeacon followed them, gloomy and haggard. Was this the Phoebus whose accursed name had been mingled with all his thoughts ever since his interview with Gringoire? He did not know it, but it was at least a Phoebus, and that magic name sufficed to make the archdeacon follow the two heedless comrades with the stealthy tread of a wolf, listening to their words and observing their slightest gestures with anxious attention. Moreover, nothing was easier than to hear everything they said, as they talked loudly, not in the least concerned that the passers-by were taken into their confidence. They talked of duels, wenches, wine pots, and folly.

At the turning of a street, the sound of a tambourine reached them from a neighboring square. Dom Claude heard the officer say to the scholar, "Thunder! Let us hasten our steps!"

"Why, Phoebus?"

"I'm afraid lest the Bohemian should see me."

"What Bohemian?"

"The little girl with the goat."

"La Esmeralda?"

"That's it, Jehan. I always forget her devil of a name. Let us make haste, she will recognize me. I don't want to have that girl accost me in the street."

"Do you know her, Phoebus?"

Here the archdeacon saw Phoebus sneer, bend down to Jehan's ear, and say a few words to him in a low voice; then Phoebus burst into a laugh, and shook his head with a triumphant air.

"Truly?" said Jehan.

"Upon my soul!" said Phoebus.

"This evening?"

"This evening."

"Are you sure that she will come?"

"Are you a fool, Jehan? Does one doubt such things?"

"Captain Phoebus, you are a happy gendarme!"

The archdeacon heard the whole of this conversation. His teeth chattered; a visible shiver ran through his whole body. He halted for a moment, leaned against a post like a drunken man, then followed the two merry knaves.

At the moment when he overtook them once more, they had changed their conversation. He heard them singing at the top of their lungs the ancient refrain:

Les enfants des Petits-Carreaux
Se font pendre cornme des veaux.

Chapter 7

The Mysterious Monk

THE ILLUSTRIOUS WINE-shop of the Pomme d'Eve was situated in the University, at the corner of the Rue de la Rondelle and the Rue de la Bâtonnier. It was a very spacious and very low hall on the ground floor, with a vaulted ceiling whose central spring rested upon a huge pillar of wood painted yellow; tables everywhere, shining pewter jugs hanging on the walls, always a large number of drinkers, plenty of wenches, a window on the street, a vine at the door, and over the door a flaring piece of sheet-iron, painted with an apple and a woman, rusted by the rain and turning with the wind on an iron pin. This species of weather-vane that looked upon the pavement was the signboard.

Night was falling; the square was dark; the wine-shop, full of candles, flamed afar like a forge in the gloom; the noise of glasses and feasting, of oaths and quarrels, which escaped through the broken panes, was audible. Through the mist that the warmth of the room spread over the window in front, a hundred confused figures could be seen swarming, and from time to time a burst of noisy laughter broke forth from it. The passers-by who were going about their business, slipped past this tumultuous window without glancing at it. Only at intervals did some little ragged boy raise himself on tiptoe as far as the ledge, and hurl into the drinking-shop, that ancient, jeering hoot, with which drunken men were then pursued: "Aux Houls, saouls, saouls, saouls!"

Nevertheless, one man paced imperturbably back and forth in front of the tavern, gazing at it incessantly, and going no further from it than a pikeman from his sentry-box. He was enveloped in a mantle to his very nose. This mantle he had just purchased of the old-clothes man, in the vicinity of the Pomme d'Eve, no doubt to protect himself from the cold of the March evening, possibly also, to conceal his costume. From time to time he paused in front of the dim window with its leaden lattice, listened, looked, and stamped his foot.

At length the door of the dram-shop opened. This was what he appeared to be waiting for. Two boon companions came forth. The ray of light that escaped from the door crimsoned for a moment their jovial faces.

The man in the mantle went and stationed himself on the watch under a porch on the other side of the street.

"*Corne et tonnerre!*" said one of the comrades. "Seven o'clock is on the point of striking. 'Tis the hour of my appointed meeting."

"I tell you," repeated his companion, with a thick tongue, "that I don't live in the Rue des Mauvaises Paroles, *indignus qui inter mala verba habitat*. I have a lodging in the Rue Jean-Pain-Mollet, *in vico Johannis Pain-Mollet.* You are more horned than a unicorn if you assert the contrary. Every one knows that he who once mounts astride a bear is never after afraid; but you have a nose turned to dainties like Saint-Jacques of the hospital."

"Jehan, my friend, you are drunk," said the other.

The other replied staggering, "It pleases you to say so, Phoebus; but it hath been proved that Plato had the profile of a hound."

The reader has, no doubt, already recognized our two brave friends, the captain and the scholar. It appears that the man who was lying in wait for them had also recognized them, for he slowly followed all the zigzags that the scholar caused the captain to make, who being a more hardened drinker had retained all his self-possession. By listening to them attentively, the man in the mantle could catch in its entirety the following interesting conversation,—

"*Corbacque!* Do try to walk straight, master bachelor; you know that I must leave you. Here it is seven o'clock. I have an appointment with a woman."

"Leave me then! I see stars and lances of fire. You are like the Chateau de Dampmartin, which is bursting with laughter."

"By the warts of my grandmother, Jehan, you are raving with too much rabidness. By the way, Jehan, have you any money left?"

"Monsieur Rector, there is no mistake; the little butcher's shop, *parva boucheria.*"

"Jehan! My friend Jehan! You know that I made an appointment with that little girl at the end of the Pont Saint-Michel, and I can only take her to the Falourdel's, the old crone of the bridge, and that I must pay for a chamber. The old witch with a white moustache would not trust me. Jehan! For pity's sake! Have we drunk up the whole of the curé's purse? Have you not a single parisis left?"

"The consciousness of having spent the other hours well is a just and savory condiment for the table."

"Belly and guts! A truce to your whimsical nonsense! Tell me, Jehan of the devil! Have you any money left? Give it to me, *Bé-Dieu!* or I will search you, were you as leprous as Job, and as scabby as Caesar!"

"Monsieur, the Rue Galiache is a street which hath at one end the Rue de la Verrerie, and at the other the Rue de la Tixeranderie."

"Well, yes! My good friend Jehan, my poor comrade, the Rue Galiache is good, very good. But in the name of heaven collect your wits. I must have a sou parisis, and the appointment is for seven o'clock."

"Silence for the rondo, and attention to the refrain:

> *Quand les rats mangeront les cas,*
> *Le roi sera seigneur d'Arras;*
> *Quand la mer, qui est grande et lee*
> *Sera a la Saint-Jean gelee,*
> *On verra, par-dessus la glace,*
> *Sortir ceux d'Arras de leur place."*

"Well, scholar of Antichrist, may you be strangled with the entrails of your mother!" exclaimed Phoebus, and he gave the drunken scholar a rough push; the latter slipped against the wall, and slid flabbily to the pavement of Philip Augustus. A remnant of fraternal pity, which never abandons the heart of a drinker, prompted Phoebus to roll Jehan with his foot upon one of those pillows of the poor, which Providence keeps in readiness at the corner of all the street posts of Paris, and which the rich blight with the name of "a rubbish-heap." The captain adjusted Jehan's head upon an inclined plane of cabbage-stumps, and on the very instant, the scholar fell to snoring in a magnificent bass. Meanwhile, all malice was not extinguished in the captain's heart. "So much the worse if the devil's cart picks you up on its passage!" he said to the poor, sleeping clerk; and he strode off.

The man in the mantle, who had not ceased to follow him, halted for a moment before the prostrate scholar, as though agitated by indecision; then, uttering a profound sigh, he also strode off in pursuit of the captain.

We, like them, will leave Jehan to slumber beneath the open sky, and will follow them also, if it pleases the reader.

On emerging into the Rue Saint-André-des-Arcs, Captain Phoebus perceived that some one was following him. On glancing sideways by chance, he perceived a sort of shadow crawling after him along the walls. He halted, it halted; he resumed his march, it resumed its march. This disturbed him not overmuch. "Ah, bah!" he said to himself, "I have not a sou."

He paused in front of the College d'Autun. It was at this college that he had sketched out what he called his studies, and, through a scholar's teasing habit which still lingered in him, he never passed the façade without inflicting on the statue of Cardinal Pierre Bertrand, sculptured to the right of the portal, the affront of which Priapus complains so bitterly in the satire of Horace, *Olim truncus eram ficulnus*. He had done this with so much unrelenting animosity that the inscription *Eduensis episcopus* had become almost effaced. Therefore, he halted before the statue according to his wont. The street was utterly deserted. At the moment when he was coolly retying his shoulder knots, with his nose in the air, he saw the shadow approaching him with slow steps, so slow that he had ample time to observe that this shadow wore a cloak and a hat. On arriving near him, it halted and remained more motionless than the statue of Cardinal Bertrand. Meanwhile, it riveted upon Phoebus two intent eyes, full of that vague light which issues in the night time from the pupils of a cat.

The captain was brave, and would have cared very little for a highwayman, with a rapier in his hand. But this walking statue, this petrified man, froze his blood. There were then in circulation, strange stories of a surly monk, a nocturnal prowler about the streets of Paris, and they recurred confusedly to his memory. He remained for several minutes in stupefaction, and finally broke the silence with a forced laugh.

"Monsieur, if you are a robber, as I hope you are, you produce upon me the effect of a heron attacking a nutshell. I am the son of a ruined family, my dear fellow. Try your hand near by here. In the chapel of this college there is some wood of the true cross set in silver."

The hand of the shadow emerged from beneath its mantle and descended upon the arm of Phoebus with the grip of an eagle's talon; at the same time the shadow spoke, "Captain Phoebus de Châteaupers!"

"What, the devil!" said Phoebus, "you know my name!"

"I know not your name alone," continued the man in the mantle, with his sepulchral voice. "You have a rendezvous this evening."

"Yes," replied Phoebus in amazement.

"At seven o'clock."

"In a quarter of an hour."

"At la Falourdel's."

"Precisely."

"The lewd hag of the Pont Saint-Michel."

"Of Saint Michel the archangel, as the Pater Noster saith."

"Impious wretch!" muttered the spectre. "With a woman?"

"*Confiteor*, I confess—"

"Who is called—?"

"La Esmeralda," said Phoebus, gayly. All his heedlessness had gradually returned.

At this name, the shadow's grasp shook the arm of Phoebus in a fury.

"Captain Phoebus de Châteaupers, thou liest!"

Any one who could have beheld at that moment the captain's inflamed countenance, his leap backwards, so violent that he disengaged himself from the grip which held him, the proud air with which he clapped his hand on his swordhilt, and, in the presence of this wrath the gloomy immobility of the man in the cloak, any one who could have beheld this would have been frightened. There was in it a touch of the combat of Don Juan and the statue.

"Christ and Satan!" exclaimed the captain. "That is a word that rarely strikes the ear of a Châteaupers! Thou wilt not dare repeat it."

"Thou liest!" said the shadow coldly.

The captain gnashed his teeth. Surly monk, phantom, superstitions—he had forgotten all at that moment. He no longer beheld anything but a man, and an insult.

"Ah, this is well!" he stammered, in a voice stifled with rage. He drew his sword, then stammering, for anger as well as fear makes a man tremble: "Here! On the spot! Come on! Swords! Swords! Blood on the pavement!"

But the other never stirred. When he beheld his adversary on guard and ready to parry, "Captain Phoebus," he said, and his tone vibrated with bitterness, "you forget your appointment."

The rages of men like Phoebus are milk-soups, whose ebullition is calmed by a drop of cold water. This simple remark caused the sword that glittered in the captain's hand to be lowered.

"Captain," pursued the man, "tomorrow, the day after tomorrow, a month hence, ten years hence, you will find me ready to cut your throat; but go first to your rendezvous."

"In sooth," said Phoebus, as though seeking to capitulate with himself, "these are two charming things to be encountered in a rendezvous, a sword and a wench; but I do not see why I should miss the one for the sake of the other, when I can have both."

He replaced his sword in its scabbard.

"Go to your rendezvous," said the man.

"Monsieur," replied Phoebus with some embarrassment, "many thanks for your courtesy. In fact, there will be ample time tomorrow for us to chop up father Adam's doublet into slashes and buttonholes. I am obliged to you for allowing me to pass one more agreeable quarter of an hour. I certainly did hope to put you in the gutter, and still arrive in time for the fair one, especially as it has a better appearance to make the women wait a little in such cases. But you strike me as having the air of a gallant man, and it is safer to defer our affair until tomorrow. So I will betake myself to my rendezvous; it is for seven o'clock, as you know." Here Phoebus scratched his ear. "Ah. *Corne Dieu!* I had forgotten! I haven't a sou to discharge the price of the garret, and the old crone will insist on being paid in advance. She distrusts me."

"Here is the wherewithal to pay."

Phoebus felt the stranger's cold hand slip into his a large piece of money. He could not refrain from taking the money and pressing the hand.

"*Vrai Dieu!*" he exclaimed, "you are a good fellow!"

"One condition," said the man. "Prove to me that I have been wrong and that you were speaking the truth. Hide me in some corner whence I can see whether this woman is really the one whose name you uttered."

"Oh!" replied Phoebus, "'tis all one to me. We will take, the Sainte-Marthe chamber; you can look at your ease from the kennel hard by."

"Come then," said the shadow.

"At your service," said the captain, "I know not whether you are Messer Diabolus in person; but let us be good friends for this evening; tomorrow I will repay you all my debts, both of purse and sword."

They set out again at a rapid pace. At the expiration of a few minutes, the sound of the river announced to them that they were on the Pont Saint-Michel, then loaded with houses.

"I will first show you the way," said Phoebus to his companion, "I will then go in search of the fair one who is awaiting me near the Petit-Châtelet."

His companion made no reply; he had not uttered a word since they had been walking side by side. Phoebus halted before a low door, and knocked roughly; a light made its appearance through the cracks of the door.

"Who is there?" cried a toothless voice.

"*Corps-Dieu! Tête-Dieu! Ventre-Dieu!*" replied the captain.

The door opened instantly, and allowed the new-comers to see an old woman and an old lamp, both of which trembled. The old woman was bent double, clad in tatters, with a shaking head, pierced with two small eyes, and coiffed with a dish clout; wrinkled everywhere, on hands and face and neck; her lips retreated under her gums, and about her mouth she had tufts of white hairs which gave her the whiskered look of a cat.

The interior of the den was no less dilapitated than she; there were chalk walls, blackened beams in the ceiling, a dismantled chimney-piece, spiders' webs in all the corners, in the middle a staggering herd of tables and lame stools, a dirty child among the ashes, and at the back a staircase, or rather, a wooden ladder, which ended in a trap door in the ceiling.

On entering this lair, Phoebus's mysterious companion raised his mantle to his very eyes. Meanwhile, the captain, swearing like a Saracen, hastened to "make the sun shine in a crown" as saith our admirable Régnier.

"The Sainte-Marthe chamber," said he.

The old woman addressed him as monseigneur, and shut up the crown in a drawer. It was the coin that the man in the black mantle had given to Phoebus. While her back was turned, the bushy-headed and ragged little boy who was playing in the ashes, adroitly approached the drawer, abstracted the crown, and put in its place a dry leaf which he had plucked from a fagot.

The old crone made a sign to the two gentlemen, as she called them, to follow her, and mounted the ladder in advance of them. On arriving at the upper story, she set her lamp on a coffer, and, Phoebus, like a frequent visitor of the house, opened a door that opened on a dark hole. "Enter here, my dear fellow," he said to his companion. The man in the mantle obeyed without a word in reply, the door closed upon him; he heard Phoebus bolt it, and a moment later descend the stairs again with the aged hag. The light had disappeared.

CHAPTER 8

The Utility of Windows That Open on the River

CLAUDE FROLLO (FOR we presume that the reader, more intelligent than Phoebus, has seen in this whole adventure no other surly monk than the archdeacon) groped about for several moments in the dark lair into which the captain had bolted him. It was one of those nooks that architects sometimes reserve at the point of junction between the roof and the supporting wall. A vertical section of this kennel, as Phoebus had so justly styled it, would have made a triangle. Moreover, there was neither window nor air-hole, and the slope of the roof prevented one from standing upright. Accordingly, Claude crouched down in the dust, and the plaster that cracked beneath him; his head was on fire; rummaging around him with his hands, be found on the floor a bit of broken glass, which he pressed to his brow, and whose coolness afforded him some relief.

What was taking place at that moment in the gloomy soul of the archdeacon? God and himself could alone know.

In what order was he arranging in his mind la Esmeralda, Phoebus, Jacques Charmolue, his young brother so beloved, yet abandoned by him in the mire, his archdeacon's cassock, his reputation perhaps dragged to la Falourdel's, all these adventures, all these images? I cannot say. But it is certain that these ideas formed in his mind a horrible group.

He had been waiting a quarter of an hour; it seemed to him that he had grown a century older. All at once be heard the creaking of the boards of the stairway; some one was ascending. The trapdoor opened once more; a light reappeared. There was a tolerably large crack in the worm-eaten door of his den; he put his face to it. In this manner he could see all that went on in the adjoining room. The cat-faced old crone was the first to emerge from the trap-door, lamp in hand; then Phoebus, twirling his moustache, then a third person, that beautiful and graceful figure, la Esmeralda. The priest beheld her rise from below like a dazzling apparition. Claude trembled, a cloud spread over his eyes, his pulses beat violently, everything rustled and whirled around him; he no longer saw nor heard anything.

When he recovered himself, Phoebus and Esmeralda were alone seated on the wooden coffer beside the lamp that made these two youthful figures and a miserable pallet at the end of the attic stand out plainly before the archdeacon's eyes.

Beside the pallet was a window, whose panes broken like a spider's web upon which rain has fallen, allowed a view, through its rent meshes, of a corner of the sky, and the moon lying far away on an eiderdown bed of soft clouds.

The young girl was blushing, confused, palpitating. Her long, drooping lashes shaded her crimson cheeks. The officer, to whom she dared not lift her eyes, was radiant. Mechanically, and with a charmingly unconscious gesture, she traced with the tip of her finger incoherent lines on the bench, and watched her finger. Her foot was not visible. The little goat was nestling upon it.

The captain was very gallantly clad; he had tufts of embroidery at his neck and wrists; a great elegance at that day.

It was not without difficulty that Dom Claude managed to hear what they were saying, through the humming of the blood, which was boiling in his temples.

(A conversation between lovers is a very commonplace affair. It is a perpetual "I love you." A musical phrase which is very insipid and very bald for indifferent listeners, when it is not ornamented with some *fioriture*; but Claude was not an indifferent listener.)

"Oh!" said the young girl, without raising her eyes, "do not despise me, monseigneur Phoebus. I feel that what I am doing is not right."

"Despise you, my pretty child!" replied the officer with an air of superior and distinguished gallantry, "despise you, *tête-Dieu*! And why?"

"For having followed you!"

"On that point, my beauty, we don't agree. I ought not to despise you, but to hate you."

The young girl looked at him in affright: "Hate me! What have I done?"

"For having required so much urging."

"Alas!" said she, "'tis because I am breaking a vow. I shall not find my parents! The amulet will lose its virtue. But what matters it? What need have I of father or mother now?"

So saying, she fixed upon the captain her great black eyes, moist with joy and tenderness.

"Devil take me if I understand you!" exclaimed Phoebus. La Esmeralda remained silent for a moment, then a tear dropped from her eyes, a sigh from her lips, and she said, "Oh, monseigneur, I love you!"

Such a perfume of chastity, such a charm of virtue surrounded the young girl that Phoebus did not feel completely at his ease beside her. But this remark emboldened him: "You love me!" he said with rapture, and he threw his arm round the gypsy's waist. He had only been waiting for this opportunity.

The priest saw it, and tested with the tip of his finger the point of a poniard that he wore concealed in his breast.

"Phoebus," continued the Bohemian, gently releasing her waist from the captain's tenacious hands, "You are good, you are generous, you are handsome; you saved me, me, who am only a poor child lost in Bohemia. I had long been dreaming of an officer who should save my life. 'Twas of you that I was dreaming, before I knew you, my Phoebus; the officer of my dream had a beautiful uniform like yours, a grand look, a sword; your name is Phoebus; 'tis a beautiful name. I love your name; I love your sword. Draw your sword, Phoebus, that I may see it."

"Child!" said the captain, and he unsheathed his sword with a smile.

The gypsy looked at the hilt, the blade; examined the cipher on the guard with adorable curiosity, and kissed the sword, saying, "You are the sword of a brave man. I love my captain." Phoebus again profited by the opportunity to impress upon her beautiful bent neck a kiss which made the young girl straighten herself up as scarlet as a poppy. The priest gnashed his teeth over it in the dark.

"Phoebus," resumed the gypsy, "let me talk to you. Pray walk a little, that I may see you at full height, and that I may hear your spurs jingle. How handsome you are!"

The captain rose to please her, chiding her with a smile of satisfaction, "What a child you are! By the way, my charmer, have you seen me in my archer's ceremonial doublet?"

"Alas, no!" she replied.

"It is very handsome!"

Phoebus returned and seated himself beside her, but much closer than before.

"Listen, my dear—"

The gypsy gave him several little taps with her pretty hand on his mouth, with a childish mirth and grace and gayety.

"No, no, I will not listen to you. Do you love me? I want you to tell me whether you love me."

"Do I love thee, angel of my life!" exclaimed the captain, half kneeling. "My body, my blood, my soul, all are thine; all are for thee. I love thee, and I have never loved any one but thee."

The captain had repeated this phrase so many times, in many similar conjunctures, that he delivered it all in one breath, without committing a single mistake. At this passionate declaration, the gypsy raised to the dirty ceiling that served for the skies a glance full of angelic happiness.

"Oh!" she murmured, "this is the moment when one should die!"

Phoebus found "the moment" favorable for robbing her of another kiss, which went to torture the unhappy archdeacon in his nook. "Die!" exclaimed the amorous captain, "What are you saying, my lovely angel? 'Tis a time for living, or Jupiter is only a scamp! Die at the beginning of so sweet a thing! *Corne-de-boeuf*, what a jest! It is not that. Listen, my dear Similar, Esmenarda—Pardon! You have so prodigiously Saracen a name that I never can get it straight. 'Tis a thicket which stops me short."

"Good heavens!" said the poor girl, "and I thought my name pretty because of its singularity! But since it displeases you, I would that I were called Goton."

"Ah! Do not weep for such a trifle, my graceful maid! 'Tis a name to which one must get accustomed, that is all. When I once know it by heart, all will go smoothly. Listen then, my dear Similar; I adore you passionately. I love you so that 'tis simply miraculous. I know a girl who is bursting with rage over it—"

The jealous girl interrupted him: "Who?"

"What matters that to us?" said Phoebus. "Do you love me?"

"Oh!" said she.

"Well, that is all! You shall see how I love you also. May the great devil Neptunus spear me if I do not make you the happiest woman in the world. We will have a pretty little house somewhere. I will make my archers parade before your windows. They are all mounted, and set at defiance those of Captain Mignon. There are *voulgiers, cranequiniers* and hand *couleveiniers*. I will take you to the great sights of the Parisians at the storehouse of Rully. Eighty thousand armed men, thirty thousand white harnesses, short coats or coats of mail; the sixty-seven banners of the trades; the standards of the parliaments, of the chamber of accounts, of the treasury of the generals, of the aides of the mint; a devilish fine array, in short! I will conduct you to see the lions of the Hôtel du Roi, which are wild beasts. All women love that."

For several moments the young girl, absorbed in her charming thoughts, was dreaming to the sound of his voice, without listening to the sense of his words.

"Oh, how happy you will be!" continued the captain, and at the same time he gently unbuckled the gypsy's girdle.

"What are you doing?" she said quickly. This "act of violence" had roused her from her revery.

"Nothing," replied Phoebus, "I was only saying that you must abandon all this garb of folly, and the street corner when you are with me."

"When I am with you, Phoebus!" said the young girl tenderly.

She became pensive and silent once more.

The captain, emboldened by her gentleness, clasped her waist without resistance; then began softly to unlace the poor child's corsage, and disarranged her tucker to such an extent that the panting priest beheld the gypsy's beautiful shoulder emerge from the gauze, as round and brown as the moon rising through the mists of the horizon.

The young girl allowed Phoebus to have his way. She did not appear to perceive it. The eye of the bold captain flashed.

Suddenly she turned toward him. "Phoebus," she said, with an expression of infinite love, "instruct me in thy religion."

"My religion!" exclaimed the captain, bursting with laughter, "I instruct you in my religion! *Corne et tonnerre!* What do you want with my religion?"

"In order that we may be married," she replied.

The captain's face assumed an expression of mingled surprise and disdain, of carelessness and libertine passion.

"Ah, bah!" said he. "Do people marry?"

The Bohemian turned pale, and her head drooped sadly on her breast.

"My beautiful love," resumed Phoebus, tenderly, "what nonsense is this? A great thing is marriage, truly! One is none the less loving for not having spit Latin into a priest's shop!"

While speaking thus in his softest voice, he approached extremely near the gypsy; his caressing hands resumed their place around her supple and delicate waist, his eye flashed more and more, and everything announced that Monsieur Phoebus was on the verge of one of those moments when Jupiter himself commits so many follies that Homer is obliged to summon a cloud to his rescue.

But Dom Claude saw everything. The door was made of thoroughly rotten cask staves, which left large apertures for the passage of his hawklike gaze. This brown-skinned, broad-shouldered priest, hitherto condemned to the austere virginity of the cloister, was quivering and boiling in the presence of this night scene of love and voluptuousness. This young and beautiful girl given over in disarray to the ardent young man, made melted lead flow in his veins; his eyes darted with sensual jealousy beneath all those loosened pins. Any one who could, at that moment, have seen the face of the unhappy man glued to the worm-eaten bars, would have thought that he beheld the face of a tiger glaring from the depths of a cage at some jackal devouring a gazelle. His eye shone like a candle through the cracks of the door.

All at once, Phoebus, with a rapid gesture, removed the gypsy's gorgerette. The poor child, who had remained pale and dreamy, awoke with a start; she recoiled hastily from the enterprising officer, and, casting a glance at her bare neck and shoulders, red, confused, mute with shame, she crossed her two beautiful arms on her breast to conceal it. Had it not been for the flame that burned in her cheeks, at the sight of her so silent and motionless, one would have declared her a statue of Modesty. Her eyes were lowered.

But the captain's gesture had revealed the mysterious amulet that she wore about her neck.

"What is that?" he said, seizing this pretext to approach once more the beautiful creature he had just alarmed.

"Don't touch it!" she replied, quickly, "'tis my guardian. It will make me find my family again, if I remain worthy to do so. Oh, leave me, monsieur le capitaine! My mother! My poor mother! My mother!

Where art thou? Come to my rescue! Have pity, Monsieur Phoebus, give me back my gorgerette!"

Phoebus retreated and said in a cold tone, "Oh, mademoiselle! I see plainly that you do not love me!"

"I do not love him!" exclaimed the unhappy child, and at the same time she clung to the captain, whom she drew to a seat beside her. "I do not love thee, my Phoebus? What art thou saying, wicked man, to break my heart? Oh, take me! Take all! Do what you will with me, I am thine. What matters to me the amulet! What matters to me my mother! 'Tis thou who art my mother since I love thee! Phoebus, my beloved Phoebus, dost thou see me? 'Tis I. Look at me; 'tis the little one whom thou wilt surely not repulse, who comes, who comes herself to seek thee. My soul, my life, my body, my person, all is one thing—which is thine, my captain. Well, no! We will not marry, since that displeases thee; and then, what am I? A miserable girl of the gutters, whilst thou, my Phoebus, art a gentleman. A fine thing, truly! A dancer wed an officer! I was mad. No, Phoebus, no; I will be thy mistress, thy amusement, thy pleasure, when thou wilt; a girl who shall belong to thee. I was only made for that, soiled, despised, dishonored, but what matters it, beloved? I shall be the proudest and the most joyous of women. And when I grow old or ugly, Phoebus, when I am no longer good to love you, you will suffer me to serve you still. Others will embroider scarfs for you; 'tis I, the servant, who will care for them. You will let me polish your spurs, brush your doublet, dust your riding-boots. You will have that pity, will you not, Phoebus? Meanwhile, take me! Here, Phoebus, all this belongs to thee, only love me! We gypsies need only air and love."

So saying, she threw her arms round the officer's neck; she looked up at him, supplicatingly, with a beautiful smile, and all in tears. Her delicate neck rubbed against his cloth doublet with its rough embroideries. She writhed on her knees, her beautiful body half naked. The intoxicated captain pressed his ardent lips to those lovely African shoulders. The young girl, her eyes bent on the ceiling, as she leaned backwards, quivered, all palpitating, beneath this kiss.

All at once, above Phoebus's head she beheld another head; a green, livid, convulsed face, with the look of a lost soul; near this face was a hand grasping a poniard. It was the face and hand of the priest; he had broken the door and he was there. Phoebus could not see him. The young girl remained motionless, frozen with terror, dumb, beneath that terrible apparition, like a dove that should raise its head at the moment when the hawk is gazing into her nest with its round eyes.

She could not even utter a cry. She saw the poniard descend upon Phoebus, and rise again, reeking.

"Maledictions!" said the captain, and fell.

She fainted.

At the moment when her eyes closed, when all feeling vanished in her, she thought that she felt a touch of fire imprinted upon her lips, a kiss more burning than the red-hot iron of the executioner.

When she recovered her senses, she was surrounded by soldiers of the watch they were carrying away the captain, bathed in his blood the priest had disappeared; the window at the back of the room which opened on the river was wide open; they picked up a cloak which they supposed to belong to the officer and she heard them saying around her,

"'Tis a sorceress who has stabbed a captain."

Book Eighth

CHAPTER 1

The Crown Changed into a Dry Leaf

GRINGOIRE AND THE entire Court of Miracles were suffering mortal anxiety. For a whole month they had not known what had become of la Esmeralda, which greatly pained the Duke of Egypt and his friends the vagabonds, nor what had become of the goat, which redoubled Gringoire's grief. One evening the gypsy had disappeared, and since that time had given no signs of life. All searches had proved fruitless. Some tormenting bootblacks had told Gringoire about meeting her that same evening near the Pont Saint-Michel, going off with an officer; but this husband, after the fashion of Bohemia, was an incredulous philosopher, and besides, he, better than any one else, knew to what a point his wife was virginal. He had been able to form a judgment as to the unconquerable modesty resulting from the combined virtues of the amulet and the gypsy, and he had mathematically calculated the resistance of that chastity to the second power. Accordingly, he was at ease on that score.

Still he could not understand this disappearance. It was a profound sorrow. He would have grown thin over it, had that been possible. He had forgotten everything, even his literary tastes, even his great work, *De figuris regularibus et irregularibus*, which it was his intention to have printed with the first money which he should procure (for he had raved over printing, ever since he had seen the "Diadascolon" of Hugues de Saint Victor, printed with the celebrated characters of Vindelin de Spire).

One day, as he was passing sadly before the criminal Tournelle, he perceived a considerable crowd at one of the gates of the Palais de Justice.

"What is this?" he inquired of a young man who was coming out.

"I know not, sir," replied the young man. "'Tis said that they are trying a woman who hath assassinated a gendarme. It appears that there is sorcery at the bottom of it, the archbishop and the official have intervened in the case, and my brother, who is the archdeacon of Josas, can think of nothing else. Now, I wished to speak with him, but I have not been able to reach him because of the throng, which vexes me greatly, as I stand in need of money."

"Alas, sir!" said Gringoire, "I would that I could lend you some, but, my breeches are worn to holes, and 'tis not crowns which have done it."

He dared not tell the young man that he was acquainted with his brother the archdeacon, to whom he had not returned after the scene in the church; a negligence that embarrassed him.

The scholar went his way, and Gringoire set out to follow the crowd that was mounting the staircase of the great chamber. In his opinion, there was nothing like the spectacle of a criminal process for dissipating melancholy, so exhilaratingly stupid are judges as a rule. The populace that he had joined walked and elbowed in silence. After a slow and tiresome march through a long, gloomy corridor, which wound through the court-house like the intestinal canal of the ancient edifice, he arrived near a low door, opening upon a hall which his lofty stature permitted him to survey with a glance over the waving heads of the rabble.

The hall was vast and gloomy, which latter fact made it appear still more spacious. The day was declining; the long, pointed windows permitted only a pale ray of light to enter, which was extinguished before it reached the vaulted ceiling, an enormous trellis-work of sculptured beams, whose thousand figures seemed to move confusedly in the shadows, many candles were already lighted here and there on tables, and beaming on the heads of clerks buried in masses of documents. The anterior portion of the hall was occupied by the crowd; on the right and left were magistrates and tables; at the end, upon a platform, a number of judges, whose rear rank sank into the shadows, sinister and motionless faces. The walls were sown with innumerable fleurs-de-lis. A large figure of Christ might be vaguely descried above the judges, and everywhere there were pikes and halberds, upon whose points the reflection of the candles placed tips of fire.

"Monsieur," Gringoire inquired of one of his neighbors, "who are all those persons ranged yonder, like prelates in council?"

"Monsieur," replied the neighbor, "those on the right are the counsellors of the grand chamber; those on the left, the councillors of inquiry; the masters in black gowns, the messires in red."

"Who is that big red fellow, yonder above them, who is sweating?" pursued Gringoire.

"It is monsieur the president."

"And those sheep behind him?" continued Gringoire, who as we have seen, did not love the magistracy, which arose, possibly, from the grudge which he cherished against the Palais de Justice since his dramatic misadventure.

"They are messieurs the masters of requests of the king's household."

"And that boar in front of him?"

"He is monsieur the clerk of the Court of Parliament."

"And that crocodile on the right?"

"Master Philippe Lheulier, advocate extraordinary of the king."

"And that big, black tom-cat on the left?"

"Master Jacques Charmolue, procurator of the king in the Ecclesiastical Court, with the gentlemen of the officialty."

"Come now, monsieur, said Gringoire, "pray what are all those fine fellows doing yonder?"

"They are judging."

"Judging whom? I do not see the accused."

"'Tis a woman, sir. You cannot see her. She has her back turned to us, and she is hidden from us by the crowd. Stay, yonder she is, where you see a group of partisans."

"Who is the woman?" asked Gringoire. "Do you know her name?"

"No, monsieur, I have but just arrived. I merely assume that there is some sorcery about it, since the official is present at the trial."

"Come!" said our philosopher, "we are going to see all these magistrates devour human flesh. 'Tis as good a spectacle as any other."

"Monsieur," remarked his neighbor, "think you not, that Master Jacques Charmolue has a very sweet air?"

"Hum!" replied Gringoire. "I distrust a sweetness which hath pinched nostrils and thin lips."

Here the bystanders imposed silence upon the two chatterers. They were listening to an important deposition.

"Messeigneurs," said an old woman in the middle of the hall, whose form was so concealed beneath her garments that one would have pronounced her a walking heap of rags; "Messeigneurs, the thing is as true as that I am la Falourdel, established these forty years at the Pont Saint Michel, and paying regularly my rents, lord's dues, and quit rents; at the gate opposite the house of Tassin-Caillart, the dyer, which is on the side up the river—a poor old woman now, but a pretty maid in former days, my lords. Some one said to me lately, 'La Falourdel, don't use your spinning-wheel too much in the evening; the devil is fond of combing the distaffs of old women with his horns. 'Tis certain that the surly monk who was round about the temple last year, now prowls in the City. Take care, La Falourdel, that he doth not knock at your door.' One evening I was spinning on my wheel, there comes a knock at my door; I ask who it is. They swear. I open. Two men enter. A man in black and a handsome officer. Of the black man nothing could be seen but his eyes, two coals of fire. All the rest was hat and cloak. They say to me, 'The Sainte-Marthe chamber.' 'Tis my upper chamber, my lords, my cleanest. They give me a crown. I put the crown in my drawer, and I say: 'This shall go to buy tripe at the slaughter-house of la Gloriette tomorrow.' We go up stairs. On arriving at the upper chamber, and while my back is turned, the black man disappears. That dazed me a bit. The officer, who was as handsome as a great lord, goes down stairs again with me. He goes out. In about the time it takes to spin a quarter of a handful of flax, he returns with a beautiful young girl, a doll who would have shone like the sun had she been coiffed. She had with her a goat; a big billy-goat, whether black or white, I no longer remember. That set me to thinking. The girl does not concern me, but the goat! I love not those beasts, they have a beard and horns. They are so like a man. And then, they smack of the Witches' Sabbath. However, I say nothing. I had the crown. That is right, is it not, Monsieur Judge? I show the captain and the wench to the upper chamber, and I leave them alone; that is to say, with the goat. I go down and set to spinning again—I must inform you that my house has a ground floor and story above. I know not why I fell to thinking of the surly monk whom the goat had put into my head again, and then the beautiful girl was rather strangely decked out. All at once, I hear a cry upstairs, and something falls on the floor and the window opens. I run to mine that is beneath it, and I behold a black mass pass before my eyes and fall into the water. It was a phantom clad like a priest. It was a moonlight night. I saw him quite plainly. He was swimming in the direction of the city. Then, all of a tremble, I call the watch. The gentlemen of the police enter, and not knowing just at the first moment what the matter was, and being merry, they beat me. I explain to them. We go up stairs, and what do we find? My poor chamber all blood, the captain stretched out at full length with a dagger in his neck, the girl pretending to be dead, and the goat all in a fright. 'Pretty work!' I say, 'I shall have to wash that floor for more than a fortnight. It will have to be scraped; it will be a terrible job.' They carried off the officer, poor young man, and the wench with her bosom all bare. But wait, the worst is that on the next day, when I wanted to take the crown to buy tripe, I found a dead leaf in its place."

The old woman ceased. A murmur of horror ran through the audience.

"That phantom, that goat—all smacks of magic," said one of Gringoire's neighbors.

"And that dry leaf!" added another.

"No doubt about it," joined in a third, "she is a witch who has dealings with the surly monk, for the purpose of plundering officers."

Gringoire himself was not disinclined to regard this as altogether alarming and probable.

"Goody Falourdel," said the president majestically, "have you nothing more to communicate to the court?"

"No, monseigneur," replied the crone, "except that the report has described my house as a hovel and stinking; which is an outrageous fashion of speaking. The houses on the bridge are not imposing, because there are such multitudes of people; but, nevertheless, the butchers continue to dwell there, who are wealthy folk, and married to very proper and handsome women."

The magistrate who had reminded Gringoire of a crocodile rose. "Silence!" said he. "I pray the gentlemen not to lose sight of the fact that a dagger was found on the person of the accused. Goody Falourdel, have you brought that leaf into which the crown that the demon gave you was transformed?

"Yes, monseigneur," she replied; "I found it again. Here it is."

A bailiff handed the dead leaf to the crocodile, who made a doleful shake of the head, and passed it on to the president, who gave it to the procurator of the king in the ecclesiastical court, and thus it made the circuit of the hall.

"It is a birch leaf," said Master Jacques Charmolue. "A fresh proof of magic.

A counsellor took up the word.

"Witness, two men went upstairs together in your house: the black man, whom you first saw disappear and afterwards swimming in the Seine, with his priestly garments, and the officer. Which of the two handed you the crown?" The old woman pondered for a moment and then said, "The officer."

A murmur ran through the crowd.

"Ah!" thought Gringoire, "this makes some doubt in my mind."

But Master Philippe Lheulier, advocate extraordinary to the king, interposed once more.

"I will recall to these gentlemen," "that in the deposition taken at his bedside, the assassinated officer, while declaring that he had a vague idea when the black man accosted him that the latter might be the surly monk, added that the phantom had pressed him eagerly to go and make acquaintance with the accused; and upon his, the captain's, remarking that he had no money, he had given him the crown which the said officer paid to la Falourdel. Hence, that crown is the money of hell."

This conclusive observation appeared to dissipate all the doubts of Gringoire and the other sceptics in the audience.

"You have the documents, gentlemen," added the king's advocate, as he took his seat; "you can consult the testimony of Phoebus de Châteaupers."

At that name, the accused sprang up, her head rose above the throng. Gringoire with horror recognized la Esmeralda.

She was pale; her tresses, formerly so gracefully braided and spangled with sequins, hung in disorder; her lips were blue, her hollow eyes were terrible. Alas!

"Phoebus!" she said, in bewilderment; "where is he? O messeigneurs, before you kill me, tell me, for pity sake, whether he still lives?"

"Hold your tongue, woman," replied the president, "that is no affair of ours."

"Oh, for mercy's sake, tell me if he is alive!" she repeated, clasping her beautiful emaciated hands; and the sound of her chains in contact with her dress, was heard.

"Well!" said the king's advocate roughly, "he is dying. Are you satisfied?"

The unhappy girl fell back on her criminal's seat, speechless, tearless, white as a wax figure.

The president bent down to a man at his feet, who wore a gold cap and a black gown, a chain on his neck and a wand in his hand.

"Bailiff, bring in the second accused."

All eyes turned toward a small door, which opened, and, to the great agitation of Gringoire, gave passage to a pretty goat with horns and hoofs of gold. The elegant beast halted for a moment on the threshold, stretching out its neck as though, perched on the summit of a rock, it had before its eyes an immense horizon. Suddenly it caught sight of the gypsy girl, and leaping over the table and the head of a clerk, in two bounds it was at her knees; then it rolled gracefully on its mistress's feet, soliciting a word or a caress; but the accused remained motionless, and poor Djali himself obtained not a glance.

"Eh, why—'tis my villanous beast," said old Falourdel, "I recognize the two perfectly!"

Jacques Charmolue interfered.

"If the gentlemen please, we will proceed to the examination of the goat." He was, in fact, the second criminal. Nothing more simple in those days than a suit of sorcery instituted against an animal. We find, among others in the accounts of the provost's office for 1466, a curious detail concerning the expenses of the trial of Gillet-Soulart and his sow, "executed for their demerits," at Corbeil. Everything is there, the cost of the pens in which to place the sow, the five hundred bundles of brushwood purchased at the port of Morsant, the three pints of wine and the bread, the last repast of the victim fraternally shared by the executioner, down to the eleven days of guard and food for the sow, at eight deniers parisis each. Sometimes, they went even further than animals. The capitularies of Charlemagne and of Louis le Débonnaire impose severe penalties on fiery phantoms that presume to appear in the air.

Meanwhile the procurator had exclaimed: "If the demon which possesses this goat, and which has resisted all exorcisms, persists in its deeds of witchcraft, if it alarms the court with them, we warn it that we shall be forced to put in requisition against it the gallows or the stake." Gringoire broke out into a cold perspiration. Charmolue took from the table the gypsy's tambourine, and presenting it to the goat, in a certain manner, asked the latter, "What o'clock is it?"

The goat looked at it with an intelligent eye, raised its gilded hoof, and struck seven blows.

It was, in fact, seven o'clock. A movement of terror ran through the crowd.

Gringoire could not endure it.

"He is destroying himself!" he cried aloud; "You see well that he does not know what he is doing."

"Silence among the louts at the end of the hall!" said the bailiff sharply.

Jacques Charmolue, by the aid of the same manoeuvres of the tambourine, made the goat perform many other tricks connected with the date of the day, the month of the year, etc., which the reader has already witnessed. And, by virtue of an optical illusion peculiar to judicial proceedings, these same spectators who had, probably, more than once applauded in the public square Djali's innocent magic were terrified by it beneath the roof of the Palais de Justice. The goat was undoubtedly the devil.

It was far worse when the procurator of the king, having emptied upon a floor a certain bag filled with movable letters, which Djali wore round his neck, they beheld the goat extract with his hoof from the scattered alphabet the fatal name of Phoebus. The witchcraft of which the captain had been the victim appeared irresistibly demonstrated, and in the eyes of all, the gypsy, that ravishing dancer, who had so often dazzled the passers-by with her grace, was no longer anything but a frightful vampire.

However, she betrayed no sign of life; neither Djali's graceful evolutions, nor the menaces of the court, nor the suppressed imprecations of the spectators any longer reached her mind.

In order to arouse her, a police officer was obliged to shake her unmercifully, and the president had to raise his voice, "Girl, you are of the Bohemian race, addicted to deeds of witchcraft. You, in complicity with the bewitched goat implicated in this suit, during the night of the twenty-ninth of March last, murdered and stabbed, in concert with the powers of darkness, by the aid of charms and underhand practices, a captain of the king's archers of the watch, Phoebus de Châteaupers. Do you persist in denying it?"

"Horror!" exclaimed the young girl, hiding her face in her hands. "My Phoebus! Oh, this is hell!"

"Do you persist in your denial?" demanded the president coldly.

"Do I deny it?" she said with terrible accents; and she rose with flashing eyes.

The president continued squarely, "Then how do you explain the facts laid to your charge?"

She replied in a broken voice, "I have already told you. I do not know. 'Twas a priest, a priest whom I do not know; an infernal priest who pursues me!"

"That is it," retorted the judge; "the surly monk."

"Oh, gentlemen, have mercy! I am but a poor girl—"

"Of Egypt," said the judge.

Master Jacques Charmolue interposed sweetly, "In view of the sad obstinacy of the accused, I demand the application of the torture."

"Granted," said the president.

The unhappy girl quivered in every limb. But she rose at the command of the men with partisans, and walked with a tolerably firm step, preceded by Charmolue and the priests of the officiality, between two rows of halberds, toward a medium-sized door which suddenly opened and closed again behind her, and which produced upon the grief-stricken Gringoire the effect of a horrible mouth which had just devoured her.

When she disappeared, they heard a plaintive bleating; it was the little goat mourning.

The sitting of the court was suspended. A counsellor having remarked that the gentlemen were fatigued, and that it would be a long time to wait until the torture was at an end, the president replied that a magistrate must know how to sacrifice himself to his duty.

"What an annoying and vexatious hussy," said an aged judge, "to get herself put to the question when one has not supped!"

CHAPTER 2

Continuation of the Crown That Was
Changed into a Dry Leaf

AFTER ASCENDING AND descending several steps in the corridors, which were so dark that they were lighted by lamps at mid-day, la Esmeralda, still surrounded by her lugubrious escort, was thrust by the police into a gloomy chamber. This chamber, circular in form, occupied the ground floor of one of those great towers, which, even in our own century, still pierce through the layer of modern edifices with which modern Paris has covered ancient Paris. There were no windows to this cellar; no other opening than the entrance, which was low, and closed by an enormous iron door. Nevertheless, light was not lacking; a furnace had been constructed in the thickness of the wall; a large fire was lighted there, which filled the vault with its crimson reflections and deprived a miserable candle, which stood in one corner, of all radiance. The iron grating which served to close the oven, being raised at that moment, allowed only a view at the mouth of the flaming vent-hole in the dark wall, the lower extremity of its bars, like a row of black and pointed teeth, set flat apart; which made the furnace resemble one of those mouths of dragons which spout forth flames in ancient legends. By the light that escaped from it, the prisoner beheld, all about the room, frightful instruments whose use she did not understand. In the centre lay a leather mattress, placed almost flat upon the ground, over which hung a strap provided with a buckle, attached to a brass ring in the mouth of a flat-nosed monster carved in the keystone of the vault. Tongs, pincers, large ploughshares, filled the interior of the furnace, and glowed in a confused heap on the coals. The sanguine light of the furnace illuminated in the chamber only a confused mass of horrible things.

This Tartarus was called simply, The Question Chamber.

On the bed, in a negligent attitude, sat Pierrat Torterue, the official torturer. His underlings, two gnomes with square faces, leather aprons, and linen breeches, were moving the iron instruments on the coals.

In vain did the poor girl summon up her courage; on entering this chamber she was stricken with horror.

The sergeants of the bailiff of the courts drew up in line on one side, the priests of the officiality on the other. A clerk, inkhorn, and a table were in one corner.

Master Jacques Charmolue approached the gypsy with a very sweet smile.

"My dear child," said he, "do you still persist in your denial?"

"Yes," she replied, in a dying voice.

"In that case," replied Charmolue, "it will be very painful for us to have to question you more urgently than we should like. Pray take the trouble to seat yourself on this bed. Master Pierrat, make room for mademoiselle, and close the door."

Pierrat rose with a growl.

"If I shut the door," he muttered, "my fire will go out."

"Well, my dear fellow," replied Charmolue, "leave it open then."

Meanwhile, la Esmeralda had remained standing. That leather bed on which so many unhappy wretches had writhed, frightened her. Terror chilled the very marrow of her bones; she stood there bewildered and stupefied. At a sign from Charmolue, the two assistants took her and placed her in a sitting posture on the bed. They did her no harm; but when these men touched her, when that leather touched her, she felt all her blood retreat to her heart. She cast a frightened look around the chamber. It seemed to her as though she beheld advancing from all quarters toward her, with the intention of crawling up her body and biting and pinching her, all those hideous implements of torture, which as compared to the instruments of all sorts she had hitherto seen, were like what bats, centipedes, and spiders are among insects and birds.

"Where is the physician?" asked Charmolue.

"Here," replied a black gown whom she had not before noticed. She shuddered.

"Mademoiselle," resumed the caressing voice of the procucrator of the Ecclesiastical court, "for the third time, do you persist in denying the deeds of which you are accused?"

This time she could only make a sign with her head.

"You persist?" said Jacques Charmolue. "Then it grieves me deeply, but I must fulfil my office."

"Monsieur le Procureur du Roi," said Pierrat abruptly, "How shall we begin?"

Charmolue hesitated for a moment with the ambiguous grimace of a poet in search of a rhyme.

"With the boot," he said at last.

The unfortunate girl felt herself so utterly abandoned by God and men, that her head fell upon her breast like an inert thing that has no power in itself.

The tormentor and the physician approached her simultaneously. At the same time, the two assistants began to fumble among their hideous arsenal.

At the clanking of their frightful irons, the unhappy child quivered like a dead frog that is being galvanized. "Oh!" she murmured, so low that no one heard her; "Oh, my Phoebus!" Then she fell back once more into her immobility and her marble silence. This spectacle would have rent any other heart than those of her judges. One would have pronounced her a poor sinful soul, being tortured by Satan beneath the scarlet wicket of hell. The miserable body which that frightful swarm of saws, wheels, and racks were about to clasp in their clutches, the being who was about to be manipulated by the harsh hands of executioners and pincers, was that gentle, white, fragile creature, a poor grain of millet which human justice was handing over to the terrible mills of torture to grind. Meanwhile, the callous hands of Pierrat Torterue's assistants had bared that charming leg, that tiny foot, which had so often amazed the passers-by with their delicacy and beauty, in the squares of Paris.

"'Tis a shame!" muttered the tormentor, glancing at these graceful and delicate forms.

Had the archdeacon been present, he certainly would have recalled at that moment his symbol of the spider and the fly. Soon the unfortunate girl, through a mist that spread before her eyes, beheld the boot approach; she soon beheld her foot encased between iron plates disappear in the frightful apparatus. Then terror restored her strength.

"Take that off!" she cried angrily; and drawing herself up, with her hair all dishevelled: "Mercy!"

She darted from the bed to fling herself at the feet of the king's procurator, but her leg was fast in the heavy block of oak and iron, and she sank down upon the boot, more crushed than a bee with a lump of lead on its wing.

At a sign from Charmolue, she was replaced on the bed, and two coarse hands adjusted to her delicate waist the strap that hung from the ceiling.

"For the last time, do you confess the facts in the case?" demanded Charmolue, with his imperturbable benignity.

"I am innocent."

"Then, mademoiselle, how do you explain the circumstance laid to your charge?"

"Alas, monseigneur, I do not know."

"So you deny them?"

"All!"

"Proceed," said Charmolue to Pierrat.

Pierrat turned the handle of the screw-jack, the boot was contracted, and the unhappy girl uttered one of those horrible cries which have no orthography in any human language.

"Stop!" said Charmolue to Pierrat. "Do you confess?" he said to the gypsy.

"All!" cried the wretched girl. "I confess! I confess! Mercy!"

She had not calculated her strength when she faced the torture. Poor child, whose life up to that time had been so joyous, so pleasant, so sweet, the first pain had conquered her!

"Humanity forces me to tell you," remarked the king's procurator, "that in confessing, it is death that you must expect."

"I certainly hope so!" said she. And she fell back upon the leather bed, dying, doubled up, allowing herself to hang suspended from the strap buckled round her waist.

"Come, fair one, hold up a little," said Master Pierrat, raising her. "You have the air of the lamb of the Golden Fleece which hangs from Monsieur de Bourgogne's neck."

Jacques Charmolue raised his voice,

"Clerk, write. Young Bohemian maid, you confess your participation in the feasts, Witches' Sabbaths, and witchcrafts of hell, with ghosts, hags, and vampires? Answer."

"Yes," she said, so low that her words were lost in her breathing.

"You confess to having seen the ram which Beelzebub causes to appear in the clouds to call together the Witches' Sabbath, and which is beheld by socerers alone?"

"Yes."

"You confess to having adored the heads of Bophomet, those abominable idols of the Templars?"

"Yes."

"To having had habitual dealings with the devil under the form of a goat familiar, joined with you in the suit?"

"Yes."

"Lastly, you avow and confess to having, with the aid of the demon, and of the phantom vulgarly known as the surly monk, on the night of the twenty-ninth of March last, murdered and assassinated a captain named Phoebus de Châteaupers?"

She raised her large, staring eyes to the magistrate, and replied, as though mechanically, without convulsion or agitation, "Yes."

It was evident that everything within her was broken.

"Write, clerk," said Charmolue. And, addressing the torturers, "Release the prisoner, and take her back to the court."

When the prisoner had been "unbooted," the procurator of the ecclesiastical court examined her foot, which was still swollen with pain. "Come," said he, "there's no great harm done. You shrieked in good season. You could still dance, my beauty!"

Then he turned to his acolytes of the officiality, "Behold justice enlightened at last! This is a solace, gentlemen! Madamoiselle will bear us witness that we have acted with all possible gentleness."

CHAPTER 3

End of the Crown That Was Turned into a Dry Leaf

WHEN SHE RE-ENTERED the audience hall, pale and limping, she was received with a general murmur of pleasure. On the part of the audience there was the feeling of impatience gratified which one experiences at the theatre at the end of the last entr'acte of the comedy, when the curtain rises and the conclusion is about to begin. On the part of the judges, it was the hope of getting their suppers sooner.

The little goat also bleated with joy. He tried to run toward his mistress, but they had tied him to the bench.

Night was fully set in. The candles, whose number had not been increased, cast so little light, that the walls of the hall could not be seen. The shadows there enveloped all objects in a sort of mist. A few apathetic faces of judges alone could be dimly discerned. Opposite them, at the extremity of the long hall, they could see a vaguely white point standing out against the sombre background. This was the accused.

She had dragged herself to her place. When Charmolue had installed himself in a magisterial manner in his own, he seated himself, then rose and said, without exhibiting too much self-complacency at his success, "The accused has confessed all."

"Bohemian girl," the president continued, "have you avowed all your deeds of magic, prostitution, and assassination on Phoebus de Châteaupers."

Her heart contracted. She was heard to sob amid the darkness.

"Anything you like," she replied feebly, "but kill me quickly!"

"Monsieur, procurator of the king in the ecclesiastical courts," said the president, "the chamber is ready to hear you in your charge."

Master Charmolue exhibited an alarming note book, and began to read, with many gestures and the exaggerated accentuation of the pleader, an oration in Latin, wherein all the proofs of the suit were piled up in Ciceronian periphrases, flanked with quotations from Plautus, his favorite comic author. We regret that we are not able to offer to our readers this remarkable piece. The orator pronounced it with marvellous action. Before he had finished the exordium, the perspiration was starting from his brow, and his eyes from his head.

All at once, in the middle of a fine period, he interrupted himself, and his glance, ordinarily so gentle and even stupid, became menacing.

"Gentlemen," he exclaimed (this time in French, for it was not in his copy book), "Satan is so mixed up in this affair, that here he is present at our debates, and making sport of their majesty. Behold!"

So saying, he pointed to the little goat, who, on seeing Charmolue gesticulating, had, in point of fact, thought it appropriate to do the same, and had seated himself on his haunches, reproducing to the best of his ability, with his forepaws and his bearded head the pathetic pantomine of the king's procurator in the ecclesiastical court. This was, if the reader remembers, one of his prettiest accomplishments. This incident, this last proof, produced a great effect. The goat's hoofs were tied, and the king's procurator resumed the thread of his eloquence.

It was very long, but the peroration was admirable. Here is the concluding phrase; let the reader add the hoarse voice and the breathless gestures of Master Charmolue, "*Ideò, domni, coram strygâ demonstratâ, crimine patente, intentione criminis existente, in nomine sanctoe ecclesiæ Nostræ-Dominæ Parisiensis quæ est in saisinâ habendi omnimodam altam et bassam justitiam in illâ hac intemeratâ Civitatis insulâ, tenore præsentium declaremus nos requirere, primo, aliquamdam pecuniariam indemnitatem; secundo, amendationem honorabilem ante portalium maximum Nostroe-Dominoe, ecclesiæ cathedralis; tertio, sententiam in virtute cujus ista styrgâ cum suâ capellâ, seu in trivio vulgariter dicto* la Grève, *seu in insulâ exeunte in fluvio Secanæ, juxta pointam juardini regalis, executatæ sint!*"

He put on his cap again and seated himself.

"*Eheu!*" sighed the broken-hearted Gringoire, "*bassa latinitas!*"

Another man in a black gown rose near the accused; he was her lawyer. The judges, who were fasting, began to grumble.

"Advocate, be brief," said the president.

"Monsieur the President," replied the advocate, "since the defendant has confessed the crime, I have only one word to say to these gentlemen. Here is a text from the Salic law; 'If a witch hath eaten a man, and if she be convicted of it, she shall pay a fine of eight thousand deniers, which amount to two hundred sous of gold.' May it please the chamber to condemn my client to the fine?"

"An abrogated text," said the advocate extraordinary of the king.

"*Nego*, I deny it," replied the advocate.

"Put it to the vote!" said one of the councillors; "the crime is manifest, and it is late."

They proceeded to take a vote without leaving the room. The judges signified their assent without giving their reasons; they were in a hurry. Their capped heads were seen uncovering one after the other, in the gloom, at the lugubrious question addressed to them by the president in a low voice. The poor accused had the appearance of looking at them, but her troubled eye no longer saw.

Then the clerk began to write; then he handed a long parchment to the president.

Then the unhappy girl heard the people moving, the pikes clashing, and a freezing voice saying to her, "Bohemian wench, on the day when it shall seem good to our lord the king, at the hour of noon, you will be taken in a tumbrel, in your shift, with bare feet, and a rope about your neck, before the grand portal of Notre-Dame, and you will there make an apology with a wax torch of the weight of two pounds in your hand, and thence you will be conducted to the Place de Grève, where you will be hanged and strangled on the town gibbet; and likewise your goat; and you will pay to the official three lions of gold, in reparation of the crimes by you committed and by you confessed, of sorcery and magic, debauchery and murder, upon the person of the Sieur Phoebus de Châteaupers. May God have mercy on your soul!"

"Oh, 'tis a dream!" she murmured; and she felt rough hands bearing her away.

CHAPTER 4

Lasciate Ogni Speranza

IN THE MIDDLE AGES, when an edifice was complete, there was almost as much of it in the earth as above it. Unless built upon piles, like Notre-Dame, a palace, a fortress, a church, had always a double bottom. In cathedrals, it was, in some sort, another subterranean cathedral, low, dark, mysterious, blind, and mute, under the upper nave that was overflowing with light and reverberating with organs and bells day and night. Sometimes it was a sepulchre. In palaces, in fortresses, it was a prison, sometimes a sepulchre also, sometimes both together. These mighty buildings, whose mode of formation and vegetation we have elsewhere explained, had not simply foundations, but, so to speak, roots which ran branching through the soil in chambers, galleries, and staircases, like the construction above. Thus churches, palaces, fortresses, had the earth half way up their bodies. The cellars of an edifice formed another edifice, into which one descended instead of ascending, and which extended its subterranean grounds under the external piles of the monument, like those forests and mountains that are reversed in the mirror-like waters of a lake, beneath the forests and mountains of the banks.

At the fortress of Saint-Antoine, at the Palais de Justice of Paris, at the Louvre, these subterranean edifices were prisons. The stories of these prisons, as they sank into the soil, grew constantly narrower and more gloomy. They were so many zones, where the shades of horror were graduated. Dante could never imagine anything better for his hell. These tunnels of cells usually terminated in a sack of a lowest dungeon, with a vat-like bottom, where Dante placed Satan, where society placed those condemned to death. A miserable human existence, once interred there; farewell light, air, life, *ogni speranza—*

every hope; it only came forth to the scaffold or the stake. Sometimes it rotted there; human justice called this "forgetting." Between men and himself, the condemned man felt a pile of stones and jailers weighing down upon his head; and the entire prison, the massive bastille was nothing more than an enormous, complicated lock, which barred him off from the rest of the world.

It was in a sloping cavity of this description, in the *oubliettes* excavated by Saint-Louis, in the *inpace* of the Tournelle, that la Esmeralda had been placed on being condemned to death, through fear of her escape, no doubt, with the colossal court-house over her head. Poor fly, who could not have lifted even one of its blocks of stone!

Assuredly, Providence and society had been equally unjust; such an excess of unhappiness and of torture was not necessary to break so frail a creature.

There she lay, lost in the shadows, buried, hidden, immured. Any one who could have beheld her in this state, after having seen her laugh and dance in the sun, would have shuddered. Cold as night, cold as death, not a breath of air in her tresses, not a human sound in her ear, no longer a ray of light in her eyes; snapped in twain, crushed with chains, crouching beside a jug and a loaf, on a little straw, in a pool of water, which was formed under her by the sweating of the prison walls; without motion, almost without breath, she had no longer the power to suffer; Phoebus, the sun, midday, the open air, the streets of Paris, the dances with applause, the sweet babblings of love with the officer; then the priest, the old crone, the poignard, the blood, the torture, the gibbet; all this did, indeed, pass before her mind, sometimes as a charming and golden vision, sometimes as a hideous nightmare; but it was no longer anything but a vague and horrible struggle, lost in the gloom, or distant music played up above ground, and which was no longer audible at the depth where the unhappy girl had fallen.

Since she had been there, she had neither waked nor slept. In that misfortune, in that cell, she could no longer distinguish her waking hours from slumber, dreams from reality, any more than day from night. All this was mixed, broken, floating, disseminated confusedly in her thought. She no longer felt, she no longer knew, she no longer thought; at the most, she only dreamed. Never had a living creature been thrust more deeply into nothingness.

Thus benumbed, frozen, petrified, she had barely noticed on two or three occasions, the sound of a trap door opening somewhere above her, without even permitting the passage of a little light, and through which a hand had tossed her a bit of black bread. Nevertheless, this periodical visit of the jailer was the sole communication that was left her with mankind.

A single thing still mechanically occupied her ear; above her head, the dampness was filtering through the mouldy stones of the vault, and a drop of water dropped from them at regular intervals. She listened stupidly to the noise made by this drop of water as it fell into the pool beside her.

This drop of water falling from time to time into that pool, was the only movement which still went on around her, the only clock which marked the time, the only noise which reached her of all the noise made on the surface of the earth.

To tell the whole, however, she also felt, from time to time, in that cesspool of mire and darkness, something cold passing over her foot or her arm, and she shuddered.

How long had she been there? She did not know. She had a recollection of a sentence of death pronounced somewhere, against some one, then of having been herself carried away, and of waking up in darkness and silence, chilled to the heart. She had dragged herself along on her hands. Then iron rings that cut her ankles, and chains had rattled. She had recognized the fact that all around her was wall, that below her there was a pavement covered with moisture and a truss of straw; but neither lamp nor air-hole. Then she had seated herself on that straw and, sometimes, for the sake of changing her attitude, on the last stone step in her dungeon. For a while she had tried to count the black minutes measured off for her by the drop of water; but that melancholy labor of an ailing brain had broken off of itself in her head, and had left her in stupor.

At length, one day, or one night (for midnight and midday were of the same color in that sepulchre), she heard above her a louder noise than was usually made by the turnkey when he brought her bread and jug of water. She raised her head, and beheld a ray of reddish light passing through the crevices in the sort of trap door contrived in the roof of the *inpace*.

At the same time, the heavy lock creaked, the trap grated on its rusty hinges, turned, and she beheld a lantern, a hand, and the lower portions of the bodies of two men, the door being too low to admit of her seeing their heads. The light pained her so acutely that she shut her eyes.

When she opened them again the door was closed, the lantern was deposited on one of the steps of the staircase; a man alone stood before her. A monk's black cloak fell to his feet, a cowl of the same color concealed his face. Nothing was visible of his person, neither face nor hands. It was a long, black shroud standing erect, and beneath which something could be felt moving. She gazed fixedly for several minutes at this sort of spectre. But neither he nor she spoke. One would have pronounced them two statues confronting each other. Two things only seemed alive in that cavern; the wick of the lantern, which sputtered on account of the dampness of the atmosphere, and the drop of water from the roof, which cut this irregular sputtering with its monotonous splash, and made the light of the lantern quiver in concentric waves on the oily water of the pool.

At last the prisoner broke the silence.

"Who are you?"

"A priest."

The words, the accent, the sound of his voice made her tremble.

The priest continued, in a hollow voice, "Are you prepared?"

"For what?"

"To die."

"Oh!" said she. "Will it be soon?"

"Tomorrow."

Her head, which had been raised with joy, fell back upon her breast.

"'Tis very far away yet!" she murmured; "why could they not have done it today?"

"Then you are very unhappy?" asked the priest, after a silence.

"I am very cold," she replied.

She took her feet in her hands, a gesture habitual with unhappy wretches who are cold, as we have already seen in the case of the recluse of the Tour-Roland, and her teeth chattered.

The priest appeared to cast his eyes around the dungeon from beneath his cowl.

"Without light! Without fire! In the water! It is horrible!"

"Yes," she replied, with the bewildered air which unhappiness had given her. "The day belongs to every one, why do they give me only night?"

"Do you know," resumed the priest, after a fresh silence, "why you are here?"

"I thought I knew once," she said, passing her thin fingers over her eyelids, as though to aid her memory, "but I know no longer."

All at once she began to weep like a child.

"I should like to get away from here, sir. I am cold, I am afraid, and there are creatures which crawl over my body."

"Well, follow me."

So saying, the priest took her arm. The unhappy girl was frozen to her very soul. Yet that hand produced an impression of cold upon her.

"Oh!" she murmured, "'tis the icy hand of death. Who are you?"

The priest threw back his cowl; she looked. It was the sinister visage which had so long pursued her; that demon's head which had appeared at la Falourdel's, above the head of her adored Phoebus; that eye which she last had seen glittering beside a dagger.

This apparition, always so fatal for her, and which had thus driven her on from misfortune to misfortune, even to torture, roused her from her stupor. It seemed to her that the sort of veil that had lain thick upon her memory was rent away. All the details of her melancholy adventure, from the nocturnal scene at la Falourdel's to her condemnation to the Tournelle, recurred to her memory, no longer vague and confused as heretofore, but distinct, harsh, clear, palpitating, terrible. These souvenirs, half effaced and almost obliterated by excess of suffering, were revived by the sombre figure which stood before her, as the approach of fire causes letters traced upon white paper with invisible ink, to start out perfectly fresh. It seemed to her that all the wounds of her heart opened and bled simultaneously.

"Hah!" she cried, with her hands on her eyes, and a convulsive trembling, "'tis the priest!"

Then she dropped her arms in discouragement, and remained seated, with lowered head, eyes fixed on the ground, mute and still trembling.

The priest gazed at her with the eye of a hawk that has long been soaring in a circle from the heights of heaven over a poor lark cowering in the wheat, and has long been silently contracting the formidable circles of his flight, and has suddenly swooped down upon his prey like a flash of lightning, and holds it panting in his talons.

She began to murmur in a low voice, "Finish! Finish the last blow!" and she drew her head down in terror between her shoulders, like the lamb awaiting the blow of the butcher's axe.

"So I inspire you with horror?" he said at length.

She made no reply.

"Do I inspire you with horror?" he repeated.

Her lips contracted, as though with a smile.

"Yes," said she, "the headsman scoffs at the condemned. Here he has been pursuing me, threatening me, terrifying me for months! Had it not been for him, my God, how happy it should have been! It was he who cast me into this abyss! Oh heavens! It was he who killed him! My Phoebus!"

Here, bursting into sobs, and raising her eyes to the priest, "Oh! wretch, who are you? What have I done to you? Do you then, hate me so? Alas, what have you against me?"

"I love thee!" cried the priest.

Her tears suddenly ceased, she gazed at him with the look of an idiot. He had fallen on his knees and was devouring her with eyes of flame.

"Dost thou understand? I love thee!" he cried again.

"What love!" said the unhappy girl with a shudder.

He resumed, "The love of a damned soul."

Both remained silent for several minutes, crushed beneath the weight of their emotions; he maddened, she stupefied.

"Listen," said the priest at last, and a singular calm had come over him; "you shall know all I am about to tell you that which I have hitherto hardly dared to say to myself, when furtively interrogating my conscience at those deep hours of the night when it is so dark that it seems as though God no longer saw us. Listen. Before I knew you, young girl, I was happy."

"So was I!" she sighed feebly.

"Do not interrupt me. Yes, I was happy, at least I believed myself to be so. I was pure, my soul was filled with limpid light. No head was raised more proudly and more radiantly than mine. Priests consulted me on chastity; doctors, on doctrines. Yes, science was all in all to me; it was a sister to me, and a sister sufficed. Not but that with age other ideas came to me. More than once my flesh had been moved as a woman's form passed by. That force of sex and blood which, in the madness of youth, I had imagined that I had stifled forever had, more than once, convulsively raised the chain of iron vows which bind me, a miserable wretch, to the cold stones of the altar. But fasting, prayer, study, the mortifications of the cloister, rendered my soul mistress of my body once more, and then I avoided women. Moreover, I had but to open a book, and all the impure mists of my brain vanished before the splendors of science. In a few moments, I felt the gross things of earth flee far away, and I found myself once more calm, quieted, and serene, in the presence of the tranquil radiance of eternal truth. As long as the demon sent to attack me only vague shadows of women who passed occasionally before my eyes in church, in the streets, in the fields, and who hardly recurred to my dreams, I easily vanquished him. Alas, if the victory has not remained with me, it is the fault of God, who has not created man and the demon of equal force. Listen. One day—"

Here the priest paused, and the prisoner heard sighs of anguish break from his breast with a sound of the death rattle.

He resumed, "One day I was leaning on the window of my cell. What book was I reading then? Oh, all that is a whirlwind in my head. I was reading. The window opened upon a Square. I heard a sound of tambourine and music. Annoyed at being thus disturbed in my revery, I glanced into the Square. What I beheld, others saw beside myself, and yet it was not a spectacle made for human eyes. There, in the middle of the pavement—it was midday, the sun was shining brightly—a creature was dancing. A creature so beautiful that God would have preferred her to the Virgin and have chosen her for his mother and have wished to be born of her if she had been in existence when he was made man! Her eyes were black and splendid; in the midst of her black locks, some hairs through which the sun shone glistened like threads of gold. Her feet disappeared in their movements like the spokes of a rapidly turning wheel. Around her head, in her black tresses, there were disks of metal, which glittered in the sun, and formed a coronet of stars on her brow. Her dress thick set with spangles, blue, and dotted with a thousand sparks, gleamed like a summer night. Her brown, supple arms twined and untwined around her waist, like two scarfs. The form of her body was surprisingly beautiful. Oh, what a resplendent figure stood out, like something luminous even in the sunlight! Alas, young girl, it was thou! Surprised, intoxicated, charmed, I allowed myself to gaze upon thee. I looked so long that I suddenly shuddered with terror; I felt that fate was seizing hold of me."

The priest paused for a moment, overcome with emotion. Then he continued, "Already half fascinated, I tried to cling fast to something and hold myself back from falling. I recalled the snares that Satan had already set for me. The creature before my eyes possessed that superhuman beauty which can come only from heaven or hell. It was no simple girl made with a little of our earth, and dimly lighted within by the vacillating ray of a woman's soul. It was an angel, but of shadows and flame, and not of light. At the moment when I was meditating thus, I beheld beside you a goat, a beast of witches, which smiled as it gazed at me. The midday sun gave him golden horns. Then I perceived the snare of the demon, and I no longer doubted that you had come from hell and that you had come thence for my perdition. I believed it."

Here the priest looked the prisoner full in the face, and added, coldly, "I believe it still. Nevertheless, the charm operated little by little; your dancing whirled through my brain; I felt the mysterious spell working within me. All that should have awakened was lulled to sleep; and like those who die in the snow, I felt pleasure in allowing this sleep to draw on. All at once, you began to sing. What could I do, unhappy wretch? Your song was still more charming than your dancing. I tried to flee. Impossible. I was nailed, rooted to the spot. It seemed to me that the marble of the pavement had risen to my knees. I was forced to remain until the end. My feet were like ice; my head was on fire. At last you took pity on me, you ceased to sing, you disappeared. The reflection of the dazzling vision, the reverberation of the enchanting music disappeared by degrees from my eyes and my ears. Then I fell back into the embrasure of the window, more rigid, more feeble than a statue torn from its base. The vesper bell roused me. I drew myself up; I fled; but alas! Something within me had fallen never to rise again, something had come upon me from which I could not flee."

He made another pause and went on, "Yes, dating from that day, there was within me a man whom I did not know. I tried to make use of all my remedies. The cloister, the altar, work, books—follies! Oh, how hollow does science sound when one in despair dashes against it a head full of passions! Do you know, young girl, what I saw thenceforth between my book and me? You, your shade, the image of the luminous apparition that had one day crossed the space before me. But this image had no longer the same color; it was sombre, funereal, gloomy as the black circle which long pursues the vision of the imprudent man who has gazed intently at the sun.

"Unable to rid myself of it, since I heard your song humming ever in my head, beheld your feet dancing always on my breviary, felt even at night, in my dreams, your form in contact with my own, I desired to see you again, to touch you, to know who you were, to see whether

I should really find you like the ideal image which I had retained of you, to shatter my dream, perchance, with reality. At all events, I hoped that a new impression would efface the first, and the first had become insupportable. I sought you. I saw you once more. Calamity! When I had seen you twice, I wanted to see you a thousand times, I wanted to see you always. Then—how stop myself on that slope of hell?—then I no longer belonged to myself. The other end of the thread that the demon had attached to my wings he had fastened to his foot. I became vagrant and wandering like yourself. I waited for you under porches, I stood on the lookout for you at the street corners, I watched for you from the summit of my tower. Every evening I returned to myself more charmed, more despairing, more bewitched, more lost!

"I had learned who you were; an Egyptian, Bohemian, gypsy, zingara. How could I doubt the magic? Listen. I hoped that a trial would free me from the charm. A witch enchanted Bruno d'Ast; he had her burned, and was cured. I knew it. I wanted to try the remedy. First I tried to have you forbidden from the square in front of Notre-Dame, hoping to forget you if you returned no more. You paid no heed to it. You returned. Then the idea of abducting you occurred to me. One night I made the attempt. There were two of us. We already had you in our power, when that miserable officer came up. He delivered you. Thus did he begin your unhappiness, mine, and his own. Finally, no longer knowing what to do, and what was to become of me, I denounced you to the official.

"I thought that I should be cured like Bruno d'Ast. I also had a confused idea that a trial would deliver you into my hands; that, as a prisoner I should hold you, I should have you; that there you could not escape from me; that you had already possessed me a sufficiently long time to give me the right to possess you in my turn. When one does wrong, one must do it thoroughly. 'Tis madness to halt midway in the monstrous! The extreme of crime has its deliriums of joy. A priest and a witch can mingle in delight upon the truss of straw in a dungeon!

"Accordingly, I denounced you. It was then that I terrified you when we met. The plot I was weaving against you, the storm I was heaping up above your head, burst from me in threats and lightning glances. Still, I hesitated. My project had its terrible sides that made me shrink back.

"Perhaps I might have renounced it; perhaps my hideous thought would have withered in my brain, without bearing fruit. I thought that it would always depend upon me to follow up or discontinue this prosecution. But every evil thought is inexorable, and insists on becoming a deed; but where I believed myself to be all powerful, fate was more powerful than I. Alas, 'tis fate which has seized you and delivered you to the terrible wheels of the machine which I had constructed doubly. Listen. I am nearing the end.

"One day—again the sun was shining brilliantly—I behold man pass me uttering your name and laughing, who carries sensuality in his eyes. Damnation! I followed him; you know the rest."

He ceased.

The young girl could find but one word:

"Oh, my Phoebus!"

"Not that name!" said the priest, grasping her arm violently. "Utter not that name! Oh, miserable wretches that we are, 'tis that name which has ruined us! Or, rather we have ruined each other by the inexplicable play of fate! You are suffering, are you not? You are cold; the night makes you blind, the dungeon envelops you; but perhaps you still have some light in the bottom of your soul, were it only your childish love for that empty man who played with your heart, while I bear the dungeon within me; within me there is winter, ice, despair; I have night in my soul.

"Do you know what I have suffered? I was present at your trial. I was seated on the officials' bench. Yes, under one of the priests' cowls, there were the contortions of the damned. When you were brought in, I was there; when you were questioned, I was there. Den of wolves! It was my crime, it was my gallows that I beheld being slowly reared over your head. I was there for every witness, every proof, every plea; I could count each of your steps in the painful path; I was still there when that ferocious beast—oh! I had not foreseen torture! Listen. I followed you to that chamber of anguish. I beheld you stripped and handled, half naked, by the infamous hands of the tormentor. I beheld your foot, that foot which I would have given an empire to kiss and die, that foot, beneath which to have had my head crushed I should have felt such rapture, I beheld it encased in that horrible boot, which converts the limbs of a living being into one bloody clod. Oh, wretch! While I looked on at that, I held beneath my shroud a dagger, with which I lacerated my breast. When you uttered that cry, I plunged it into my flesh; at a second cry, it would have entered my heart. Look! I believe that it still bleeds."

He opened his cassock. His breast was in fact, mangled as by the claw of a tiger, and on his side he had a large and badly healed wound.

The prisoner recoiled with horror.

"Oh!" said the priest, "young girl, have pity upon me! You think yourself unhappy; alas, alas! You know not what unhappiness is. Oh, to love a woman! To be a priest! To be hated! To love with all the fury of one's soul; to feel that one would give for the least of her smiles, one's blood, one's vitals, one's fame, one's salvation, one's immortality and eternity, this life and the other; to regret that one is not a king, emperor, archangel, God, in order that one might place a greater slave beneath her feet; to clasp her night and day in one's dreams and one's thoughts, and to behold her in love with the trappings of a soldier and to have nothing to offer her but a priest's dirty cassock, which will inspire her with fear and disgust! To be present with one's jealousy and one's rage, while she lavishes on a miserable, blustering imbecile, treasures of love and beauty! To behold that body whose form burns you, that bosom which possesses so much sweetness, that flesh palpitate and blush beneath the kisses of another! Oh heaven! To love her foot, her arm, her shoulder, to think of her blue veins, of her brown skin, until one writhes for whole nights together on the pavement of one's cell, and to behold all those caresses which one has dreamed of, end in torture! To have succeeded only in stretching her upon the leather bed! Oh! These are the veritable pincers, reddened in the fires of hell. Oh, blessed is he who is sawn between two planks, or torn in pieces by four horses! Do you know what that torture is, which is imposed upon you for long nights by your burning arteries, your bursting heart, your breaking head, your teeth-gnawed hands; mad tormentors which turn you incessantly, as upon a red-hot gridiron, to a thought of love, of jealousy, and of despair! Young girl, mercy! A truce for a moment! A few ashes on these live coals! Wipe away, I beseech you, the perspiration that trickles in great drops from my brow! Child, torture me with one hand, but caress me with the other! Have pity, young girl! Have pity upon me!"

The priest writhed on the wet pavement, beating his head against the corners of the stone steps. The young girl gazed at him, and listened to him.

When he ceased, exhausted and panting, she repeated in a low voice, "Oh my Phoebus!"

The priest dragged himself toward her on his knees.

"I beseech you," he cried, "if you have any heart, do not repulse me! Oh! I love you! I am a wretch! When you utter that name, unhappy girl, it is as though you crushed all the fibres of my heart between your teeth. Mercy! If you come from hell I will go thither with you. I have done everything to that end. The hell where you are, shall be paradise; the sight of you is more charming than that of God! Oh, speak! You will have none of me? I should have thought the mountains would be shaken in their foundations on the day when a woman would repulse such a love. Oh! If you only would! Oh, how happy we might be. We would flee—I would help you to flee—we would go somewhere, we would seek that spot on earth, where the sun is brightest, the sky the bluest, where the trees are most luxuriant. We would love each other, we would pour our two souls into each other, and we would have a thirst for ourselves which we would quench in common and incessantly at that fountain of inexhaustible love."

She interrupted with a terrible and thrilling laugh.

"Look, father, you have blood on your fingers!"

The priest remained for several moments as though petrified, with his eyes fixed upon his hand.

"Well, yes!" he resumed at last, with strange gentleness, "insult me, scoff at me, overwhelm me with scorn! But come, come. Let us make haste. It is to be tomorrow, I tell you. The gibbet on the Grève, you know it? It stands always ready. It is horrible to see you ride in that tumbrel! Oh mercy! Until now I have never felt the power of my love for you. Oh, follow me! You shall take your time to love me after I have saved you. You shall hate me as long as you will. But come. Tomorrow, tomorrow! The gallows! Your execution! Oh, save yourself! Spare me!"

He seized her arm, he was beside himself, he tried to drag her away.

She fixed her eye intently on him.

"What has become of my Phoebus?"

"Ah!" said the priest, releasing her arm, "you are pitiless."

"What has become of Phoebus?" she repeated coldly.

"He is dead!" cried the priest.

"Dead!" said she, still icy and motionless, "then why do you talk to me of living?"

He was not listening to her.

"Oh, yes!" said he, as though speaking to himself. "He certainly must be dead. The blade pierced deeply. I believe I touched his heart with the point. Oh! My very soul was at the end of the dagger!"

The young girl flung herself upon him like a raging tigress, and pushed him upon the steps of the staircase with supernatural force.

"Begone, monster! Begone, assassin! Leave me to die! May the blood of both of us make an eternal stain upon your brow! Be thine, priest! Never, never! Nothing shall unite us! Not hell itself! Go, accursed man! Never!"

The priest had stumbled on the stairs. He silently disentangled his feet from the folds of his robe, picked up his lantern again, and slowly began the ascent of the steps that led to the door; he opened the door and passed through it.

All at once, the young girl beheld his head reappear; it wore a frightful expression, and he cried, hoarse with rage and despair, "I tell you he is dead!"

She fell face downwards upon the floor, and there was no longer any sound audible in the cell than the sob of the drop of water that made the pool palpitate amid the darkness.

CHAPTER 5

The Mother

I DO NOT believe that there is anything sweeter in the world than the ideas which awake in a mother's heart at the sight of her child's tiny shoe; especially if it is a shoe for festivals, for Sunday, for baptism, the shoe embroidered to the very sole, a shoe in which the infant has not yet taken a step. That shoe has so much grace and daintiness, it is so impossible for it to walk, that it seems to the mother as though she saw her child. She smiles upon it, she kisses it, she talks to it; she asks herself whether there can actually be a foot so tiny; and if the child be absent, the pretty shoe suffices to place the sweet and fragile creature before her eyes. She thinks she sees it, she does see it, complete, living, joyous, with its delicate hands, its round head, its pure lips, its serene eyes whose white is blue. If it is in winter, it is yonder, crawling on the carpet, it is laboriously climbing upon an ottoman, and the mother trembles lest it should approach the fire. If it is summer time, it crawls about the yard, in the garden, plucks up the grass between the paving-stones, gazes innocently at the big dogs, the big horses, without fear, plays with the shells, with the flowers, and makes the gardener grumble because he finds sand in the flower-beds and earth in the paths. Everything laughs, and shines and plays around it, like it, even the breath of air and the ray of sun that vie with each other in disporting among the silky ringlets of its hair. The shoe shows all this to the mother, and makes her heart melt as fire melts wax.

But when the child is lost, these thousand images of joy, of charms, of tenderness, which throng around the little shoe, become so many horrible things. The pretty broidered shoe is no longer anything but an instrument of torture that eternally crushes the heart of the mother. It is always the same fibre that vibrates, the tenderest and most sensitive; but instead of an angel caressing it, it is a demon who is wrenching at it.

One May morning, when the sun was rising on one of those dark blue skies against which Garofolo loves to place his Descents from the Cross, the recluse of the Tour-Roland heard a sound of wheels, of horses and irons in the Place de Grève. She was somewhat aroused by it, knotted her hair upon her ears in order to deafen herself, and resumed her contemplation, on her knees, of the inanimate object which she had adored for fifteen years. This little shoe was the universe to her, as we have already said. Her thought was shut up in it, and was destined never more to quit it except at death. The sombre cave of the Tour-Roland alone knew how many bitter imprecations, touching complaints, prayers and sobs she had wafted to heaven in connection with that charming bauble of rose-colored satin. Never was more despair bestowed upon a prettier and more graceful thing.

It seemed as though her grief were breaking forth more violently than usual; and she could be heard outside lamenting in a loud and monotonous voice which rent the heart.

"Oh my daughter!" she said, "my daughter, my poor, dear little child, so I shall never see thee more! It is over! It always seems to me that it happened yesterday! My God! My God! It would have been better not to give her to me than to take her away so soon. Did you not know that our children are part of ourselves, and that a mother who has lost her child no longer believes in God? Ah, wretch that I am to have gone out that day! Lord! Lord! To have taken her from me thus; you could never have looked at me with her, when I was joyously warming her at my fire, when she laughed as she suckled, when I made her tiny feet creep up my breast to my lips? Oh! If you had looked at that, my God, you would have taken pity on my joy; you would not have taken from me the only love that lingered, in my heart! Was I then, Lord, so miserable a creature, that you could not look at me before condemning me? Alas! Alas! Here is the shoe; where is the foot? Where is the rest? Where is the child? My daughter! My daughter! What did they do with thee? Lord, give her back to me. My knees have been worn for fifteen years in praying to thee, my God! Is not that enough? Give her back to me one day, one hour, one minute; one minute, Lord! And then cast me to the demon for all eternity! Oh, if I only knew where the skirt of your garment trails, I would cling to it with both hands, and you would be obliged to give me back my child! Have you no pity on her pretty little shoe? Could you condemn a poor mother to this torture for fifteen years? Good Virgin!

Good Virgin of heaven! My infant Jesus has been taken from me, has been stolen from me; they devoured her on a heath, they drank her blood, they cracked her bones! Good Virgin, have pity upon me. My daughter, I want my daughter! What is it to me that she is in paradise? I do not want your angel, I want my child! I am a lioness, I want my whelp. Oh! I will writhe on the earth, I will break the stones with my forehead, and I will damn myself, and I will curse you, Lord, if you keep my child from me! You see plainly that my arms are all bitten, Lord! Has the good God no mercy? Oh! Give me only salt and black bread, only let me have my daughter to warm me like a sun! Alas! Lord my God. Alas! Lord my God, I am only a vile sinner; but my daughter made me pious. I was full of religion for the love of her, and I beheld you through her smile as through an opening into heaven. Oh, if I could only once, just once more, a single time, put this shoe on her pretty little pink foot, I would die blessing you, good Virgin. Ah! Fifteen years! She will be grown up now! Unhappy child! What! It is really true then I shall never see her more, not even in heaven, for I shall not go there myself. Oh, what misery to think that here is her shoe, and that that is all!"

The unhappy woman flung herself upon that shoe; her consolation and her despair for so many years, and her vitals were rent with sobs as on the first day; because, for a mother who has lost her child, it is always the first day. That grief never grows old. The mourning garments may grow white and threadbare, the heart remains dark.

At that moment, the fresh and joyous cries of children passed in front of the cell. Every time that children crossed her vision or struck her ear, the poor mother flung herself into the darkest corner of her sepulchre, and one would have said, that she sought to plunge her head into the stone in order not to hear them. This time, on the contrary, she drew herself upright with a start, and listened eagerly. One of the little boys had just said, "They are going to hang a gypsy today."

With the abrupt leap of that spider which we have seen fling itself upon a fly at the trembling of its web, she rushed to her air-hole, which opened as the reader knows, on the Place de Grève. A ladder had, in fact, been raised up against the permanent gibbet, and the hangman's assistant was busying himself with adjusting the chains that had been rusted by the rain. There were some people standing about.

The laughing group of children was already far away. The sacked nun sought with her eyes some passer-by whom she might question.

All at once, beside her cell, she perceived a priest making a pretext of reading the public breviary, but who was much less occupied with the "lectern of latticed iron," than with the gallows, toward which he cast a fierce and gloomy glance from time to time. She recognized monsieur the archdeacon of Josas, a holy man.

"Father," she inquired. "Who are they about to hang yonder?"

The priest looked at her and made no reply; she repeated her question. Then he said, "I know not."

"Some children said that it was a gypsy," went on the recluse.

"I believe so," said the priest.

Then Paquette la Chantefleurie burst into hyena-like laughter.

"Sister," said the archdeacon, "do you then hate the gypsies heartily?"

"Do I hate them!" exclaimed the recluse, "they are vampires, stealers of children! They devoured my little daughter, my child, my only child! I have no longer any heart, they devoured it!"

She was frightful. The priest looked at her coldly.

"There is one in particular whom I hate, and whom I have cursed," she resumed; "it is a young one, of the age which my daughter would be if her mother had not eaten my daughter. Every time that that young viper passes in front of my cell, she sets my blood in a ferment."

"Well, sister, rejoice," said the priest, icy as a sepulchral statue; "that is the one whom you are about to see die."

His head fell upon his bosom and he moved slowly away.

The recluse writhed her arms with joy.

"I predicted it for her, that she would ascend thither! Thanks, priest!" she cried.

And she began to pace up and down with long strides before the grating of her window, her hair dishevelled, her eyes flashing, with her shoulder striking against the wall, with the wild air of a female wolf in a cage, who has long been famished, and who feels the hour for her repast drawing near.

CHAPTER 6

Three Human Hearts Differently Constructed

PHOEBUS WAS NOT dead, however. Men of that stamp die hard. When Master Philippe Lheulier, advocate extraordinary of the king, had said to poor Esmeralda; "He is dying," it was an error or a jest. When the archdeacon had repeated to the condemned girl, "He is dead," the fact is that he knew nothing about it, but that he believed it, that he counted on it, that he did not doubt it, that he devoutly hoped it. It would have been too hard for him to give favorable news of his rival to the woman whom he loved. Any man would have done the same in his place.

It was not that Phoebus's wound had not been serious, but it had not been as much so as the archdeacon believed. The physician, to whom the soldiers of the watch had carried him at the first moment, had feared for his life during the space of a week, and had even told him so in Latin. But youth had gained the upper hand; and, as frequently happens, in spite of prognostications and diagnoses, nature had amused herself by saving the sick man under the physician's very nose. It was while he was still lying on the leech's pallet that he had submitted to the interrogations of Philippe Lheulier and the official inquisitors, which had annoyed him greatly. Hence, one fine morning, feeling himself better, he had left his golden spurs with the leech as payment, and had slipped away. This had not, however, interfered with the progress of the affair. Justice, at that epoch, troubled itself very little about the clearness and definiteness of a criminal suit. Provided that the accused was hung, that was all that was necessary. Now the judge had plenty of proofs against la Esmeralda. They had supposed Phoebus to be dead, and that was the end of the matter.

Phoebus, on his side, had not fled far. He had simply rejoined his company in garrison at Queue-en-Brie, in the Isle-de-France, a few stages from Paris.

After all, it did not please him in the least to appear in this suit. He had a vague feeling that be should play a ridiculous figure in it. On the whole, he did not know what to think of the whole affair. Superstitious, and not given to devoutness, like every soldier who is only a soldier, when he came to question himself about this adventure, he did not feel assured as to the goat, as to the singular fashion in which he had met la Esmeralda, as to the no less strange manner in which she had allowed him to divine her love, as to her character as a gypsy, and lastly, as to the surly monk. He perceived in all these incidents much more magic than love, probably a sorceress, perhaps the devil; a comedy, in short, or to speak in the language of that day, a very disagreeable mystery, in which he played a very awkward part, the role of blows and derision. The captain was quite put out of countenance about it; he experienced that sort of shame which our La Fontaine has so admirably defined—

Ashamed as a fox who has been caught by a fowl.

Moreover, he hoped that the affair would not get noised abroad, that his name would hardly be pronounced in it, and that in any case it would not go beyond the courts of the Tournelle. In this he was not mistaken, there was then no "Gazette des Tribunaux"; and as not a week passed which had not its counterfeiter to boil, or its witch to hang, or its heretic to burn, at some one of the innumerable justices of Paris, people were so accustomed to seeing in all the squares the ancient feudal Themis, bare armed, with sleeves stripped up, performing her duty at the gibbets, the ladders, and the pillories, that they hardly paid any heed to it. Fashionable society of that day hardly knew the name of the victim who passed by at the corner of the street, and it was the populace at the most who regaled themselves with this coarse fare. An execution was a common incident of the public highways, like the braising-pan of the baker or the slaughter-house of the knacker. The executioner was only a sort of butcher of a little deeper dye than the rest.

Hence Phoebus's mind was soon at ease on the score of the enchantress Esmeralda, or Similar, as he called her, concerning the blow from the dagger of the Bohemian or of the surly monk (it mattered little which to him), and as to the issue of the trial. But as soon as his heart was vacant in that direction, Fleur-de-Lys returned to it. Captain Phoebus's heart, like the physics of that day, abhorred a vacuum.

Queue-en-Brie was a very insipid place to stay at then, a village of farriers, and cow-girls with chapped hands, a long line of poor dwellings and thatched cottages, which borders the grand road on both sides for half a league; a tail, in short, as its name imports.

Fleur-de-Lys was his last passion but one, a pretty girl, a charming dowry; accordingly, one fine morning, quite cured, and assuming that, after the lapse of two months, the Bohemian affair must be completely finished and forgotten, the amorous cavalier arrived on a prancing horse at the door of the Gondelaurier mansion.

He paid no attention to a tolerably numerous rabble which had assembled in the Place du Parvis, before the portal of Notre-Dame; he remembered that it was the month of May; he supposed that it was some procession, some Pentecost, some festival, hitched his horse to the ring at the door, and gayly ascended the stairs to his beautiful betrothed.

She was alone with her mother.

The scene of the witch, her goat, her cursed alphabet, and Phoebus's long absences, still weighed on Fleur-de-Lys's heart. Nevertheless, when she beheld her captain enter, she thought him so handsome, his doublet so new, his baldrick so shining, and his air so impassioned, that she blushed with pleasure. The noble damsel herself was more charming than ever. Her magnificent blond hair was plaited in a ravishing manner, she was dressed entirely in that sky blue which becomes fair people so well, a bit of coquetry which she had learned from Colombe, and her eyes were swimming in that languor of love which becomes them still better.

Phoebus, who had seen nothing in the line of beauty, since he left the village maids of Queue-en-Brie, was intoxicated with Fleur-de-Lys, which imparted to our officer so eager and gallant an air, that his peace was immediately made. Madame de Gondelaurier herself, still maternally seated in her big arm-chair, had not the heart to scold him. As for Fleur-de-Lys's reproaches, they expired in tender cooings.

The young girl was seated near the window still embroidering her grotto of Neptune. The captain was leaning over the back of her chair, and she was addressing her caressing reproaches to him in a low voice.

"What has become of you these two long months, wicked man?"

"I swear to you," replied Phoebus, somewhat embarrassed by the question, "that you are beautiful enough to set an archbishop to dreaming."

She could not repress a smile.

"Good, good, sir. Let my beauty alone and answer my question. A fine beauty, in sooth!"

"Well, my dear cousin, I was recalled to the garrison."

"And where is that, if you please? And why did not you come to say farewell?"

"At Queue-en-Brie."

Phoebus was delighted with the first question, which helped him to avoid the second.

"But that is quite close by, monsieur. Why did you not come to see me a single time?"

Here Phoebus was rather seriously embarrassed.

"Because—the service—and then, charming cousin, I have been ill."

"Ill!" she repeated in alarm.

"Yes, wounded!"

"Wounded!"

She, poor child, was completely upset.

"Oh, do not be frightened at that," said Phoebus, carelessly, "it was nothing. A quarrel, a sword cut; what is that to you?"

"What is that to me?" exclaimed Fleur-de-Lys, raising her beautiful eyes filled with tears. "Oh! You do not say what you think when you speak thus. What sword cut was that? I wish to know all."

"Well, my dear fair one, I had a falling out with Mahè Fédy, you know, the lieutenant of Saint-Germain-en-Laye, and we ripped open a few inches of skin for each other. That is all."

The mendacious captain was perfectly well aware that an affair of honor always makes a man stand well in the eyes of a woman. In fact, Fleur-de-Lys looked him full in the face, all agitated with fear, pleasure, and admiration. Still, she was not completely reassured.

"Provided that you are wholly cured, my Phoebus!" said she. "I do not know your Mahè Fédy, but he is a villanous man. And whence arose this quarrel?"

Here Phoebus, whose imagination was endowed with but mediocre power of creation, began to find himself in a quandary as to a means of extricating himself for his prowess.

"Oh! How do I know? A mere nothing, a horse, a remark! Fair cousin," he exclaimed, for the sake of changing the conversation, "what noise is this in the Cathedral Square?"

He approached the window.

"Oh! *Mon Dieu*, fair cousin, how many people there are on the Place!"

"I know not," said Fleur-de-Lys; "it appears that a witch is to do penance this morning before the church, and thereafter to be hung."

The captain was so thoroughly persuaded that la Esmeralda's affair was concluded, that he was but little disturbed by Fleur-de-Lys's words. Still, he asked her one or two questions.

"What is the name of this witch?"

"I do not know," she replied.

"And what is she said to have done?"

She shrugged her white shoulders.

"I know not."

"Oh, *mon Dieu* Jesus!" said her mother; "there are so many witches nowadays that I dare say they burn them without knowing their names. One might as well seek the name of every cloud in the sky. After all, one may be tranquil. The good God keeps his register." Here the venerable dame rose and came to the window. "Good Lord! You are right, Phoebus," said she. "The rabble is indeed great. There are people on all the roofs, blessed be God! Do you know, Phoebus, this reminds me of my best days. The entrance of King Charles VII, when, also, there were many people. I no longer remember in what year that was. When I speak of this to you, it produces upon you the effect—does it not?—the effect of something very old, and upon me of something very young. Oh, the crowd was far finer than at the present day! They even stood upon the machicolations of the Porte Sainte-Antoine. The king had the queen on a pillion, and after their highnesses came all the ladies mounted behind all the lords. I remember that they laughed loudly, because beside Amanyon de Garlande, who was very short of stature, there rode the Sire Matefelon, a chevalier of gigantic size, who had killed heaps of English. It was very fine. A procession of all the gentlemen of France, with their oriflammes waving red before the eye. There were some with pennons and some with banners. How can I tell the Sire de Calm with a pennon; Jean de Châteaumorant with a banner; the Sire de Courcy with a banner, and a more ample one than any of the others except the Duc de Bourbon? Alas, 'tis a sad thing to think that all that has existed and exists no longer!"

The two lovers were not listening to the venerable dowager. Phoebus had returned and was leaning on the back of his betrothed's chair, a charming post whence his libertine glance plunged into all the openings of Fleur-de-Lys's gorget. This gorget gaped so conveniently, and allowed him to see so many exquisite things and to divine so many more, that Phoebus, dazzled by this skin with its gleams of satin, said to himself, "How can any one love anything but a fair skin?"

Both were silent. The young girl raised sweet, enraptured eyes to him from time to time, and their hair mingled in a ray of spring sunshine.

"Phoebus," said Fleur-de-Lys suddenly, in a low voice, "we are to be married three months hence; swear to me that you have never loved any other woman than myself."

"I swear it, fair angel!" replied Phoebus, and his passionate glances aided the sincere tone of his voice in convincing Fleur-de-Lys.

Meanwhile, the good mother, charmed to see the betrothed pair on terms of such perfect understanding, had just quitted the apartment to attend to some domestic matter; Phoebus observed it, and this so emboldened the adventurous captain that very strange ideas mounted to his brain. Fleur-de-Lys loved him, he was her betrothed; she was alone with him; his former taste for her had re-awakened, not with all its freshness but with all its ardor; after all, there is no great harm in tasting one's wheat while it is still in the blade; I do not know whether these ideas passed through his mind, but one thing is certain, that Fleur-de-Lys was suddenly alarmed by the expression of his glance. She looked round and saw that her mother was no longer there.

"Good heavens!" said she, blushing and uneasy, "how very warm I am?"

"I think, in fact," replied Phoebus, "that it cannot be far from midday. The sun is troublesome. We need only lower the curtains."

"No, no," exclaimed the poor little thing, "on the contrary, I need air."

And like a fawn who feels the breath of the pack of hounds, she rose, ran to the window, opened it, and rushed upon the balcony.

Phoebus, much discomfited, followed her.

The Place du Parvis Notre-Dame, upon which the balcony looked, as the reader knows, presented at that moment a singular and sinister spectacle that caused the fright of the timid Fleur-de-Lys to change its nature.

An immense crowd, which overflowed into all the neighboring streets, encumbered the Place, properly speaking. The little wall, breast high, which surrounded the Place, would not have sufficed to keep it free had it not been lined with a thick hedge of sergeants and hackbuteers, culverines in hand. Thanks to this thicket of pikes and arquebuses, the Parvis was empty. Its entrance was guarded by a force of halberdiers with the armorial bearings of the bishop. The large doors of the church were closed, and formed a contrast with the innumerable windows on the Place, which, open to their very gables, allowed a view of thousands of heads heaped up almost like the piles of bullets in a park of artillery.

The surface of this rabble was dingy, dirty, earthy. The spectacle that it was expecting was evidently one of the sort that possess the privilege of bringing out and calling together the vilest among the populace. Nothing is so hideous as the noise that was made by that swarm of yellow caps and dirty heads. In that throng there were more laughs than cries, more women than men.

From time to time, a sharp and vibrating voice pierced the general clamor.

"Hey, Mahiet Baliffre! Is she to be hung yonder?"

"Fool! 'Tis here that she is to make her apology in her shift! The good God is going to cough Latin in her face! That is always done here, at midday. If 'tis the gallows that you wish, go to the Grève."

"I will go there, afterwards."

"Tell me, la Boucanbry? Is it true that she has refused a confessor?"

"It appears so, la Bechaigne."

"You see what a pagan she is!"

"'Tis the custom, monsieur. The bailiff of the courts is bound to deliver the malefactor ready judged for execution if he be a layman, to the provost of Paris; if a clerk, to the official of the bishopric."

"Thank you, sir."

"Oh, God!" said Fleur-de-Lys, "the poor creature!"

This thought filled with sadness the glance that she cast upon the populace. The captain, much more occupied with her than with that pack of the rabble, was amorously rumpling her girdle behind. She turned round, entreating and smiling.

"Please let me alone, Phoebus! If my mother were to return, she would see your hand!"

At that moment, midday rang slowly out from the clock of Notre Dame. A murmur of satisfaction broke out in the crowd. The last vibration of the twelfth stroke had hardly died away when all heads surged like the waves beneath a squall, and an immense shout went up from the pavement, the windows, and the roofs,

"There she is!"

Fleur-de-Lys pressed her hands to her eyes, that she might not see.

"Charming girl," said Phoebus, "do you wish to withdraw?"

"No," she replied; and she opened through curiosity, the eyes which she had closed through fear.

A tumbrel drawn by a stout Norman horse, and all surrounded by cavalry in violet livery with white crosses, had just debouched upon the Place through the Rue Saint-Pierre-aux-Boeufs. The sergeants of the watch were clearing a passage for it through the crowd, by stout blows from their clubs. Beside the cart rode several officers of justice and police, recognizable by their black costume and their awkwardness in the saddle. Master Jacques Charmolue paraded at their head.

In the fatal cart sat a young girl with her arms tied behind her back, and with no priest beside her. She was in her shift; her long black hair (the fashion then was to cut it off only at the foot of the gallows) fell in disorder upon her half-bared throat and shoulders.

Athwart that waving hair, more glossy than the plumage of a raven, a thick, rough, gray rope was visible, twisted and knotted, chafing her delicate collar-bones and twining round the charming neck of the poor girl, like an earthworm round a flower. Beneath that rope glittered a tiny amulet ornamented with bits of green glass, which had been left to her no doubt, because nothing is refused to those who are about to die. The spectators in the windows could see in the bottom of the cart her naked legs that she strove to hide beneath her, as by a final feminine instinct. At her feet lay a little goat, bound. The condemned girl held together with her teeth her imperfectly fastened shift. One would have said that she suffered still more in her misery from being thus exposed almost naked to the eyes of all. Alas! Modesty is not made for such shocks.

"Jesus!" said Fleur-de-Lys hastily to the captain. "Look fair cousin, 'tis that wretched Bohemian with the goat."

So saying, she turned to Phoebus. His eyes were fixed on the tumbrel. He was very pale.

"What Bohemian with the goat?" he stammered.

"What!" resumed Fleur-de-Lys, "do you not remember?"

Phoebus interrupted her.

"I do not know what you mean."

He made a step to re-enter the room, but Fleur-de-Lys, whose jealousy, previously so vividly aroused by this same gypsy, had just been re-awakened, Fleur-de-Lys gave him a look full of penetration and distrust. She vaguely recalled at that moment having heard of a captain mixed up in the trial of that witch.

"What is the matter with you?" she said to Phoebus, "one would say, that this woman had disturbed you."

Phoebus forced a sneer. "Me! Not the least in the world! Ah, yes, certainly!"

"Remain, then!" she continued imperiously, "and let us see the end."

The unlucky captain was obliged to remain. He was somewhat reassured by the fact that the condemned girl never removed her eyes from the bottom of the cart. It was but too surely la Esmeralda. In this last stage of opprobrium and misfortune, she was still beautiful; her great black eyes appeared still larger, because of the emaciation of her cheeks; her pale profile was pure and sublime. She resembled what she had been, in the same degree that a virgin by Masaccio, resembles a virgin of Raphael—weaker, thinner, more delicate.

Moreover, there was nothing in her which was not shaken in some sort, and which with the exception of her modesty, she did not let go at will, so profoundly had she been broken by stupor and despair. Her body bounded at every jolt of the tumbrel like a dead or broken thing; her gaze was dull and imbecile. A tear was still visible in her eyes, but motionless and frozen, so to speak.

Meanwhile, the lugubrious cavalcade has traversed the crowd amid cries of joy and curious attitudes. But as a faithful historian, we must state that on beholding her so beautiful, so depressed, many were moved with pity, even among the hardest of them.

The tumbrel had entered the Parvis.

It halted before the central portal. The escort ranged themselves in line on both sides. The crowd became silent, and, in the midst of this silence full of anxiety and solemnity, the two leaves of the grand door swung back, as of themselves, on their hinges, which gave a creak like the sound of a fife. Then there became visible in all its length, the deep, gloomy church, hung in black, sparely lighted with a few candles gleaming afar off on the principal altar, opened in the midst of the Place which was dazzling with light, like the mouth of a cavern. At the very extremity, in the gloom of the apse, a gigantic silver cross was visible against a black drapery that hung from the vault to the pavement. The whole nave was deserted. But a few heads of priests could be seen moving confusedly in the distant choir stalls, and, at the moment when the great door opened, there escaped from the church a loud, solemn, and monotonous chanting, which cast over the head of the condemned girl, in gusts, fragments of melancholy psalms—

"*Non timebo millia populi circumdantis me: exsurge, Domine; salvum me fac, Deus!*"

"*Salvum me fac, Deus, quoniam intraverunt aquœ usque ad animam meam.*

"*Infixus sum in limo profundi; et non est substantia.*"

At the same time, another voice, separate from the choir, intoned upon the steps of the chief altar, this melancholy offertory,

"*Qui verbum meum audit, et credit ei qui misit me, habet vitam œternam et in judicium non venit; sed transit a morte in vitam.*"

This chant, which a few old men buried in the gloom sang from afar over that beautiful creature, full of youth and life, caressed by the warm air of spring, inundated with sunlight was the mass for the dead.

The people listened devoutly.

The unhappy girl seemed to lose her sight and her consciousness in the obscure interior of the church. Her white lips moved as though in prayer, and the headsman's assistant who approached to assist her to alight from the cart, heard her repeating this word in a low tone, "Phoebus."

They untied her hands, made her alight, accompanied by her goat, which had also been unbound, and which bleated with joy at finding itself free: and they made her walk barefoot on the hard pavement to the foot of the steps leading to the door. The rope about her neck trailed behind her. One would have said it was a serpent following her.

Then the chanting in the church ceased. A great golden cross and a row of wax candles began to move through the gloom. The halberds of the motley beadles clanked; and, a few moments later, a long procession of priests in chasubles, and deacons in dalmatics, marched gravely toward the condemned girl, as they drawled their song, spread out before her view and that of the crowd. But her glance rested on the one who marched at the head, immediately after the cross-bearer.

"Oh!" she said in a low voice, and with a shudder, "'tis he again! The priest!"

It was in fact, the archdeacon. On his left he had the sub-chanter, on his right, the chanter, armed with his official wand. He advanced with head thrown back, his eyes fixed and wide open, intoning in a strong voice,—

"*De ventre inferi clamavi, et exaudisti vocem meam.*

"*Et projecisti me in profundum in corde mans, et flumem circumdedit me*★."

At the moment when he made his appearance in the full daylight beneath the lofty arched portal, enveloped in an ample cope of silver barred with a black cross, he was so pale that more than one person in the crowd thought that one of the marble bishops who knelt on the sepulchral stones of the choir had risen and was come to receive upon the brink of the tomb, the woman who was about to die.

She, no less pale, no less like a statue, had hardly noticed that they had placed in her hand a heavy, lighted candle of yellow wax; she had not heard the yelping voice of the clerk reading the fatal contents of the apology; when they told her to respond with Amen, she responded Amen. She only recovered life and force when she beheld the priest make a sign to her guards to withdraw, and himself advance alone toward her.

Then she felt her blood boil in her head, and a remnant of indignation flashed up in that soul already benumbed and cold.

The archdeacon approached her slowly; even in that extremity, she beheld him cast an eye sparkling with sensuality, jealousy, and desire, over her exposed form. Then he said aloud,—

"Young girl, have you asked God's pardon for your faults and shortcomings?"

He bent down to her ear, and added (the spectators supposed that he was receiving her last confession): "Will you have me? I can still save you!"

She looked intently at him: "Begone, demon, or I will denounce you!"

★ "Out of the belly of hell cried I, and thou heardest my voice. For thou hadst cast me into the deep in the midst of the seas, and the floods compassed me about."

He gave vent to a horrible smile: "You will not be believed. You will only add a scandal to a crime. Reply quickly! Will you have me?"

"What have you done with my Phoebus?"

"He is dead!" said the priest.

At that moment the wretched archdeacon raised his head mechanically and beheld at the other end of the Place, in the balcony of the Gondelaurier mansion, the captain standing beside Fleur-de-Lys. He staggered, passed his hand across his eyes, looked again, muttered a curse, and all his features were violently contorted.

"Well, die then!" he hissed between his teeth. "No one shall have you." Then, raising his hand over the gypsy, he exclaimed in a funereal voice:—"*I nunc, anima anceps, et sit tibi Deus misenicors!*" [Go now, soul, trembling in the balance, and God have mercy upon thee].

This was the dread formula with which it was the custom to conclude these gloomy ceremonies. It was the signal agreed upon between the priest and the executioner.

The crowd knelt.

"*Kyrie eleison,*" said the priests, who had remained beneath the arch of the portal.

"*Kyrie eleison,*" repeated the throng in that murmur which runs over all heads, like the waves of a troubled sea.

"Amen," said the archdeacon.

He turned his back on the condemned girl, his head sank upon his breast once more, he crossed his hands and rejoined his escort of priests, and a moment later he was seen to disappear, with the cross, the candles, and the copes, beneath the misty arches of the cathedral, and his sonorous voice was extinguished by degrees in the choir, as he chanted this verse of despair,—

"*Omnes gurgites tui et fluctus tui super me transierunt*" [All thy waves and thy billows have gone over me].

At the same time, the intermittent clash of the iron butts of the beadles' halberds, gradually dying away among the columns of the nave, produced the effect of a clock hammer striking the last hour of the condemned.

The doors of Notre-Dame remained open, allowing a view of the empty desolate church, draped in mourning, without candles, and without voices.

The condemned girl remained motionless in her place, waiting to be disposed of. One of the sergeants of police was obliged to notify

Master Charmolue of the fact, as the latter, during this entire scene, had been engaged in studying the bas-relief of the grand portal which represents, according to some, the sacrifice of Abraham; according to others, the philosopher's alchemical operation: the sun being figured forth by the angel; the fire, by the fagot; the artisan, by Abraham.

There was considerable difficulty in drawing him away from that contemplation, but at length he turned round; and, at a signal which he gave, two men clad in yellow, the executioner's assistants, approached the gypsy to bind her hands once more.

The unhappy creature, at the moment of mounting once again the fatal cart, and proceeding to her last halting-place, was seized, possibly, with some poignant clinging to life. She raised her dry, red eyes to heaven, to the sun, to the silvery clouds, cut here and there by a blue trapezium or triangle; then she lowered them to objects around her, to the earth, the throng, the houses; all at once, while the yellow man was binding her elbows, she uttered a terrible cry, a cry of joy. Yonder, on that balcony, at the corner of the Place, she had just caught sight of him, of her friend, her lord, Phoebus, the other apparition of her life!

The judge had lied! The priest had lied! It was certainly he, she could not doubt it; he was there, handsome, alive, dressed in his brilliant uniform, his plume on his head, his sword by his side!

"Phoebus!" she cried, "my Phoebus!"

And she tried to stretch toward him arms trembling with love and rapture, but they were bound.

Then she saw the captain frown, a beautiful young girl who was leaning against him gazed at him with disdainful lips and irritated eyes; then Phoebus uttered some words which did not reach her, and both disappeared precipitately behind the window opening upon the balcony, which closed after them.

"Phoebus!" she cried wildly, "can it be you believe it?" A monstrous thought had just presented itself to her. She remembered that she had been condemned to death for murder committed on the person of Phoebus de Châteaupers.

She had borne up until that moment. But this last blow was too harsh. She fell lifeless on the pavement.

"Come," said Charmolue, "carry her to the cart, and make an end of it."

No one had yet observed in the gallery of the statues of the kings, carved directly above the arches of the portal, a strange spectator, who had, up to that time, observed everything with such impassiveness, with a neck so strained, a visage so hideous that, in his motley accoutrement of red and violet, he might have been taken for one of those stone monsters through whose mouths the long gutters of the cathedral have discharged their waters for six hundred years. This spectator had missed nothing that had taken place since midday in front of the portal of Notre-Dame. And at the very beginning he had securely fastened to one of the small columns a large knotted rope, one end of which trailed on the flight of steps below. This being done, he began to look on tranquilly, whistling from time to time when a blackbird flitted past. Suddenly, at the moment when the superintendent's assistants were preparing to execute Charmolue's phlegmatic order, he threw his leg over the balustrade of the gallery, seized the rope with his feet, his knees and his hands; then he was seen to glide down the façade, as a drop of rain slips down a window-pane, rush to the two executioners with the swiftness of a cat which has fallen from a roof, knock them down with two enormous fists, pick up the gypsy with one hand, as a child would her doll, and dash back into the church with a single bound, lifting the young girl above his head and crying in a formidable voice,—

"Sanctuary!"

This was done with such rapidity, that had it taken place at night, the whole of it could have been seen in the space of a single flash of lightning.

"Sanctuary! Sanctuary!" repeated the crowd; and the clapping of ten thousand hands made Quasimodo's single eye sparkle with joy and pride.

This shock restored the condemned girl to her senses. She raised her eyelids, looked at Quasimodo, then closed them again suddenly, as though terrified by her deliverer.

Charmolue was stupefied, as well as the executioners and the entire escort. In fact, within the bounds of Notre-Dame, the condemned girl could not be touched. The cathedral was a place of refuge. All temporal jurisdiction expired upon its threshold.

Quasimodo had halted beneath the great portal, his huge feet seemed as solid on the pavement of the church as the heavy Roman pillars. His great, bushy head sat low between his shoulders, like the heads of lions, who also have a mane and no neck. He held the young girl, who was quivering all over, suspended from his horny hands like a white drapery; but he carried her with as much care as though he feared to break her or blight her. One would have said that he felt that she was a delicate, exquisite, precious thing, made for other hands than his. There were moments when he looked as if not daring to touch her, even with his breath. Then, all at once, he would press her forcibly in his arms, against his angular bosom, like his own possession, his treasure, as the mother of that child would have done. His gnome's eye, fastened upon her, inundated her with tenderness, sadness, and pity, and was suddenly raised filled with lightnings. Then the women laughed and wept, the crowd stamped with enthusiasm, for, at that moment Quasimodo had a beauty of his own. He was handsome; he, that orphan, that foundling, that outcast, he felt himself august and strong, he gazed in the face of that society from which he was banished, and in which he had so powerfully intervened, of that human justice from which he had wrenched its prey, of all those tigers whose jaws were forced to remain empty, of those policemen, those judges, those executioners, of all that force of the king which he, the meanest of creatures, had just broken, with the force of God.

And then, it was touching to behold this protection which had fallen from a being so hideous upon a being so unhappy, a creature condemned to death saved by Quasimodo. They were two extremes of natural and social wretchedness, coming into contact and aiding each other.

Meanwhile, after several moments of triumph, Quasimodo had plunged abruptly into the church with his burden. The populace, fond of all prowess, sought him with their eyes, beneath the gloomy nave, regretting that he had so speedily disappeared from their acclamations. All at once, he was seen to re-appear at one of the extremities of the gallery of the kings of France; he traversed it, running like a madman, raising his conquest high in his arms and shouting: "Sanctuary!" The crowd broke forth into fresh applause. The gallery passed, he plunged once more into the interior of the church. A moment later, he re-appeared upon the upper platform, with the gypsy still in his arms, still running madly, still crying, "Sanctuary!" and the throng applauded. Finally, he made his appearance for the third time upon the summit of the tower where hung the great bell; from that point he seemed to be showing to the entire city the girl whom he had saved, and his voice of thunder, that voice which was so rarely heard, and which he never heard himself, repeated thrice with frenzy, even to the clouds: "Sanctuary! Sanctuary! Sanctuary!"

"Noel! Noel!" shouted the populace in its turn; and that immense acclamation flew to astonish the crowd assembled at the Grève on the other bank, and the recluse who was still waiting with her eyes riveted on the gibbet.

Book Ninth

CHAPTER 1

Delirium

CLAUDE FROLLO WAS no longer in Notre-Dame when his adopted son so abruptly cut the fatal web in which the archdeacon and the gypsy were entangled. On returning to the sacristy he had torn off his alb, cope, and stole, had flung all into the hands of the stupefied beadle, had made his escape through the private door of the cloister, had ordered a boatman of the Terrain to transport him to the left bank of the Seine, and had plunged into the hilly streets of the University, not knowing whither he was going, encountering at every step groups of men and women who were hurrying joyously toward the Pont Saint-Michel, in the hope of still arriving in time to see the witch hung there, pale, wild, more troubled, more blind and more fierce than a night bird let loose and pursued by a troop of children in broad daylight. He no longer knew where he was, what he thought, or whether he might be dreaming. He went forward, walking, running, taking any street at haphazard, making no choice, only urged ever onward away from the Grève, the horrible Grève, which he felt confusedly, to be behind him.

In this manner he skirted Mount Sainte-Geneviève, and finally emerged from the town by the Porte Saint-Victor. He continued his flight as long as he could see, when he turned round, the turreted enclosure of the University, and the rare houses of the suburb; but, when, at length, a rise of ground had completely concealed from him that odious Paris, when he could believe himself to be a hundred leagues distant from it, in the fields, in the desert, he halted, and it seemed to him that he breathed more freely.

Then frightful ideas thronged his mind. Once more he could see clearly into his soul, and he shuddered. He thought of that unhappy girl who had destroyed him, and whom he had destroyed. He cast a haggard eye over the double, tortuous way which fate had caused their two destinies to pursue up to their point of intersection, where it had dashed them against each other without mercy. He meditated on the folly of eternal vows, on the vanity of chastity, of science, of religion, of virtue, on the uselessness of God. He plunged to his heart's content in evil thoughts, and in proportion as he sank deeper, he felt a Satanic laugh burst forth within him.

And as he thus sifted his soul to the bottom, when he perceived how large a space nature had prepared there for the passions, he sneered still more bitterly. He stirred up in the depths of his heart all his hatred, all his malevolence; and, with the cold glance of a physician who examines a patient, he recognized the fact that this malevolence was nothing but vitiated love; that love, that source of every virtue in man, turned to horrible things in the heart of a priest, and that a man constituted like himself, in making himself a priest, made himself a demon. Then he laughed frightfully, and suddenly became pale again, when he considered the most sinister side of his fatal passion, of that corrosive, venomous malignant, implacable love, which had ended only in the gibbet for one of them and in hell for the other; condemnation for her, damnation for him.

And then his laughter came again, when he reflected that Phoebus was alive; that after all, the captain lived, was gay and happy, had handsomer doublets than ever, and a new mistress whom he was conducting to see the old one hanged. His sneer redoubled its bitterness when he reflected that out of the living beings whose death he had desired, the gypsy, the only creature whom he did not hate, was the only one who had not escaped him.

Then from the captain, his thought passed to the people, and there came to him a jealousy of an unprecedented sort. He reflected that the people also, the entire populace, had had before their eyes the woman whom he loved exposed almost naked. He writhed his arms with agony as he thought that the woman whose form, caught by him alone in the darkness would have been supreme happiness, had been delivered up in broad daylight at full noonday, to a whole people, clad as for a night of voluptuousness. He wept with rage over all these mysteries of love, profaned, soiled, laid bare, withered forever. He wept with rage as he pictured to himself how many impure looks had been gratified at the sight of that badly fastened shift, and that this beautiful girl, this virgin lily, this cup of modesty and delight, to which he would have dared to place his lips only trembling, had just been transformed into a sort of public bowl, whereat the vilest populace of Paris, thieves, beggars, lackeys, had come to quaff in common an audacious, impure, and depraved pleasure.

And when he sought to picture to himself the happiness which he might have found upon earth, if she had not been a gypsy, and if he had not been a priest, if Phoebus had not existed and if she had loved him; when he pictured to himself that a life of serenity and love would have been possible to him also, even to him; that there were at that very moment, here and there upon the earth, happy couples spending the hours in sweet converse beneath orange trees, on the banks of brooks, in the presence of a setting sun, of a starry night; and that if God had so willed, he might have formed with her one of those blessed couples,—his heart melted in tenderness and despair.

Oh, she! Still she! It was this fixed idea that returned incessantly, which tortured him, which ate into his brain, and rent his vitals. He did not regret, he did not repent; all that he had done he was ready to do again; he preferred to behold her in the hands of the executioner rather than in the arms of the captain. But he suffered; he suffered so that at intervals he tore out handfuls of his hair to see whether it was not turning white.

Among other moments there came one, when it occurred to him that it was perhaps the very minute when the hideous chain that he had seen that morning, was pressing its iron noose closer about that frail and graceful neck. This thought caused the perspiration to start from every pore.

There was another moment when, while laughing diabolically at himself, he represented to himself la Esmeralda as he had seen her on that first day, lively, careless, joyous, gayly attired, dancing, winged, harmonious, and la Esmeralda of the last day, in her scanty shift, with a rope about her neck, mounting slowly with her bare feet, the angular ladder of the gallows; he figured to himself this double picture in such a manner that he gave vent to a terrible cry.

While this hurricane of despair overturned, broke, tore up, bent, uprooted everything in his soul, he gazed at nature around him. At his feet, some chickens were searching the thickets and pecking, enamelled beetles ran about in the sun; overhead, some groups of dappled gray clouds were floating across the blue sky; on the horizon, the spire of the Abbey Saint-Victor pierced the ridge of the hill with its slate obelisk; and the miller of the Copeaue hillock was whistling as he watched the laborious wings of his mill turning. All this active, organized, tranquil life, recurring around him under a thousand forms, hurt him. He resumed his flight.

He sped thus across the fields until evening. This flight from nature, life, himself, man, God, everything, lasted all day long. Sometimes he flung himself face downward on the earth and tore up the young blades of wheat with his nails. Sometimes he halted in the deserted street of a village, and his thoughts were so intolerable that he grasped his head in both hands and tried to tear it from his shoulders in order to dash it upon the pavement.

Toward the hour of sunset, he examined himself again, and found himself nearly mad. The tempest which had raged within him ever since the instant when he had lost the hope and the will to save the gypsy—that tempest had not left in his conscience a single healthy idea, a single thought which maintained its upright position. His reason lay there almost entirely destroyed. There remained but two distinct images in his mind, la Esmeralda and the gallows; all the rest was blank. Those two images united, presented to him a frightful group; and the more he concentrated what attention and thought was left to him, the more he beheld them grow, in accordance with a fantastic progression, the one in grace, in charm, in beauty, in light, the other in deformity and horror; so that at last la Esmeralda appeared to him like a star, the gibbet like an enormous, fleshless arm.

One remarkable fact is, that during the whole of this torture, the idea of dying did not seriously occur to him. The wretch was made so. He clung to life. Perhaps he really saw hell beyond it.

Meanwhile, the daylight continued to decline. The living being which still existed in him reflected vaguely on retracing its steps. He believed himself to be far away from Paris; on taking his bearings, he perceived that he had only circled the enclosure of the University. The spire of Saint-Sulpice, and the three lofty needles of Saint Germain-des-Prés, rose above the horizon on his right. He turned his steps in that direction. When he heard the brisk challenge of the men-at-arms of the abbey, around the crenelated, circumscribing wall of Saint-Germain, he turned aside, took a path which presented itself between the abbey and the lazar-house of the bourg, and at the expiration of a few minutes found himself on the verge of the Pré-aux-Clercs. This meadow was celebrated by reason of the brawls which went on there night and day; it was the hydra of the poor monks of Saint-Germain: *quod monachis Sancti-Germaini pratensis hydra fuit, clericis nova semper dissidiorum capita suscitantibus*. The archdeacon was afraid of meeting some one there; he feared every human countenance; he had just avoided the University and the Bourg Saint-Germain; he wished to re-enter the streets as late as possible. He skirted the Pré-aux-Clercs, took the deserted path that separated it from the Dieu-Neuf, and at last reached the water's edge. There Dom Claude found a boatman, who, for a few farthings in Parisian coinage, rowed him up the Seine as far as the point of the city, and landed him on that tongue of abandoned land where the reader has already beheld Gringoire dreaming, and which was prolonged beyond the king's gardens, parallel to the Ile du Passeur-aux-Vaches.

The monotonous rocking of the boat and the ripple of the water had, in some sort, quieted the unhappy Claude. When the boatman had taken his departure, he remained standing stupidly on the strand, staring straight before him and perceiving objects only through magnifying oscillations that rendered everything a sort of phantasmagoria to him. The fatigue of a great grief not infrequently produces this effect on the mind.

The sun had set behind the lofty Tour-de-Nesle. It was the twilight hour. The sky was white, the water of the river was white. Between these two white expanses, the left bank of the Seine, on which his eyes were fixed, projected its gloomy mass and, rendered ever thinner and thinner by perspective, it plunged into the gloom of the horizon like a black spire. It was loaded with houses, of which only the obscure outline could be distinguished, sharply brought out in shadows against the light background of the sky and the water. Here and there windows began to gleam, like the holes in a brazier. That immense black obelisk thus isolated between the two white expanses of the sky and the river, which was very broad at this point, produced upon Dom Claude a singular effect, comparable to that which would be experienced by a man who, reclining on his back at the foot of the tower of Strasburg, should gaze at the enormous spire plunging into the shadows of the twilight above his head. Only, in this case, it was Claude who was erect and the obelisk which was lying down; but, as the river, reflecting the sky, prolonged the abyss below him, the immense promontory seemed to be as boldly launched into space as any cathedral spire; and the impression was the same. This impression had even one stronger and more profound point about it, that it was indeed the tower of Strasbourg, but the tower of Strasbourg two leagues in height; something unheard of, gigantic, immeasurable; an edifice such as no human eye has ever seen; a tower of Babel. The chimneys of the houses, the battlements of the walls, the faceted gables of the roofs, the spire of the Augustines, the tower of Nesle, all these projections which broke the profile of the colossal obelisk added to the illusion by displaying in eccentric fashion to the eye the indentations of a luxuriant and fantastic sculpture.

Claude, in the state of hallucination in which he found himself, believed that he saw, that he saw with his actual eyes, the bell tower of hell; the thousand lights scattered over the whole height of the terrible tower seemed to him so many porches of the immense interior furnace; the voices and noises which escaped from it seemed so many shrieks, so many death groans. Then he became alarmed, he put his hands on his ears that he might no longer hear, turned his back that he might no longer see, and fled from the frightful vision with hasty strides.

But the vision was in himself.

When he re-entered the streets, the passers-by elbowing each other by the light of the shop-fronts, produced upon him the effect of a constant going and coming of spectres about him. There were strange noises in his ears; extraordinary fancies disturbed his brain. He saw neither houses, nor pavements, nor chariots, nor men and women, but a chaos of indeterminate objects whose edges melted into each other. At the corner of the Rue de la Barillerie, there was a grocer's shop whose porch was garnished all about, according to immemorial custom, with hoops of tin from which hung a circle of wooden candles, which came in contact with each other in the wind, and rattled like castanets. He thought he heard a cluster of skeletons at Montfauçon clashing together in the gloom.

"Oh!" he muttered, "the night breeze dashes them against each other, and mingles the noise of their chains with the rattle of their bones! Perhaps she is there among them!"

In his state of frenzy, he knew not whither he was going. After a few strides he found himself on the Pont Saint-Michel. There was a light in the window of a ground-floor room; he approached. Through a cracked window he beheld a mean chamber which recalled some confused memory to his mind. In that room, badly lighted by a meagre lamp, there was a fresh, light-haired young man, with a merry face, who amid loud bursts of laughter was embracing a very audaciously attired young girl; and near the lamp sat an old crone spinning and singing in a quavering voice. As the young man did not laugh constantly, fragments of the old woman's ditty reached the priest; it was something unintelligible yet frightful—

> Bark, Grève, grumble, Grève!
> Spin, spin, my distaff, spin her rope
> for the hangman, who is whistling in the meadow.
> What a beautiful hempen rope!
> Sow hemp, not wheat, from Issy to Vanvre.
> The thief hath not stolen the beautiful hempen rope.
> Grumble, Grève, bark, Grève!
> To see the dissolute wench hang on the blear-eyed gibbet,
> windows are eyes.

Thereupon the young man laughed and caressed the wench. The crone was la Falourdel; the girl was a courtesan; the young man was his brother Jehan.

He continued to gaze. That spectacle was as good as any other.

He saw Jehan go to a window at the end of the room, open it, cast a glance on the quay, where in the distance blazed a thousand lighted casements, and he heard him say as he closed the sash,

"'Pon my soul! How dark it is; the people are lighting their candles, and the good God his stars."

Then Jehan came back to the hag, smashed a bottle standing on the table, exclaiming,

"Already empty, *cor-boeuf*! and I have no more money! Isabeau, my dear, I shall not be satisfied with Jupiter until he has changed your two white nipples into two black bottles, where I may suck wine of Beaune day and night."

This fine pleasantry made the courtesan laugh, and Jehan left the room.

Dom Claude had barely time to fling himself on the ground in order that he might not be met, stared in the face and recognized by his brother. Luckily, the street was dark, and the scholar was tipsy. Nevertheless, he caught sight of the archdeacon prone upon the earth in the mud.

"Oh, oh!" said he; "here's a fellow who has been leading a jolly life, today."

He stirred up Dom Claude with his foot, and the latter held his breath.

"Dead drunk," resumed Jehan. "Come, he's full. A regular leech detached from a hogshead. He's bald," he added, bending down, "'tis an old man! *Fortunate senex!*"

Then Dom Claude heard him retreat, saying,

"'Tis all the same, reason is a fine thing, and my brother the archdeacon is very happy in that he is wise and has money."

Then the archdeacon rose to his feet, and ran without halting, toward Notre-Dame, whose enormous towers he beheld rising above the houses through the gloom.

At the instant when he arrived, panting, on the Place du Parvis, he shrank back and dared not raise his eyes to the fatal edifice.

"Oh!" he said, in a low voice, "is it really true that such a thing took place here, today, this very morning?"

Still, he ventured to glance at the church. The front was sombre; the sky behind was glittering with stars. The crescent of the moon, in her flight upward from the horizon, had paused at the moment, on the summit of the right hand tower, and seemed to have perched itself, like a luminous bird, on the edge of the balustrade, cut out in black trefoils.

The cloister door was shut; but the archdeacon always carried with him the key of the tower in which his laboratory was situated. He made use of it to enter the church.

In the church he found the gloom and silence of a cavern. By the deep shadows that fell in broad sheets from all directions, he recognized the fact that the hangings for the ceremony of the morning had not yet been removed. The great silver cross shone from the depths of the gloom, powdered with some sparkling points, like the milky way of that sepulchral night. The long windows of the choir showed the upper extremities of their arches above the black draperies, and their painted panes, traversed by a ray of moonlight had no longer any hues but the doubtful colors of night, a sort of violet, white and blue, whose tint is found only on the faces of the dead. The archdeacon, on perceiving these wan spots all around the choir, thought he beheld the mitres of damned bishops. He shut his eyes, and when he opened them again, he thought they were a circle of pale visages gazing at him.

He started to flee across the church. Then it seemed to him that the church also was shaking, moving, becoming endued with animation, that it was alive; that each of the great columns was turning into an enormous paw, which was beating the earth with its big stone spatula, and that the gigantic cathedral was no longer anything but a sort of prodigious elephant, which was breathing and marching with its pillars for feet, its two towers for trunks and the immense black cloth for its housings.

This fever or madness had reached such a degree of intensity that the external world was no longer anything more for the unhappy man than a sort of Apocalypse—visible, palpable, terrible.

For one moment, he was relieved. As he plunged into the side aisles, he perceived a reddish light behind a cluster of pillars. He ran toward it as to a star. It was the poor lamp that lighted the public breviary of Notre-Dame night and day, beneath its iron grating. He flung himself eagerly upon the holy book in the hope of finding some consolation, or some encouragement there. The hook lay open at this passage of Job, over which his staring eye glanced, "And a spirit passed before my face, and I heard a small voice, and the hair of my flesh stood up."

On reading these gloomy words, he felt that which a blind man feels when he feels himself pricked by the staff that he has picked up. His knees gave way beneath him, and he sank upon the pavement, thinking of her who had died that day. He felt so many monstrous vapors pass and discharge themselves in his brain, that it seemed to him that his head had become one of the chimneys of hell.

It would appear that he remained a long time in this attitude, no longer thinking, overwhelmed and passive beneath the hand of the demon. At length some strength returned to him; it occurred to him to take refuge in his tower beside his faithful Quasimodo. He rose; and, as he was afraid, he took the lamp from the breviary to light his way. It was a sacrilege; but he had got beyond heeding such a trifle now.

He slowly climbed the stairs of the towers, filled with a secret fright which must have been communicated to the rare passers-by in the Place du Parvis by the mysterious light of his lamp, mounting so late from loophole to loophole of the bell tower.

All at once, he felt a freshness on his face, and found himself at the door of the highest gallery. The air was cold; the sky was filled with hurrying clouds, whose large, white flakes drifted one upon another like the breaking up of river ice after the winter. The crescent of the moon, stranded in the midst of the clouds, seemed a celestial vessel caught in the ice-cakes of the air.

He lowered his gaze, and contemplated for a moment, through the railing of slender columns which unites the two towers, far away, through a gauze of mists and smoke, the silent throng of the roofs of Paris, pointed, innumerable, crowded and small like the waves of a tranquil sea on a summer night.

The moon cast a feeble ray, which imparted to earth and heaven an ashy hue.

At that moment the clock raised its shrill, cracked voice. Midnight rang out. The priest thought of midday; twelve o'clock had come back again.

"Oh!" he said in a very low tone, "she must be cold now."

All at once, a gust of wind extinguished his lamp, and almost at the same instant, he beheld a shade, a whiteness, a form, a woman, appear from the opposite angle of the tower. He started. Beside this woman was a little goat, which mingled its bleat with the last bleat of the clock.

He had strength enough to look. It was she.

She was pale, she was gloomy. Her hair fell over her shoulders as in the morning; but there was no longer a rope on her neck, her hands were no longer bound; she was free, she was dead.

She was dressed in white and had a white veil on her head.

She came toward him, slowly, with her gaze fixed on the sky. The supernatural goat followed her. He felt as though made of stone and too heavy to flee. At every step she took in advance, he took one backwards, and that was all. In this way he retreated once more beneath the gloomy arch of the stairway. He was chilled by the thought that she might enter there also; had she done so, he would have died of terror.

She did arrive, in fact, in front of the door to the stairway, and paused there for several minutes, stared intently into the darkness, but without appearing to see the priest, and passed on. She seemed taller to him than when she had been alive; he saw the moon through her white robe; he heard her breath.

When she had passed on, he began to descend the staircase again, with the slowness which he had observed in the spectre, believing himself to be a spectre too, haggard, with hair on end, his extinguished lamp still in his hand; and as he descended the spiral steps, he distinctly heard in his ear a voice laughing and repeating,—

"A spirit passed before my face, and I heard a small voice, and the hair of my flesh stood up."

CHAPTER 2

Hunchbacked, One-Eyed, Lame

EVERY CITY DURING the Middle Ages, and every city in France down to the time of Louis XII. had its places of asylum. These sanctuaries, in the midst of the deluge of penal and barbarous jurisdictions that inundated the city, were a species of islands that rose above the level of human justice. Every criminal who landed there was safe. There were in every suburb almost as many places of asylum as gallows. It was the abuse of impunity by the side of the abuse of punishment; two bad things which strove to correct each other. The palaces of the king, the hotels of the princes, and especially churches, possessed the right of asylum. Sometimes a whole city that stood in need of being repeopled was temporarily created a place of refuge. Louis XI made all Paris a refuge in 1467.

Once he was within the asylum, the criminal was sacred; but he must beware of leaving it; one step outside the sanctuary, and he fell back into the flood. The wheel, the gibbet, the strappado, kept good guard around the place of refuge, and lay in watch incessantly for their prey, like sharks around a vessel. Hence, condemned men were to be seen whose hair had grown white in a cloister, on the steps of a palace, in the enclosure of an abbey, beneath the porch of a church; in this manner the asylum was a prison as much as any other. It sometimes happened that a solemn decree of parliament violated the asylum and restored the condemned man to the executioner; but this was of rare occurrence. Parliaments were afraid of the bishops, and when there was friction between these two robes, the gown had but a poor chance against the cassock. Sometimes, however, as in the affair of the assassins of Petit-Jean, the headsman of Paris, and in that of Emery Rousseau, the murderer of Jean Valleret, justice overleaped the church and passed on to the execution of its sentences; but unless by virtue of a decree of Parliament, woe to him who violated a place of asylum with armed force! The reader knows the manner of death of Robert de Clermont, Marshal of France, and of Jean de Châlons, Marshal of Champagne; and yet the question was only of a certain Perrin Marc, the clerk of a money-changer, a miserable assassin; but the two marshals had broken the doors of St. Méry. Therein lay the enormity.

Such respect was cherished for places of refuge that, according to tradition, animals even felt it at times. Aymoire relates that a stag, being chased by Dagobert, having taken refuge near the tomb of Saint-Denis, the pack of hounds stopped short and barked.

Churches generally had a small apartment prepared for the reception of supplicants. In 1407, Nicolas Flamel caused to be built on the vaults of Saint-Jacques de la Boucherie, a chamber that cost him four livres six sous, sixteen farthings, parisis.

At Notre-Dame it was a tiny cell situated on the roof of the side aisle, beneath the flying buttresses, precisely at the spot where the wife of the present janitor of the towers has made for herself a garden, which is to the hanging gardens of Babylon what a lettuce is to a palm-tree, what a porter's wife is to a Semiramis.

It was here that Quasimodo had deposited la Esmeralda, after his wild and triumphant course. As long as that course lasted, the young girl had been unable to recover her senses, half unconscious, half awake, no longer feeling anything, except that she was mounting through the air, floating in it, flying in it, that something was raising her above the earth. From time to time she heard the loud laughter, the noisy voice of Quasimodo in her ear; she half opened her eyes; then below her she confusedly beheld Paris checkered with its thousand roofs of slate and tiles, like a red and blue mosaic, above her head the frightful and joyous face of Quasimodo. Then her eyelids drooped again; she thought that all was over, that they had executed her during her swoon, and that the misshapen spirit which had presided over her destiny, had laid hold of her and was bearing her away. She dared not look at him, and she surrendered herself to her fate. But when the bellringer, dishevelled and panting, had deposited her in the cell of refuge, when she felt his huge hands gently detaching the cord which bruised her arms, she felt that sort of shock which awakens with a start the passengers of a vessel which runs aground in the middle of a dark night. Her thoughts awoke also, and returned to her one by one. She saw that she was in

Notre-Dame; she remembered having been torn from the hands of the executioner; that Phoebus was alive, that Phoebus loved her no longer; and as these two ideas, one of which shed so much bitterness over the other, presented themselves simultaneously to the poor condemned girl; she turned to Quasimodo, who was standing in front of her, and who terrified her, and said to him, "Why have you saved me?"

He gazed at her with anxiety, as though seeking to divine what she was saying to him. She repeated her question. Then he gave her a profoundly sorrowful glance and fled. She was astonished.

A few moments later he returned, bearing a package that he cast at her feet. It was clothing that some charitable women had left on the threshold of the church for her.

Then she dropped her eyes upon herself and saw that she was almost naked, and blushed. Life had returned.

Quasimodo appeared to experience something of this modesty. He covered his eyes with his large hand and retired once more, but slowly.

She made haste to dress herself. The robe was a white one with a white veil—the garb of a novice of the Hôtel-Dieu.

She had barely finished when she beheld Quasimodo returning. He carried a basket under one arm and a mattress under the other. In the basket there was a bottle, bread, and some provisions. He set the basket on the floor and said, "Eat!" He spread the mattress on the flagging and said, "Sleep."

It was his own repast, it was his own bed, which the bellringer had gone in search of.

The gypsy raised her eyes to thank him, but she could not articulate a word. She dropped her head with a quiver of terror.

Then he said to her, "I frighten you. I am very ugly, am I not? Do not look at me; only listen to me. During the day you will remain here; at night you can walk all over the church. But do not leave the church either by day or by night. You would be lost. They would kill you, and I should die."

She was touched and raised her head to answer him. He had disappeared. She found herself alone once more, meditating upon the singular words of this almost monstrous being, and struck by the sound of his voice, which was so hoarse yet so gentle.

Then she examined her cell. It was a chamber about six feet square, with a small window and a door on the slightly sloping plane of the roof formed of flat stones. Many gutters with the figures of animals seemed to be bending down around her, and stretching their necks in order to stare at her through the window. Over the edge of her roof she perceived the tops of thousands of chimneys that caused the smoke of all the fires in Paris to rise beneath her eyes. A sad sight for the poor gypsy, a foundling, condemned to death, an unhappy creature, without country, without family, without a hearthstone.

At the moment when the thought of her isolation thus appeared to her more poignant than ever, she felt a bearded and hairy head glide between her hands, upon her knees. She started (everything alarmed her now) and looked. It was the poor goat, the agile Djali, which had made its escape after her, at the moment when Quasimodo had put to flight Charmolue's brigade, and which had been lavishing caresses on her feet for nearly an hour past, without being able to win a glance. The gypsy covered him with kisses.

"Oh, Djali!" she said, "how I have forgotten thee! And so thou still thinkest of me! Oh, thou art not an ingrate!"

At the same time, as though an invisible hand had lifted the weight which had repressed her tears in her heart for so long, she began to weep, and, in proportion as her tears flowed, she felt all that was most acrid and bitter in her grief depart with them.

Evening came, she thought the night so beautiful that she made the circuit of the elevated gallery that surrounds the church. It afforded her some relief, so calm did the earth appear when viewed from that height.

Chapter 3

Deaf

On the following morning, she perceived on awaking, that she had been asleep. This singular thing astonished her. She had been so long unaccustomed to sleep! A joyous ray of the rising sun entered through her window and touched her face. At the same time with the sun, she beheld at that window an object that frightened her, the unfortunate face of Quasimodo. She involuntarily closed her eyes again, but in vain; she fancied that she still saw through the rosy lids that gnome's mask, one-eyed and gap-toothed. Then, while she still kept her eyes closed, she heard a rough voice saying, very gently,

"Be not afraid. I am your friend. I came to watch you sleep. It does not hurt you if I come to see you sleep, does it? What difference does it make to you if I am here when your eyes are closed! Now I am going. Stay, I have placed myself behind the wall. You can open your eyes again."

There was something more plaintive than these words, and that was the accent in which they were uttered. The gypsy, much touched, opened her eyes. He was, in fact, no longer at the window. She approached the opening, and beheld the poor hunchback crouching in an angle of the wall, in a sad and resigned attitude. She made an effort to surmount the repugnance with which he inspired her. "Come," she said to him gently. From the movement of the gypsy's lips, Quasimodo thought that she was driving him away; then he rose and retired limping, slowly, with drooping head, without even daring to raise to the young girl his gaze full of despair. "Do come," she cried, but he continued to retreat. Then she darted from her cell, ran to him, and grasped his arm. On feeling her touch him, Quasimodo trembled in every limb. He raised his suppliant eye, and seeing that she was leading him back to her quarters, his whole face beamed with joy and tenderness. She tried to make him enter the cell; but he persisted in remaining on the threshold. "No, no," said he; "the owl enters not the nest of the lark."

Then she crouched down gracefully on her couch, with her goat asleep at her feet. Both remained motionless for several moments, considering in silence, she so much grace, he so much ugliness. Every moment she discovered some fresh deformity in Quasimodo. Her glance travelled from his knock knees to his humped back, from his humped back to his only eye. She could not comprehend the existence of a being so awkwardly fashioned. Yet there was so much sadness and so much gentleness spread over all this, that she began to become reconciled to it.

He was the first to break the silence. "So you were telling me to return?"

She made an affirmative sign of the head, and said, "Yes."

He understood the motion of the head. "Alas!" he said, as though hesitating whether to finish, "I am—I am deaf."

"Poor man!" exclaimed the Bohemian, with an expression of kindly pity.

He began to smile sadly.

"You think that that was all that I lacked, do you not? Yes, I am deaf, that is the way I am made. 'Tis horrible, is it not? You are so beautiful!"

There lay in the accents of the wretched man so profound a consciousness of his misery, that she had not the strength to say a word. Besides, he would not have heard her. He went on, "Never have I seen my ugliness as at the present moment. When I compare myself to you, I feel a very great pity for myself, poor unhappy monster that I am! Tell me, I must look to you like a beast. You, you are a ray of sunshine, a drop of dew, the song of a bird! I am something frightful, neither man nor animal, I know not what, harder, more trampled under foot, and more unshapely than a pebble stone!"

Then he began to laugh, and that laugh was the most heartbreaking thing in the world. He continued, "Yes, I am deaf; but you shall talk to me by gestures, by signs. I have a master who talks with me in that way. And then, I shall very soon know your wish from the movement of your lips, from your look."

"Well!" she interposed with a smile, "tell me why you saved me."

He watched her attentively while she was speaking.

"I understand," he replied. "You ask me why I saved you. You have forgotten a wretch who tried to abduct you one night, a wretch to whom you rendered succor on the following day on their infamous pillory. A drop of water and a little pity; that is more than I can repay with my life. You have forgotten that wretch, but he remembers it."

She listened to him with profound tenderness. A tear swam in the eye of the bellringer, but did not fall. He seemed to make it a sort of point of honor to retain it.

"Listen," he resumed, when he was no longer afraid that the tear would escape; "our towers here are very high, a man who should fall from them would be dead before touching the pavement; when it shall please you to have me fall, you will not have to utter even a word, a glance will suffice."

Then he rose. Unhappy as was the Bohemian, this eccentric being still aroused some compassion in her. She made him a sign to remain.

"No, no," said he. "I must not remain too long. I am not at my ease. It is out of pity that you do not turn away your eyes. I shall go to some place where I can see you without your seeing me: it will be better so."

He drew from his pocket a little metal whistle.

"Here," said he, "when you have need of me, when you wish me to come, when you will not feel too much horror at the sight of me, use this whistle. I can hear this sound."

He laid the whistle on the floor and fled.

CHAPTER 4

Earthenware and Crystal

DAY FOLLOWED DAY. Calm gradually returned to the soul of la Esmeralda. Excess of grief, like excess of joy, is a violent thing that lasts but a short time. The heart of man cannot remain long in one extremity. The gypsy had suffered so much, that nothing was left her but astonishment. With security, hope had returned to her. She was outside the pale of society, outside the pale of life, but she had a vague feeling that it might not be impossible to return to it. She was like a dead person, who should hold in reserve the key to her tomb.

She felt the terrible images that had so long persecuted her, gradually departing. All the hideous phantoms, Pierrat Torterue, Jacques Charmolue, were effaced from her mind, all, even the priest.

And then, Phoebus was alive; she was sure of it, she had seen him. To her the fact of Phoebus being alive was everything. After the series of fatal shocks which had overturned everything within her, she had found but one thing intact in her soul, one sentiment—her love for the captain. Love is like a tree; it sprouts forth of itself, sends its roots out deeply through our whole being, and often continues to flourish greenly over a heart in ruins.

And the inexplicable point about it is that the more blind is this passion, the more tenacious it is. It is never more solid than when it has no reason in it.

La Esmeralda did not think of the captain without bitterness, no doubt. No doubt it was terrible that he also should have been deceived; that he should have believed that impossible thing, that he could have conceived of a stab dealt by her who would have given a thousand lives for him. But, after all, she must not be too angry with him for it; had she not confessed her crime? Had she not yielded, weak woman that she was, to torture? The fault was entirely hers. She should have allowed her finger nails to be torn out rather than such a word to be wrenched from her. In short, if she could but see Phoebus once more, for a single minute, only one word would be required, one look, in order to undeceive him, to bring him back. She did not doubt it. She was astonished also at many singular things, at the accident of Phoebus's presence on the day of the penance, at the young girl with whom he had been. She was his sister, no doubt. An unreasonable explanation, but she contented herself with it, because she needed to believe that Phoebus still loved her, and loved her alone. Had he not sworn it to her? What more was needed, simple and credulous as she was? And then, in this matter, were not appearances much more against her than against him? Accordingly, she waited. She hoped.

Let us add that the church, that vast church, which surrounded her on every side, which guarded her, which saved her, was itself a sovereign tranquillizer. The solemn lines of that architecture, the religious attitude of all the objects that surrounded the young girl, the serene and pious thoughts that emanated, so to speak, from all the pores of that stone, acted upon her without her being aware of it. The edifice had also sounds fraught with such benediction and such majesty, that they soothed this ailing soul. The monotonous chanting of the celebrants, the responses of the people to the priest, sometimes inarticulate, sometimes thunderous, the harmonious trembling of the painted windows, the organ, bursting forth like a hundred trumpets, the three belfries, humming like hives of huge bees, that whole orchestra on which bounded a gigantic scale, ascending, descending incessantly from the voice of a throng to that of one bell, dulled her memory, her imagination, her grief. The bells, in particular, lulled her. It was something like a powerful magnetism that those vast instruments shed over her in great waves.

Thus every sunrise found her more calm, breathing better, less pale. In proportion as her inward wounds closed, her grace and beauty blossomed once more on her countenance, but more thoughtful, more reposeful. Her former character also returned to her, somewhat even of her gayety, her pretty pout, her love for her goat, her love for singing, her modesty. She took care to dress herself in the morning in the corner of her cell for fear some inhabitants of the neighboring attics might see her through the window.

When the thought of Phoebus left her time, the gypsy sometimes thought of Quasimodo. He was the sole bond, the sole connection, the sole communication that remained to her with men, with the living. Unfortunate girl, she was more outside the world than Quasimodo! She understood not in the least the strange friend whom chance had given her. She often reproached herself for not feeling a gratitude that should close her eyes, but decidedly, she could not accustom herself to the poor bellringer. He was too ugly.

She had left the whistle he had given her lying on the ground. This did not prevent Quasimodo from making his appearance from time to time during the first few days. She did her best not to turn aside with too much repugnance when he came to bring her her basket of provisions or her jug of water, but he always perceived the slightest movement of this sort, and then he withdrew sadly.

Once he came at the moment when she was caressing Djali. He stood pensively for several minutes before this graceful group of the goat and the gypsy; at last he said, shaking his heavy and ill-formed head, "My misfortune is that I still resemble a man too much. I should like to be wholly a beast like that goat."

She gazed at him in amazement.

He replied to the glance, "Oh! I well know why," and he went away.

On another occasion he presented himself at the door of the cell (which he never entered) at the moment when la Esmeralda was singing an old Spanish ballad, the words of which she did not understand, but which had lingered in her ear because the gypsy women had lulled her to sleep with it when she was a little child. At the sight of that villanous form which made its appearance so abruptly in the middle of her song, the young girl paused with an involuntary gesture of alarm. The unhappy bellringer fell upon his knees on the threshold, and clasped his large, misshapen hands with a suppliant air. "Oh!" he said, sorrowfully, "continue, I implore you, and do not drive me away." She did not wish to pain him, and resumed her lay, trembling all over. By degrees, however, her terror disappeared, and she yielded herself wholly to the slow and melancholy air she was singing. He remained on his knees with hands clasped, as in prayer, attentive, hardly breathing, his gaze riveted upon the gypsy's brilliant eyes.

On another occasion, he came to her with an awkward and timid air. "Listen," he said, with an effort; "I have something to say to you."

She made him a sign that she was listening. Then he began to sigh, half opened his lips, appeared for a moment to be on the point of speaking, then he looked at her again, shook his head, and withdrew slowly, with his brow in his hand, leaving the gypsy stupefied. Among the grotesque personages sculptured on the wall, there was one to whom he was particularly attached, and with which he often seemed to exchange fraternal glances. Once the gypsy heard him saying to it, "Oh! why am not I of stone, like you!"

At last, one morning, la Esmeralda had advanced to the edge of the roof, and was looking into the Place over the pointed roof of Saint-Jean le Rond. Quasimodo was standing behind her. He had placed himself in that position in order to spare the young girl, as far as possible, the displeasure of seeing him. All at once the gypsy started, a tear and a flash of joy gleamed simultaneously in her eyes, she knelt on the brink of the roof and extended her arms toward the Place with anguish, exclaiming: "Phoebus, come, come! A word, a single word in the name of heaven! Phoebus! Phoebus!" Her voice, her face, her gesture, her whole person bore the heartrending expression of a shipwrecked man who is making a signal of distress to the joyous vessel which is passing afar off in a ray of sunlight on the horizon.

Quasimodo leaned over the Place, and saw that the object of this tender and agonizing prayer was a young man, a captain, a handsome cavalier all glittering with arms and decorations, prancing across the end of the Place, and saluting with his plume a beautiful lady who was smiling at him from her balcony. However, the officer did not hear the unhappy girl calling him; he was too far away.

But the poor deaf man heard. A profound sigh heaved his breast; he turned round; his heart was swollen with all the tears he was swallowing; his convulsively clenched fists struck against his head, and when he withdrew them there was a bunch of red hair in each hand.

The gypsy paid no heed to him. He said in a low voice as he gnashed his teeth, "Damnation! That is what one should be like! 'Tis only necessary to be handsome on the outside!"

Meanwhile, she remained kneeling, and cried with extraordinary agitation, "Oh, there he is alighting from his horse! He is about to enter that house! Phoebus! He does not hear me! Phoebus! How wicked that woman is to speak to him at the same time with me! Phoebus! Phoebus!"

The deaf man gazed at her. He understood this pantomime. The poor bellringer's eye filled with tears, but he let none fall. All at once he pulled her gently by the border of her sleeve. She turned round. He had assumed a tranquil air; he said to her, "Would you like to have me bring him to you?"

She uttered a cry of joy.

"Oh, go! Hasten! Run! Quick! That captain! That captain! Bring him to me! I will love you for it!"

She clasped his knees. He could not refrain from shaking his head sadly.

"I will bring him to you," he said, in a weak voice. Then he turned his head and plunged down the staircase with great strides, stifling with sobs.

When he reached the Place, he no longer saw anything except the handsome horse hitched at the door of the Gondelaurier house; the captain had just entered there.

He raised his eyes to the roof of the church. La Esmeralda was there in the same spot, in the same attitude. He made her a sad sign with his head; then he planted his back against one of the stone posts of the Gondelaurier porch, determined to wait until the captain should come forth.

In the Gondelaurier house it was one of those gala days that precede a wedding. Quasimodo beheld many people enter, but no one come out. He cast a glance toward the roof from time to time; the gypsy did not stir any more than himself. A groom came and unhitched the horse and led it to the stable of the house.

The entire day passed thus, Quasimodo at his post, la Esmeralda on the roof, Phoebus, no doubt, at the feet of Fleur-de-Lys.

At length night came, a moonless night, a dark night. Quasimodo fixed his gaze in vain upon la Esmeralda; soon she was no more than a whiteness amid the twilight; then nothing. All was effaced, all was black.

Quasimodo beheld the front windows from top to bottom of the Gondelaurier mansion illuminated; he saw the other casements in the Place lighted one by one, he also saw them extinguished to the very last, for he remained the whole evening at his post. The officer did not come forth. When the last passers-by had returned home, when the windows of all the other houses were extinguished, Quasimodo was left entirely alone, entirely in the dark. There were at that time no lamps in the square before Notre-Dame.

Meanwhile, the windows of the Gondelaurier mansion remained lighted, even after midnight. Quasimodo, motionless and attentive, beheld a throng of lively, dancing shadows pass athwart the many-colored painted panes. Had he not been deaf, he would have heard more and more distinctly, in proportion as the noise of sleeping Paris died away, a sound of feasting, laughter, and music in the Gondelaurier mansion.

Toward one o'clock in the morning, the guests began to take their leave. Quasimodo, shrouded in darkness watched them all pass out through the porch illuminated with torches. None of them was the captain.

He was filled with sad thoughts; at times he looked upwards into the air, like a person who is weary of waiting. Great black clouds, heavy, torn, split, hung like crape hammocks beneath the starry dome of night. One would have pronounced them spiders' webs of the vault of heaven.

In one of these moments he suddenly beheld the long window on the balcony, whose stone balustrade projected above his head, open mysteriously. The frail glass door gave passage to two persons, and closed noiselessly behind them; it was a man and a woman.

It was not without difficulty that Quasimodo succeeded in recognizing in the man the handsome captain, in the woman the young lady whom he had seen welcome the officer in the morning from that very balcony. The place was perfectly dark, and a double crimson curtain which had fallen across the door the very moment it closed again, allowed no light to reach the balcony from the apartment.

The young man and the young girl, so far as our deaf man could judge, without hearing a single one of their words, appeared to abandon themselves to a very tender tête-a-tête. The young girl seemed to have allowed the officer to make a girdle for her of his arm, and gently repulsed a kiss.

Quasimodo looked on from below at this scene that was all the more pleasing to witness because it was not meant to be seen. He contemplated with bitterness that beauty, that happiness. After all, nature was not dumb in the poor fellow, and his human sensibility, all maliciously contorted as it was, quivered no less than any other. He thought of the miserable portion that Providence had allotted to him; that woman and the pleasure of love, would pass forever before his eyes, and that he should never do anything but behold the felicity of others. But that which rent his heart most in this sight, that which mingled indignation with his anger, was the thought of what the gypsy would suffer could she behold it. It is true that the night was very dark, that la Esmeralda, if she had remained at her post (and he had no doubt of this), was very far away, and that it was all that he himself could do to distinguish the lovers on the balcony. This consoled him.

Meanwhile, their conversation grew more and more animated. The young lady appeared to be entreating the officer to ask nothing more of her. Of all this Quasimodo could distinguish only the beautiful clasped hands, the smiles mingled with tears, the young girl's glances directed to the stars, the eyes of the captain lowered ardently upon her.

Fortunately, for the young girl was beginning to resist but feebly, the door of the balcony suddenly opened once more and an old dame appeared; the beauty seemed confused, the officer assumed an air of displeasure, and all three withdrew.

A moment later, a horse was champing his bit under the porch, and the brilliant officer, enveloped in his night cloak, passed rapidly before Quasimodo.

The bellringer allowed him to turn the corner of the street, then he ran after him with his ape-like agility, shouting: "Hey there, captain!"

The captain halted.

"What wants this knave with me?" he said, catching sight through the gloom of that hipshot form which ran limping after him.

Meanwhile, Quasimodo had caught up with him, and had boldly grasped his horse's bridle: "Follow me, captain; there is one here who desires to speak with you!"

"*Corne-mahom!*" grumbled Phoebus, "here's a villanous, ruffled bird which I fancy I have seen somewhere. Oh master, will you let my horse's bridle alone?"

"Captain," replied the deaf man, "do you not ask me who it is?"

"I tell you to release my horse," retorted Phoebus, impatiently. "What means the knave by clinging to the bridle of my steed? Do you take my horse for a gallows?"

Quasimodo, far from releasing the bridle, prepared to force him to retrace his steps. Unable to comprehend the captain's resistance, he hastened to say to him, "Come, captain, 'tis a woman who is waiting for you." He added with an effort: "A woman who loves you."

"A rare rascal!" said the captain, "who thinks me obliged to go to all the women who love me! Or who say they do. And what if, by chance, she should resemble you, you face of a screech-owl? Tell the woman who has sent you that I am about to marry, and that she may go to the devil!"

"Listen," exclaimed Quasimodo, thinking to overcome his hesitation with a word, "come, monseigneur! 'Tis the gypsy whom you know!"

This word did, indeed, produce a great effect on Phoebus, but not of the kind the deaf man expected. It will be remembered that our gallant officer had retired with Fleur-de-Lys several moments before Quasimodo had rescued the condemned girl from the hands of Charmolue. Afterwards, in all his visits to the Gondelaurier mansion he had taken care not to mention that woman, the memory of whom was, after all, painful to him; and on her side, Fleur-de-Lys had not deemed it politic to tell him that the gypsy was alive. Hence Phoebus believed poor "Similar," as he called her, to be dead, and that a month or two had elapsed since her death. Let us add that for the last few moments the captain had been reflecting on the profound darkness of the night, the supernatural ugliness, the sepulchral voice of the strange messenger; that it was past midnight; that the street was deserted, as on the evening when the surly monk had accosted him; and that his horse snorted as it looked at Quasimodo.

"The gypsy!" he exclaimed, almost frightened. "Look here, do you come from the other world?"

And he laid his hand on the hilt of his dagger.

"Quick, quick," said the deaf man, endeavoring to drag the horse along; "this way!"

Phoebus dealt him a vigorous kick in the breast.

Quasimodo's eye flashed. He made a motion to fling himself on the captain. Then he drew himself up stiffly and said, "Oh! how happy you are to have some one who loves you!"

He emphasized the words "some one" and, loosing the horse's bridle, went on. "Begone!"

Phoebus spurred on in all haste, swearing. Quasimodo watched him disappear in the shades of the street.

"Oh!" said the poor deaf man, in a very low voice; "to refuse that!"

He re-entered Notre-Dame, lighted his lamp and climbed to the tower again. The gypsy was still in the same place, as he had supposed.

She flew to meet him as far off as she could see him. "Alone!" she cried, clasping her beautiful hands sorrowfully.

"I could not find him," said Quasimodo coldly.

"You should have waited all night," she said angrily.

He saw her gesture of wrath, and understood the reproach.

"I will lie in wait for him better next time," he said, dropping his head.

"Begone!" she said to him.

He left her. She was displeased with him. He preferred to have her abuse him rather than to have afflicted her. He had kept all the pain to himself.

From that day forth, the gypsy no longer saw him. He ceased to come to her cell. At the most she occasionally caught a glimpse at the summit of the towers, of the bellringer's face turned sadly to her. But as soon as she perceived him, he disappeared.

We must admit that she was not much grieved by this voluntary absence on the part of the poor hunchback. At the bottom of her heart she was grateful to him for it. Moreover, Quasimodo did not deceive himself on this point.

She no longer saw him, but she felt the presence of a good genius about her. Her provisions were replenished by an invisible hand during her slumbers. One morning she found a cage of birds on her window. There was a piece of sculpture above her window that frightened her. She had shown this more than once in Quasimodo's presence. One morning, for all these things happened at night, she no longer saw it, it had been broken. The person who had climbed up to that carving must have risked his life.

Sometimes, in the evening, she heard a voice, concealed beneath the wind screen of the bell tower, singing a sad, strange song, as though to lull her to sleep. The lines were unrhymed, such as a deaf person can make.

> Look not at the face,
> young girl, look at the heart.
> The heart of a handsome young man is often deformed.
> There are hearts in which love does not keep.
>
> Young girl, the pine is not beautiful;
> it is not beautiful like the poplar,
> but it keeps its foliage in winter.
> Alas! What is the use of saying that?
> That which is not beautiful has no right to exist;

beauty loves only beauty;
April turns her back on January.

Beauty is perfect,
beauty can do all things,
beauty is the only thing that does not exist by halves.
The raven flies only by day,
the owl flies only by night,
the swan flies by day and by night.

One morning, on awaking, she saw on her window two vases filled with flowers. One was a very beautiful and very brilliant but cracked vase of glass. It had allowed the water with which it had been filled to escape, and the flowers that it contained were withered. The other was an earthenware pot, coarse and common, but which had preserved all its water, and its flowers remained fresh and crimson.

I know not whether it was done intentionally, but la Esmeralda took the faded nosegay and wore it all day long upon her breast.

That day she did not hear the voice singing in the tower.

She troubled herself very little about it. She passed her days in caressing Djali, in watching the door of the Gondelaurier house, in talking to herself about Phoebus, and in crumbling up her bread for the swallows.

She had entirely ceased to see or hear Quasimodo. The poor bellringer seemed to have disappeared from the church. One night, nevertheless, when she was not asleep, but was thinking of her handsome captain, she heard something breathing near her cell. She rose in alarm, and saw by the light of the moon, a shapeless mass lying across her door on the outside. It was Quasimodo asleep there upon the stones.

CHAPTER 5

The Key to the Red Door

IN THE MEANTIME, public rumor had informed the archdeacon of the miraculous manner in which the gypsy had been saved. When he learned it, he knew not what his sensations were. He had reconciled himself to la Esmeralda's death. In that matter he was tranquil; he had reached the bottom of personal suffering. The human heart (Dom Claude had meditated upon these matters) can contain only a certain quantity of despair. When the sponge is saturated, the sea may pass over it without causing a single drop more to enter it.

Now, with la Esmeralda dead, the sponge was soaked, all was at an end on this earth for Dom Claude. But to feel that she was alive, and Phoebus also, meant that tortures, shocks, alternatives, life, were beginning again. And Claude was weary of all this.

When he heard this news, he shut himself in his cell in the cloister. He appeared neither at the meetings of the chapter nor at the services. He closed his door against all, even against the bishop. He remained thus immured for several weeks. He was believed to be ill. And so he was, in fact.

What did he do while thus shut up? With what thoughts was the unfortunate man contending? Was he giving final battle to his formidable passion? Was he concocting a final plan of death for her and of perdition for himself?

His Jehan, his cherished brother, his spoiled child, came once to his door, knocked, swore, entreated, gave his name half a score of times. Claude did not open.

He passed whole days with his face close to the panes of his window. From that window, situated in the cloister, he could see la Esmeralda's chamber. He often saw herself with her goat, sometimes with Quasimodo. He remarked the little attentions of the ugly deaf man, his obedience, his delicate and submissive ways with the gypsy. He recalled, for he had a good memory, and memory is the tormentor of the jealous, he recalled the singular look of the bellringer, bent on the dancer upon a certain evening. He asked himself what motive could have impelled Quasimodo to save her. He was the witness of a thousand little scenes between the gypsy and the deaf man, the pantomime of which, viewed from afar and commented on by his passion, appeared very tender to him. He distrusted the capriciousness of women. Then he felt a jealousy which be could never have believed possible awakening within him, a jealousy which made him redden with shame and indignation: "One might condone the captain, but this one!" This thought upset him.

His nights were frightful. As soon as he learned that the gypsy was alive, the cold ideas of spectre and tomb that had persecuted him for a whole day vanished, and the flesh returned to goad him. He turned and twisted on his couch at the thought that the dark-skinned maiden was so near him.

Every night his delirious imagination represented la Esmeralda to him in all the attitudes that had caused his blood to boil most. He beheld her outstretched upon the poniarded captain, her eyes closed, her beautiful bare throat covered with Phoebus's blood, at that moment of bliss when the archdeacon had imprinted on her pale lips that kiss whose burn the unhappy girl, though half dead, had felt. He beheld her, again, stripped by the savage hands of the torturers, allowing them to bare and to enclose in the boot with its iron screw, her tiny foot, her delicate rounded leg, her white and supple knee. Again he beheld that ivory knee which alone remained outside of Torterue's horrible apparatus. Lastly, he pictured the young girl in her shift, with the rope about her neck, shoulders bare, feet bare, almost nude, as he had seen her on that last day. These images of voluptuousness made him clench his fists, and a shiver run along his spine.

One night, among others, they heated so cruelly his virgin and priestly blood, that he bit his pillow, leaped from his bed, flung on a surplice over his shirt, and left his cell, lamp in hand, half naked, wild, his eyes aflame.

He knew where to find the key to the red door, which connected the cloister with the church, and he always had about him, as the reader knows, the key of the staircase leading to the towers.

Chapter 6

Continuation of the Key to the Red Door

THAT NIGHT, LA Esmeralda had fallen asleep in her cell, full of oblivion, of hope, and of sweet thoughts. She had already been asleep for some time, dreaming as always, of Phoebus, when it seemed to her that she heard a noise near her. She slept lightly and uneasily, the sleep of a bird; a mere nothing waked her. She opened her eyes. The night was very dark. Nevertheless, she saw a figure gazing at her through the window; a lamp lighted up this apparition. The moment that the figure saw that la Esmeralda had perceived it, it blew out the lamp. But the young girl had had time to catch a glimpse of it; her eyes closed again with terror.

"Oh!" she said in a faint voice, "the priest!"

All her past unhappiness came back to her like a flash of lightning. She fell back on her bed, chilled.

A moment later she felt a touch along her body that made her shudder so that she straightened herself up in a sitting posture, wide awake and furious.

The priest had just slipped in beside her. He encircled her with both arms.

She tried to scream and could not.

"Begone, monster! Begone, assassin!" she said, in a voice which was low and trembling with wrath and terror.

"Mercy, mercy!" murmured the priest, pressing his lips to her shoulder.

She seized his bald head by its remnant of hair and tried to thrust aside his kisses as though they had been bites.

"Mercy!" repeated the unfortunate man. "If you but knew what my love for you is! 'Tis fire, melted lead, a thousand daggers in my heart."

She stopped his two arms with superhuman force.

"Let me go," she said, "or I will spit in your face!"

He released her. "Vilify me, strike me, be malicious! Do what you will! But have mercy! Love me!"

Then she struck him with the fury of a child. She made her beautiful hands stiff to bruise his face. "Begone, demon!"

"Love me! Love me pity!" cried the poor priest returning her blows with caresses.

All at once she felt him stronger than herself.

"There must be an end to this!" he said, gnashing his teeth.

She was conquered, palpitating in his arms, and in his power. She felt a wanton hand straying over her. She made a last effort, and began to cry: "Help! Help! A vampire! A vampire!"

Nothing came. Djali alone was awake and bleating with anguish.

"Hush!" said the panting priest.

All at once, as she struggled and crawled on the floor, the gypsy's hand came in contact with something cold and metallic; it was Quasimodo's whistle. She seized it with a convulsive hope, raised it to her lips and blew with all the strength that she had left. The whistle gave a clear, piercing sound.

"What is that?" said the priest.

Almost at the same instant he felt himself raised by a vigorous arm. The cell was dark; he could not distinguish clearly who it was that held him thus; but he heard teeth chattering with rage, and there was just sufficient light scattered among the gloom to allow him to see above his head the blade of a large knife.

The priest fancied that he perceived the form of Quasimodo. He assumed that it could be no one but he. He remembered to have stumbled, as he entered, over a bundle that was stretched across the door on the outside. But, as the newcomer did not utter a word, he knew not what to think. He flung himself on the arm that held the knife, crying: "Quasimodo!" He forgot, at that moment of distress, that Quasimodo was deaf.

In a twinkling, the priest was overthrown and a leaden knee rested on his breast.

From the angular imprint of that knee he recognized Quasimodo; but what was to be done? How could he make the other recognize him? The darkness rendered the deaf man blind.

He was lost. The young girl, pitiless as an enraged tigress, did not intervene to save him. The knife was approaching his head; the moment was critical. All at once, his adversary seemed stricken with hesitation.

"No blood on her!" he said in a dull voice.

It was, in fact, Quasimodo's voice.

Then the priest felt a large hand dragging him feet first out of the cell; it was there that he was to die. Fortunately for him, the moon had risen a few moments before.

When they had passed through the door of the cell, its pale rays fell upon the priest's countenance. Quasimodo looked him full in the face, a trembling seized him, and he released the priest and shrank back.

The gypsy, who had advanced to the threshold of her cell, beheld with surprise their roles abruptly changed. It was now the priest who menaced, Quasimodo who was the suppliant.

The priest, who was overwhelming the deaf man with gestures of wrath and reproach, made the latter a violent sign to retire.

The deaf man dropped his head, then he came and knelt at the gypsy's door. "Monseigneur," he said, in a grave and resigned voice, "you shall do all that you please afterwards, but kill me first."

So saying, he presented his knife to the priest. The priest, beside himself, was about to seize it. But the young girl was quicker than be; she wrenched the knife from Quasimodo's hands and burst into a frantic laugh. "Approach," she said to the priest.

She held the blade high. The priest remained undecided.

She would certainly have struck him.

Then she added with a pitiless expression, well aware that she was about to pierce the priest's heart with thousands of red-hot irons, "Ah! I know that Phoebus is not dead!"

The priest overturned Quasimodo on the floor with a kick, and, quivering with rage, darted back under the vault of the staircase.

When he was gone, Quasimodo picked up the whistle that had just saved the gypsy.

"It was getting rusty," he said, as he handed it back to her; then he left her alone.

The young girl, deeply agitated by this violent scene, fell back exhausted on her bed, and began to sob and weep. Her horizon was becoming gloomy once more.

The priest had groped his way back to his cell.

It was settled. Dom Claude was jealous of Quasimodo!

He repeated with a thoughtful air his fatal words: "No one shall have her."

Book Tenth

CHAPTER 1

Gringoire Has Many Good Ideas in Succession

As SOON AS Pierre Gringoire had seen how this whole affair was turning, and that there would decidedly be the rope, hanging, and other disagreeable things for the principal personages in this comedy, he had not cared to identify himself with the matter further. The outcasts with whom he had remained, reflecting that, after all, it was the best company in Paris, had continued to interest themselves in behalf of the gypsy. He had thought it very simple on the part of people who had, like herself, nothing else in prospect but Charmolue and Torterue, and who, unlike himself, did not gallop through the regions of imagination between the wings of Pegasus. From their remarks, he had learned that his wife of the broken crock had taken refuge in Notre-Dame, and he was very glad of it. But he felt no temptation to go and see her there. He meditated occasionally on the little goat, and that was all. Moreover, he was busy executing feats of strength during the day for his living, and at night he was engaged in composing a memorial against the Bishop of Paris, for he remembered having been drenched by the wheels of his mills, and he cherished a grudge against him for it. He also occupied himself with annotating the fine work of Maudry-le-Rouge, Bishop of Noyon and Tournay, *De Cupâ Petrarum*, which had given him a violent passion for architecture, an inclination which had replaced in his heart his passion for hermeticism, of which it was, moreover, only a natural corollary, since there is an intimate relation between hermeticism and masonry. Gringoire had passed from the love of an idea to the love of the form of that idea.

One day he had halted near Saint Germain-l'Auxerrois, at the corner of a mansion called "For-l'Evêque" (the Bishop's Tribunal), which stood opposite another called "For-le-Roi" (the King's Tribunal).

At this For-l'Evêque, there was a charming chapel of the fourteenth century, whose apse was on the street. Gringoire was devoutly examining its exterior sculptures. He was in one of those moments of egotistical, exclusive, supreme, enjoyment when the artist beholds nothing in the world but art, and the world in art. All at once he feels a hand laid gravely on his shoulder. He turns round. It was his old friend, his former master, monsieur the archdeacon.

He was stupefied. It was a long time since he had seen the archdeacon, and Dom Claude was one of those solemn and impassioned men, a meeting with whom always upsets the equilibrium of a sceptical philosopher.

The archdeacon maintained silence for several minutes, during which Gringoire had time to observe him. He found Dom Claude greatly changed; pale as a winter's morning, with hollow eyes, and hair almost white. The priest broke the silence at length, by saying, in a tranquil but glacial tone, "How do you do, Master Pierre?"

"My health?" replied Gringoire. "Eh! Eh, one can say both one thing and another on that score. Still, it is good, on the whole. I take not too much of anything. You know, master, that the secret of keeping well, according to Hippocrates; *id est: cibi, potus, somni, venus, omnia moderata sint.*"

"So you have no care, Master Pierre?" resumed the archdeacon, gazing intently at Gringoire.

"None, i' faith!"

"And what are you doing now?"

"You see, master. I am examining the chiselling of these stones, and the manner in which yonder bas-relief is thrown out."

The priest began to smile with that bitter smile which raises only one corner of the mouth.

"And that amuses you?"

"'Tis paradise!" exclaimed Gringoire. And leaning over the sculptures with the fascinated air of a demonstrator of living phenomena: "Do you not think, for instance, that yon metamorphosis in bas-relief is executed with much adroitness, delicacy and patience? Observe that slender column. Around what capital have you seen foliage more tender and better caressed by the chisel. Here are three raised bosses of Jean Maillevin. They are not the finest works of this great master. Nevertheless, the naivete, the sweetness of the faces, the gayety of the attitudes and draperies, and that inexplicable charm which is mingled with all the defects, render the little figures very diverting and delicate, perchance, even too much so. You think that it is not diverting?"

"Yes, certainly!" said the priest.

"And if you were to see the interior of the chapel!" resumed the poet, with his garrulous enthusiasm. "Carvings everywhere. 'Tis as thickly clustered as the head of a cabbage! The apse is of a very devout, and so peculiar a fashion that I have never beheld anything like it elsewhere!"

Dom Claude interrupted him. "You are happy, then?"

Gringoire replied warmly, "On my honor, yes! First I loved women, then animals. Now I love stones. They are quite as amusing as women and animals, and less treacherous."

The priest laid his hand on his brow. It was his habitual gesture. "Really?"

"Stay!" said Gringoire, "one has one's pleasures!" He took the arm of the priest, who let him have his way, and made him enter the staircase turret of For-l'Evêque. "Here is a staircase! Every time that I see it I am happy. It is of the simplest and rarest manner of steps in Paris. All the steps are bevelled underneath. Its beauty and simplicity consist in the interspacing of both, being a foot or more wide, which are interlaced, interlocked, fitted together, enchained enchased, interlined one upon another, and bite into each other in a manner that is truly firm and graceful."

"And you desire nothing?"

"No."

"And you regret nothing?"

"Neither regret nor desire. I have arranged my mode of life."

"What men arrange," said Claude, "things disarrange."

"I am a Pyrrhonian philosopher," replied Gringoire, "and I hold all things in equilibrium."

"And how do you earn your living?"

"I still make epics and tragedies now and then; but that which brings me in most is the industry with which you are acquainted, master; carrying pyramids of chairs in my teeth."

"The trade is but a rough one for a philosopher."

"'Tis still equilibrium," said Gringoire. "When one has an idea, one encounters it in everything."

"I know that," replied the archdeacon.

After a silence, the priest resumed, "You are, nevertheless, tolerably poor?"

"Poor, yes; unhappy, no."

At that moment, a trampling of horses was heard, and our two interlocutors beheld defiling at the end of the street, a company of the king's unattached archers, their lances borne high, an officer at their head. The cavalcade was brilliant, and its march resounded on the pavement.

"How you gaze at that officer!" said Gringoire, to the archdeacon.

"Because I think I recognize him."

"What do you call him?"

"I think," said Claude, "that his name is Phoebus de Châteaupers."

"Phoebus! A curious name! There is also a Phoebus, Comte de Foix. I remember having known a wench who swore only by the name of Phoebus."

"Come away from here," said the priest. "I have something to say to you."

From the moment of that troop's passing, some agitation had pierced through the archdeacon's glacial envelope. He walked on. Gringoire followed him, being accustomed to obey him, like all who had once approached that man so full of ascendency. They reached in silence the Rue des Bernardins, which was nearly deserted. Here Dom Claude paused.

"What have you to say to me, master?" Gringoire asked him.

"Do you not think that the dress of those cavaliers whom we have just seen is far handsomer than yours and mine?"

Gringoire tossed his head.

"I' faith! I love better my red and yellow jerkin, than those scales of iron and steel. A fine pleasure to produce, when you walk, the same noise as the Quay of Old Iron, in an earthquake!"

"So, Gringoire, you have never cherished envy for those handsome fellows in their military doublets?"

"Envy for what, monsieur the archdeacon? Their strength, their armor, their discipline? Better philosophy and independence in rags. I prefer to be the head of a fly rather than the tail of a lion."

"That is singular," said the priest dreamily. "Yet a handsome uniform is a beautiful thing."

Gringoire, perceiving that he was in a pensive mood, quitted him to go and admire the porch of a neighboring house. He came back clapping his hands.

"If you were less engrossed with the fine clothes of men of war, monsieur the archdeacon, I would entreat you to come and see this door. I have always said that the house of the Sieur Aubry had the most superb entrance in the world."

"Pierre Gringoire," said the archdeacon, "What have you done with that little gypsy dancer?"

"La Esmeralda? You change the conversation very abruptly."

"Was she not your wife?"

"Yes, by virtue of a broken crock. We were to have four years of it. By the way," added Gringoire, looking at the archdeacon in a half bantering way, "are you still thinking of her?"

"And you think of her no longer?"

"Very little. I have so many things. Good heavens, how pretty that little goat was!"

"Had she not saved your life?"

"'Tis true, pardieu!"

"Well, what has become of her? What have you done with her?"

"I cannot tell you. I believe that they have hanged her."

"You believe so?"

"I am not sure. When I saw that they wanted to hang people, I retired from the game."

"That is all you know of it?"

"Wait a bit. I was told that she had taken refuge in Notre-Dame, and that she was safe there, and I am delighted to hear it, and I have not been able to discover whether the goat was saved with her, and that is all I know."

"I will tell you more," cried Dom Claude; and his voice, hitherto low, slow, and almost indistinct, turned to thunder. "She has in fact, taken refuge in Notre-Dame. But in three days justice will reclaim her, and she will be hanged on the Grève. There is a decree of parliament."

"That's annoying," said Gringoire.

The priest, in an instant, became cold and calm again.

"And who the devil," resumed the poet, "has amused himself with soliciting a decree of reintegration? Why couldn't they leave parliament in peace? What harm does it do if a poor girl takes shelter under the flying buttresses of Notre-Dame, beside the swallows' nests?"

"There are Satans in this world," remarked the archdeacon.

"'Tis devilish badly done," observed Gringoire.

The archdeacon resumed after a silence. "So, she saved your life?"

"Among my good friends the outcasts. A little more or a little less and I should have been hanged. They would have been sorry for it today."

"Would not you like to do something for her?"

"I ask nothing better, Dom Claude; but what if I entangle myself in some villanous affair?"

"What matters it?"

"Bah, what matters it? You are good, master, that you are! I have two great works already begun."

The priest smote his brow. In spite of the calm that he affected, a violent gesture betrayed his internal convulsions from time to time.

"How is she to be saved?"

Gringoire said to him; "Master, I will reply to you; *Il padelt*, which means in Turkish, 'God is our hope.'"

"How is she to be saved?" repeated Claude dreamily.

Gringoire smote his brow in his turn.

"Listen, master. I have imagination; I will devise expedients for you. What if one were to ask her pardon from the king?"

"Of Louis XI! A pardon!"

"Why not?"

"To take the tiger's bone from him!"

Gringoire began to seek fresh expedients.

"Well, stay! Shall I address to the midwives a request accompanied by the declaration that the girl is with child!"

This made the priest's hollow eye flash.

"With child! Knave! Do you know anything of this?"

Gringoire was alarmed by his air. He hastened to say, "Oh, no, not I! Our marriage was a real *forismaritagium*. I stayed outside. But one might obtain a respite, all the same."

"Madness! Infamy! Hold your tongue!"

"You do wrong to get angry," muttered Gringoire. "One obtains a respite; that does no harm to any one, and allows the midwives, who are poor women, to earn forty deniers parisis."

The priest was not listening to him!

"But she must leave that place, nevertheless!" he murmured. "The decree is to be executed within three days. Moreover, there will be no decree; that Quasimodo! Women have very depraved tastes!" He raised his voice: "Master Pierre, I have reflected well; there is but one means of safety for her."

"What? I see none myself."

"Listen, Master Pierre, remember that you owe your life to her. I will tell you my idea frankly. The church is watched night and day; only those are allowed to come out, who have been seen to enter. Hence you can enter. You will come. I will lead you to her. You will change clothes with her. She will take your doublet; you will take her petticoat."

"So far, it goes well," remarked the philosopher, "and then?"

"And then? She will go forth in your garments; you will remain with hers. You will be hanged, perhaps, but she will be saved."

Gringoire scratched his ear, with a very serious air. "Stay!" said he, "that is an idea which would never have occurred to me unaided."

At Dom Claude's proposition, the open and benign face of the poet had abruptly clouded over, like a smiling Italian landscape, when an unlucky squall comes up and dashes a cloud across the sun.

"Well! Gringoire, what say you to the means?"

"I say, master, that I shall not be hanged, perchance, but that I shall be hanged indubitably."

"That concerns us not."

"The deuce!" said Gringoire.

"She has saved your life. 'Tis a debt that you are discharging."

"There are a great many others which I do not discharge."

"Master Pierre, it is absolutely necessary."

The archdeacon spoke imperiously."

"Listen, Dom Claude," replied the poet in utter consternation. "You cling to that idea, and you are wrong. I do not see why I should get myself hanged in some one else's place."

"What have you, then, which attaches you so strongly to life?"

"Oh! A thousand reasons!"

"What reasons, if you please?"

"What? The air, the sky, the morning, the evening, the moonlight, my good friends the thieves, our jeers with the old hags of go-betweens, the fine architecture of Paris to study, three great books to make, one of them being against the bishops and his mills; and how can I tell all? Anaxagoras said that he was in the world to admire the sun. And then, from morning till night, I have the happiness of passing all my days with a man of genius, who is myself, which is very agreeable."

"A head fit for a mule bell!" muttered the archdeacon. "Oh, tell me who preserved for you that life which you render so charming to yourself? To whom do you owe it that you breathe that air, behold that sky, and can still amuse your lark's mind with your whimsical nonsense and madness? Where would you be, had it not been for her? Do you then desire that she through whom you are alive, should die? That she should die, that beautiful, sweet, adorable creature, who is necessary to the light of the world and more divine than God, while you, half wise, and half fool, a vain sketch of something, a sort of vegetable, which thinks that it walks, and thinks that it thinks, you will continue to live with the life which you have stolen from her, as useless as a candle in broad daylight? Come, have a little pity, Gringoire; be generous in your turn; it was she who set the example."

The priest was vehement. Gringoire listened to him at first with an undecided air, then he became touched, and wound up with a grimace that made his pallid face resemble that of a new-born infant with an attack of the colic.

"You are pathetic!" said he, wiping away a tear. "Well! I will think about it. That's a queer idea of yours.

"After all," he continued after a pause, "who knows? Perhaps they will not hang me. He who becomes betrothed does not always marry. When they find me in that little lodging so grotesquely muffled in petticoat and coif, perchance they will burst with laughter. And then, if they do hang me, well, the halter is as good a death as any! 'Tis a death worthy of a sage who has wavered all his life; a death which is neither flesh nor fish, like the mind of a veritable sceptic; a death all stamped with Pyrrhonism and hesitation, which holds the middle station betwixt heaven and earth, which leaves you in suspense. 'Tis a philosopher's death, and I was destined thereto, perchance. It is magnificent to die as one has lived."

The priest interrupted him: "Is it agreed."

"What is death, after all?" pursued Gringoire with exaltation. "A disagreeable moment, a toll-gate, the passage of little to nothingness. Some one having asked Cercidas, the Megalopolitan, if he were willing to die: 'Why not?' he replied; 'for after my death I shall see those great men, Pythagoras among the philosophers, Hecataeus among historians, Homer among poets, Olympus among musicians.'"

The archdeacon gave him his hand: "It is settled, then? You will come tomorrow?"

This gesture recalled Gringoire to reality.

"Ah, in faith no!" he said in the tone of a man just waking up. "Be hanged! 'Tis too absurd. I will not."

"Farewell, then!" and the archdeacon added between his teeth: "I'll find you again!"

"I do not want that devil of a man to find me," thought Gringoire; and he ran after Dom Claude. "Stay, monsieur the archdeacon, no ill-feeling between old friends! You take an interest in that girl, my wife, I mean, and 'tis well. You have devised a scheme to get her out of Notre-Dame, but your way is extremely disagreeable to me, Gringoire. If I had only another one myself! I beg to say that a luminous inspiration has just occurred to me. If I possessed an expedient for extricating her from a dilemma, without compromising my own neck to the extent of a single running knot, what would you say to it? Will not that suffice you? Is it absolutely necessary that I should be hanged, in order that you may be content?"

The priest tore out the buttons of his cassock with impatience: "Stream of words! What is your plan?"

"Yes," resumed Gringoire, talking to himself and touching his nose with his forefinger in sign of meditation, "that's it! The thieves are brave fellows! The tribe of Egypt love her! They will rise at the first word! Nothing easier! A sudden stroke. Under cover of the disorder, they will easily carry her off! Beginning tomorrow evening. They will ask nothing better.

"The plan! Speak," cried the archdeacon shaking him.

Gringoire turned majestically toward him: "Leave me! You see that I am composing." He meditated for a few moments more, then began to clap his hands over his thought, crying: "Admirable! Success is sure!"

"The plan!" repeated Claude in wrath.

Gringoire was radiant.

"Come, that I may tell you that very softly. 'Tis a truly gallant counter-plot, which will extricate us all from the matter. Pardieu, it must be admitted that I am no fool."

He broke off.

"Oh, by the way! Is the little goat with the wench?"

"Yes. The devil take you!"

"They would have hanged it also, would they not?"

"What is that to me?"

"Yes, they would have hanged it. They hanged a sow last month. The headsman loveth that; he eats the beast afterwards. Take my pretty Djali! Poor little lamb!"

"Malediction!" exclaimed Dom Claude. "You are the executioner. What means of safety have you found, knave? Must your idea be extracted with the forceps?"

"Very fine, master, this is it."

Gringoire bent his head to the archdeacon's head and spoke to him in a very low voice, casting an uneasy glance the while from one end to the other of the street, though no one was passing. When he had finished, Dom Claude took his hand and said coldly: "'Tis well. Farewell until tomorrow."

"Until tomorrow," repeated Gringoire. And, while the archdeacon was disappearing in one direction, he set off in the other, saying to himself in a low voice: "Here's a grand affair, Monsieur Pierre Gringoire. Never mind! 'Tis not written that because one is of small account one should take fright at a great enterprise. Bitou carried a great bull on his shoulders; the water-wagtails, the warblers, and the buntings traverse the ocean."

CHAPTER 2

Turn Vagabond

ON RE-ENTERING THE cloister, the archdeacon found at the door of his cell his brother Jehan du Moulin, who was waiting for him, and who had beguiled the tedium of waiting by drawing on the wall with a bit of charcoal, a profile of his elder brother, enriched with a monstrous nose.

Dom Claude hardly looked at his brother; his thoughts were elsewhere. That merry scamp's face whose beaming had so often restored serenity to the priest's sombre physiognomy, was now powerless to melt the gloom which grew more dense every day over that corrupted, mephitic, and stagnant soul.

"Brother," said Jehan timidly, "I am come to see you."

The archdeacon did not even raise his eyes.

"What then?"

"Brother," resumed the hypocrite, "you are so good to me, and you give me such wise counsels that I always return to you."

"What next?"

"Alas! Brother, you were perfectly right when you said to me, "Jehan! Jehan, *cessat doctorum doctrina, discipulorum disciplina*. Jehan, be wise, Jehan, be learned, Jehan, pass not the night outside of the college without lawful occasion and due leave of the master. Cudgel not the Picards: *noli, Joannes, verberare Picardos*. Rot not like an unlettered ass, *quasi asinus illitteratus*, on the straw seats of the school. Jehan, allow yourself to be punished at the discretion of the master. Jehan go every evening to chapel, and sing there an anthem with verse and orison to Madame the glorious Virgin Mary. Alas! what excellent advice was that!"

"And then?"

"Brother, you behold a culprit, a criminal, a wretch, a libertine, a man of enormities! My dear brother, Jehan hath made of your counsels straw and dung to trample under foot. I have been well chastised for it, and God is extraordinarily just. As long as I had money, I feasted, I lead a mad and joyous life. Oh, how ugly and crabbed behind is debauch which is so charming in front! Now I have no longer a blank; I have sold my napery, my shirt and my towels; no more merry life! The beautiful candle is extinguished and I have henceforth, only a wretched tallow dip which smokes in my nose. The wenches jeer at me. I drink water. I am overwhelmed with remorse and with creditors."

"The rest?" said the archdeacon.

"Alas! My very dear brother, I should like to settle down to a better life. I come to you full of contrition, I am penitent. I make my confession. I beat my breast violently. You are quite right in wishing that I should some day become a licentiate and sub-monitor in the college of Torchi. At the present moment I feel a magnificent vocation for that profession. But I have no more ink and I must buy some; I have no more paper, I have no more books, and I must buy some. For this purpose, I am greatly in need of a little money, and I come to you, brother, with my heart full of contrition."

"Is that all?"

"Yes," said the scholar. "A little money."

"I have none."

Then the scholar said, with an air which was both grave and resolute: "Well, brother, I am sorry to be obliged to tell you that very fine offers and propositions are being made to me in another quarter. You will not give me any money? No. In that case I shall become a professional vagabond."

As he uttered these monstrous words, he assumed the mien of Ajax, expecting to see the lightnings descend upon his head.

The archdeacon said coldly to him, "Become a vagabond."

Jehan made him a deep bow, and descended the cloister stairs, whistling.

At the moment when he was passing through the courtyard of the cloister, beneath his brother's window, he heard that window open, raised his eyes and beheld the archdeacon's severe head emerge.

"Go to the devil!" said Dom Claude. "Here is the last money which you will get from me."

At the same time, the priest flung Jehan a purse, which gave the scholar a big bump on the forehead, and with which Jehan retreated, both vexed and content, like a dog who had been stoned with marrow bones.

CHAPTER 3

Long Live Mirth

THE READER HAS probably not forgotten that a part of the Cour de Miracles was enclosed by the ancient wall which surrounded the city, a goodly number of whose towers had begun, even at that epoch, to fall to ruin. One of these towers had been converted into a pleasure resort by the vagabonds. There was a drain-shop in the underground story, and the rest in the upper stories. This was the most lively, and consequently the most hideous, point of the whole outcast den. It was a sort of monstrous hive, which buzzed there night and day. At night, when the remainder of the beggar horde slept, when there was no longer a window lighted in the dingy façades of the Place, when not a cry was any longer to be heard proceeding from those innumerable families, those ant-hills of thieves, of wenches, and stolen or bastard children, the merry tower was still recognizable by the noise which it made, by the scarlet light which, flashing simultaneously from the air-holes, the windows, the fissures in the cracked walls, escaped, so to speak, from its every pore.

The cellar then, was the dram-shop. The descent to it was through a low door and by a staircase as steep as a classic Alexandrine. Over the door, by way of a sign there hung a marvellous daub, representing new sons and dead chickens, with this, pun below: *Aux sonneurs pour les trépassés*: the wringers for the dead.

One evening when the curfew was sounding from all the belfries in Paris, the sergeants of the watch might have observed, had it been granted to them to enter the formidable Court of Miracles, that more tumult than usual was in progress in the vagabonds' tavern, that more drinking was being done, and louder swearing. Outside in the Place, there, were many groups conversing in low tones, as when some great plan is being framed, and here and there a knave crouching down engaged in sharpening a villanous iron blade on a paving-stone.

Meanwhile, in the tavern itself, wine and gaming offered such a powerful diversion to the ideas that occupied the vagabonds' lair that evening, that it would have been difficult to divine from the remarks of the drinkers, what was the matter in hand. They merely wore a gayer air than was their wont, and some weapon could be seen glittering between the legs of each of them—a sickle, an axe, a big two-edged sword or the hook of an old hackbut.

The room, circular in form, was very spacious; but the tables were so thickly set and the drinkers so numerous, that all that the tavern contained, men, women, benches, beer-jugs, all that were drinking, all that were sleeping, all that were playing, the well, the lame, seemed piled up pell-mell, with as much order and harmony as a heap of oyster shells. There were a few tallow dips lighted on the tables; but the real luminary of this tavern, that which played the part in this dram-shop of the chandelier of an opera house, was the fire. This cellar was so damp that the fire was never allowed to go out, even in midsummer; an immense chimney with a sculptured mantel, all bristling with heavy iron andirons and cooking utensils, with one of those huge fires of mixed wood and peat which at night, in village streets make the reflection of forge windows stand out so red on the opposite walls. A big dog gravely seated in the ashes was turning a spit loaded with meat before the coals.

Great as was the confusion, after the first glance one could distinguish in that multitude, three principal groups which thronged around three personages already known to the reader. One of these personages, fantastically accoutred in many an oriental rag, was Mathias Hungadi Spicali, Duke of Egypt and Bohemia. The knave was seated on a table with his legs crossed, and in a loud voice was bestowing his knowledge of magic, both black and white, on many a gaping face which surrounded him. Another rabble pressed close around our old friend, the valiant King of Thunes, armed to the teeth. Clopin Trouillefou, with a very serious air and in a low voice, was regulating the distribution of an enormous cask of arms, which stood wide open in front of him and from whence poured out in profusion, axes, swords, bassinets, coats of mail, broadswords, lance-heads, arrows, and viretons, like apples and grapes from a horn of plenty. Every one took something from the cask, one a morion, another a long, straight sword, another a dagger with a cross-shaped hilt. The very children were arming themselves, and there were even cripples in bowls who, in armor and cuirass, made their way between the legs of the drinkers, like great beetles.

Finally, a third audience, the most noisy, the most jovial, and the most numerous, encumbered benches and tables, in the midst of which harangued and swore a flute-like voice, which escaped from beneath a heavy armor, complete from casque to spurs. The individual who had thus screwed a whole outfit upon his body, was so hidden by his warlike accoutrements that nothing was to be seen of his person save an impertinent, red, snub nose, a rosy mouth, and bold eyes. His belt was full of daggers and poniards, a huge sword on his hip, a rusted cross-bow at his left, and a vast jug of wine in front of him, without reckoning on his right, a fat wench with her bosom uncovered. All mouths around him were laughing, cursing, and drinking.

Add twenty secondary groups, the waiters, male and female, running with jugs on their heads, gamblers squatting over taws, merelles, dice, vachettes, the ardent game of tringlet, quarrels in one corner, kisses in another, and the reader will have some idea of this whole picture, over which flickered the light of a great, flaming fire, which made a thousand huge and grotesque shadows dance over the walls of the drinking shop.

As for the noise, it was like the inside of a bell at full peal.

The dripping-pan, where crackled a rain of grease, filled with its continual sputtering the intervals of these thousand dialogues, which intermingled from one end of the apartment to the other.

In the midst of this uproar, at the extremity of the tavern, on the bench inside the chimney, sat a philosopher meditating with his feet in the ashes and his eyes on the brands. It was Pierre Gringoire.

"Be quick! Make haste, arm yourselves! We set out on the march in an hour!" said Clopin Trouillefou to his thieves.

A wench was humming:

> Good night, father and mother,
> The last cover up the fire.

Two card players were disputing. "Knave!" cried the reddest faced of the two, shaking his fist at the other; "I'll mark you with the club. You can take the place of Mistigri in the pack of cards of monseigneur the king."

"Ugh!" roared a Norman, recognizable by his nasal accent. "We are packed in here like the saints of Caillouville!"

"My sons," the Duke of Egypt was saying to his audience, in a falsetto voice, "sorceresses in France go to the Witches' Sabbath without broomsticks, or grease, or steed, merely by means of some magic words. The witches of Italy always have a buck waiting for them at their door. All are bound to go out through the chimney."

The voice of the young scamp armed from head to foot, dominated the uproar.

"Hurrah, hurrah!" he was shouting. "My first day in armor! Outcast! I am an outcast. Give me something to drink. My friends, my name is Jehan Frollo du Moulin, and I am a gentleman. My opinion is that if God were a gendarme, he would turn robber. Brothers, we are about to set out on a fine expedition. Lay siege to the church, burst in the doors, drag out the beautiful girl, save her from the judges, save her from the priests, dismantle the cloister, burn the bishop in his palace—all this we will do in less time than it takes for a burgomaster to eat a spoonful of soup. Our cause is just, we will plunder Notre-Dame and that will be the end of it. We will hang Quasimodo. Do you know Quasimodo, ladies? Have you seen him make himself breathless on the big bell on a grand Pentecost festival! *Corne du Père*! 'Tis very fine! One would say he was a devil mounted on a man. Listen to me, my friends; I am a vagabond to the bottom of my heart, I am a member of the slang thief gang in my soul, I was born an independent thief. I have been rich, and I have devoured all my property. My mother wanted to make an officer of me; my father, a sub-deacon; my aunt, a councillor of inquests; my grandmother, prothonotary to the king; my great aunt, a treasurer of the short robe—and I have made myself an outcast. I said this to my father, who spit his curse in my face; to my mother, who set to weeping and chattering, poor old lady, like yonder fagot on the and-irons. Long live mirth! I am a real Bicêtre. Waitress, my dear, more wine. I have still the wherewithal to pay. I want no more Surène wine. It distresses my throat. I'd as lief—*cor-boeuf*!—gargle my throat with a basket."

Meanwhile, the rabble applauded with shouts of laughter; and seeing that the tumult was increasing around him, the scholar cried, "Oh, what a fine noise! *Populi debacchantis populosa debacchatio*!" Then he began to sing, his eye swimming in ecstasy, in the tone of a canon intoning vespers, "*Quoe cantica! Quoe organa! Quoe cantilenoe! Quoe melodioe hic sine fine decantantur! Sonant melliflua hymnorum organa, suavissima angelorum melodia, cantica canticorum mira!*" He broke off: "Tavern-keeper of the devil, give me some supper!"

There was a moment of partial silence, during which the sharp voice of the Duke of Egypt rose, as he gave instructions to his Bohemians.

"The weasel is called Adrune; the fox, Blue-foot, or the Racer of the Woods; the wolf, Gray-foot, or Gold-foot; the bear the Old Man, or Grandfather. The cap of a gnome confers invisibility, and causes one to behold invisible things. Every toad that is baptized must be clad in red or black velvet, a bell on its neck, a bell on its feet. The godfather holds its head, the godmother its hinder parts. 'Tis the demon Sidragasum who hath the power to make wenches dance stark naked."

"By the mass!" interrupted Jehan, "I should like to be the demon Sidragasum."

Meanwhile, the vagabonds continued to arm themselves and whisper at the other end of the dram-shop.

"That poor Esmeralda!" said a Bohemian. "She is our sister. She must be taken away from there."

"Is she still at Notre-Dame?" went on a merchant with the appearance of a Jew.

"Yes, pardieu!"

"Well, comrades!" exclaimed the merchant, "to Notre-Dame! So much the better, since there are in the chapel of Saints Féréol and Ferrution two statues, the one of John the Baptist, the other of Saint-Antoine, of solid gold, weighing together seven marks of gold and fifteen estellins; and the pedestals are of silver-gilt, of seventeen marks, five ounces. I know that; I am a goldsmith."

Here they served Jehan with his supper. As he threw himself back on the bosom of the wench beside him, he exclaimed, "By Saint Voult-de-Lucques, whom people call Saint Goguelu, I am perfectly happy. I have before me a fool who gazes at me with the smooth face of an archduke. Here is one on my left whose teeth are so long that they hide his chin. And then, I am like the Marshal de Gié at the siege of Pontoise, I have my right resting on a hillock. *Ventre-Mahom!* Comrade, you have the air of a merchant of tennis-balls; and you come and sit yourself beside me! I am a nobleman, my friend! Trade is incompatible with nobility. Get out of that! Hey, there! You others, don't fight! What, Baptiste Croque-Oison, you who have such a fine nose are going to risk it against the big fists of that lout! Fool! *Non ciquam datum est habere nasum*—not every one is favored with a nose. You are really divine, Jacqueline Ronge-Oreille! 'Tis a pity that you have no hair! Hallo! My name is Jehan Frollo, and my brother is an archdeacon. May the devil fly off with him! All that I tell you is the truth. In turning vagabond, I have gladly renounced the half of a house situated in paradise, which my brother had promised me. *Dimidiam domum in paradiso.* I quote the text. I have a fief in the Rue Tirechappe, and all the women are in love with me, as true as Saint Eloy was an excellent goldsmith, and that the five trades of the good city of Paris are the tanners, the tawers, the makers of cross-belts, the purse-makers, and the sweaters, and that Saint Laurent was burnt with eggshells. I swear to you, comrades.

> That I will drink no spiced, honeyed wine for a year,
> if I am lying now.

"'Tis moonlight, my charmer; see yonder through the window how the wind is tearing the clouds to tatters! Even thus will I do to your gorget. Wenches, wipe the children's noses and snuff the candles. Christ and Mahom! What am I eating here, Jupiter? Oh, innkeeper! The hair that is not on the heads of your hussies one finds in your omelettes. Old woman! I like bald omelettes. May the devil confound you! A fine hostelry of Beelzebub, where the hussies comb their heads with the forks!

> "*Et je n'ai moi,*
> *Par la sang-Dieu!*
> *Ni foi, ni loi,*
> *Ni feu, ni lieu,*
> *Ni roi,*
> *Ni Dieu.*"

In the meantime, Clopin Trouillefou had finished the distribution of arms. He approached Gringoire, who appeared to be plunged in a profound revery, with his feet on an andiron.

"Friend Pierre," said the King of Thunes, "what the devil are you thinking about?"

Gringoire turned to him with a melancholy smile.

"I love the fire, my dear lord. Not for the trivial reason that fire warms the feet or cooks our soup, but because it has sparks. Sometimes

I pass whole hours in watching the sparks. I discover a thousand things in those stars that are sprinkled over the black background of the hearth. Those stars are also worlds."

"Thunder, if I understand you!" said the outcast. "Do you know what o'clock it is?"

"I do not know," replied Gringoire.

Clopin approached the Duke of Egypt.

"Comrade Mathias, the time we have chosen is not a good one. King Louis XI is said to be in Paris."

"Another reason for snatching our sister from his claws," replied the old Bohemian.

"You speak like a man, Mathias," said the King of Thunes. "Moreover, we will act promptly. No resistance is to be feared in the church. The canons are hares, and we are in force. The people of the parliament will be well balked tomorrow when they come to seek her! Guts of the pope I don't want them to hang the pretty girl!"

Chopin quitted the dram-shop.

Meanwhile, Jehan was shouting in a hoarse voice:

"I eat, I drink, I am drunk, I am Jupiter! Eh! Pierre, the Slaughterer, if you look at me like that again, I'll fillip the dust off your nose for you."

Gringoire, torn from his meditations, began to watch the wild and noisy scene which surrounded him, muttering between his teeth: "*Luxuriosa res vinum et tumultuosa ebrietas*. Alas, what good reason I have not to drink, and how excellently spoke Saint-Benoit: '*Vinum apostatare facit etiam sapientes!*'"

At that moment, Clopin returned and shouted in a voice of thunder: "Midnight!"

At this word, which produced the effect of the call to boot and saddle on a regiment at a halt, all the outcasts, men, women, children, rushed in a mass from the tavern, with great noise of arms and old iron implements.

The moon was obscured.

The Cour des Miracles was entirely dark. There was not a single light. One could make out there a throng of men and women conversing in low tones. They could be heard buzzing, and a gleam of all sorts of weapons was visible in the darkness. Clopin mounted a large stone.

"To your ranks, Argot!" he cried. "Fall into line, Egypt! Form ranks, Galilee!"

A movement began in the darkness. The immense multitude appeared to form in a column. After a few minutes, the King of Thunes raised his voice once more, "Now, silence to march through Paris! The password is, 'Little sword in pocket!' The torches will not be lighted till we reach Notre-Dame! Forward, march!"

Ten minutes later, the cavaliers of the watch fled in terror before a long procession of black and silent men that was descending toward the Pont an Change, through the tortuous streets which pierce the close-built neighborhood of the markets in every direction.

CHAPTER 4

An Awkward Friend

THAT NIGHT, QUASIMODO did not sleep. He had just made his last round of the church. He had not noticed, that at the moment when he was closing the doors, the archdeacon had passed close to him and betrayed some displeasure on seeing him bolting and barring with care the enormous iron locks which gave to their large leaves the solidity of a wall. Dom Claude's air was even more preoccupied than usual. Moreover, since the nocturnal adventure in the cell, he had constantly abused Quasimodo, but in vain did he ill treat, and even beat him occasionally, nothing disturbed the submission, patience, the devoted resignation of the faithful bellringer. He endured everything on the part of the archdeacon, insults, threats, blows, without murmuring a complaint. At the most, he gazed uneasily after Dom Claude when the latter ascended the staircase of the tower; but the archdeacon had abstained from presenting himself again before the gypsy's eyes.

On that night, accordingly, Quasimodo, after having cast a glance at his poor bells which he so neglected now, Jacqueline, Marie, and Thibauld, mounted to the summit of the Northern tower, and there setting his dark lanturn, well closed, upon the leads, he began to gaze at Paris. The night, as we have already said, was very dark. Paris which, so to speak was not lighted at that epoch, presented to the eye a confused collection of black masses, cut here and there by the whitish curve of the Seine. Quasimodo no longer saw any light with the exception of one window in a distant edifice, whose vague and sombre profile was outlined well above the roofs, in the direction of the Porte Sainte-Antoine. There also, there was some one awake.

As the only eye of the bellringer peered into that horizon of mist and night, he felt within him an inexpressible uneasiness. For several days he had been upon his guard. He had perceived men of sinister mien, who never took their eyes from the young girl's asylum, prowling constantly about the church. He fancied that some plot might be in process of formation against the unhappy refugee. He imagined that there existed a popular hatred against her, as against himself, and that it was very possible that something might happen soon. Hence he remained upon his tower on the watch, "dreaming in his dream-place," as Rabelais says, with his eye directed alternately on the cell and on Paris, keeping faithful guard, like a good dog, with a thousand suspicions in his mind.

All at once, while he was scrutinizing the great city with that eye which nature, by a sort of compensation, had made so piercing that it could almost supply the other organs which Quasimodo lacked, it seemed to him that there was something singular about the Quay de la Vieille-Pelleterie, that there was a movement at that point, that the line of the parapet, standing out blackly against the whiteness of the water was not straight and tranquil, like that of the other quays, but that it undulated to the eye, like the waves of a river, or like the heads of a crowd in motion.

This struck him as strange. He redoubled his attention. The movement seemed to be advancing toward the City. There was no light. It lasted for some time on the quay; then it gradually ceased, as though that which was passing were entering the interior of the island; then it stopped altogether, and the line of the quay became straight and motionless again.

At the moment when Quasimodo was lost in conjectures, it seemed to him that the movement had re-appeared in the Rue du Parvis, which is prolonged into the city perpendicularly to the façade of Notre-Dame. At length, dense as was the darkness, he beheld the head of a column debouch from that street, and in an instant a crowd—of which nothing could be distinguished in the gloom except that it was a crowd—spread over the Place.

This spectacle had a terror of its own. It is probable that this singular procession, which seemed so desirous of concealing itself under profound darkness, maintained a silence no less profound. Nevertheless, some noise must have escaped it, were it only a trampling. But this noise did not even reach our deaf man, and this great multitude, of which he saw hardly anything, and of which he heard nothing, though it was marching and moving so near him, produced upon him the effect of a rabble of dead men, mute, impalpable, lost in a smoke. It seemed to him, that he beheld advancing toward him a fog of men, and that he saw shadows moving in the shadow.

Then his fears returned to him, the idea of an attempt against the gypsy presented itself once more to his mind. He was conscious, in a confused way, that a violent crisis was approaching. At that critical moment he took counsel with himself, with better and prompter reasoning than one would have expected from so badly organized a brain. Ought he to awaken the gypsy? To make her escape? Whither? The streets were invested, the church backed on the river. No boat, no issue! There was but one thing to be done; to allow himself to be killed on the threshold of Notre-Dame, to resist at least until succor arrived, if it should arrive, and not to trouble la Esmeralda's sleep. This resolution once taken, he set to examining the enemy with more tranquillity.

The throng seemed to increase every moment in the church square. Only, he presumed that it must be making very little noise, since the windows on the Place remained closed. All at once, a flame flashed up, and in an instant seven or eight lighted torches passed over the heads of the crowd, shaking their tufts of flame in the deep shade. Quasimodo then beheld distinctly surging in the Parvis a frightful herd of men and women in rags, armed with scythes, pikes, billhooks and partisans, whose thousand points glittered. Here and there black pitchforks formed horns to the hideous faces. He vaguely recalled this populace, and thought that he recognized all the heads who had saluted him as Pope of the Fools some months previously. One man who held a torch in one hand and a club in the other, mounted a stone post and seemed to be haranguing them. At the same time the strange army executed several evolutions, as though it were taking up its post around the church. Quasimodo picked up his lantern and descended to the platform between the towers, in order to get a nearer view, and to spy out a means of defence.

Clopin Trouillefou, on arriving in front of the lofty portal of Notre-Dame had, in fact, ranged his troops in order of battle. Although he expected no resistance, he wished, like a prudent general, to preserve an order that would permit him to face, at need, a sudden attack of the watch or the police. He had accordingly stationed his brigade in such a manner that, viewed from above and from a distance, one would have pronounced it the Roman triangle of the battle of Ecnomus, the boar's head of Alexander or the famous wedge of Gustavus Adolphus. The base of this triangle rested on the back of the Place in such a manner

as to bar the entrance of the Rue du Parvis; one of its sides faced
Hôtel-Dieu, the other the Rue Saint-Pierre-aux-Boeufs. Clopin
Trouillefou had placed himself at the apex with the Duke of Egypt,
our friend Jehan, and the most daring of the scavengers.

An enterprise like that which the vagabonds were now undertaking
against Notre-Dame was not a very rare thing in the cities of the Middle
Ages. What we now call the "police" did not exist then. In populous
cities, especially in capitals, there existed no single, central, regulating
power. Feudalism had constructed these great communities in a singular
manner. A city was an assembly of a thousand seigneuries, which
divided it into compartments of all shapes and sizes. Hence, a thousand
conflicting establishments of police; that is to say, no police at all. In
Paris, for example, independently of the hundred and forty-one lords
who laid claim to a manor, there were five and twenty who laid claim to
a manor and to administering justice, from the Bishop of Paris, who had
five hundred streets, to the Prior of Notre-Dame des Champs, who had
four. All these feudal justices recognized the suzerain authority of the
king only in name. All possessed the right of control over the roads. All
were at home. Louis XI, that indefatigable worker, who so largely began
the demolition of the feudal edifice, continued by Richelieu and Louis
XIV for the profit of royalty, and finished by Mirabeau for the benefit of
the people, Louis XI had certainly made an effort to break this network
of seignories which covered Paris, by throwing violently across them
all two or three troops of general police. Thus, in 1465, an order to the
inhabitants to light candles in their windows at nightfall, and to shut up
their dogs under penalty of death; in the same year, an order to close
the streets in the evening with iron chains, and a prohibition to wear
daggers or weapons of offence in the streets at night. But in a very
short time, all these efforts at communal legislation fell into abeyance.
The bourgeois permitted the wind to blow out their candles in the
windows, and their dogs to stray; the iron chains were stretched only
in a state of siege; the prohibition to wear daggers wrought no other
changes than from the name of the Rue Coupe-Gueule to the name
of the Rue-Coupe-Gorge [cut-throat] which is an evident progress.
The old scaffolding of feudal jurisdictions remained standing; an immense
aggregation of bailiwicks and seignories crossing each other all over the
city, interfering with each other, entangled in one another, enmeshing
each other, trespassing on each other; a useless thicket of watches, sub-
watches and counter-watches, over which, with armed force, passed

brigandage, rapine, and sedition. Hence, in this disorder, deeds of violence on the part of the populace directed against a palace, a hotel, or house in the most thickly populated quarters, were not unheard-of occurrences. In the majority of such cases, the neighbors did not meddle with the matter unless the pillaging extended to themselves. They stopped up their ears to the musket shots, closed their shutters, barricaded their doors, allowed the matter to be concluded with or without the watch, and the next day it was said in Paris, "Etienne Barbette was broken open last night. The Marshal de Clermont was seized last night, etc." Hence, not only the royal habitations, the Louvre, the Palace, the Bastille, the Tournelles, but simply seignorial residences, the Petit-Bourbon, the Hôtel de Sens, the Hôtel d'Angoulême, etc., had battlements on their walls, and machicolations over their doors. Churches were guarded by their sanctity. Some, among the number Notre-Dame, were fortified. The Abbey of Saint-Germain-des-Pres was castellated like a baronial mansion, and more brass expended about it in bombards than in bells. Its fortress was still to be seen in 1610. Today, barely its church remains.

Let us return to Notre-Dame.

When the first arrangements were completed, and we must say, to the honor of vagabond discipline, that Clopin's orders were executed in silence, and with admirable precision, the worthy chief of the band, mounted on the parapet of the church square, and raised his hoarse and surly voice, turning toward Notre-Dame, and brandishing his torch whose light, tossed by the wind, and veiled every moment by its own smoke, made the reddish façade of the church appear and disappear before the eye.

"To you, Louis de Beaumont, bishop of Paris, counsellor in the Court of Parliament, I, Clopin Trouillefou, king of Thunes, grand Coësre, prince of Argot, bishop of fools, I say: Our sister, falsely condemned for magic, hath taken refuge in your church, you owe her asylum and safety. Now the Court of Parliament wishes to seize her once more there, and you consent to it; so that she would be hanged tomorrow in the Grève, if God and the outcasts were not here. If your church is sacred, so is our sister; if our sister is not sacred, neither is your church. That is why we call upon you to return the girl if you wish to save your church, or we will take possession of the girl again and pillage the church, which will be a good thing. In token of which I here plant my banner, and may God preserve you, bishop of Paris,"

Quasimodo could not, unfortunately, hear these words uttered with a sort of sombre and savage majesty. A vagabond presented his banner to Clopin, who planted it solemnly between two paving-stones. It was a pitchfork from whose points hung a bleeding quarter of carrion meat.

That done, the King of Thunes turned round and cast his eyes over his army, a fierce multitude whose glances flashed almost equally with their pikes. After a momentary pause, "Forward, my Sons!" he cried. "To work, locksmiths!"

Thirty bold men, square shouldered, and with pick-lock faces, stepped from the ranks, with hammers, pincers, and bars of iron on their shoulders. They betook themselves to the principal door of the church, ascended the steps, and were soon to be seen squatting under the arch, working at the door with pincers and levers; a throng of vagabonds followed them to help or look on. The eleven steps before the portal were covered with them.

But the door stood firm. "The devil! 'Tis hard and obstinate!" said one. "It is old, and its gristles have become bony," said another. "Courage, comrades!" resumed Clopin. "I wager my head against a dipper that you will have opened the door, rescued the girl, and despoiled the chief altar before a single beadle is awake. Stay! I think I hear the lock breaking up."

Clopin was interrupted by a frightful uproar that re-sounded behind him at that moment. He wheeled round. An enormous beam had just fallen from above; it had crushed a dozen vagabonds on the pavement with the sound of a cannon, breaking in addition, legs here and there in the crowd of beggars, who sprang aside with cries of terror. In a twinkling, the narrow precincts of the church parvis were cleared. The locksmiths, although protected by the deep vaults of the portal, abandoned the door and Clopin himself retired to a respectful distance from the church.

"I had a narrow escape!" cried Jehan. "I felt the wind, of it, *tête-de-boeuf*! but Pierre the Slaughterer is slaughtered!"

It is impossible to describe the astonishment mingled with fright that fell upon the ruffians in company with this beam.

They remained for several minutes with their eyes in the air, more dismayed by that piece of wood than by the king's twenty thousand archers.

"Satan!" muttered the Duke of Egypt, "this smacks of magic!"

"'Tis the moon which threw this log at us," said Andry the Red.

"Call the moon the friend of the Virgin, after that!" went on François Chanteprune.

"A thousand popes!" exclaimed Clopin, "you are all fools!" But he did not know how to explain the fall of the beam.

Meanwhile, nothing could be distinguished on the façade, to whose summit the light of the torches did not reach. The heavy beam lay in the middle of the enclosure, and groans were heard from the poor wretches who had received its first shock, and who had been almost cut in twain, on the angle of the stone steps.

The King of Thunes, his first amazement passed, finally found an explanation that appeared plausible to his companions.

"Throat of God! Are the canons defending themselves? To the sack, then, to the sack!"

"To the sack!" repeated the rabble, with a furious hurrah. A discharge of crossbows and hackbuts against the front of the church followed.

At this detonation, the peaceable inhabitants of the surrounding houses woke up; many windows were seen to open, and nightcaps and hands holding candles appeared at the casements.

"Fire at the windows," shouted Clopin. The windows were immediately closed, and the poor bourgeois, who had hardly had time to cast a frightened glance on this scene of gleams and tumult, returned, perspiring with fear to their wives, asking themselves whether the Witches' Sabbath was now being held in the parvis of Notre-Dame, or whether there was an assault of Burgundians, as in '64. Then the husbands thought of theft; the wives, of rape; and all trembled.

"To the sack!" repeated the thieves' crew; but they dared not approach. They stared at the beam; they stared at the church. The beam did not stir, the edifice preserved its calm and deserted air; but something chilled the outcasts.

"To work, locksmiths!" shouted Trouillefou. "Let the door be forced!"

No one took a step.

"Beard and belly!" said Clopin. "Here be men afraid of a beam."

An old locksmith addressed him. "Captain, 'tis not the beam which bothers us, 'tis the door, which is all covered with iron bars. Our pincers are powerless against it."

"What more do you want to break it in?" demanded Clopin.

"Ah! We ought to have a battering ram."

The King of Thunes ran boldly to the formidable beam, and placed his foot upon it: "Here is one!" he exclaimed; "'tis the canons who send it to you." And, making a mocking salute in the direction of the church, "Thanks, canons!"

This piece of bravado produced its effects; the spell of the beam was broken. The vagabonds recovered their courage; soon the heavy joist, raised like a feather by two hundred vigorous arms, was flung with fury against the great door that they had tried to batter down. At the sight of that long beam, in the half-light which the infrequent torches of the brigands spread over the Place, thus borne by that crowd of men who dashed it at a run against the church, one would have thought that he beheld a monstrous beast with a thousand feet attacking with lowered head the giant of stone.

At the shock of the beam, the half metallic door sounded like an immense drum; it was not burst in, but the whole cathedral trembled, and the deepest cavities of the edifice were heard to echo.

At the same moment, a shower of large stones began to fall from the top of the façade on the assailants.

"The devil!" cried Jehan. "Are the towers shaking their balustrades down on our heads?"

But the impulse had been given, the King of Thunes had set the example. Evidently, the bishop was defending himself, and they only battered the door with the more rage, in spite of the stones that cracked skulls right and left.

It was remarkable that all these stones fell one by one; but they followed each other closely. The thieves always felt two at a time, one on their legs and one on their heads. There were few that did not deal their blow, and a large layer of dead and wounded lay bleeding and panting beneath the feet of the assailants who, now grown furious, replaced each other without intermission. The long beam continued to belabor the door, at regular intervals, like the clapper of a bell, the stones to rain down, the door to groan.

The reader has no doubt divined that this unexpected resistance that had exasperated the outcasts came from Quasimodo.

Chance had, unfortunately, favored the brave deaf man.

When he had descended to the platform between the towers, his ideas were all in confusion. He had run up and down along the gallery for several minutes like a madman, surveying from above, the compact mass of vagabonds ready to hurl itself on the church, demanding the safety of the gypsy from the devil or from God. The thought had occurred to him of ascending to the southern belfry and sounding the alarm, but before he could have set the bell in motion, before Marie's voice could have uttered a single clamor, was there not time to burst in the door of the church ten times over? It was precisely the moment when the locksmiths were advancing upon it with their tools. What was to be done?

All at once, he remembered that some masons had been at work all day repairing the wall, the timber-work, and the roof of the south tower. This was a flash of light. The wall was of stone, the roof of lead, the timber-work of wood. (That prodigious timber-work, so dense that it was called "the forest.")

Quasimodo hastened to that tower. The lower chambers were, in fact, full of materials. There were piles of rough blocks of stone, sheets of lead in rolls, bundles of laths, heavy beams already notched with the saw, heaps of plaster.

Time was pressing; the pikes and hammers were at work below. With a strength which the sense of danger increased tenfold, he seized one of the beams—the longest and heaviest. He pushed it out through a loophole, then, grasping it again outside of the tower, he made it slide along the angle of the balustrade which surrounds the platform, and let it fly into the abyss. The enormous timber, during that fall of a hundred and sixty feet, scraping the wall, breaking the carvings, turned many times on its centre, like the arm of a windmill flying off alone through space. At last it reached the ground, the horrible cry arose, and the black beam, as it rebounded from the pavement, resembled a serpent leaping.

Quasimodo beheld the outcasts scatter at the fall of the beam, like ashes at the breath of a child. He took advantage of their fright, and while they were fixing a superstitious glance on the club which had fallen from heaven, and while they were putting out the eyes of the stone saints on the front with a discharge of arrows and buckshot, Quasimodo was silently piling up plaster, stones, and rough blocks of stone, even the sacks of tools belonging to the masons, on the edge of the balustrade from which the beam had already been hurled.

Thus, as soon as they began to batter the grand door, the shower of rough blocks of stone began to fall, and it seemed to them that the church itself was being demolished over their heads.

Any one who could have beheld Quasimodo at that moment would have been frightened. Independently of the projectiles that he had piled upon the balustrade, he had collected a heap of stones on the platform itself. As fast as the blocks on the exterior edge were exhausted, he drew on the heap. Then he stooped and rose, stooped and rose again with incredible activity. His huge gnome's head bent over the balustrade, then an enormous stone fell, then another, then another. From time to time, he followed a fine stone with his eye, and when it did good execution, he said, "Hum!"

Meanwhile, the beggars did not grow discouraged. The thick door on which they were venting their fury had already trembled more than twenty times beneath the weight of their oaken battering-ram, multiplied by the strength of a hundred men. The panels cracked, the carved work flew into splinters, the hinges, at every blow, leaped from their pins, the planks yawned, the wood crumbled to powder, ground between the iron sheathing. Fortunately for Quasimodo, there was more iron than wood.

Nevertheless, he felt that the great door was yielding. Although he did not hear it, every blow of the ram reverberated simultaneously in the vaults of the church and within it. From above he beheld the vagabonds, filled with triumph and rage, shaking their fists at the gloomy façade; and both on the gypsy's account and his own he envied the wings of the owls which flitted away above his head in flocks.

His shower of stone blocks was not sufficient to repel the assailants.

At this moment of anguish, he noticed, a little lower down than the balustrade whence he was crushing the thieves, two long stone gutters that discharged immediately over the great door; the internal orifice of these gutters terminated on the pavement of the platform. An idea occurred to him; he ran in search of a fagot in his bellringer's den, placed on this fagot a great many bundles of laths, and many rolls of lead, munitions which he had not employed so far, and having arranged this pile in front of the hole to the two gutters, he set it on fire with his lantern.

During this time, since the stones no longer fell, the outcasts ceased to gaze into the air. The bandits, panting like a pack of hounds who are forcing a boar into his lair, pressed tumultuously round the great door, all disfigured by the battering ram, but still standing. They were waiting with a quiver for the great blow that should split it open.

They vied with each other in pressing as close as possible, in order to dash among the first, when it should open, into that opulent cathedral, a vast reservoir where the wealth of three centuries had been piled up. They reminded each other with roars of exultation and greedy lust, of the beautiful silver crosses, the fine copes of brocade, the beautiful tombs of silver gilt, the great magnificences of the choir, the dazzling festivals, the Christmasses sparkling with torches, the Easters sparkling with sunshine—all those splendid solemneties wherein chandeliers, ciboriums, tabernacles, and reliquaries, studded the altars with a crust of gold and diamonds. Certainly, at that fine moment, thieves and pseudo sufferers, doctors in stealing, and vagabonds, were thinking much less of delivering the gypsy than of pillaging Notre-Dame. We could even easily believe that for a goodly number among them la Esmeralda was only a pretext, if thieves needed pretexts.

All at once, at the moment when they were grouping themselves round the ram for a last effort, each one holding his breath and stiffening his muscles in order to communicate all his force to the decisive blow, a howl more frightful still than that which had burst forth and expired beneath the beam, rose among them. Those who did not cry out, those who were still alive, looked. Two streams of melted lead were falling from the summit of the edifice into the thickest of the rabble. That sea of men had just sunk down beneath the boiling metal, which had made, at the two points where it fell, two black and smoking holes in the crowd, such as hot water would make in snow. Dying men, half consumed and groaning with anguish, could be seen writhing there. Around these two principal streams there were drops of that horrible rain, which scattered over the assailants and entered their skulls like gimlets of fire. It was a heavy fire that overwhelmed these wretches with a thousand hailstones.

The outcry was heartrending. They fled pell-mell, hurling the beam upon the bodies, the boldest as well as the most timid, and the parvis was cleared a second time.

All eyes were raised to the top of the church. They beheld there an extraordinary sight. On the crest of the highest gallery, higher than the central rose window, there was a great flame rising between the two towers with whirlwinds of sparks, a vast, disordered, and furious flame, a tongue of which was borne into the smoke by the wind, from time to time. Below that fire, below the gloomy balustrade with its trefoils showing darkly against its glare, two spouts with monster throats were vomiting forth unceasingly that burning rain, whose silvery stream stood out against the shadows of the lower façade. As they approached the earth, these two jets of liquid lead spread out in sheaves, like water springing from the thousand holes of a watering-pot. Above the flame, the enormous towers, two sides of each of which were visible in sharp outline, the one wholly black, the other wholly red, seemed still more vast with all the immensity of the shadow which they cast even to the sky.

Their innumerable sculptures of demons and dragons assumed a lugubrious aspect. The restless light of the flame made them move to the eye. There were griffins that had the air of laughing, gargoyles that one fancied one heard yelping, salamanders that puffed at the fire, tarasques that sneezed in the smoke. And among the monsters thus roused from their sleep of stone by this flame, by this noise, there was one who walked about, and who was seen, from time to time, to pass across the glowing face of the pile, like a bat in front of a candle.

Without doubt, this strange beacon light would awaken far away, the woodcutter of the hills of Bicêtre, terrified to behold the gigantic shadow of the towers of Notre-Dame quivering over his heaths.

A terrified silence ensued among the outcasts, during which nothing was heard, but the cries of alarm of the canons shut up in their cloister, and more uneasy than horses in a burning stable, the furtive sound of windows hastily opened and still more hastily closed, the internal hurly-burly of the houses and of the Hôtel-Dieu, the wind in the flame, the last death-rattle of the dying, and the continued crackling of the rain of lead upon the pavement.

In the meanwhile, the principal vagabonds had retired beneath the porch of the Gondelaurier mansion, and were holding a council of war.

The Duke of Egypt, seated on a stone post, contemplated the phantasmagorical bonfire, glowing at a height of two hundred feet in the air, with religious terror. Clopin Trouillefou bit his huge fists with rage.

"Impossible to get in!" he muttered between his teeth.

"An old, enchanted church!" grumbled the aged Bohemian, Mathias Hungadi Spicali.

"By the Pope's whiskers!" went on a sham soldier, who had once been in service, "here are church gutters spitting melted lead at you better than the machicolations of Lectoure."

"Do you see that demon passing and repassing in front of the fire?" exclaimed the Duke of Egypt.

"Pardieu, 'tis that damned bellringer, 'tis Quasimodo," said Clopin.

The Bohemian tossed his head. "I tell you, that 'tis the spirit Sabnac, the grand marquis, the demon of fortifications. He has the form of an armed soldier, the head of a lion. Sometimes he rides a hideous horse. He changes men into stones, of which he builds towers. He commands fifty legions. 'Tis he indeed; I recognize him. Sometimes he is clad in a handsome golden robe, figured after the Turkish fashion."

"Where is Bellevigne de l'Etoile?" demanded Clopin.

"He is dead."

Andry the Red laughed in an idiotic way: "Notre-Dame is making work for the hospital," said he.

"Is there, then, no way of forcing this door," exclaimed the King of Thunes, stamping his foot.

The Duke of Egypt pointed sadly to the two streams of boiling lead that did not cease to streak the black façade, like two long distaffs of phosphorus.

"Churches have been known to defend themselves thus all by themselves," he remarked with a sigh. "Saint-Sophia at Constantinople, forty years ago, hurled to the earth three times in succession, the crescent of Mahom, by shaking her domes, which are her heads. Guillaume de Paris, who built this one was a magician."

"Must we then retreat in pitiful fashion, like highwaymen?" said Clopin. "Must we leave our sister here, whom those hooded wolves will hang tomorrow."

"And the sacristy, where there are wagon-loads of gold!" added a vagabond, whose name, we regret to say, we do not know.

"Beard of Mahom!" cried Trouillefou.

"Let us make another trial," resumed the vagabond.

Mathias Hungadi shook his head.

"We shall never get in by the door. We must find the defect in the armor of the old fairy; a hole, a false postern, some joint or other."

"Who will go with me?" said Clopin. "I shall go at it again. By the way, where is the little scholar Jehan, who is so encased in iron?"

"He is dead, no doubt," some one replied; "we no longer hear his laugh."

The King of Thunes frowned: "So much the worse. There was a brave heart under that ironmongery. And Master Pierre Gringoire?"

"Captain Clopin," said Andry the Red, "he slipped away before we reached the Pont-aux-Changeurs,"

Clopin stamped his foot. "Gueule-Dieu! 'Twas he who pushed us on hither, and he has deserted us in the very middle of the job! Cowardly chatterer, with a slipper for a helmet!"

"Captain Clopin," said Andry the Red, who was gazing down Rue du Parvis, "yonder is the little scholar."

"Praised be Pluto!" said Clopin. "But what the devil is he dragging after him?"

It was, in fact, Jehan, who was running as fast as his heavy outfit of a Paladin, and a long ladder which trailed on the pavement, would permit, more breathless than an ant harnessed to a blade of grass twenty times longer than itself.

"Victory! *Te Deum*!" cried the scholar. "Here is the ladder of the longshoremen of Port Saint-Landry."

Clopin approached him.

"Child, what do you mean to do, *corne-Dieu* with this ladder?"

"I have it," replied Jehan, panting. "I knew where it was under the shed of the lieutenant's house. There's a wench there whom I know, who thinks me as handsome as Cupido. I made use of her to get the ladder, and I have the ladder, *Pasque-Mahom*! The poor girl came to open the door to me in her shift."

"Yes," said Clopin, "but what are you going to do with that ladder?"

Jehan gazed at him with a malicious, knowing look, and cracked his fingers like castanets. At that moment he was sublime. On his head he wore one of those overloaded helmets of the fifteenth century, which frightened the enemy with their fanciful crests. His bristled with ten iron beaks, so that Jehan could have disputed with Nestor's Homeric vessel the redoubtable title of δεχέμβολος.

"What do I mean to do with it, august king of Thunes? Do you see that row of statues which have such idiotic expressions, yonder, above the three portals?"

"Yes. Well?"

"'Tis the gallery of the kings of France."

"What is that to me?" said Clopin.

"Wait! At the end of that gallery there is a door which is never fastened otherwise than with a latch, and with this ladder I ascend, and I am in the church."

"Child let me be the first to ascend."

"No, comrade, the ladder is mine. Come, you shall be the second."

"May Beelzebub strangle you!" said surly Clopin. "I won't be second to anybody."

"Then find a ladder, Clopin!"

Jehan set out on a run across the Place, dragging his ladder and shouting: "Follow me, lads!"

In an instant the ladder was raised, and propped against the balustrade of the lower gallery, above one of the lateral doors. The throng of vagabonds, uttering loud acclamations, crowded to its foot to ascend. But Jehan maintained his right, and was the first to set foot on the rungs. The passage was tolerably long. The gallery of the kings of France is today about sixty feet above the pavement. The eleven steps of the flight before the door, made it still higher. Jehan mounted slowly, a good deal incommoded by his heavy armor, holding his crossbow in one hand, and clinging to a rung with the other. When he reached the middle of the ladder, he cast a melancholy glance at the poor dead outcasts, with which the steps were strewn. "Alas!" said he, "here is a heap of bodies worthy of the fifth book of the Iliad!" Then he continued his ascent. The vagabonds followed him. There was one on every rung. At the sight of this line of cuirassed backs, undulating as they rose through the gloom, one would have pronounced it a serpent with steel scales, which was raising itself erect in front of the church. Jehan who formed the head, and who was whistling, completed the illusion.

The scholar finally reached the balcony of the gallery, and climbed over it nimbly, to the applause of the whole vagabond tribe. Thus master of the citadel, he uttered a shout of joy, and suddenly halted, petrified. He had just caught sight of Quasimodo concealed in the dark, with flashing eye, behind one of the statues of the kings.

Before a second assailant could gain a foothold on the gallery, the formidable hunchback leaped to the head of the ladder, without uttering a word, seized the ends of the two uprights with his powerful hands, raised them, pushed them out from the wall, balanced the long and pliant ladder, loaded with vagabonds from top to bottom for a moment, in the midst of shrieks of anguish, then suddenly, with superhuman force, hurled this cluster of men backward into the Place. There was a moment when even the most resolute trembled. The ladder, launched backwards, remained erect and standing for an instant, and seemed to hesitate, then wavered, then suddenly, describing a frightful arc of a circle eighty feet in radius, crashed upon the pavement with its load of ruffians, more rapidly than a drawbridge when its chains break. There arose an immense imprecation, then all was still, and a few mutilated wretches were seen, crawling over the heap of dead.

A sound of wrath and grief followed the first cries of triumph among the besiegers. Quasimodo, impassive, with both elbows propped on the balustrade, looked on. He had the air of an old, bushy-headed king at his window.

As for Jehan Frollo, he was in a critical position. He found himself in the gallery with the formidable bellringer, alone, separated from his companions by a vertical wall eighty feet high. While Quasimodo was dealing with the ladder, the scholar had run to the postern that he believed to be open. It was not. The deaf man had closed it behind him when he entered the gallery. Jehan had then concealed himself behind a stone king, not daring to breathe, and fixing upon the monstrous hunchback a frightened gaze, like the man, who, when courting the wife of the guardian of a menagerie, went one evening to a love rendezvous, mistook the wall which he was to climb, and suddenly found himself face to face with a white bear.

For the first few moments, the deaf man paid no heed to him; but at last he turned his head, and suddenly straightened up. He had just caught sight of the scholar.

Jehan prepared himself for a rough shock, but the deaf man remained motionless; only he had turned toward the scholar and was looking at him.

"Ho, ho!" said Jehan. "What do you mean by staring at me with that solitary and melancholy eye?"

As he spoke thus, the young scamp stealthily adjusted his crossbow.

"Quasimodo!" he cried. "I am going to change your surname: you shall be called the blind man."

The shot sped. The feathered arrow whizzed and entered the hunchback's left arm. Quasimodo appeared no more moved by it than by a scratch to King Pharamond. He laid his hand on the arrow, tore it from his arm, and tranquilly broke it across his big knee; then he let the two pieces drop on the floor, rather than threw them down. But Jehan had no opportunity to fire a second time. The arrow broken,

Quasimodo breathing heavily, bounded like a grasshopper, and he fell upon the scholar, whose armor was flattened against the wall by the blow.

Then in that gloom, wherein wavered the light of the torches, a terrible thing was seen.

Quasimodo had grasped with his left hand the two arms of Jehan, who did not offer any resistance, so thoroughly did he feel that he was lost. With his right hand, the deaf man detached one by one, in silence, with sinister slowness, all the pieces of his armor, the sword, the daggers, the helmet, the cuirass, the leg pieces. One would have said that it was a monkey taking the shell from a nut. Quasimodo flung the scholar's iron shell at his feet, piece by piece. When the scholar beheld himself disarmed, stripped, weak, and naked in those terrible hands, he made no attempt to speak to the deaf man, but began to laugh audaciously in his face, and to sing with his intrepid heedlessness of a child of sixteen, the then popular ditty:—

> *"Elle est bien habillée,*
> *La ville de Cambrai;*
> *Marafin l'a pillée . . ."*

He did not finish. Quasimodo was seen on the parapet of the gallery, holding the scholar by the feet with one hand and whirling him over the abyss like a sling; then a sound like that of a bony structure in contact with a wall was heard, and something was seen to fall which halted a third of the way down in its fall, on a projection in the architecture. It was a dead body that remained hanging there, bent double, its loins broken, its skull empty.

A cry of horror rose among the vagabonds. "Vengeance!" shouted Clopin.

"To the sack!" replied the multitude. "Assault! assault!"

There came a tremendous howl, in which were mingled all tongues, all dialects, all accents. The death of the poor scholar imparted a furious ardor to that crowd. It was seized with shame, and the wrath of having been held so long in check before a church by a hunchback. Rage found ladders, multiplied the torches, and, at the expiration of a few minutes, Quasimodo, in despair, beheld that terrible ant heap mount on all sides to the assault of Notre-Dame. Those who had no ladders had knotted ropes; those who had no ropes climbed by the projections of the carvings. They hung from each other's rags. There were no means of resisting that rising tide of frightful faces; rage made these fierce countenances ruddy; their clayey brows were dripping with sweat; their eyes darted lightnings; all these grimaces, all these horrors laid siege to Quasimodo. One would have said that some other church had despatched to the assault of Notre-Dame its gorgons, its dogs, its drées, its demons, its most fantastic sculptures. It was like a layer of living monsters on the stone monsters of the façade.

Meanwhile, the Place was studded with a thousand torches. This scene of confusion, till now hid in darkness, was suddenly flooded with light. The parvis was resplendent, and cast a radiance on the sky; the bonfire lighted on the lofty platform was still burning, and illuminated the city far away. The enormous silhouette of the two towers, projected afar on the roofs of Paris, and formed a large notch of black in this light. The city seemed to be aroused. Alarm bells wailed in the distance. The vagabonds howled, panted, swore, climbed; and Quasimodo, powerless against so many enemies, shuddering for the gypsy, beholding the furious faces approaching ever nearer and nearer to his gallery, entreated heaven for a miracle, and wrung his arms in despair.

CHAPTER 5

The Retreat in Which Monsieur Louis
of France Says His Prayers

THE READER HAS not, perhaps, forgotten that one moment before catching sight of the nocturnal band of vagabonds, Quasimodo, as he inspected Paris from the heights of his bell tower, perceived only one light burning, which gleamed like a star from a window on the topmost story of a lofty edifice beside the Porte Saint-Antoine. This edifice was the Bastille. That star was the candle of Louis XI.

King Louis XI had, in fact, been two days in Paris. He was to take his departure on the next day but one for his citadel of Montilz-les-Tours. He made but seldom and brief appearance in his good city of Paris, since there he did not feel about him enough pitfalls, gibbets, and Scotch archers.

He had come, that day, to sleep at the Bastille. The great chamber, five toises square, which he had at the Louvre, with its huge chimney-piece loaded with twelve great beasts and thirteen great prophets, and his grand bed, eleven feet by twelve, pleased him but little. He felt himself lost amid all this grandeur. This good bourgeois king preferred the Bastille with a tiny chamber and couch. And then, the Bastille was stronger than the Louvre.

This little chamber, which the king reserved for himself in the famous state prison, was also tolerably spacious and occupied the topmost story of a turret rising from the donjon keep. It was circular in form, carpeted with mats of shining straw, ceiled with beams, enriched with fleurs-de-lis of gilded metal with interjoists in color; wainscoted with rich woods sown with rosettes of white metal, and with others painted a fine, bright green, made of orpiment and fine indigo.

There was only one window, a long pointed casement, latticed with brass wire and bars of iron, further darkened by fine colored panes with the arms of the king and of the queen, each pane being worth two and twenty sols.

There was but one entrance, a modern door, with a fiat arch, garnished with a piece of tapestry on the inside, and on the outside by one of those porches of Irish wood, frail edifices of cabinet-work curiously wrought, numbers of which were still to be seen in old houses a hundred and fifty years ago. "Although they disfigure and embarrass the places," says Sauvel in despair, "our old people are still unwilling to get rid of them, and keep them in spite of everybody."

In this chamber, nothing was to be found of what furnishes ordinary apartments, neither benches, nor trestles, nor forms, nor common stools in the form of a chest, nor fine stools sustained by pillars and counter-pillars, at four sols apiece. Only one easy armchair, very magnificent, was to be seen; the wood was painted with roses on a red ground, the seat was of ruby Cordovan leather, ornamented with long silken fringes, and studded with a thousand golden nails. The loneliness of this chair made it apparent that only one person had a right to sit down in this apartment. Beside the chair, and quite close to the window, there was a table covered with a cloth with a pattern of birds. On this table stood an inkhorn spotted with ink, some parchments, several pens, and a large goblet of chased silver. A little further on was a brazier, a praying stool in crimson velvet, relieved with small bosses of gold. Finally, at the extreme end of the room, a simple bed of scarlet and yellow damask, without either tinsel or lace; having only an ordinary fringe. This bed, famous for having borne the sleep or the sleeplessness of Louis XI, was still to be seen two hundred years ago, at the house of a councillor of state, where it was seen by old Madame Pilou, celebrated in *Cyrus* under the name "Arricidie" and of "la Morale Vivante."

Such was the chamber that was called "the retreat where Monsieur Louis de France says his prayers."

At the moment when we have introduced the reader into it, this retreat was very dark. The curfew bell had sounded an hour before; night was come, and there was only one flickering wax candle set on the table to light five persons variously grouped in the chamber.

The first on which the light fell was a seigneur superbly clad in breeches and jerkin of scarlet striped with silver, and a loose coat with half sleeves of cloth of gold with black figures. This splendid costume, on which the light played, seemed glazed with flame on every fold. The man who wore it had his armorial bearings embroidered on his breast in vivid colors; a chevron accompanied by a deer passant. The shield was flanked, on the right by an olive branch, on the left by a deer's antlers. This man wore in his girdle a rich dagger whose hilt, of silver gilt, was chased in the form of a helmet, and surmounted by a count's coronet. He had a forbidding air, a proud mien, and a head held high. At the first glance one read arrogance on his visage; at the second, craft.

He was standing bareheaded, a long roll of parchment in his hand, behind the armchair in which was seated, his body ungracefully doubled up, his knees crossed, his elbow on the table, a very badly accoutred personage. Let the reader imagine in fact, on the rich seat of Cordova leather, two crooked knees, two thin thighs, poorly clad in black worsted tricot, a body enveloped in a cloak of fustian, with fur trimming of which more leather than hair was visible; lastly, to crown all, a greasy old hat of the worst sort of black cloth, bordered with a circular string of leaden figures. This, in company with a dirty skullcap, which hardly allowed a hair to escape, was all that distinguished the seated personage. He held his head so bent upon his breast, that nothing was to be seen of his face thus thrown into shadow, except the tip of his nose, upon which fell a ray of light, and which must have been long. From the thinness of his wrinkled hand, one divined that he was an old man. It was Louis XI.

At some distance behind them, two men dressed in garments of Flemish style were conversing, who were not sufficiently lost in the shadow to prevent any one who had been present at the performance of Gringoire's mystery from recognizing in them two of the principal Flemish envoys, Guillaume Rym, the sagacious pensioner of Ghent, and Jacques Coppenole, the popular hosier. The reader will remember that these men were mixed up in the secret politics of Louis XI.

Finally, quite at the end of the room, near the door, in the dark, stood, motionless as a statue, a vigorous man with thickset limbs, a military harness, with a surcoat of armorial bearings, whose square face pierced with staring eyes, slit with an immense mouth, his ears concealed by two large screens of flat hair, had something about it both of the dog and the tiger. All were uncovered except the king.

The gentleman who stood near the king was reading him a sort of long memorial to which his majesty seemed to be listening attentively. The two Flemings were whispering together.

"Cross of God!" grumbled Coppenole. "I am tired of standing; is there no chair here?"

Rym replied by a negative gesture, accompanied by a discreet smile.

"*Croix-Dieu!*" resumed Coppenole, thoroughly unhappy at being obliged to lower his voice thus. "I should like to sit down on the floor, with my legs crossed, like a hosier, as I do in my shop."

"Take good care that you do not, Master Jacques."

"Heyday, Master Guillaume! Can one only remain here on his feet?"

"Or on his knees," said Rym.

At that moment the king's voice was uplifted. They held their peace.

"Fifty sols for the robes of our valets, and twelve livres for the mantles of the clerks of our crown! That's it! Pour out gold by the ton! Are you mad, Olivier?"

As he spoke thus, the old man raised his head. The golden shells of the collar of Saint-Michael could be seen gleaming on his neck. The candle fully illuminated his gaunt and morose profile. He tore the papers from the other's hand.

"You are ruining us!" he cried, casting his hollow eyes over the scroll. "What is all this? What need have we of so prodigious a household? Two chaplains at ten livres a month each, and, a chapel clerk at one hundred sols! A valet-de-chambre at ninety livres a year. Four head cooks at six score livres a year each! A spit-cook, an herb-cook, a sauce-cook, a butler, two sumpter-horse lackeys, at ten livres a month each! Two scullions at eight livres! A groom of the stables and his two aids at four and twenty livres a month! A porter, a pastry-cook, a baker, two carters, each sixty livres a year! And the farrier six score livres! And the master of the chamber of our funds, twelve hundred livres! And the comptroller five hundred. And how do I know what else? 'Tis ruinous. The wages of our servants are putting France to the pillage! All the ingots of the Louvre will melt before such a fire of expenses! We shall have to sell our plate! And next year, if God and our Lady (here he raised his hat) lend us life, we shall drink our potions from a pewter pot!"

So saying, he cast a glance at the silver goblet that gleamed upon the table. He coughed and continued. "Master Olivier, the princes who reign over great lordships, like kings and emperors, should not allow sumptuousness in their houses; for the fire spreads thence through the province. Hence, Master Olivier, consider this said once for all. Our expenditure increases every year. The thing displeases us. How, *pasque-Dieu,* when in '79 it did not exceed six and thirty thousand livres, did it attain in '80, forty-three thousand six hundred and nineteen livres? I have the figures in my head. In '81, sixty-six thousand six hundred and eighty livres, and this year, by the faith of my body, it will reach eighty thousand livres! Doubled in four years! Monstrous!"

He paused breathless, then resumed energetically, "I behold around me only people who fatten on my leanness! You suck crowns from me at every pore."

All remained silent. This was one of those fits of wrath that are allowed to take their course. He continued. "'Tis like that request in Latin from the gentlemen of France, that we should re-establish what they call the grand charges of the Crown! Charges in very deed! Charges that crush! Ah! gentlemen! you say that we are not a king to reign *dapifero nullo, buticulario nullo*! We will let you see, *pasque-Dieu,* whether we are not a king!"

Here he smiled, in the consciousness of his power; this softened his bad humor, and he turned toward the Flemings. "Do you see, Gossip Guillaum, the grand warden of the keys, the grand butler, the grand chamberlain, the grand seneschal are not worth the smallest valet. Remember this, Gossip Coppenole. They serve no purpose, as they stand thus useless round the king; they produce upon me the effect of the four Evangelists who surround the face of the big clock of the palace, and which Philippe Brille has just set in order afresh. They are gilt, but they do not indicate the hour; and the hands can get on without them."

He remained in thought for a moment, then added, shaking his aged head. "Ho, ho! By our Lady, I am not Philippe Brille, and I shall not gild the great vassals anew. Continue, Olivier."

The person whom he designated by this name, took the papers into his hands again, and began to read aloud. "To Adam Tenon, clerk of the warden of the seals of the provostship of Paris; for the silver, making, and engraving of said seals, which have been made new because the others preceding, by reason of their antiquity and their worn condition, could no longer be successfully used, twelve livres parisis.

"To Guillaume Frère, the sum of four livres, four sols parisis, for his trouble and salary, for having nourished and fed the doves in the two dove-cots of the Hôtel des Tournelles, during the months of January, February, and March of this year; and for this he hath given seven sextiers of barley.

"To a gray friar for confessing a criminal, four sols parisis."

The king listened in silence. From time to time be coughed; then he raised the goblet to his lips and drank a draught with a grimace.

"During this year there have been made by the ordinance of justice, to the sound of the trumpet, through the squares of Paris, fifty-six proclamations. Account to be regulated.

"For having searched and ransacked in certain places, in Paris as well as elsewhere, for money said to be there concealed; but nothing hath been found: forty-five livres parisis."

"Bury a crown to unearth a sou!" said the king.

"For having set in the Hôtel des Tournelles six panes of white glass in the place where the iron cage is, thirteen sols; for having made and delivered by command of the king, on the day of the musters, four shields with the escutcheons of the said seigneur, encircled with garlands of roses all about, six livres; for two new sleeves to the king's old doublet, twenty sols; for a box of grease to grease the boots of the king, fifteen deniers; a stable newly made to lodge the king's black pigs, thirty livres parisis; many partitions, planks, and trap-doors, for the safekeeping of the lions at Saint-Paul, twenty-two livres."

"These be dear beasts," said Louis XI. "It matters not; it is a fine magnificence in a king. There is a great red lion whom I love for his pleasant ways. Have you seen him, Master Guillaume? Princes must have these terrific animals; for we kings must have lions for our dogs and tigers for our cats. The great befits a crown. In the days of the pagans of Jupiter, when the people offered the temples a hundred oxen and a hundred sheep, the emperors gave a hundred lions and a hundred eagles. This was wild and very fine. The kings of France have always had roarings round their throne. Nevertheless, people must do me this justice, that I spend still less money on it than they did, and that I possess a greater modesty of lions, bears, elephants, and leopards. Go on, Master Olivier. We wished to say thus much to our Flemish friends."

Guillaume Rym bowed low, while Coppenole, with his surly mien, had the air of one of the bears of which his majesty was speaking. The king paid no heed. He had just dipped his lips into the goblet, and he spat out the beverage, saying: "Foh! What a disagreeable potion!"

The man who was reading continued: "For feeding a rascally footpad, locked up these six months in the little cell of the flayer, until it should be determined what to do with him, six livres, four sols."

"What's that?" interrupted the king; "feed what ought to be hanged! *Pasque-Dieu!* I will give not a sou more for that nourishment. Olivier, come to an understanding about the matter with Monsieur d'Estouteville, and prepare me this very evening the wedding of the gallant and the gallows. Resume."

Olivier made a mark with his thumb against the article of the "rascally foot soldier," and passed on.

"To Henriet Cousin, master executor of the high works of justice in Paris, the sum of sixty sols parisis, to him assessed and ordained by monseigneur the provost of Paris, for having bought, by order of the said sieur the provost, a great broad sword, serving to execute and decapitate persons who are by justice condemned for their demerits, and he hath caused the same to be garnished with a sheath and with all things thereto appertaining; and hath likewise caused to be repointed and set in order the old sword, which had become broken and notched in executing justice on Messire Louis de Luxembourg, as will more fully appear ."

The king interrupted: "That suffices. I allow the sum with great good will. Those are expenses I do not begrudge. I have never regretted that money. Continue."

"For having made over a great cage . . ."

"Ah!" said the king, grasping the arms of his chair in both hands, "I knew well that I came hither to this Bastille for some purpose. Hold, Master Olivier; I desire to see that cage myself. You shall read me the cost while I am examining it. Messieurs Flemings, come and see this; 'tis curious."

Then he rose, leaned on the arm of his interlocutor, made a sign to the sort of mute who stood before the door to precede him, to the two Flemings to follow him, and quitted the room.

The royal company was recruited, at the door of the retreat, by men of arms, all loaded down with iron, and by slender pages bearing flambeaux. It marched for some time through the interior of the gloomy donjon, pierced with staircases and corridors even in the very thickness of the walls. The captain of the Bastille marched at their head, and caused the wickets to be opened before the bent and aged king, who coughed as he walked.

At each wicket, all heads were obliged to stoop, except that of the old man bent double with age. "Hum," said he between his gums, for he had no longer any teeth, "we are already quite prepared for the door of the sepulchre. For a low door, a bent passer."

At length, after having passed a final wicket, so loaded with locks that a quarter of an hour was required to open it, they entered a vast and lofty vaulted hall, in the centre of which they could distinguish by the light of the torches, a huge cubic mass of masonry, iron, and wood. The interior was hollow. It was one of those famous cages of prisoners of state, which were called "the little daughters of the king." In its walls there were two or three little windows so closely trellised with stout iron bars; that the glass was not visible. The door was a large flat slab of stone, as on tombs; the sort of door which serves for entrance only. Only here, the occupant was alive.

The king began to walk slowly round the little edifice, examining it carefully, while Master Olivier, who followed him, read aloud the note.

"For having made a great cage of wood of solid beams, timbers and wall-plates, measuring nine feet in length by eight in breadth, and of the height of seven feet between the partitions, smoothed and clamped with great bolts of iron, which has been placed in a chamber situated in one of the towers of the Bastille Saint-Antoine, in which cage is placed and detained, by command of the king our lord, a prisoner who formerly inhabited an old, decrepit, and ruined cage. There have been employed in making the said new cage, ninety-six horizontal beams, and fifty-two upright joists, ten wall-plates three toises long; there have been occupied nineteen carpenters to hew, work, and fit all the said wood in the courtyard of the Bastille during twenty days."

"Very fine heart of oak," said the king, striking the woodwork with his fist.

"There have been used in this cage," continued the other, "two hundred and twenty great bolts of iron, of nine feet, and of eight, the rest of medium length, with the rowels, caps and counterbands appertaining to the said bolts; weighing, the said iron in all, three thousand, seven hundred and thirty-five pounds; beside eight great squares of iron, serving to attach the said cage in place with clamps and nails weighing in all two hundred and eighteen pounds, not reckoning the iron of the trellises for the windows of the chamber wherein the cage hath been placed, the bars of iron for the door of the cage and other things."

"'Tis a great deal of iron," said the king, "to contain the light of a spirit."

"The whole amounts to three hundred and seventeen livres, five sols, seven deniers."

"*Pasque-Dieu!*" exclaimed the king.

At this oath, which was the favorite of Louis XI, some one seemed to awaken in the interior of the cage; the sound of chains was heard, grating on the floor, and a feeble voice, which seemed to issue from the tomb was uplifted. "Sire, sire! Mercy!" The one who spoke thus could not be seen.

"Three hundred and seventeen livres, five sols, seven deniers," repeated Louis XI.

The lamentable voice that had proceeded from the cage had frozen all present, even Master Olivier himself. The king alone wore the air of not having heard. At his order, Master Olivier resumed his reading, and his majesty coldly continued his inspection of the cage.

"In addition to this there hath been paid to a mason who hath made the holes wherein to place the gratings of the windows, and the floor of the chamber where the cage is, because that floor could not support this cage by reason of its weight, twenty-seven livres fourteen sols parisis."

The voice began to moan again.

"Mercy, sire! I swear to you that 'twas Monsieur the Cardinal d'Angers and not I, who was guilty of treason."

"The mason is bold!" said the king. "Continue, Olivier."

Olivier continued, "To a joiner for window frames, bedstead, hollow stool, and other things, twenty livres, two sols parisis."

The voice also continued. "Alas, sire! Will you not listen to me? I protest to you that 'twas not I who wrote the matter to Monseigneur do Guyenne, but Monsieur le Cardinal Balue."

"The joiner is dear," quoth the king. "Is that all?"

"No, sire. To a glazier, for the windows of the said chamber, forty-six sols, eight deniers parisis."

"Have mercy, sire! Is it not enough to have given all my goods to my judges, my plate to Monsieur de Torcy, my library to Master Pierre Doriolle, my tapestry to the governor of the Roussillon? I am innocent. I have been shivering in an iron cage for fourteen years. Have mercy, sire! You will find your reward in heaven."

"Master Olivier," said the king, "the total?"

"Three hundred sixty-seven livres, eight sols, three deniers parisis.

"Notre-Dame!" cried the king. "This is an outrageous cage!"

He tore the book from Master Olivier's hands, and set to reckoning it himself upon his fingers, examining the paper and the cage alternately. Meanwhile, the prisoner could be heard sobbing. This was lugubrious in the darkness, and their faces turned pale as they looked at each other.

"Fourteen years, sire! Fourteen years now since the month of April, 1469. In the name of the Holy Mother of God, sire, listen to me! During all this time you have enjoyed the heat of the sun. Shall I, frail creature, never more behold the day? Mercy, sire! Be pitiful! Clemency is a fine, royal virtue, which turns aside the currents of wrath. Does your majesty believe that in the hour of death it will be a great cause of content for a king never to have left any offence unpunished? Besides, sire, I did not betray your majesty, 'twas Monsieur d'Angers; and I have on my foot a very heavy chain, and a great ball of iron at the end, much heavier than it should be in reason. Eh, sire! Have pity on me!"

"Olivier," cried the king, throwing back his head, "I observe that they charge me twenty sols a hogshead for plaster, while it is worth but twelve. You will refer back this account."

He turned his back on the cage, and set out to leave the room. The miserable prisoner divined from the removal of the torches and the noise, that the king was taking his departure.

"Sire, sire!" he cried in despair.

The door closed again. He no longer saw anything, and heard only the hoarse voice of the turnkey, singing in his ears this ditty—

> "Maître Jehan Balue,
> Has lost out of view
> His good bishoprics all:
> Monsieur de Verdun
> Cannot now boast of one;
> They are gone, one and all."

The king re-ascended in silence to his retreat, and his suite followed him, terrified by the last groans of the condemned man. All at once his majesty turned to the Governor of the Bastille. "By the way," said he, "was there not some one in that cage?"

"Pardieu, yes sire!" replied the governor, astounded by the question.

"And who was it?"

"Monsieur the Bishop of Verdun."

The king knew this better than any one else. But it was a mania of his.

"Ah!" said he, with the innocent air of thinking of it for the first time, "Guillaume de Harancourt, the friend of Monsieur the Cardinal Balue. A good devil of a bishop!"

At the expiration of a few moments, the door of the retreat had opened again, then closed upon the five personages whom the reader has seen at the beginning of this chapter, and who resumed their places, their whispered conversations, and their attitudes.

During the king's absence, several despatches had been placed on his table, and he broke the seals himself. Then he began to read them promptly, one after the other, made a sign to Master Olivier who appeared to exercise the office of minister, to take a pen, and without communicating to him the contents of the despatches, he began to dictate in a low voice, the replies which the latter wrote, on his knees, in an inconvenient attitude before the table.

Guillaume Rym was on the watch.

The king spoke so low that the Flemings heard nothing of his dictation, except some isolated and rather unintelligible scraps, such as:

"To maintain the fertile places by commerce, and the sterile by manufactures....To show the English lords our four bombards, London, Brabant, Bourg-en-Bresse, Saint-Omer....Artillery is the cause of war being made more judiciously now.... To Monsieur de Bressuire, our friend.... Armies cannot be maintained without tribute, etc."

Once he raised his voice: "*Pasque-Dieu!* Monsieur the King of Sicily seals his letters with yellow wax, like a king of France. Perhaps we are in the wrong to permit him so to do. My fair cousin of Burgundy granted no armorial bearings with a field of gules. The grandeur of houses is assured by the integrity of prerogatives. Note this, friend Olivier."

Again. "Oh, oh!" said he. "What a long message! What doth our brother the emperor claim?" And running his eye over the missive and breaking his reading with interjection: "Surely, the Germans are so great and powerful, that it is hardly credible! But let us not forget the old proverb: 'The finest county is Flanders; the finest duchy, Milan; the finest kingdom, France.' Is it not so, Messieurs Flemings?"

This time Coppenole bowed in company with Guillaume Rym. The hosier's patriotism was tickled.

The last despatch made Louis XI frown. "What is this?" he said. "Complaints and fault finding against our garrisons in Picardy! Olivier, write with diligence to M. the Marshal de Rouault: That discipline is relaxed. That the gendarmes of the unattached troops, the feudal nobles, the free archers, and the Swiss inflict infinite evils on the rustics. That the military, not content with what they find in the houses of the rustics, constrain them with violent blows of cudgel or of lash to go and get wine, spices, and other unreasonable things in the town. That monsieur the king knows this. That we undertake to guard our people against inconveniences, larcenies and pillage. That such is our will, by our Lady! That in addition, it suits us not that any fiddler, barber, or any soldier varlet should be clad like a prince, in velvet, cloth of silk, and rings of gold. That these vanities are hateful to God. That we, who are gentlemen, content ourselves with a doublet of cloth at sixteen sols the ell, of Paris. That messieurs the camp-followers can very well come down to that, also. Command and ordain. To Monsieur de Rouault, our friend. Good."

He dictated this letter aloud, in a firm tone, and in jerks. At the moment when he finished it, the door opened and gave passage to a new personage, who precipitated himself into the chamber, crying in affright: "Sire, sire! There is a sedition of the populace in Paris!" Louis XI's grave face contracted; but all that was visible of his emotion passed away like a flash of lightning. He controlled himself and said with tranquil severity, "Gossip Jacques, you enter very abruptly!"

"Sire, sire! There is a revolt!" repeated Gossip Jacques breathlessly.

The king, who had risen, grasped him roughly by the arm, and said in his ear, in such a manner as to be heard by him alone, with concentrated rage and a sidelong glance at the Flemings, "Hold your tongue, or speak low!"

The new comer understood, and began in a low tone to give a very terrified account, to which the king listened calmly, while Guillaume Rym called Coppenole's attention to the face and dress of the new arrival, to his furred cowl (*caputia fourrata*), his short cape (*epitogia curta*), his robe of black velvet, which bespoke a president of the court of accounts.

Hardly had this personage given the king some explanations, when Louis XI exclaimed, bursting into a laugh, "In truth? Speak aloud, Gossip Coictier! What call is there for you to talk so low? Our Lady knoweth that we conceal nothing from our good friends the Flemings."

"But sire . . ."

"Speak loud!"

Gossip Coictier was struck dumb with surprise.

"So," resumed the king, "speak sir. There is a commotion among the louts in our good city of Paris?"

"Yes, sire."

"And which is moving you say, against monsieur the bailiff of the Palais de Justice?"

"So it appears," said the gossip, who still stammered, utterly astounded by the abrupt and inexplicable change which had just taken place in the king's thoughts.

Louis XI continued: "Where did the watch meet the rabble?"

"Marching from the Grand Truanderie, toward the Pont-aux-Changeurs. I met it myself as I was on my way hither to obey your majesty's commands. I heard some of them shouting: 'Down with the bailiff of the palace!'"

"And what complaints have they against the bailiff?"

"Ah!" said Gossip Jacques, "because he is their lord."

"Really?"

"Yes, sire. They are knaves from the Cour des Miracles. They have been complaining this long while, of the bailiff, whose vassals they are. They do not wish to recognize him either as judge or as keeper of the highways?"

"Yes, certainly!" retorted the king with a smile of satisfaction which he strove in vain to disguise.

"In all their petitions to the Parliament, they claim to have but two masters. Your majesty and their God, who is the devil, I believe."

"Eh, eh!" said the king.

He rubbed his hands, he laughed with that inward mirth which makes the countenance beam; he was unable to dissimulate his joy, although he endeavored at moments to compose himself. No one understood it in the least, not even Master Olivier. He remained silent for a moment, with a thoughtful but contented air.

"Are they in force?" he suddenly inquired.

"Yes, assuredly, sire," replied Gossip Jacques.

"How many?"

"Six thousand at the least."

The king could not refrain from saying: "Good!" He went on, "Are they armed?"

"With scythes, pikes, hackbuts, pickaxes. All sorts of very violent weapons."

The king did not appear in the least disturbed by this list. Jacques considered it his duty to add, "If your majesty does not send prompt succor to the bailiff, he is lost."

"We will send," said the king with an air of false seriousness. "It is well. Assuredly we will send. Monsieur the bailiff is our friend. Six thousand! They are desperate scamps! Their audacity is marvellous, and we are greatly enraged at it. But we have only a few people about us tonight. Tomorrow morning will be time enough."

Gossip Jacques exclaimed, "Instantly, sire! There will be time to sack the bailiwick a score of times, to violate the seignory, to hang the bailiff. For God's sake, sire, send before tomorrow morning."

The king looked him full in the face. "I have told you tomorrow morning." It was one of those looks to which one does not reply. After a silence, Louis XI raised his voice once more, "You should know that, Gossip Jacques. What was—" He corrected himself. "What is the bailiff's feudal jurisdiction?"

"Sire, the bailiff of the palace has the Rue Calendre as far as the Rue de l'Herberie, the Place Saint-Michel, and the localities vulgarly known as the Mureaux, situated near the church of Notre-Dame des Champs (here Louis XI raised the brim of his hat), which hotels number thirteen, plus the Cour des Miracles, plus the Maladerie, called the Banlieue, plus the whole highway which begins at that Maladerie and ends at the Porte Sainte-Jacques. Of these divers places he is voyer, high, middle, and low, justiciary, full seigneur."

"Bless me!" said the king, scratching his left ear with his right hand, "that makes a goodly bit of my city! Ah, monsieur the bailiff was king of all that!"

This time he did not correct himself. He continued dreamily, and as though speaking to himself, "Very fine, monsieur the bailiff! You had there between your teeth a pretty slice of our Paris."

All at once he broke out explosively, "*Pasque-Dieu!* What people are those who claim to be voyers, justiciaries, lords and masters in our domains? Who have their tollgates at the end of every field? Their gallows and their hangman at every cross-road among our people? So that as the Greek believed that he had as many gods as there were fountains, and the Persian as many as he beheld stars, the Frenchman counts as many kings as he sees gibbets! Pardieu! 'Tis an evil thing, and the confusion of it displeases me. I should greatly like to know whether it be the mercy of God that there should be in Paris any other lord than the king, any other judge than our parliament, any other emperor than ourselves in this empire! By the faith of my soul! The day must certainly come when there shall exist in France but one king, one lord, one judge, one headsman, as there is in paradise but one God!"

He lifted his cap again, and continued, still dreamily, with the air and accent of a hunter who is cheering on his pack of hounds: "Good, my people! Bravely done! Break these false lords! Do your duty! At them! Have at them! Pillage them! Take them! Sack them! . . . Ah, you want to be kings, messeigneurs? On, my people on!"

Here he interrupted himself abruptly, bit his lips as though to take back his thought which had already half escaped, bent his piercing eyes in turn on each of the five persons who surrounded him, and suddenly grasping his hat with both hands and staring full at it, he said to it: "Oh! I would burn you if you knew what there was in my head."

Then casting about him once more the cautious and uneasy glance of the fox re-entering his hole, "No matter! We will succor monsieur the bailiff. Unfortunately, we have but few troops here at the present moment, against so great a populace. We must wait until tomorrow. The order will be transmitted to the City and every one who is caught will be immediately hung."

"By the way, sire," said Gossip Coictier, "I had forgotten that in the first agitation, the watch have seized two laggards of the band. If your majesty desires to see these men, they are here."

"If I desire to see them!" cried the king. "What! *Pasque-Dieu!* You forget a thing like that! Run quick, you, Olivier! Go, seek them!"

Master Olivier quitted the room and returned a moment later with the two prisoners, surrounded by archers of the guard. The first had a coarse, idiotic, drunken and astonished face. He was clothed in rags, and walked with one knee bent and dragging his leg. The second had a pallid and smiling countenance, with which the reader is already acquainted.

The king surveyed them for a moment without uttering a word, then addressing the first one abruptly, "What's your name?"

"Gieffroy Pincebourde."

"Your trade."

"Outcast."

"What were you going to do in this damnable sedition?"

The outcast stared at the king, and swung his arms with a stupid air. He had one of those awkwardly shaped heads where intelligence is about as much at its ease as a light beneath an extinguisher.

"I know not," said he. "They went, I went."

"Were you not going to outrageously attack and pillage your lord, the bailiff of the palace?"

"I know that they were going to take something from some one. That is all."

A soldier pointed out to the king a billhook that he had seized on the person of the vagabond.

"Do you recognize this weapon?" demanded the king.

"Yes; 'tis my billhook; I am a vine-dresser."

"And do you recognize this man as your companion?" added Louis XI, pointing to the other prisoner.

"No, I do not know him."

"That will do," said the king, making a sign with his finger to the silent personage who stood motionless beside the door, to whom we have already called the reader's attention.

"Gossip Tristan, here is a man for you."

Tristan l'Hermite bowed. He gave an order in a low voice to two archers, who led away the poor vagabond.

In the meantime, the king had approached the second prisoner, who was perspiring in great drops: "Your name?"

"Sire, Pierre Gringoire."

"Your trade?"

"Philosopher, sire."

"How do you permit yourself, knave, to go and besiege our friend, monsieur the bailiff of the palace, and what have you to say concerning this popular agitation?"

"Sire, I had nothing to do with it."

"Come, now! You wanton wretch, were not you apprehended by the watch in that bad company?"

"No, sire, there is a mistake. 'Tis a fatality. I make tragedies. Sire, I entreat your majesty to listen to me. I am a poet. 'Tis the melancholy way of men of my profession to roam the streets by night. I was passing there. It was mere chance. I was unjustly arrested; I am innocent of this civil tempest. Your majesty sees that the vagabond did not recognize me. I conjure your majesty—"

"Hold your tongue!" said the king, between two swallows of his drink. "You split our head!"

Tristan l'Hermite advanced and pointing to Gringoire, "Sire, can this one be hanged also?"

This was the first word that he had uttered.

"Phew!" replied the king, "I see no objection."

"I see a great many!" said Gringoire.

At that moment, our philosopher was greener than an olive. He perceived from the king's cold and indifferent mien that there was no other resource than something very pathetic, and he flung himself at the feet of Louis XI, exclaiming, with gestures of despair, "Sire, will your majesty deign to hear me! Sire! Break not in thunder over so small a thing as myself. God's great lightning doth not bombard a lettuce. Sire, you are an august and, very puissant monarch; have pity on a poor man who is honest, and who would find it more difficult to stir up a revolt than a cake of ice would to give out a spark! Very gracious sire, kindness is the virtue of a lion and a king. Alas! Rigor only frightens minds; the impetuous gusts of the north wind do not make the traveller lay aside his cloak; the sun, bestowing his rays little by little, warms him in such ways that it will make him strip to his shirt. Sire, you are the sun. I protest to you, my sovereign lord and master, that I am not an outcast, thief, and disorderly fellow. Revolt and brigandage belong not to the outfit of Apollo. I am not the man to fling myself into those clouds that break out into seditious clamor. I am your majesty's faithful vassal. That same jealousy which a husband cherisheth for the honor of his wife, the resentment that the son hath for the love of his father, a good vassal should feel for the glory of his king; he should pine away for the zeal of this house, for the aggrandizement of his service. Every other passion that should transport him would be but madness. These, sire, are my maxims of state: then do not judge me to be a seditious and thieving rascal because my garment is worn at the elbows. If you will grant me mercy, sire, I will wear it out on the knees in praying to God for you night and morning! Alas! I am not extremely rich, 'tis true. I am even rather poor. But not vicious on that account. It is not my fault. Every one knoweth that great wealth is not to be drawn from literature, and that those who are best posted in good books do not always have a great fire in winter. The advocate's trade taketh all the grain, and leaveth only straw to the other scientific professions. There are forty very excellent proverbs anent the hole-ridden cloak of the philosopher. Oh, sire! Clemency is the only light which can enlighten the interior of so great a soul. Clemency beareth the torch before all the other virtues. Without it they are but blind men groping after God in the dark. Compassion, which is the same thing as clemency, causeth the love of subjects, which is the most powerful bodyguard to a prince. What matters it to your majesty, who dazzles all faces, if there is one poor man more on earth, a poor innocent philosopher spluttering amid the shadows of calamity, with an empty pocket which resounds against his hollow belly? Moreover, sire, I am a man of letters. Great kings make a pearl for their crowns by protecting letters. Hercules did not disdain the title of Musagetes. Mathias Corvin favored Jean de Monroyal, the ornament of mathematics. Now, 'tis an ill way to protect letters to hang men of letters. What a stain on Alexander if he had hung Aristoteles! This act would not be a little patch on the face of his reputation to embellish it, but a very malignant ulcer to disfigure it. Sire! I made a very proper epithalamium for Mademoiselle of Flanders and Monseigneur the very august Dauphin. That is not a firebrand of rebellion. Your majesty sees that I am not a scribbler of no reputation, that I have studied excellently well, and that I possess much natural eloquence. Have mercy upon me, sire! In so doing you will perform a gallant deed to our Lady, and I swear to you that I am greatly terrified at the idea of being hanged!"

So saying, the unhappy Gringoire kissed the king's slippers, and Guillaume Rym said to Coppenole in a low tone: "He doth well to drag himself on the earth. Kings are like the Jupiter of Crete, they have ears only in their feet." And without troubling himself about the Jupiter of Crete, the hosier replied with a heavy smile, and his eyes fixed on Gringoire: "Oh! That's it exactly! I seem to hear Chancellor Hugonet craving mercy of me."

When Gringoire paused at last, quite out of breath, he raised his head tremblingly toward the king, who was engaged in scratching a spot on the knee of his breeches with his finger-nail; then his majesty began to drink from the goblet of drink. But he uttered not a word, and this silence tortured Gringoire. At last the king looked at him. "Here is a terrible bawler!" said he. Then, turning to Tristan l'Hermite, "Bah! Let him go!"

Gringoire fell backwards, quite thunderstruck with joy.

"At liberty!" growled Tristan "Doth not your majesty wish to have him detained a little while in a cage?"

"Gossip," retorted Louis XI, "think you that 'tis for birds of this feather that we cause to be made cages at three hundred and sixty-seven livres, eight sous, three deniers apiece? Release him at once, the wanton (Louis XI was fond of this word which formed, with *Pasque-Dieu*, the foundation of his joviality), and put him out with a buffet."

"Ugh!" cried Gringoire, "what a great king is here!"

And for fear of a counter order, he rushed toward the door, which Tristan opened for him with a very bad grace. The soldiers left the room with him, pushing him before them with stout thwacks, which Gringoire bore like a true stoical philosopher.

The king's good humor since the revolt against the bailiff had been announced to him, made itself apparent in every way. This unwonted clemency was no small sign of it. Tristan l'Hermite in his corner wore the surly look of a dog who has had a bone snatched away from him.

Meanwhile, the king thrummed gayly with his fingers on the arm of his chair, the March of Pont-Audemer. He was a dissembling prince, but one who understood far better how to hide his troubles than his joys. These external manifestations of joy at any good news sometimes proceeded to very great lengths thus, on the death, of Charles the Bold, to the point of vowing silver balustrades to Saint Martin of Tours; on his advent to the throne, so far as forgetting to order his father's obsequies.

"Hey, sire!" suddenly exclaimed Jacques Coictier, "what has become of the acute attack of illness for which your majesty had me summoned?"

"Oh!" said the king, "I really suffer greatly, my gossip. There is a hissing in my ear and fiery rakes rack my chest."

Coictier took the king's hand, and begun to feel of his pulse with a knowing air.

"Look, Coppenole," said Rym, in a low voice. "Behold him between Coictier and Tristan. They are his whole court. A physician for himself, a headsman for others."

As he felt the king's pulse, Coictier assumed an air of greater and greater alarm. Louis XI watched him with some anxiety. Coictier grew visibly more gloomy. The brave man had no other farm than the king's bad health. He speculated on it to the best of his ability.

"Oh, oh!" he murmured at length, "this is serious indeed."

"Is it not?" said the king, uneasily.

"*Pulsus creber, anhelans, crepitans, irregularis,*" continued the leech.

"*Pasque-Dieu!*"

"This may carry off its man in less than three days."

"Our Lady!" exclaimed the king. "And the remedy, gossip?"

"I am meditating upon that, sire."

He made Louis XI put out his tongue, shook his head, made a grimace, and in the very midst of these affectations, "Pardieu, sire," he suddenly said, "I must tell you that there is a receivership of the royal prerogatives vacant, and that I have a nephew."

"I give the receivership to your nephew, Gossip Jacques," replied the king; "but draw this fire from my breast."

"Since your majesty is so clement," replied the leech, "you will not refuse to aid me a little in building my house, Rue Saint-André-des-Arcs."

"Heugh!" said the king.

"I am at the end of my finances," pursued the doctor; and it would really be a pity that the house should not have a roof; not on account of the house, which is simple and thoroughly bourgeois, but because of the paintings of Jehan Fourbault, which adorn its wainscoating. There is a Diana flying in the air, but so excellent, so tender, so delicate, of so ingenuous an action, her hair so well coiffed and adorned with a crescent, her flesh so white, that she leads into temptation those who regard her too curiously. There is also a Ceres. She is another very fair divinity. She is seated on sheaves of wheat and crowned with a gallant garland of wheat ears interlaced with salsify and other flowers. Never were seen more amorous eyes, more rounded limbs, a nobler air, or a more gracefully flowing skirt. She is one of the most innocent and most perfect beauties whom the brush has ever produced."

"Executioner!" grumbled Louis XI, "what are you driving at?"

"I must have a roof for these paintings, sire, and, although 'tis but a small matter, I have no more money."

"How much doth your roof cost?"

"Why a roof of copper, embellished and gilt, two thousand livres at the most."

"Ah, assassin!" cried the king, "He never draws out one of my teeth which is not a diamond."

"Am I to have my roof?" said Coictier.

"Yes; and go to the devil, but cure me."

Jacques Coictier bowed low and said, "Sire, it is a repellent which will save you. We will apply to your loins the great defensive composed of cerate, Armenian bole, white of egg, oil, and vinegar. You will continue your drink and we will answer for your majesty."

A burning candle does not attract one gnat alone. Master Olivier, perceiving the king to be in a liberal mood, and judging the moment to be propitious, approached in his turn.

"Sire—"

"What is it now?" said Louis XI.

"Sire, your majesty knoweth that Simon Radin is dead?"

"Well?"

"He was councillor to the king in the matter of the courts of the treasury."

"Well?"

"Sire, his place is vacant."

As he spoke thus, Master Olivier's haughty face quitted its arrogant expression for a lowly one. It is the only change which ever takes place in a courtier's visage. The king looked him well in the face and said in a dry tone, "I understand."

He resumed. "Master Olivier, the Marshal de Boucicaut was wont to say, 'There's no master save the king, there are no fishes save in the sea.' I see that you agree with Monsieur de Boucicaut. Now listen to this; we have a good memory. In '68 we made you valet of our chamber: in '69, guardian of the fortress of the bridge of Saint-Cloud, at a hundred livres of Tournay in wages (you wanted them of Paris). In November, '73, by letters given to Gergeole, we instituted you keeper of the Wood of Vincennes, in the place of Gilbert Acle, equerry; in '75, gruyer of the forest of Rouvray-lez-Saint-Cloud, in the place of Jacques le Maire; in '78, we graciously settled on you, by letters patent sealed doubly with green wax, an income of ten livres parisis, for you and your wife, on the Place of the Merchants, situated at the School Saint-Germain; in '79, we made you gruyer of the forest of Senart, in place of that poor Jehan Daiz; then captain of the Château of Loches; then governor of Saint-Quentin; then captain of the bridge of Meulan, of which you cause yourself to be called comte. Out of the five sols fine paid by every barber who shaves on a festival day, there are three sols for you and we have the rest. We have been good enough to change your name of le Mauvais (the Evil), which resembled your face too closely. In '76, we granted you, to the great displeasure of our nobility, armorial bearings of a thousand colors, which give you the breast of a peacock. *Pasque-Dieu!* Are not you surfeited? Is not the draught of fishes sufficiently fine and miraculous? Are you not afraid that one salmon more will make your boat sink? Pride will be your ruin, gossip. Ruin and disgrace always press hard on the heels of pride. Consider this and hold your tongue."

These words, uttered with severity, made Master Olivier's face revert to its insolence.

"Good!" he muttered, almost aloud, "'tis easy to see that the king is ill today; he giveth all to the leech."

Louis XI far from being irritated by this petulant insult, resumed with some gentleness, "Stay, I was forgetting that I made you my ambassador to Madame Marie, at Ghent. Yes, gentlemen," added the king turning to the Flemings, "this man hath been an ambassador. There, my gossip," he pursued, addressing Master Olivier, "let us not get angry; we are old friends. 'Tis very late. We have terminated our labors. Shave me."

Our readers have not, without doubt, waited until the present moment to recognize in Master Olivier that terrible Figaro whom Providence, the great maker of dramas, mingled so artistically in the long and bloody comedy of the reign of Louis XI. We will not here undertake to develop that singular figure. This barber of the king had three names. At court he was politely called Olivier le Daim (the Deer); among the people Olivier the Devil. His real name was Olivier le Mauvais.

Accordingly, Olivier le Mauvais remained motionless, sulking at the king, and glancing askance at Jacques Coictier.

"Yes, yes, the physician!" he said between his teeth.

"Ah, yes, the physician!" retorted Louis XI, with singular good humor; "the physician has more credit than you. 'Tis very simple; he has taken hold upon us by the whole body, and you hold us only by the chin. Come, my poor barber, all will come right. What would you say and what would become of your office if I were a king like Chilperic, whose gesture consisted in holding his beard in one hand? Come, gossip mine, fulfil your office, shave me. Go get what you need therefore."

Olivier perceiving that the king had made up his mind to laugh, and that there was no way of even annoying him, went off grumbling to execute his orders.

The king rose, approached the window, and suddenly opening it with extraordinary agitation: "Oh! yes!" he exclaimed, clapping his hands, "yonder is a redness in the sky over the City. 'Tis the bailiff burning. It can be nothing else but that. Ah, my good people! Here you are aiding me at last in tearing down the rights of lordship!"

Then turning toward the Flemings: "Come, look at this, gentlemen. Is it not a fire which gloweth yonder?"

The two men of Ghent drew near.

"A great fire," said Guillaume Rym.

"Oh!" exclaimed Coppenole, whose eyes suddenly flashed, "that reminds me of the burning of the house of the Seigneur d'Hymbercourt. There must be a goodly revolt yonder."

"You think so, Master Coppenole?" And Louis XI's glance was almost as joyous as that of the hosier. "Will it not be difficult to resist?"

"Cross of God! Sire! Your majesty will damage many companies of men of war thereon."

"Ah! I! 'Tis different," returned the king. "If I willed."

The hosier replied hardily, "If this revolt be what I suppose, sire, you might will in vain."

"Gossip," said Louis XI, "with the two companies of my unattached troops and one discharge of a serpentine, short work is made of a populace of louts."

The hosier, in spite of the signs made to him by Guillaume Rym, appeared determined to hold his own against the king.

"Sire, the Swiss were also louts. Monsieur the Duke of Burgundy was a great gentleman, and he turned up his nose at that rabble rout. At the battle of Grandson, sire, he cried: 'Men of the cannon! Fire on the villains!' and he swore by Saint-George. But Advoyer Scharnachtal hurled himself on the handsome duke with his battle-club and his people, and when the glittering Burgundian army came in contact with these peasants in bull hides, it flew in pieces like a pane of glass at the blow of a pebble. Many lords were then slain by low-born knaves; and Monsieur de Château-Guyon, the greatest seigneur in Burgundy, was found dead, with his gray horse, in a little marsh meadow."

"Friend," returned the king, "you are speaking of a battle. The question here is of a mutiny. And I will gain the upper hand of it as soon as it shall please me to frown."

The other replied indifferently, "That may be, sire; in that case, 'tis because the people's hour hath not yet come."

Guillaume Rym considered it incumbent on him to intervene. "Master Coppenole, you are speaking to a puissant king."

"I know it," replied the hosier, gravely.

"Let him speak, Monsieur Rym, my friend," said the king; "I love this frankness of speech. My father, Charles the Seventh, was accustomed to say that the truth was ailing; I thought her dead, and that she had found no confessor. Master Coppenole undeceiveth me."

Then, laying his hand familiarly on Coppenole's shoulder, "You were saying, Master Jacques?"

"I say, sire, that you may possibly be in the right, that the hour of the people may not yet have come with you."

Louis XI gazed at him with his penetrating eye. "And when will that hour come, master?"

"You will hear it strike."

"On what clock, if you please?"

Coppenole, with his tranquil and rustic countenance, made the king approach the window.

"Listen, sire! There is here a donjon keep, a belfry, cannons, bourgeois, soldiers; when the belfry shall hum, when the cannons shall roar, when the donjon shall fall in ruins amid great noise, when bourgeois and soldiers shall howl and slay each other, the hour will strike."

Louis's face grew sombre and dreamy. He remained silent for a moment, then he gently patted with his hand the thick wall of the donjon, as one strokes the haunches of a steed.

"Oh! no!" said he. "You will not crumble so easily, will you, my good Bastille?"

And turning with an abrupt gesture toward the sturdy Fleming, "Have you never seen a revolt, Master Jacques?"

"I have made them," said the hosier.

"How do you set to work to make a revolt?" said the king.

"Ah!" replied Coppenole, "'tis not very difficult. There are a hundred ways. In the first place, there must be discontent in the city. The thing is not uncommon. And then, the character of the inhabitants. Those of Ghent are easy to stir into revolt. They always love the prince's son; the prince, never. Well! One morning, I will suppose, some one enters my shop, and says to me: 'Father Coppenole, there is this and there is that, the Demoiselle of Flanders wishes to save her ministers, the grand bailiff is doubling the impost on shagreen, or something else'—what you will. I leave my work as it stands, I come out of my hosier's stall, and I shout: 'To the sack!' There is always some smashed cask at hand. I mount it, and I say aloud, in the first words that occur to me, what I have on my heart; and when one is of the people, sire, one always has something on the heart: Then people troop up, they shout, they ring the alarm bell, they arm the louts with what they take from the soldiers, the market people join in, and they set out. And it will always be thus, so long as there are lords in the seignories, bourgeois in the bourgs, and peasants in the country."

"And against whom do you thus rebel?" inquired the king; "against your bailiffs? Against your lords?"

"Sometimes; that depends. Against the duke, also, sometimes."

Louis XI returned and seated himself, saying, with a smile, "Ah! Here they have only got as far as the bailiffs."

At that instant Olivier le Daim returned. He was followed by two pages, who bore the king's toilet articles; but what struck Louis XI was that he was also accompanied by the provost of Paris and the chevalier of the watch, who appeared to be in consternation. The spiteful barber also wore an air of consternation, which was one of contentment beneath, however. It was he who spoke first.

"Sire, I ask your majesty's pardon for the calamitous news which I bring."

The king turned quickly and grazed the mat on the floor with the feet of his chair. "What does this mean?"

"Sire," resumed Olivier le Daim, with the malicious air of a man who rejoices that he is about to deal a violent blow, "'tis not against the bailiff of the courts that this popular sedition is directed."

"Against whom, then?"

"Against you, sire?"

The aged king rose erect and straight as a young man. "Explain yourself, Olivier! And guard your head well, gossip; for I swear to you by the cross of Saint-Lô that, if you lie to us at this hour, the sword which severed the head of Monsieur de Luxembourg is not so notched that it cannot yet sever yours!"

The oath was formidable; Louis XI had only sworn twice in the course of his life by the cross of Saint-Lô.

Olivier opened his mouth to reply. "Sire—"

"On your knees!" interrupted the king violently. "Tristan, have an eye to this man."

Olivier knelt down and said coldly, "Sire, a sorceress was condemned to death by your court of parliament. She took refuge in Notre-Dame. The people are trying to take her from thence by main force. Monsieur the provost and monsieur the chevalier of the watch, who have just come from the riot, are here to give me the lie if this is not the truth. The populace is besieging Notre-Dame."

"Yes, indeed!" said the king in a low voice, all pale and trembling with wrath. "Notre-Dame! They lay siege to our Lady, my good mistress in her cathedral! Rise, Olivier. You are right. I give you Simon Radin's charge. You are right. 'Tis I whom they are attacking. The witch is under the protection of this church, the church is under my protection. And I thought that they were acting against the bailiff! 'Tis against myself!"

Then, rendered young by fury, he began to walk up and down with long strides. He no longer laughed, he was terrible, he went and came; the fox was changed into a hyena. He seemed suffocated to such a degree that he could not speak; his lips moved, and his fleshless fists were clenched. All at once he raised his head, his hollow eye appeared full of light, and his voice burst forth like a clarion: "Down with them, Tristan! A heavy hand for these rascals! Go, Tristan, my friend! Slay, slay!"

This eruption having passed, he returned to his seat, and said with cold and concentrated wrath, "Here, Tristan! There are here with us in the Bastille the fifty lances of the Vicomte de Gif, which makes three hundred horse: you will take them. There is also the company of our unattached archers of Monsieur de Châteaupers: you will take it. You are provost of the marshals; you have the men of your provostship: you will take them. At the Hôtel Saint-Pol you will find forty archers of monsieur the dauphin's new guard: you will take them. And, with all these, you will hasten to Notre-Dame. Ah! Messieurs, louts of Paris, do you fling yourselves thus against the crown of France, the sanctity of Notre-Dame, and the peace of this commonwealth! Exterminate, Tristan! Exterminate! And let not a single one escape, except it be for Montfauçon."

Tristan bowed. "'Tis well, sire."

He added, after a silence, "And what shall I do with the sorceress?"

This question caused the king to meditate.

"Ah!" said he, "the sorceress! Monsieur d'Estouteville, what did the people wish to do with her?"

"Sire," replied the provost of Paris, "I imagine that since the populace has come to tear her from her asylum in Notre-Dame, 'tis because that impunity wounds them, and they desire to hang her."

The king appeared to reflect deeply: then, addressing Tristan l'Hermite, "Well, gossip, exterminate the people and hang the sorceress."

"That's it," said Rym in a low tone to Coppenole, "punish the people for willing a thing, and then do what they wish."

"Enough, sire," replied Tristan. "If the sorceress is still in Notre-Dame, must she be seized in spite of the sanctuary?"

"*Pasque-Dieu!* The sanctuary!" said the king, scratching his ear. "But the woman must be hung, nevertheless."

Here, as though seized with a sudden idea, he flung himself on his knees before his chair, took off his hat, placed it on the seat, and gazing devoutly at one of the leaden amulets which loaded it down, "Oh!" said he, with clasped hands, "our Lady of Paris, my gracious patroness, pardon me. I will only do it this once. This criminal must be punished. I assure you, madame the virgin, my good mistress, that she is a sorceress who is not worthy of your amiable protection. You know, madame, that many very pious princes have overstepped the privileges of the churches for the glory of God and the necessities of the State. Saint Hugues, bishop of England, permitted King Edward to hang a witch in his church. Saint-Louis of France, my master, transgressed, with the same object, the church of Monsieur Saint-Paul; and Monsieur Alphonse, son of the king of Jerusalem, the very church of the Holy Sepulchre. Pardon me, then, for this once. Our Lady of Paris, I will never do so again, and I will give you a fine statue of silver, like the one that I gave last year to Our Lady of Ecouys. So be it."

He made the sign of the cross, rose, donned his hat once more, and said to Tristan, "Be diligent, gossip. Take Monsieur Châteaupers with you. You will cause the tocsin to be sounded. You will crush the populace. You will seize the witch. 'Tis said. And I mean the business of the execution to be done by you. You will render me an account of it. Come, Olivier, I shall not go to bed this night. Shave me."

Tristan l'Hermite bowed and departed. Then the king, dismissing Rym and Coppenole with a gesture, "God guard you, messieurs, my good friends the Flemings. Go, take a little repose. The night advances, and we are nearer the morning than the evening."

Both retired and gained their apartments under the guidance of the captain of the Bastille. Coppenole said to Guillaume Rym, "Hum! I have had enough of that coughing king! I have seen Charles of Burgundy drunk, and he was less malignant than Louis XI when ailing."

"Master Jacques," replied Rym, "'tis because wine renders kings less cruel than does barley water."

Chapter 6

Little Sword in Pocket

On emerging from the Bastille, Gringoire descended the Rue Saint-Antoine with the swiftness of a runaway horse. On arriving at the Baudoyer gate, he walked straight to the stone cross that rose in the middle of that place, as though he were able to distinguish in the darkness the figure of a man clad and cloaked in black, who was seated on the steps of the cross.

"Is it you, master?" said Gringoire.

The personage in black rose.

"Death and passion! You make me boil, Gringoire. The man on the tower of Saint-Gervais has just cried half-past one o'clock in the morning."

"Oh," retorted Gringoire, "'tis no fault of mine, but of the watch and the king. I have just had a narrow escape. I always just miss being hung. 'Tis my predestination."

"You lack everything," said the other. "But come quickly. Have you the password?"

"Fancy, master, I have seen the king. I come from him. He wears fustian breeches. 'Tis an adventure."

"Oh! Distaff of words! What is your adventure to me! Have you the password of the outcasts?"

"I have it. Be at ease. 'Little sword in pocket.'"

"Good. Otherwise, we could not make our way as far as the church. The outcasts bar the streets. Fortunately, it appears that they have encountered resistance. We may still arrive in time."

"Yes, master, but how are we to get into Notre-Dame?"

"I have the key to the tower."

"And how are we to get out again?"

"Behind the cloister there is a little door which opens on the Terrain and the water. I have taken the key to it, and I moored a boat there this morning."

"I have had a beautiful escape from being hung!" Gringoire repeated.

"Eh, quick! Come!" said the other.

Both descended toward the city with long strides.

CHAPTER 7

Châteaupers to the Rescue

THE READER WILL, perhaps, recall the critical situation in which we left Quasimodo. The brave deaf man, assailed on all sides, had lost, if not all courage, at least all hope of saving, not himself (he was not thinking of himself), but the gypsy. He ran distractedly along the gallery. Notre-Dame was on the point of being taken by storm by the outcasts. All at once, a great galloping of horses filled the neighboring streets, and, with a long file of torches and a thick column of cavaliers, with free reins and lances in rest, these furious sounds debouched on the Place like a hurricane, "France! France! cut down the louts! Châteaupers to the rescue! Provostship! Provostship!"

The frightened vagabonds wheeled round.

Quasimodo who did not hear, saw the naked swords, the torches, the irons of the pikes, all that cavalry, at the head of which he recognized Captain Phoebus; he beheld the confusion of the outcasts, the terror of some, the disturbance among the bravest of them, and from this unexpected succor he recovered so much strength, that he hurled from the church the first assailants who were already climbing into the gallery.

It was, in fact, the king's troops who had arrived. The vagabonds behaved bravely. They defended themselves like desperate men. Caught on the flank, by the Rue Saint-Pierre-aux-Boeufs, and in the rear through the Rue du Parvis, driven to bay against Notre-Dame, which they still assailed and Quasimodo defended, at the same time besiegers and besieged, they were in the singular situation in which Comte Henri Harcourt, *Taurinum obsessor idem et obsessus*, as his epitaph says, found himself later on, at the famous siege of Turin, in 1640, between

Prince Thomas of Savoy, whom he was besieging, and the Marquis de Leganez, who was blockading him.

The battle was frightful. There was a dog's tooth for wolf's flesh, as P. Mathieu says. The king's cavaliers, in whose midst Phoebus de Châteaupers bore himself valiantly, gave no quarter, and the slash of the sword disposed of those who escaped the thrust of the lance. The outcasts, badly armed, foamed and bit with rage. Men, women, children, hurled themselves on the cruppers and the breasts of the horses, and hung there like cats, with teeth, finger nails and toe nails. Others struck the archers in the face with their torches. Others thrust iron hooks into the necks of the cavaliers and dragged them down. They slashed in pieces those who fell.

One was noticed who had a large, glittering scythe, and who, for a long time, mowed the legs of the horses. He was frightful. He was singing a ditty, with a nasal intonation, he swung and drew back his scythe incessantly. At every blow he traced around him a great circle of severed limbs. He advanced thus into the very thickest of the cavalry, with the tranquil slowness, the lolling of the head and the regular breathing of a harvester attacking a field of wheat. It was Chopin Trouillefou. A shot from an arquebus laid him low.

In the meantime, windows had been opened again. The neighbors hearing the war cries of the king's troops, had mingled in the affray, and bullets rained upon the outcasts from every story. The Parvis was filled with a thick smoke, which the musketry streaked with flame. Through it one could confusedly distinguish the front of Notre-Dame, and the decrepit Hôtel-Dieu with some wan invalids gazing down from the heights of its roof all checkered with dormer windows.

At length the vagabonds gave way. Weariness, the lack of good weapons, the fright of this surprise, the musketry from the windows, the valiant attack of the king's troops, all overwhelmed them. They forced the line of assailants, and fled in every direction, leaving the Parvis encumbered with dead.

When Quasimodo, who had not ceased to fight for a moment, beheld this rout, he fell on his knees and raised his hands to heaven; then, intoxicated with joy, he ran, he ascended with the swiftness of a bird to that cell, the approaches to which he had so intrepidly defended. He had but one thought now; it was to kneel before her whom he had just saved for the second time.

When he entered the cell, he found it empty.

Book Eleventh

CHAPTER 1

The Little Shoe

LA ESMERALDA WAS sleeping at the moment when the outcasts assailed the church.

Soon the ever-increasing uproar around the edifice, and the uneasy bleating of her goat which had been awakened, had roused her from her slumbers. She had sat up, she had listened, she had looked; then, terrified by the light and noise, she had rushed from her cell to see. The aspect of the Place, the vision which was moving in it, the disorder of that nocturnal assault, that hideous crowd, leaping like a cloud of frogs, half seen in the gloom, the croaking of that hoarse multitude, those few red torches running and crossing each other in the darkness like the meteors which streak the misty surfaces of marshes, this whole scene produced upon her the effect of a mysterious battle between the phantoms of the Witches' Sabbath and the stone monsters of the church. Imbued from her very infancy with the superstitions of the Bohemian tribe, her first thought was that she had caught the strange beings peculiar to the night, in their deeds of witchcraft. Then she ran in terror to cower in her cell, asking of her pallet some less terrible nightmare.

But little by little the first vapors of terror had been dissipated; from the constantly increasing noise, and from many other signs of reality, she felt herself besieged not by spectres, but by human beings. Then her fear, though it did not increase, changed its character. She had dreamed of the possibility of a popular mutiny to tear her from her asylum. The idea of once more recovering life, hope, Phoebus, who was ever present in her future, the extreme helplessness of her condition, flight cut off, no support, her abandonment, her isolation— these thoughts and a thousand others overwhelmed her. She fell upon her knees, with her head on her bed, her hands clasped over her head, full of anxiety and tremors, and, although a gypsy, an idolater, and a pagan, she began to entreat with sobs, mercy from the good Christian God, and to pray to our Lady, her hostess. For even if one believes in nothing, there are moments in life when one is always of the religion of the temple that is nearest at hand.

She remained thus prostrate for a very long time, trembling in truth, more than praying, chilled by the ever-closer breath of that furious multitude, understanding nothing of this outburst, ignorant of what was being plotted, what was being done, what they wanted, but foreseeing a terrible issue.

In the midst of this anguish, she heard some one walking near her. She turned round. Two men, one of whom carried a lantern, had just entered her cell. She uttered a feeble cry.

"Fear nothing," said a voice that was not unknown to her, "it is I."

"Who are you?" she asked.

"Pierre Gringoire."

This name reassured her. She raised her eyes once more, and recognized the poet in very fact. But there stood beside him a black figure veiled from head to foot, which struck her by its silence.

"Oh!" continued Gringoire in a tone of reproach, "Djali recognized me before you!"

The little goat had not, in fact, waited for Gringoire to announce his name. No sooner had he entered than it rubbed itself gently against his knees, covering the poet with caresses and with white hairs, for it was shedding its hair. Gringoire returned the caresses.

"Who is this with you?" said the gypsy, in a low voice.

"Be at ease," replied Gringoire. "'Tis one of my friends." Then the philosopher setting his lantern on the ground, crouched upon the stones, and exclaimed enthusiastically, as he pressed Djali in his arms, "Oh! 'tis a graceful beast, more considerable no doubt, for its neatness than for its size, but ingenious, subtle, and lettered as a grammarian! Let us see, my Djali, hast thou forgotten any of thy pretty tricks? How does Master Jacques Charmolue?. . ."

The man in black did not allow him to finish. He approached Gringoire and shook him roughly by the shoulder.

Gringoire rose.

"'Tis true," said he: "I forgot that we are in haste. But that is no reason master, for getting furious with people in this manner. My dear and lovely child, your life is in danger, and Djali's also. They want to hang you again. We are your friends, and we have come to save you. Follow us."

"Is it true?" she exclaimed in dismay.

"Yes, perfectly true. Come quickly!"

"I am willing," she stammered. "But why does not your friend speak?"

"Ah!" said Gringoire, "'tis because his father and mother were fantastic people who made him of a taciturn temperament."

She was obliged to content herself with this explanation. Gringoire took her by the hand; his companion picked up the lantern and walked on in front. Fear stunned the young girl. She allowed herself to be led away. The goat followed them, frisking, so joyous at seeing Gringoire again that it made him stumble every moment by thrusting its horns between his legs.

"Such is life," said the philosopher, every time that he came near falling down; "'tis often our best friends who cause us to be overthrown."

They rapidly descended the staircase of the towers, crossed the church, full of shadows and solitude, and all reverberating with uproar, which formed a frightful contrast, and emerged into the courtyard of the cloister by the red door. The cloister was deserted; the canons had fled to the bishop's palace in order to pray together; the courtyard was empty, a few frightened lackeys were crouching in dark corners. They directed their steps toward the door that opened from this court upon the Terrain. The man in black opened it with a key that he had about him. Our readers are aware that the Terrain was a tongue of land enclosed by walls on the side of the City and belonging to the chapter of Notre-Dame, which terminated the island on the east, behind the church. They found this enclosure perfectly deserted. There was here less tumult in the air. The roar of the outcasts' assault reached them more confusedly and less clamorously. The fresh breeze that follows the current of a stream, rustled the leaves of the only tree planted on the point of the Terrain, with a noise that was already perceptible. But they were still very close to danger. The nearest edifices to them were the bishop's palace and the church. It was plainly evident that there was great internal commotion in the bishop's palace. Its shadowy mass was all furrowed with lights that flitted from window to window; as, when one has just burned paper, there remains a sombre edifice of

ashes in which bright sparks run a thousand eccentric courses. Beside
them, the enormous towers of Notre-Dame, thus viewed from behind,
with the long nave above which they rise cut out in black against
the red and vast light which filled the Parvis, resembled two gigantic
andirons of some cyclopean fire-grate.

What was to be seen of Paris on all sides wavered before the eye
in a gloom mingled with light. Rembrandt has such backgrounds to
his pictures.

The man with the lantern walked straight to the point of the
Terrain. There, at the very brink of the water, stood the worm-eaten
remains of a fence of posts latticed with laths, whereon a low vine
spread out a few thin branches like the fingers of an outspread hand.
Behind, in the shadow cast by this trellis, a little boat lay concealed.
The man made a sign to Gringoire and his companion to enter. The
goat followed them. The man was the last to step in. Then he cut the
boat's moorings, pushed it from the shore with a long boat-hook, and,
seizing two oars, seated himself in the bow, rowing with all his might
toward midstream. The Seine is very rapid at this point, and he had a
good deal of trouble in leaving the point of the island.

Gringoire's first care on entering the boat was to place the goat on
his knees. He took a position in the stern; and the young girl, whom
the stranger inspired with an indefinable uneasiness, seated herself
close to the poet.

When our philosopher felt the boat sway, he clapped his hands
and kissed Djali between the horns.

"Oh!" said he, "now we are safe, all four of us."

He added with the air of a profound thinker, "One is indebted
sometimes to fortune, sometimes to ruse, for the happy issue of great
enterprises."

The boat made its way slowly toward the right shore. The young
girl watched the unknown man with secret terror. He had carefully
turned off the light of his dark lantern. A glimpse could be caught of
him in the obscurity, in the bow of the boat, like a spectre. His cowl,
which was still lowered, formed a sort of mask; and every time that he
spread his arms, upon which hung large black sleeves, as he rowed, one
would have said they were two huge bat's wings. Moreover, he had not
yet uttered a word or breathed a syllable. No other noise was heard in
the boat than the splashing of the oars, mingled with the rippling of
the water along her sides.

"On my soul!" exclaimed Gringoire suddenly, "we are as cheerful and joyous as young owls! We preserve the silence of Pythagoreans or fishes! *Pasque-Dieu*. My friends, I should greatly like to have some one speak to me. The human voice is music to the human ear. 'Tis not I who say that, but Didymus of Alexandria, and they are illustrious words. Assuredly, Didymus of Alexandria is no mediocre philosopher. One word, my lovely child! Say but one word to me, I entreat you. By the way, you had a droll and peculiar little pout; do you still make it? Do you know, my dear, that parliament hath full jurisdiction over all places of asylum, and that you were running a great risk in your little chamber at Notre-Dame? Alas, the little bird trochylus maketh its nest in the jaws of the crocodile. Master, here is the moon re-appearing. If only they do not perceive us. We are doing a laudable thing in saving mademoiselle, and yet we should be hung by order of the king if we were caught. Alas! Human actions are taken by two handles. That is branded with disgrace in one that is crowned in another. He admires Cicero who blames Catiline. Is it not so, master? What say you to this philosophy? I possess philosophy by instinct, by nature, *ut apes geometriam*. Come! No one answers me. What unpleasant moods you two are in! I must do all the talking alone. That is what we call a monologue in tragedy. *Pasque-Dieu*! I must inform you that I have just seen the king, Louis XI, and that I have caught this oath from him, *Pasque-Dieu*! They are still making a hearty howl in the city. 'Tis a villanous, malicious old king. He is all swathed in furs. He still owes me the money for my epithalamium, and he came within a nick of hanging me this evening, which would have been very inconvenient to me. He is niggardly toward men of merit. He ought to read the four books of Salvien of Cologne, *Adversits Avaritiam*. In truth! 'Tis a paltry king in his ways with men of letters, and one who commits very barbarous cruelties. He is a sponge, to soak money raised from the people. His saving is like the spleen that swelleth with the leanness of all the other members. Hence complaints against the hardness of the times become murmurs against the prince. Under this gentle and pious sire, the gallows crack with the hung, the blocks rot with blood, the prisons burst like over full bellies. This king hath one hand that grasps, and one which hangs. He is the procurator of Dame Tax and Monsieur Gibbet. The great are despoiled of their dignities, and the little incessantly overwhelmed with fresh oppressions. He is an exorbitant prince. I love not this monarch. And you, master?"

The man in black let the garrulous poet chatter on. He continued to struggle against the violent and narrow current, which separates the prow of the City and the stem of the island of Notre-Dame, which we call today the Isle St. Louis.

"By the way, master!" continued Gringoire suddenly. "At the moment when we arrived on the Parvis, through the enraged outcasts, did your reverence observe that poor little devil whose skull your deaf man was just cracking on the railing of the gallery of the kings? I am near sighted and I could not recognize him. Do you know who he could be?"

The stranger answered not a word. But he suddenly ceased rowing, his arms fell as though broken, his head sank on his breast, and la Esmeralda heard him sigh convulsively. She shuddered. She had heard such sighs before.

The boat, abandoned to itself, floated for several minutes with the stream. But the man in black finally recovered himself, seized the oars once more and began to row against the current. He doubled the point of the Isle of Notre-Dame, and made for the landing-place of the Port au Foin.

"Ah!" said Gringoire, "yonder is the Barbeau mansion. Stay, master, look: that group of black roofs which make such singular angles yonder, above that heap of black, fibrous grimy, dirty clouds, where the moon is completely crushed and spread out like the yolk of an egg whose shell is broken. 'Tis a fine mansion. There is a chapel crowned with a small vault full of very well carved enrichments. Above, you can see the bell tower, very delicately pierced. There is also a pleasant garden, which consists of a pond, an aviary, an echo, a mall, a labyrinth, a house for wild beasts, and a quantity of leafy alleys very agreeable to Venus. There is also a rascal of a tree which is called 'the lewd,' because it favored the pleasures of a famous princess and a constable of France, who was a gallant and a wit. Alas! We poor philosophers are to a constable as a plot of cabbages or a radish bed to the garden of the Louvre. What matters it, after all? Human life, for the great as well as for us, is a mixture of good and evil. Pain is always by the side of joy, the spondee by the dactyl. Master, I must relate to you the history of the Barbeau mansion. It ends in tragic fashion. It was in 1319, in the reign of Philippe V, the longest reign of the kings of France. The moral of the story is that the temptations of the flesh are pernicious and malignant. Let us not rest our glance too long on our neighbor's wife, however gratified our senses may be by her beauty. Fornication is a very libertine thought. Adultery is a prying into the pleasures of others. Oh, the noise yonder is redoubling!"

The tumult around Notre-Dame was, in fact, increasing. They listened. Cries of victory were heard with tolerable distinctness. All at once, a hundred torches, the light of which glittered upon the helmets of men at arms, spread over the church at all heights, on the towers, on the galleries, on the flying buttresses. These torches seemed to be in search of something; and soon distant clamors reached the fugitives distinctly: "The gypsy! The sorceress! Death to the gypsy!"

The unhappy girl dropped her head upon her hands, and the unknown began to row furiously toward the shore. Meanwhile our philosopher reflected. He clasped the goat in his arms, and gently drew away from the gypsy, who pressed closer and closer to him, as though to the only asylum which remained to her.

It is certain that Gringoire was enduring cruel perplexity. He was thinking that the goat also, "according to existing law," would be hung if recaptured; which would be a great pity, poor Djali! That he had thus two condemned creatures attached to him; that his companion asked no better than to take charge of the gypsy. A violent combat began between his thoughts, in which, like the Jupiter of the Iliad, he weighed in turn the gypsy and the goat; and he looked at them alternately with eyes moist with tears, saying between his teeth: "But I cannot save you both!"

A shock informed them that the boat had reached the land at last. The uproar still filled the city. The unknown rose, approached the gypsy, and endeavored to take her arm to assist her to alight. She repulsed him and clung to the sleeve of Gringoire, who, in his turn, absorbed in the goat, almost repulsed her. Then she sprang alone from the boat. She was so troubled that she did not know what she did or whither she was going. Thus she remained for a moment, stunned, watching the water flow past; when she gradually returned to her senses, she found herself alone on the wharf with the unknown. It appears that Gringoire had taken advantage of the moment of debarcation to slip away with the goat into the block of houses of the Rue Grenier-sur-l'Eau.

The poor gypsy shivered when she beheld herself alone with this man. She tried to speak, to cry out, to call Gringoire; her tongue was dumb in her mouth, and no sound left her lips. All at once she felt the stranger's hand on hers. It was a strong, cold hand. Her teeth chattered, she turned paler than the ray of moonlight that illuminated her. The man spoke not a word. He began to ascend toward the Place de Grève, holding her by the hand.

At that moment, she had a vague feeling that destiny is an irresistible force. She had no more resistance left in her, she allowed herself to be dragged along, running while he walked. At this spot the quay ascended. But it seemed to her as though she were descending a slope.

She gazed about her on all sides. Not a single passer-by. The quay was absolutely deserted. She heard no sound, she felt no people moving save in the tumultuous and glowing city, from which she was separated only by an arm of the Seine, and whence her name reached her, mingled with cries of "Death!" The rest of Paris was spread around her in great blocks of shadows.

Meanwhile, the stranger continued to drag her along with the same silence and the same rapidity. She had no recollection of any of the places where she was walking. As she passed before a lighted window, she made an effort, drew up suddenly, and cried out, "Help!"

The bourgeois who was standing at the window opened it, appeared there in his shirt with his lamp, stared at the quay with a stupid air, uttered some words which she did not understand, and closed his shutter again. It was her last gleam of hope extinguished.

The man in black did not utter a syllable; he held her firmly, and set out again at a quicker pace. She no longer resisted, but followed him, completely broken.

From time to time she called together a little strength, and said, in a voice broken by the unevenness of the pavement and the breathlessness of their flight, "Who are you? Who are you?" He made no reply.

They arrived thus, still keeping along the quay, at a tolerably spacious square. It was the Grève. In the middle, a sort of black, erect cross was visible; it was the gallows. She recognized all this, and saw where she was.

The man halted, turned toward her and raised his cowl.

"Oh!" she stammered, almost petrified, "I knew well that it was he again!"

It was the priest. He looked like the ghost of himself; that is an effect of the moonlight, it seems as though one beheld only the spectres of things in that light.

"Listen!" he said to her; and she shuddered at the sound of that fatal voice which she had not heard for a long time. He continued speaking with those brief and panting jerks, which betoken deep internal convulsions. "Listen! We are here. I am going to speak to you. This is the Grève. This is an extreme point. Destiny gives us to one another. I am going to decide as to your life; you will decide as to my soul. Here is a place, here is a night beyond which one sees nothing. Then listen to me. I am going to tell you ... In the first place, speak not to me of your Phoebus. (As he spoke thus he paced to and fro, like a man who cannot remain in one place, and dragged her after him.) Do not speak to me of him. Do you see? If you utter that name, I know not what I shall do, but it will be terrible."

Then, like a body that recovers its centre of gravity, he became motionless once more, but his words betrayed no less agitation. His voice grew lower and lower.

"Do not turn your head aside thus. Listen to me. It is a serious matter. In the first place, here is what has happened. All this will not be laughed at. I swear it to you. What was I saying? Remind me! Oh! There is a decree of Parliament which gives you back to the scaffold. I have just rescued you from their hands. But they are pursuing you. Look!"

He extended his arm toward the City. The search seemed, in fact, to be still in progress there. The uproar drew nearer; the tower of the lieutenant's house, situated opposite the Grève, was full of clamors and light, and soldiers could be seen running on the opposite quay with torches and these cries, "The gypsy! Where is the gypsy! Death! Death!"

"You see that they are in pursuit of you, and that I am not lying to you. I love you. Do not open your mouth; refrain from speaking to me rather, if it be only to tell me that you hate me. I have made up my mind not to hear that again. I have just saved you. Let me finish first. I can save you wholly. I have prepared everything. It is yours at will. If you wish, I can do it."

He broke off violently. "No, that is not what I should say!"

As he went with hurried step and made her hurry also, for he did not release her, he walked straight to the gallows, and pointed to it with his finger, "Choose between us two," he said, coldly.

She tore herself from his hands and fell at the foot of the gibbet, embracing that funereal support; then she half turned her beautiful head, and looked at the priest over her shoulder. One would have said that she was a Holy Virgin at the foot of the cross. The priest remained motionless, his finger still raised toward the gibbet, preserving his attitude like a statue. At length the gypsy said to him, "It causes me less horror than you do."

Then he allowed his arm to sink slowly, and gazed at the pavement in profound dejection.

"If these stones could speak," he murmured, "yes, they would say that a very unhappy man stands here."

He went on. The young girl, kneeling before the gallows, enveloped in her long flowing hair, let him speak on without interruption. He now had a gentle and plaintive accent that contrasted sadly with the haughty harshness of his features.

"I love you. Oh, how true that is! So nothing comes of that fire which burns my heart! Alas, young girl, night and day—yes, night and day I tell you—it is torture. Oh! I suffer too much, my poor child. 'Tis a thing deserving of compassion, I assure you. You see that I speak gently to you. I really wish that you should no longer cherish this horror of me. After all, if a man loves a woman, 'tis not his fault! Oh, my God! What! So you will never pardon me? You will always hate me? All is over then. It is that which renders me evil, do you see? And horrible to myself. You will not even look at me! You are thinking of something else, perchance, while I stand here and talk to you, shuddering on the brink of eternity for both of us! Above all things, do not speak to me of the officer!—I would cast myself at your knees, I would kiss not your feet, but the earth which is under your feet; I would sob like a child, I would tear from my breast not words, but my very heart and vitals, to tell you that I love you—all would be useless, all! And yet you have nothing in your heart but what is tender and merciful. You are radiant with the most beautiful mildness; you are wholly sweet, good, pitiful, and charming. Alas! You cherish no ill will for any one but me alone! Oh, what a fatality!"

He hid his face in his hands. The young girl heard him weeping. It was for the first time. Thus erect and shaken by sobs, he was more miserable and more suppliant than when on his knees. He wept thus for a considerable time.

"Come!" he said, these first tears passed, "I have no more words. I had, however, thought well as to what you would say. Now I tremble and shiver and break down at the decisive moment, I feel conscious of something supreme enveloping us, and I stammer. Oh! I shall fall upon the pavement if you do not take pity on me, pity on yourself. Do not condemn us both. If you only knew how much I love you! What a heart is mine! Oh! What desertion of all virtue! What desperate abandonment of myself! A doctor, I mock at science; a gentleman, I tarnish my own name; a priest, I make of the missal a pillow of sensuality, I spit in the face of my God! All this for thee, enchantress! To be more worthy of thy hell! And you will not have the apostate! Oh, let me tell you all! More still, something more horrible, oh! Yet more horrible! . . ."

As he uttered these last words, his air became utterly distracted. He was silent for a moment, and resumed, as though speaking to himself, and in a strong voice, "Cain, what hast thou done with thy brother?"

There was another silence, and he went on—"What have I done with him, Lord? I received him, I reared him, I nourished him, I loved him, I idolized him, and I have slain him! Yes, Lord, they have just dashed his head before my eyes on the stone of thine house, and it is because of me, because of this woman, because of her."

His eye was wild. His voice grew ever weaker; he repeated many times, yet, mechanically, at tolerably long intervals, like a bell prolonging its last vibration: "Because of her. Because of her."

Then his tongue no longer articulated any perceptible sound; but his lips still moved. All at once he sank together, like something crumbling, and lay motionless on the earth, with his head on his knees.

A touch from the young girl, as she drew her foot from under him, brought him to himself. He passed his hand slowly over his hollow cheeks, and gazed for several moments at his fingers, which were wet. "What!" he murmured, "I have wept!"

And turning suddenly to the gypsy with unspeakable anguish, "Alas! You have looked coldly on at my tears! Child, do you know that those tears are of lava? Is it indeed true? Nothing touches when it comes from the man whom one does not love. If you were to see me die, you would laugh. Oh! I do not wish to see you die! One word! A single word of pardon! Say not that you love me, say only that you will do it; that will suffice; I will save you. If not—oh! The hour is passing. I entreat you by all that is sacred, do not wait until I shall have turned to stone again, like that gibbet which also claims you! Reflect that I hold the destinies of both of us in my hand, that I am mad—it is terrible— that I may let all go to destruction, and that there is beneath us a bottomless abyss, unhappy girl, whither my fall will follow yours to all eternity! One word of kindness! Say one word! Only one word!"

She opened her mouth to answer him. He flung himself on his knees to receive with adoration the word, possibly a tender one, which was on the point of issuing from her lips. She said to him, "You are an assassin!"

The priest clasped her in his arms with fury, and began to laugh with an abominable laugh.

"Well, yes, an assassin!" he said, "and I will have you. You will not have me for your slave, you shall have me for your master. I will have you! I have a den, whither I will drag you. You will follow me, you will be obliged to follow me, or I will deliver you up! You must die, my beauty, or be mine! Belong to the priest! Belong to the apostate! Belong to the assassin! This very night, do you hear? Come, joy; kiss me, mad girl! The tomb or my bed!"

His eyes sparkled with impurity and rage. His lewd lips reddened the young girl's neck. She struggled in his arms. He covered her with furious kisses.

"Do not bite me, monster!" she cried. "Oh, the foul, odious monk! Leave me! I will tear out thy ugly gray hair and fling it in thy face by the handful!"

He reddened, turned pale, then released her and gazed at her with a gloomy air. She thought herself victorious, and continued, "I tell you that I belong to my Phoebus, that 'tis Phoebus whom I love, that 'tis Phoebus who is handsome! You are old, priest! You are ugly! Begone!"

He gave vent to a horrible cry, like the wretch to whom a hot iron is applied. "Die, then!" he said, gnashing his teeth. She saw his terrible look and tried to fly. He caught her once more, he shook her, he flung her on the ground, and walked with rapid strides toward the corner of the Tour-Roland, dragging her after him along the pavement by her beautiful hands.

On arriving there, he turned to her, "For the last time, will you be mine?"

She replied with emphasis, "No!"

Then he cried in a loud voice, "Gudule! Gudule! Here is the gypsy! Take your vengeance!"

The young girl felt herself seized suddenly by the elbow. She looked. A fleshless arm was stretched from an opening in the wall, and held her like a hand of iron.

"Hold her well," said the priest; "'tis the gypsy escaped. Release her not. I will go in search of the sergeants. You shall see her hanged."

A guttural laugh replied from the interior of the wall to these bloody words—"Hah! hah! hah!" The gypsy watched the priest retire in the direction of the Pont Notre-Dame. A cavalcade was heard in that direction.

The young girl had recognized the spiteful recluse. Panting with terror, she tried to disengage herself. She writhed, she made many starts of agony and despair, but the other held her with incredible strength. The lean and bony fingers which bruised her, clenched on her flesh and met around it. One would have said that this hand was riveted to her arm. It was more than a chain, more than a fetter, more than a ring of iron, it was a living pair of pincers endowed with intelligence, which emerged from the wall.

She fell back against the wall exhausted, and then the fear of death took possession of her. She thought of the beauty of life, of youth, of the view of heaven, the aspects of nature, of her love for Phoebus, of all that was vanishing and all that was approaching, of the priest who was denouncing her, of the headsman who was to come, of the gallows which was there. Then she felt terror mount to the very roots of her hair and she heard the mocking laugh of the recluse, saying to her in a very low tone: "Hah! hah! hah! You are going to be hanged!"

She turned a dying look toward the window, and she beheld the fierce face of the sacked nun through the bars.

"What have I done to you?" she said, almost lifeless.

The recluse did not reply, but began to mumble with a singsong irritated, mocking intonation: "Daughter of Egypt! Daughter of Egypt! Daughter of Egypt!"

The unhappy Esmeralda dropped her head beneath her flowing hair, comprehending that it was no human being she had to deal with.

All at once the recluse exclaimed, as though the gypsy's question had taken all this time to reach her brain—"'What have you done to me?' you say! Ah, what have you done to me, gypsy! Well, listen. I had a child! You see! I had a child! A child, I tell you—a pretty little girl! My Agnes!" she went on wildly, kissing something in the dark. "Well, do you see, daughter of Egypt? They took my child from me; they stole my child; they ate my child. That is what you have done to me."

The young girl replied like a lamb, "Alas! Perchance I was not born then!"

"Oh, yes!" returned the recluse. "You must have been born. You were among them. She would be the same age as you! So! I have been here fifteen years; fifteen years have I suffered; fifteen years have I prayed; fifteen years have I beat my head against these four walls—I tell you that 'twas the gypsies who stole her from me, do you hear that? And who ate her with their teeth. Have you a heart? Imagine a child playing, a child sucking; a child sleeping. It is so innocent a thing! Well, that, that is what they took from me, what they killed. The good God knows it well! Today, it is my turn; I am going to eat the gypsy. Oh! I would bite you well, if the bars did not prevent me! My head is too large! Poor little one! While she was asleep! And if they woke her up when they took her, in vain she might cry; I was not there! Ah! Gypsy mothers, you devoured my child! Come see your own."

Then she began to laugh or to gnash her teeth, for the two things resembled each other in that furious face. The day was beginning to dawn. An ashy gleam dimly lighted this scene, and the gallows grew more and more distinct in the square. On the other side, in the direction of the bridge of Notre-Dame, the poor condemned girl fancied that she heard the sound of cavalry approaching.

"Madam," she cried, clasping her hands and falling on her knees, dishevelled, distracted, mad with fright; "madam, have pity! They are coming. I have done nothing to you. Would you wish to see me die in this horrible fashion before your very eyes? You are pitiful, I am sure. It is too frightful. Let me make my escape. Release me! Mercy. I do not wish to die like that!"

"Give me back my child!" said the recluse.

"Mercy! Mercy!"

"Give me back my child!"

"Release me, in the name of heaven!"

"Give me back my child!"

Again the young girl fell; exhausted, broken, and having already the glassy eye of a person in the grave.

"Alas!" she faltered, "you seek your child, I seek my parents."

"Give me back my little Agnes!" pursued Gudule. "You do not know where she is? Then die! I will tell you. I was a woman of the town, I had a child, they took my child. It was the gypsies. You see plainly that you must die. When your mother, the gypsy, comes to reclaim you, I shall say to her: 'Mother, look at that gibbet! Or, give me back my child.' Do you know where she is, my little daughter? Stay! I will show you. Here is her shoe, all that is left me of her. Do you know where its mate is? If you know, tell me, and if it is only at the other end of the world, I will crawl to it on my knees."

As she spoke thus, with her other arm extended through the window, she showed the gypsy the little embroidered shoe. It was already light enough to distinguish its shape and its colors.

"Let me see that shoe," said the gypsy, quivering. "God! God!"

And at the same time, with her hand that was at liberty, she quickly opened the little bag ornamented with green glass, which she wore about her neck.

"Go on, go on!" grumbled Gudule. "Search your demon's amulet!"

All at once, she stopped short, trembled in every limb, and cried in a voice which proceeded from the very depths of her being: "My daughter!"

The gypsy had just drawn from the bag a little shoe absolutely similar to the other. To this little shoe was attached a parchment on which was inscribed this charm:

> When thou shalt find its mate,
> thy mother will stretch out her arms to thee.

Quicker than a flash of lightning, the recluse had laid the two shoes together, had read the parchment and had put close to the bars of the window her face beaming with celestial joy as she cried, "My daughter! My daughter!"

"My mother!" said the gypsy.

Here we are unequal to the task of depicting the scene. The wall and the iron bars were between them. "Oh, the wall!" cried the recluse. "Oh, to see her and not to embrace her! Your hand! Your hand!"

The young girl passed her arm through the opening; the recluse threw herself on that hand, pressed her lips to it and there remained, buried in that kiss, giving no other sign of life than a sob which heaved her breast from time to time. In the meanwhile, she wept in torrents, in silence, in the dark, like a rain at night. The poor mother poured out in floods upon that adored hand the dark and deep well of tears, which lay within her, and into which her grief had filtered, drop by drop, for fifteen years.

All at once she rose, flung aside her long gray hair from her brow, and without uttering a word, began to shake the bars of her cage cell, with both hands, more furiously than a lioness. The bars held firm. Then she went to seek in the corner of her cell a huge paving stone, which served her as a pillow, and launched it against them with such violence that one of the bars broke, emitting thousands of sparks. A second blow completely shattered the old iron cross which barricaded the window. Then with her two hands, she finished breaking and removing the rusted stumps of the bars. There are moments when woman's hands possess superhuman strength.

A passage broken, less than a minute was required for her to seize her daughter by the middle of her body, and draw her into her cell. "Come let me draw you out of the abyss," she murmured.

When her daughter was inside the cell, she laid her gently on the ground, then raised her up again, and bearing her in her arms as though she were still only her little Agnès, she walked to and fro in her little room, intoxicated, frantic, joyous, crying out, singing, kissing her daughter, talking to her, bursting into laughter, melting into tears, all at once and with vehemence.

"My daughter! My daughter!" she said. "I have my daughter! Here she is! The good God has given her back to me! Ha! Come all of you! Is there any one there to see that I have my daughter? Lord Jesus, how beautiful she is! You have made me wait fifteen years, my good God, but it was in order to give her back to me beautiful. Then the gypsies did not eat her! Who said so? My little daughter! My little daughter! Kiss me. Those good gypsies! I love the gypsies! It is really you! That was what made my heart leap every time that you passed by. And I took that for hatred! Forgive me, my Agnès, forgive me. You thought me very malicious, did you not? I love you. Have you still the little mark on your neck? Let us see. She still has it. Oh! You are beautiful! It was I who gave you those big eyes, mademoiselle. Kiss me. I love you. It is nothing to me that other mothers have children; I scorn them now. They have only to come and see. Here is mine. See her neck, her eyes, her hair, her hands. Find me anything as beautiful as that! Oh! I promise you she will have lovers, that she will! I have wept for fifteen years. All my beauty has departed and has fallen to her. Kiss me."

She addressed to her a thousand other extravagant remarks, whose accent constituted their sole beauty, disarranged the poor girl's garments even to the point of making her blush, smoothed her silky hair with her hand, kissed her foot, her knee, her brow, her eyes, was in raptures over everything. The young girl let her have her way, repeating at intervals and very low and with infinite tenderness, "My mother!"

"Do you see, my little girl," resumed the recluse, interspersing her words with kisses, "I shall love you dearly? We will go away from here. We are going to be very happy. I have inherited something in Reims, in our country. You know Reims? Ah, no, you do not know it; you were too small! If you only knew how pretty you were at the age of four months! Tiny feet that people came even from Epernay, which is seven leagues away, to see! We shall have a field, a house. I will put you to sleep in my bed. My God! My God! Who would believe this? I have my daughter!"

"Oh, my mother!" said the young girl, at length finding strength to speak in her emotion, "the gypsy woman told me so. There was a good gypsy of our band who died last year, and who always cared for me like a nurse. It was she who placed this little bag about my neck. She always said to me: 'Little one, guard this jewel well! 'Tis a treasure. It will cause thee to find thy mother once again. Thou wearest thy mother about thy neck.' The gypsy predicted it!"

The sacked nun again pressed her daughter in her arms.

"Come, let me kiss you! You say that prettily. When we are in the country, we will place these little shoes on an infant Jesus in the church. We certainly owe that to the good, holy Virgin. What a pretty voice you have! When you spoke to me just now, it was music! Ah! My Lord God! I have found my child again! But is this story credible? Nothing will kill one—or I should have died of joy."

And then she began to clap her hands again and to laugh and to cry out: "We are going to be so happy!"

At that moment, the cell resounded with the clang of arms and a galloping of horses that seemed to be coming from the Pont Notre-Dame, amid advancing farther and farther along the quay. The gypsy threw herself with anguish into the arms of the sacked nun.

"Save me! Save me! Mother! They are coming!"

"Oh, heaven! What are you saying? I had forgotten! They are in pursuit of you! What have you done?"

"I know not," replied the unhappy child; "but I am condemned to die."

"To die!" said Gudule, staggering as though struck by lightning. "To die!" she repeated slowly, gazing at her daughter with staring eyes.

"Yes, mother," replied the frightened young girl, "they want to kill me. They are coming to seize me. That gallows is for me! Save me! Save me! They are coming! Save me!"

The recluse remained for several moments motionless and petrified, then she moved her head in sign of doubt, and suddenly giving vent to a burst of laughter, but with that terrible laugh which had come back to her, "Ho, ho, no! 'Tis a dream of which you are telling me. Ah, yes! I lost her, that lasted fifteen years, and then I found her again, and that lasted a minute! And they would take her from me again! And now, when she is beautiful, when she is grown up, when she speaks to me, when she loves me; it is now that they would come to devour her, before my very eyes, and I her mother! Oh, no! These things are not possible. The good God does not permit such things as that."

Here the cavalcade appeared to halt, and a voice was heard to say in the distance, "This way, Messire Tristan! The priest says that we shall find her at the Rat-Hole." The noise of the horses began again.

The recluse sprang to her feet with a shriek of despair. "Fly! Fly! My child! All comes back to me. You are right. It is your death! Horror! Maledictions! Fly!"

She thrust her head through the window, and withdrew it again hastily.

"Remain," she said, in a low, curt, and lugubrious tone, as she pressed the hand of the gypsy, who was more dead than alive. "Remain! Do not breathe! There are soldiers everywhere. You cannot get out. It is too light."

Her eyes were dry and burning. She remained silent for a moment; but she paced the cell hurriedly, and halted now and then to pluck out handfuls of her gray hairs, which she afterwards tore with her teeth.

Suddenly she said: "They draw near. I will speak with them. Hide yourself in this corner. They will not see you. I will tell them that you have made your escape. That I released you, in faith!"

She set her daughter down (for she was still carrying her) in one corner of the cell that was not visible from without. She made her crouch down, arranged her carefully so that neither foot nor hand projected from the shadow, untied her black hair which she spread over her white robe to conceal it, placed in front of her her jug and her paving stone, the only articles of furniture which she possessed, imagining that this jug and stone would hide her. And when this was finished she became more tranquil, and knelt down to pray. The day, which was only dawning, still left many shadows in the Rat-Hole.

At that moment, the voice of the priest, that infernal voice, passed very close to the cell, crying, "This way, Captain Phoebus de Châteaupers."

At that name, at that voice, la Esmeralda, crouching in her corner, made a movement.

"Do not stir!" said Gudule.

She had barely finished when a tumult of men, swords, and horses halted around the cell. The mother rose quickly and went to post herself before her window, in order to stop it up. She beheld a large troop of armed men, both horse and foot, drawn up on the Grève.

The commander dismounted, and came toward her.

"Old woman!" said this man, who had an atrocious face. "We are in search of a witch to hang her; we were told that you had her."

The poor mother assumed as indifferent an air as she could, and replied, "I know not what you mean."

The other resumed, "*Tête-Dieu!* What was it that frightened archdeacon said? Where is he?"

"Monseigneur," said a soldier, "he has disappeared."

"Come, now, old madwoman," began the commander again, "do not lie. A sorceress was given in charge to you. What have you done with her?"

The recluse did not wish to deny all, for fear of awakening suspicion, and replied in a sincere and surly tone, "If you are speaking of a big young girl who was put into my hands a while ago, I will tell you that she bit me, and that I released her. There! Leave me in peace."

The commander made a grimace of disappointment. "Don't lie to me, old spectre!" said he. "My name is Tristan l'Hermite, and I am the king's gossip. Tristan the Hermit, do you hear?" He added, as he glanced at the Place de Grève around him, "'Tis a name which has an echo here."

"You might be Satan the Hermit," replied Gudule, who was regaining hope, "but I should have nothing else to say to you, and I should never be afraid of you."

"*Tête-Dieu,*" said Tristan, "here is a crone! Ah! So the witch girl hath fled! And in which direction did she go?"

Gudule replied in a careless tone, "Through the Rue du Mouton, I believe."

Tristan turned his head and made a sign to his troop to prepare to set out on the march again. The recluse breathed freely once more.

"Monseigneur," suddenly said an archer, "ask the old elf why the bars of her window are broken in this manner."

This question brought anguish again to the heart of the miserable mother. Nevertheless, she did not lose all presence of mind.

"They have always been thus," she stammered.

"Bah!" retorted the archer, "only yesterday they still formed a fine black cross, which inspired devotion."

Tristan cast a sidelong glance at the recluse.

"I think the old dame is getting confused!"

The unfortunate woman felt that all depended on her self-possession, and, although with death in her soul, she began to grin. Mothers possess such strength.

"Bah!" said she, "the man is drunk. 'Tis more than a year since the tail of a stone cart dashed against my window and broke in the grating. And how I cursed the carter, too."

"'Tis true," said another archer, "I was there."

Always and everywhere people are to be found who have seen everything. This unexpected testimony from the archer re-encouraged the recluse, whom this interrogatory was forcing to cross an abyss on the edge of a knife. But she was condemned to a perpetual alternative of hope and alarm.

"If it was a cart that did it," retorted the first soldier, "the stumps of the bars should be thrust inwards, while they actually are pushed outwards."

"Ho, ho!" said Tristan to the soldier. "You have the nose of an inquisitor of the Châtelet. Reply to what he says, old woman."

"Good heavens!" she exclaimed, driven to bay, and in a voice that was full of tears in despite of her efforts, "I swear to you, monseigneur, that 'twas a cart which broke those bars. You hear the man who saw it. And then, what has that to do with your gypsy?"

"Hum!" growled Tristan.

"The devil!" went on the soldier, flattered by the provost's praise. "These fractures of the iron are perfectly fresh."

Tristan tossed his head. She turned pale.

"How long ago, say you, did the cart do it?"

"A month, a fortnight, perhaps, monseigheur, I know not."

"She first said more than a year," observed the soldier.

"That is suspicious," said the provost.

"Monseigneur!" she cried, still pressed against the opening, and trembling lest suspicion should lead them to thrust their heads through and look into her cell. "Monseigneur, I swear to you that 'twas a cart which broke this grating. I swear it to you by the angels of paradise. If it was not a cart, may I be eternally damned, and I reject God!"

"You put a great deal of heat into that oath," said Tristan, with his inquisitorial glance.

The poor woman felt her assurance vanishing more and more. She had reached the point of blundering, and she comprehended with terror that she was saying what she ought not to have said.

Here another soldier came up, crying, "Monsieur, the old hag lies. The sorceress did not flee through the Rue de Mouton. The street chain has remained stretched all night, and the chain guard has seen no one pass."

Tristan, whose face became more sinister with every moment, addressed the recluse, "What have you to say to that?"

She tried to make head against this new incident,

"That I do not know, monseigneur; that I may have been mistaken. I believe, in fact, that she crossed the water."

"That is in the opposite direction," said the provost, "and it is not very likely that she would wish to re-enter the city, where she was being pursued. You are lying, old woman."

"And then," added the first soldier, "there is no boat either on this side of the stream or on the other."

"She swam across," replied the recluse, defending her ground foot by foot.

"Do women swim?" said the soldier.

"*Tête-Dieu*, old woman! You are lying!" repeated Tristan angrily. "I have a good mind to abandon that sorceress and take you. A quarter of an hour of torture will, perchance, draw the truth from your throat. Come! You are to follow us."

She seized on these words with avidity.

"As you please, monseigneur. Do it. Do it. Torture. I am willing. Take me away. Quick, quick! Let us set out at once! During that time," she said to herself, "my daughter will make her escape."

"'S death!" said the provost, "what an appetite for the rack! I understand not this madwoman at all."

An old, gray-haired sergeant of the guard stepped out of the ranks, and addressing the provost, "Mad in sooth, monseigneur. If she released the gypsy, it was not her fault, for she loves not the gypsies. I have been of the watch these fifteen years, and I hear her every evening cursing the Bohemian women with endless imprecations. If the one of whom we are in pursuit is, as I suppose, the little dancer with the goat, she detests that one above all the rest."

Gudule made an effort and said, "That one above all."

The unanimous testimony of the men of the watch confirmed the old sergeant's words to the provost. Tristan l'Hermite, in despair at extracting anything from the recluse, turned his back on her, and with unspeakable anxiety she beheld him direct his course slowly toward his horse.

"Come!" he said, between his teeth "March on! Let us set out again on the quest. I shall not sleep until that gypsy is hanged."

But he still hesitated for some time before mounting his horse. Gudule palpitated between life and death, as she beheld him cast about the Place that uneasy look of a hunting dog that instinctively feels that the lair of the beast is close to him, and is loath to go away. At length he shook his head and leaped into his saddle. Gudule's horribly compressed heart now dilated, and she said in a low voice, as she cast a glance at her daughter, whom she had not ventured to look at while they were there, "Saved!"

The poor child had remained all this time in her corner, without breathing, without moving, with the idea of death before her. She had lost nothing of the scene between Gudule and Tristan, and the anguish of her mother had found its echo in her heart. She had heard all the successive snappings of the thread by which she hung suspended over the gulf; twenty times she had fancied that she saw it break, and at last she began to breathe again and to feel her foot on firm ground. At that moment she heard a voice saying to the provost: "*Corboeuf*! Monsieur le Prevôt, 'tis no affair of mine, a man of arms, to hang witches. The rabble of the populace is suppressed. I leave you to attend to the matter alone. You will allow me to rejoin my company, who are waiting for their captain."

The voice was that of Phoebus de Châteaupers; that which took place within her was ineffable. He was there, her friend, her protector, her support, her refuge, her Phoebus. She rose, and before her mother could prevent her, she had rushed to the window, crying, "Phoebus! Aid me, my Phoebus!"

Phoebus was no longer there. He had just turned the corner of the Rue de la Coutellerie at a gallop. But Tristan had not yet taken his departure.

The recluse rushed upon her daughter with a roar of agony. She dragged her violently back, digging her nails into her neck. A tigress mother does not stand on trifles. But it was too late. Tristan had seen.

"Ha!" he exclaimed with a laugh that laid bare all his teeth and made his face resemble the muzzle of a wolf. "Two mice in the trap!"

"I suspected as much," said the soldier.

Tristan clapped him on the shoulder, "You are a good cat! Come!" he added, "where is Henriet Cousin?"

A man who had neither the garments nor the air of a soldier, stepped from the ranks. He wore a costume half gray, half brown, flat hair, leather sleeves, and carried a bundle of ropes in his huge hand. This man always attended Tristan, who always attended Louis XI.

"Friend," said Tristan l'Hermite, "I presume that this is the sorceress of whom we are in search. You will hang me this one. Have you your ladder?"

"There is one yonder, under the shed of the Pillar-House," replied the man. "Is it on this justice that the thing is to be done?" he added, pointing to the stone gibbet.

"Yes."

"Ho," continued the man with a huge laugh, which was still more brutal than that of the provost. "We shall not have far to go."

"Make haste!" said Tristan, "you shall laugh afterwards."

In the meantime, the recluse had not uttered another word since Tristan had seen her daughter and all hope was lost. She had flung the poor gypsy, half dead, into the corner of the cellar, and had placed herself once more at the window with both hands resting on the angle of the sill like two claws. In this attitude she was seen to cast upon all those soldiers her glance that had become wild and frantic once more. At the moment when Rennet Cousin approached her cell, she showed him so savage a face that he shrank back.

"Monseigneur," he said, returning to the provost, "which am I to take?"

"The young one."

"So much the better, for the old one seemeth difficult."

"Poor little dancer with the goat!" said the old sergeant of the watch.

Rennet Cousin approached the window again. The mother's eyes made his own droop. He said with a good deal of timidity, "Madam—"

She interrupted him in a very low but furious voice, "What do you ask?"

"It is not you," he said, "it is the other."

"What other?"

"The young one."

She began to shake her head, crying, "There is no one! There is no one! There is no one!"

"Yes, there is!" retorted the hangman, "and you know it well. Let me take the young one. I have no wish to harm you."

She said, with a strange sneer, "Ah, so you have no wish to harm me!"

"Let me have the other, madam; 'tis monsieur the provost who wills it."

She repeated with a look of madness, "There is no one here."

"I tell you that there is!" replied the executioner. "We have all seen that there are two of you."

"Look then!" said the recluse, with a sneer. "Thrust your head through the window."

The executioner observed the mother's finger-nails and dared not.

"Make haste!" shouted Tristan, who had just ranged his troops in a circle round the Rat-Hole, and who sat on his horse beside the gallows.

Rennet returned once more to the provost in great embarrassment. He had flung his rope on the ground, and was twisting his hat between his hands with an awkward air.

"Monseigneur," he asked, "where am I to enter?"

"By the door."

"There is none."

"By the window."

"'Tis too small."

"Make it larger," said Tristan angrily. "Have you not pickaxes?"

The mother still looked on steadfastly from the depths of her cavern. She no longer hoped for anything, she no longer knew what she wished, except that she did not wish them to take her daughter.

Rennet Cousin went in search of the chest of tools for the night man, under the shed of the Pillar-House. He drew from it also the

double ladder, which he immediately set up against the gallows. Five or
six of the provost's men armed themselves with picks and crowbars, and
Tristan betook himself, in company with them, toward the window.

"Old woman," said the provost, in a severe tone, "deliver up to us
that girl quietly."

She looked at him like one who does not understand.

"*Tête-Dieu!*" continued Tristan, "why do you try to prevent this
sorceress being hung as it pleases the king?"

The wretched woman began to laugh in her wild way.

"Why? She is my daughter."

The tone in which she pronounced these words made even
Henriet Cousin shudder.

"I am sorry for that," said the provost, "but it is the king's good
pleasure."

She cried, redoubling her terrible laugh, "What is your king to
me? I tell you that she is my daughter!"

"Pierce the wall," said Tristan.

In order to make a sufficiently wide opening, it sufficed to dislodge
one course of stone below the window. When the mother heard the
picks and crowbars mining her fortress, she uttered a terrible cry; then
she began to stride about her cell with frightful swiftness, a wild beasts'
habit which her cage had imparted to her. She no longer said anything,
but her eyes flamed. The soldiers were chilled to the very soul.

All at once she seized her paving stone, laughed, and hurled it with
both fists upon the workmen. The stone, badly flung (for her hands
trembled), touched no one, and fell short under the feet of Tristan's
horse. She gnashed her teeth.

In the meantime, although the sun had not yet risen, it was broad
daylight; a beautiful rose color enlivened the ancient, decayed chimneys
of the Pillar-House. It was the hour when the earliest windows of the
great city open joyously on the roofs. Some workmen, a few fruit-sellers
on their way to the markets on their asses, began to traverse the Grève;
they halted for a moment before this group of soldiers clustered round
the Rat-Hole, stared at it with an air of astonishment and passed on.

The recluse had gone and seated herself by her daughter, covering
her with her body, in front of her, with staring eyes, listening to the
poor child, who did not stir, but who kept murmuring in a low voice,
these words only, "Phoebus! Phoebus!" In proportion as the work of
the demolishers seemed to advance, the mother mechanically retreated,

and pressed the young girl closer and closer to the wall. All at once, the recluse beheld the stone (for she was standing guard and never took her eyes from it), move, and she heard Tristan's voice encouraging the workers. Then she aroused from the depression into which she had fallen during the last few moments, cried out, and as she spoke, her voice now rent the ear like a saw, then stammered as though all kind of maledictions were pressing to her lips to burst forth at once.

"Ho, ho, ho! Why this is terrible! You are ruffians! Are you really going to take my daughter? Oh, the cowards! Oh, the hangman lackeys! The wretched, blackguard assassins! Help! Help! Fire! Will they take my child from me like this? Who is it then who is called the good God?"

Then, addressing Tristan, foaming at the mouth, with wild eyes, all bristling and on all fours like a female panther, "Draw near and take my daughter! Do not you understand that this woman tells you that she is my daughter? Do you know what it is to have a child? Eh, lynx, have you never lain with your female? Have you never had a cub? And if you have little ones, when they howl have you nothing in your vitals that moves?"

"Throw down the stone," said Tristan. "It no longer holds."

The crowbars raised the heavy course. It was, as we have said, the mother's last bulwark.

She threw herself upon it, she tried to hold it back; she scratched the stone with her nails, but the massive block, set in movement by six men, escaped her and glided gently to the ground along the iron levers.

The mother, perceiving an entrance effected, fell down in front of the opening, barricading the breach with her body, beating the pavement with her head, and shrieking with a voice rendered so hoarse by fatigue that it was hardly audible, "Help! Fire! Fire!"

"Now take the wench," said Tristan, still impassive.

The mother gazed at the soldiers in such formidable fashion that they were more inclined to retreat than to advance.

"Come, now," repeated the provost. "Here you, Rennet Cousin!"

No one took a step.

The provost swore, "*Tête de Christ*! My men of war! Afraid of a woman!"

"Monseigneur," said Rennet, "do you call that a woman?"

"She has the mane of a lion," said another.

"Come!" repeated the provost, "the gap is wide enough. Enter three abreast, as at the breach of Pontoise. Let us make an end of it, death of Mahom! I will make two pieces of the first man who draws back!"

Placed between the provost and the mother, both threatening, the soldiers hesitated for a moment, then took their resolution, and advanced toward the Rat-Hole.

When the recluse saw this, she rose abruptly on her knees, flung aside her hair from her face, then let her thin flayed hands fall by her side. Then great tears fell, one by one, from her eyes; they flowed down her cheeks through a furrow, like a torrent through a bed that it has hollowed for itself.

At the same time she began to speak, but in a voice so supplicating, so gentle, so submissive, so heartrending, that more than one old convict-warder around Tristan who must have devoured human flesh wiped his eyes.

"Messeigneurs! Messieurs the sergeants, one word. There is one thing that I must say to you. She is my daughter, do you see? My dear little daughter whom I had lost! Listen. It is quite a history. Consider that I knew the sergeants very well. They were always good to me in the days when the little boys threw stones at me, because I led a life of pleasure. Do you see? You will leave me my child when you know! I was a poor woman of the town. It was the Bohemians who stole her from me. And I kept her shoe for fifteen years. Stay, here it is. That was the kind of foot she had. At Reims! La Chantefleurie! Rue Folle-Peine! Perchance, you knew about that. It was I. In your youth, then, there was a merry time, when one passed good hours. You will take pity on me, will you not, gentlemen? The gypsies stole her from me; they hid her from me for fifteen years. I thought her dead. Fancy, my good friends, believed her to be dead. I have passed fifteen years here in this cellar, without a fire in winter. It is hard. The poor, dear little shoe! I have cried so much that the good God has heard me. This night he has given my daughter back to me. It is a miracle of the good God. She was not dead. You will not take her from me, I am sure. If it were myself, I would say nothing; but she, a child of sixteen! Leave her time to see the sun! What has she done to you? Nothing at all. Nor have I. If you did but know that she is all I have, that I am old, that she is a blessing that the Holy Virgin has sent to me! And then, you are all so good! You did not know that she was my daughter; but now you do know it. Oh! I love her! Monsieur, the grand provost. I would prefer a stab in my own vitals to a scratch on her finger! You have the air of such a good lord! What I have told you explains the matter, does it not? Oh! If you have had a mother, monsiegneur! You are the captain, leave me my child! Consider that I pray you on my knees, as one prays to Jesus Christ! I ask nothing of any one; I am from Reims, gentlemen; I own a little field inherited from my uncle, Mahiet Pradon. I am no beggar. I wish nothing, but I do want my child! Oh, I want to keep my child! The good God, who is the master, has not given her back to me for nothing! The king! You say the king! It would not cause him much pleasure to have my little daughter killed! She is my daughter! She is my own daughter! She belongs not to the king! She is not yours! I want to go away! We want to go away! And when two women pass, one a mother and the other a daughter, one lets them go! Let us pass! We belong in Reims. Oh, you are very good, messieurs the sergeants, I love you all. You will not take my dear little one, it is impossible! It is utterly impossible, is it not? My child, my child!"

We will not try to give an idea of her gestures, her tone, of the tears which she swallowed as she spoke, of the hands which she clasped and then wrung, of the heart-breaking smiles, of the swimming glances, of the groans, the sighs, the miserable and affecting cries which she mingled with her disordered, wild, and incoherent words. When she became silent Tristan l'Hermite frowned, but it was to conceal a tear that welled up in his tiger's eye. He conquered this weakness, however, and said in a curt tone, "The king wills it."

Then he bent down to the ear of Rennet Cousin, and said to him in a very low tone, "Make an end of it quickly!" Possibly, the redoubtable provost felt his heart also failing him.

The executioner and the sergeants entered the cell. The mother offered no resistance, only she dragged herself toward her daughter and threw herself bodily upon her. The gypsy beheld the soldiers approach. The horror of death reanimated her. "Mother!" she shrieked, in a tone of indescribable distress, "Mother! They are coming! Defend me!"

"Yes, my love, I am defending you!" replied the mother, in a dying voice; and clasping her closely in her arms, she covered her with kisses. The two lying thus on the earth, the mother upon the daughter, presented a spectacle worthy of pity.

Rennet Cousin grasped the young girl by the middle of her body, beneath her beautiful shoulders. When she felt that hand, she cried, "Heuh!" and fainted. The executioner who was shedding large tears upon her, drop by drop, was about to bear her away in his arms. He tried to detach the mother, who had, so to speak, knotted her hands around her daughter's waist; but she clung so strongly to her child, that it was impossible to separate them. Then Rennet Cousin dragged the young girl outside the cell, and the mother after her. The mother's eyes were also closed.

At that moment, the sun rose, and there was already on the Place a fairly numerous assembly of people who looked on from a distance at what was being thus dragged along the pavement to the gibbet. For that was Provost Tristan's way at executions. He had a passion for preventing the approach of the curious.

There was no one at the windows. Only at a distance, at the summit of that one of the towers of Notre-Dame which commands the Grève, two men outlined in black against the light morning sky, and who seemed to be looking on, were visible.

Rennet Cousin paused at the foot of the fatal ladder, with that which he was dragging, and, barely breathing, with so much pity did the thing inspire him, he passed the rope around the lovely neck of the young girl. The unfortunate child felt the horrible touch of the hemp. She raised her eyelids, and saw the fleshless arm of the stone gallows extended above her head. Then she shook herself and shrieked in a loud and heartrending voice: "No! No! I will not!" Her mother, whose head was buried and concealed in her daughter's garments, said not a word; only her whole body could be seen to quiver, and she was heard to redouble her kisses on her child. The executioner took advantage of this moment to hastily loose the arms with which she clasped the condemned girl. Either through exhaustion or despair, she let him have his way. Then he took the young girl on his shoulder, from which the charming creature hung, gracefully bent over his large head. Then he set his foot on the ladder in order to ascend.

At that moment, the mother who was crouching on the pavement opened her eyes wide. Without uttering a cry, she raised herself erect with a terrible expression; then she flung herself upon the hand of the executioner, like a beast on its prey, and bit it. It was done like a flash of lightning. The headsman howled with pain. Those near by rushed up. With difficulty they withdrew his bleeding hand from the mother's teeth. She preserved a profound silence. They thrust her back with much brutality, and noticed that her head fell heavily on the pavement. They raised her, she fell back again. She was dead.

The executioner, who had not loosed his hold on the young girl, began to ascend the ladder once more.

CHAPTER 2

The Beautiful Creature Clad in White

WHEN QUASIMODO SAW that the cell was empty, that the gypsy was no longer there, that while he had been defending her she had been abducted, he grasped his hair with both hands and stamped with surprise and pain; then he set out to run through the entire church seeking his Bohemian, howling strange cries to all the corners of the walls, strewing his red hair on the pavement. It was just at the moment when the king's archers were making their victorious entrance into Notre-Dame, also in search of the gypsy. Quasimodo, poor, deaf fellow, aided them in their fatal intentions, without suspecting it; he thought that the outcasts were the gypsy's enemies. He himself conducted Tristan l'Hermite to all possible hiding-places, opened to him the secret doors, the double bottoms of the altars, the rear sacristries. If the unfortunate girl had still been there, it would have been he himself who would have delivered her up.

When the fatigue of finding nothing had disheartened Tristan, who was not easily discouraged, Quasimodo continued the search alone. He made the tour of the church twenty times, length and breadth, up and down, ascending and descending, running, calling, shouting, peeping, rummaging, ransacking, thrusting his head into every hole, pushing a torch under every vault, despairing, mad. A male who has lost his female is no more roaring nor more haggard.

At last when he was sure, perfectly sure that she was no longer there, that all was at an end, that she had been snatched from him, he slowly mounted the staircase to the towers, that staircase which he had ascended with so much eagerness and triumph on the day when he had saved her. He passed those same places once more with drooping head, voiceless, tearless, almost breathless. The church was again deserted, and had fallen back into its silence. The archers had quitted it to track the sorceress in the city. Quasimodo, left alone in that vast Notre-Dame, so besieged and tumultuous but a short time before, once more betook himself to the cell where the gypsy had slept for so many weeks under his guardianship.

As he approached it, he fancied that he might, perhaps, find her there. When, at the turn of the gallery which opens on the roof of the side aisles, he perceived the tiny cell with its little window and its little door crouching beneath a great flying buttress like a bird's nest under a branch, the poor man's heart failed him, and he leaned against a pillar to keep from falling. He imagined that she might have returned thither, that some good genius had, no doubt, brought her back, that this chamber was too tranquil, too safe, too charming for her not to be there, and he dared not take another step for fear of destroying his illusion. "Yes," he said to himself, "perchance she is sleeping, or praying. I must not disturb her."

At length he summoned up courage, advanced on tiptoe, looked, entered. Empty. The cell was still empty. The unhappy deaf man walked slowly round it, lifted the bed and looked beneath it, as though she might be concealed between the pavement and the mattress, then he shook his head and remained stupefied. All at once, he crushed his torch under his foot, and, without uttering a word, without giving vent to a sigh, he flung himself at full speed, head foremost against the wall, and fell fainting on the floor.

When he recovered his senses, he threw himself on the bed and rolling about, he kissed frantically the place where the young girl had slept and which was still warm; he remained there for several moments as motionless as though he were about to expire; then he rose, dripping with perspiration, panting, mad, and began to beat his head against the wall with the frightful regularity of the clapper of his bells, and the resolution of a man determined to kill himself. At length he fell a second time, exhausted; he dragged himself on his knees outside the cell, and crouched down facing the door, in an attitude of astonishment.

He remained thus for more than an hour without making a movement, with his eye fixed on the deserted cell, more gloomy, and more pensive than a mother seated between an empty cradle and a full coffin. He uttered not a word; only at long intervals, a sob heaved his body violently, but it was a tearless sob, like summer lightning that makes no noise.

It appears to have been then, that, seeking at the bottom of his lonely thoughts for the unexpected abductor of the gypsy, he thought of the archdeacon. He remembered that Dom Claude alone possessed a key to the staircase leading to the cell; he recalled his nocturnal attempts on the young girl, in the first of which he, Quasimodo, had assisted, the second of which he had prevented. He recalled a thousand details, and soon he no longer doubted that the archdeacon had taken the gypsy. Nevertheless, such was his respect for the priest, such his gratitude, his devotion, his love for this man had taken such deep root in his heart, that they resisted, even at this moment, the talons of jealousy and despair.

He reflected that the archdeacon had done this thing, and the wrath of blood and death which it would have evoked in him against any other person, turned in the poor deaf man, from the moment when Claude Frollo was in question, into an increase of grief and sorrow.

At the moment when his thought was thus fixed upon the priest, while the daybreak was whitening the flying buttresses, he perceived on the highest story of Notre-Dame, at the angle formed by the external balustrade as it makes the turn of the chancel, a figure walking. This figure was coming toward him. He recognized it. It was the archdeacon.

Claude was walking with a slow, grave step. He did not look before him as he walked, he was directing his course toward the northern tower, but his face was turned aside toward the right bank of the Seine, and he held his head high, as though trying to see something over the roofs. The owl often assumes this oblique attitude. It flies toward one point and looks toward another. In this manner the priest passed above Quasimodo without seeing him.

The deaf man, who had been petrified by this sudden apparition, beheld him disappear through the door of the staircase to the north tower. The reader is aware that this is the tower from which the Hôtel-de-Ville is visible. Quasimodo rose and followed the archdeacon.

Quasimodo ascended the tower staircase for the sake of ascending it, for the sake of seeing why the priest was ascending it. Moreover, the poor bellringer did not know what Quasimodo should do, what he should say, what he wished. He was full of fury and full of fear. The archdeacon and the gypsy had come into conflict in his heart.

When he reached the summit of the tower, before emerging from the shadow of the staircase and stepping upon the platform, he cautiously examined the position of the priest. The priest's back was turned to him. There is an openwork balustrade that surrounds the platform of the bell tower. The priest, whose eyes looked down upon the town, was resting his breast on that one of the four sides of the balustrades which looks upon the Pont Notre-Dame.

Quasimodo, advancing with the tread of a wolf behind him, went to see what he was gazing at thus. The priest's attention was so absorbed elsewhere that he did not hear the deaf man walking behind him.

Paris is a magnificent and charming spectacle, and especially at that day, viewed from the top of the towers of Notre-Dame, in the fresh light of a summer dawn. The day might have been in July. The sky was perfectly serene. Some tardy stars were fading away at various points, and there was a very brilliant one in the east, in the brightest part of the heavens. The sun was about to appear; Paris was beginning to move. A very white and very pure light brought out vividly to the eye all the outlines that its thousands of houses present to the east. The giant shadow of the towers leaped from roof to roof, from one end of the great city to the other. There were several quarters from which were already heard voices and noisy sounds. Here the stroke of a bell, there the stroke of a hammer, beyond, the complicated clatter of a cart in motion.

Already several columns of smoke were being belched forth from the chimneys scattered over the whole surface of roofs, as through the fissures of an immense sulphurous crater. The river, which ruffles its waters against the arches of so many bridges, against the points of so many islands, was wavering with silvery folds. Around the city, outside the ramparts, sight was lost in a great circle of fleecy vapors through which one confusedly distinguished the indefinite line of the plains, and the graceful swell of the heights. All sorts of floating sounds were dispersed over this half-awakened city. Toward the east, the morning breeze chased a few soft white bits of wool torn from the misty fleece of the hills.

In the Parvis, some good women, who had their milk jugs in their hands, were pointing out to each other, with astonishment, the singular dilapidation of the great door of Notre-Dame, and the two solidified streams of lead in the crevices of the stone. This was all that remained of the tempest of the night. The bonfire lighted between the towers by Quasimodo had died out. Tristan had already cleared up the Place, and had the dead thrown into the Seine. Kings like Louis XI are careful to clean the pavement quickly after a massacre.

Outside the balustrade of the tower, directly under the point where the priest had paused, there was one of those fantastically carved stone gutters with which Gothic edifices bristle, and, in a crevice of that gutter, two pretty wallflowers in blossom, shaken out and vivified, as it were, by the breath of air, made frolicsome salutations to each other. Above the towers, on high, far away in the depths of the sky, the cries of little birds were heard.

But the priest was not listening to, was not looking at, anything of all this. He was one of the men for whom there are no mornings, no birds, no flowers. In that immense horizon, which assumed so many aspects about him, his contemplation was concentrated on a single point.

Quasimodo was burning to ask him what he had done with the gypsy; but the archdeacon seemed to be out of the world at that moment. He was evidently in one of those violent moments of life when one would not feel the earth crumble. He remained motionless and silent, with his eyes steadily fixed on a certain point; and there was something so terrible about this silence and immobility that the savage bellringer shuddered before it and dared not come in contact with it. Only, and this was also one way of interrogating the archdeacon, he followed the direction of his vision, and in this way the glance of the unhappy deaf man fell upon the Place de Grève.

Thus he saw what the priest was looking at. The ladder was erected near the permanent gallows. There were some people and many soldiers in the Place. A man was dragging a white thing, from which hung something black, along the pavement. This man halted at the foot of the gallows.

Here something took place that Quasimodo could not see very clearly. It was not because his only eye had not preserved its long range, but there was a group of soldiers that prevented his seeing everything. Moreover, at that moment the sun appeared, and such a flood of light overflowed the horizon that one would have said that all the points in Paris, spires, chimneys, gables, had simultaneously taken fire.

Meanwhile, the man began to mount the ladder. Then Quasimodo saw him again distinctly. He was carrying a woman on his shoulder, a young girl dressed in white; that young girl had a noose about her neck. Quasimodo recognized her.

It was she.

The man reached the top of the ladder. There he arranged the noose. Here the priest, in order to see the better, knelt upon the balustrade.

All at once the man kicked away the ladder abruptly, and Quasimodo, who had not breathed for several moments, beheld the unhappy child dangling at the end of the rope two fathoms above the pavement, with the man squatting on her shoulders. The rope made several gyrations on itself, and Quasimodo beheld horrible convulsions run along the gypsy's body. The priest, on his side, with outstretched neck and eyes starting from his head, contemplated this horrible group of the man and the young girl—the spider and the fly.

At the moment when it was most horrible, the laugh of a demon, a laugh which one can only give vent to when one is no longer human, burst forth on the priest's livid face.

Quasimodo did not hear that laugh, but he saw it.

The bellringer retreated several paces behind the archdeacon, and suddenly hurling himself upon him with fury, with his huge hands he pushed him by the back over into the abyss over which Dom Claude was leaning.

The priest shrieked: "Damnation!" and fell.

The spout, above which he had stood, arrested him in his fall. He clung to it with desperate hands, and, at the moment when he opened his mouth to utter a second cry, he beheld the formidable and avenging face of Quasimodo thrust over the edge of the balustrade above his head.

Then he was silent.

The abyss was there below him. A fall of more than two hundred feet and the pavement.

In this terrible situation, the archdeacon said not a word, uttered not a groan. He merely writhed upon the spout, with incredible efforts to climb up again; but his hands had no hold on the granite, his feet slid along the blackened wall without catching fast. People who have ascended the towers of Notre-Dame know that there is a swell of the stone immediately beneath the balustrade. It was on this retreating angle that miserable archdeacon exhausted himself. He had not to deal with a perpendicular wall, but with one that sloped away beneath him.

Quasimodo had but to stretch out his hand in order to draw him from the gulf; but he did not even look at him. He was looking at the Grève. He was looking at the gallows. He was looking at the gypsy.

The deaf man was leaning, with his elbows on the balustrade, at the spot where the archdeacon had been a moment before, and there, never detaching his gaze from the only object which existed for him in the world at that moment, he remained motionless and mute, like a man struck by lightning, and a long stream of tears flowed in silence from that eye which, up to that time, had never shed but one tear.

Meanwhile, the archdeacon was panting. His bald brow was dripping with perspiration, his nails were bleeding against the stones, his knees were flayed by the wall.

He heard his cassock, which was caught on the spout, crack and rip at every jerk that he gave it. To complete his misfortune, this spout ended in a leaden pipe that bent under the weight of his body. The archdeacon felt this pipe slowly giving way. The miserable man said to himself that, when his hands should be worn out with fatigue, when his cassock should tear asunder, when the lead should give way, he would be obliged to fall, and terror seized upon his very vitals. Now and then he glanced wildly at a sort of narrow shelf formed, ten feet lower down, by projections of the sculpture, and he prayed heaven, from the depths of his distressed soul, that he might be allowed to finish his life, were it to last two centuries, on that space two feet square. Once, he glanced below him into the Place, into the abyss; the head that he raised again had its eyes closed and its hair standing erect.

There was something frightful in the silence of these two men. While the archdeacon agonized in this terrible fashion a few feet below him, Quasimodo wept and gazed at the Grève.

The archdeacon, seeing that all his exertions served only to weaken the fragile support that remained to him, decided to remain quiet. There he hung, embracing the gutter, hardly breathing, no longer stirring, making no longer any other movements than that mechanical convulsion of the stomach, which one experiences in dreams when one fancies himself falling. His fixed eyes were wide open with a stare. He lost ground little by little, nevertheless, his fingers slipped along the spout; he became more and more conscious of the feebleness of his arms and the weight of his body. The curve of the lead that sustained him inclined more and more each instant toward the abyss.

He beheld below him, a frightful thing, the roof of Saint-Jean le Rond, as small as a card folded in two. He gazed at the impressive carvings, one by one, of the tower, suspended like himself over the precipice, but without terror for themselves or pity for him. All was stone around him; before his eyes, gaping monsters; below, quite at the bottom, in the Place, the pavement; above his head, Quasimodo weeping.

In the Parvis there were several groups of curious good people, who were tranquilly seeking to divine who the madman could be who was amusing himself in so strange a manner. The priest heard them saying, for their voices reached him, clear and shrill: "Why, he will break his neck!"

Quasimodo wept.

At last the archdeacon, foaming with rage and despair, understood that all was in vain. Nevertheless, he collected all the strength that remained to him for a final effort. He stiffened himself upon the spout, pushed against the wall with both his knees, clung to a crevice in the stones with his hands, and succeeded in climbing back with one foot, perhaps; but this effort made the leaden beak on which he rested bend abruptly. His cassock burst open at the same time. Then, feeling everything give way beneath him, with nothing but his stiffened and failing hands to support him, the unfortunate man closed his eyes and let go of the spout. He fell.

Quasimodo watched him fall.

A fall from such a height is seldom perpendicular. The archdeacon, launched into space, fell at first head foremost, with outspread hands; then he whirled over and over many times; the wind blew him upon the roof of a house, where the unfortunate man began to break up. Nevertheless, he was not dead when he reached there. The bellringer saw him still endeavor to cling to a gable with his nails; but the surface sloped too much, and he had no more strength. He slid rapidly along the roof like a loosened tile, and dashed upon the pavement. There he no longer moved.

Then Quasimodo raised his eyes to the gypsy, whose body he beheld hanging from the gibbet, quivering far away beneath her white robe with the last shudderings of anguish, then he dropped them on the archdeacon, stretched out at the base of the tower, and no longer retaining the human form, and he said, with a sob which heaved his deep chest, "Oh! All that I have ever loved!"

CHAPTER 3

The Marriage of Phoebus

TOWARD EVENING ON that day, when the judiciary officers of the bishop came to pick up from the pavement of the Parvis the dislocated corpse of the archdeacon, Quasimodo had disappeared.

A great many rumors were in circulation with regard to this adventure. No one doubted but that the day had come when, in accordance with their compact, Quasimodo, that is to say, the devil, was to carry off Claude Frollo, that is to say, the sorcerer. It was presumed that he had broken the body when taking the soul, like monkeys who break the shell to get at the nut.

This is why the archdeacon was not interred in consecrated earth.

Louis XI died a year later, in the month of August, 1483.

As for Pierre Gringoire, he succeeded in saving the goat, and he won success in tragedy. It appears that, after having tasted astrology, philosophy, architecture, hermetics—all vanities, he returned to tragedy, vainest pursuit of all. This is what he called "coming to a tragic end." This is what is to be read, on the subject of his dramatic triumphs, in 1483, in the accounts of the "Ordinary": "To Jehan Marchand and Pierre Gringoire, carpenter and composer, who have made and composed the mystery made at the Châtelet of Paris, at the entry of Monsieur the Legate, and have ordered the personages, clothed and dressed the same, as in the said mystery was required; and likewise, for having made the scaffoldings thereto necessary; and for this deed—one hundred livres."

Phoebus de Châteaupers also came to a tragic end. He married.

Chapter 4

The Marriage of Quasimodo

We have just said that Quasimodo disappeared from Notre-Dame on the day of the gypsy's and of the archdeacon's death. He was not seen again, in fact; no one knew what had become of him.

During the night that followed the execution of la Esmeralda, the night men had detached her body from the gibbet, and had carried it, according to custom, to the cellar of Montfauçon.

Montfauçon was, as Sauval says, "the most ancient and the most superb gibbet in the kingdom." Between the faubourgs of the Temple and Saint Martin, about a hundred and sixty toises from the walls of Paris, a few bow shots from La Courtille, there was to be seen on the crest of a gentle, almost imperceptible eminence, but sufficiently elevated to be seen for several leagues round about, an edifice of strange form, bearing considerable resemblance to a Celtic cromlech, and where also human sacrifices were offered.

Let the reader picture to himself, crowning a limestone hillock, an oblong mass of masonry fifteen feet in height, thirty wide, forty long, with a gate, an external railing and a platform; on this platform sixteen enormous pillars of rough hewn stone, thirty feet in height, arranged in a colonnade round three of the four sides of the mass which support them, bound together at their summits by heavy beams, whence hung chains at intervals; on all these chains, skeletons; in the vicinity, on the plain, a stone cross and two gibbets of secondary importance, which seemed to have sprung up as shoots around the central gallows; above all this, in the sky, a perpetual flock of crows; that was Montfauçon.

At the end of the fifteenth century, the formidable gibbet that dated from 1328, was already very much dilapidated; the beams were worm-eaten, the chains rusted, the pillars green with mould; the layers of hewn stone were all cracked at their joints, and grass was growing on that platform which no feet touched. The monument made a horrible profile against the sky; especially at night when there was a little moonlight on those white skulls, or when the breeze of evening brushed the chains and the skeletons, and swayed all these in the darkness. The presence of this gibbet sufficed to render gloomy all the surrounding places.

The mass of masonry that served as foundation to the odious edifice was hollow. A huge cellar had been constructed there, closed by an old iron grating, which was out of order, into which were cast not only the human remains, which were taken from the chains of Montfauçon, but also the bodies of all the unfortunates executed on the other permanent gibbets of Paris. To that deep charnel-house, where so many human remains and so many crimes have rotted in company, many great ones of this world, many innocent people, have contributed their bones, from Enguerrand de Marigni, the first victim, and a just man, to Admiral de Coligni, who was its last, and who was also a just man.

As for the mysterious disappearance of Quasimodo, this is all that we have been able to discover.

About eighteen months or two years after the events which terminate this story, when search was made in that cavern for the body of Olivier le Daim, who had been hanged two days previously, and to whom Charles VIII had granted the favor of being buried in Saint Laurent, in better company, they found among all those hideous carcasses two skeletons, one of which held the other in its embrace. One of these skeletons, which was that of a woman, still had a few strips of a garment which had once been white, and around her neck was to be seen a string of adrézarach beads with a little silk bag ornamented with green glass, which was open and empty. These objects were of so little value that the executioner had probably not cared for them. The other, which held this one in a close embrace, was the skeleton of a man. It was noticed that his spinal column was crooked, his head seated on his shoulder blades, and that one leg was shorter than the other. Moreover, there was no fracture of the vertebrae at the nape of the neck, and it was evident that he had not been hanged. Hence, the man to whom it had belonged had come thither and had died there. When they tried to detach the skeleton that he held in his embrace, he fell to dust.

Note Added to the Definitive Edition

It is by mistake that this edition was announced as augmented by many new chapters. The word should have been unpublished. In fact, if by new, newly made is to be understood, the chapters added to this edition are not new. They were written at the same time as the rest of the work; they date from the same epoch, and sprang from the same thought, they have always formed a part of the manuscript of *Notre-Dame-de-Paris*. Moreover, the author cannot comprehend how fresh developments could be added to a work of this character after its completion. This is not to be done at will. According to his idea, a romance is born in a manner that is, in some sort, necessary, with all its chapters; a drama is born with all its scenes. Think not that there is anything arbitrary in the numbers of parts of which that whole, that mysterious microcosm which you call a drama or a romance, is composed. Grafting and soldering take badly on works of this nature, which should gush forth in a single stream and so remain. The thing once done, do not change your mind, do not touch it up. The book once published, the sex of the work, whether virile or not, has been recognized and proclaimed; when the child has once uttered his first cry he is born, there he is, he is made so, neither father nor mother can do anything, he belongs to the air and to the sun, let him live or die, such as he is. Has your book been a failure? So much the worse. Add no chapters to an unsuccessful book. Is it incomplete? You should have completed it when you conceived it. Is your tree crooked? You cannot straighten it up. Is your romance consumptive? Is your romance not capable of living? You cannot supply it with the breath it lacks. Has your drama been born lame? Take my advice, and do not provide it with a wooden leg.

Hence the author attaches particular importance to the public knowing for a certainty that the chapters here added have not been made expressly for this reprint. They were not published in the preceding editions of the book for a very simple reason. At the time when *Notre-Dame-de-Paris* was printed the first time, the manuscript of these three chapters had been mislaid. It was necessary to rewrite them or to dispense with them. The author considered that the only two of these chapters which were in the least important, owing to their extent, were chapters on art and history which in no way interfered with the groundwork of the drama and the romance, that the public would not notice their loss, and that he, the author, would alone be in possession of the secret. He decided to omit them, and then, if the whole truth must be confessed, his indolence shrunk from the task of rewriting the three lost chapters. He would have found it a shorter matter to make a new romance.

Now the chapters have been found, and he avails himself of the first opportunity to restore them to their place.

This now, is his entire work, such as he dreamed it, such as he made it, good or bad, durable or fragile, but such as he wishes it.

These recovered chapters will possess no doubt, but little value in the eyes of persons, otherwise very judicious, who have sought in *Notre-Dame-de-Paris* only the drama, the romance. But there are perchance, other readers, who have not found it useless to study the aesthetic and philosophic thought concealed in this book, and who have taken pleasure, while reading *Notre-Dame-de-Paris*, in unravelling beneath the romance something else than the romance, and in following (may we be pardoned these rather ambitious expressions), the system of the historian and the aim of the artist through the creation of the poet.

For such people especially, the chapters added to this edition will complete *Notre-Dame-de-Paris*, if we admit that *Notre-Dame-de-Paris* was worth the trouble of completing.

In one of these chapters on the present decadence of architecture, and on the death (in his mind almost inevitable) of that king of arts, the author expresses and develops an opinion unfortunately well rooted in him, and well thought out. But he feels it necessary to say here that he earnestly desires that the future may, some day, put him in the wrong. He knows that art in all its forms has everything to hope from the new generations whose genius, still in the germ, can be heard gushing forth in our studios. The grain is in the furrow, the harvest will certainly be fine. He merely fears, and the reason may be seen in the second volume of this edition, that the sap may have been withdrawn from that ancient soil of architecture that has been for so many centuries the best field for art.

Nevertheless, there are today in the artistic youth so much life, power, and, so to speak, predestination, that in our schools of architecture in particular, at the present time, the professors, who are detestable, produce, not only unconsciously but even in spite of themselves, excellent pupils; quite the reverse of that potter mentioned by Horace, who dreamed amphorae and produced pots. *Currit rota, urcens exit.*

But, in any case, whatever may be the future of architecture, in whatever manner our young architects may one day solve the question of their art, let us, while waiting for new monument, preserve the ancient monuments. Let us, if possible, inspire the nation with a love for national architecture. That, the author declares, is one of the principal aims of this book; it is one of the principal aims of his life.

Notre-Dame-de-Paris has, perhaps opened some true perspectives on the art of the Middle Ages, on that marvellous art which up to the present time has been unknown to some, and, what is worse, misknown by others. But the author is far from regarding as accomplished, the task he has voluntarily imposed on himself. He has already pleaded on more than one occasion, the cause of our ancient architecture, he has already loudly denounced many profanations, many demolitions, many impieties. He will not grow weary. He has promised himself to recur frequently to this subject. He will return to it. He will be as indefatigable in defending our historical edifices as our iconoclasts of the schools and academies are eager in attacking them; for it is a grievous thing to see into what hands the architecture of the Middle Ages has fallen, and in what a manner the botchers of plaster of the present day treat the ruin of this grand art, it is even a shame for us intelligent men who see them at work and content ourselves with hooting them. And we are not speaking here merely of what goes on in the provinces, but of what is done in Paris at our very doors, beneath our windows, in the great city, in the lettered city, in the city of the press, of word, of thought. We cannot resist the impulse to point out, in concluding this note, some of the acts of vandalism that are every day planned, debated, begun, continued, and successfully completed under the eyes of the artistic public of Paris, face to face with criticism, which is disconcerted by so much audacity. An archbishop's palace has just been demolished, an edifice in poor taste, no great harm is done; but in a block with the archiepiscopal palace a bishop's palace has been demolished, a rare fragment of the fourteenth century, which the demolishing architect could not distinguish from the rest. He has torn up the wheat with the tares; 'tis all the same. They are talking of razing the admirable chapel of Vincennes, in order to make, with its stones, some fortification, which Daumesnil did not need, however. While the Palais Bourbon, that wretched edifice, is being repaired at great expense, gusts of wind and equinoctial storms are allowed to destroy the magnificent painted windows of the Sainte-Chapelle. For the last few days there has been a scaffolding on the tower of Saint Jacques de la Boucherie; and one of these mornings the pick will be laid to it. A mason has been found to build a little white house between the venerable towers of the Palais-de-Justice. Another has been found willing to prune away Saint-Germain-des-Pres, the feudal abbey with three bell towers. Another will be found, no doubt, capable of pulling down Saint-Germain l'Auxerrois. All these masons claim to be architects, are paid by the prefecture or from the petty budget, and wear green coats. All the harm which false taste can inflict on good taste, they accomplish. While we write, deplorable spectacle! One of them holds possession of the Tuileries, one of them is giving Philibert Delorme a scar across the middle of his face; and it is not, assuredly, one of the least of the scandals of our time to see with what effrontery the heavy architecture of this gentleman is being flattened over one of the most delicate façades of the Renaissance!

PARIS, October 20, 1832